CRANIUM FILL PART 1

Dedicated to my Mother, Father, Rick, SBO, Charlie Brown and Sun-Sun

To Mom
Thank you for
all that you do and
have done for me and
for others!
love
Stan

CRANIUM FILL

Part One

By

C.F. Hutton

TABLE OF CONTENTS

Please remember that a story includes both oral and aural attention and that renegade truths and faded beliefs are often wound so tight around perception that a reader can't begin to fathom where facts end and fable continues. Even though this saga occurs beyond where we are considering now, know this, that accomplishment, that is unbelievable in its origin, can, in review, be judged inevitable in the end.

Years after a seminal event occurs, it can take on a peculiar enchantment, an almost wishful blindness that masks the spitting truth that now is not as good as then. As a firm believer that there is no age limit on ambition or adventure and that the critical arch of time, place and luck is history's powerful and perverted key to the success of any great endeavor pursued by and with the diligence and intent of a clear mind and a good heart, I will share my knowledge of people of sincere singularity who acted during the loud times before and after the election of 2016 in which third became first, and wherein these individuals distinctive actions truly merit your respect now and in the future.

Today, in your place on the face of this earth, the time is nigh to hear me clearly and properly use what you come to learn and have purpose to perfect to the best of your abilities the world around you and make sure that nothing can ever be as it has been if it has been wrong for so long.

In the ebb and flow of the tides between the ruled and the rulers, the rulers do not always finish with the prize.

Prelude
"HIDDEN GIVINGS"
"Were I to await perfection, my book would never be finished."
Tai T'ung 13th Century author, History of Chinese Writing

Date July - mid 1970's

They were unmarried, frightened, inexperienced in the harsher realities of life, a pair of teens driving on to their goal of leaving their guilt on the altar of forgiveness, hopefully to soften dismay. But neither the sweet smell of sage freshen by rain nor the dark of the early morning hour could mask the anxiousness, nor soften the fact that neither knew their final destination, just an approximation that might assist in their need to escape, regroup, and then return to what was then considered normal for their era. They were alone in the flatlands, during the seventies, heading north towards a gathering of lights situated on an apparent rise barely discernible in the feint moonlight, doing what they thought best for their families still living in the fifties.

He continued on Highway 50 then turned onto the uneven brick laden street named Central. A train whistle sounded behind and broke through the loud clattering beneath them. She spotted a sign for the high school which taught the children of this town of 14,000 souls and she found it amusing in a sick manner that the teams name were the Demons. She tried to soft sing, hum, as signs of awakening were happening in her arms. Damn those bricks! Damn my tears. They had been in hiding just before the event, their only contact with kin being a letter, a scribbled 'balm' implying 'they had eloped'. The mid-wife had been sworn to secrecy and paid with part of his savings to secure her agreement. They had done their best with this recent, most responsible, most stressful longest week of their lives, but they knew this final act was their only option. He saw San Jose and turned right to the east.

The Sisters of Saint Joseph had operated Saint Mary of the Plains College in some capacity since 1913. The good ladies had taken over the grounds and buildings of the original campus, which had been run by both Presbyterians and Methodists. These Protestants had called the early learning center, Soule College, named after a patent medicine millionaire, Asa T. Soule, who was known worldwide as the "Hop Bitters King" and who, more importantly in 1886, endowed $50,000 to the fledgling school. Hop Bitters was an elixir promoted with gusto and with the announced purpose to 'cure what ails ya', seemingly, an odd but good match for a religious academy. On Sunday, May 10th, 1942, God let it be known that he was in the area. The campus was observing a world-wide solidarity day, students and faculty had gathered around the statue of Our Lady of the Plains. Then the ceremony moved into the Chapel to perform the May crowning of the Blessed Virgin Mary. About a quarter of eight that evening, shortly after the ceremonies had wrapped up, a tornado struck the campus, destroying the old buildings. Locals considered it a miracle that no one had perished in the disaster. The school finally recovered in 1952 as the new Saint Mary of the Plains began construction. Modern in design, the four story building of salmon colored brick included a chapel wing on the west, featuring a campanile rising over a hundred feet from a stone relief sculpture of the Holy Family at its base. And now, the building known as Hennessy Hall was about to witness another sad but wonderful twist of fate miracle, the 'act' remaining the center of attention for weeks to follow. Neither students nor the sister-teachers saw nor heard as the furtive couple left the large wicker basket, its note "Need Milk, please! Thank you. God Bless" pinned to the pink security blanket covering the baskets beautiful tiny wonderments sitting on the entry block beneath the stone plaque with 'AD 1952' etched into it, none of the occupants heard as the teenagers, turned and ran down the five steps, hurrying, the young man helping the tearful young mother into the passenger side of the vehicle, carefully but quickly closing the door, then racing around the front to get in behind the wheel, a slight splish-splash of footsteps on dampened asphalt, the only notice of their presence. They were off, heading around the western side of the now silhouetted by dawns first hints cathedral swinging onto San Jose, a major move in their lives that would follow them forever. The two had heard no cries as adrenaline can simultaneously calm and excite and lend a hand to what is directly in front and needs attendance. They were turning south on Central when the first lights in the Hall were switching on to see what sounded at first like a mountain lion cub crying, certainly an alien noise to dawns usual arrival and subtlety. He tried to maintain the speed over the noisier than ever bricks but he was contesting with a leaden foot And her cries seemed an accelerant to the situation. Just about the time the two parents had reached the first rows of the "leaning to the east" wind pushed phone poles on the highway south of Dodge City, the first Sister, then another are bending down to soothe the now loud babies on the stone entry of the Hall. Before the age of the eternal electronic eye, no one was witness then to mother's mournful wail nor the teen male's valiant attempt to act as he believes a man should act in this moment ...temperate words and expressions of portrayed certainty which would assure himself later that he had assisted in doing the right thing while at the same time competing with the thought of what his and her lives really were like a bare twenty five minutes ago and what they were to be in a now new future.

It is said that The Sisters, after the first shock and first actions to comfort the newborns and approaching the list of who to call first, proceeded to nurture and prepare for the long haul by, within the hour of the babies arrival, selecting options for names for the little bundles of love from names of Saints, local street names and one Sister's suggested the actual use of a contraband Ouija board.

Chapter 1

"And That Goes For Every Other Bastard In The Universe Too"

"1000 friends are not enough, but one enemy is too many."

Vietnam saying

September 11th, 2015

"To misquote Jesus, fuck em!"

The recollection of Yoggee's closing words on the phone while Sean had waited at DIA to embark, prompts a smile.

Amused not only at the unusual yet familiar method and meaning often originating from Yoggee, aka Leonard Samson Drummerman, one of the most unique, intelligent but obtuse humans on earth, Sean Linden is also tickled by the serendipitous feel as simultaneously, as if God was delivering a one liner, Train's "Calling All You Angels" is playing in his headset, a suitable mix for saviors he supposed, as the flight descended into Williston, the destination for what he and his fellow savior traveler and friend, Halas, hoped would be the starting point for one more successful mission, which on this occasion, was to keep their friend and business partner from being shot and or put in jail and to keep their business still intact and still theirs. Unfortunately, Yoggee had the habit of keeping bad news deep within until the almost irretrievable last minute, for fear that it would harm those closest to him and because his pride frequently settled for less than common sense.

Sean recalled during Yoggee's call earlier that morning, 8 a.m. District of Columbia time, as he had said that the "agents of the poachers of posterity" which meant the Williams County Sheriff's Department, were at the The Fill trying to serve Yoggee, as best as the still groggy Sean could discern, something akin to a final summons to appear in court. Sean initially responded with, "What in the Hell? What summons?" Within seconds though, Sean was fully alert as he realized that it was Mr. Drummerman on the other end of the line and that questions would be a waste of precious seconds. Activating a rapid deployment response was priority one and Sean was on his way to the shower, phone in hand, as he told Yoggee to hang on to whatever he had by the tail , that he would contact Moah and they would get to North Dakota ASAP. He had told Yoggee to inform law enforcement that the businesses attorneys would be flying in too and for everyone to await their arrival and all would be taken care of, to which Yoggee expectedly exclaimed, "Lawyers! The Hell you say. We don't need those Mother suckers of sympathy and serenity here!" Sean had interrupted the expected volcanic about attorneys with a terse, "Quiet. Just do it."

"But, Sean, this doesn't require polite and reasoned rhetoric, these..."

"Stop wasting time, Leonard" the use of Leonard was intended to let Yoggee know Sean was serious and upset. "We're partners and whatever you've involved in, we should have been told, damn it." Sean recalled the silence. It was pretty loud.

He knew that Yoggee had specifically chosen North Dakota to live in, one, because of the family homestead and two, because it was the state with the least amount of lawyers per capita in America,..... lawyers, which equaled in Yoggee's thinking, the origin of all mental and ethical pollution and he would never miss the opportunity to quote a now very dated survey; "national survey, my son" he would say, to give it the weight of certainty that national surveys were intended to convey, "in which 95.2%.. "Yoggee never left the point two out as it lent more credibility and effect to the overwhelming truthfulness of his position," that this majority, 95.2% of people, wind up feeling that they didn't get their money's worth after they hired lawyers."

Sean wasn't a usually snippy, biting personality, especially to a friend or mentor, but that morning was an exception. "Listen, just tell your Sheriff friend to be patient. Hold your ground but do not, and I repeat, do not antagonize the law, you hear me?"

"But Sean, this has gone on..."

"No. Don't care. You should have told us, whatever this is, Yoggee...."

"Land grabs, Sean, thievery as art..."

"Yoggee, Focus! Good bye!"

Sean had next dialed Moah Halas and arranged to meet him in Denver. Then he speed dialed Cade and asked if Cade could spare Giddings for the day.

Ah, September 11th, wouldn't have it any other way.

The plane was still thirty miles away from Sloulin Field. Sean had grown weary of flying. He had jumped out of some planes for business reasons, as had Moah, and once, Sean had jumped out of a chopper to save his life let alone twice from birds for purposes that were never to be discussed if one was fortunate to return from those specific endeavors. Moah was staring out the window. Silent. Serious. His usual demeanor, Sean reflected. Their friendship is near ancestral; not by blood, but by shared duty that called for blood, for honor and for the trust that's fostered by success in execution of them.

Moah glanced at Sean. "Why doesn't he think to tell us when he needs help? Or that the business is on the table in a sticky ante of shit?"

Sean laughed, "He's a cruel master of the heart, isn't he" "The funkiest of the funky."

"We'll be alright. Giddings's flying in on Cade's jet."

"Let's pray that Yoggee doesn't go any more Yoggee on the cops than he already has." Sean nodded and retightened his seatbelt as the pilot announced to prepare for landing. Moah chuckled "Not bad, five hours to get from bed to the land of legal flim-flam and the still loveable, galloping mayhem known as Leonard Samson Drummerman."

Sean returned the smile and thought of Drummerman's sometime opinion of Mr. Halas. Yoggee contended that Moah was more "fire on fire than ever. Love him so like a little brother, but he's a damn beer angry pissed off level of a one man embroil." Strange, opposites do not attract after all. Or do they?

And all this to protect a property and the rights of said property north of Williston, North Dakota, off highway 85 in the vicinity of Zahl and Bone Tail or as Mr. Drummerman would describe the place he lived in or deliver directions to as "The Cranium Fill Saloon and Automobile Emporium, an establishment as far from matrimonial bliss and as close to Satan as you could legally get, a building not far northeast from the confluence of the Missouri and Yellowstone Rivers, a haven for the mind if you have the time and you have the dime, a locale about 130 miles West of Rugby, the measured geographical center of the North American continent, a tavern of well earned repute, just a skip on the water rock throw away from the intersection of the Little Muddy River and the 1,600 miles of shoreline of beautiful Lake Sakakawea, a structure constructed for well brewed memories, just about 20 to 30 miles east of the Montana line in the general neighborhood of Good Gawd Fun. It's The Cranium Fill, my friends, the Fill, with the present and only ever owner, moi, Yoggee, a man, a distinct mark on the skin of humanity, unforgettable as a rainbow and as harmless as a migraine, at your service."

But, as Moah and Sean would come to learn, the point of contention this fine September day was not what was on the surface or in the air of the Cranium Fill, but what was beneath it, the Bakken Shale Formation, a rich deposit the U.S. Geological Survey calls the largest continuous oil accumulation it ever assessed.

Yoggee's continuous refusals to even listen or give moment's notice to any of the suitors bids to explore let alone drill on even a gnats ass sized section of his inherited 640 acres of prairie eventually brought on the usual attempted tricks and chicanery of the well connected to push the locally purchased or those more commonly known by the deserved tag, bought and paid politicians, to massage and manipulate the codes, the zoning and the condemnation rules for their mutual benefit and to fulfill their merged desire of profit for government coffers and for campaign funding and for corporate bottom lines and for lord sized bonuses.

"Hell, there are nearly 5,000 wells now," Yoggee would argue, "and millions of barrels, why do you need mine, you Philistine pigs of petro." "There will be no trucks, no mud and no bribes will change me or my land." He did not want the rig noise, nor the degradation for his neighbors, the bison, the prairie dogs, the mule and white tailed deer, coyotes and most certainly not the sharp-tailed grouse.

On the one occasion in town when he was stopped by a persistent land man who argued that "wasn't it nuts that fortune was but a signature away and wasn't it a fools game to care about this barren place?" Yoggee, with forced calmness, countered with, "Yes, its' blustery here, but, son, the average temperature is 70, did you know that? But I did not move here for just the clime, but I moved here for the distance from the flocks of legal asses's and people like you, a paradise with a state motto that sealed the deal for me, "Liberty and Union, Now and Forever, One and Inseparable." This, as usual, was followed in an almost aside delivery, a casual mention of the fact that his inheritance of 640 acres from his father's Swedish side of the family also had something to do with his love of the place. Yoggee farmed barley, beans, sunflowers and wheat on the land and while susceptible to the same vagaries of nature that his fellow farmers were wise to and planned for, he was secure because of the constant four season, no matter the weather cash flow of a thriving watering hole set in the middle of roustabouts, bikers and tourists, bored and otherwise.

He had fended off feints, empty threats and condemnation attempts by bureaucrats and their masters simply by ignoring all correspondence and demands which Yoggee viewed as mere scribbling by scoundrels, not worth a syllable of response. Nor had he thought these pieces of pulp and circumstance worth the time or trouble to mention to Mr. Halas or Mr. Linden, until now.

Yoggee, with the help of his two bouncers, had delayed and held his own for going on three plus hours. He wondered if he could soften the moment with the offer of a truce pitcher of lemonade to the group. A meadowlark calls in the American elm to the south of the building. He remembered a memory.

He smiled and yelled to the gathering of Williams County's finest.

"Gentlemen and Nancy Katy, you are wasting taxpayer's money and you are also smashing my wild prairie roses with your vehicles and boots. Now we go back..." "Yoggee, it's our job to enforce the orders of the court, whether we like it or not. You got to respond to legal requests for information or appearances so that..."

"Whoa up there, Tom Tisdale. You straight shot know that this government of greedy horn dogs has gone downhill ever since your dad left as Mayor. It's become a shysters Shangri-La, an Eden without ethics for the well connected and you cannot truthfully dispute this, can you? Can you? No."

The silence was authoritative, and affirmation of what was said.

Sheriff Tisdale offered another semi plea, "Jesus almighty, Yoggee, you just can't ignore a judge. Just sue, why don't you?"

"Sue, shit! Spend money with idiots that don't give a rat's ass about how much you are spending nor the outcome of what you are spending boatloads for...Sue? You know me, Tom, long enough to know I do not associate with lawyers...except maybe for today." Sheriff Tisdale and the other officer's mouths drop. Yoggee and an attorney! Mark the day, month and year. "Are you telling me, Yoggee, that you are going to resolve this today with legal assistance? That we can all go..."

Yoggee interrupted Tisdale's hopeful inquiry.

"I have help on the way. But no lawsuit! Ha, I'd have my raccoon or my pig, Soy Blossom, or Clementine for that matter, sue for me before I'd let a two legged pissant stand good for me in this zoo of a mess dealing with suits too arrogant to be insulted and too mentally infirmed to have a clue.."

"Then what the..."

"My partners, Sean Linden and ..."

The sheriffs were stunned at the mention of Sean Linden's name. "Sean Linden's a partner of yours, Yoggee? When? How?"

"..And my other partner, Moah Halas, should be landing at Sloulin bout now. And they said that they had council coming with them. Listen, Brad and Bart and the animals are weary of this standoff, just as you are. And they are on overtime helping me hold off you underpaid, and this is not an imprecation as I still love you, peons. And as you all well know, I have known most of you for, well, since your formative years."

A sudden breeze caused the turquoise aluminum sign with the "Tetanus is the Devil" white lettered warning hanging over the open garage door to swing and squeak, emphasizing the strange tenderness of the moment. Tetanus was the Greek God of rust and Yoggee thought it appropriate to assign the placard a place over an entry to what usually served as the home for the modem metal beast known as an automobile. "Listen, guys, no insult intended, Nancy Katy,"

"None took, Yoggee."

"Do you want me and what might happen here on your minds for the rest of your lives all because of MAGI Inc. and its desires? Chester Chishum or did I say "jissum", which brought laughter from the yard...Yoggee had an unusual and usually successful way of de-intensifying, as he put it, any rock hard situation and it seemed to be working again. Even Chester was smiling.

"I knew your daddy's daddy when you were a mere sperm in your daddy's dreams and son, you and the other's have quaffed more here at the Fill than almost any other gun - toting fools I have ever known. Why, I know you down to the flavors of snow cones you each liked coming up to my trailer at the park after your little league games in your baggy uniforms and your one size too big caps, made even your losses taste sweet, didn't I? And this is how you now intend to treat a friend? This is how you earn your money, your blood currency at the behest of people you don't even know, stealing a man's manse. Boys and Nancy Kate, I may have served you ices long ago but that sure as sin doesn't mean you get to serve me shit today!

I need time Tisdale. My relationship with you, well, hell, with all of you, is almost always antemundane. And most certainly irenic, the majority of the time...but I am giving notice and now my truculence level is at maximum. The Fill is not for the taking and is not only mine but it's my friends, my partners, it's my animals and it's yours too, when your tabs are paid."

Yoggee punctuated his statement amidst the responding guffaws and laughter with a blast skyward from his shotgun, Mabel. The sheriffs ducked and a few "God damns" and "Jesus, Yoggee's" were uttered as the pellets ricocheted off the Fills weathervane above the main entry, just missing the sign at the vanes base, "Serving Drafts, Not Flats", but spinning the oversized weathercock styled in the form of a cockerel and painted in a bright taxi cab yellow and cherry red which resulted in an abnormal occurrence on the bar's roof of not being able to tell which way the prevailing wind was blowing until finally, the pellet induced motion twirled to a stop.

All eyes were on Yoggee and on the interior of the garage to the right of Mr. Drummerman. The Cranium Fill and Automobile Emporium got the second half of its name not for the owner's talent with cars but for what was inside the garage whose door was open for nearly six months of the year or longer as weather permitted for marketing purposes only. Yoggee preferred the door up because inside in the bay was the Jaguar, a gold hussy, an eye grabber and conversation prompter, that sat on a jack where usually the left rear wheel would normally reside. This did not detract from the notoriety as the vehicle always appeared balanced, perfectly presentable no matter the preceptor's stance or location. The fact was that Yoggee knew jack about automobiles but he figured the car would draw all mechanics, self appointed aficionados of haughty rides, oil rowdies, Jag addicts and the like who were within drinking distance of the Fill. Upon cursory inspection, the assembled group agreed that no stray pellet had marred the thing and so they focused back on each other.

Sheriff Tisdale waved his hand. "Yoggee, no need to do that again. Shoot your mouth off all you want, my friend, but no more guns, you hear?"

The gathered officers knew well the kindness of the man in front of them. They knew of Yoggee's charitable heart to the native tribes, to children of need, white, red, black...it did not matter, he had done a lot of good for those that had not known good for a long time. Besides that, the Fills glasses and beer were always iced and frosty and he was commonly recognized as an intelligent, talented individual who was the best at sorting out and finding what Yoggee himself called, deventricular ventriloquisms, a feckless, heartless speaking out of both sides of the mouth without any meaning to be found between the words, faster than any other human or lie detector could in all of western North Dakota.

The wheels touched down but memories are still in the air.

"The Cranium Fill Where Surrealism Escapes To Reality" This was the headline that titled the first page of Mr. Drummermans's business plan leading off his presentation of proffered partnership with Moah and Sean.

"Gentlemen," which was about the only time Sean could recall his partner using this term, "I have conducted business research and development in this industry with hours upon hours of investigation in many a watering oasis's of fine alcohol, taking in the crème de le crème of white lightening from the backwoodsiest of taverns and invested many a minute sipping the coldest beer from the hoppiest of joints in America, all observed, of course, in the controlled study atmosphere of various laboratories of the liquored up, where even Dali and Gene Autry would feel at ease. I dare say as a practicing, certifiable Sans Compos Mentis...having full control of one's mind..." Moah had intervened. "Mensa Maniac?"

... undeterred as usual, Yoggee continues, "of absolutus (freed) acumen and born with the delicate, deft ability of how to wonk things through and wring dollars out of fun that I can deliver on this approach to"....

Sean remembered that both he and Moah at this point in the meeting, uninterrupted with, 'we're in,' not only because they knew Yoggee's marketing abilities, but it also saved them from the prospect of drawn out mentoring and messaging which they both knew they would in the end not be able to refuse. Additionally, Yoggee already had the building, the land and the constitution it would require to manage what Yoggee would tag as the eclectic ecstasy otherwise known as The Cranium Fill.

People, place, purpose; if all are blended to near perfection and then throw in the high markup and the salability in bad times and good times of liquor , viola, profit follows. And so it was with the Fill.

As one entered the Fill, signs were in preponderance, expensively carved ones, metal ones, some hand scribbled, all causing patrons to stop, maybe scratch their heads and then continue in further beneath the large treated lodge pole beams to the cedar and knotty pined walls and green slate floors of what could only be described palette of pandemonium for the eye, with tacked to the wood leopard skin velvet tapestries surrounding the corner booths and blacked gold streaked mirror panels flanking the remaining ones. There was space enough for round tables seating six and for large open areas if dancing to the jukebox or an occasional band required it. Two pool tables and one video Craps game placed as far away from the two large bars dance and seating areas, netted huge profits for such a small amount of square footage.

The first sign at the entry or "lush lobby" as Y called it, read "There will be no repining here, gizmos!" which Sean thought so acutely on target for the activity of this day...and next to it, as you came through the massive red swinging doors (which had cost them all more premium dollars on the premises liability insurance but Yoggee had been insistent on this), hung another sign that had caused a local ladies rights group to clamor during the first week of the bars operation which stated, "No Rebarbative Females Allowed!". Yoggee took the marketing opportunity to maximum effect when he responded to the "professionally indignant", as he called the group, with a succinct letter to the Editor in the local paper with the disclaimer that, "All ladies are allowed in my establishment, hence all ladies are beautiful. Sincerely, Leonard Samson Drummerman, a fatally attracted fan of the fairer sex for the fairer part of my life."

Behind the one hundred foot long south bar and above the stocked shelves of spirits suitable for ruffians and royalty, shined the blue gassed neon announcement in beautifully cursively designed tubes, "The Saloon and Roost That Only Madams, Outlaws and Authors Can Savor; Which Are You?"

Sean mused over their friend and partner's habit of frequently welcoming a newcomer to the establishment because there never any strangers with Yoggee. "I'm the owner of this one of a kind legal un-Shebeen... (Irish place where illegal liquor is sold) I'm the system analysts, your bartender, for what ails you, I'm the extremely pleased to meet you proprietor of this cock-a-hoop, whose origin, in all likelihood, meant the action of turning on a tap and allowing the liquor to flow and the fun to grow." Yoggee promoted drink specials on special Cock-a-Hoop days which actually were any day he felt particularly amicable to the group gathered at the moment or for on the rare occasion when he spied an easy to recognize down in the boondocks patron or a couple that were obviously too serious, too uptight to enjoy themselves in a place that was meant to be a romper room for the mind, he officially pronounced that the Cock-a-Hoop special of the day was. and then he would lean in or go over to ask the object or objects of his genuine concern what his or hers or their favorite liquid pleasure was and that libation would be the special of the day and would be free for the first few rounds to the individual or couple in evidential need of a pick me up, provided as a kick-start for attitudinal re-Feng Shueing and given from the heart of another "been there, done that" soul who happen to own a bar.

Along with bouncer/tenders and the "Babe Stars" as Yoggee called the hard working and loyal women who served in The Fill, his pet raccoon, Sage, was a walking center of attention whenever Sage decided to make an appearance. Well trained to the manners of humans and knowledgeable of his limits and that his usual territory was in the rear of the bar near the storage area. In fact, Sage, as well as Yoggee's other on site corporate officers, Clementine the porcupine, and Keno, the lutino cockatiel with an attitude, had been the objects and targets of numerous health board citations and claims of violations of zoning and code ordinances and other quasi legal attempts by the bureaucracies and other powers of the opaque to wedge protests and basically harass Yoggee into acceptance and submission to their real ambition of gaining expanded tax revenues by Yoggee okaying the erection of derricks on his land to which Yoggee always responded".. That if there was any erectioneering going on on my land, it will be my own!"

The pot bellied beautiful ursine Soy Blossom was never allowed in the public area of the bar; as she was not listed as one of the official corporate board members; she mostly loved the confines of her Taj Mahal of a sty in the expanse of Yoggee's back yard. But Keno, Sean's favorite co member of the board of directors was different. His massive cage was fastened up high by the north view window. "My little hooked billed bastard" Yoggee lovingly called him. "He's one hell of a sippin', biting' lemon chiffon beau, Keno, a male with orange rouge on his cheeks, but I don't hold that against him because of his natural acidic guile and talent for possessing a checks and balance system of reading personalities with experienced watchfulness etched in edginess, a crooked billed straight shooter who lets me know immediately which people entering our confines love animals and those who don't. If Keno screeches in your direction, odds are that you burnt ants with magnifying glass or you beat puppies as a child. And we know early on to keep a more careful watch on you."

Usually, Sean recalled, you could not hear Keno's noise above the bar's general strum and drang except when the bird would loudly respond to when Yoggee would bang the large bronze plate hanging up behind the second cash register, The Golgotha Gong so named by the proprietor, in an act of visual and aural acknowledgement, to celebrate a patron's generous tip for one of the Bar Star's, and hopefully also as an inducement for others to follow suit... or upon the occasion when the inspiration would well up in the owner and he would go into his, "Listen up, my banty bacchanalias, the bell tolls for thee and thee, yes, indeed, my gathered libationists, from you smiling smurfs to you Cheshire's reserved and grizzled, the Golgotha is your metronome for the now, for the heavy handed past and for the still echoing warning ring of your futures going, going, good bye, long gone.", and with the studied flourish of a master provocateur and profiteer, he would conclude, "Drink hearty, mates and mattresses, for the morrow is on the lamb",

And with this, he'd swing and bang the Golgotha again, to which Keno in response would loudly screech, thus, establishing the perfect piratical ambiance to draw forth cheers and elicit more requests for that required tool of successful toasts and loosening of inhibitions worldwide, more liquor and more beer.

While the raccoon, the pot bellied pig, the cockatiel and the porcupine were constant moveable topics of conversation and careful eye; they were the frosting on top of the ensemble chocolate for the senses that was the rest of the bar.

Yoggee had full control, interior, exterior, everything. Moah and Sean stayed out of the way. Of course, except for times like this day.

Yoggee had made sure that the expansion of the original building ran up and was constructed on the hillock so that from his usual standard operating position in the bar, (behind the bar and cash register) he would never feel closed in, no matter the crowd count, by demanding picture windows aplenty. He also knew that on the busiest of nights, those on the outside would be patient but anxious with anticipation and all important thirst for the swirling dynamics they were witnessing on the inside through the big, expensive but productive, panes of glass. These windows on humanity as Yoggee called them, also allowed him to "view the flatlands of my mind, to see Them (whomever Them were at the time, the Feds, the cops, the organic and changing crowds, just Them) before they come in the door, those of skeletal ethics, the diva dilettantes, the dancing trust funders of deceit, all the ass suckers of America who mistake scorn for respect, yes, I want to see from afar the sad, sad sacks of the delusion and dishevelment, the purveyors of trap door schemes and woeful stories of the ilk that only the insecure and insincere can conjure and execute with shameless aplomb ..Them I want to see long before they find me and their destiny with my drinks and their grimy fisted dreams..."

Sean and Moah, half jokingly felt blessed to have a man, a partner like Mr. Leonard Samson Drummerman in their lives, a man of obvious social skills and love for his fellow man. Even with the current status of apparent disarray as they both knew it was a 24 hour duty being Yoggee's best friends and that it was actually worth it.

What else can be said for an uncanny saloon owner and master abroacher?

Whose best bouncer is a porcupine, has a raccoon for an alarm system, and whose background checks are conducted by a cockatiel...all for minimal cost to the company except to state that there is genius in his stride and style of management. Why the raccoon was dexterous enough to turn door knobs and did not care about the graveyard shift or overtime pay while the assistant enforcer of quality control, Clementine the porcupine, a thirty five pound connoisseur of carrots and fruits, mostly nocturnal like her brother board member, Sage, who only enforced action if threatened or if Yoggee commanded her into action with the code yell, "Bamboozle!", which had never had to have been commanded.

The biggest bikers would keep an angels countenance in Clementine's presence, they being made aware by her occasional vocalizing and by her hard not to notice quills hairs which patrons incorrectly believed could be projected at them if she was disturbed or if Yoggee asked, a prickly peacekeeper, an insurance against brawl or misplaced pride. Clem lived in the back with Sage in a large cage with high cross beams with crooks for both to sleep within. Only once had the quilled one become irked, as she had turned and began to back towards the object of her discontent, a loud mouth patron that was obviously bothering Yoggee in a badgering and belligerent manner..Yoggee had spotted her movement and calmed her with the yells of "TINE, TINE!" which halted her advance on the now docile man before she could lash him with her heavily quilled tail or produce a noxious odor...ah,. The Fill, one of...

Moah interrupted the reminiscence, "You know, Sean, my favorite philosophical statement in life is on a sign just to the right of the Fill's men's room..."

"Sounds appropriate," Sean chided.

It's a quote by Paulo Coelho. He wrote The Alchemist. It says, "When you seek out your own personal legend, the universe conspires."

"And do you recall that right below that quote is where Yoggee scribbled in green kaylo marker ink his oft repeated comment ..." "I get so sick and tired of being perfect all the time. Signed Leonard Samson Drummerman, circa, who knows"?

Moah laughed, "Yes.." and continued, "and this from the man whose initial contact and as he himself would tantalizingly tease, 'for possible future contact work', opening "bar line" is, when confronted with mystery that is the presence of a beautiful woman, "Madam, thank you for the singular honor of presenting me with the gracious gift of your indulgence and with the heaven sent opportunity for me to deliver on and to exceed your grandest libational and libidinous thirsts in the most professional, humble and adoring manner that is within the human realm and that you will ever, ever possibly taste. Will that be cash or credit?"

They laughed and finished their drinks.

The Fill's neighbors and friends had taken up the cause of the animals and the man they had come to view as rare and exceptional, almost extinct examples of defenders of freedom and individualism who stood out in a world now diseased, almost strangled into lemminghood by the creeping holier than thou twisting vile kudzu vine of political correctness. The community showed up and threatened, at early hearings, to throw any elected officials out that acted against the people's favorites and eventually, the habitual foolishness's of those wrapped up in tape-itis rojo and equally afflicted by the misshapen, warped by insecurity, pride of authority that ol' so many governments and ol' so many student body presidents bathe in, ended.

But, continued occasional requests within the past year for Yoggee to appear before someone merely to come in to notarize and sign off on some official paperwork in someone's office in some official capacity that would officially close the book on the previous silliness that occupied a lot of official time, had piled up and were unofficially ignored by Yoggee, as he believed the extra officiating to be offensive and nothing more serious than the remaining act of a system that customarily took a long time to officially close out in an efficient manner official business. As the events of that September day were revealing, it was the wrong move and wrong assumption by their friend most knew as Yoggee or Yoggeemeister, but never as Leonard or Mr. Drummerman.

The plane taxied. The angels were on the ground. Get to pay phone as they both did not like or use cells, except in emergencies. Probably, if overused, an agent of cancer and definitely too easy to track one's movement and life ways.

Moah nudged Sean and pointed out the window to a cat running across the tarmac. They laughed because the cat was black. At least it hadn't crossed their path.

"I know, I know." The feline's presence mutually conjured up another mini billboard's of Yoggee's thinking, and in chorus, "Robinson Crusoe shot the cats, not the dogs!" Somehow, the crass symmetry of coming to the rescue of someone who presented the posture of preferring yapping to meowing, someone which completed the common public expectation of a bar owner comfortable in the usual mayhem of the trade they plied, was someone, yet, no matter the appearance of mob congeniality, who was never easily read nor predictable, but who was in fact an individual of warmed milk gentleness, perfectly sweetened with the sugar cube of a hero's concern for his fellow man, someone conflicted like most of us by the simultaneous nurture and torment of the eternal play of right and wrong. Yoggee was always on perimeter duty for his heart, only allowing exposure to molten emotions, this weakness in the mace of his feelings, rarely, and only to and with a handful of fortunate friends.

And now, this two-legged irascible nicety was in the circle of need again. It did not matter though nor would it ever. He had always been there for the both of us and even though he was a lackey in the art of nuance, he was our company's pied piper of profit and more to the bottom line issue, our brother by another mother.

Walking to the terminal, Moah releases small tension, "On Dixon, on Blitzen, onward to save our cash cow of retirement, our favorite utterer of udder oddity, our factual madman of mirth and merriment. Our one and only, Sean. Sell the smell, he says, the yin, the yang, the aroma, the odor, the dash and the board, sell the smell, gentlemen, because bars aren't gray areas for the brittle, boys. Remember when he said, 'Planning ahead is key to business, war and love. You have Hectors and you have Achilles at the barstools and an owner's priority then is to watch out for all the becoming-more-attractive-by-the-drink Helens that the aforementioned heroes in the making are eyeballing even more closely with probably less than chivalrous intent, plan ahead, right?" Sean joined in... "And he was right about the drinks too. Gentlemen, just like smells and music are the best provocateurs of memory, you must have drinks with names hard to forget." Moah smiled and nodded. The Gerrymander was one of the Fill's festive liquids, served in large glasses reminiscent of an O'Brien's Hurricane glass, they had sold many. Named after Elbridge Gerry of Massachusetts and for the salamander because of the animals shape and its similarity with the awkward shape of a voting district created when old Elbridge was in office. "Who would name their kid, Elbridge, for god's sake," Yoggee derisory exclaims. The concoction was a conception of Yoggee's that mixed Kuala, Baileys, yes, then more Leche el Pero as Yoggee called the final shot of 151 Wild Turkey capped by a celery stick for stirring purposes and for vague nutritional value and forgiveness...

"My, my, how far from the muddy world of the salamander have our pseudo representatives advanced." Moah quickly put thumbs down, adding, "Here's to the progeny of impropriety, the stench, I mean the politico's we're stuck with and to Elmo too." Sean smiled, but he knew the depth of his friend's statement and that it was from Moah's heart.

"When we get to the Fill, I suggest we settle the scene and then settle into a few "Sine Qua Non's" (without which not) with the man the drinks named for."

"Right on. Mix one half grapefruit juice for the Hell in life and one half of any alcohol you want from the top shelf for Heaven, and viola, you have the drink tagged by Yoggee with the Latin name and always accompanied by the funmaster's reframe before one dared put the concoction to one's lips,." which Sean repeated ... 'Admire this, you mere balls of mortal flesh, it's the God's ale, its Sine Qua Non, it's that without which not air, no life, that without which not war, no strife, that without which not love, solo flight, that without which not the cock within the hen, no sin, yeah, no bumpkin kin, yes, it's the Sine Qua Non, that without which not you pucker up and miss the cherry on top of a maidens kiss, that o so mighty forbidden caress of sultry lips, that without which not, my thirsty crew, life really, truly, is the pitiful, pitiful shits." Then, "Glasses unite, and drink, drink as if it's a last fight, fast, furious, battling hard, till finally you fall prey, yet another victim, overcome within the sad vicious lair of the Sine Qua Non of the never ending night."

****

At same moment Moah and Sean were heading to baggage claim, a shot was fired skyward, bringing the gathering at the Fill to a sharper level of focus, a trigger pull executed by the shooter for the measured effect of reminding the surrounders that the surroundee was armed and that surroundee, while well liked, even loved, was still unpredictable and still noticeably irritated at the now hours long standoff. Besides, Yoggee had to continue to stall. Fortunately, Mr. Drummerman' oeuvre was the talent of taking the measure of place, time and people and fully engaging the mix to his benefit. A shot followed by silence could say a lot and Yoggee believed that the unsaid or "loud empty" as he called it, showed undisputable intelligence and control, whether in a book, on a stage, or in this present circumstance, a pause could do a lot for the cause. Hemingway was his author, the master of the unwritten, a writer who let readers fill in the asides and stew over hidden assumptions and massive what ifs. On the stage and screen, Yoggee was partial to Hopkins, whom he praised for the raw edge art of portraying "thought." From Lechter to John Adams, Yoggee would brook no negation that in this, Sir Anthony was supreme. This was Yoggee's deep felt kneel down definition and example of eruditeness and this was noted by the Fill's proprietor as a barometer of the bearing of a person, as anyone lacking this necessity was a Cro-Magnon, barely past Neanderthal graduation. Would seem to Yoggee's view as a precise estimation of the potential and possibilities for the future of the drinker in front of him. Yoggee's was aware of the peaks and valleys of people because of his prejudices and loss memories of his own Neanderthal moments. The owner was fond of the Kabuki in life and believed that a civilized person would and should know that without uttering aloud or even breaking the wind with an "ah", female or male, did not matter to him, the common civility of treasured silence and its knack for never allowing unbridled ignorance to appear, was lost forever for whomever spoke first at the measured bar of the Cranium Fill.

Thirty-eight, thirty-nine, forty... all right, Yoggee concluded that the proper amount of significant quiet had elapsed and would allow him to go against the grain and he began, "Let's pow-wow a truce. You promise no takee Yoggee or attempt to screwee with us, and..."

Sheriff Tisdale cut in, "Yoggee, we're all friends, you know that. Just don't shoot off the gun again, you damn fool, alright? You'll have all those yahoos over the hill itching to get here for the news and then things might really become uncivil and..."

"Uncivil? Good Hell, Sheriff This is civil? Civil, when friends surround and harass friends at the behest of no one heres friends from god knows from which state and from god knows where? Tell me that, Tis!'

"Well, Yogg..."

"Yogg's this, Tis. as he grabbed, well, you know where.

"Now here's the deal. Give me your, and this goes for all of you, your words of honor, no tricks, no serving of worthless pieces of shit papers, no nothing or acts that would cause your children or your children to be, to hate you certain for the rest of your lives, and one at a time, mind you, you are free to use the restrooms. We've also fixed up some lemonade and coffee if you care to. All to go, of course, no meandering inside. What do you say? As Dakotans, do we have a successful parlay here? No tricks."

Tisdale looked around at his associates. "Not a word to the desk messiah's, understood?" Nodded agreement was enough. Thank heaven the news mavens were being kept at bay back at the entry gate by

Watts and Cameron and that a flyover ban had been imposed. Sheriff would send relief to them as soon as his team had taken advantage of the surroundee's offer. The local media also knew well enough not to get involved with any schemes of trespassing through the barbed wire barrier of Yoggees' lands as they knew the owner might actually follow through with the trespassing warning of being shot if it was ignored. It had crossed a few of the reporter's minds when they had heard the shot and echo in the distance when Yoggee had hit the cockerel vane, but the prospect of questionable notoriety, bail money and with no prospect of achieving their most desired of goals, that of finally dislodging the firmly ensconced and well-liked anchors sitting on their highly paid rears back at their stations, through this, in their warped view, intrepid act of gallant reportage on this once in a ratings period story, the anxious smell of an "exclusive" upward fame, eventually drifted away to its final resting place on the level plains of discretion.

Tisdale knew nature called and the warmth of the day and added to the thirst collective and lemonade was the kicker.

"It's agreed. You heard the man. One at a time. And can I have creme in my java, Mr. Drummerman?"

"Come talk to me, Tis. Katy, you're first. Bart will accompany you. You all watch out...Clementine is loose for her morning constitutional and mornings are not the best time for her better nature to come out and as you all know Sage is Sage, so potty direct, alright. No dallying."

Brett brings coffee and lemonade on a tray. Sheriff Tisdale and Yoggee meet midway in the yard.

"Let's have a new start to our day, shall we Tis, a beginning based on an old friendship and a new strategy. This is a procedure of farce and you know it. Did you know that in Estonia ..."

"Estonia?"

"Yes, in Estonia a few years ago, farmers received tax notices for methane emissions from their cows, their cows for Christ sake, Tis! Cows belch, cows are flatulent machines and Euro eco P.C. yahoos saw this natural occurrence as a ripe revenue enhancement section. It's no different here! Tax the air, why don't we? Hell, they tried that with the asinine cap and trade slight of hand and now they have you trying to enforce my signature on some meaningless piece of paper because it makes it easier to close the book on their initial greed inspired stupidities and their culpability in the dark side of blithering, suffocating red tape! Now, dammit, Sheriff, would you sacrifice common sense on the pompous alter of officialdom, if you were an Estonian, or even, even gamble injury in order to uphold the law of the ignoramus ignorattae, all for taxing a cow's ass?" The sheriff knew from experience not to attempt to interfere when Yoggee was on a roll. "Among us, you all muddle all too frequently in the muddy waters of obfuscation and obstruction for others, don't you? For the others to make money on issues just as lame as taxing the passing of gas out of a cow's anus or for this instance, to attempt to seize through maneuver and guile, to force me to accept the wishes of the buccaneers of the almighty buck?

All I stand for, Tis, or would die for, is here, this bar, this land... in essence, I'm fighting this pernicious cancer in our country because I am looked upon as the everyman, an simple Simon dewdrop target in someone else's gun site, and you and officers are the triggers for this misslaw, used in behalf of some other behind-the-curtain scumbag who can pay for the biggest ammo, and who can bribe the most and the weakest of the rotten apples in the political barrel? And you know it's a fact. Just look at America and tell me any otherwise? Hell no, you can't!"

Sheriff Tisdale silently sipped his coffee as he well knew and surmised that no thoughtful patriot could muster a retort to what Yoggee said and he also had to get to the urinal soon and exchange would only prolong Yoggee's resourceful and considered mantra. He was thankful when his friend's cell phone rang.

Yoggee flipped it open and responded in his usual way, "Cotton and Increase Mather's proud relative here; what's your sermon!" No one knew if this heredity was true, but it did stop unwanted salespeople in their tracks.

"Sean!"

Sheriff Tisdale left with Bart to relieve himself.

"You're on your way?"

"Yes, Yoggee, we're getting the rental. Still in standoff mode?"

"Yes, Sheriff and I are having a spot of tea and"

"Tea! Wha..."

"Sean, its okay but get here lick split as everyone is getting thick and antsy."

"Moah's coming up now with the car. Be on 85 soon."

"You know, Sean, this country's lost the ability to search for and own its destinies anymore...hey, is Giddings landed yet? I only got about another thirty or forty minutes of bullshit left in my barrels."

"No. He'll be in about twenty or thirty and we've set his rental up so he'll hit the ground running. And Yoggee?"

"Yeah, Sean?"

"You never run on empty as far as the BS tank, so keep it on the road till we get there."

"Yea...whoo, what the, oh crap." Sean hears commotion in the transmission. "Listen, Sean," wind and muffling, "See ya, got to ru.. Oh.."

"Yoggee? Yoggee?, Are yo..."

More garbled noise.

"Sean, sounds like Sage is ..." Sean could hear the breathing of Yoggee bounding up the stairs of the bar, and thru the doors to noise and echoes of a commotion within.

"SAGE, you settle..." muffle sound as Yoggee apparently had the cell in clinched palm..

"Sheriff, don't move. Clementine, get off the bar, NOW! Bart, you and the sheriff back out behind me here and I'll.." Sean than heard the metallic sound of a pan or other utensil clanging against something...

"YOGGEE?" then he and Moah packed hurriedly and he jumped in the rental as Moah gunned it.

"What' the hell, Sean?"

"Sounds like the zoo is distinctly pissed, Moah."

"Love pets, don't you?" as they both laughed and raced north past the golf course and Spring Lake Park towards the high noon now playing out in the rangeland home where the deer and the antelope roam and the raccoons and the porcupines storm.

The now safely on the outside Sheriff is joined by Yoggee as he responded to the radio alert by Watts as to the arrival of Sean and Moah at the entry gate.

Local satellite camera feeds taped their vehicle heading up the road to the Fill's premises, with the accompanying reporting by the talking heads of Sean Linden's noteworthy presence at the scene.

Moah was first to see the weathervane as they came up and over the knoll. Then the surrounding circle of police vehicles came into view and finally as they pulled up to the edge of the scene, two figures standing midway between what would pass as the front yard of the Fill and its parking area. One of the men was in uniform and had a red or sunburned face and the other is their easily recognizable partner, the man with a beard that never seemed to grow nor never seemed to have experienced a razor either.

Both walked towards the rental as Sean and Moah came to a halt.

"Well, good to see you both alive but this too will pass," the rough faced one joked as he hugged the objects of his loving derision and then turned. "Sheriff Tisdale, my partners, Sean Linden and Moah Halas."

The Sheriff smiled at both and shook hands. "My pleasure, gentlemen. Yoggee says your attorney will be here soon. Can we then possibly resolve this with his help? I just need a legal pink slip to finish up here."

"Attorney Tell will..."

"Giddings Tell?" the sheriff inquired.

"Yes." Sean noticed that the sheriff had a bar towel wrapped around his left hand.

Yoggee picked up on this. "Clementine and Sage kind of joined into this day's soiree and well, Sheriff..."

Tisdale cut in.. "Ah, hell; my fault. I just slammed the lemonade glass down a might too hastily when Sage reared up and Tine started to turn around on us..."

Yoggee added, "Tine was slow though and Sage had just started his snarl dance..."

"On his hinds, Yogg?" Moah interjected.

"Yes," Tisdale responded, "but it wasn't the kids fault. I just came out of the restroom a little too fast and it startled them."

Sean got back to the subject of the day." Sheriff, Giddings has a release form, a written release for Yoggee to sign, some kind of estoppels, I guess, I do not know for sure, but a piece of legalese that will move this situation to an end for today and on to more important things."

"Jumping King of Judah!" Yoggee was on alert with the mention of signing anything. "Sean, this regamastuff that Giddings is bringing..." with a noticeable pitch and tone almost on the edge of cantankerous elidings, Yoggee not being a practicing apothegmatic (A terse practical instructed saying) when riled, "it damn well doesn't admit to nothing, right, Sean? Moah, you know what Giddings got?"

"Damn it Yoggee, stiff the bitch right now, ya hear! Then Moah turned as red as Tisdale's face when he noticed Katie over the sheriffs shoulder. "No offense, maam." Then Moah returned to Yoggee. "This is your mess, brother, because you always definitely march to the sound of your own beat and unfortunately, you're the only man in the damn band and the tune is usually out of key! Listen, Giddings will set the tempo back to what the lyrics require. Got it?"

The sheriff couldn't resist. "Well, I'll be, a flummoxed Yoggee! I can't believe." The laughter was interrupted by the crackle of the radio with Officer Cameron informing the group that attorney Tell was at the properties gate. "Let him in so we can get out of here." Attorney Giddings Tell arrived and without allowing any stuttering or stalling or pontification by Yoggee, made him sign and date on the necessary lines. Good byes were exchanged with Yoggee promising a few rounds to the officers for their troubles. Before the authorities left, they requested Sean's autograph and to shake his hand which he somewhat embarrassingly obliged.

Tisdale closed with, "Mr. Linden, Mr. Halas, please keep him somewhat respectable, tame, will you, at least until we can satisfy the suits," Moah added, "and the robes." When the authorities had left, Giddings turned to the partners," I'm air worn, dusty, and definitely in need of hydration with heft, but don't get me wrong...always' happy to be of service to Cade's friends."

"As about the only lawyer I will ever circumambulate the topic of any day with, welcome. Let's adjourn, gentlemen, to water our holes, shall we." Yoggee continued," How is Cade doing?"

Lawyer Tell brought them up to speed as they moved in to a table where Brett brought them frosted glasses of Heineken. "He's sorry he couldn't come. You know he loves any excuse to leave Washington, any excuse to jump in the middle of anything with you." "To Cade." Moah toasted and then touched Tell on the arm, "Really appreciate you hurrying out here to help."

"Moah, you guys are some of the few clients I have, Cade included, that renew, that kick start my hope again in humanity and the profession I chose." For a moment, no one said anything, as they realized that the attorney wasn't meaning to be lighthearted.

Yoggee brought the atmosphere back to congenial, "Well, I'll be flipped, an attorney with a live bitih conscience."

Giddings tried to scowl at Yoggee, but the beer got in the way. And the games of gosh and josh began around Yoggee's table.

"No doomsday virgins here, right?" Yoggee raised his mug," Here's to the sacrifice, the will, the attitude of pirates, men with half crocodile, half stallion for their mother and their father and lightening for their blood." Mugs met. Beers drained.

Yoggee guided the conversation through various bogs of the brain as he was wont to do; from inquiring of lawyer Tell of whether or not would Yoggee be able to get out of a DUI charge, by jumping out of the car when stopped by the cops, pulling out a bottle of Jack Daniels, take swigs from it in front of the officers, and thereby, whether or not this act would negate the law's ability to categorically state whether or not he had been drinking before getting behind the wheel to then Yoggee throwing out for discussion, why Matthias was the apostle chosen by lot to replace, to succeed, Judas Iscariot?

His method, semi Socratic in origin, though sometimes grammatically traumatized, would often swerve near the solecismistic ditch, but in the nick of time, he would turn the wheel of the nonsensical to the almost knowledgeable, and you always would be happy that you had gone along for the provocative ride.

"In the current cult of 'Right Now', people will read what they see." The beer was kicking into 2nd gear. Yoggee's dissertation continued. "Bias irises occur. Why, it's as natural as having rods and cones in the eye."

Giddings Tell couldn't resist. "Here's to you, my friend of Gabby Hayseian projection, while frequently non- sufferen' succotash in delivery, is in fact, succinctly correct almost, why, almost 49 per cent of the time!"

Moah nudged Sean, "And that's how you can tell when he's high."

"Bart, get some buffalo wings going and make sure the kids are alright, okay?" Yoggee's living quarters were in the rear, three bedrooms couple of baths, a den and the kids area consisted of a large aviary like enclosure within which were large cross beam logs for both Sage and Clementine to sleep in. An oversized doggy door was close for when nature called. Yoggee had painstakingly trained them to be somewhat respectful to humans and always respectful of their dad's house by accepting housebreaking as part of the deal. This exit allowed them to head out to the back yard which was large with a couple of shrubs, a large dirt berm for digging and exploration, all surrounded by a high slick steel fence that neither could scale or dig beneath.

"And Bart, would you please make sure that they are covered for now. They probably need their rest from the tiresome events of our day. Thanks, Barty."

Yoggee turned back to the table. "You know, Keno the cockatiel was the only sane one today." The beautiful lutino chirped from his cage at hearing the mention of his name from his papa.

"The guard bird with an attitude wasn't a significant contributor to the mayhem, good son that he is."

Keno was usually free to roam during the day, a rare bird indeed, as he had been housebroken too, a one in a million shot with a cockatiel. But that day had been different. He had remained quiet throughout the standoff in his cage without the usual squawking protest against confinement. The bar curtains were still drawn in his area of the bar which was the usual A.M. procedure as Keno had the propensity to desire to fly into the windows, apparently in Yoggee's opinion, believing he had found a portal to new adventure and freedom. It had stunned Keno the first and only time he had flown towards the welcoming plains and had run beak first into the hard sand barrier of the picture window. This had upset and scared Yoggee to tears as he had run to the ground and picked Keno up and helped him back to the cage where it took a while for the bird to come back to his senses.

Now, Keno was fully engaged, chirping in, adding to the general hum of conversation at the table of friends and to the usual hubbub of the bar prepping for afternoon and evening business.

"So thank you one and all, you too, Bart, for coming to my aid. The Fill appreciates it." Clinking of glasses in toasts. " Skol and Scat." Yoggee smacks his lips. "Mr. do Tell, this paperwork you flew in with, it just puts a stop to this peck, peck, peck nonsense, right?" Yoggee had just signed and not read the papers. Giddings Tell was the only attorney he trusted emphatically, ever.

"Yes, Yoggee, all you need to do is acknowledge that the judge and his court are in existence."

Moah was more direct." In other words, SHOW UP when the appearance notices start to become more than a fist full, right?"

"But guys, these nothing more than gnat ass sized bothers about code violations or the animals or anything else that is at variance with what these neatniks of normalcy, these house gangs of pc pushers decide what is right and wrong here, waste my time, waste my life with their indulgent inadequacies. Screw em'. I pay good taxes, if there is such a thing. Paid their fricking fines to give them some reason to falsely believe they have a purpose for being..."

Attorney Tell then reasoned "But these add up, Yoggee, and over time, the authorities do tire of having your, well, not yours, but problems, issues atop their desktop blotters, sticky notes with your name on them, attached and prominent enough on their bureaucratically structured calendars of prim and proper that are really pink two inch by two inch squares of alarm, which attract attention of their bosses, their chiefs and thereby upset the nice, the usual don't make waves in their daily existence, if they are not eventually dealt with...and by you ignoring their, what you see as Babbitt like protests, may lead them to being tempted to listen to outside saviors with promises of bigger bags of revenues, more tax funds to play God with and to get you off their desks, off their date books and out of their hair with..."

"Drillers, land men and other corporations of the devil..."

"Yes, and you can slug it out with them during these small feints and tests on principals for maybe six, seven innings, but there might be something lurking in the bullpen, patiently waiting, consistently beseeching the manager, the judge, that they are warm and ready to come in and throw high and tight to lay you low for once and for all...and the manager might listen to this, even allow a spitball here or there, if it means his contract is good for the long term.."

Sean jumped in "Almighty reelection."

"..With no extra innings and with the promise of enlarged licensing agreements..." Moah snipes "the lagniappe of lobbyist's cash."

"The result being he gets to keep his team together into a well funded future and you, you are headed to the dugout, never able to even get to play on your own diamond again as your opponents round your bases and steal home. So, little nicks, here and there, do mean something, Yoggee, and can..."

Moah interrupted

"Can add up to big pricks."

Sean added "and to loopholes becoming the Fill's sinkhole."

"And, Tell concluded "and the future drilling hole for the favored burrowers of the month club."

Keno signaled that the silence was too thoughtful and unnatural for his liking.

"Keno's like a yodel dog in a cage..."

"Kind of like the thoughts in your head, right?" Sean kidded.

Yoggee responded in his usual non sequined manner. "Unlike the rest of this country, gentlemen, there aren't many Starbucks in North Dakota. Most are in Bismarck. But even without these noted dispensaries of caffeine, North Dakota is not slumberous, although I did spy two way too obese but pretty women strolling into Callard's feed store last week which in an odd way made all too much sense to me, but I digress.."

"When don't you?" Moah got in between sips.

"What I am stating is that North Dakota is singular among the mighty forty nine other sister states in so many ways."

Moah, Sean and Giddings knew not to interrupt further the philosopher of the plains, besides; it provided ample time for the pedagogue's unorthodoxies to unfold and for the students to sip on the cool fuel of ale well done.

"This beautiful place is known for its long straight roads and not hurvy-curvy streets but speaking of hurvy-curvy..." the fourth brew was kicking in and the Padron hadn't been an impediment either, "Peggy Lee sang here on local stations, before she went out to the hinterlands of stardom. And Phil Jackson, Hall of Fame coach, born here too, graduated from the school in Williston...and people say North Dakota is short on stature. Hell, we live longer here, in fact, we have the largest proportions of people 85 and older than elsewhere and there are two reasons."

The attorney cautiously went against his training and asks "Why" to a question he did not have the answer to.

"Because, my legitimate eagle, one, there's a scarcity of lawyers and two, there's a butt load of beer."

Giddings, in response to the crack about his profession, "While I have read that North Dakota ranked highest on extroversion and agreeableness, and you, my friend, I propose is the reason why the Bell curve here is so wide, so fat in those subjects....I must note that in that same article, I also read that North Dakotans are, in fact, rated last in openness, which would suggest to me that your study might really be walking in the realm of facade...while the good folks of Utah, were rated the least neurotic and dealt in reality more than most!"

"UTAH!? Why, my misled councilor of the silly and the insane, Utah ranks last in beer consumption, a drastic commentary on any state if there ever was one, and Utah has one of the highest rates in the USA of sexual harassment claims filed by MEN ..Either because, I am sure, women get sparse attention by their men who can't hold up their end of the bargain on a consistent basis. Or, too many wives gang nagging them, perhaps I would file too! I also heard that Utah is the most depressed state in the Union." Giddings shot back "Listen, Dakota fares better dealing with depression..."

"By drinking more..."

"No, because the Dakotans have move psychiatrists and social workers per capita than any other states. And I bet you keep yours on 24/7 alert, don't you?"

"My what?"

"Your psychiatrist, who probably needs a psychiatrist just for dealing with you, you loveable old loon..."

Yoggee laughed, "Skol and Scat" and all drained the beers and a request for more rounds is made.

"By the way, it's taxis for everyone or Bart or Brent will shuttle you when we done..." "And at least, Yoggee, Utahans behave themselves when they do drink; fewer than twenty per cent of their traffic fatalities involve drunk drivers while in this state, even with all your ramrod straight roads, you come in dead last with nearly fifty per cent of your fatalities involving a driver who's over the limit."

Yoggee's habit of increasing fillips with increasing agitation was noticeable and loud on the wood table top. "Giddings, you recall that case in Texas, I think, where the kids of a Mormon enclave were taken away by authorities to see if there was child abuse?" Giddings, with skilled trepidation, "Yes, the Jeffords thing."

"Yes, well your brothers in Lawyering were in mid-season form running up the bill by time extortion and..."

"Time extortion?" Moah was angry at himself for jumping in.

"Yes, by mid-day of the first day of hearings, each kid, each kid, mind you, each Mom, each dog, even, had an attorney..."

Giddings smiling reflected "Representation is vital to democracy..."

"..that by noon or so, only two witnesses had testified and only about the foundation for documents to be admitted later in the proceedings...God Damn, one Texas State trooper was cross examined by hordes of these attorneys, each asking him the same damn question in the same damn words on behalf of a child, a parent or the dog...and each of these bill by the minute for repetitive minutia lawyers got the exact same answer from the poor trooper...and you say attorneys have a soul...but don't get me wrong, I love you, Gidds, just as Cade and these boys do, because I do respect the toughness you must have to choose a career path where nothing is beyond the pale."

All laughed as it is understood that this is how men show affection for each other, by degradation and dismissal.

Sean had been lean on participation and interjected. "I've read where we have become so litigious a sad sack society in this once great land, I feel that there's a constant screech, a never ending noise perfume of the absurd...for example, a friend mentioned a case to me where clients of some business have filed complaints, legal complaints, over being served coffee in plastic cups and then feeling slighted by witnessing other clients being served the same coffee in a porcelain or some other high faulting demitasse ass container!

People do not have a right to not be offended."

"But, "Yoggee entered in," your fellow practitioners, Mr. do Tell, will still try to find a path to litigate if coin can be made in behalf of people too ignorant to be ashamed or insulted by their own idiotic choices and actions. What's wrong with this cartoon, councilor?"

Again, laughter cut the moment in half with the soft edged knife of jagged male bonding, a puzzle piece place women never enter, and where insults traded is the commodity of comradeship and affection.

"By the way, Giddy, I've never asked, "Yoggee continued, "where the hell are you from?" Sean and Moah smiled as they knew the answer.

"Fifth generation Mormon from Orem."

Yoggee's expression was worthy of a ticket. Almost spitting beer but not quite, "Jesus H. and Brigham Young too! A Mormon lawyer! I rest my case for the assumed and the amazed. But that's the bigness of the Fill. It takes all types and all types are welcomed. A toast, my blood friends. Bring some fresh cold grog, will ya, Brad?"

"Yes, sir."

"And bring frosted ones for Bart and yourself too. Got prep done, right?"

"Of course, Yoggee."

With fresh fun fuel in hand, Yoggee stood for another dedication, "To the Cranium Fill, where the world comes to throw caution and concern to the four winds of nonchalance, where that which once was understood possibly as important is now matter of fact, where chivalry is not seen as a weakness, where beautiful is a woman's bottom and not the bottom line. It's Fill time, a Fill for all against the slings and arrows of a world gone upside down. To the Cranium Fill, a happy synaptic zippy do dah adventure to a sparkling thinking' place, a train off the known track for oil rowdies, for the convicted and the unconvinced, for clean bikers and biker babes who aren't, a haven for the hurting and the hunting, it's the from the heart all in the head chill of an over the fence thrill of a surprise solution, yes, here's to the ever active, never dormant den of equity, the ever loving' Cranium Fill. Skol and Scat! Bart, Brad, and Brent, a few more please but no more for you as you need to stay deferential enough to handle tonight. And the kids are okay?

"They are covered and resting."

"Good. Good, thank you. And please round up more fixings than these wings, boys. We will eat and then we'll get you taxied to your rooms."

Moah dug into the original gist of their present gathering. "What big boy have you pissed off besides these local aficionado's, Yoggee?"

Giddings jumped in, "Oil, obviously."

Sean added, "You're the thorn in the lions paw and the lion's not used to not being free to prowl wherever it wants. Listen, Yogg, is there any other issue we need to know about?" "Hell, no. You nailed it. They want the land."

Giddings clarified "No, they want what's beneath."

"Other people's possessions, other people's money," Moah sneered "for the least expense incurred, as usual."

Yoggee focuses on the attorney. "Giddy, as my favorite master and practiced purveyor of gadgets of gullibility and slobbering morality plays..."

"Thank you for the compliment and shared insight."

"I've not had the time recently to find the sum of this predicament, now, mind you, I have had queries, what ifs, thrown my way by various idea schemers, pretty land women, even an attorney like yourself, but much more handsome, of course.."

"Of course."

"And he said that he represented Lambs and Lions Development Limited..."

"Come on!" Moah disparaged.

"Really had a card with that name on it and bold enough to give it to me..."

Moah added, "Awash in syrupy Christianity, with the too slick by half quality only a Swaggert or a Clinton could envy, I'm sure."

"Or a Mormon." Giddings continued, "He wanted to deal you in to a lease for drilling, right?"

"Of course."

"This is a veneer company doing recon for..."

Moah sneered, finishing Tell's sentence "Hawkins-Burke."

"Magi?" Sean blurted.

"Magi, Inc. Indeed." Giddings agreed.

"Well, well. Two plus two still equals four." Yoggee continued on the theme of the obvious "The almighty pursuit of whatever it takes, executed by the hired anal cavities of others without standards or strength of character or regard to what's left in their ugly wake."

Keno chirped at the difference in the tone of his master's voice.

"Boys, start raising my bail money now because I'll need it if one of these quirks of birth comes in the Fill again. It's our bar and it's my section land. Long family held and my inherited families, yours too. These jackals can seize these," as Yoggee grabbed his crotch just as Bart delivered the sub sandwiches, "and I'll make them enjoy it before I cut theirs off!"

Sean Linden had yet to contribute much to the verbal jousting, as the beer had proved a pleasing calm to the semi-roughhouse mentality of the day. A trained listener and studious observer of emotions and the language of the body under threat or duress, he now jumped in before the others could respond. "Yoggee, level it all out now. Moah, Gidds and I don't want any more roller coaster days for the business. Nor do you, I know. This property, this business is ours. It's protections, its rights, and correct me, Gidds, if I am wrong, goes back to, why, the field of Runnymede, centuries ago..."

The others were glad to see that they were not alone speaking in tongues, otherwise recognized outside of the walls of a church, as communication, dappled and nuanced, perfected only by distance from the proximity of a saloon and, once entered, the time elapsed within said confines "..When King John acknowledged that he did not have absolute power over his lords, subjects, whatever they went by in England when he, John, signed the Magna Charta. The U.S. Bill of Rights, written because the barnacles of their day, the Red Coats, had abused the Colonies. Provides that property can't be taken for public use or private use, without just cause and just compensation, right Gidds?"

Moah "Not today it isn't, Sean." Then turning to Gidds, "Define public use, define it, Gidds, define it in this day of rigged wording, where pledges and signatures are not worth the ink spilled, and these times of legalized bribery. Clear it up for Pollyanna here." Sean shot a grimace at Moah but before he could vocalize his feelings, Giddings broke in. "It used to mean the community good would be served. A road, a school, as long as an arms length fair price was agreed to, it was considered proper. Then the Supremes fucked it up decades ago and abuse became the ready, willing and able order of the day. "Public use" was then redefined in the ambiguous and slippery swamp of something called "Public purpose".

Yoggee raised his new frosted beer "Thank you, old holy robes," Moah corrected the toast with, "Holy robbers, don't you mean?"

Yoggee continued "yes, for..." but Giddings edged in with "and for later redefining "public purpose" to the even hairier can't argue against without gobs of money term, "public benefit". I want yours because it benefits my people. Soo sad, soo fiendishly friendly, a hopeful carapace against attack..." Giddings was now perhaps over the legal limit but he and the others were in give no quarter moods and he raised his mug, "To my CEO's, the Supremes!"

"Up theirs!" Moah vocalized with true intent.

"No, Moah, unfortunately, up ours. as these judges have brought forth and allowed "public benefit" to be morphed by financial Frankenstein's into..."

Moah interrupted Gidds again "Attorneys and politicians, no slight intended, Gidds..." "Yes, they allowed this thing on the table, to twist into a deformed meaning that permitted real estate promoters and developers with enough political clout to pull the strings of the puppets in their purchased government to do the dirty work of scattering, legally scaring off home and business owners who stood in the way of their desires, satiating this gluttonous drive for higher tax revenues by these hyenas of incumbency to use and to continue their legislative feasts for them and their friends on the carrion of those they initially promised to protect and not roast." Mr. Tell paused to sip on the very un-Mormon like liquid. "From my earliest days, gentlemen" and turning to Keno," and guard bird, I've fought in what was once thought a noble profession, a bulwark against instances such as where political groupies and sniveling snipers labeled neighborhoods as blighted to justify seizing said blighted areas for quote, public benefit, unquote,. thereby transferring homes and business's from rightful owners to their friends, the thieves who wanted to erect the stacked luxury of expensive condos or to be allowed to promote enhanced revenue structures as their co-desperado's, the politicos, saw them because "swank" means "bank" to hold up artists of all stripes..."

Sean commented, "Horizontal stripes would be the best fit" Moah added,

"These bastards covet their neighbors land more than their neighbor's wives, don't they?" Yoggee jumped back into it "Bullshit. Both!"

"As you are well aware, these defects of humanity, reward their favorite corporations and developers and what do you know! These objects of their attention also happen to be the anointed group's biggest contributors, do ya think?" Gidds paused. "The third rail of this, the Supremes inspired skunk works, is the sad fact that the lifeblood of these vote gathering vampires is the tax bonanzas derived from these despicable acts perpetrated on the broken backs, the broken dreams and the broken homes of others.

I've witnessed attempts to declare eminent domain against churches, churches who offer no monetary reward to the great enactors, solely in order that the chosen few can turn the property over to subsidized, kiss their big ass companies who promise to provide cities with pockets full of that good old keep incumbency rolling lubrication, cash. Now Vaseline of another sort is blight. Blight is a concept that is so open to interpretation, to manipulation and to big money it just waits to be misused. Why, I once was involved in defending an area of a city that was declared blighted because some of the buildings were found by, guess who, that's right, city inspectors, to have had chipped paint. For chipped paint, a building can be demolished! Welcome to my loophole nightmare!"

Moah, astonished. "That can't be. That is ins..."

"Oh, yessiree! " Yoggee was in the thick of it again. "Never underestimate a bureaucrat's ability to stoop lower than dearly departed six feet under dead and buried."

"And they tax them too," noted Sean.

"Public benefit has come to mean whatever politicians say it is and since the 1950's it has mainly been the mechanism of the maniacal to grab land on the cheap. No joke. I know where a used car dealer was cleared out for an Audi dealership. In fact, the definition of blight is so broad now, my fellow imbibers, that I have had to defend against insidious term for what all of us would consider, when sober, as well maintained, neat properties. Make no mistake. Private entities benefit from the perversion of justice. The Supremes abdicated their watchdog roles..."

Sean interrupted "Gidds, I thought blight meant hazardous, falling down, dilapidated, even something abandoned."

"With enough money, Sean, meaning has no meaning."

"The definition of "is" strikes again" recollected Moah.

"Blight, gentlemen, now means any place of, and I quote, any place of economic underutilization, unquote. Yoggee," as Giddings turned to him, "if the Fill paid less in taxes than say a 7-11..." Moah cut in, "or a whorehouse", Giddings finished, "it could be or maybe qualify as blighted."

"Jumping Judah!"

"Or a nice place for an oil patch "Moah surmised.

"Count on Mr. Halas for a reality check" noted Sean.

Giddings stayed on track. "Sandra Day O'Connor, on the day the gutless wonders decided in the most fuckable way possible in the Kelo v New London case, she said, "The specter of condemnation hangs over all property. Nothing is to prevent the state from replacing any Motel 6 with a Ritz-Carlton, any home with a shopping mall or any farm with a factory."

To which Yoggee responded "HA, got them there! This country doesn't have farms or factories left!"

Moah conjectured "Giddings, that means any fool group of the bought and the paid for who serve those other than those that elected them, may evict some poor slob citizen to benefit someone richer who pays them, contributes to them to commit the robbery under the guise of acting in some municipalities best concerns, and this is all legal? This is today what is considered right? I'm damn sure that Jesse James and the Sheriff of Nottingham are surely pissed that they aren't alive now, I betcha!"

"Fortunately, one redeeming quality of the vocation I have chosen is that I have had the opportunity to defend people, citizens, against forces of what common sensed people would say are evil and indefensible and I have, thank God, won more often that I've lost."

Sean's cut to the quick training honed in. "But you have lost."

Before Giddings could respond, Moah mused, "That Kelso thing eviscerated the Fifth Amendment. A government without limits is a government to be destroyed, isn't it?" Yoggee pounded the table, "I suggest we drink faster and increase the economic utilization of these premises. We don't have a moment to lose. Brad, bring another round of Padron, poor favor! Remember, Happy Hour must be maintained at all costs. And Bart, would you pull the curtains. I want to look out on what this day's been about."

And then answering his own question, "Even with the Bakken thing, we still bank on the soil. That's how I am and will always be."

Even with the annual 20 inches of northern plains rain and snowmelt, Yoggee had successfully cultivated spring wheat, barley, flax and sunflower seeds from the dark soils. Farms in the Dakota's have been halved since World War II, but farm size doubled. In the mid to late 1800's, Yoggee's Scandinavian relatives bought options on tracks from the railroads and the government, filing land claims under the Homestead Act of 1862 and the Timber Culture Law of 1873, accumulating enough acreage for the section which Yoggee now proudly owned.

They followed Yoggee's gaze towards the West. "Distance is a good thing when distance means too far from materials, too far from markets...this limited industry on the plains and until recently, this meant insulation from my neighbor's noise and swirl. The high rolling plains, the buttes, the crew cut mesas, this is my reality and I think it's a good grip on what quality is about."

The padron is served. "Although for the life of me, I cannot figure out why half of the radio stations in Williston are contemporary Christian and yet, you all, well, almost all, know our bottom line, we're a cash cow nourished at the engorged teat of sinner's weaknesses.

But, this is the land where cows meander into towns and graze in gardens, break satellite dishes and are then charged with cow-at-large misdemeanors, so I ask, why the amazement at paradox in a particularly peculiar place with particularly peculiar people. What'd you expect?"

Then Yoggee swerved to serious again "The thing the new money's chasing is a mixture of black shale, silt and sandstone, formed during Late Devonian to Early Mississippian ages, now called the Bakken Formation and said by the know it ails to be one of the largest oil finds the US Geo boys have ever surveyed and fracking makes it so."

"Late De fracking what?" Moah spat out.

"It's horizontal drilling, not vertical. Means fracken more profits" Giddings continued "Hydro fracturing produces increased porosity in rock that eases movement of oil or gas to the well. One well drains more volume, produces more resources than before..."

"And more freaking concerns."

"Yes, it can, Yoggee. Horizontal drilling means one well can cross beneath several properties and any owner who owns less than a good piece of property, has to divvy up royalties with several other owners; both drillers and owners deal with more bookkeeping, more negotiations, more lawsuit potential, .."

"For spills? What?' Sean asked.

Yoggee beat Giddings "Spills are the least how about water contamination? Hell, they use chemical mix, methanol, God knows what else for fracturing, Giddings, and our friend's property is a number one prospect for those bent on drilling," bent" because..."

Moah cuts in, "Because Yogg's section is one large mother load off land, matched with just one mother'f er to deal with, they gain control without all the hassles of most deals. No wonder the appetite to feed here is calling all vultures. It doesn't matter what the bar tab is to Lions and Lamb, Magi or whatever other name is on the rock they crawl out from under, it's worth any bribe, any act to control."

"I know I'm a knot in the wood. Plenty of my neighbor Dakotans are making more than they ever would in wheat. Building's up. Employment's up. What do you expect when the state issues drilling permits in less time than it takes to wipe your ass? Little less hubbub now, but." Yoggee paused to reflect. "I don't want junk pumped into my groundwater. I don't want flares of burning gas warming my sky or spoiling my views, and I damn well don't want the dust of progress I distrust kicked up on gravel roads I never want built. Is truth only a myth today? If even an air ace from Nam, a Republican activist, mind you, can be turned bribable, burpable, and branded by the hot iron of greed for life, it can happen to anyone. Why, today, Diogenes would be wandering these wastelands holding his flame in hand at high noon, still looking for an honest man and still found wanting, I'd bet you that!" Yoggee recovered the mood from the reflective silent and pushed it to the lighthearted "It's a good thing that people seek relief from the crust and rust in their days and come here for little bits of happy and lots of draft beer to clear the funnel ways of thought, agree?"

But Moah stayed serious "Deceit can hang in the air. Had a Nam vet sergeant once, he'd been a tunnel rat, brave son of a bitch, and he shared his experience of how smell saves lives. He shared how his group would know of ambushes before they were trapped by catching a whiff of the enemy before they would see them. It seems the V.C. used kerosene for illumination in their caves and when they would come topside, the smell remained with them and alerted serge and his guys to their presence. But the Cong would sometimes smell the weeks of "jungle" on the Americans before they came in view too...so whoever caught a whiff of the aroma of deceit first would handle the situation the best. Just like business or dating, good to know about something going wrong before it does..."

"Our technologies have made our connections a slender thing and our true senses scatter to the winds." Sean suggested. "Something horrible happens and after the initial shock, it's just another three minute package on the news. The next morning, we turn on our internet, we scan another account of another diseased act, a question without an acceptable answer, implicating us all in its horror and its attraction and its morbid connection to our own mortality, and then we escape to the comfort of another website and another abomination or cause ??? and the treadmill of mind numbing stimuli continues until at the end of your day, you realize, you have wasted it on the meaningless and the profane and it's time for bed." This was surprising commentary from Sean Linden, as the others saw him as a positive light no matter how dark the perception of the moment.

Attorney Tell quickly and figuratively took the floor while still, in fact, physically very much attached to the bar chair "Today's informational breeding pools are nothing more than styled interruptions designed to keep common sense attached to the supercilious and the routine. Why? Because never question what's legal and what's not. Why? Because there's a different set of laws for each level of status in America's caste system, that's why. There is one set of laws for the corporate board member and one set of laws for the woman using food stamps, one set of laws for a juvenile delinquent and one for the molester priest, one set of laws for the pimp, another for the prostitute. Overwhelm people with laws and give the power of deferential judgment to a select untouchable few, and law whores up all meaning as a communal, equal reference point for any decision and general respect for the law is justly lost."

"Amen and Hallelujah, brother!" Moah yelled. Sean nodded and smiled at the sad wisdom of what was just said. Yoggee appeared stunned.

"And I quote" Giddings now stood. "The whole aim of practical politics is to keep the populace alarmed-and hence clamorous to be led to safety-by menacing it with an endless series of hobgoblins, all of them imaginary, unquote."

Yoggee stood too. "Skol and scat!" After the toast was downed he yelled to Brad, "Call the taxi and make sure the Bar Stars are going to be here for opening at five, alright."

A "yes sir" came from the kitchen and before Yoggee could speak, the attorney continued, "I tell you, a guilty person has the odds, has the angels in his favor of walking out and getting parole than an innocent person has of being found not guilty and going to jail. It's true. I went after a child killer in my early career. The killer had over 20, 25 federally protected constitutional rights and the parents of the murdered kid had zero. What a country? What a law, huh? The kicker is, this beast had been arrested 10 times before, all arrests and convictions and costs of parole paid for by taxpayers, mind you, but the biggest sabotage by the justice system was the sick twist, you ready, that because the defendant's attorney was ill and had been granted the okay to step out of the courtroom for a five minute recovery break and during this absence, the bastard muttered aloud, "I did it" Said it twice to the amazed crowd. I immediately requested summary judgment but the judge was taken aback by the action and before she could think and respond, the defense attorney entered and when apprised of the situation, asked for a mistrial. This to my gut sickness, the judge, upon finding her ability to speak, said yes and threw the confession out!" To the "what the's and "bullshit" pronouncements of his friends disbelief, attorney Tell responded, "She threw it out because of a Supreme Court judgment that a defendants lawyer must be in the room when a confession is made!" "Come on!"

"Kid you not! I still don't know if it was planned." Giddings looked down at the table. "And I have never been able to erase the faces of those parents from my mind."

Moah stood up too" What happened to the freak?"

"Well, he was retried, avoided the death penalty, cost more trauma to the family again and more dollars to the sucker taxpayers and did serve time but under the law, something at the time called mandatory parole law, he was required to serve no more than half of his sentence and he ended up serving what I guess judges see as the value of an eight year old girl's life, 13 years, six months and 13 days."

"I have read somewhere" Sean broke the painful silence "that killers are five times more likely than over convicts to kill someone after they are released."

"Didn't follow much on this guy after that." Gidds mused. "Put him as far away from my thinking as possible but will never forget his quote; one of the officers sent me a clipping of when the shit was let out. He said, "Some of you all might say I am lucky. I say you all are wrong. I am not lucky. But what I can say for sure though is that the stooges that came up with this rule, why, they are just stupid pricks."

They spotted the taxi coming up the drive.

Yoggee walked them out to meet it and told them he would drive the rental into town in the morning and that they would all have breakfast before Moah flew back to work and Giddings left for D.C. Sean had decided to stay a few days.

As Moah had opened the door of the cab, he turned and hugged Yoggee and said " Except for us and a few other noble fool friends of ours, never forget, that in our world, today, we must all tread carefully because now, trust is only in the dust, a crushed reminder of where greatness use to trod. Skol and scat!"

The taxi turned south and as it was close to 5 o'clock, animals were ready and humans were arriving to be fed and their thirsts quenched, signaling another evening was about to commence at the good time gathering place formally known as the Cranium Fill And Automobile Emporium.

Chapter 2

Stellae Errantes
(Wandering stars)

"There are as many painters as morning stars but artists are few."

Tu Fu, Chinese poet Tang Dynasty

September 17, 2015

On Yom Kipper, Williston's Laughing Garter Shopping Center witnessed the timeless act of systems colliding and destinies uniting in the eternal recess yard of universal happenstance, where haphazardness teeter totters with randomness and within which the heart and the mind cling to the galactic jungle gym of emotion whose heights are limited only by the restless law of serendipitous bliss. All because of a parking space.

Sean and the other car saw the one available space at the same time. Sean waved for the woman to go ahead. As the sedan pulled into the spot, Sean glanced from the profile of attractiveness moving in front of him to his rear view mirror just in time to see the red car speeding towards him but not quickly enough to brace for the impact. He heard the siren just as he felt the giant shove. His rental spun. As she jumped in her seat, she glanced towards the origin of the smashing metal. She glimpsed the door of the compact opening through the crust of the scene, saw the door of the rammer open, noticed the black and white braking then saw the gentleman jump up and over the Audi's hood and onto the about to run driver and cause of the melee. The leap knocked the disheveled almost homeless looking man to the ground and then fists punished the culprit. She had never seen punches thrown with the rapidity of the man on top. The cop rushed in, pulled them apart and snapped the cuffs on the bloodied one on the pavement. She jumped out and rushed to the other man now prone on the pavement.

He was massaging his forehead. She heard the cop asking if he was alright and thanking him too. "This son of a bitch escaped the 7-11, held em up and stole the car." Another patrol car was pulling into the lot. "I'll call in an ambu..."

"No, no, I'm fine." She thought his voice calm and beautiful. "Maam, I will need you as a witness, please stay here."

"Yes, officer." The policeman noticed a familiarity with the voice but could not place the lady in the worn jeans and T-shirt or the face behind the big sunglasses.

"Thanks. Call this in and be back in moment" He left with the stunned robber to meet the other officer.

She turned and stared down and saw that the man was covering his eyes and that the rest of him was handsome. He was blurry eyed and the sun blinded as he squinted up. He tried to focus and after a few seconds he centered in on the longest, loveliest four legs he had ever seen close up.

"Are you all right? God! Don't talk. Don't move. I've got some wipes that will. .."

"I'm all ...I'm a little knocked down but"

"Shush, let me wipe your brow." She saw his eyes. His vision cleared.

They looked at each other. Mouths were open but silent, momentarily deprived of the power of speech as they stared.

As he looked up into her concerned continence he swore an iridescent almost mother of pearl halo circled her and thought that he must have been whip lashed harder than he first thought. Her sunglasses were now pulled back and up over her brow.

"I hate to sound simple but has anyone told you that you bear a striking and wonderful, I might add resemblance to Odessa Gabriel?"

She laughed and smiled, "Yes." She knew his features from somewhere too. Knowing the pain of indecent familiarity with someone you have never met before, it was avoidance at first glance, a momentary turn away time for both.

Sean Linden had lost all reasonable faculties when he first spotted this beauty of the kliegs. Odessa was not prepared to meet the man of her real life dreams, but when is one ever. In the flesh, in front of her now. He noticed her tremble.

"Do I look that bad?" He was finally over the accident and sitting up.

She hesitated at the thoughts streaming forth, heart to head as she quickly recalled the only other man or so called man to twix her ever, bewitch beyond anyone before as the man on the asphalt awed her now. The other man had taken months for her to see the star potential beyond the starting sparks. But this one, oh my.

"No. You look great dirty." Their laughter was cut short by the officer.

"Great job, sir. This fugitive was wanted for murder in Iowa."

"What?"

"Yeah, APB for him from yesterday. He just admitted it. Killed his wife and said it was because the marriage had grown inadequate."

"Inadequate!" Odessa is in disbelief.

"And robbing a 7-11 made it all adequate?"

"Well, Mr. Linden, yes, I recognize you, sorry, but he also, get this, said that he and his lady just had a lack of similar interests. Some people, huh?" Odessa now knew her prince.

"Look, officer, when you and the other officer report this in, neither of us wishes the glare of publicity. As a favor..."

"No problem, Sean. And as a friend of Yoggee's, short term memory is now SOP. You and Ms. Gabriel, we'll keep you out of it as long as we can. You better get as the press is around the corner."

So it was her. She smiled at him as she and the officer helped him to his feet.

"Get in my car, Sean. Thanks, officer. I'm not, neither of us were part of your day, right?"

Yes maam, yes maam....ah, could you sign this please? You too, Sean? "Quickly, quickly."

They signed and Sean asked if he could arrange a tow for rental back to agency. "Will do." As they hopped into Odessa's car and started the engine. They heard an ambulance as they backed up and began to exit the Laughing Garter Shopping Center as Odessa asked; "Can I treat you to coffee, tea..." the "or me" was left unsaid.

They laughed. Sean suggested, "I'm sure we can find something on the bypass or University..." "That's discreet..."

"You are who I thought you were even without makeup, hair wrapped in a bun and the big dark glasses, Ms. Gabriel."

"Odessa, Sean, its Odessa."

"It's my pleasure."

"And you, Mr. Linden, are hard not to notice or forget too..."

Parking wasn't a problem as the cafe was almost empty. The booth leather made the loudest noise in the establishment as they sat. It overcame the waitress bussing bottles and the sad country song playing on the static enhanced overhead speakers.

"The excuses to kill are a dime a dozen these days. No common interests!

What horseshit! Justice, Sean, is an unworthy bitch living on past glories. We pay for murderers and molesters to breath and then set them free while druggies stay locked up."

"There's a thin membrane between crazy and sane..." "..And attorneys paid to keep it so."

"No family is immune from low tides. Even Einstein, one of his sons, he was diagnosed with schizophrenia and ended up in a psychiatric ward." Odessa liked this man. "I know you must be sane, Mr. Linden."

"And why is that, Ms. Gabriel?"

"Because from what I have read, seen, you shun celebrity, trappings and tricks." Sean almost blushed.

"But I, on the other hand bleed celebrity or I die." "So opposites might just attract after all."

Odessa did blush but recovered quickly, "Celebrity is not about being seen...it's about fans coming to see me so I can see them. They want my recognition of their existence. They want to think that their image, that special "look" by me at them standing in the smiling mass, that I will remember what I say forever, that I will recall their face, their smile or some other singular peculiarity that they believe all their lives makes them special or different. Sad so sad that this is so human, so frail a thing, that means so much to so many, recognition that, hey, I'm different and you, me, took notice of my existence...ha, little do they understand that I barely remember who I am, let alone recall any of them. It's a brittle game of gotcha, got me where both seer and be seener deal in foolish realms of fantasy and artful neglect, the wonderful waltz of the crazy and the sane."

The waitress brought their coffees. Sean takes a slow, 'thoughtful' sip. He likes it black. Odessa stirs the sugar in hers. Cream closes the deal for her.

"Dark and light?" "Men and women" "Crazy and sane?" "God's punch line" "What?"

"Relationships" Odessa was deep in his eyes. "Dostoevsky, I studied him in a review about his plot, his story, The Idiot, and in it he says all relationships have problems, they're eternal, unsolvable, beyond reason and dependant on non conformance and abnormal behavior, kinky cool, huh? Do you agree moncherie?"

Sean was taken aback by the actress's reference to one of his favorite authors, to Dostoevsky, a man who had come within a nudge of death by firing squad, a balancing moment Sean could touch with experience, and then glancing from the surprising depth of her eyes to over her right shoulder as a vehicle was flying, left to right, through the air turning once mid flight, Odessa turned to see the where and the why of Sean's widening eyes, she gasped too as she and the 6 or 7 other people in the establishment collectively held their breath as the car hit the vacant lot across the street, rolled once, dust rising, coming to rest on its drivers side and the loud groan/sigh of the collective audience released, no one moved except Sean , who rose, but halted as he and the others saw a hand rise up and through the open window of the crumpled passenger door, followed by a tousled blond tufted head. People stood in place as the man pulled himself out of the Volvo and shook himself off, waved to two pedestrians approaching the scene and then came towards the cafe and through the door to the amazement of the diners and coffee fiend and asked if he could use the phone since he couldn't find his cell and he needed a tow truck. The stunned cashier gave him her phone.

Odessa called to him, "What happened?" The man waved to her and the others with a humble dismissiveness. "Got hit from behind, ran up a trailer ramp in front of me and trapeze time, here we go!"

Sean could not see if the man was in shock. He could have been as he was working at behaving normally. "Did you see who hit you?"

"No, but..."

Another man hurriedly entered. He was the driver of the truck that was towing the trailer ramp that had been the launching pad for the accident. He had circled back, parked his rig and was now next to the survivor. "Brother, I couldn't do. I didn't see, it was a red rig and is still heading north, I think. Didn't get license as I was watching you in the. Well, I mean, you were flying..." "It's okay, man, I..."

"But I did get company name and..."

Sean turned back to the real center of his attention. Odessa turned to him as he said, "Powerful brain chemical, adrenaline."

"Yes, pheromones a popping everywhere today, wouldn't you say, Mr. Linden?" Nearly two thirds of us believe in love at first sight, some within the first hour of meeting the other. There must be mystery though; that there is so much more adventure to follow in finding out more about each other. It has been called a chemical rainbow, a kaleidoscopic "rush" of relation and touch.

"Come on, man. I'll get you a tow buddy of mine and your Volvo to a body man of mine. You need to call insurance too." The accident victim turned from the helpful but excited trucker and tipped the cashier. "What's this? I don't ..."

"Take it. I need to cover all my bases today, Maam. I still have to get to the shop." The cashier interrupted, "But you need to see a doctor or at least..."

"I'm alright, Maam. God didn't laugh at me today. He smiled."

And with that the men left and the cafe settled in to normal again, dishes pinging, orders called and a new country song of woe on the radio.

Still happy at the fact of their privacy, Odessa and Sean returned the mutual escape of each other's disguise.

"It's rare that you get to redo, to retake the big, the money shot in real life." Odessa is musing aloud about what had happened. "We all should be able to dance at the ball at least once, shouldn't we Sean?"

"Something about Sinbad the sailor, not the comedian..." She smiled affectionately. "I read years ago, stuck. It said that Sinbad, quote, 'used life joyously, eating prime meats, drinking delicately, lying soft and dressing rich."

She savored these wonderful words and the man before her. Was he racy too?

"I have a favorite quote." "Yes?"

"Would you take it lying down or would you lie down first and bait the hook?"

She laughed with the giggle of a schoolgirl who had been around the playground more than once and he liked it.

"Who said that?" "I did and I do."

It was a moment tantalized in which speed and time are lost as well as the occasional heart. Many topics were covered. She joked about her marriages and vowed she believed in monandry to which Sean teased that in botany that meant 'the condition of possessing only one perfect stamen.' Ah, she noted, he could be provocative.

They both would remember later that this was one of those precise times etched in Rembrandt sepia light and dark play, forever brilliant in detail and fondness.

She felt comfortable enough to respond to his inquiry of why of all places was she in Williston? She responded 'destiny', than responded honestly, "Sean, I have an autistic son in a private clinic not far from here. His dad, well, we never married, but he loves and supports him too. We both visit frequently but secretly. Only our agents ..."she hesitated, "yes, he is in the frickin business too...only our agents know."

Before Sean could recover, Odessa continued, "His name is Robert and he is my truth, my song of love. I do have him with me sometimes in Hollywood, not enough as it is hard for me and my assistant to care for him 24/7." Anticipating his next question, 'He is almost 16."

Sean looked at this screen enigma and was honored by her quick read of him. She knew her "other side" was secure with him.

"Legends are a dime a dozen these days, aren't they?" Curious statement by her, he felt.

"Twenty four seven means value is not as weighty as before and mystery is all but gone." Odessa mentioned Madame Curie as an icon of hers since childhood. "She still doesn't get the credit she deserves ...what she inspired, well, she, her celebrity eventually was nowhere to be found, replaced by others idols of desires and aspirations, sacrificed at the false alter of ersatz accomplishment. In other words, women often get screwed and men brag about it." Ah, an earthy philosopher and Sean loved it.

Sean opened up to her as she was naked to him. He shared that in his teens, he was ingrained with a sense of otherhood, almost biblical, he said, in the concept of 'standing for those that can't', loving those that others would not, a quiet bully pulpit for the dispossessed, a Kennedy approach to the future of if not, why not...from the early time of school recesses of elementary grades when the boys played 'tackle the guy with the football,' only a vague myth in the litigious school grounds of today he added, all against one and the ball carrier had to run the gauntlet and when tackled in a pile on, still cling, like a heroic prince of lore, to the ball no matter the tugs of the hair or the scratching and clawing, no way give up the ball until the bell rang for classes. Odessa now understood why this man was the way he was, with this tenacity, fire from the schoolyards of his youth, remained in him, the man who had continued on in the dangerous playground of the adult world of the hardened stances of play for keeps killing fields of tyrants and international tugs and tirades delivered in real blood and dangerous bluff. Odessa was emotionally overdrawn. She believed she was in the rare presence of a pleasurable man, unafraid of his own skin and she felt that true guardian angels of the public work overtime and the actual ones dismiss the hoopla surrounding their contributions to the events secured by their efforts and this one, Sean, was a genuine and humble soul, who indeed despised the modern style notoriety that cascades, that comes with what was once considered the common, and not of the singularity for its present rarity of as she heard Sean now saying, "simply doing what is right for others; without the present amoral calculation of how such acts can benefit the self, bitter commentary," Sean continued, "on our times of guessing on what is ethical to misplaced acclaim and opinions of dismaying and paper-thin cliche.

If angels had a union, Odessa, they would have gone on strike for better working conditions decades ago."

She sat back comfortably in the booth as he shared the ride of his life and she was pleased for the trek and knew it was a rare revelation of the routes this man had taken, and she was honored by his willingness to open up to her. He told her that he left Omaha as soon as he graduated and gravitated to the military and special Opps. He shared that Robin Hood was his first hero, his first love in literature, as this figure of his youth lived to 'have things right for the most; to get off the horse of high handedness, get down on the muddy ground to help the lonely, the forlorn, the silent cries of the forgotten ones in a world gone sour. He laughed and smiled towards her as he shared that, with age, he knew this 'knightly' approach was viewed as passé, but he never let on as to his sadness of this knowledge, nor would he yield to the concept of sarcasm and distain for those who would actually behave selflessly. He took pleasure that his way made others queasy in their modern miasma of self promotion and aggrandizement...He marveled at the nervousness by the modern weak masses, the aversion to value and honor in their midst and this was proclaimed by their acts for all to see by the vehemence in their efforts at distancing themselves by all means available to as far away as possible from what in the past would be taught and look to as an example to follow. "Shameless vacuous herd mentality for survival in our high tech- low touch world, wouldn't you agree, Ms. Gabriel?"

They toasted mugs and she told him to continue. She wanted to know all about whom she had fallen in love with.

Sean told her that he recently was semi-retired from the military but qualified this that one never quits what's in their DNA, from the only family he had really known in adulthood, the service. 2015, he said, was another pivot point in a life framed by more than a few abrupt moves. He pondered aloud about the quiet deeds in desperate moments during the hard acts of patriotism, most of which no one would ever know whom to thank.

He spurns the limelight. His nature demanded this for purpose of longevity. His natural inclination had no doubt led to the desire of being the director in the chair and never the player in front of the lens. This recent play in front of the public at the Fill was aggravating much like the Colorado episode which had brought the full focus of media and other bothersome arcade accolades. The weight of heroism had stunned him. Both he and the Navaho had felt like specimens on the Petri dish of governmental promotion and misplaced public adoration. His innate shyness and evenhanded clarity of self and purpose kept his balance. He believed that John the Navaho was fine too. This new stage on life of crossroads to choose from, consulting or something else would be a welcomed break from the unevenness of previous years. Yeah, right. With Odessa Gabriel as your present moment? She was ordering a late breakfast special and he nodded to make it "two".

He had worked briefly for Blackwater, but regretfully resigned; knew it was not for him, his first step away from non civilian life, not wanting to be the lone wolf howling for others in pack hunts. He wanted more, to investigate how to succeed with his evolved tenacity, to put his talents towards still helping those that cannot help themselves and making a living at it. Is this a child's whim, a Quiotesques view of things?

Odessa excused herself and left for the restroom. Sean watched as any male with a pulse would. The 'it' of a Mae West with the eyes of a Joule. Even in make-upless, patch work clothed disguise, big screen worthy.

His mind meandered to his first book, second favorite to Robin Hood. It was Sir Walter Scott's 'Prince Valiant'. Ah, chivalry, iconic romance, these were still alive and possible, right; although he never admitted this hopeful wish to anyone. He had training in acute understanding of body language and planning next moves. Only with women had his training sometimes led to mistaken intent. Their notions and motions had often befuddled him, this usually studied philosopher warrior in cameo as to what was to action out next. Now, he had more time to trudge through reflection and quietude, a vastly different experience from the tenor of most of his life where action/reaction in the tumble rumble of death and concrete results measured success. He pondered the possibilities on topics he'd never given a second of consideration to previously, of writing a declassified account of his adrenaline ridden life and selling it. He had a working title of "Adventure, Glory and a Girl." Two thirds of the title he had hands on knowledge of, but the mystery and diverse results of the remaining third, women, insured that it would be a fictional brew rimmed by the porcelain thin edge of reality. The title was all Sean had inked on the legal pad stored in his roll top in his D.C. townhome. His editor, his Siamese, 'the cat', Thucydides, was now one year old, full of vinegar and cat spunk. Sean got him the day after his full on dive into change. The feline behaved well for Sean's caretakers, the elderly neighbor couple, who took care of Mr. T. during Sean's travels. Of course, in a consistent pattern of feline defiance, the T cat would snob day for a day after Sean's return and then after the appropriate time of dismissal, settle into the man/cat buddy-hood until Sean's next departure or until the rarity of an intruder in the house, especially a female.

"Sean?" The actress had returned. "Tell me about dam thing."

God help me. Beautiful and direct. And he would now open up to her as he never had except in debriefing.

"I remember reading the first paragraphs in the Times." Odessa's voice was now whispery, almost conspiratorial, not that the still meager amount of patrons in the diner would notice. "It led off with a quote by a witness and I'm paraphrasing now...the guy was sitting on a, ah, a wooden bench with a metal plague molded over its top rung with the dedication, burnished smooth by so many backs leaning against it, the thing said "one of our favorite views", donated by ah, what were their names, oh, yes, I remember, the irony; a Kent and Meri Christianson, Christianson; and this guy on their bench was about to witness your fight with the Islamic terrorists! Wild, huh?"

"I never really..."

"It said he watched the attack on the Glory Hole and the Roberts Tunnel building. Saw the missile fired at the dam, that it caused him to jump and stumble over a beetle-kill stump next to the bench and as he got up he heard the explosion to the left. Shook him again. He heard the pops of the shots fired by the Water Board patrol. Saw rescue helicopter jerk from the recoil of a second attack. Saw a figure fall from the chopper. Heard another explosion at the Roberts building and said that then he heard sirens sounding from all directions. He said he froze as he felt part of a 3-D movie and was afraid." Sean just listened to her. Silent and intense. She barely took a breath.

"The lady then said she saw the chopper on the lake arch up and to the left. As she looked back to the south, she saw a green ranger truck heading down the gravel road, about a half mile from the sound of another explosion at the fenced in area of the mechanical warehouse for the Roberts. She said two or three dark figures started away from the garage and house area back towards the approaching truck...pops of bullets echoed across the waters...the truck swerved and went off the road. The figures ran out the destroyed gate and up the slope to the south....Sean, I'm sorry." Odessa had noticed the smile behind the folded hands. She stopped. "That couple was like Zapruder without the film." She reached out and folded her hands over his. It was warm and both would never later forget the sense of that first touch, the electricity never faded with time. "I asked you and blatherpuss takes over. Do you, can you share? I apologize." "No apology accepted." Odessa then realized that she was clasping his hands maybe a little too long and as she really wanted this man to respect her so she gently released and shyly retreated.

"I will share what I can." His straightforwardness continued the capture.

"There were four groups of three. I and another associate had tracked the leader in country for some months. He was the architect, an engineer, the politically correct choice for the usually politically correct of political Denver, which he had counted on, I'm sure. And had worked his way into the planning group studying the possible expansion of a tramway on the highway, I-70.

I was with him on a hired chopper to fly from Denver up to the Eisenhower Tunnel to study the location and the feasibility of a third bore hole through the mountain for the tram. A second squad staged an emergency on Quandary Peak which required the search and rescue chopper. Fortunately my associate infiltrated as a guide for these so called day trip hikers and confidant that could assist in target recognition. The third group had stayed at a rental home in the Summerwood area. They attacked the Roberts.

And the fourth group was the diversion." "Sean, why that day, the time?"

"They wanted to one, shock America from the center, the heartland. They wanted to match the awe inspiring attack on Ben-Laden. That they could get us anywhere too. They wanted to block the rising waters of the runoff from release, maybe because major problem for the dam, and for the Eisenhower, a blast if that missile had entered the portal would have horrible consequences. As for timing, hell as simple as the Brinks truck usually doing the City Market pickup at 4:00 o'clock. This fourth squad timed it when the guard walked out, one of the women is walking a baby carriage and trips and spills a doll in front of the guard and as he goes to help, the terrorist pulls a large knife out and wraps her arm around the guard and the shiny edge to his throat. In her imperfect English she tells him to tell the shocked driver to open the truck door or, "Or I will slit your infidel head off."

"My God. How can..."

Sean continued as his train of thought was on track and he knew he would not ride this rail of conscientiousness with her or anyone else ever again. "Her two other members ran from across the path, ignoring the screams of shoppers, and put AK's to the driver's window. As they were forcing the armored truck driver to comply, they surely heard the explosions to the south on Lake Dillon and knew that their last Jihad was well underway.

"Why the truck? Money, hostages?"

"They did not give a shit about the bags of money. It was about the dramatics, diversion, and terror. As the sheriff's later said that they were throwing money out the bag door as they fired at them. They stabbed the first guard and were trying to force the driver to engage the truck to ram it out of there.

Meanwhile, I had knocked the pilot out on the west portal and grabbed the stick and had Mamoud by the neck as he tried to fire the hand held at the tunnel."

Sean paused. "I remember seeing the stone of the mountain, the spit of his mouth as I knocked him from the cockpit and bits of orange ...had to of been the tunnel personnel running through the swirl. Don't remember hitting the ground. Do remember a hard hat looming over me. And dragging me from flames. Chopper had hit hard and some smoke and flame were kicking up from instrument panel and from behind I think. Mamoud had broken his neck in the fall.

Same time John was lifting the rescue chopper up and away from the patrols shots at the Glory. He had knocked the gun out of the passenger seat terrorist hand and banged his head on the dash panel, knocking him out. He said that he broke his arm knocking the missile firer off target as he reloaded for second missile attack. He said he raised the stick up abruptly to the left and this terrorist lost his balance and he and the weapon fell to the water below." Sean looked at Odessa's food. "Hey, the eggs are getting cold, don't you...?"

"Damn, Sean, please more..."

He took a bite of sausage and gravy. "Those ones at the Roberts really didn't do much damage either as the concrete blocks in front of the door were problematic and after they shot the unfortunate but timely ranger, they set a charge that did not go off and high tailed back up the Ridge Trail meadow gulch to their rental. They nearly made it but the two Summit Sheriffs cut them off and shot them before they could make it to the garage. Those officers, felt bad for them because they were shocked to pull the black ski hoods off the bodies to find two of the dead were women."

"I remember the report of three of them, the shock that women..."

"Two of them had had husbands killed and who knows, revenge mixed with religion and viola, the feminine side of jihad."

Odessa finally put a fork to her eggs and nibbled.

"Really a mess at the Quandary site. John has had a hard time tempering the memory of the three search members shooting. He said that when the rescue group landed, he felt helpless as he one, had a gun in his back as he posed as leaned over the fake injury, the terrorist lying on the trail and two, because our orders were to track to conclusion what was the reason for this many frickin terrorists in the area. And we were not aware of the team at the market until they announced it by the storming of the money truck."

Odessa took a sip of the cold coffee not knowing what to do or say next.

"Strange, I always know when it's four o'clock in the afternoon, Mountain Time, no matter where I am in the world."

The actress pushed her meal across the table, got up and came around to the hero's side of the booth and sat down and hugged him.

Terrorists stopped thinking about mountain targets after Sean and The Navaho had thwarted their Summit County mission. Oddly, mountain properties values went up even higher as buyers viewed high country property as one, not a metropolitan area, other words, not a target area, and two, the up and away perception that the heights offered more security than the flatlands. Sean fought hard against the celebrity and stupendous falsehood as he saw it of fame. He did not participate in many more off the books engagements after that. He rarely shared that his impressions of that day. The image from the day in Israel enters his memory; the bus explosion. He was a block away. He raced to the scene. Parts were everywhere. Metal and people pieces strewn everywhere and amidst the hellish milieu, Sean's most acute memory were not the arms, legs or heads but the I-phones and cells, tucked in what remained of some of the torsos breast shirt pockets, ringing their individual tunes, an incessant death dirge, a composition by the living calling for their loved ones as news spread of the bombing. Sean kept his cell phone on vibrate for just this reason.

Odessa kept side glancing at his profile. They are now back to smiling like kids without knowing why. Here, she thought, was a man who knew life was primal and that all three acts can be brutal, but he was a man equal to the required dialogue and delivery. She almost sighed.

He wondered her spiritual beliefs. They would get into that later, he was sure. He leaned towards Deist, almost Jefferson in pondering the 'what ifs', worship the almighty, be a good man, empirical and tolerant, capable of encouraging virtuous living, Sally Hemming's or not. He laughed inside and then outwardly as he turned into her and kissed her cheek. Rewards and punishments would have to come later.

Chapter 3

"Intended Consequences"

"These are the times that try men's souls. The summer soldier and the sunshine Patriot will, in this crisis, shrink from the service of their country; but he that stands it now, deserves the love of man and woman. Tyranny, like hell, is not easily conquered; yet we have this consolation with us, that the harder the conflict, the more glorious the triumph. What we obtain too cheap, we esteem too lightly: It is dearness only that gives everything its value. Heaven knows how to put a proper price upon its goods; and it would be strange indeed if so celestial an article as Freedom should not be highly rated."

Thomas Paine
"The American Crisis"
December 23rd, 1776

September 23rd, 2015

Never one to shy away from leveraging to maximum benefit the circumstances of any presented opportunity, and with a masters talent for adroitness (with acknowledged apologies to the alarm system otherwise known as the guard cockatiel, Keno) in killing two birds with one stone that would humble a Barnum, Yoggee master stroked the anniversary celebration of the Cranium Fill with the big muscle cherry on top combination of the appearance of the "Life, take it all in" actress coupled with the reluctant hero, all framed and underlined with the added allure of it all happening, all being for charity, an event for the all encompassing needy. The bar's birthday now became the Yoggee proclaimed "Festival of Feistiness, Foam and Funds" to benefit the children of the reservations and the children of the police and fire personal that had been injured or killed in the line of duty. He nicknamed it the "Raise The Bar For Those Too Young To Rendezvous". The partners, Moah, Sean and Yoggee, had pledged all profits to the cause and had spent their own money hiring extra help for the caravan tents, draft stations, and the extra off duty police for security and extra parking requirements and control. Yoggee made sure that applicable approvals were obtained, permits paid and that all legal hurdles and concerns were expedited with the prodding's of Giddings Tell, somewhat orchestrated with the goal of achieving almost godlike armor against any bureaucratically induced abuse or corporate induced harassment for at least a few more years. But not all was Machiavellian in the plan. Yoggee sincerely wanted to continue what he had done for years. Unknown to many, Mr. Drummerman had generously and privately donated money to the less fortunate in the state and in neighboring reservations.

The donor's nee drinkers began to show early. Moah had flown back in after his most recent Air Marshal stint, and became Yoggee's early object of loving derision. "Moah, that studio you have in Wheat Ridge is so small that if you shut the knife drawer the place would appear expansive!" Moah smiled. "It suits my life now, old man." Sean knew it was on. He was alert to Odessa coming back out to the front from freshening up in Yoggee's residence.

"Well, good luck and cheap sin to you too, youngster."

"That's like saying there's a happy Wal-Mart for hell somewhere, Yogg." as both he and Yoggee entered into the front of the Fill behind Sean as he went to meet Odessa who had just come from the residence area and was now professionally handling the growing crowd of males and assorted women gathering around her. One of the Bar Stars brought them their drinks. "Thank you, Cindy." Yoggee turned and poked Moah in the ribs. "I told him," Yoggee was pointing to Sean as Sean was taking Odessa's arm, "Remember, Sean, things aren't what they are cranking up to be when it comes to women. Moah, it reminds me of my wife." Moah almost rolled his eyes. "I told her, I said, Honey, I'm just trying to get through my dreams with you. And she said, Yoggee.." and Yoggee paused as he watch the crowd follow Sean and Odessa to the front bar area.. "What did your wife say, man?" Yoggee came back to Moah. "I say, I told her that I am no anarchist of love, not chaotic in amore, but, baby, I am just someone that dreams in the 3 dimensions of you, doll; backwards, forwards and upside down."

"Oh, and I wonder why she left."

"She said she was tired of the hurt, the masochism of being my mate. And as I shared with Sean..."

"Oh, God."

"..I said to him, Sean, mark your territory well and remember this, is this infatuation, or is this just another matter of scrambled love?...and proceed accordingly, my son, and go cautiously into what lays ahead."

Before Moah could laugh or comment, Yoggee stated, "But you know what, Moah, I haven't figured out how to miss them yet." They both looked over to their obviously happy partner and the object of his pleased attention. "She is beautiful. Seemed pleasant when Sean introduced her. Listen, Moah, if you're not turned on by that you are definitely a low wage earner." And then in the very familiar and very expected meanderings of the Fill's practicing muse he added what was for Yoggee his daily pontification and for others, his obliquetory non-sequitor, "We always need forks. Stuck with way too many spoons, way too many for our own good."

Moah refused to let Yoggee see his puzzlement.

"What makes you jump up, your hairs go on edge, Moah? Your gut get pissed off, go luan on something? That's Chinese for 'chaos', luan."

"Whiskey and women, Yoggee, the two w's."

"Yes, Moah, I know what you mean. But sometimes, my friend, too much to drink is not enough to do the job...but then, sometimes, ah sweet ataraxia and the mind is at calm. Skol and scat!" The two friends downed the shots that had accompanied their now empty beer mugs. And then Yoggee jumped up on a table and began discourse with the assembling crowd, "Whiskey, its origin is from Irish and Scottish Gaelic. it meant "water of life" so breathe in its sacred aroma, my fellow donors, and drink up, drink up as we have taxi's and shuttles too for you to ride home and as equally as important, we have children that need "water for life" to have a chance to ride into their futures too." The applause and sound of toasting mugs and champagne glasses filled the room. The Fill's birthday bash was popular and pictures were aplenty. Sean and Odessa patiently stood with many for pictures and autographs, of course if requests for photos were accompanied by donations in the big glass vase standing next to them. The actress was used to bothersome intrusions and she helped Sean manage it by sharing with him her humor and graciousness, gained through years of "appearance" demeanor and ploy. He thought he was happy. But he later shared that during it all, he envisioned himself above the bar, above the crowd, floating as an omniscient narrator at his own unwanted coming out party and the actress's premier. He laughed as he could not believe that she was there in person, in his bar. He questioned the scene and the Fellini of it all. The group had moved on and taken a break from the picture taking. Yoggee was saddling up to conversation central. "Before my SAD times..."

Odessa looked quizzical. Yoggee noticed as he had hardly taken his eyes off of her since her entrance. "Before my System Analyst Days, S, A, D's...I had some problems in required studies, like biology; until it dawned on me to use icon memory, I recalled that from overhead, the Y chromosome appears as a man at full mast, yes? And opposite this the X chromosome to me at least, is a nun with her habit in a wad and her legs crossed. Viola, iconphony, connecting dots, to make systems easy to adapt and understand. You put full mast man with crossed legged nun and you have a new system, theory of chaos, I think..." As Yoggee noticed that his wit had not really left the ground, he did as was his want in such situations and continued on to another of his topical islands of mental hoola hoops, " I was birthed and as of that year, I began my seemingly hi-polarized search for my quiddity, essential nature of a person, Moi revealed, and quietude..."

Simultaneously, a tray of glassware apparently found the ground with a significant smashing, crashing reverberation from depths of the back room, "Sounds like I am still searching. He paused for the customary downbeat of laughter and added. "The trek has been fun, if not cautionary."

Sean had moved next to Odessa, gently nudging her arm to which she responded with a smile.

Moah and the surrounding others listened too as Yoggee was on a Fill roll. In loud voice to overcome the din of the seemingly non-maddening group, "My friends and friends yet to be made, I serve ale, quaff to various a many archetypes, primitive models such as yours truly, and I have found that money ages like wine and both in time can lose their "kick", their verity, and then snideville-lite happens and poof, you're old, an archetypal entity gone to seed. Nevertheless, I am proud that I speak the occasional Shelta, a language used by Irish and Welsh gypsies, "Deviant vocabularis," Moah added, "in plain English, which I might add, is rare in these confines, the words of a tipsy gypsy." And Moah, in exaggerated grandness, bowed at the hip towards his partner. Not amused and unfazed, Mr. Drummerman continued to his own beat.

"I only take busman's holidays, leisure time spent doing the same thing that one should always do at work, enjoying the art of life to its fullest for I ask you, how can one work at something they do not like and be an honest contributor to anything of worth or value? How?"

"More imperfect imitations for the album." Moah chided.

"Poppycock, Moah. In all its' meaning, from Dutch, pap, means "soft", and with noted emphasis, "and 'kak', which means dung. Poppycock. Look Moah and you the other children of the corn, I'm a privileged professor of ontology two point 0 'Nature of Being' and all I study, all I ask, it to serve my base carnal needs, always extra large, please."

Sean pointed to another wall hanging and script, "And now ladies and gentlemen, you are in understanding of the author of such theorems as this," The gathered looked at the wall above the jute box. The enamel maple sign had carved into it, almost rune like, 'Where Dakotans come to Drink. Affordable, Adorable Quaffability.' The group toasted and Odessa was asked to join for more pictures and autographs for charity which she gladly accommodated.

Yoggee studied Sean as his friend followed her with his glance. "How do you say bad about a good thing, right Sean?"

"What?"

"Women." Sean smirked at him.

"Yes, remember, son, don't eat anything whose name you can't pronounce!"

"Good God, man, I'm surprised that you haven't starved, Yoggee," Moah was attempting to buffer...but Yoggee continued," Carry yourself always like a movie star, everyone should, but never forget to still see through a pauper's eyes."

Sean looked at Yoggee and shook his head.

"Her heart is in the right place, don't get me wrong, helping the kids and all, but Sean, and I shut down after this...."

"There is a God." Moah, still attempting to keep it light.

"and she certainly is a pukka pulchritude, means 'excellent beauty', but maybe with a wee bit of wrongness within, pulsating problems beneath the surface, a sexy samba of sour waiting to happen if you are not careful." Sean had turned to his friend to hear this last bit of proffered caution and desperately wanted to tell his favorite know it all about Odessa's son, and her love for him and her tenderness towards Sean so far, but as he had promised her to keep her wish of silence on the matter, he just stared at Yoggee, a little more intensely as Yoggee said, "The only French I know is femme fatale which now means an attractive and seductive woman."

Moah had positioned himself between his two partner's as he could read the level of alcohol starting to babble forth from the older one and the level of non receptivity rising in the brow and eyes of now not smiling other younger one.

"The original French," Yoggee was entering Yellow light territory, "meaning, it meant 'disastrous woman."

Moah turned to Sean, "You know this dust bin means well and I know you love Sean, Yoggee. You flake head, don't let the drink and don't let your record with women color your thoughts for Sean, alright?" It was rare that Moah Halas acted as pacifier.

Usually, except in the angry reverberations of bitter memories and occasional disgust with the state of the nation he loved and had sacrificed much for, his gray eyes betrayed nothing. Moah's father had combined his parent's names with the two of his Czechoslovakian Catholic wife's parent's names to name his son, Moah. When Moah's father's Polish parents had arrived in America, they traveled west with most of the Halas clan claiming a stake in the Wilson Lake area of Kansas, which today is noted not only for the body of water and stone post fencing, but the large fields of wind generators, looming over a few homesteads, some occupied, with now stilled windmills still standing, as if proudly marking the olden needs of the past and to remind their metal progeny of their origins. Moah's mother left her Czechoslovakian clansmen in Kansas when she moves with Mr. Halas when Moah was thirteen to Denver where Mr. Halas opened a liquor store. Tall and in excellent health, when Moah was of age, he had enlisted and tested into the green berets and then participated in select Special Ops missions requiring small, efficient, highly trained groups of calculating and dangerous men. Still chiseled at 43, Moah Halas now split his time as TSA air marshal and as an advocate for veterans. Close friends were few, with the two he was now standing between, Sean and Yoggee, the closest and an African friend from his past right up there with the other two as well. As was his nature, he bristled at the paid by greed elitists as he phrased the objects of his scorn, politicians and their ilk including in his ire the military pencil pushers and lobbyists in general and perhaps the most galling of his objects for ridicule, a wayward with the truth press and media, whom, in his very high contrast black and white world perception were mouth puppets for one agenda of shit or another.

His only vanity concerned his feeling of having abnormally long arms. Moah consciously attempted to mask this by frequently wearing surf baggies, a 1960's beach attire, colorful, almost neon but longed legged and in Moah's mind, the perfect balance for his arms. When casual called, 'baggies' won. When advocacy was the order of the day, he treated himself to Armani, tailored to suit his 6'3" frame and to visually state the seriousness of his stance. He wore standard travel fare in his capacity as an air marshal to blend in.

A small lacuna drew attention to his left ear lobe, compliments of a near fatal bullet from a firefight in the Megreb. Moah credited his survival with death brush to his habit, his superstition bordering on fetish, of his learned trait from one of his hero's, Crazy Horse, the Sioux warrior. Crazy Horse always went into battle with a totem, a charm, which was a river smoothed pebble, a stone which he tucked behind his ear for luck and protection. Moah taped a black marble within the fold of his ear and in this instance in the desert of Africa, it had deflected but in so doing, was smashed by the round, sending the projectile off by a fraction of God blessed geometry as he called it, saving his skull, leaving the small tear in the lobe as the only physical reminder of his horse sense of emulating his hero, the master horseman.

Although he was polar opposite to their political tenets, Moah was inwardly amused at himself for his honest, almost reverential admiration for the Clintons: he was closed to aweship of their dueling egos in their constant battles for the front row, amazed in his respect for their semi raunchy audacity to fabricate, malign and their ability to dismiss with a leer or sarcastic practiced smile their many opponents and still skate away no matter the refuse or debris left in the wake of their efforts, to go on to more astoundments and outragements as Moah coined most politicians acts, especially these two. The Clintons, though, were indeed different. They had the balls to enact the "how dare they" posture at the drop of a hint of negativity towards them and they presented themselves with the perfection of master artists, with a look of disgust as they asked people to remember "all that we have done for humanity" with the correct posture and presumed stance of trustworthiness and a with body language that was the perfect frame of reference for victimhood, that again and again showed the couples complete disdain for shame or self blame. Real Beauts. No looking back, always a new easel to paint the future on. Moah admired their effrontery and aspired to their level of detachment but he knew he still faced a steep rocky incline to reaching this summit of self preservation, aloofness and lord-over-ness. But he would keep trying. But Moah's real world losses and inner agitations of his present and past made clear to him that he never would achieve this possessive apex. His hobbies of surfing, coin collecting and music, were momentary pleasure Isles from seas of troubles. Metallica, Led Zepp, Hendrix and African percussion led him to a soothing place helping to keep the loud nature of his thinking drowned out by the audio level on his amps. Strangely, and Sean had taken note of this as "cosmic odd", Cole Porter was Moah's most favored lyrical rhythmic balm and Moah called the composer "cool, cool hand Cole."

Moah's dad, Mr. Halas, and apropos, Halas was Czech slang for "a noisy person" which derived from Czech 'halas' "uproar". In the Polish language of his deceased mother, whom Moah adored, 'halas' meant "noise" and Moah laughed at this as his dad's life and his life had rarely, if not ever, been a quiet stroll in the garden of goodies except in his father's case with his mother and for him, the rainbow time of Maria, his wife.

Moah politely acted as if he was still listening to the banter of Yoggee, Sean and the others but he was now in memory sphere and he took a big gulp from his glass.

Maria had died on Cinco de Mayo in a SWAT raid that had come to their address by mistake. Moah was now staring into one of the neon's above the bar. When Moah's door was broken down in a search for supposed cache of cartel drugs, Mariah was shot as she had screamed and threw a kitchen knife at the dark clad intruders. She did not hear the screams of "police," "freeze" and other orders in the confusion and surprise as she stopped the first shot fired by the rookie member of the squad. In the night suck commotion of that tragic morning, Moah had raced downstairs, yelling, screaming at peak that he was "Green Beret, Green Be. what the Hell," and then he could never erase the sound or her scream as she was hit nor how far he had jumped to the ground floor by her body as she fell to the carpet. He remembered knocking one of the barrels away and yelling and the rifle but to the head, he still was conscious and grabbed another barrel as he was gang tackled, how slow mo things are in review, how the sound is erased except for the silent yell he saw from his wife' mouth, framed in lipstick and blood, her eyes, her baby blues looking at him, and crying too. The memory then blurred as if God intervened at these times with mini segments to hold back pain. The blue and yellow gas tubes did not block his recalled vision of the waiting room of the EMTs as Maria was wheeled in on Sunday morning, 1:00 a.m. …the crowds of what appeared to him as mass gatherings of Hispanics, some blacks and a white in the comer of the turquoise walled room...the cops and EMTs had to push and shove the crowds out of the way as the regular emergency exit doors had not worked, they had jammed, they had God Damned jamb! People where yelling in Spanish and English and the florescent lights grayed the whole play of the thing. The chattering and crying babies, it all still whirled, a churning ball of emotional shit as he replayed it for the thousandth time, finally, free of the drunks and injured, racing down the pea green linoleum floor of the hallway leading to pushing through the swinging doors of the emergency room, he felt her grip lesson. He later felt that weakness in his hand, her fading touch from that night of evils, felt her tiny fingers loosen.

During fights and even while killing time with the tube, she was still there. Through the doors they had gone, the beeping of the heart machine, the hum of the authorities and the green garbed, the final constant peel of the flat line sound, the high pitch voices, the "Stand back's the electric pads of shock, the flat line alert still sounding, the sound of now over, the shot of adrenaline, the pads again, the colorless look of it all now, the deep grips of the arms around Moah, restraining as best they could his frantic efforts to reach the only love he had ever trusted or known, the faces of failure in their now pulled down masks and bloodied smocks, their gloves just as red, the slow motion of tears, tension and his bride dead on the pink sheets of one of those still torturous uncomfortable hospital beds.

The 'why' never came and he took another drink. The same as he always had. He momentarily faded back into the now of things. He took deep breath and turned towards the group again. "Moah, Moah, don't you agree?" Yoggee was asking his vote for his position on some thing or another and Moah responded with a forced smile and a drink raise and turned back to the lights and his memories.

His dad's retirement in the foothills rest of Denver shuttled back into recallville. Then his younger brother, Lech, his mother had named him after her hero. And Lech's smile brought a sigh to his hardened heart brother, the Soldier Joe as Lech called him. Wonder if he is still designing sets? Damn, Dad! Moah knew he was lonely and no matter how much he and Lech tried to be in their father's life, Mr. Halas could not reason them into his heart, his passionate wife was gone, and to quell the tremor's, the pain, Mr. Halas's solace was from a iced tumbler of Jack, early and often a liquid agent of mildness from recall and bitterness.

Moah just did not understand the instructions for being God, how to bring peace to this once giant of a man, now shrunk by circumstance and choice. Moah was always thankful that his parents had driven on another 300 miles west from where the rest of the family had stopped. His dad would not have lasted long if he didn't have the Rocky Mountains to view and not the wind generators, the highest things in the horizontal only world of Kansas.

Ah, Denver. He had met Maria there. He and some friends had dropped into the Schosh Inn on a Ladies Night and he was surprised to see her there. She was a teller in his bank and he understood her to be a married woman. Or so he thought. He had been too shy to converse with her as he was dazzled by her and silenced by the diamond on her finger. They only talked bank talk. But there she was with another women and Moah laughed as he remembered her turndown of numerous offers to dance or other cravings. She had filled him in on these male banalities after they had dated for some time. Sean could see it all. The moment he thought of how to meet her and how to gather the courage still tickled him. He and his friends had taken note of how many men had sauntered up to the two attractive women and had been shooed away by both, although what turned out to be Maria's roommate did get up and accept one offer to shake it on the dance floor, but Maria never budged. After one of Moah's friends had tried to ask her to get up and join him on the floor and he like the others before was caste adrift in the humble sea of a bar turn down, Moah turned to his friends and bet them $5 each that he would be the one to get the beauty in the corner to dance. His offer was quickly taken up and accompanied by the standard challenges to his manhood and his sanity. He got up. Went to her table. He knew the eyes of his buddies were almost searing his back. The bank teller recognized her bashful customer and he recognized her as beautiful as ever.

"Hi, Sean," she had begun.

"Maria, I may call you Maria?"

"Of course."

"This is going to sound strange but take it the right way. Do you want to make some money and laugh too?"

Moah remembered as if yesterday her big laugh and smiling "Yes. What's up?"

"If you casually look over my right shoulder at those three yahoos I came in with..." "One of them ask me to dance, yes, I see them..."

"Well, I know, and I thought it would be funny if I came over , and mind you I would understand if you say no, but I bet them each that I would come over and get you to dance with me....I will split the winnings with you if you do, $5 from each."

Maria's eyes had answered first. And she had reached out in dramatic fashion and stood to take him to the dance floor, glancing appropriately towards the astonished losers four tables away. "Why, Moah," she had said loudly, "I'd love to."

The two went to the floor and their first dance together was a slow Three Dog Night song, "Easy to Be Hard." He remembered their catching up on her now being in the process of divorcing her husband, their secret until then fondness for each other and then leaving the Inn, of course only after collecting the winnings from the sheepish trio, and heading to a late night diner to spend the money on coffee and on getting to know about who they would each spend the rest of their lives with.

Moah had proceeded to the pool table area which still afforded some elbow room as the players needed stick space. His mind went to his spaces. In marriage and now. Maria and he bought a nice ranch home outside town. They had a survival garden now overrun with weeds but still producing zucchinis, watermelons and rabbits for the tenants he had leased it to since his wife's death.

The main floor had been "neater than a nun's ass" as Yoggee would describe it. The basement had been Moah's area and it was generally messy in an organized "I-know-where-everything-is- don't-touch-anything" managerial approach. She allowed him cigars down there. Moah knew it was the only time he had felt fulfilled. He wouldn't let the tear forming to show. He took another sip. The cautious optimism of those times hurt and pleased at the same time. He still battled with the notion of Heaven calling in the note and hating the Almighty for it. The authorities were mistaken and admitted it. Sorry with reparations or whatever those bastard attorneys had called it. We're nothing but reconfigured dust, and we'll never be anything more, no matter how we sweep it. His dad entered again. He remembered him telling his mother before their move west that he wanted to move to a place where " the locals weren't afraid of drinking dandelion wine and where the first question asked of newcomers to a town isn't "what church do you belong to?". His father disliked elegant lightheartedness and extravagant praise which to him equaled something akin to pissing against the wind.

The barstar, Kendra interrupted his stream of consciousness. "Do you want another, Mr. Halas? And Mr. Drummerman wants to know if you're ready for some wings?" Moah smiled at her and said yes to both and tried not to stare too intently at her as she reminded him of Maria. He had mentioned this to Sean once and Sean had hugged him as if that would squeeze the memory and the comparison out of Moah. He watched her walk to others for orders and to semi strut for her tips...the capitalist way is truly beautiful then Moah thought of his dad's distinct distaste for banks and for certain politicians. Mr. Halas railed against many laws but one in particular he found devilishly hypocritical, something called bankruptcy reform pushed by the whores in Congress and Corporations, same bordello, his dad noted, "Just different entrances and exits". "The law", his dad would continue, "made it more difficult for John Q. Public to file for bankruptcy but allowed the dirt dogs in the plush leather chairs to file no matter what, even when the failure is the result of their own incompetence, deception and often illegal acts and slight of hand accounting. What monsters of destruction!" His dad often thought a few of these white collared crooks should be "Mussolinied, mistresses and all, and then we might actually get a few to pay attention to us, the groundlings, the ever present and bitter reminders of their origins. I could not say it better, Dad."

Kendra brought the fresh one and told Moah that the wings would be ready in a few minutes at the front bar. Moah thanked her. Again, her best attributes were in motion and the action reminded him of his dad's name for Pelosi, Madame Flutterfly he had called her. He did not like Nixon either nor Harry Reid of Nevada, who had insulted Mr. Halas for life when it was reported that Senator Reid had complained about the smell of his fellow American's that were touring their Capitol. Mr. Halas called Reid "Senator Hold Your Nose," ever after.

Sean came up and grabbed him to join them for wings. They walked to the bar. Odessa waved to them as they came up and they sheepishly grinned and waved. Yoggee had her ear and the others so Sean and Moah had some space to themselves and they were offered two stools by Bart who had saved them.

"What a mob, huh? How you doing?" Sean could read his friend. Years long friendships do this. "Sean, do you ever doubt what's good and what's bad?"

"You mean, am I sure about who and what I do is right, Hell, not always. My middle name's not Jesus." Sean thought Moah a portmanteau personality, even as direct as Moah Halas was, Sean saw him as morpheme man, a person whose form and meaning derive from a complicated blending of emotions like smoke and smog combining to produce fog, Moah's inners were disguised well and shared rarely and unevenly.

"You know, I was reading something last week and this piece talked about government mistakes, intentionally and otherwise. Did you know that way back in 63 when those little black girls were killed in that bombing in Birmingham, Hoover's FBI withheld evidence for decades? According to this article, these upstanding public servants even admitted that they withheld thousands of pages of documents from that McVeigh's defense team. Although I am glad they screwed those hump boys of the law and I would have gladly done the dude dead myself, it's still the wrong of it all that disturbs, and I say, destroys this country."

Sean took another sip and remained noncommittal but friendly to the discussion.

"FBI has continued to rely on crooks as informants. Look at how they protected that Irish mob boss, some Boston politicians brother, of course, and even, again using the data of snitches', these G-men put a citizen, an innocent American for Christ's sake, in prison for decades for a murder the man did not commit. And these were just singular examples of a symptomatic system of ethical dodge ball, a sickness that ails not only the law, but the military, business, education, religion...nothing is off limits, Sean. There's a plague of personality gone interstellar narcissistic. Each of us must be a star which can only shine if we catch this bug, this disease of success at all costs, no matter the body count, the tentacles are far reaching and rarely allow escape." Moah downed his drink and hailed Bart to hustle up two more for them.

"Whoa, I'm still with, Bubba." as Sean held his drink up.

Moah looked beyond Sean to Odessa and Sean followed his glance.

"You sure are."

And Sean knew he had touched a 'wayback' in his friend's heart and was uncomfortable, but Moah ignored the feeling of his friend's obvious connection and disquiet. The Padron was delivered and the observation continued.

"How can people trust in the integrity of a system where these things, these purchased bungles are now commonplace? How?"

"You miss Africa, don't you?"

"I miss the openness and my friends in Mali, Niger, and the desert. Everything there seems so clear. It is understood by everyone that governments are weak and easily bought. They don't preach the crusade of doing something for others while screwing them at the same time. Refreshing. Our brothers there, now sisters too, I know you feel this too; they are, the frontline military, they are all I have ever found worthy of my heart, my blood or my precious time." Sean raised his glass. "Skol and Scat!" They clinked and drank it down.

"Sean, remember that Colonel, the one our C.O. from Carson would name as his mentor?"

"The one Gallatin would quote when he did not want to state his own beliefs?"

"Yeah, Gallatin would say, Colonel, what was his name, Smuck? Was that it?

"You know, Moah, it was Smuck. I never forgot that Gallatin swore that was this guy's real name. I still question that."

"Yeah, well, using Smuck for his thoughts, remember Gallatin said Smuck had two brilliant ideas for dealing with our two biggest problems, remember, Sean, terrorists and illegal's?" "Noise on, my brother, noise on."

"Smuck said simple way to defeat Al-Qaida was to arm all the Arab women who have been treated worse than dung though hundreds of decades; from Lebanon to Libya, arm them and help them get a change in their husbands thinking that treats them as slaves.

Gallatin said Smuck might have something there. I had some problems with that as you remember. I have Muslim friends who are better than most men I know here. And they treat their wives well from what I have seen. But I did agree with Smuck's idea of female liberation for the really dangerous bastards...why, as .Gallatin said, Smuck emphasized, it would extend our fighting force without extending our fatalities and the propaganda benefit, whoa, we would have terrorists everywhere wearing cups and hiding their wives silverware!"

"What would the anti-waterboarders do with that?"

"Oh, they would probably attack this just like they would attack Smuck's nee Gallatin's number two solution to the illegal problem."

"You mean the Mexico Plaza Square drop?"

"You remember that one too?"

"God, how could someone forget that?"

"What's not to like? The president calls for thousands of truck owners to volunteer to pick up volunteer illegal's and take them to bases to hop on choppers, and then have our boys supply the Mexican patriots with weapons and the air support to invade Mexico City, the cartel hacienda's and have these hard working, and even I recognize this, Sean." Sean had frowned at Moah words as he well knew his friends ire at the illegal problem. "They work their asses off when they show up. We would just force them to show up to take their country back and, a recon Questa of their own land, not ours. I liked Gallatin's, I mean the Smuckese of it all. A good people get a country back, the Mexicans and us. But, Sean, you and I both know we are scarce in politicians with the foresight, the power to promote either of these two solutions..."

"That sounds a little too Neitzesque, doesn't it?"

Ignoring Sean's comment, Moah moved on, "We need a Putin, still in office by maneuver, fiat and by his uncanny ability to impress in his quiet ruthlessness and presentable Russianess...and yes, what we have, we have a Congress which is the only brothel that doesn't make money for the pimps, the people." Sean thought it best to change topic and maybe get he and his friend up and away from the big bar.

"Let's head over to Yoggee and the lady, what do you say?"

"Lady? Lady. You know, Sean, that also means the grinding organ in the stomach of a lobster, don't you?"

Sean Linden is viewed as a leader with intrepid nerve, cool, lucid judgment in the hottest of life and death contests but he now finds himself caught between the most dangerous of tugs, the beautiful beckoning of a new relationship versus the fidelity needed of standing by an old friend, literally, as Moah was listing just a bit to the left. Sean turned and smiled to Odessa with that shrug of a smile that woman easily recognize as the cave man without the club stare, the "I can't be there yet but I am working on it" look of a man perplexed with purpose as of yet to be defined.

Moah noticed their look. "No saddle. No stirrups."

Sean turned back, "What?" Moah began again, "Alexander's father, Philip one, laid the groundwork for his son's greatness all because of cavalry, horse sense, Sean. I suggest studying maneuvering bareback. Phillip did it. He beat Greece and their bitter rivals, the Thessalonians," and Moah then pointed towards the actress and her fans, Yoggee and the two bodyguards in close proximity that had flown in on a leased jet ordered by Odessa's agent when she had been informed of Odessa's desire to attend the charity event and to stay longer than originally planned, "...and not the Thespians."

Sean laughed, "Yes, there were a thousand of them with Leonidas at Thermopylae, I know the difference."

Moah continued his alert, "Thessaly's elite appointed Philip the One their ruler of their League and along with their money, King Phil also got Thessaly's thousands count cavalry. These horse soldiers fought in diamond shaped formations and were unbeatable and these troops were loyal to Philip and his son, Alex the Greatest, for over 32 years, without saddles, without spurs, until Alexander shooed them away at the Oxus River in Asia when they tired of each other.

Diamond configurations, a gem of an attack scheme for armies or for women, wouldn't you say, Sean, and no spurs, no saddles, hang on tight as bucking is projected."

"Your point being, my tipsy sated bastard?"

"The point being, my infatuated and obviously head over heels brother, is that this is a horse with no name, spirited beyond description and while the ride will be of epic proportions, this bronc ain't meant for breaking, except your heart." And before Sean could muster protest Moah finished, "The point being is, I love you, Sean, you, Yoggee are the closest, and except for what family I have, to me. I care about starts and stops."

Yoggee hollered to them, "Come on, boys, get over here. No board meetings without me!" They acknowledge him, and Odessa who was staring with what appeared a practiced smile in their direction too. Moah and Sean raised their glasses and indicated that they would finish them and then come back to their friends.

"Starts and stops. Wars. How to start and how to stop them; that is the question. Romans thought wars were the domain, the concern of the Gods and the Romans handled fights in two idiosyncratic traditions or means, one at a war's initiation in which they would search for oracles or omens for the success of the venture and then, with conquest still steaming fresh and jealousy lurking amid the columns, another touch the God's moment would occur when the fearful powers, the robed ones, would forcefully, at the conclusion of the battles, through the guise of tradition and obligation, remind the hero that he, 'you, are a mere mortal.' The process allowed that the almighty Senate gave permission and only with their okay, must maintain the allusion of superiority, mind you, they gave permission for a conquering general to be honored with a triumph, a celebration where the hero could bring his legions and booty into the sacred margins of Rome to the roars and protestations of a loyal and adoring public. But, as you know, swords have two edges." Moah paused to take big drink and Sean joined and tried to initiate motion towards the other end of the bar, but Moah held him with his free hand. "The hero, his face was painted red for the day, don't know if it meant blood or embarrassment, probably enforced humility...it did relate to Jupiter, the statue of Jupiter at the Capitol was painted red. The general wore special ceremonial attire and he had a sword of state, a scepter in hand. As he rode towards the Capitol, his troops shouted obscenities and obnoxious remarks at him from the sides, all from custom and love, of course, but the kicker, the break on someone getting a swelled head or ego was that all along the parade rout, a ditch dirt slave would ride in the chariot at his side and whisper to him that 'you are dust, you are a man, you will always be mortal' and other such reminders of the inconsequential of this pageant for fools."

"Is this where 'sidekicks' comes from?"

"Brother Sean; war makes you wise in a hurry and angry forever." Moah finishes his drink. "Sean, Odessa is the Senate and unbridled. She will celebrate you with contingencies." Frowning, Sean pushed away from the long rail.

"Sean, never forget your place and the ride may last longer than others have ever galloped with her but never lose sight or grasp of your lifespan in her world. There's a time limit."

"God damn it, Moah, you really can drag the mud of sobriety into anything, don't you." "Hey, before we calypso over there, one other thing. Serious."

"As if this hasn't been?"

"Listen. Something happens to me ..."

"What the?"

"Something goes down, I pass, here's a bit for you and Yoggee."

"Good God, double downer time it sounds. Let's get ov..."

"Wait! Just remember this, this rhyme or riddle I guess. It leads to location of what I can leave you both as appreciation for true friendship and..."

"Are you really trying to piss me off? What is this about...?"

"You will find material good, share with others, if you follow Clint kicking a Shuttle into the very tip of Hope's nose."

"Jesus, what is that?"

"Directions for you and the Y man in case I check out before either of you. And" "Get your drunken ass up. We're joining reality again."

Sean put both their drinks on the counter and turns Moah in the right direction.

"Hollywood and Yoggee! Reality? Ha!" The partners headed towards the unwelcome brio of glamour and grog, acting as if all were usual and the atmosphere, standard operating procedure. Odessa hailed Sean, "There you laggards are." And he smiled at her, but inwardly, he struggled against the Bard of Avon's observation that "Life is but a stage", this, as she hugged him and he felt the contour of her against him and the eyes of Moah on them both.

****

"Their re-elections are at stake. They know this, don't they Jansen? Their balls are ours, right?" The head of Magi Corporation wanted the word that he had got the bid, that the government lagniappe was his and he could mark another 'to do' off his list so he could more quickly get down to the business of enjoying himself in his new Naples mansion which had been constructed on the site of another ex rich person home lost through foreclosure during the sad market of the late 2000's in Florida. The previous home had been worth 15 million but the new owner had it demolished and built a 30 million dollar rather rectangular, rather ordinary appearing home in its place. Modem, stucco, coral in color with easy maintenance and modem accoutrement as its architectural frosting, the dune and teal tiles, the rounded edges almost hacienda like, fitting projections for the proud owner, a modem day Don, calculating and untouched by sentimentality or attachment. "Finish it or finish them. I will call you later, Jansen. Have a good day."

Stuart Hawkins-Burke had grown up in a noted acting family; both parents proud of their names, hence, the hyphenated surname which he grew fonder of through the years after initial rebellion common to early adolescent selfishness and expected absorption of narcissism, although these traits still wandered the mind ways of the 41 year old CEO-CFO of one of the nation's largest companies, MAGI INC. Olive colored eyes, thick mane of dishwater blond, Hawkins-Burke is a clean freak, a lover of art; a purposed devil may care appearance with a well disguised strictness for detail and execution.

After graduating a year ahead of normal from the University of California at Santa Barbara with a Masters in Business Administration, Hawkins-Burke, immediately and forever after, desired control and obsequiousness and wide recognition for his achievements. Hard driving, no time for the minutiae of social chit chat without reward or glad handing without deal making, he had invested his substantial inheritance smartly. Always distraught at the concept of a lack of success or the inkling of failure, he was constantly on guard and ever cunning. Not many individuals in his world were close to him, except on and off again for his sister. Hawkins-Burke, for all his talent, had an amateur's time of trying to get a handle on the meaning of trust. A psychoanalyst might surmise that this guidance system for survival, emotionally and professionally, emanated from his and his sister being step children. After their parent's deaths, he was estranged from his sister, but loved her dearly and occasionally, they communicated in summer via Fed Ex on what they believed each other's birthday was and during the Holidays too. Hawkins-Burke's attire, except when occasion or fundraiser required otherwise, was 'sparse mod' as he described it, Levi's, rumpled short sleeved cotton shirts, which he joked was to show that 'nothing was up the sleeves', which one acquaintance joked was like 'a priest saying he didn't notice the alter boys or the rather young, rather comely habit wrapped nun either.'

Hawkins-Burke laughingly mentioned once to his closest of his own ilk, his triggerman in chief as he tapped him, his featmed lobbyist lawyer, a redundancy if ever there was one, Jansen Hyde that "you know you're in the top tier when you wear bullet proof vests, ride in the bullet proof limos and Escalades and leave the Rolls at home."

Jansen Hyde had assisted in most of Stuart's and Magi's successful ventures, with above the table activities in international currencies and exchanges in the developing world, gold ; and under the radar trade in overseas human organ harvesting, extensive investments with high returns in the deforested Amazon of lumber and potential natural healing wonder plants of the great jungle, smuggled out of countries without tax or tariffs or concern for the long term damage to the environment or the impoverished citizens of these areas who get next to nothing while companies like MAGI, the middle men, the cartels reap billions in profit. "The packagers and shippers," as Hyde framed it, "there lies the vig, the juice and that's where we want to be." Nothing seemed beyond their possible grasp. Oil to mining, they knew the angle of approach, money and threat of ending politicians careers usually eventuated in the companies successful dealings. Hyde had worked many profitable land acquisitions from the Bureau of Land Management with dirt cheap, almost give away land swaps and purchases permitted under the 1872 federal Mining Act. The BLM lands, national forest and open lands evaporated under a tidal wave of sales to companies, MAGI, chief among them. They cared not a wit that the lands exchanged were fittingly valued or that the public interest was protected by the agencies of the federal government. As Jansen saw it, "To break the will, own the plow."

Hawkins-Burke and Hyde were ecstatic when the Kelso ruling gave their eminent domain weapon even more vicious a fire power and, in most cases, MAGI got the 'blight' they needed to demand compliance and destroy lives that stood in the path of their voracious appetite for the in- the-black beauty of the bottom line. Hyde frequently commented on and scoffed at the dirty state of America's union, a nodded acceptance of sleaze, established and maintained by the legislature for hire mentality that enabled him in his early days as corporate attorney to have helped many worldwide business's set up shop in the tax avoiding Cayman's, in a five-story office building on a nice, almost Hardy Boys setting tree-lined street, called the Ugland House. Nearly 19,000 corporate entities listed this Ugland residence as headquarters at a time in the mid 2000's, some 900 American businesses among them, and Hyde proved one of the most able of gatekeepers for his "needy babies" as he called these, his earliest clients. Hawkins-Burke noted Hyde's talents and hired him away for MAGI's benefit. Jansen had been seduced by Hawkins- Burke's forthrightfulness. Stuart had opened their negotiations with, "I never heard poorly of anyone without discovering it less than had been said, except in your case." Jansen loved that and the money offered was not an amount to say no to. He had always believed that the more the money, the more the virtue.

Stuart Hawkins-Burke got back to now. He went to the new granite top bar area and mixed up a strawberry health drink in his new deluxe mixer. He looked out the picture window towards the turquoise gulf waters and debated whether to take the boat out and challenge the dark blue gray clouds approaching from the west. Have to call the guards to make it ready. No, stay put.

Hyde would get the job done. And why not. Stuart Hawkins-Burke finished the drink and thought, 'why worry.' He was a lord over a giant fiefdom in an age where the yoke of paying taxes had switched gradually more and more to the backs of the serfs, while the benefits of government had shifted more and more to the royal realms of the day, to corporations. "God, it's good to be the king." And Stuart Hawkins-Burke headed back to the bar to make another smoothie.

Chapter 4

"In The Same Sunlight Under The Same Sky"

"Man is by nature a social animal; and an unsocial person who is unsocial naturally and not accidentally is either unsatisfactory or superhuman...Society is a natural phenomenon and is prior to the individual...And anyone who is unable to live a common life or who is so self-sufficient that he has no need to do so is no member of Society, which means that he is either a beast or a god."

Aristotle   "Politics"

September 24 2015

The gunmen, as usual, were paid more than most in Mexico, employed to spray messages in blood. They were the Los Ni-Nis, the "neither-nors", young males who claimed they neither "study nor work", except in the capacity as killers, torturers and errand tenders for the cartels. Their path to success in their mission had been cleared by the usual threats and bribes. The victims supposed security had faded at the proper minute; only two of the Don's guard's had been unreachable and now they, like their master, were sangre el mundo, communiques in the sand delivered by unsentimental men of little note or concern, sent by vicious, sinister lords of destruction fueled by pathological pride. Thankfully, for the one undead among the slain, the amateur expendable shooters were anxious to leave and masked by the dust and smoke, they did not see the slight movement of an elbow nor the blinking of the lids of the barely alive boy covered over by the bodies of two of his siblings. He fought not to vomit and give away a hint of his existence to the lobos locos circling the pile of what was five minutes before his family. The boy watched from beneath his sister's arm as one of the murderers leaned down about ten feet away and shot his father at close range one more time. He felt a small throbbing on the side of his head. His sister had fallen against him and as soon as they had hit the ground he had frozen. He remained silent. He struggled to hold his breath even though adrenaline was fighting his attempt to be still. He panted through barely open lips.

Someone yelled "Vamanos". Doors slammed. Tires spun, gravel kicked up and the boy stayed still as pebbles hit his face. He watched as the three Escalades raced away. He wondered if he was the only one alive. Fear kept him motionless and he only moved to get up when he saw the last vehicle drop down and out of sight on the horizon. It was time to rise from the dead. Adjusting to the light took a moment as he carefully moved his sister's arm away and rose up. He heard gurgling. He knew that it wasn't a spring. The air smelled of gasoline and lead. His head ached and then his heart as he begin to focus. He now remembered the noise before the pain. The wheels, his father's curse, his mother's wail, the gunfire, the plops and thuds of metal tearing into flesh, the scream's, bodies falling into him, the dust ..the suffocating haze of smoke and dirt. There were no calls for help. He knew his sister was dead. And as he looked beyond her, he knew he was alone and that life was now more precarious than just 50 seconds before.

At the same moment of this family's destruction, many miles north of the hacienda, John Truefellow is doing his job as auxiliary sheriff chasing a wife beater down a nameless dirt road in a forgotten area of a forgotten people's reservation. Similarly, as the survivor is presently standing, still in shock, as the lawmen is closing in on the erratically driven rusted Chevy of a drunken coward, in Denver, Cade is in session with his accountant, a friend for years who had consistently proven his worth by reporting positive and true figures and by not feeding the IRS anymore than its voracious appetite required. Cade smiles as he stares out the window south towards the apparent storm clouds and he smiles, amused that this man talking asset preservation to him was in therapy for years and truly hated numbers which Cade believes caused his friends inner tumult.

Little did the Mexican boy now upright amid disaster sitting in the same light as shines on the Navaho in pursuit and the same brightness that attracts the wandering thoughts of the Mogul, little would he or could he know that all would connect; that both the Navaho and the Mogul would enter his life...this young frightened life, which minutes before, had existed as expected, peaceful under the shining light of a beautiful day, a life abruptly changed, all recognition of what was or what could be, cut down to the scaring reality of a moment gone horribly, horribly wrong.

The survivor knew his existence meant danger, constant and suffocating. The tears were dry now. Adrenaline softened shock. Metallic smell was overwhelming. He strained to move but still hesitated as he listened for pleas for help but there were none. He was mesmerized by the sight of his father's body, bloodied, a purple not red appearance on his white shirt, his frame covering his older sisters body. He finally unfroze and went to his mother's side. She was face down; her blond hair framing the hole in the center of her head, blood was still coming out. He snapped out of his mental back and forth of whether or not to turn her over as his tortured thoughts were interrupted by his father's instructions for what to do in an emergency. "Water, weapon, way." "Water, weapon, way." His father's voice got him moving towards the garage. He entered and grabbed the dedicated emergency cell phone from the top shelf. The phone had remained in its cradle, charged and never used with only one number programmed into it. The teenager picked up the backpack, stocked with side packs of water, gorp, flashlight and an unregistered hand gun.

The boy opened the small envelope lying atop the two day provisions packed in the canvas pack. His father's handwriting begun to smear as tears from the boy overwhelming emotions streaked the ink. He held it away for a minute as he struggled to get it together again. He knew it wouldn't be long until someone would be coming. And whatever came, he anticipated that it would not be good. His emotions settled and he read the instructions.

He dialed the number on the sheet. He waited for the described voicemail response and then stated the code word required and closed the phone.

He was seven miles from the border. He had to stay away from the road and remain on the back arroyos and he had to stay moving. His father's words told him that he would have approximately 10 hours at the most to walk and run to the rendezvous. He made sure the safety was off, left the garage and headed north. If he followed the route his father had set out he would be alright as small caches of backup food and water were hidden along the way, marked by easily recognized landmarks. An old boyhood non-cartel friend of his father's was his first contact target. Through the years, his father had paid this man well to be ready for this day. And by the time the son had walked over the first hill a couple of hundred yards behind his shattered household, all need to know parties were in action. As he picked up the pace, the boy pondered who did it. Which rival cartel murdered his past and killed his approachable future? The Sinaloa, the Juarez group, the remaining Zeta's from Tamaulipas? A disgruntled "El Jefe" wanabe? That would wait. Now he focused on the Sonora, Aqua Prieta and across the border to the vicinity of Douglas. All he was sure of was that his father's maverick moods and methodologies had finally punctured someone's prickly insecurities and had scorched someone's paper thin pride. The son smirked to himself as he knew that these were replacement words for the real culprit behind the remains of his tragic day...greed.

****

The music automatically played when she entered her home. "Wish You Were Here" by Floyd was on. Odessa Gabriel mused over her agent's parting words about the scripts possible title, "The Beautiful and The Profane". She had responded to him with her view, "You mean, "Beautifully Profane", don't you, Digger?" She had continued in exaggerated exasperation, "...Jesus, I'm trapped; I feel cornered by my image, the portrayal of what I see on the screen, Digs. I dream of breaking this saran wrap to something, anything else that's mine, all mine...but, dammit, I know not what "mine" really is!" Digs had appropriately listened as if what she said made sense to him, but Odessa had recognized this countenance before and she knew he was doing his job of just 'being there' and nothing more would be forthcoming.

Her home decor was "early American carnival" as she described her eclectic tastes but it was her true haven from her employment in a real carnival, Hollywood.

It was afternoon on the coast and as she past the granite kitchen counters her motion detector coffee brewer went into gear and that was alright with her. She was a caffeine freak. She drank Indonesian Kopi Luwak beans, expensive in price, of course, and exotic in its production. The beans are consumed by small civet cats which then excrete them. The result is packaged and sold at nearly $450 per pound. "Expensive shit" a date had joked. Their sense of humor polar opposite, they had gone out only for a week.

Her maid, Melinda, had dutifully placed strands of saffron from crocus flowers in an urn Odessa had purchased from the Black Sea area while on location a few years previously. From Kashmir, Saffron is the world's most costly spice, with an acre only yielding a few pounds. Odessa looked above the garnet strands to her framed quote by dance company owner, Eliot Feld. "Art is always a New York argument with the past." Before Odessa had the thought framed, she had scribbled in raging red lipstick at the bottom, "Fuckin Ay", and then put it in glass surrounded by mahogany. She moved to the tete-a-tete, the S shaped sofa which forces people to face each other but which allowed for easy escape if necessary. She recalled the director joking with her after the actress had shared her excitement about meeting Sean. Karen had teased Odessa that Odessa at least before," believed in monandry, the custom of only one husband at a time and now she saw Odessa" practicing, botany; the condition of possessing only one perfect stamen!" Odessa had rejoined that at least she did not believe..." in gynarchy like Karen did." The tete-a-tete sat in what Odessa called her "Medieval Umber" room, not a sizeable space, den like, indefinite, on the shade side with no bright hum in color or sound to remind her of the outside drone she labored within. Ah, Melinda. A sweetheart, my little adjuvant as she affectionately called her assistant slash maid, who also the head of a midsized staff, all collectively referred to as "my toot suite adjuvant"....always a language off from being heard right. ..Her staff properly gathered as if the meeting was non chazzans and not the punctual thing it always was. Her staff kept her supplied in her secrets. A few select staff had assisted with the medical...any substance added to a drug or remedy to assist or heighten its actions and their proficiency in this and the mastery of silence as an allegiance test and which is a quantum requirement for hefty Christmas bonuses. Melinda had been the actress's friend before the actress was an actress. Melinda knew how to manage. She gave space and allows her boss to work to a point of sitting down with Melinda and sharing what is really on the bosses mind. Then tears, always the tears as apology, so the same rare but seemingly incipient dismissiveness would be excused the next time, as it always was. And the bonuses always increase each year.

While Odessa was the person in charge in the toy house of the industry she was employed in, Melinda was the actual Chatelaine of the household.

The actress was now extemporizing," this potential relationship is in it's, oh, what is that.

..ah, insitu, the natural or original position, my second favorite to missionary as you know, and this, stage one is the most charming part of meeting someone new." Melinda smiled at her friend. The actress Odessa Gabriel sat at the kitchen counter. Melinda poured another strawberry 'rita and Odessa sucked a drink in and kept the mix at the top of her mouth because that is where she liked to taste her sweets, the mix of sugar and cold, the swishing, the swigging and then the gulp, had been, since her first memories, her second favorite sensation.

As it now stood at about a quarter past 5:00p.m., she toasted with Melinda, and the assistant, childhood friend could go back to defcon 3. Odessa looks towards the many hued west, the newest man in her world, his smile centered just to the left of the sun setting behind the Pacific, genuine and frightfully embracing.

****

"What is your answer?"

The boy had followed his father's instructions. This was the right door to knock on...the face on the man asking the question is the one on the photo.

The inquisitor revealed nothing but contempt. His brow was furrowed.

"Do you intend to answer me within this century, mi amigo, or should I plan for the long haul."

The man boy knew the answer. It was the delivery of his response that was crucial. Delay lent weight to what he was about to say.

"It was the Martinez group. Eight of his worms shot us." "You saw this?"

"Saw this? I was this." He leaned towards the inquisitor to show the bullet crease above his left ear. The boy had forgotten about the ooze wound. The blood line was purple now, with dust caked in, about three inches in length.

There. It was out. Was the boy playing in the right game? Was this man the man paid by the boys' father to be ready for this day for over twenty years? Or was he dealing with the cartels enforcement authority, the bribed and typical big Ciudad cop, counting the bounty for turning in this survivor before him?

The policeman stilled waded in the pool of right and wrong, someone who remembered his catholic upbringing and the mother that made him different from the other material whores in his district force. He smiled at the boy. He thought about the power in his possession, the power over life and death, both his and the individual staring at him.

He knew he must act. "I am sorry about your father and family." He grabbed the boy' shoulder firmly, not too hard, but to show a bond with the son of the man who had helped the policeman live well for his family and future. The policeman's duty was set. The boy would meet his northern compadre and then it would be the Indian's concern.

"We will have to interact a few times. I will do the talking. Listen, Chico, do not, if we get separated for any reason, do not give up who you are, not even if Jesus Christ asks you...no answers. Serious times now, son. I know you are trained to understand."

The policeman found an almost clean pink rag and ran hot water over it and then daubed at the head wound.

"You did not really feel this early?"

"I only noticed the throbbing a little while ago."

It would later be discovered that this mixture of luck and theatre, a grazing wound as everyone else around died, that particles of the bullet remained in the skull after treatment and continued to contribute to visions and perceived prophetic abilities which the boy never took seriously even while many thought him prescient, without alliteration or gloss.

The policeman had eased them towards the appointment with the North. A direct pay way to border it! Everyone got a cut. They encounter nada, except at the border. The next stage of his father's plan again engaged trusted others to participate in the preservation of his life. The man wore a uniform. Sheriff, may be. It was apparent the policeman and the Norte Americano knew each other. The boy man took a breath as he felt the days gasp ending.

The new one turned to him and asked, "El Faco Baca?"

"Nine lives." Snorted the teen. Tired of proving himself as if, "who else could it be?"

"I pray you are the son of Don de Mejas?"

"I pray you are the right Indian? Sorry, my Ingles, esta, is, in improvisinal stages."

The policeman shook the Indian's hand, pivoted south and rapidly double timed it back to his federales vehicle to radio in, acting as normal as was still possible in Mexico.

The evening is upon them and a relief from the day. It is a short walk to the second hidden cop car.

The Indian told the boy to get in the back seat. Told him to lie down and cover up with blanket as evenings in September can be cool. The boy found Hostess Twinkies, chocolate bars and a liter of orange juice in a cooler. He was so hungry; he forgot how orange juice tastes after chocolate.

"Indian? Who are you? Why are you here?"

"How do I answer that to make the truth happy?" The Indian pushed back from the steering wheel not realizing how tight he had been holding it.

The teen inquired again, "Where are you from?"

Checks and balances had kept the Indian alive. And he wanted to keep his track record of not allowing unsullied emotions to interfere with thinking, still unmarked upon.

"Never forget that one day, one hour, one minute can remain forever and matter much for the remainder of a lifetime. Memory can be the crutches needed for a stigma or the signature needed for strength." The Indian glanced at his rear view mirror. "Hey, backseat?! Tell me again, your full name?"

The teen looked at the perihelion west, the rainbow of the sundog now going dark fast. "Alejandro Buddha Jesus Simon de Mejas. My father was a man who usually did not take chances and this issue, a son's blessed name, he wanted to cover as many bases as possible to secure protection and best wishes for his children as a way of the father's atonement for his father's early vile ways as he had begun his criminal path while only thirteen. Buddha Jesus' father did not want it held against his family. His real family."

The Indian had been listening but is paying attention to the dusty road and the way ahead and casually responds, "I know your background. Your father loved you dearly and by your presence, something terrible has happened." The teen nodded. "And you will share when you..."

"They were all killed."

The Indian tried to muffle a gasp only partially succeeding. Thank God the Don banked for this day.

"Don't really know who? Don't really know why." The teen shivered.

"You're safe now, Jesus Buddha ...aw, hell...dry those eyes. This day you are a man. You have survived the fallen and for a purpose only you will find.

First, I am sorry. Second, for the miracle of your arrival and for brevity, I will call you 'Godboy'."

Alejandro Jesus Buddha Simon de Bolivar y San Martin de Mejas is puzzled. The Indian laughed, "It's perfect! "Godboy" In Spanish too, NinoDios????" The teen laughed and then nervously "Is that blasphemy?"

"No. It's fact. You being alive is miracle. We are children of God, remember."

"Ah, Diosnino..." The last descendant of the de Mejas hacienda smiled as he recognized the blessing of this name in this most crisp time of his life.

"Yes, Godboy, it is only the Great Spirit that could have this happen."

The sheriff pulled the vehicle to a rock outcrop and parked beneath its ledge. "Take a standup break. Bathroom. We need to wait for satellite to pass."

"Thank you for your charity."

The Indian acted like he didn't hear the comment.

"What's your favorite bible lesson?"

This got the Indian's attention. Not one to be caught off guard, he was quick to recover.

"Well. Dignity. Yourself and others. It's in Leviticus. Jesus encounters a man with leprosy. The law of the day required such afflicted people to call out and alert others to their presence. "Unclean. Unclean. But on this occasion, the leper did not shout warnings as he headed towards Jesus. He stopped and dropped at Jesus feet, head to ground and begged for Jesus help. Not only did Jesus respond by destroying the affliction, but he restored the more important...the man's worth and dignity."

The sheriff's radio crackled. He still had interference with link to base. He hit talk button twice, resulting in two blasts of static at the other end of the transmission, alerting base that all was well, common. It also was beneficial that a last minute technical demand required down time for security....a secret "need to know" only ten minutes off line real time request from somewhere up the official looking food chain manifest of how things get done, order. It appeared official. ...and the watchers.. .deaf and dumb precisely at the right time and the needed place...never recorded the darken vehicle managing the crossing as if in daylight, guided by another watchful eye and benefactor of Godboy's father's magnanimity and careful attention to his proveable around the bend foresight ...except for once.

The driver noticed the correct arroyo south of Douglas, Arizona, turned left into it and knew the first stage of the mission was finished on what would otherwise be just another night in the quiet pandemonium known as the border lands.

John Hummingbird Truefellow is a part time tribal councilor, part time advocate/lobbyist for his tribe and other Native Americans, as well as a part time volunteer Sheriff for the Navaho Nation.

Broad shouldered, just under six feet tall, handsome, soft spoken, three scars; one, a bullet from Iraq, one, a bullet from a teenage mental adjustment session in a bar and the third wound, a knife, was from a wife who tired of the distance, mentally and physically between the husband and the wife when the husband was away on two tours of Saddam's land. She wanted more than red dirt for the rest of her life. It initially hurt Truefellow hard, and then softened into an occasional pang. John was in more familiar terrain among men. Women, to John Hummingbird Truefellow were as close to walking peyote as ever found and personal peace came from avoiding them for every reason but two. He was a praying man, mostly for his people, the Navaho Nation, to prosper. He viewed the Bureau of Indian Affairs and ignorance as twins. He owned a nice sized Hogan he named 'Casa de Top Sky', and is co owner with Sean Linden in a Washington D.C. condominium that acted as a haven during some of their heavy traveling to and from the District; a good location for him, as he traveled frequently in the east advocating native American rights and seeking funds and donations for education and aid for battling addictions and abuse that are prevalent on tribal lands. As his mother could not wait until the next depot, he was born in Mexican Hat, Utah, on a Greyhound bus, New Year's Eve. His dad, an alcoholic, after his service in the Persian Gulf conflict, left his mother when John was thirteen. His mother had willed them through it with somber courage that John witnessed and by her giving of her body for cash that he never saw nor heard about until after high school.

He was expert at archery.. "what'd you think an Indian would be good at, white boy?!" being his usual friendly rejoinder to the funny 'unspoken' in the air. Poetry was a weak spot as were the History Channel, Fellini, Lead Zeppelin and the masterpiece, "A River Runs Through It". He cried every time Pitt and the Bear charged each other. His grandfather had been a decorated Windtalker and John had named his pet Gila monster, Fred, after him.

Notoriously private, even in front of groups on stage as advocate for a cause, he never revealed much...he had not shared his feint hope for a child with even Sean Linden, his non blood brother, but it was never far away similarly to the occasional other stone in his moccasin, the memory of his wife.

But now, viola, enter stage of life downstage full center...light speed change and now you have a new nephew...the story had been set years ago...as John was known to have relatives living in Mexico...perfectly hooked for the day it would be finally pulled off the shelf and used. Jesus Buddha's father, a very benevolent with purpose lord had donated and invested with Truefellow in the causes the Navaho cherished with the understanding, a clear understanding of what was expected in return. For two decades, the needs of the Dineh, whether school needs, clothing, health care improvement, Godboy's dad gave the Navaho to use how he saw fit. "Just stand ready to help my family if ever the day comes." This is all Mr. de Mejas demanded. And it was the only time that the Indian and the Mexican spoke.

The Navaho's debt was now to be paid back in life changing spades. Alejandro Buddha Jesus' adrenaline had something to say, not specifically to the Indian, just aloud in the forum of the rocks, "Genius is without virtue these days you know." The Navaho stared at the sentinel saguaros. He wondered which among them were the oldest. They can live a couple of centuries. "The desert is literally a trash bin. Each person crossing these lands leaves an average of eight pounds of garbage. Sorry, this is not meant as comment on Mexico or you or anything except the madness of men and these hidden freeways of misery. Nature has seen it all."

"That's left standing, right?"

"That wound holding up?"

"Wound? Fine. Just a scrape."

"No headache?"

"I'm alright." The tiny particles of bullet remained imbedded and the young man did not ponder them much thereafter. Later, confidents would somewhat tease, somewhat inquire, as to the boy's hints of prophetical touch and how these traits were related to his "lead in the head..." He did not come to the conclusion until after he was shot that intuition rather than intellect demonstrated certain truths to be fundamental and that the tragedy, always at home on some synaptic cul-de-sac which his head could not unmap, bringing him to a place of habitual perspicacity which had imbued a gallant gentleness for the defenseless and for the unlucky.

"Come on. Sit up front. Time to get going."

The teen sat passenger.

As the Sheriff shut his door, Jesus Buddha mused, "Vision. Seen it all. And yet, I can't believe what I saw...I had science tutor, el professor Hidalgo...and one lesson of his always stuck..."

The Sheriff knew it was good that the boy released as shock wore off and adrenaline went to maintenance mode.

"What a difference a few inches makes."

Truefellow stared ahead.

"Our eyes, whether crossed, blue, green, bloodshot are separated by the nose, at least a couple inches between them." Godboy glanced to his left to see if he was being listened to. He was. "Senor Hidalgo said that each eye receives a vaguely different image from the other. The magical house we know as the brain then mingles these pieces of light together to shape a three dimensional version of our reality."

The teen looked to his right and up. The moon... He focused to see the man on its surface.

"Since the likeness in each eye is actually two dimensional, the three D look we comprehend is really a convincing illusion."

Officer Truefellow considered this latest epiphany. He threw a smile towards his most recent relative.

"Vision is a learned set of more than twenty separate skills."

The sheriff had witnessed many reservation children coming from broken homes. Some were tougher than others. He handed advice and the canteen to the passenger. "Here's to the funkiness of our failures and our fanfares, right, Muchacho?"

The sheriff later confided to Linden, Moah and to Buddha Jesus himself, the Indian's thoughts of that night, which he, in typical Native Americanese condensed into an operating statement with only the necessary, necessary.

"This sapling has more ring count than normal for the size of his roots."

This is the Navaho's way of commenting positively on his new found, new molded out of whole cloth, nephew. It was also the advocate's way of noting and approving of Godboy's apparent blend of a "going for more than you're told is possible now" philosophy with a genial approach, singular and refreshing. Provocation with a smile. The teen had the potential of becoming quite an antagonist for good. And he could be the thorn in the paw of the lion.

"You are familiar with Immanuel Kant, right?"

Sheriff cut him a glance that said don't insult me again so the passenger continued.

"Kant said this. Another tidbit from Hildalgo. Quote, 'If God is perfect, he had no need to create a world; if he is imperfect he is not God. If God were good, and had divine powers, he could not possibly have created so imperfect a world, so rich in suffering, so certain in death.' unquote."

"You are aware that length means strength and that about half the Bible writers completed their writings before the birth of both Confucius and your Siddhartha Gautama? For hundreds of centuries...length...strength...why? Because this is a God that gives a damn for those of us most subject to abuse. This is an almighty that many have lain down for." Young de Mejas was slightly taken aback by the forcefulness of Truefellow.

"Yes, he's kind!" de Mejas responded dismissively, almost robotically, as he visioned his Mother's smile in death.

"The Bible makes the extraordinary ordinary and vice versa." The sheriff paused as he checked his rear view and spotted only one pair of distant headlights. It gave Buddha Jesus time to recover.

"You know, Sheriff, the first memory I have of learning a verse from the good book...my, Mother, of course, is, and was from Psalms. Get this, the Jehovah God instructs people not to return for the leftovers from the grain harvests and the vineyards, not to gather the remainder, the gleanings, for God wanted, and the almighty was rock on in this, hombre, God demanded that, and I remember this from oh, about five or so, he told the people of Israel to let, to leave lone the excess crops, the residue of the fields, because the Lord commanded that this bounty" should stay for the alien resident, for the fatherless boy, and for the widow."

The gravel kicking against the undercarriage was exaggerated by the patentable silence in the cab.

The young undocumented spoke and humored the moment. "Well, two out of three, not bad, but a widow would have made it a trifecta and a much, much better memory and a much much stranger coincidence."

Sensing the need to turn the current away from torment, the Indian returned to the softer subject of science and religion. Antagonism can be trendy. And aid in the short term need to forget.

"Galileo's contemporaries, not all, but most, were so wobbly kneed at the prospect of a comfortable dogma being destroyed by what their colleague expounded and Galileo proven by what the G man had invented, so distraught that a good lot of them would not look through the looking glass to the new heavens above since the device exposed the heavens revealed to be way different than what the approved teachings of the Church had spewed out for centuries....Ptolemy got a kick in the Aswan too."

Godboy laughed.

"Things evolve. Your life is now in this change. And from what I've seen, you will be fine."

Godboy quickly wanted to get away from the serious and back to the irreligious.

"In Mexico, the Indian ball games were strenuous, tended to brutality and the decidedly sinful and losing was a one time thing. Then came Cortez and Teoteotetlan became an island city fit for schoolmarms and churches."

Sheriff Truefellow gave his passenger an apple from his travel bag and said, "Here's to God and gold, the snake eyes of history."

De Mejas took a bite. The Navaho gnawed on a stick of beefjerky.

Similar to the yellow lines racing alongside each other in the no passing lanes, neither the Indian or the Mexican would remember the origin of their parallelism, their coming together during the baby steps of synchronicity; gravel to pavement, body to mind, and with a kindly kismet initiated that September evening/morning, a till dying breath do part friendship began.

$$***********************$$

"Occupation: Actress. Time of day: Who knows?" The author laughed at her latest entry in... Da-Da The Diary...a daily exploration of an actress's method, mind and madness'es...to be reviewed and edited later for subsequent publication and profit, a fact which Odessa had in mind as she laid the groundwork for the next decade of her career. With a diamond cutters precision and the analism of an artist, the "Actress of Desiring Minds" (This was not her favorite description of herself) as the Hollywood and Viners tended to tag her and as was also promoted by the star's almost as dazzling as Odessa herself, agent , Vanessa Riks, a constant in all press releases, appearances, contracts, commitments, whether one hour or one year, everything that wrapped around her clients world, Vanessa would be the one to put her finger on the ribbon and complete the bow., Ms. Gabriel had carefully prepared a response for any prolonged downward trend in her popularity or her ability to leverage outrageous contracts, both, possible catastrophe's that may arise asp-like and bite her on her Cleopatra career arse as she was wont to cackle. Possible discomfitures, such as age and an inability to turn as many heads as before, need, in their infancy, quick attention and the discipline of pre-planning if they are not to inflict long term damage to the image.

She turned to the front of the small book, well, maybe a midsized diary; actresses have more to share and purge. On the first page she read the date from a couple of year previous and "Be crazy and keep honest track of it. It's a better bottom line."

Her credo could read; Set the metronome to the profitable beat and serenade of the expected but never forget to always pay the orchestra to improve the tempo and strengthen the tonal texture to reach memorable heights and crescendos of gossip, a two step finale of airy suspicions and gutsy flirtations delicately blended and professionally positioned within the cacophony sphere of twenty four hour cycle of Schadenfreude that always needs salting and "cooking" concerns and protestations that always require stirring., and you will always be on the lips of the public for better or for worse. And worse sells better.

Project shamelessness in the bold and brazen way of the young Madonna. Not the one in the church. And keep this going for as long as the years on her would permit. With the mannerisms of a good hearted pirate and the predator habits of an owl on nocturnal wanderlust and prowl, she had the required attention wherever she went. When on the set or on a man, she knew her lines.

Born on the border in Fabens, Texas, youngest of seven daughters in a Catholic family, Odessa, unlike the other newly arrived pop up starlets in the furnace fanfare of Hollywood dreams, was not dazed by the electric fire of potential fame, because Odessa had learned at an early age in an uncanny way for a then just turned 18 year old beautiful girl from a land of sage and spice, about the human condition of meanness and the eternal search for escape from boredom.

She well knew the survival tact that got one through bitter moments and near death disappointments by watching groups and learning early, studying and mastering management against the herd's instincts for selfishness and general propensity to celebrate in the false glory of the intimidation of others.

The Texan loved her mother, who resided in Gardena and played poker to pass her time. She never forgot how nonplussed or unfazed her mother had seemed when her father died while she was still in high school and Mr. Gabriel's name rarely came up in conversation thereafter in her or her sister's presence. In girlhood, she preferred the classical movies of the type she would eventually star in, strong woman, loved by many, respected by most if not all, an emotionally stranded individual who understood that she would never again meet another lover of merit, mirth, and moments of mighty memory after experiencing a lifetime long love from a once in a lifetime man. The female "unrequited thing" one of the makeup women tagged it. "Or maybe she got requited but never felt the oomph of the moment again with any other swinging dude." another had chimed in with obvious primal knowledge of how frustrating that could be.

The femme fatale ending up on the wrong side of falling in love with a once in a lifetime man had made Odessa wealthy and many others in the cine pit envious and snide in their approach or commentary towards her. Odessa had done her spade work early, getting down into the dirty and the ugly of getting ahead in Hollywood, subjecting herself to her first agents passes and sexual metaphors when she realized that these were not idle percolations as he was in fact successful at securing, over a shorter than usual time, tapping into his multifarious contacts in casting laybacks and come due paybacks.

The agent had taught her to make as much of the press a friend as possible...friends without benefits but ever available for a properly timed quip or career advancing tidbit of knowledge to feed the consumer... She learned fast as she channeled Mae West with a quote that made the inside of People but not the cover she fronted. She had been asked at one of her first premiers which sport was she a fan of and she responded that her favorite sport was "...Watching the men behind her". The fuses of the fireworks of controversy and scandal were lit then and the show had continued for years mostly without too many embers falling on too many of the wrong people.

The actress wondered if the military man would like her style. Her preferred clothes were haphazard and lovely; rich rags, she called them. Ragged tank tops and jeans were the usual when she was not on set.

As she had become "wiser" (Odessa's word for "older"), she was more acutely dialed in to her market with the ease of familiarity that a parent has with their child whether it was the ubiquitous cocktailing and gatherings of the shiny few to hitting the marks on location, she nailed it. An additional benefit of the 'wisering' process was that her voice became even more tempting, full and unforgettable, so much so that she was paid the highest rate for 30 seconds of recording for a commercial that all but one other male announcer, called the 'Balls Grande of Beverly Hills' for more reasons than just voice work, had been paid.

She always believed 19 to be her lucky numeric charm. She loved the letter "S" as it was the 19th letter in the alphabet and now that she had meant Sean it all seemed just as should be. But no matter your perception of this, Lord help you if you called the actress, no matter how chummy you thought the relationship to be, "oh Susanna", as exile was in your future. The "S" in Odessa S. Gabriel was for Susanna who was a Jewish captive in Babylon falsely accused of adultery, and whose life Daniel saved. Daniel intrigued her further when she learned that Daniel means 'God is my judge.'

Odessa made as much time in her schedule and life as an actress for one child by mistake and one child by choice. Ms. G. had had decided at age 30 to gain "forever stardom" by having a child the easy way and in the very public forum of humility and selflessness, adopted a one year old girl, renamed Sophia by Ms. 0., which the actress had learned while on location in Athens meant "wisdom" in Greek. Miss Gabriel's child by blood was born when the star was twenty and just nine months after her first hit movie and fathered by an older man who was the only man since Sean that had swept her up through heights she had never known.

Autistic, living in secret, Aaron is her love too and she visits the care facility frequently, always in disguise and always with kind words for the nurses and caregivers who she paid bonuses to of such measure as to insure her privacy and their attentive regard to her son. Besides, she would sue them privately and corporately to oblivion and back if they screwed up on patient doctor privilege and confidentiality.

Once, when the press snooping came close to discovery of Aaron, one of Odessa's sister's claimed the child as hers and credited and thanked Odessa for her love and support of her nephew. The Gabriel clan, mother and sisters, never wavered in having the back of their beloved breadwinner nor she theirs. Equally, her nannies were well compensated, as was Ricks, to show Odessa's love to Sophia when the actress was absent.

The actress was about to write a little more in Da Diary about her recent time when Sean walked on stage. Literally. He had visited her while filming script about Jean Rio Baker, American pioneer woman, a British convert to Mormonism and a widow that traveled the west with a brood of kids and a fearless determination of the nature that only religious zealotry can replicate. Odessa might still have been in character. Independency. Women. And, it was another hot day in Utah.

She recalled teasing his shyness. "Talk about double standards," The actress and her friend were alone under the trailer sunshade, sipping lemonade. "No language, Sean, none in this world has ever had a word for a virgin man." She spit out ice cube and had caught Sean's look and reddened cheeks and they both had laughed. Glasses were raised to empowered women in history. "To the Delphi Oracle. How could a link between humans and Gods not be at the top of the list! The Pythia, my God what a devil sounding name, she was one powerful higher than a kite bitch. She could end wars, cause construction of new cities or the halting of their plans; she could even be the origin of government policies. The oracle for the God Apollo. Hell of a calling card."

Sean deadpans, "In ancient Israel, Beulah was the word for wife. And it meant "owned". Odessa had fawned and switching the gear of the moment said, "Don't forget, that this Baker woman was disheartened by male leadership and the tyranny of the church they ran. Abuse and polygamy."

"Sounds like subject matter for treatments out here." Sean's comment did not illicit the humorous response he had hoped for.

"Gynarchy Alert. Gynaikos 'women,' plus Kraterin "to rule." And I am still pissed about Mary Magdalene. Those old padres made her a person of lewdness, shiftiness, elusive motivations, lasciviousness, in short, an actress!" Through the laughter, she had continued and invited Sean to Hollywood party or as she had called it, "an event for the epigrammatically challenged and the soiled visions of the many would of-could of's in attendance that usually stay longer than the rest of the professional revelers. It's an opportunity for pushing the panache and I want you to abet me in it."

The Diarist then thought of the two laughing after the Leveetra moment. The ad had come on and Odessa commented, "In case an erection lasts four or more hours with us, I'll call my horny self loathing friends so a good boner doesn't go to waste, so you also perform a community service for dysfunctional parts of humanity, kind of an early Christmas gift for you and them." His obvious discomfiture signaled that she had achieved her silly goal of keeping him in his manly place, a waiting or rumpus room until he got the cue to her readiness for the next step.

Celebrities are addicted to response. They show antipathy towards their enslavement in numerous outbursts of being human by acting out being real, instigating headline grabbing activities and" Oh, yes I can!" moments to know, to reaffirm, that they are alive and have value in both worlds.

She remembered the eyes, always the eyes; his smile often. And as obstructions were her security and his talent, she wanted his walk beside her.

They had teased on the phone in long conversations, ambling through getting to know each other talks.

"I'm considered a talented degenerate by the devoted hounds of the holy/hellish press." Sean joked and the light of that day was on his face and Odessa recalled its look perfectly, "Great product line."

Odessa had almost horse laughed and choked at the same time. "Don't make me wet myself." She had becalmed, and, "Yes, I went to college."

Sean leaned in. He had not read anything about university time for the star.

"I'm a graduate of the ecoele de fuck me now, fuck me "wow" of loving way of hard knocks and double locks, survival tools for my world, soldier boy." She had thought him aroused but later told him that she could not tell. She recalled the celery she bit into. Crisp. Noisy. "When I'm on mark, on the lens, I just take it all in; put it all out so that after one take or twenty, I'm satisfied with the sweat of my intent."

Odessa looked out to the lights of L. A... It is the wayward time of the morning.

She calls him. It was close to when he usually arose. She wanted to share with Sean about the new personal development class she'd enrolled in and to also establish that they could talk at any time about anything. "According to Master Talker, Olivier, women have regressed into repositories of reaction. In Vedic times the status, in Vedic times, the Indo- Aryan women were respected. Held high. Esteemed. And there were three modes of getting married."

"This is definitely better than Good Morning America."

"The three ways, get the gals consent, two, purchase her like Sissy Spacek in Prime Cut or Time or whatever that Lee Marvin movie was.. and three, by the seizure of the bride. The last method was considered a great tribute by women."

"So Flintstone my way to your heart? Is that it, screen girl?" "Bonk and bang, babbie doll, bonk and bang."

****

"You will be in fine hands. My mother, one of her earliest admonitions that I recall, was about the frailty of resistance to gossip and its evil results for both provider and abider."

The sheriff had poured a cup of coffee for himself and for Godboy. They were stopped atop a paved lookout parking lot on a mesa that afforded a good look both east and west.

"Mom held a box filled with white packing balls out at arms length. The top four cardboard flaps had been closed and she said, 'if pop these flaps open, the balls will fly every which way but to a good place and I could never get all of these scattered things back into the package.' She said that is how it gets when you broaden on the truth or spread a lie about someone. So she, and please, Poquito, do not take this wrong..." John continued as he saw Godboy wave that concern off. "..Your mother and mine are probably very alike in the good things they..." The Indian stopped.

"Ah, kindness. A good location." Godboy smiled at Truefellow's respect. "The kind of places you put in ink on a map for a friend." Godboy expanded. "My mom, she taught me that the Bible susses this perfectly..."

"Suss what?"

"Gets the good out in front. Get after it with helping orphans. Wow, is that what I am?" The Indian did not look in the teen's direction.

"Widows and orphans and to keep yourself from being contaminated by the infected world we live in."

The Navaho thought of the boy's father's business model, but then, the father had greatly aided him and debt repayment is due, so no looking rearward now.

De Mejas felt Truefellow's slight discomfort. "Jesus goes after the soul beneath, the hidden part of every ugly duckling. He desired the undesirables, showing that God's grace doesn't give a damn about stigma."

The sheriff started to leave the overlook. Coffee needed refilling so he stopped in the middle of the exit, turned his lights on, and as he filled their cups, "People and possessions, they are the weaker that need things, do without for a change,.....there's a, whoa , wait, let's get going again." Overheads were shut down and they headed back onto the highway. "Haves and have nots; history, over and over again."

"Alex the Great came across a guy who was naked it is said, sitting in a barrel or something and the man in the barrel challenge the greatest on earth at that time with the following posit, 'I am much greater than you,' the pauper began to the prince of the world, 'greater because I have despised more things than you have owned. What you, oh prince, consider great to possess or worship or something like that, can't remember the professor on this verbatim, the beggar said, 'is too small for me to despise."

"So do not need anything is the moral of this?"

"No. Do not need anything or anyone." The bitter edge of the run together day broke a hole in the border of proximity and propriety and John saw Buddha Jesus sigh and slightly slump. Truefellow thought again about his new charge's family. They were killed in a business decision. Buddha Jesus' father had donated to Truefellows causes up to the last moment of Mr. de Mejas's life. Complex personality. The Don had reminded the Indian the one time they had met, of the devil may care actor, Gilbert Roland, same 'stache and ruggedness about them both. And now, his son.

"Papa is probably haggling with Malverde."

The sheriff glanced away from the road. "What? Mal what?"

"The patron saint of drug traffickers, Jesus Malverde. Mi Padre, he would want a refund on his deal."

"Patron Saint of dru..?"

"Yes!" The young de Mejas stared ahead. "Ah, yes, he is wanting a refund on his gift." Truefellow noticed the first tear he had seen from the young man.

"In Culiacan, on the Pacific, there's a shrine, a chapel that is Malverde's. The locals, they leave donations, prayers for protection, you name it. The economy there relies on the dirty thing, smuggling. Malverde is considered a Robin Hood..."

"Like the Medellin Hood, Escobar?"

"More so. Two billion dollars floats around the area. A good chunk of the economy is supplied by drugs; smuggling has been their balm for decades. And my father, he had read everything he could on Malverde as he did envisioned himself a little, I see this now, as a Malverde, a champion for the poor who might do, should we say, naughty things for ah, good people who are in bad ways. Is that how you say it?"

The sheriff flashed his high beams at an approaching obviously speeding pickup and the vehicle slowed as it spotted the law car.

"The people there, the devoted poor as my mother called them, they claim, and have for years, that Malverde robbed rich politicians and gave to the poor. This was at the beginning of the 20th century, 1910, 1909 maybe?"

The sheriff interrupted, "Malverde, that means..."

"Si, perfectmento. Green evil, marijuana...Amazing, isn't it, how serious serendipity plays a part, things just seem to fit like Lego blocks...."

"Or a reminder that God likes to laugh too." As soon as he had said this, the Indian regretted it as he noted his companion's face turn more dour and jaw set hard. "I'm sorry, that's a lit..."

"No, no. Es bien. Bien. You see, my father took me with him to Culiacan. We all were dressed in near peon. We went in an old station wagon. Did not want to draw attention that de Mejas was in another cartel's hood; is that how you say it, hood?"

The Navaho smiled. "Yes, hood's fine."

"My father remained half block away, hat and shades and unlit, untidy fat cigar in mouth. He told me later that if anyone were to look his way, their eyes would go to the crappy looking thing in his mouth and not focus on the rest of him. A cartel lord would never chomp down on something like this, would they? He watched as Antonio and myself ...ah, shit, Antonio!"

"What? What is it? Antonio what?"

Buddha Jesus' lower lip danced. "I just remembered his, his yell, scream really, that's when I felt the thud. Bullet hit my grandfather's eagle and snake belt buckle, mi padre just had given it to me, and I fell back and, yes, yes, I got hit on the side of the head before the ground? Don't really know...but Antonio's painful wail was the last, and I did not recall this until now, his sound overwhelms my opaqueness of the thing." He works to regain composure. "My father watched me and Antonio walk down the street and we went into shrine. Antonio cut us in to the front of the pilgrims and you know, Sheriff, amazing how the people, those poor people, they backed off without dissent and it seemed they sensed by Antonio's demeanor, that they better not. I witnessed their wonderment at me, the 'who was I, what am I' kind of stares one never forgets. I slipped my father's fat manila envelope in the offering box and Antonio and I turned and made our way out and back to the waiting wagon. I remember no one said a word. My father only moved to lift the shades and he thanked me with his eyes and a nod. We went around the block to the McDonald's, got cheeseburgers to go, and headed back home." Godboy paused. "Yes, Papa is definitely squaring things with Malverde".

They let that settle in the air. The radio crackled for the first time in a half hour. Sometimes discemable words and noticeable static is all that came through. As the sheriff turned down the volume he squinted towards the horizon. A hint of faint pillow light suggested dawn's arrival an hour away. The focus of the sheriff's attention is the somewhat weaving used green Camaro ahead of them. And the right tail light which is burned out. And the license plate number which he all too well knew. He flips the lights on but not the siren. "I know this driver. Stay here."

Buddha Jesus watched the sheriff's giant sized shadow cast by the high beams get smaller on the yucca and stone backdrop as the officer approached the passenger's side of the Chevy.

Truefellow opened the door and leaned in. "Look, Joseph, we c..."

"Howdy, Sheriff," responded Truefellow's friend since grade school.

"Joe, you've ..."

"Grown? I know."

"Dammit! I will be behind you running hazards and get you to your turnoff. You have a taillight out and you smell slightly wary of sobriety don't you think?"

Joseph looked down quickly and said, "Thank you. 'Bout a half mile more than right ..."

"..To the red dirt road home," Truefellow interjected. He returned to the police car.

"All he needs to do is to turn onto the right dirt road, then only a couple of cactus and a few drop-offs is all he should have to mess with and importantly, we get him to his road and he can only nick himself up and nobody else."

The sheriff's friend had been a star in athletics, well-liked, and now...

Both were watching the Camaro maintain a fairly straight ahead approach, no swerving...and at twenty two miles per hour rate of movement, not bad.

"I've known him almost from my earliest memories." John rubbed his sleepless eyes. "One day, all is reasonable, sound, and the world is round and full. Then, lightning quick, boom...and I mean no disrespect to your own moment now in life, son."

Godboy brushed that away with a 'as if ' look. "Doesn't need explanation, sheriff." Truefellow continued, "Then from who knows where, the world is flat and there is no time for reason. Joseph Walks Ahead Of Day, that's him, the one light guy, good hearted as they come." He leaned out his window and yelled, "Alright, man, you are going great. Few more football fields and we'll be there!" The occupant in the Chevy did not respond for a half beat and then a hand popped out, a newly lit Camel flicking sparks as Joseph Walks Ahead Of Day waved his appreciation in return.

"His scholarship was jerked up in Utah. Dated Caucasian girl which stirred the tribal pot a little. Stood up for Native rights as a freshman. I sent him some of my early tenets, suggestions, and helped him occasionally."

Sheriff looked in rear view to check if traffic was coming up from behind. Still early, so not much on single lane road to be of concern.

"I still know he was; I knew he was set up. Blackmail. Got slammed around by some who first entertained casinos as the 'be-all' for tribal benefits and tribal future. Joseph Walks Ahead Of Day is the American Native, small triumphs and massive tribulations. He is Dineh. And you now shall know learn a little about," the Navaho looked at Godboy, "...your tribe." Buddha Jesus arched his eyebrow and a small smile says go ahead.

"When Columbus turned up, there were probably 5 million of us in Norte Americana. Diseases, massacres, relocation, removal to dead end reservations even sterilization like we were Master Coyote who, to them, does not deserve to live and bingo, 100 years ago there are now maybe a quarter million Indians. Here's a kicker though. Today, ten million Americans are proud to claim to have a pint or so of Indian blood running through them, a status boost on the heritage of a discarded people, now honored and sought after by the very vermin, at least their ancestors that caused the demise. There are maybe two million of us now."

"The Navaho?"

Truefellow laughed. "I wish. No. That's total natives. Our biggest enemy in recent years, maybe longer, has been the Bureau of Indian Affairs and the Interior Department. Misplaced trust accounts for tribes, oil and gas leases, billions of dollars lost, slightly misplaced maybe, or misspent; these are the excuses, Nino, a dismissive manner that borders on a to the death insult because of the lack of remorse shown in the delivered explanations."

"I know my country treats Indians ...there's still a caste system." Godboy thought of the reports he had heard about the difficulties on Mexico's southern border with the illegals. "I once smiled at an Indian teenager sitting in a mall who was apparently on vacation with his family from the countryside. He looked shocked that I acknowledged his presence. He noticeably hesitated, and then returned the greeting and on we both went."

"We believe our land and we are in Utah, New Mexico and Arizona, it is the cradle of civilization. The reservation's about 27,000 square miles and there's three hundred thousand of us. We do excellent silver work and weaving, focusing the mass of it on rugs purchased by tourists. You will see Navaho men with long hair tied into a knot we call a tsiiyeel."

"Yours isn't."

Still a teenager, aren't we?"

"Well?"

"Shaved my head for football, never changed since and this is long for me, " as the sheriff raised his cap with one hand and ran his other over the butch waxed crew cut. "Also, I can't tie the knot. And never call a woman a squaw and never mention Kit Carson! He caused the 'Long Walk', which you will learn more about later."

"What?"

"You might be followed in white stores in towns. Situation is poor at times and some people do steal. I have hard time blaming either party." Storeowners hate the loss."

"But there is no excuse for bigotry."

"No." The sheriff called in a status report. He finished and said, "We have meth, rape, abuse problems. Do not, I repeat, you will never, while with me, I will be knowledgeable of your whereabouts, you hear? At least, until you are of age. Strike that. I'm sorry. You came of age today, Godboy, in a manner I can never fathom but will always respect." Truefellow looked back to the road.

"You can be made sick by the ghosts of your slain enemies so we have sweat lodges. The whole earth is sacred to us. In wintertime, we have tender raindrops, light precept Navaho's call the "female rains" and July, after scorching days and bone dry nights, in July, the angry "male rains" come down hard, ferocious torrents. The clearest days of the year come after these storms. The stones, the orange and the purple and the shiny layers of ocher, they are so nice and new looking that you think they were made on a movie set. The blue sky is almost eye closing in its radiance and a stunning trim to the rainbow in rock during the summer storms." The Navaho looked over to see if his companion was still with him and Buddha Jesus was staring back at him. "And when you are older, here, on the reservation, it is a good thing to know that the Navaho believe the stars are in the up above because a First Woman, with capable letters, put them there. Always try to begin with admiration for First Woman if your lady is pissed at you and it may soften the blows. And never forget that Navaho descent is traced through the mother, but I digress."

They laughed.

"Listen, she, First Woman, she emblazoned the laws of the universe on the walls of heaven. Then, the Trickster, the coyote, grabbed the First Woman's blanket of stardust and swung it skywards and created the Milky Way. Big deal babe, got it!"

"Yes."

"Poverty is an open wound on the reservations in this country." The Navaho had a penchant for abrupt changes of subject. "Our Federal government is in need of a refill. New fuel that changes policies that reward those who are already set apart and blessed by those who are paid to do just such a thing and thereby insuring the existence of the both of them, the lobbied and the lobbyist."

"But it's still better than Mexico's."

"There are weeks that that's debatable."

"I will share with you the beautiful heroes we call the Code Talkers. They devised an unbreakable secret communication system using Navaho language which kept us ahead of the Japs in the Second World War. Best weapon we had in the South Pacific. About 420 of them. First action was Guadalcanal. Indians have enlisted in military in higher percentages than other groups."

"Even with the treatment you have received for centuries?" "Yes, we're Americans, the real ones."

Walks Ahead of Day reached his turnoff, slowed and started down his red dirt road home. He flashed his brights and honked his appreciation as he kick up dust. The sheriff answered in kind. He stopped the patrol car and Godboy and he watched the Camaro make it the first few hundred yards as Walks Ahead maneuvered the familiar path with ease.

"The Dineh believe that our land is the cradle of civilization. Our civilization, not the white man's. The do-gooders, missionaries and teachers, white ones, of course, they tried to ban our language, our youngsters had their mouths washed out with soap if they spoke a word of their blood language..."

"Talk English, or not at all?"

"Yeah. Now I ask you, where would we be if they had succeeded? No code talk and how many more Americans would have died in WW2, if Navaho did not resist and had been forced to swallow their own words forever, to get white or die?"

Godboy remained silent. The sheriffs' passion had surprised him yet it hadn't. He knew the steady, shabby way the United States had treated the Indian states. He admired this unbridled "bloodspeak," as his father had called it. Anything said from the heart and caressed by the soul; guts without the frosting of equivocation or the fringe of retreat, that's bloodspeak.

"Walks Ahead is almost home." The sheriff pointed towards the tiny red dot of the surviving taillight as its bouncy passage through the granite and the cacti disappeared. Then the sheriff, as if to no one in particular, said, "His countenance, windswept. His complexion, ruddy pointless." They started down the pavement again.

"Only a couple more hours and we'll be done with patrol."

De Mejas was silent for a mile and then the enormity of the past 18 hours swarmed over him. "Thank you, John Truefellow."

The Navaho was not one to take kindness and compliment easily. "Does your wound hurt? Is it throbbing?" I'll give it a quick clean again at the rest stop."

Godboy smiled at his friend's stoic attempt at casualness. His head did not hurt even as his mind waged war with disparate thoughts. Buddha Jesus thought of his parents, his childhood, and his mother's admonition to make a mark for good in the world; how his life was now new land. His father's contribution to Truefellow for the tribal schools or for how the sheriff saw as best use for his people, yes, it was penance for the rest of his father's affairs, illicit and otherwise, but now, the seeding had ripen into a lifeline for the last de Mejas. He fights to keep revenge from the forefront of his current contemplation. It is hard as he still had the blood of his kin on his skin. He loathed his father's career choice and now his head begins to pulse with echo and meaning of the day as the small bit of lead bullet still embedded just above his left ear, nudged for attention a little more forcefully than before. Godboy noticed his 'savior's' occasional glances of concern on his periphery or what was left of it, but he did not acknowledge them as he instead focused as best as the circumstances of the day and the more noticeable pain allowed on what was good for the present and not the evil he hated that seemed to be now more assertively edging to the foreground of his thinking. He concentrated on movies he preferred: his mother's favorite things especially her quirky advocacy for anything that questioned organized religion but not the existence of a higher being; his father's love of flamenco, baseball and his children; his dead sister and the other's. His green eyes were teared out and now scratchy dry. His brown hair is caked with the dirt of his family courtyard.

"Have some more water, Nino."

Godboy nodded to the Navaho and took the offered bent metal canteen cup. The cool steel and refreshing liquid were pleasing diversions until Buddha Jesus recalled the stilled body of his hiking companion, Vincent Van Pawgh; that's the way his mother had spelled it on the orange collar of the golden retriever that his mother had given him. She brought "V" dog home when the pup was a week and a half old. How odd it is that he thought of Vincent first, and then came the image, the nightmare in daytime of his twin sisters, Alena and Guadalupe's in fearful final embrace, their bodies, their pink dresses splotched in the purple red logos, all too familiar, now iconic, of the Mexican disaster known as Anos de Muerte, the years of death in the age of the Cartels. Shouldn't he have thought of them before the family pet? And his mother, oh dear God, my God. His mother now gone. She was Swedish or Irish, Buddha Jesus was never certain as his mother never spoke much about her past. A beautiful blond that captured many an eye, Mrs. De Mejas was charismatic, a romanticist with steely convictions and an affinity for forgiveness. Godboy's loving angel on earth had just returned from visiting friends in California when she was gunned down with the rest of his world. She rushed at him in an emotional roller coaster of jagged imagery and bittersweet memory. The young De Mejas bit hard on lower lip as he recalled his mother's insistence on Swedish origins, probably a loving lie for his father's apparent predilection for fantasy and as a manner for her to keep the marital pot stirring and his father on his toes. She rarely backed down, talented at instigating conversations that, in her opinion, demanded response, a skillful agent provocateur of passion and persistence, able to light his father's fire in more than a few ways, targeting as a wrestler the throw weight of her opponent and using it for her purposes and when really agitated, feeding into her husbands rebellious way against his own family upbringing; guarded, private and Catholic and turning favor her way. His father was ardent in evocation of machismo, but it was evident to all, that Don De Mejas was in love with a fiercely independent female, physical and feisty, that challenged the Don's sense of manly traditionalism without quarter, and besides, as his father was wont to express in willful surrender, "She is blond."

The Navaho looked over to the source of the heavy sigh and Godboy glanced one eye opened back at him and then closed it again.

The policeman contemplated the shift. The kid had worn well and now out. Hour or two of rest would return wonders. Truefellow leaned in and turned the radio audio down to almost not noticeable. Until the young Mexican could adapt to this new walk, this new past, this fresh circle of adults in close proximity, it would be challenging for even this obviously talented individual. But he is of grounded stock. Most Mexicans are.

Godboy chuckled inside.

"What?" the sheriff questioned.

"I laughed at the fact that my mother allowed my father to think he was the head of the house and he loved her so for allowing this to be."

The sheriff smiled and focused again on the highway ahead. Now dawn and beauty time as cinematographers call it. Many of the Hollywood tribe around here years ago. Special 'look' for film is dawn and dusk and never high noon. Or so the guys with the oversized lens draped around their necks said. He thought of the color very likely now reflecting off his mix of adobe, wood, metal and tile modern Hogan. It would be in full pink orange rant on the porch patio and almost to the extent of blinding on the copper platted front door as it faced the rising day with obnoxious brilliance.

Godboy remembered the sheriff mentioning something about breakfast and bed in an hour or so and then another mention about being glad when this graveyard shift would be ending as he only had taken this as a two week favor to a new sheriff, a first time father and mother. Truefellow had told the newbie that he would owe the Navaho and to get his rear home for...and then as the boy would later relate, the thought of "Oh God, What now?" closed him down and finally, officially, Buddha Jesus Simon de Bolivar de Mejas shut down and slept during what remained of that particular early morning hour and continued peacefully through into what would be the first two hours of the start down the new but bumpy path to his peculiar, one might even say rare, future place in the universe.

****

She is awake staring up at the gold flaked black glass mirror, pondering her barely discernible figure in the dim hint of light in the purposely made dark interior of the master "playroom" as the star called her bedroom suite.

Before they had hung up earlier that morning, both Sean and the lady of the screen had laughed at Odessa's lament that she "always gets invited to all the A list weddings. Damn expensive and not always the best champagnes. And then I am called, no in true Hollywoooood," the actress had drawn out the pronunciation of the word like the Japanese submariner in Spielberg's "1942", "preference ...for casual remoteness in relationships, professional and otherwise, I am subpoenaed via text that I might be called in as witness in the happy as of last year couples present divorce proceedings. Attorney's offices aren't what they used to be, either. More Red Bull than alcohol."

"It's attention, though." Sean had interjected with a not too feint whiff of disdain in his voice. Odessa, as a trained reader of body language and stance, just by the sound and cadence of one's voice, she could read the momentum of the moment, continued, "Yes, dear, I do live in the ugly duckling world of what's in it for me, Sean. And I have learned how to get through this pond even if it is top heavy with scum. Randy means ratings, darlink." Or as the actress called the world of "her" as she in private called "life", to be successful in dog eat dog business's, one must honed an almost centrifugal preciseness in maintaining a tricky balance on the fine line of ardor and abandonment. Ms. Gabriel was most proficient at playing with the prickly panicky toy of public opinion, no assembly required.

This early morning was singular in its notoriety because the star did not have to be on set. She had to do some lip sync in a few days but it was now for a couple of days, in her favorite language, "desporter" time, 'carry away' in old French, which meant to the actor to enjoy without restraint her time without an audience or a crew. She laughed at how surprised she was to sense how comfortable her bed really was without company.

At last, a break from her usual eclat at useable knowledge of who to bed, who to wed or who to keep deliciously well fed in order to be on the short list for the next great script. She found the remote on the end table and flipped on the television for aural distraction to soften the sudden cri de Coeur that would fragrant her mind occasionally, a mental bouquet of intemperate thinking and wonderment that usually reached a crescendo just after she left her son at the care facility or when she was alone. The heartbreak of her son's condition, and her inner questioning other decision to keep this side life of hers a secret for as long as possible for, and she knew this, the pitiful reason of protecting her own image and not the proffered up reason she would provide to her assistant, Melinda, of protecting the boy. Her true ache was that this was an act to justify selfishness, her own survival habit whenever she faced situations beyond her control. She did not want the "there but for the grace of God" public sentiment to focus on her son. Her back alley upbringing caused her to view culture and presence as tools of manipulation for survival and not much else.

As she had said to Sean on the phone, "Hollywood events are manufactured pieces of uppity panache and divertissement Nobliege, cage match sized egos on 'roids bouncing around the edges of making sense or giving a damn, vain attempts at intellectual magnificence, forgotten as soon as the utterance no longer panders the air." Odessa remembered what Sean had then said to her. "You know, Miss, every moment with you has the potential for a big fat memory, good or bad, right?"

She liked this man as he made her laugh without prompting. She recalled that she had continued on with a little more French in and out as she had noticed how this tic of hers had caused his face to smirk and she thoroughly enjoyed his peaceful agitation. She understood from experience that keeping men on their toes was never a bad thing for a woman.

"Seannie, my dear," the actress had softly mouthed with an exaggerated Diamond Lil lilt, "You must scent the room with intended recherche to keep the attention train rolling and on track."

"Recher what?"

"Little known or unusual items or words and therefore not easily understood by the unwashed masses..."

"Shitty shibboleths!"

"...Exactly!" They had laughed and she knew that she truly loved his voice.

The rays of the day were filtering in between the closed pull slats and draw down blinds. Odessa sat up in bed and squinted towards the TV to see what the breaking news on Fox was about...Ha; her friends in the business would cry foul if they knew that she watched Fox along with the proscribed networks of the left and their stepchildren in cable. It was a well known mandate that every well rounded good liberal, cum progressive, cum whatever the next name on the next rock that this far left menagerie in Los Angeles next crawls out from under, that one must join, bow to, wearing proud, strutting in fact, their announced credentials as truly giving, selfless, the "perfectly impassioned" as Odessa tagged them, if you were to have any future in the town of Tinsel. Odessa had told Sean that her best acting occurred off screen as she had effectively made a clear path in her career around the studio eddies of political correctness and had not allowed her to be damaged by the constant drain of groupthink that's prevalent in studio world. She easily maintained her fade of being one of them, a card carrying member of the magnificently uninformed and massively mocked, the persona of celebrity that more than a few of the great national unwashed noted with derision and astonishment, was vapid and revelatory to the core about the arrogant ignorance of those enamored with easy answer and sophomoric display. She fit in with this melange of brisk edicts and bountiful pontifications because, well, she knew how to give believable performances and she knew that she was playing to a friendly house.

As she focused on the screen, she was not surprised that the "breaking news" was not really worth a second glance. The term had become ubiquitous, stripped of its attention grabbing power because of media's non discrimination in its use. In the unfortunate era of the pursuit of the banal and the elevation of the mundane, everything is "Breaking News", so much so that now nary a head turns when this term flashes across the screen. This morning, the breaking news was a feed of an early rush hour carjacking on the Santa Ana and the requisite helicopter tracking from the air. She switched to The Comedy Channel to see if there was anything more enlightening on. She liked Stewart but she felt like a shower and to the steam she went. She sat on the black marble ledge as moisture caressed her. This was her haven. No phones. No best boys or understudies, whatever they used to be and no breaking news. Her mom was probably getting ready for bus trip to Gardena. Odessa would call her later to see if she had cleaned up on the felt that day. Was Sean still asleep? No, of course not. His military cut would not allow a sleep-in unless there was something worth staying in the sheets for ...at least she hoped to find out if this were true in the very near future together. Damn, she had already had some testing questions from some of her female acquaintances as the couples meeting and interest in each other was in the public domain and a topical curiosity for many who could not a fathom a match between a straight arrow and such a curve like herself. She stood and reached for the organic shampoo and massaged in the lavender colored liquid with steady circular movement and with a little more firmness as she considered just who these friends were. They were super rich, by marriage or by birth for the most part, fighting their own bouts of depression, boredom, low self esteem and addictive narcissism by living outrageously, always seeking the next great happy pill and feigning empathy whenever complimentary or convenient. Odessa laughed as she rinsed. With friends like these, right? God, when they weren't actually caught doing something good, they tended to cling to the "actress" Odessa, the star's constructed persona of shallowness, vindictiveness, shamelessness and noticeable disdain for propriety, an untamed toughness her friends admired and rarely, if ever, separated from the true soul of, the gut innards of, the real O.G.

Odessa pressed the steam shower button to off and began to towel.

Sean Linden was the first man that she felt had penetrated her mask and it had been so damn easy for him. Would he be the one, the poetry and the calm of a true companionship that she had craved for most of her life? Her looks had served her well but beauty can isolate too. Would she ever learn to let her guard down? For real?

Her usual insouciance was absent in the Laughing Garter parking lot. She recalled her surprise at her initial reaction to the man lying on the asphalt. She wanted to know more about him and this was not Odessa being Odessa as she tended to stick to people that were interested in her and not the other way around. Odessa thought of her mother and hers early life; a single mother rearing a near starveling on her own and now, the once puny ugly duck is a swan, awash in almost numinous celebrity, all because her mom was no quitter and her girl wasn't either. Must give her a call before moms out the door. Odessa switched channels to the local news as she looked for the cell phone and a hair brush.

The anchor was loud and grating. "Breaking News. Cartel lord and family gunned down. Details to follow after this word from Metamucil."

Probably be a movie later the actress muses as she waits for her mother to pick up the phone.

Chapter 5

"Gnothi Seauton"
(Know Thyself) Greek

*"We must do everything that lies in our power to obtain
to virtue and wisdom in this life. The prize is so splendid
and the hope is so great."*

Plato 'Respublica'

September 26, 2015

The senator is a survivor. Enemies fail in dislodging him. They hadn't mastered how to compete with the legislator's artful use of Socratic irony or his common sense approach to communication nor the Oklahoman's proven concern for the people of his state. And opponents in his party and in the DNC had the scars that remained in public memory long after the fight that caused them. The senator would approach a debate with an affectation of ignorance, assuming the posture in argument or horse trading and then, at the exact moment for perfection, when most would be watching and most certainly in time for the eastern network news shows to air the argument, the bumbling Okie would transform into a man of charm and perspicacity, exposing with wit and precisely targeted disdain, the uninspiring, lethargic, almost primeval errors in his rival's reasoning...always ending his entertaining but factual dissertation with "..And that is spelled... r..e..a..s..o..n..i..n..g. for those among us who have wearied of thinking. Remember. money can't always buy smarts but it can always be found in a deal with the devil."

Brisk, pragmatic and prickly when needed, Senator Bruce well understood the delicate patterns and perfidious undertows of Congress. Adept at tapping into the subterfuge available in the purposeful arcane rules of the institution and using them to his constituents benefit, he was as equally masterful in identifying "the tell", zeroing in on a chink in style or presentation that gave away the true depth of his opponents resistance. He would use this identifiable weakness to massage vulnerable egos or to stoke rivalries when necessary to his success. And then send all a gift at the Holidays. In the epoch of Wi-Fi intellect and collective bargaining for the ethical high ground, he stood alone and above the legislative sty, his name for the Senate, and railed at the injustice of a position or sounded the clarion call for proposal he supported with equal, powerful weapons, irony and revulsion, delivered with a professorial eyes above the glasses rim look of disdain if you did not agree the argument now hanging in the air... you were not worth another second of any seriously educated person's time. Professor Sorentsen, over many a training cocktail or cognac, had fined tuned the Senator's delivery style to the point that the politician was nearly as crafted in the "how dare you question the sense of what I say" stare as the professor.

"You remember the construction on doc's street, right?"

"Yes sir."

The senator smiled at the face in the rear view mirror. "Come on, Dakota, dad's fine. And thanks for stepping in when I needed you. And keep your eyes on the road." They both laughed.

The senator's step son, a veteran, had quickly responded when the legislator called saying he needed a driver as the senators usual bodyguard cum driver, Chambers, was in emergency surgery, and Dakota's brothers were working so "what time will you be here?" meant "move it, son," and as the son knew the senator never appreciated the randomness of being late as the old man called it, the son had one foot in the shower as he had closed the cell phone.

One of many of colorful names for the original larger than just one building hamlets proclaimed as towns by the proud handfuls of white occupants in the Indian Territory of Oklahoma is Pink, Oklahoma, and it's most famous son, was Senator Dunleavy Bruce. As he explained, "Pink is 18 miles east of Norman in Pottawatomie County, a community where Redbud trees are never true red, but instead, mostly purple and white, where countryside churches, Baptist, nearly always, compete with carports, tin roofs and barns and radio towers cutting through the black oak domain, salvage yards too; better pieces of metal than most, not as much rust, yes, Pink is white picket fences, prettiest thing on some properties and then there's obviously rethought gazebos tilting by creeks named Pecan or Bullfrog, garish but happy fireworks stands, cattle and horse trailers, hand-scrawled 'moving sale' signs mixed in with gospel meeting placards announcing the next time God needs talking to...this is the vicinity of Pink, my home sweet home." Then the Senator would joke, "At least I'm not from Cement!," another distinctly Oklahoman town that was not offended by the well known quip as the Senator had always remembered the denizens of Cement and it's county of Caddo when someone with hip high trough trousers and a master's knowledge of the feed lot was called for to insure that Cementians and Pinkers did not go wanting when funding time was nigh and when any mention of re-election was considered rude among the polite company of gathered accomplices.

The senator's father was a banker. The elder Bruce was proud of the athletic but somewhat rebellious son. Dunleavy was groomed to follow the steps of the father in the financial world but the younger saw it as a harness and he felt his introduction to banking smothering in expectation and even though he enjoyed math, the younger Bruce despised the potential palette of his future if it meant walking the path his father did. He pleaded with his father not to expect him to go where his father and his father's father had gone. With the accumulation of some youthful embarrassments that had brought unwanted attention to the Bruce name and aura of respectability that had been maintained for years, the rift widened between father and son, resulting in the son leaving after his senior year to work in the oil patch and eventually earning enough to pay for his education at the University of Oklahoma. His parents concern did not lessen as he was their only child after the death in Vietnam of the senator's older brother, Lance, and no one had fully recovered from it. And, in that his Scottish father and his one half Cherokee, one half Irish mother had met and graduated from Oklahoma State University, this caused another small degree of separation, a somewhat teasing mechanism to lighten a particular burdensome moment but still relied upon as an affable excuse to tamp down any current discord.

Distance between parents and son ensued until "Dunsey", as his student friends called him, during his sophomore year returned home, fresh with high grades in Petroleum Engineering and a recognized maturity. During the separation, the parties had communicated by letter and occasional tense phone call.

There had been good reason, Mrs. Angelica Bruce, had named her second son, Strong Bull, attesting to this in most visible manner available by making the baby Dunleavy's middle name legal to satisfy Mrs. Bruce's ancestors.

It was at the initial session of familial reproachmont that Dunleavy revealed a new interest in politics in the Carter administration, the intricacy of "real politic, from the barn to the bank, locally and worldwide, how to get things done for the most."

"Without getting any blowback for taking from others, right?"

"Oh, come on, Dad."

"Holy Hell of the Highlands, you've been hanging out with Marxist professors, haven't you, or at least sat in one too many Socialist infested fern bars I've read about."

His father had then espied Angelica's on the warpath stare and promptly shut up.

This was her unspoken reminder to the father that they did not want to lose contact again with their remaining son and flexibility by Mr. Bruce would immediately be the replacement part for stoic rigid propriety which Mr. Bruce had been taught was the essence of strength and right conviction.

The father recovered quickly in the Mother's eye when he said, "Yes, you are right. Must sample all aspects of a viewpoint, wage into the muck and mayhem of political bluster and balls and target the kernel, the guts of a need and the circumstances of the people with the needs and how one would best go about filling in the many holes in a desperate, despoiled humanity, agreed? Mother?"

Angelica and Dunleavy had stared in amazed silence. The Senator still laughed at this image. It was so opposite the nature of the father he was accustomed to. It had also been the most emotion, most expression of passion that his father had shown since the first mournful days after Lance's funeral. Then the father of his youth came back into the room.

"Graduate in your field of present study, Dunleavy, and then, with this fallback vocation secured, in two years, come back and pursue what is in your blood, son. I know, I sensed from the peaks and valleys of your youthful revolt and rants against the inequities of our times, that you wanted to eventually dance across the lily pads to the fresh water and provide substance to as many frogs in the pond as you could...and I understand as I was a dreamer when I was your age too..." to which the Senator recalled his mother responding with a knowing smile and this had soften Dunleavy's first defensive posture and he listened further without interruption...." I will support you in this, we will, that is,"... amazing that stare and its results. "First, of course, graduate."

The Christmas nog in the crystal mugs with the Bruce crest etched into them, were raised and toasts made.

Nearing 62, Dunleavy Bruce's green eyes could still see clearly without the need for eyewear and his hair, Reaganesque and natural, would never see coloring if it ever began to show gray. Not his style.

The car was now stopped by a flagman. Dakota is small talking with the construction worker. The worker barely looked legal. God, teenagers are so older in experience and so hardened by societal drift and misplay than he was at their age. Yes, he remembered his first taste of angst of early romance gone bad in his expeditious and perilous live forever approach of his youth and he had lived with a girl or two in his Junior and Senior years which had widened the chasm between father and son but surprisingly had shown his mother to be more of a liberated women than either of the Bruce males had anticipated. God, mother was saint, even when her son was boot high in bullshit, she was ready with the shovel. Dad was too, but he wanted to use the tool in a manner totally opposite of the manner his mother desired.

The senator's pager sounds. He looks at sender. It could wait and turned the "intruder" off as he called the evil icon of an age he hadn't found a nice name for. As he watched his stepson and the still hint of pimples teen with the construction flag talk sports, he slumps as he ponders the unthinkable but now very possible concern, that the deep sixing of another American generation was about to commence. Geeze, we cannot waste this generation. They are our fighters, our dreamers, the seams of our future and yet, with this era of serial meism, the Senator contemplated the odds of success lowering with each news cycle.

Kennedy had pushed volunteerism and this was an 'attractive'. While not in agreement with the Democrat's politics, young Bruce was fond of the Camelot man and had responded to the president's clarion call for action by volunteering in a Republican youth group and assisting in what would be his first baby steps in campaigning, and what would be the first occasion since his brother's death that he felt he had actually pleased his father. The Senator-to-be efforts were noticed by important GOP hands, experts aware of the party's problem which was a desperately needed infusion of youth, of 'star blood', and plenty of it, if the grand old thinker's of the grand old party were ever again to see any hope of a viable future for "elephants" in an America run amok with jackasses as the seventies did indeed appear to the stale old guard of a stale old political party.

The Senator leaned forward and tapped his son on shoulder, "Ask him how much longer, okay?" Dakota followed instructions and "maybe five more minutes or so" was the response. "Thank you" the Senator yelled to the worker as he smiled at the thought of being later than usual with his old friend. The professor would bitch at him and then they would get into the business of a lifelong friendship again and move on.

Professor Benjamin Elliot Sorentsen was the Senator's most trusted confidant except for that home town girl of summers past, the one, after various breakups and makeup's and against her parents desires, that he'd finally married long after the most opportune time for such an event had past. While they truly loved each other, the red headed, head turning beauty, Katherine S. Mulhane, (the "S" was for Starr, as Katherine's father had the randy sense of humor and irony that most oilmen from Bartlesville had in those days and also because her father had truly prayed for a boy and upon the discovery of an apparent miscommunication with the almighty, Mr. Mulhane thought it best to give his daughter the Starr tag, from the cantankerous Belle, as a hopeful amulet in name that would protect and brand his baby girl as tough and as rowdy as any man and hopefully give her a leg up in dealing with the idiots that he well knew inhabited a man's world and that he well knew would try to tame her, in other words as Kate would joke later, men just like her father.)

As can happen within the hard but dazzling glow of ardor gone rogue between distinctly ardent but private individuals, and after tremendous weeks but tumultuous months, divorce barged in as the sensible response for reclaiming sanity. It was a survival mechanism for two, still obviously in love, good people, that eventually allowed continuance of the relationship without the harness of a marriage license which had been used by both as a false arbiter that only seemed to spur on the hurt and the rage that comes with one too many "how could you'!" arguments that often result in a cancerous devaluation of the estimation that matters the most to each impassioned petitioner, that of the other they are in discourse against now and with whom they would sleep with later. This divorce was atypical and rare because it had truly saved a once in a lifetime relationship from complete destruction.

The public saw them as one even though they themselves legally didn't. Both occasionally dated to keep their separateness fresh, up front and close to desired story line. Frequently asked about the other's acquaintances, both would feign pleasure at the prospect of the other finding their true soul mate, even though Kate and Dunsey knew that they had already discovered theirs years ago.

They helped in each other's charitable efforts and events and Kate jumped at the opportunity to assist the Senator in 1991 in the adoption and caring for the Senator's four orphan sons, Cody, Josey, Dakota and Shane, as if she had some skin in the game and they were her own. They were proud of "the tribe" as the senator called them as all four had served in Iraq and Afghanistan and Josey, Shane, and Cody within the last year had joined the Capitol Police. Dakota was almost finished with his vetting.

Katherine would occasionally accompany the senator to bring attention to their causes. Both enjoyed the tiusting presence of a loving friend in the public arena. He called her "my page three girl" and she called him "my favorite mistake." When security concerns allowed, he would drive them to events in his red El Camino and during the Holidays, they load up the vehicle with gifts and go to Acostia and give them to the amazed children. A couple of seasons, they rented a truck to follow the El Camino, filled with bikes, basketballs and dolls, which were handed out by security and marines. The press had to track the couple down as the senator and the lady despised promotion at the expense of others. Both viewed this as an overwhelmingly tragic statement about the cult of "me" that had permeated the vernacular and style of the politically crass and as the two "old" schoolers saw it, had given society a ruinous permission to accept narcissism as normal; a permissible trait for success, a touchstone for revealed "genius." As Kate's mother had taught, never announce a good deed as God will cry if you do.

The Senator saw the flagmen start to back away from the car, and Dakota put it in gear, Bruce dialed the professor's number to update him on their progress, but of course, the teacher had forgotten again to turn his answering system on. The ringer was always shut off so the Senator's odds against hope was that his friend would be walking by the phone and notice the red light flashing and pick up the receiver. Another mini lecture about promptness was now in the offering to which the Senator would respond with his customary, "The work of the people is not on a time clock, good sir, but it is indeed a mighty thirsty and thankless endeavor that would almost be hopeless without the proper amount of lubrication to sooth the lamentations common to such employment,"...upon which the professor would duly pour from his private stock his choice of fine vino, cognac or whiskey, to assist the student in quickly reaching the professors refined level of discourse that had been elevated even further by the teacher's fine tuning of the liquid lesson plan while waiting for the tardy one to arrive.

God, he was lucky to have two trusted friends when many a man has none. Both Kate and the Prof had been there when the weight of his office almost crushed him as it would anyone with a heart living in the rude, crude world of lip service ethics and ghastly greed that the liar's haven otherwise known as the District of Columbia had become.

The Senator's worst fear was losing effectiveness and the energy necessary to continue his trenchant, almost irritating, pursuit for truth and the subsequent diminution of the original vividness that got him where he was today. It troubled him that he might one day not be able to deliver on his terms and instead, become a metaphor for fading away or appearing worn, as a color too long in the sun or a struggling memory angling for detail and worth.

Dakota parked in front of the Professor's townhome. He tries to jump out the driver's door to open his dad's door but the Senator had beaten him to it.

"Thanks, Dakota. I'll call in awhile."

"Give Mr. Sorenson my best, sir."

The senator was about to respond when a car horn honked behind them. They both turned to see a cab door open and Sean Linden get out.

"Look what the cat refused!" Dakota yells at Sean, a man he respects and loves as a fellow warrior.

Sean smiled and waved him off as the Senator jumped in, "From what I have read recently, I thought you might be studying your lines with your new drama coach, kid." "Bite me, Socrates."

They shake hands.

"Prof called and suggested it would be good to come by and "chill" with the old dudes."

"Yeah, right." Mr. Bruce looked at Mr. Linden as they approached the front door and it was apparent to the Senator that Linden looked more weathered than he remembered, but what could one expect of a man of arms transitioning from full time military to the arms of a movie queen and the tactical maneuvers that required.

Professor Benjamin Elliot Sorentsen the Fourth opens the front door.

"Ah, Benji." The senator hailed his lifelong thorn in paw and best friend.

"Dunce, how are ya?," then to Sean, who had been a student of his, the teacher, as was his nature with favorite pupils, fires off a quote to see if Sean still practices the art of retention, "Young men are easily deceived, for they are quick to hope." Without hesitation, Sean replied, "Aristotle," as the Senator guesses, "Mae West?"

"Gunner" to his friends, (Dunleavy often inquired if there were really three Gunners before this recent incarnation of familial hot shots), Professor Sorentson's reserve was found only in what he kept in his liquor cabinet and not much else. He battled academic hypocrisy, bias and the hyperventilation over political correctness spawned by the lord over liberal faculties he, in his opinion, has had to contend with for decades. But he had liberal friends too as he was recognized by them as almost even-handed in that "Gunner" also never brooked or gave quarter to the over bearing, holier than thouness of the dinosaur right either, the "talk to any good hookers recently," side of the aisle crowd as he tagged them. His battles in academia rose to white hot levels, enough to attract the moths of the media and enough to be electronically knighted with the title of "notorious person," which, in the age of 24 hour debased chastisements and roaring righteousness's, the professor proudly wore as a mortar board of gold.

The ram-rod straight not unattractive man with the ancient Roman or now Hubie Brown haircut drove a purple Karmen Gia with a personalized license plate which read SCATAR, a literal moving statement, in his opinion, of the nature of things in general. He was pleased that there were still no Greeks at the Division of Motor Vehicles in Washington.

The professor's voice is an aural mixture of Abe Lincoln high pitch and an occasional soundsplash of Jeffersonian stammer, not a frequent occurrence in the latter case, but just enough to turn heads such as those that faced him three days out of five workdays in the classroom of higher learning; the now decade long "vampire" generation who believe you are turning in way too early if it's only one in the morning, and who also are most attentive to that which is most like a video game, or that which has deep punitive possibilities if ignored such as receiving an "F" for a grade. Gunner's success as a history professor in an age when history seems passe was due to, as he labels it, the ability to perform "theatrics with a purpose" that leads to retention within the pseudo sacred ground of familiarity of today's technically inclined, and contrary to claims otherwise, socially disinclined leaders of tomorrow.

Dozing in Dr. Sorentsens lecture was not an explainable act. Adding to the attentive atmosphere in the professor's stadium style room of knowledge transfusion was his ban on lap top computers. The teacher knew multitasking as myth. Focus, feedback and a little foolishness did a good lecture make. His affected curmudgeon stance kept most fools at bay "with politicians the exception, of course" as he often chided his favorite bureaucrat. His peeves, stated with clarity on the first day of class and whenever the professor sensed compassion coming his way, were tardiness and the costly hobby of fabrication, lying. With a keep your distance preference, Benjamin Elliot Sorentsen's friends knew his deep seeds which were college football, special editions of Homer and any book about Heinrich Schliemann, music by Elvis, Glenn Miller and the Stones, but not the Beatles which he considered just a tad soft.

A Rhodes Scholar in History and a Time Magazine "Person of The Year" runner-up noted for the maelstrom this provocateur of conservatism caused within the ocean of liberal tranquility that universities had nurtured for decades and the waves of opprobrium, foamy with protest and facile esoterica, which resulted. The mincing observation that sinners make the best saints could well be apropos as an instigative factor for the teacher. Only one friend knew of the professor's affair with a student in the early eighties three months after the teachers wife had died. Senator Bruce could easily commiserate with his best friend in this estimation of adage cum real as the legislator had had his own fits of humanity and useless bouts of striving for imperviousness, errands even Prometheus would cackle at.

"There are times when things need to move more quickly and I thought this would be opportune time for you both to get to know each other informally instead of through the chatty nothingness prevalent at charity events or the cuddleling testimony of congressional speak devised for CSPAN and insomniacs. I say you both deserve the better knowledge of the other."

The professor took measure of his friends and their response to what he had said. The senator and the soldier just stared.

"Look, you of few but precise words and you," as the teacher pointed towards the older man, "you, of verbosity as a tool fame, you're both my friends and I do not friend easily, mind you, so no cameras, no urgencies, just us and since it's past noon and the country still seems to be running in spite of our absence from the halls of Montezuma or the slot machine on The Hill. Say, care for a shot, shake or smashed grape, what'd you have?" Everyone laughed. The professor left to gather the libation requests.

"He's a beauty, isn't he? But I'm glad he got us together. I know I have never thanked you except for expert testimony that is, for what you have done for country and I now thank you, Mr. Linden, and I pray that more will follow like you and that you are not the last of a kind."

Sean was uncomfortable whenever complimented and barely motioned a thank you. He sensed he had found a friend in the making and it pleased him even if it was a bureaucrat. The professor returned and with an exaggerated solemnity, half bowing to each guest as he offered the drinks.

"Why the sobriety, Gunner?

"Because, Senator, I dare say we'll need it for the future." He raised his glass and the others did too. "I do know the good Senator and no, Sean, that's not an oxymoron, holds opinions close to mine and I suspect maybe close to yours too."

Sean permitted a slight smile.

"Typical lifespan of great civilizations is two centuries. One of your kilted clansmen, Dunsey, a Scot, Sean, name of Alexander Tytler; was elegant in explaining why the mighty fall. He said democracy isn't permanent. It cannot be because its demise is caused by the most wicked of human traits besides murder and this of course, is greed. Tyler said that when the attitude is monetary guidelines are damned, it follows light speed quickly thereafter that electors discover that they can vote themselves or vote for politicians who promise to give the electorate the bounty of the country, the collapse of democracy has always been assured. He said you can chart from history the stages of decline..."

"Stages?"

"Yes, Tytler coined the word 'agnosticism' too. Yes, like a merciless cradle to death spiral from which there is no escaping. Tyler's last stages of before total decline were abundance to selfishness; selfishness to complacency; from complacency to apathy; from apathy to dependency; from dependency to bondage. Where do you think we are now, gentlemen?" "From what I have witnessed, we live in the era of the authenticity of illusion."

Both older men eyed the speaker carefully.

"And I don't know how Tytler missed the stage when reasonableness and honesty become troublesome and substance becomes victim to facade, because that's the world I feel I have walked back into."

"The era of empirical empathy, huh?"

"Yes, Doctor, I..."

"PHD will do for short, but go on."

Sean laughed at the professors' stab at cliche and continued. "It's just a quirky barometer of mine that is now on a path to red alert that requires attention." The teacher and bureaucrat leaned in.

"It's simple, really. What's the daily rate of how many people are beginning to believe that they are Jesus? I know it's going up. This is my only explanation so far for the thickness of thought and oiliness of orthodoxy I've experienced since returning to, quote, the civilized world. Too many gods in the making for a country to survive."

"Very sobering view, Mr. Linden," the PHDer observed. "Especially for one I thought might be too busy studying lines with a new drama coach to be serious about anything else for a while."

The attempt at humor caused only the Senator to smile.

Sean pretended irritation and then continued. "I guess I am wondering when did clear-headiness become passé, what date did that happen? The Tea Party made anger acceptable because it was the only tool left in the box to construct, to increase access to the process of governing. They had no other choice. And as far as I see it, the Occupy group is right there with them, if not on the same verse, it's the same song."

The senator jiggled the ice in his drink and glanced out the professor's window as if the street and the brick and mortar buildings offered answers. He turned back to the soldier and the teacher. "No recent fact thin, fat feel good flaw laws as I tag em have made a dent in the corrosive knack for lack of a more indecent word to describe it..."

"How bout bribeburree," the educator chimed.

"....no containment of the well-heeled and the well-coupled to procure puppets for profit and gain...dammit, Gunner, you know the inequalities in election power is pampered with by a fawning press and pushed aside after ratings are over or an election is won! Then substance is conveniently forgotten again and any mention of reform is scooted out the back door until the next auction for action cycle comes around. You know I have fought this for years and have been called every name imaginable in Webster's and some I can't even mention to a sailor for doing so!"

"Yes, that's why we pray, Dunsey, and that's why we drink, Sean. More ice for the propellant, gentlemen?"

"Sean," the Senator addressed the soldier as the professor added more energy and more coolant to their glasses, "the country has been stuck on dumb looking in all the wrong places for leadership for too many years. All we have to show for this piss against the wind exercise are professors, pimps and pushers who win because they possess the largest mainline to those with the most juice."

Sean considered the Senator's obvious contempt and knew he was in the presence of a kindred soul. "Senator, in the service, trust is everything or you die. I am sickened at sensing the slow death of democracy because the ability to trust is, as I see it, now considered, now promoted as a fact of being for fools only...a messy liability if you are ever to be considered of serious mettle. Good God, look at how far many have gone in this government because they were talented at the art of deceit, denial and the destruction and twisting of ethics into where the mere mention of morals is now considered a laugh line. It is a wonder to me that our children have not gone madder than they have!"

"Pardon the interruption but the place you work is the problem. Weaken the influence of the Senate by controlling the budget and by this bodies instinct to persuade by withholding of gifts or punishing by withholding options forcing obedience to its desires. Scrutiny of the common man and woman into the hidden ways and smug motives of Congress must be revealed and reviled; Honest Interlocutors required". The senator was motionless taking in his good friend's commentary.

Sean Linden weighed in "Truth can be a paralyzing agent, a cleanser that stops all motion and madness."

Sen. Bruce's response was knowledgeable, "emergency, emergency, I'm running out of campaign contributions what I mean by this you understand that a preponderance of discretionary supplemental spending, they are labeled emergencies that can be brought late into the session when no one is looking and the weak are in charge."

"When are the weak never in charge in your workplace, Senator?"

Sean stared at his friend as the memory of one of the professors lessons came to mind, from the Upanishads, that true liberation involved during the process of the soul, the inner soul's journey to divine calling and somehow Confucius jumped into the gray matter fray about issues with honoring elders. "The in God We Trust roller coaster is now open for that ride without safety bars and for that fulfillment of amusement most cannot resist."

Prof. Sorentson was pleased with the students among him. "A Parisian attorney, name of Montebourg, I believe, says that corruptions like a heavy pollution that weighs on people's spirits." Seeing no noticeable disagreement with his comment, he continued, "throw so much at Americans that all results in confusion masking, blanking the perspective collective memories of previous corruption in order to continue with the current crop of corrupters, the new incompetent clerisy adorned in the fine fresh garments of exquisite excuse and wash and wear behavior." The Prof. was of the bartender generation where cocktails like oxygen, lubricated the days efforts and moral relativity poured forth from every bottle until one could handle no more philosophy for the day. In the Professors case, he had finally faced up to this liquid fade raw when he began to grip less bottles of wine during those long unteachable moments between classes. "Frances Bacon said that causes and motives of sedition are 'innovation in religion, taxes: alteration of customs and laws' something to that effect, oh yes and 'the breaking up of privileges.' These are some of what he said was or were causes for revolt as best I recall the quote went on about, uh, yes.. 'unworthy persons, strangers, disbanded soldiers, factions grown desperate and whatsoever invaded and offended peoples' lives caused them to as he said' joineth and knitteth them in a common cause."

The professor again surveyed his audience, continuing, "Bacon zeroed in on the main items that needed prevention, needed removal by all means possible to maintain the status quo, and these were, to keep sedation at bay. I mean, these were,' want and poverty."

"That man was quite a seamstress, wasn't he?"

"Yes, Sean," Sen. Bruce came back to life, "he was." Sen. Bruce paused, "You have it in you. Sean, you ought to go into office." Sean was not pleased and his scowl said so.

"The time is there, the time is right, and you have the capabilities to make it fit right." "There's nothing been tailored in my life and I'm not ready for alterations now, although Senator, you, you are right that I'm in the in between Netherlands, first time in years." The educator couldn't resist, "Heart and head I would surmise, insult not intended."

Sean shook it off.

The professor, proficient at deciphering the mood of any classroom, committee meeting or bar, exclaimed, "Good Gawd Gabrielle and you!". The professor had used the actress's sobriquet. "It's the end times."

"Then we go down the hatch," and Sean drained his drink.

"What the snarling scholar is trying to present, sans histrionics, is to consider the alternatives, yours, and the countries." Sen. Bruce leaned a little closer towards Sean. "Its manifest what's dear to you. You don't fake humbleness and you are proof that dignity is not a commodity. Shit, son, you're the preponderance of evidence that honor still has a grip on the good among us, Sean."

Sean was moving around in his chair, trying to find a less uncomfortable position.

The senator offered final commentary, "Politics is theatrics with a purpose. Just like it is in law or in love, I daresay."

"You daresay?" Sean challenged.

"Consider as you have throughout your life, the country, Sean. You have the constitution of our forefathers and it may well be your dirty little destiny to continue in pursuit of sacred vows beyond and bigger than self in civilian life too."

The senator leaned back in his chair. "This government is, well, the people's expectations are being ground to bits on purpose by the government's mantra which is I'm the government and basically I'm out for me. How dare you think "you", you outsiders ... you, you citizens! Hell, in this era, good government is the stuff of fables."

Sean scanned his watch then, "Thank you, Prof. Sen. This has been invigorating, but I've never considered politics as a way to go about things nor has it ever attracted me. Actually, it's AAAC."

"What?"

"Avoid at all costs."

"But Sean, if it is...."

Sean, interrupting, "No, but it's and no slights intended, but it's time for a cab for me. I do appreciate both of yours insight and effort, but I'm indecisive about everything in front of me now and I have found that's never a productive time to select a path.

The senator stood up and addressed Sean, "I'll split the taxi with you and I promise not to discuss this further on the ride."

Sean nodded and a cab was contacted.

Professor Sorentsen wrapped up the situation as he usually would with a quote. It was a quote he used in the last class of every semester.

"From an anonymous Athenian author known as the Old Oligarch, probably scrawled out sometime in 425 BC or thereabouts, and I quote, 'Then, there is something which some people find amazing in every area, the Athenians assigned more to the wicked and the poor and the populists than to the Good. In this way, they are actually preserving the democracy. In every land on earth, the Best are opposed to democracy,' unquote. Then I say to the class itching to get to the break..'T, his old humbug, not your teacher but the other ancient commentator, as you can see, he really was against giving the mob an as he saw it an undeserved voice in the doings of the State to which I say to you avid pupils...go out and do not make waves but instead go ahead and shake, rattle and roll the craggy nearsightedness of the Status Quo. Hail Columbia and have a masterful playtime. Class dismissed,' and the cheers would, well, Sean, you remember."

The "student", the senator, and the professor smiled wordless goodbyes as they, the possibly pompous, the certainly irascible and the clearly humble, readied to close down the night in the welcomed privacy of their own concerns.

Chapter 6

"Do You Remember Your Myth?"

"A crown is merely a hat that lets the rain in."

Frederick the Great

October 7, 2015

He could only handle all the publicity attendant to such events maybe twice, three times a year; that is, if they were not sponsored by him.

She could handle any publicity. Charities were her favorite forums for recognition, but opposite his obvious reluctance, her heart drove her money while his money drove his heart. And while both understood the splendor of conspicuous success and renowned notoriety and how to function through both, until they accidentally bumped into each other's back, they had never met.

Stuart Hawkins-Burke appeared stunned as he turned to face Senator Lilith" Lullaby" Langtree, so named for how adeptly she put legislation to bed and as equally for how many senators desired to hear sweet nothings from those lips in her bed.

They stood wordless in Cade Bartharlomew's main studio, the location for the moguls fund-raising gala. The key lights were perfect.

He rued he had not met this woman many years before. He felt he had missed everything. She knew the future had changed.

"It has been said that the world of money and the world of elegance should never touch but I now know this to be a lie. Don't you agree?"

She did not respond. She was occupied speculating on the arcana of the man and the arc of his desires, which is necessary for survival in her line of work. She also knew this would keep him unbalanced and still the prey.

"Doesn't everyone want to know that they are alive, alive, not insignificant and that it actually would be nice if one is as ubiquitous as the oxygen you breathe, don't you agree?"

"Wrong is your persistent pest, isn't it, Mr. Hawkins-Burke, being mistaken, I mean, don't you agree?"

His countenance revealed that she had come too close to the post and she liked it.

The senator bit down even harder," Latin, the word 'meticulosus'?",she raised her brows to see if it registered; not waiting for reply, she continued," The ending, 'osus', means 'full of.'" She paused. "Then you pucker up and add the tiny little 'ul', add it to 'metus', meaning 'fear' and you get 'meticulosus'; 'full of little fears,' which is Latin for 'your reality', don't you agree?"

Stuart was turned on by the thought of conquering his equal flower; dazzling, dangerous and extremely risky for the wrong pollinator.

"Nature is the cue card for every act. It is God yakking at us to get in the light and dance." He still couldn't read her.

Ms. Langtree pressed him closer with her eyes and, "Of course, in these digital days of humans playing God anything is possible; lionize and lying eyes are way too frequent occurrences. I've read about your proclivities."

The target warily answered, "Really?"

"Yes, you apparently appreciate art. Even nature's prime example for beauty. You're attached to it. Read it in a "People" story about, well that's why I thought of meticulous."

"Chinese painting and penmanship is what you remember from the magazine interview?" Hawkins

Burke smiled bigger. "Sung is magical. No mistakes allowed. You do only once each brushstroke on silk. Each moment in ink is final. The universe, nature is large, grand, in Sung discipline and if a human being is part of the composition the figure of the human is miniscule. Kind of an afterthought in the communication between the artist and soul of the artist and, 'between the pen and the ink."

Her eyes sunk through him. "And your love affair with flora too."

"You mean the orchids?"

"Scented reminders of the Almighty. Sight, smell, beauty, all combined in a bloom. It's the heart primeval, our deepest thoughts sunning themselves."

Stuart broke the spell, "I appreciate the orchid's ability to deceive, to manipulate for its own survival. Individual species call forth only certain, shall I call them pollinators, protecting their purity from others, other types of orchids I mean. They manipulate bees, wasps by appearance, fragrance and mimicry, ensuring great age, great endurance."

She didn't flutter a lid. "Orchids do remind us of us, don't they, Mr. Hawkins-Burke? They have two pedals on either side, a landing pad for pollination. Their sensuality keeps the breeding going because they offer anticipation," Hawkins-Burke hoped his tongue remained still..."and the type of fun that memories never avoid."

As were his ilk, whenever nerves were about to fail and reveal his humanity, he attempted turning attention from self and pushing the focus to another topic. Hawkins-Burke nodded to Lilith, motioning with his head for her to turn towards Cade Bartholomew and Senator Dunleavy Bruce. "What a raspy pair there, huh".

"You mean the mogul and the mongrel?"

"Yes, the orotund or oro rotunda and..."

"With rounded mouth."

Hawkins-Burke was stunned by his growing attraction for this person with a penchant for Latin as the preferred method of belittlement. He stared at the ocean eyed, Elizabeth Hurley cheeked, Titian haired beauty with the stiletto smile.... and crowning all this, she knew how to make sausage. He was awed. She looked past the flaws.

It was antinomian attraction, at delicate stage, yes; nevertheless, it was advancing through mirage to the oasis of playful mayhem and merriment they both so frequently had sought but both had so rarely found.

She wondered if she were insane to consider the power of being powerless. He intruded, "Are you amazed like me at the fact of our existence?"

Sen. Langtree rapidly turned point, "Tell me your lies now, mix up your mysteries for me a little will you please, because, yeah, I've heard almost all of them from way too many tellers of tall tales with way too many quick endings and way too many a bad taste left in my mouth." "Oscar Wilde said that one's real life is often the life one does not lead."

"I agree with the boy, but like him, it's men that have always caused problems, but give time a wide berth and you can sanctify just about anything, can't you?"

"It must be a sincere brainmess when one has a Republican mind stalked by a Democratic heart." "Ah, Mister Magi man" with gritted purr, "you had me at 'what's in it for me!' His speculations previous to their meeting were confirmed. This woman, this shiniest jewel beneath the Thesaurus's dome, did know when, where, and why the doors of the treasure house were opened and why they were closed.

Senator Langtree was equally pleased at detecting actual shyness behind the handsomeness and beneath the portrayed aloofness. Jesus, his photographers must all be shutter flukes," amateurs.

Slow the throttle, you ass. Stuart, get hold and close down the innards talk, you fool. Breathe, ah, say, yoga may be helping after all.

He watched as she smiled at a waiter bringing adult beverages, as she thanked him, as he smiled in return, as she delicately took a small sip of the rose.

From what he had read, her pet peeve were people, mostly pols, who paid only lip service to the expanding needs, the true concerns of the downtrodden, the " growing forgotten" as Senator Bruce had called them...Hawkins-Burke remembered that she essentially had joined with the older Senator, a rarity for the parties, in calling out her colleagues, party didn't matter, tagging them as " knobby kneed weaklings, sarsaparilla Suzies who avoid the hard work it takes to do more than just giving a damn holier than thou speech in front of cameras about 'needs' .no, instead they eat up a veritable mountain of valuable time filling it with tug at your heartstrings posturing and profiling and then, then they scoot on down the highway of Hell to the next chicken dinner, the next donor butt kissing session without ever effecting meaningful legislature that matters in the care, in the daily urgencies of the unfortunate among us, the citizens without hope, the people without even the capacity to dream, because you see, Greta, this, the poor feel, is something that other people have the time to do but not them. The street and the screech won't allow it." Hawkins-Burke had seen the passion in her, watched the compassion on fire in the Fox interview. He knew then that he must meet her...sometime...

"Stuart?"

'Sometime' was present and accounted for.

"Yes, my Senator."

"Your business practices and investments have drawn many as suspicious eye and a lot of Monday morning quarterbacking.."

"Sore losers, squawking from the tribe of little big nothings, so ashamed of never being noticed, except for their shortcomings."

"Well, Mr. Magi, Inc..."

"You can call me, Mac"

"...The Knife?"

The laughter was mutual and real.

"What about the business of energy and Magi?"

Hawkins-Burke measured possible adversaries and possible allies versus his own tendentiousness. Finally, he had found one worthy: the medal was in hand. It was gold.

Before his response, the Senator continued, "Wasn't the original meaning of Magi, ah, sorcerers with astrology on the side, glorified shamans," Ms. Langtree moved slightly forward, "casting spells?"

"Hero, of first century Alexandria said that his main premise for science was quote, producing bewilderment and awe."

He eyed her more closely if that was even possible. "You see, I've made much fortune on this Hellenistic geniuses' thesis. I bewildered the masses with the awe of my magi nano tech cell work. The comedian of a few years ago what was his name, Robin Williams, yes, well he had a show way back.."

"Mork and Mindy?"

"Yes, that's it. He said 'nano nano' for some laughter provoking reason, not knowing that that little four letter word would take on new meaning as another four letter word."

"Which is?"

"Rich."

It crossed Lilith's mind that his smile reminder her of a pirate, a pleased swashbuckler, at that.

"So you fancy yourself a modern-day "Hee-row", 2000 years hence: a capital 'H' Hero from the vicinity of Alexandria,... Virginia, not Egypt, right?" She unbalanced him with her teasing sincerity. Again.

"You do charge up the down staircase frequently don't you?"

"I like anything that charges."

"Up the hill or down?"

"Downhill with the sun at my back, Sparky."

"No power shortage here, I assure you."

"Why, Mr. Hawkins-Burke, I would never assume that your grid has been ground down, never." She took another sip of the red and after a tiny swallow, "In fact, I believe that it's probably been overloaded for way, way too long, hasn't it?"

Delicate men could make the 'lullaby' lady physically ill. She appreciated gentlemen able to wield authority under pressure but still with needs. They were in her field of operations then as she had mastered the talent of listening to men, a key factor in maintaining control.

He was silent, perhaps even slightly stunned, but obviously happy, if that's the proper description for the grin upon his face...so she moved in deeper." How have you made Magi grow so exponentially large?"

Stuart Hawkins-Burke was rarely at a loss for words, so he struggled and he managed with effort to recover, to show life. "I invest in markets most likely to be effected, are projected to be decimated by climate heat up; coffee, corn, hedges on crop losses, floods, gods little tweaks on issues with His classical throwdown's, the all-time winners, pestilence and disease and then, voila, Senator, Magi gains 'nets' that are as high and as beautiful as the endless azure of the heavens, producing that same elation and elevation I feel when 1 experience the powder blue yonder of your sweet Jesus eyes."

She strained to appear unaffected.

He did not hesitate. "Water scarcity, that's the ring to snatch; maybe 200-300 million Africans will face water stress because of contamination and another one of those God pot sweeteners, drought. Bottled water, water pumps, irrigation equipment, planning of cloud seeding, your hybrid seeds for the poor and the destitute that can only be purchased from Magi's division of agricultural studies, charities, nonprofits of course, at least most of them; yes, these are a few of my favorite thing's.. At least I keep most of the facilities in-country, honestly, only because Jansen Hyde knows where the bodies are buried and where the loopholes have been designed for..."

"Either for your grand entry or your grand escape, right?" "Well, I..."

"So marinade all these efforts with government subsidies, University studies and, shazaam, taxes are a memory and everything is politically palatable to Boards of Directors as well as those smelly stockyards of bored politicians?" She allowed the silence to linger before, "I like our convergence, don't you?"

The Magi man revealed shyness, confusion by his red blush bordered by pale cheeks which pleased her greatly as she knew it was infrequent that this man was thrown around an emotional romper room of the heart by a provocative individual such as herself. She drove it home, "How to get the seed out when the rows are not plowed; that's the basic crux of it all, isn't it, Mr. Hawkins hyphen Burke?"

Was that a signal? Brutally humbling, this sweet anguish of uncertainty.

"We are from distinctly different schools, Mr. H B. You are from the classroom of 'easy knocks'... whilst I, on the other palm, "Lilith sampled more rose," I am from the school of 'run before you crawl', the never kneel curricula in which desire denied is considered gauche and unhealthy, a failing grade guaranteed if ones goal is long-term joy and long lived satisfaction, and even though you spawned from a lily pad of another pond, we do swim in the same currents, don't we, Mr. H B?"

Stuart stared at her, the 'bad, very bad girl' Senator. His lips attempted sound but there was not a smidgen of a syllable.

"And in that school of breezy dreaming, did they train you that the vulnerability of love is an acquired taste, Stuart, or did they fail you in that as well?"

Was the bridge down, the moat beneath not an impediment anymore?

"Did you know, Stuart, a University study, a real University, discovered that narcissists are the most prone to have casual sex, more than anyone else." She enjoyed the flummoxed male nearly as dearly as the subject she was discussing. "As your life implies, it's all about getting the power, isn't it, babe?"

He understood the cauldrons of boiling ebony still roiled above the battlements. "Perhaps you are not aware the fact of nature that the fields exposure to the seed, even its' close proximity, can improve the vitality, even the mood of the yard, vastly improving her prospects for fertility and expanded bounty?" He gently took her left hand, raised it to his lips, kissed it, and equally as gentlemanly, released it and slightly bowed.

"Mind your manners, you rogue. Considering the circumstances of our meeting such talk as we talk, is it fitting at an event for, for..."

"Children, my dear?"

"Yes, children, children are why we..."

"Meet?"

"Oh, what's the name of this damned gathering, you fool! It escapes me."

"Nothing escapes fait acompli, my dearest, or should I say, the loveliest field of dreams I've ever encountered?"

And The Keep was kept no more.

In his column, Tripp Bellows included this meeting of gush and blush as well as his perceptions of D.C.'s other 'eventees' attending his friend Cade Bartholomew's passion, the networks annual studio charity auction. "First, disclaimer numero uno; most of the idolized individuals are my friends. Disclaimer numero dos; this doesn't matter as charity often brings strange bedfellows together. After all, it's a one night gala to honor those in need of more than the shallow comfort of a slam bam, thank you, maam, one night satisfaction; but I digress. The before mentioned, Mr. Bartholomew, seeded the pot with a $100,000 check and immediately thereafter, in his only comment for publication, Mr. Hawkins-Burke announced, "I will double that!" and the auction went joyously north after that with pledges and cash approaching over $1 million in contributions for Mr. Bartholomew's fab five, The Make A Wish Foundation, St. Jude's' Children Hospital, The Wounded Warrior Project, The Paralyzed Veterans of America and The Habitat For Humanity.

My college teacher, Mr. Sorentsen, distinguished professor with the patience of a rehabilitated Job, donated a signed by the author copy of Mark Twain's Huckleberry Finn. Senator Dunleavy, 'the Bruce is loose', contributed a $5.000 gift certificate to Toys Are Us, or, as the good Senator jokingly said, "Could be mistaken for an offer of a personal tour of the Senate."

'Oh My Gawd' Gabriel provided a signed script from her first starring role, "Deadly Alive" for the bidding. I might add that Miss Odessa was escorted by the Patriots' Patriot, Sean Linden (He'll hate this).

When Senator 'Lullaby' Langtree wasn't busy turning Mr. Hawkins hypen Burke into a 'cudlelicious' awe hyphen struck lad (He'll hate this too), she promoted her contribution, which was a dinner date with her, followed by a flight for her and the donor to New York to see the Broadway Show of the donors' choice... whereupon, of course, Mr. Magi Man outbid anyone that dared to even hint at an offer. I note here that the usually poker-faced right hand palm of the Magi CEO-CFO, one Mr. Jansen Hyde, appeared disquieted, fidgety, not unlike a makeup-less clown gone down, you know, the one who falls way before the flower on the lapel squirts the 'gag' out; you know the type. This correspondent contributed a personal item of mine as well. I'm auctioning, well, not me, but through Mr. Bartholomew's efforts, the hand written lyrics to "Thank You Through The Tears", scribbled on three slightly yellowed bar napkins that come from a now defunct drinking establishment that worked its magic for many years in Albuquerque, New Mexico. It's set in a 14 karat gold frame and my Cures band mates all signed it with me. Cade and I agreed to leave the bidding open on this item until day after tomorrow. Check it out on Networks web page.

Bids are getting to the scary silly level.

I would be remiss if I failed to note that standing in for the Native American activist and my very dear Navajo friend, John Truefellow, was his nephew, the handsome, the intelligent and the tall for his teenage years, Mr.de Mejas, (And he'll hate this as well) a senorita swooner, if ever there were one.

I will bring the tent down with this... while Mr.Bartholomew, (he of the monster new ratings for his studios) likes to present himself as one tough hombre; I tell you, citizens, (with apologies to Tweety), "I taught I saw a Puddy Cat. I Did!, I Did! And his name is Cade Bartholomew the Third, the beast-sized broadcaster with the Kraken-sized heart. (He very well may punch me in my face just to prove me wrong because I definitely know that he will thoroughly detest this)."

Within five years of the stations inception, the father of the host, Mr. Bartholomew the Second, had brought the fledgling Network to viable challenger status for major league sized ratings and profitable demographics. As whiffs of Alzheimer's evolved into more than just clues, Second had turned the reins over to The Third earlier than the pundits and the son had anticipated. And this occurred only two years after Cade juniors' mother died from an allergic reaction to a drug. The Third was 21 when the world tumbled for both father and son. Then "Corn", as Junior was known to close friends, was 22 when Senior Bartholomew was properly diagnosed.

The studio quickly expanded from Denver to, as Senior called it, "The pool hall for unpithy pit vipers, D.C."

Seniors' love for Cade junior proved justworthy as junior weathered the aforementioned most difficult years of his life as the son propelled the reach of his father's vision as the son became a full throttled competitor to the other major mouthpieces of the airwaves.

A glaring difference between the Second and the Third was that, all too frequently, The Third wore his concerns not only on his sleeve but virtually clothed himself in the now seemingly unfashionable fullness of a passionate heart. Just after Mrs. Bartholomews shocking death, Cade never forgot, a few days after her funeral, his father's stern admonishment. After seeing a segment on the local ABC affiliate about a noted charitable event and "the considerate souls involved", Junior told Senior, "Dad, I want to be a secret Santa Claus; help unfortunate kids, help those vagrants on Colfax, their fantasies come true; their efforts, their opportunities expand to their," upon which Senior interrupted, "Son, I'm proud that you have your mother's kindness in your blood. God bless her deeply. But steel yourself for the future. There are those and they are numerous, son, that will take advantage of you every blessed time that they can, will smell you out fast, beat up your feelings with pugilistic precision, break your heart, take your wealth with not an nth of degree of remorse or concern for the filthy mess they make of you as you lay prone in all your misplaced kindness, your expectations ambushed, oozing out on a beggars turf. Never stand still, Cade. You cannot afford to become a stationary target. This business of ours is the number one attention getter for all those who use bull's-eyes as guidance systems for their goals. Never forget your purpose here and never let the help see you weep. Charity you can do on your vacations, far from the publicity of misplaced scrutiny, which believe me you will know by its duly decimal depth and hair trigger recriminations; for son, you are always on stage and the groundlings will always try to reach out and touch you hard and there are never enough tugs in the world for them to be satisfied." The discussion over, the fiery media magnet had wheeled on his heels and headed out the door in the direction of his next appointment.

Now, during his umteenth charitable event, momentarily alone in the stations' master control, Junior managed a grin as he recalled another of the many differences between father and son, pretty much summing up how far the apple had strayed from the branch. Senior adored Winston Churchill and Corn loved Theodore Roosevelt. Ah, the ancient duel of head and heart buzz sawing again.

The mogul leaned against the sound board and drained the contents of his glass. Forty years old, a few inches over 6 feet, green eyes, a tuff of thick Michael McDonald-like premature gray hair; add to this mix his wealth and it is easy to see why it had never been a problem for Cade Bartholomew to ever fail to attract the female's which had ever since those awkward self- awareness pushy days of adolescence posed, in polite terms, a plethora of situational hazards. He'd survived a plenitude of relationships gone to seedless (mostly of his doings) and one expensive failed marriage. He ruminated on the rummage from his early student days when he partied so hard and so publicly that he was expelled from the nation's most favored party school, the University of Colorado in Boulder. Corn brought many of his college binge pals home to Cherry Creek, always when senior was away on business, to chill out and to introduce them to the real power within the realm of Bartholomew, the matriarch, "Lady Anne" Bartholomew. As she had kept Senior honest and kept him in love, Anne Bartholomew always worked her motherly magic to keep Junior ever progressing down the smooth fairways of life, ever cognizant of her sons propensity to burrow into the rough of misplaced affections and the sand traps of hopeless designs. Unquestionably, his mother was his fiercest defender and forever his greatest love; forever until the saddest day of Junior's life, the day the prescriptions went horribly sour, that messy maddening Fall day, the day of his Mothers death.

Understanding with virgin clarity the severity of the situation, Junior had transferred to the University of Oklahoma, and in two years graduated in Management; the result of refocused attention of giving his all, of doing everything Cade could to ease the walk of the widowers way, that sullen shaded path ahead when one loses the companion of their life as his father had. Cade occasionally speculated among friends that this period was probably the origin of his later problems with carpel tunnel syndrome in that it was then " when I indulged in the frequent bending of the wrist to achieve the proper angle for the bangles of ice to not get in the way of the perfect flow rate for a well-aged scotch to perform its expectant duty of soothing an aching mind." He would further share, " This priming-the-pump exercise quickly familiarize myself with the absolute two necessities required for all lead dogs; first class alcohol and the near providential ability to fade to black on any bad memories."

Once, when the then young Isaac 'Chaz' Bellows asked his friend from college," What music do you prefer, master Bartholomew?", and the former responded," Any pole dance music that leads to the climbing up of more than just the charts is instantly a favorite of mine," the latter, the future front man for one of America's major rock bands, knew that they would be friends for life.

In fact, Mr. Bellows witnessed often the validation of their kinship through the many nice moves, both monetarily and otherwise, that Mr. Bartholomew preformed in service and aid to others; a man always desirous of leaving no trace of his kindness, a man's' actions as Tripp would come to understand that were in actuality, simple, silent dedications to the only angel Junior had ever believed in, 'Lady Anne' Bartholomew.

The master control room elevator doors opened. Cade turned his attention to his friend. Sean nodded as he walked towards him.

"Welcome to the Pasha suite."

Cade lifted his drink and Sean met the media mans' glass with his.

"Salute to you ol' baron of broadcasting!"

"The Pasha's playground, more precisely, where I oversee that overturned sandbox down there, that playground, otherwise referred to as the main studio and my oh my, Seannee," Cade directed their eyes down to the crowded floor of donors and bidders, "My God, Sean, Miss Odessa Gabrielle herself! Whatever on the planet got into her beautiful head to even glance at the likes of you!"

"She's a highlight in real life too, Junior."

"So she's cornered another fallen angel, has she?"

"Enough. This isn't keg days."

"Yes, a memorable week of bacchanalia that; I recall parts of it fondly."

"We're apparently doomed to be friends forever. It's my bane. I, who bought you your first pair of Levis, as your wardrobe consisted of suits; suits which were, well, a bit too much for any roommate of mine's closet and you, you..."

"Lucky sperm?"

"God damn right."

They clink their glasses again. Cade's face became slightly more serious. "You know I'm alone now because I'm too known, can't trust too easily, and I feel God is paying me back for my youthful, should I say times, when women were girls, and in my eyes, girls were also women and I liked them both, but then I didn't rally to the point of discernment in the differences between one and the other. I liked both at different times, but didn't...but didn't know that until.."

"Post keg days?"

"Oh, no, no; much later than that"

"Figures."

"Sean, it has been a situational pinch since my sophomore year of higher learning. Did you know that I was absolutely the last person on campus to try pot?"

"And what does that have to do with... "

"Did not think it was worth the hype until one time at a party, I tried it and I saw God, Sean, in deified digital color in front of me on the cinderblock wall of my apartment."

"Mother Theresa would be proud."

"You know, Sean, that nobody ever screened my mouth at the airport of confessional flight patterns, don't you?"

"Better than most."

Cade portrayed the look of close scrutiny as he leaned in towards his friend. "My dear dad said something others have said. He said, quote, assume, the old saying goes, makes an, quote, ass, unquote, out of "u" quote and "me". Cade leaned just 2 inches closer, saying, "You don't mind my dad talk, do you?"

Sean turned to the monitor with the image of the moguls' latest national evening news anchor. "Sean, you know, I have never been your standard grade Lothario and that I will never fail in giving the "look" the public wants, right?"

"She's apparently intelligent, so you have broken your pattern, I would say."

"Remember, Sean, you win by distraction."

"Anything to maintain the rights of people such as yourself in exercising freedom of speech, right?"

"Partial attention of the world's multitudes of distracted tribes can become very expensive to maintain." Cade's paused, then continuing, "With tablets, bonsai breaking news, WI, and watches that watch you, confusion maintains the reign and all is well for the 0.00 1% and it's, good night, John boy."

"You attract the heavy hearted, don't you?"

"No need for interpreters that way, right, Sean, you know, those real helpful words, the language of assistance, that's purposely lost in the daily scribbles of the absurd, the absolute, and the absolved, don't you, the unholy trilogy devised solely for the status quo in society, care packages for the witless to keep the "few", the gooey good, maintained in comfortable expectations as any Zeus or Athena would expect, right?"

"Whatever you say, Ghengis, whatever you say." Sean took a drink of his imbibetation and then, "Negotiated ethics will break down any society, won't it?"

"All but the finest among us."

"A relentless barrage of dreadful circumstances makes everyone feel better about their dreary way of going about things, doesn't it, Corn?"

"I knew you would agree. Drink, Sean, drink to the finest among us, right?" Cade then practiced what he preached and downed his liquid sacrament." Welcome to the shell game."

"No matter what you try, my dear friend, I remember what truly lonely entails, since I met Odessa." And as Sean turned to exit, he implored, "Come, come, my mighty one: let's see what the common folk endure, shall we?", but Sean stopped his move upon hearing his friends retort as Cade said, "Been to any of those Hollywood parties yet, my man?"

Cade continued. "Ah, Cinema Verite; ah, those go twitter hipper things, those Facebook things, those go skinny dipping things, those tell-all things, those corporate ties, those deputize yourself emanations by the pool, those Hollywood Shuffles and the ensuing tabloid wonder of it all, this German drama of bitch and bite, ah, the aroma of swollen success, almost suffocates you as you enter the hallowed hallways, don't you know."

Sean recognizes what was coming with the impish look on Cades face. "Tell me, Sean, have you ridden the best ride in Disneyland yet?"

Sean shook his head and feigns disgust.

"It's sad to witness, to see that you're the same old tight-assed person still swimming upstream in a rapidly looser world." Cade waited a beat, then, "Get with the flow, bro, get with the flow."

"Corn, sometimes a personality is strong enough to send history in a new direction."

Mr. Bartholomew was surprised at Sean's reply, knowing Sean to be the least self-centered of anyone Cade had feelings for. Was this a changed Sean; was he being serious? What had Odessa Gabrielle done to his friend!

"Seeing the good professor Sorentsen down there among the others, I'm wondering if any of them besides Tripp and the Senator know what a piece of good medicine he really is, " "Yes, he is that, certainly."

"..One of his teachings reverberates, Cade, a Hemingway tome; Sorentsen quoting it, artfully in his inevitable manner, yes, the last time I remembered it before now was a chilly evening patrol with Moah in the Sahara, an ordered thing that had suckers odds for survival or success but a, ah, a thing which could not be avoided....Funny, but maybe not, what comes to a man in desolated place under the stars: those bright shots of eternity, those heavenly touchstones, yes, these candles of God which, if you are a realist, you understand that you may never see another sky such as this night full of these shiny reminders of the dearness of life. Yes, Cade; Hemingway, Sorentsen; they intruded then too."

Cade attempted composure but knew it not.

"Hemingway says something, pretty much line for line, I've got it, but as I recall it's begins mid-sentence, quoting, "a son will die, and the mother of a man that has died for his country should be the proudest woman in the world, and the happiest. And how much better to die in all the happy period of un-disillusioned youth, to go out in a blaze of light, then to have your body worn out and old and illusions shattered."

"Senior quoted Hemingway to me frequently."

"Citing Hemingway can only go so far."

"Why go further?"

"Well played number two, I mean, number three."

They laughed. Cade bent down in front of what appeared to be a box of wires and cables, pressed a red button marked "escape", upon which the false panel opened up revealing a mid-sized refrigerator within, stocked with four bottles of cold champagne.

"This is the producers private" in case of emergency" rescue stash, which I, as owner, under no articles of the FCC rules, have right to commandeer whenever I deem necessary." The mogul gave one bottle to Sean and taking another said." Will you accompany me downstairs to the auction floor, kind sir, as we must keep the bids rolling tippingly off their well heeled tongues as there are children to help, homes to build and.."

"Warriors to heal"

"Indeed, Sean, indeed."

"Exiting the elevator, Sean saw Sen. Bruce waving to him to come hither. Cade went in opposite direction to mingle with the moneyed many. They had popped the corks in the elevator before Cade press the Floor One button so both were ready for action.

Sean grabbed a glass from a passing server and poured it for the Senator before the Senator could say anything but, finally, "Thank you for being a mind reader, Mr. Linden." Sean joined him with his fresh glass, also eyeing to see if Odessa, whom he spotted across the studio, was enjoying herself, which apparently she was as she was in animated conversation with Senator Langtree. Both were smiling so Sean felt comfortable stopping to chat with "the Bruce is Loose."

The Senator noticed the younger mans initial focus. "Ah, you know, Sean, on those occasions when I've been seeking donations; both for my good causes and for those not so good, I ha.." "The political ones?"

"Well, yes, of course. But the point being; I have found myself in stelliferous company too, you know those sparkling West Coast gatherings abundant with pitiful pulsars of promotion, Malibu quarks with quirks, novas of no distinction but naughtiness and oh, yes, rounding out this universe of the wealthy but strange, those ever present white dwarfs that so long ago and so many premieres before sucked the air out of everyone else's honesty and essence." The 'Bruce' took a quick breath and before Sean could blink, "Sean, as your friend, just one more word from this old 'been there before bastard', lo to the navigator without a map in this most cynical system of starry, starry nights. It isn't that..."

"This is the second time in five minutes that I have been questioned about the mystery of motives. Enough already."

"Oh, don't get me wrong Sean. She could be another Theodora, the Byzantine actress; the wife of Justinian. Theodora was the brains behind that throne." "Do you mean bizarre or Byzantium, which is it?"

They smiled together and stared across the studio together at the subject of their exchange; Odessa, radiant, standing firm, elegantly arrayed in an extremely complimentary form-fitting azure fashion; a woven adornment of appeal, an attraction which neither man could then resist, nor for that matter, for which neither man would ever in a lifetime be able to come up with the name of the designer responsible for this presently beautiful moment in mind.

Senator couldn't help himself. "You know the song about the devil in the blue dress; I'm..."

"You josh just a bit much, Senator."

"And you dost protest too much, kind sir, because, you see, history, in religion, 'blue' signifies truths that were frequently associated with the Almighty herself. Some cultures thought the color blue stood for constancy, fidelity; so Odessa; I assume this is the subject we discuss..."

"Never assume."

"Yes, well, even, Mr. Linden, even the mariners of fabled saga, ancient voyagers, those men of respected song and storied verse, yes, they too believed that the color 'blue' represented a positive, a, well, almost angelically inspired celestial ceiling of forever that blanketed their pathways and protected them from those mean oceans which they thought were mostly composed of discordant froth and foam; so verily to them, that 'blue' above, you see, was as calming an agent as the softness of a grandmothers comforter and to them also, it was a sign, an azure-hued omen, a portent of freedom from intemperate weather and deadly storm, a heavenly symbol of safe passage in the most precarious of adventures...yes, Mr. Linden, it was the color 'blue' that got them through, and so, as I humbly proclaimed at the outset of our observation of the dear lady over there awash in powder blue perfection.....you bitch too much!"

They laughed as relatives at rarely held reunions do; heartily, unrestrained and without any concern for pesky pieces of Grandma's potato salad still hanging out on their happy lips.. Some attendees noticed them, and just as quickly, returned to their own being noticed.

"Say, you two, "Cade passed by, restocked, fresh full bottle of bubbly in hand, "don't go getting hooked up with any burdens of bedizenment... Be clean, be proficient in productive pleasure; the fruits will be plentiful and penetrating to the senses and women will willingly help you harvested it all. Bye." The mogul moved on to the next collection of empty flutes.

The senator recovered first, "In spite of himself, I know him to be a nice man and most importantly, one of my most favored lunatics; of course, how could it be otherwise, he's one of your friends."

Sean grinned, as he sincerely adored the older man, who now added," Hollywood and Washington is inhabited by the same child beasts, Sean. Anthropophagous people by choice, preachers of faithful mendacity, practitioners of clockwork orange shenanigans and heists; and their progeny for posterity being? Why polyglot ethics, brain numbing exudations and remorseless excuses, of course."

"Sean watched the senator's eyes move from Sean to over Sean's left shoulder. He turned to follow the senator's gaze in time to see Senator Langtree lift her glass in acknowledgement of the senators' nod, smiling at them both, obviously and purposefully ignoring her most recent admirer by her side, Hawkins-Burke, as Hawkins-Burke attempted indifference, but was betrayed, in fact, by his glowering pitch-perfect 'look' of unimpeachable disdain; complemented by a stance, a publicized attitude only practicing sociopaths can execute with such professional expertise.

'We've been targeted by Hawkins-Burkes' latest project, and Seanee, I love how it agitates him, so much so that he's become the target, not she. Please, please, Sean, lift your glass in returned acknowledgment to the dear lady, won't you?"

Mr. Linden acted on the senators' terse request.

"Ah, great, Sean, a double shot at that prick, huh? Now smile, son, for the kill shot. Yes, there you go. Yes, good, very good. Look at the Magi man's puzzlement, and yet Stuart still attempts to act as if he doesn't care, what a mockery of a real man, huh?"

"Most men are, Senator, most are," as Sean continued to give response to the captivating ladies positive inferences towards the senator and himself. He joined the senator and being pleased by Hawkins-Burke obvious discomfort, but didn't know why. He'd save that for later.

Odessa turned and saw him. Sean's smile became real.

The Senator slightly bowed, waved his unfettered hand with gentle flourish, then, without pause, he straightened and percolated into another topic as if everything previous never happened. "Congress is a field of schemes."

Sean winked at Odessa; she winked back as she turned to meet another fan, while simultaneously he pivoted to hear the rest of Mr. Bruce's wisdom.

"Never forget that it is critical to one's career to be on speaking terms with the architects." Sean remembered one of Prof. Sorentsen's able descriptions of the man.

"When aroused, Sean, he can be one distinctively nasty combination of Samuel Clemens and Foghorn Leghorn busting on a tear and to those that are foolish enough to mistake the punch lines or the vinegar in his veins for an innocent old man's batch of frostings and sweet foolishness, brother, that's when you best be getting on Kevlar and a helmet too."

Senator Dunleavy Bruce was speaking again, "You must understand the dynamics of any parlor game. Don't say much early, if at all. Then, in those beginning stages, suggest that you, well, 'might' possibly talk to the opponents. Then propagandize their faults everywhere. Next, ask for the moon in negotiations, the more absurd; the better. Then, Lord Almighty, behold the metamorphosis; become the biggest benevolent S.O.B. in the room and agree to what you wanted all along, a compromise that's not a compromise."

"Are we still talking politics or about women?"

"Well, something akin to both; prison."

"Sean, would you help me with awareness and promotion persistence and call to action cards, just help me dealing with improvements in our prison conditions, our prison systems?"

"Well, I'd like," Sean hesitated.

"They're like women..." "... to, but I'm not..." ".. throughout the world; a captive workforce beneath private wardens and administrations that extract all they can from the incarcerated; the early ages to the old cons, 'slaves', all without hope or cause to breathe for. The meals they serve, that hyena avoiding slop reminds me of the stuff the king served his prisoners in 'The Wizard of Id'. Geez, I miss Johnny Hart, a cartoonist unparalleled in poignant but humorous revelations about the sorrowful condition of humanity. Was the only thing worth reading in the Washington Post, I might add." The senator squinted at Sean. "No, is not acceptable, right?"

"I will help where I can best help, but... "

"No, they will listen to you. You have all levels of society's very best wishes. And, because you are almost Neil Armstrongnian in avoiding publicity or self promotion ... "Senator Bruce playfully indicated towards the actress, "except maybe for now. Kidding, kidding, but Sean, it's your messaging moment..."

"I'm never in the market for some messaging or whatever the crap it's called, so, Sena..."

"Why, the law today is a Hooters girl, a beautiful person, an attractive concept, who's actually nice, who tries hard every day to approach everything in life as morally, as evenly as possible but, but, in the required territory of her daily travels to survive, she consistently scrapes up against the hoary outside, her body and mind forced to be subject to all the shades of the dirty due diligences of sloppy eyed attorneys, the majority of whom believe she is just like them in that she charges just like they do... by the hour."

"You just body-slammed Solomon, didn't you?" "Justice, nor the lack of it, is no jesters stage!"

Dunleavy's sudden forcefulness surprised the younger man but Sean eased as the Senator continued,... "Even though, laughter, yes, laughter may be the best coping mechanism, the only balm for the living, and by the living, I mean the tinier-by-the-minute truly thoughtful among us, Sean, type individuals that which, on a daily, if not hourly basis, must combat the waves, the multitudes of dead-ended excremental walking, breathing excuses that parade around as human beings, those propped up personas tossed out in society as mini-messiahs, you know, those speaking the sermons of easy answers, those flesh and blood bumptious occurrences I frequently define as being the result of the vulgar vagaries of disastrous ovulations, those to which the masses, the maddening "give it all to me on a silver platter" populace, happily and foolhardily hail as the "wise and farsighted ", these centers of the "selfie" generations affections, these glorified "must haves" which possess not a smidgeon of "must have" serviceable sense; these are the real jailors of our times, our minds, and I tell you, Sean, recidivism's the bitch of the thing; we've got to break this anarchy of turnstile justice and exonerations to the highest bidders, Mr. Linden, or the comfortably unconcerned will wear down the uncomfortably concerned." The Senator took a breath, then, "Most importantly though, help from people like you, it means the world to those that need noticing the most; those men and women stuck in shithole situations of life, yes, whether their fault or otherwise, but these crushed souls beg for what we all crave, Sean. the God given grace of the gift of human touch. Will you help me help them, son?"

Sean's right hand met the Senator's outstretched paw; the grasp of agreement, ancient in origin, no notaries' necessary, sealed Sean's support.

"I'll help you where and when I can. Thank you for the opportunity." He spotted his house guest standing by the makeup rooms entrances and thought it best to check on the young man, see how he was faring..."Please excuse me, Senator."

"Of course, and thank you again."

"Yes, need to see how The Navaho's nephew is doing. "

"Good idea as I see 'Lady Lullabies' lad approaching the nearby vicinity."

The week previous to the present event, Stuart Hawkins-Burke was overseas enjoying a strictly low profile (meaning only two body guards) vacation; hiking, sightseeing, and tasting the cuisine of Spain. Desirous of privacy, he and his 'associates', dressed ragged-rugged man style, remaining unshaved, letting hair do the disheveled thing, projecting a bon vivant of overstated 'averageness'; all of which achieved the Magi Mans' goal of below-the-radar relaxation and privacy. During this sojourn de Espana, Hawkins-Burke had avoided all electronic connection with the world outside his immediate location; no news, no informacio nada, including no contact from Jansen Hyde, which, in hindsight, Mr. Hyde was immensely thankful for now as circumstances of that week of the bosses absence did not all go as planned. Hyde more than anyone in the company, understood the imperative need, during Hawkins-Burkes' trip, for the man to remain unfettered by even a scent of trial or tribulation, because Hyde and

Magi required the boss to be well rested and at Hawkins - Burkes superior best for the upcoming business week as Magi was scheduled to begin the most important of negotiations with their most important of largest suppliers...

Hyde thanked whatever Titans that rule the unknown for the timely 'zone of solitude' that had surrounded Stuart in Spain, especially because the leader of Magi wasn't able to receive any news of his estranged sister's demise. Word of her death would have sent Mr. Hawkins-Burke into a tailspin at the most inauspicious of important corporate moments, and this, in the opinion of the ultimate business hound, Hyde, would have proven disastrous per the penultimate corporate goal of "closing the deal."

After both left their step-parents, Hawkins-Burke and his sister did not agree on much. An occasional note or telegram without a return of address, were the only form of contact. But it provided both with the value most cherished by siblings; validation of each others existence. Neither spoke or wrote to the other of their private lives.

On his return from the studio men's room, Hawkins-Burke spotted a handsome teenager. ... 'Must be Lindens' and The Navahos houseguest,' whom Hawkins-Burke had duly been informed about during the pre-event 'review' conference conducted by Hyde.

He didn't know why, but Hawkins-Burke smelled opportunity, and strutted forward.

Jansen Hyde lurked nearby, doing his job, attempting to insure that a "private moment", wouldn't became an iconic negative image of "publicized hypocrisy or worse', he, the watchful worrier guarding against anything that could result in damaging, deep slices to Magi's corporate currency and promoted persona.

"How do you do? I'm Mr. Hawkins-Burke, and you?"

"I'm staying with Mr. Linden and my Uncle, John Truefellow. I'm Mr. de Mejas. Jesus."

"So staying with the living hero, Linden, are you... and Truefellows' nephew too... part of the tribe, are you, huh?"

Godboy had been made aware of Hawkins-Burkes style. Not sure whether from The Navaho or from Sean or the newspapers. He recovered quickly from what most would consider a quarrelsome inquiry.

"Logic and genetics would answer that in the 'affirmative', wouldn't you agree?

Emblematic of his fathers' feistiness, the young man continued, "I've heard of you and your ways and your worries."

Hawkins-Burke straightened, a more serious demeanor, bodily announced. "Worry? What a strange comment, especially in our first. . ."

"You aren't the only bold one here, Mr. Hawkins-Burke."

Mr. Hyde grimaced.

The CEO-CFO of Magi, Inc., amused, laughed a genuine guffaw.

Jensen Hyde made a motion to touch Hawkins-Burke's arm, but stopped as he notice that all the people within range were watching, attentive to this unfolding scene; in Hyde's estimation, a veritable gawkers gourmet.

"Young man of such strange, old thoughts."

Sen. Langtree returns with Odessa Gabriel, and the Senator is obviously intrigued in her newest flames level of repartee as she hears him say, "And your parents, son?"

"They're not here. "

Mr. Hyde calculated that more than a 'comfortable' amount of people were turning their attention towards Mr. Hyde's boss. Hyde sensed what, to him, was an all-too-familiar 'taint' forming; an odiferous thing, the kind of which lobbyists of Hyde's particular, shall we say, caliber and talent, readily identified with; the aroma of billowing bad news storms building, gathering on seemingly endless horizons of hubbub; always, so always, pungent with potential for the very unwanted and the very worst of airs, the smelliest of all things to those in Jansen Hyde's profession, scrutiny. Hyde moved within elbow-nudging range.

Delayed by another well wisher after leaving the company of Senator Bruce, Sean Linden finally joined the 'watch party', smiling a 'hello' to the actress as she blew him a small kiss in return. He was just in time to hear Hawkins-Burke.

"Do you not want the prize of the good life, my friend, and do you not understand that achieving the good life, that it doesn't arrive without efforts or concerns or 'worries' as some would call it?" Alejandro Buddha Jesus Simon de Mejas replied, "As someone much smarter than the both of us said, 'worry gives a small thing a big shadow'. Is this not so?"

Hawkins-Burke glanced at Hyde, then Lilith, and then returned attention to the young de Mejas. "For any age, you have an unusual approach for understatement and understanding, little Truefellow."

"As I mentioned, you can call me Jesus."

Except for Hyde, everyone laughed, including Jesus.

"Don't you believe, too, that this country is the 'what', the 'when', and the 'where' for the survival of the dreams of the world, yes?"

Godboy barely hesitated before, "Yes, but I also know that location, the origins of one's essence, the 'where' you are in the time and space of life, that's the source of meaningful guidance, the purpose behind the ability of doing things when you can. Don't you see that where you are dictates the when you can, the when you can do the undoable; to electrify and charge up the seriously nonchalant; to sear into them, to burn into these furiously uncurious the 'want to' to instead becoming the courageously concerned?"

Hyde smelled 'upstage', that, if not already arrived, was certainly circling, asking for landing coordinates.

"My mother taught me that a Greek, an old Greek sage, name of Solon, said thousands of years ago, said that Justice is a principle of the abstract that can be rationalized only through the sweat and tears and the acts and works of man. To Solon, Mom said, reasoning, thinking through the muddled mess of small minded platitudes is only honestly debated when there is a stirring in the heart, and as this Greek also said,' and without inciting the wrath of the Gods,' meaning no High- On commands or bullying orders to line up this way or that way or decrees to cater to old appetites, that the most courageously concerned should and do find so distasteful and so, so wrong, and so dreadfully passe."

"Your mother is a brilliant woman."

"Yes, she, she is, Mr. Hawkins-Burke." The young man hoped no one took note of the stutter. "Unfortunately, from the little I've read, it matters not whether a man is a demigod or a horse's ass, is it not the truth that justice is for sale like a common commodity? In fact, I more than suggest that it is far from blind or impartial, and that it's near outrageously impossible in our times to discover equitable remedy when Lady Liberty herself is so very aware, as very knowledgeable as to the difference between the weight of a feather and the weight of a bar of gold."

"You really believe in these attempts, these superficial silhouettes of 'what is' and 'what isn't'? Are you going for sainthood, son?"

An inaudible gasp, the type of silence noticeable for its unbearable presence, nearly caused arrhythmia in Mr. Hyde.

Godboy turned away from the insidious unctuousness of the businessman, but upon hearing the soft wind chime voice of Senator 'Lullaby', reversed course.

"Passion's admirable, compadre, but it alone will not get you to shore. You see, what Stuart is attempting to convey... "

Hawkins-Burke maintained his smile. Jensen Hyde settled into fresh levels of displeasure with deeper wrinkles and redder brow.

"... is that rocky reality squeezes in on you everywhere and while it's majestic to suggest one align their course by the charitable disposition of the stars or be guided by the beatified buoys of forgiveness and grace, check your charts frequently, Mr.de Mejas, as the shitty shoals of 'slam you down hard' are forever lurking just below the surface of your presumptions; smug, poised with powerful currents, ready to suck you dry, so deeply, so steeply, so rapidly so completely that surfacing for air is long past being part of any of your equations..."

So quiet the aftermath, Sean could swear that he heard the footfall of shadows; until, in best British stage accent, "Oh My Gawd", exclaimed," Oh, come now, Lilith!"

"What?"

"I say, egad, old girl: couldn't you be a trite more specific, what!"

"Well," Sen. Langtree playfully cackled, "I'm no bloody Mary Poppins and I dare say that by the looks of you, you are no Mother Teresa either" The women laughed, the men relaxed.

Hawkins-Burke spotted him first but before Stuart could greet him with the first salvo...

"Hello Mr. Lowbrow-Highbrow, how are we?"

"Sen. Hop-Scotch, still sober are we?"

Mr. Hyde finally nudged Mr. Hawkins-Burke on the arm. Mr. Hawkins-Burke ignored Mr. Hyde. Sen. Bruce took a sip of champagne and then with exaggerated smack of his lips, "Ah, Dionysius, see what you've wrought, a mordant parasite within the woodworks of the vats of life, drink anyone?"

"Oh, you're into sharing your life's blood now?"

"You agree, I am sure, that lawyers and CPAs," Mr. Bruce focused on Mr. Hyde, "that they should be the guarantors of taxation and justice and not, how should I say, the intelligent designers, the hired guns of the hierarchy, properly positioned to circumvent, to collude, to play dirty for those at the other end of their chain... Doggy is what, that's what it's called, right Mr. Hyde?"

Hyde sneered, professionally, "What preachy pooh porn, you drooling maniac."

Mr. Bartholomew, along with Prof. Sorentsen, gathering Godboy, Odessa and Sean..., "And this, coming from a mere sternutation in the scheme of things; now I'll imbibe to that."...

..led them away from the forming tempest to the other side of the studio.

Prof. Sorentsen asked the teenager, "Have you thought of becoming a teacher, or perhaps," with a laugh," a politician, my friend?"

Godboy returned the smile to the obviously friendly adult.

Sean patted the teachers shoulder. "This is Prof. Sorentsen, Nino. And he's a good tall person. And don't answer his question, Nino, as we already have way too many politicians and look what teaching has done to him!"

Prof. Sorentsen, looking at Cade, deadpanned, "I didn't have you in any of my courses, did I?"

"Why yes, those classes that that I can remember, yes."

"Well, you've come some distance with the help of my lectures, haven't you?"

The cacophony between the senator and the lobbyist had moved to The Troubleshooter set of the studio, still within range to hear snippets of, 'Senator Sanctimony!" and "Illustrious Ingrate!" as Prof. Sorentsen indicated towards the area of discord, "In earlier times, generals and Kings would fight each other, often to the death. Today, some senators, not necessarily my vocal friend over yonder, but other ones and representatives and representatives of representatives claim, through statements written by God knows whom, about the glory of their time here on earth and their many heroic acts, when, in reality, they are nothing more than proud peacocks of faux-pau persuasions and injudicious pursuits."

"Third-rate people with first-rate digs," Odessa observed. "Sounds like my 'hood." "I concur, Miss Gabriel."

"You can call me Odessa, Professor. Formality's definitely not a branch from my family tree." "As you taught me, Doctor, to grab the luster of legacy, one must rewrite history first, correct?" "Cade, you must have listened more in my class that I've ever imagined, but, yes, the true method of dragging history through the toilet is biblioclasm, the deliberate destructive acts of cultural insult and inflammatory stereotyping: among the best being, the Pol Pots, the Red Guards of Mao, Stalin and Hitler. Nothing but the grandest of incinerators with the biggest flamethrowers to destroy most of the tree rings of mans history in so small amount of time." "That's why the best are found among the wellborn, right?"

Dr. Sorentsen, knowing that Cade was being his usual impish self played along.

"Well, it is true that Aristotle thought that the noble, the wealthy, and the sage among us should rule, yes."

"And the aged among us too?"

"No matter your irritating stabs at hilarity, as this, apparently for you, must be included in your daily requirements for succor... I thoroughly believe, Sean, Odessa, Godboy, that the democratic power within the common among us, the mom with nowhere to turn and seemingly with no time for considerations beyond the next meal for their children or the young blacks, the Hispanics too, and others which appear to cast no shadows. Yes, I say they all, if not albeit faintly, still hear the rumble, the heartbeats of their dreams through the unvarnished sirens of history, the beckoning bloody reference points of right and wrong harkens to their better natures as well as their heartbreaking pleas. I say they are waiting for their collective urges to be heeded; the wellsprings of their aspirations to finally be unencumbered, unleashed, and all they need for a change is an honest appraisal of theirs and the countries situation and their recognition of a ready heart of a ready leader to make it so. Whether a sage, a pauper or a prince ignites this, does it really matter? You know, the British have a moment in their history, we would be wise to perhaps follow, act on now."

"Monty Python?"

"You really are miscast as a human, aren't you, Cade?" Sean wasn't teasing his friend. Professor Sorentsen took a hearty gulp of liquid invigoration, then, "In the first Parliament of Edward Ill, the knights set apart from the barons, joining the regular class, the citizens. It was the pivotal point in English history. If all these landed classes had group together, their front would've meant disaster to the development of broader liberties, which, sooner than later, allowed the masses of the unheralded to prevail over the 'heralded."

"I say we need another mixing of the breeds, today, don't you?"

"Like the one that's in progress over by the troubleshooter's desk, right?"

"Yes!" Odessa shouted, "Mark one for the de Mejas clan."

"I sincerely choose that what you say is positive, Professor. Somewhere in that mischievous heart of yours, you know this."

The professor suggested a nod towards Cade.

"Doc, I do fight against the prevailing 'positrons' of progressivism as equally as I do against squawking bombastics of the surer than right, Right. Whatever you do, though, don't let Tripp know that." All smiled. "You see that, don't you? I strive for clean news and I clearly sign in and it's, well, like the old days when station managers at local affiliates did do editorials in studios, standing in front of what some said was supposed to represent 'smarts' with the manager posed in front of a thick oak desk surrounded in the background with a bunch of thick books on thick shelves with the author's names, Greek mostly, prominent and busts of long dead philosophers spaced perfectly between these literary 'props' as these guys stood for something; these managers, they spoke out, they cleared the air of any misconceptions about what they thought was right, without nary a passing thought as to what some ascot decorated salivating consultant behind the camera had to say. Most of these dudes today think it would cost them money, ad revenues or minutes of 'gotcha time' in their piss and moan newscasts. I think it costs them their souls."

It is said that you can reach the marrow of a man and perceive the passion within the heart of that man by entering the fane that the man inhabits; 'fane' being an archaic term for 'sanctuary' or 'temple'. As a bona fide enthusiast of the 'archaic', Prof. Sorentsens' sacred lair/ home office presents guests/visitors (those allowed to enter, of course) with a riotous eye play, a messy visual menagerie of obviously seasoned older tattered books, chiseled stone works, artifacts of the arcane; all surrounded on three sides by dark wooded walls upon which hang glass covered mahogany framed quotes and exclamations (exotic and otherwise): the composition perfectly complimented by the 'fanes' near frumpy decor and the oeuvre is tangentially complete with the totality of the essence of the individual on full display, no apologies offered, proudly exposed, for all who wish to see the 'core' within the environs displayed.

The oak desk, usually topped with a mess of papers and pearls of wisdom, competed with a green apple that was always placed in its spot in the maelstrom of wood pulp and yellow magic markers, as the teacher thought that it, the apple, (he'd read this somewhere), that it calmed nerves. Professor Sorentsens' used his favorite funky ancient saying, which is displayed on the wall behind where he sat, he used it as a "tell"... that is, if, a guest read what was written in Latin up behind the professor on and the guest laughed because the guest could read Latin; the Professor marked the person as someone the professor could relate to as a human with two important criteria; a sense of humor and, two, the good taste to understand Latin. The quote in question reads, "Quid enim est ubi ponit galas?", which is a quote by Marcus Antonius, Caesars buddy, which, in English says, "What did it matter where a man stuck his cock?" Next to the daily reminder of Johnny Appleseed is a brass paperweight (which is frequently overwhelmed by what it is meant to control) which has etched, in near cuneiform perfection, the motto from the great seal of the United States, reading, "Nevus Ordo Seclorum", in English, "A new order of the ages". Sitting next to this, a good-sized geode is placed, and etched into the purple above its depressed center, "Cave Ganem", translated meaning, "Beware of the dog."

Prof. Sorentsen did not have a large screen television in his large living room because, as he had once shared with 'The Bruce is on the Loose', "a large room with a large-screen only amplifies the grand scale loneliness of a single viewer." His D.C. townhome; four bedrooms, four baths, three extra 'whatever' rooms, he described as styled in Northumbrian, and as the good teacher elaborated further," Retro' Steak and Ale' pewter cozy."

Additionally, Elliott Sorentsen the third had a strange kinship to the comedian, W. C. Fields. Both educators had lost a son to drowning. Only Sen. Bruce and the professor's ex-wife were privy to this mournful memory. This father kept a footnote from Arnold Toynbee taped to the inside cover of his Day-Timer, a poignant testimony to the agony of losing a child. He'd almost memorized it as equally clean and clear as his Everett visualization of never forgetting the outline of his sons tiny face. The yellowed clipping, still legible through the scotch tape, read: 'In the life of the Helenic Society, in which parents were committed by social convention, and not forbidden by law, to repudiate responsibility for new-born children, and to expose them either to perish or to be brought up by some compassionate passerby, it was the custom to leave the exposed child some tokens of identity in order that a possibility of re-establishing relations between child and parents might be kept open to meet the perhaps improbable contingency of the child surviving.

He fought for children, against unreasonable abortions, teachers unions were anathema, all he viewed as the modern compatriots of Hellenistic parents, the ones that believed that the children were nothing more than matters of consequences that could harm the parents, the type of people who measured their progeny only by society's evaluation and comparison to themselves, the parents; the growth and creativity of the children be damned,' we've got status and power to be maintained.'

The professor read and graded students' papers without a teacher's aide. During post graduation years, he maintained contact with many; Cade Bartholomew, being one of his favorite corresponding 'miscreants', as the professor adoringly tagged the media man. Both enjoyed updating the other. The aforementioned mogul reciprocated the adoration, often recalling in dialogue standout examples of his mentors' mien, short sermonic responses recalling the older man's class instructions about" The first cloth presented is not always the finest of garments, make sure you check the stitching", as well as, "The wariness of accepting the meaning of a first glance" or the lesson warning about," Easy acquiescence to the well rounded verse of the most vicious among us." One of Mr. Bartholomew's favorite lessons from Dr. Sorentsen dealt with the fighter Max Schmeling and his enduring relationship with the fighter, Joe Louis. Hitler tried to portray Schmeling as Superman, an Aryan Mighty Mouse and Cade remembered the professor, even only a few years ago, mentioning in email conversation, a quote from Schmeling about those times which went as follows, "I don't want anyone to say I was a good athlete, but worth nothing as a human being- 1 couldn't bear that." This, as Cade had highlighted to Sorentsen, from a man that had hid Jews from the Nazi monsters and had later helped the persecuted, the hunted, to escape the horrors of the camps of death; a man seen as an enemy by America, whom, in later years, after the Nazi's demise, aided the American icon and supposed foe, Joe Louis. Quietly and without fanfare and with an oh so respectful knowledge of another proud mans needs; and all this without a hint of the personal need we so frequently witness from the average 'heroes' of today, all too often seen as grasping at self-serving satisfactions, in actuality smallish acts writ large and promoted as grand gestures always accompanied by the requisite blaring announcements of an opponent's disposal. Through the years, Max Schmeling, provided monetary and spiritual assistance to his once competitor, now life-long compatriot; the type of assistance, without promotion or hoopla, the kind any real hero would wish for another real champion. "Wow, what a real he-man, huh, professor!",. Cade had typed. The professor thought the mogul a good soul, perhaps put on earth as reminder of Sorentsens cherished son; but never, not once, did Professor Sorentsens patterns of thought allow him to ever reveal this 'thinking' to the wayward student from, God forbid, Colorado; not once, oh God, never, no how! Cade frequently brought up the times when the Professor and the student met in some now forgotten bar in Campus Corner, discussing heritage and the heretical. Recalling his father, Cade had shared with the 'teach' about what Cades father thought about those particular business associates of Cades father whom, initially, did not 'think' as clearly as they were required to satisfy Cades father's desires. "Altitude sickness, mixed with alcohol or other diversions, eventually pacify the unbelieving, the ones not ready to bend to your desires." Dad taught me that negotiations at elevation can always be 'your serve; son; always." Cade furthered shared with the professor that, based on his fathers' recommendations, Cade would consistently schedule business meetings in the Fall or the Winter because the son understood things learned from Senior about cold weather that his competition didn't know, the lack of knowledge of which frequently upset the competition's mental state, let alone their digestion, all based on a false fear, that being which, that colds and flu do not come with the climate; they come from virus.. As Cade senior taught, "If properly executed, 'Third', the fools will accept anything just to catch the next flight home." Within the industry, 'Swayed, Filleted, and Bartholomade' became the figurative designation for anyone foolish enough to conduct negotiations at altitude in Denver with first, The Second, and later, The Third.

"It grabs you where it counts, Colorado," and Cade took another sip of champagne before, "a place beyond any humans ability to properly describe, Doc."

Godboy leaned even a little closer to hear more as the professor raised his glass in agreement with his 'students' pronouncement and the two men commenced to commiserate further. Odessa had excused herself to greet and urge upping bids on her signed script. Now undivided, Sean's attention played through the back nine of his thoughts, zeroing in one of the men in his presence; the instinctive, the rebellious, and the very talented royal pain in the ass man-child, his ex-college roommate, Cade The Third, who Sean privately but affectionately dubbed, the Colorado 'Whiplash', a justly deserved name as represented by the day in 2008 when Cades' divorce was final. That afternoon Cade picked up a drop-dead breathtaking neon Gold 2008 Rolls-Royce Phantom Coupe, decorated as gaudy good in gold leaf plated, with massive aspen leaf serving as the hood mount, and as Sean recalled Cade saying that day, "The better to ride the washboard back ways of the great Stony Mountains, my buddy, and the better to bump that Baptist, God forgive me... not!, 'bitch', right out of my hair, out of my checking accounts, out of my fantasies and out of my fears. Dude, (Sean still despised this thoughtless term) this baby's top speed is 130 mph, on pavement of course. I ordered custom hybrid snow tires which even your half tracks will envy." Sean's continued amusement increased as Cade then had seemingly turned serious, with the proud exclamation, "I have a body shop in Silverthorne on retainer." Then, as swiftly as lightning fires blasts from the ground, the topic had changed from an elegant coupe to an inelegant ex, "Jesus, Sean, Kirsten, the Norwegian nasty, I tell you, Sean, I should've jumped ship when she said, "I want to be married in Hell, Caddee Darling,". Sean remember how perplexed he felt as Cade went on, "And I agreed, Sean, because, you see, Mr. Linden, because 'Hell' is the word over there for 'prosperity', some kind of good luck; Kirsten assured me of this..

So we flew to Hell, Norway! Yes, striking terrain, steaming mesmerizing."

"Yes, as she is", Sean remember the jiving then recovering just a bit with," or was."

None of which phased the TV man as he had continued, "Yes, smartass, the fjords were awed- jawed dropping beauties, yes, but equally as momentous and as terrifying and potentially, note, I say potentially, as ball-smashing as were this woman's ability to do such jaw smashing damage to one's psyche, but, damn, Sean, I never thought so much havoc could ensue for being in love with a holier than thou Viking for just a week and a half! God, Sean, the problem was, that for the remaining 50 1/2 weeks, she didn't understand the responsibility of having big money and what this entails."

"Listen, Junior, if you were my teacher then about anything financial, I'd be screaming at Odin too!"

Cade had ignored Sean, saying, as if to conclude the issue," Really fired up the approaching demise of our 'dreamy coupling' for life when I told Kirsten, I say to her,' Do you, dearest deranged of mine, know that I have become bored with your attempts at highbrow bullshit gone to Hell because, as the Gods would have it, you were struck at birth with such a delinquent embarrassing excuse of a mind?". By the way, I could tell she hated them, 'of mine' part and I enjoyed it immensely."

Sean recalled his response, "I can see that quite possibly as a watershed moment, yes."

And then Cade had replied, "Buckle up buckaroo, we're going threads out, dash bash 1-70 style, a test drive for the wild, not the mild; hallelujah, the Phantoms about to fly, alert the decent among us, if there are any! Yeah! " On the way 'up the hill,' as Cade always described the start in the foothills of the six thousand foot approach up to his home in Summit County; the talk between buddies, began with Red Rocks on the South and Coors Brewery on the North, and did not slow down until reaching the east portal of the Eisenhower Tunnel. Cade's expose ranged wide, as this was (and is) 'Thirds' preferred methodology of 'cooking' his views. At the Genesee Park exit mile marker 254 near where the State buffalo herd roam, the young magnet had freely delved into his, 'ever so evolved', approach to broadcast management. Sean remembered wondering then about Cades sanity again.

As Cade described it, on the rare occasion when the self described CFO, CEO grand pasha was needed for a critical employment interview, Cade would briskly enter the office, calmly shake potential employees hands, and just as calmly, he would then just pace back and forth in front of the people with his zipper down. If the interviewee did not say anything, acted properly as they viewed the situation required, Cade hired them as anchors or sales managers. If instead, the interviewee spoke up and pointed out what would be an embarrassment to most humans on this planet except to Bartholomew the Third, the

CFO, CEO Gen. Grand Pasha of the network offered to these people either the position of being a director in the studio or a board member on the Board of Directors." Of course, according to Cade, this was for male applicants only, as the station attorneys would never allow him to interview a female job applicant as they feared that Cade would be prone to hire them all and to be just as equally prone to becoming a target of sexual harassment lawsuits; the attorneys rightfully fearing that ladies would never understand the, as Cade said," The finer points of my nuance-cees nor the etiquette behind my pronounced desires to push them up the ladder of success... Hell, Sean, their career advancements were hard not to notice!"

As he stood now, staring at his friend, his teacher and his 'houseguest', Sean grinned, picturing that blur of a day in that fast Phantom of a vehicle with the admittedly 'adorable' Pasha of Cherry Creek at the wheel and happy.

Sean was aware, only because Senator "The Bruce is Loose" had shared with him that, in recent years, the professor often joined the mogul in Cades charitable efforts, which were very different from most of today's 'most charitable' People Magazines People', in that Cade demanded anonymity for what he considered, 'his treasured times'. Professor Sorentsen watched and assisted, monetarily and otherwise, in his 'students' direct methods, as the young Bartholomew went into the hospitals, the hurting orphanages, into the streets to help the people "who wouldn't know what to do with decent meals as it's almost mythic to them." Cade, more than once, reminded Mr. Sorentsen," Dammit, Doc, you taught me that self esteem is the most hurting kind of loss." The pasha's hidden unchaperoned good nature was, as he demanded, unpublicized. Only Sorentsen was to know when Mr. Bartholomew was about, tossing seed money, "bundles of unburdening" as The Third himself termed it, "to people in wheelchairs, to young mothers with babes in arms, to nursing homes to cheer them that need cheerin' to remember that it's not all done yet!"

Cade had once shared with Sean," Doing for others is the Big Time, Sean. The key is, and I know you know this as I know you well, the key is to never make a big thing about your own big time." Cade never failed to understand the frailty of dignity or fame nor how rapidly one can fall so far, so fast, as he would often referred to Moah Halas's repeated refrain, "Icarus, anyone?", to which, on one occasion, Sean replied, "Yes, if all the cue balls are aligned, you can never climb high enough to escape the insistent possibility of a Royal face plant.", to which Cade had asked," Yoggeeism, right?"., and Sean had acknowledged, "Absolutely."

The 'present' intruded.

"Ah, the aroma of vanilla bean good; almost overwhelming." Hawkins-Burke was standing next to Sean Linden.

Sean measured the man Yoggee judged as the 'reason' for the fiasco at The Fill. Hawkins-Burke was reportedly a hypochondriac so, "Ah, Mr. Hawkins-Burke. Little pale, are you well?"

"So the young Rajah staying with you..."

"Navajo's cousin," Sean interrupted.

"Oh yes, the other native son."

It was the first meeting between two notoriously private individuals. The battery cables appeared crossed. Odessa and Lilith stood by the men, quietly observing, as were the others.

"Democracy is a fraud. Every sensible person knows it. We stick to our rules, so long as they are serviceable to our needs, and we break them the moment they don't do what we want."

Mr. Linden continued sampling his drink while Mr. Hawkins-Burke elaborated, "So it's really useful fraud, like patriotism..."

"Or plastic surgery," Odessa interjected.

"It's so easy to co-opt the world, isn't it, Ms. Gabrielle?"

"Behold everyone, a walking, talking Taoist; enjoy life to the fullest, self is center, is that what you are, Mr. Hawkins-Burke, an egoist for modern times? Beware, though, that there are serious weaknesses in such habits of enjoying the pleasures of one's every impulse."

"I'll champagne to that, Odessa,"

"Thank you, Lilith."

Sean sensed insecurity in Stuart's eyes, and then it was gone. Sean pondered, 'Is this pity I feel? No. Can't be.'

"Have I missed anything?" Tripp Bellows, finished with intrepid recording of interpretations of the festivities, joined the ensemble, center stage. "I've concluded, dear acquaintances, after making my rounds of these heady Washingtoneese, present company excluded, certainly, that we are nothing more than attendees to a Thyestean banquet where there's no count as to the number of courses served or the meals devoured or whether or not we really want to know the ingredients within the feast; just swallow and go with the flow."

"No taste' is the best revenge, right, Tripp?"

"Cade, as you well know, revenge causes people to clothe themselves in the most uncomplimentary of fashions, and by the way, what is that you're wearing, leisure lounge lizard?" Sen. Bruce let loose, "By their nature, egotists fear of failure outweigh their fear of the unknown, and emotions, well, in that it is so rare that egotists have any, emotions are the greatest cause of their mistakes, don't you agree, Mr. Hawkins-Burke?"

"You might say that, Senator, and some, as you yourself most assuredly know, some even reach the heights of inane cupidity, actually believing that the Lord God himself is in sacred and unalterable agreement with all their starry-starry plans and with all their wishy-wishy wonderments."

"It might serve you well, Mr. H-B," Senator Bruce, near snorting, "..if you would recognize that irony is a mistress without guise or guile. You might do yourself a huge favor by updating your adornments."

Prof. Sorentsen jumped in to referee, "The poet and philosopher, Li Po, accepted the view that it was desirable to be followed by two servants; one with wine, the other with a spade to bury him where he fell." The Professor stared at both combatants. "You two can at least agree on this, can't you, that merriment is cherished only because it can perish at any moment, and that we should live in peace, because, as effervescent as life is, we never know the date and time of that one last smile, do we, yes?"

Mr. Linden assisted, "That satisfies the possibility of greatness in both of you, doesn't it, Stuart?"

"Good luck to you, Sean. And I do respect your service. Thank you." Hawkins-Burke turned, but turned back to Linden, "Remember this; I do not envy anyone who dares to go deep with me." Sen. Langtree gently squeezed his arm, prompting him to follow her elsewhere.

Professor Sorentsen and Mr. Bellows gravitated away from the others towards the last of the auction tables, finding their way to the promotions set, beneath the boom microphone, which fortunately, wasn't 'hot'.

Student-Teacher, Teacher-Student; this interchangeable argumentative couple, intractably bound in the only way they ever possibly could survive the aggravating touchstones of their mutual history; through humor, grudging respect, and by either never once admitting affection of the genuine kind.

As Prof. Elliot Sorentsen saw it, part of the problem was that Mr. Bellows had dropped out of his class, twice!

As Mr. 'Tripp' Bellows saw it, part of the problem was that Mr. Sorentsen was upset because no student had ever dropped out a class of the professors except for pregnancy, felony or death. "Glad this is for a good cause, right doc?" Tripp sipped more gulp juice, then, "Because we both, at the least, must appear respectful of the situation, another sip,... even though I see billboard sized barbs building behind those disappointed eyes of yours and..."

"It is still remarkable to me, Master Bellows, that you make a dime scribbling your jumbled thoughts down for all to see."

"And to 'hear' as well, don't forget that."

"You mean the noise traffic? Yes, that childish raucousness too."

As is frequent during male verbal jousting, Tripp devalued Elliot's comment by ignoring it, and then by switching subjects. "Can kids, who do kids have as heroes today, Doc? No-one. No one, except for our blessed military men and women, and maybe strong lyrics that are tuned in to the angst... so don't get on music's ass as it can be a relief, a guide for... "

"Around 100 BC thereabouts, Asclepiades of Bithynia; he was a physician. and, as most 'docs' were then as opposed to today, he was highly respected and renowned for his abilities. He implored, my dear Chaz, that when treating the sick, it was critical for their recovery that a construct, their schedule for treatment should include proper diet, exercise, bathing, and here's the kicker, insert drum roll here, Asclepiades prescribed for the insane... music! Yes, 'music' for the really, really sick."

"That is 'sick', doc, and your face now tells me that you really don't have a clue what 'sick' means in today's lingo, do you?"

Professor Sorentsen remained quiet as he was indeed, confused.

"Let me tell you what I see as really 'sick', very 'sick' in this country today, Doc. Did you know that truckers are hairdressers on asphalt? No, I didn't think so. Yes, truckers on CB's talk truth just like hairdressers doing hair hear everything too; and pass it on... that's where the truth is, riding the roads and dyeing the luscious manes of American honeys. Both truckers and hairdressers tell it as it is because they live it as it is. And in all these forgotten parts of the country, truth, like water, finds the easiest path. What's really 'sick' today, Doc, is that down on the pavement running beneath the truckers, down to the roots beneath the colored hairs, clarity is found, found in the truck stops and found in the salons... the true incubators, the documented constituencies of veracity, whom, if ever you are , if ever we are going to tap into anything of importance ever again in this 'sick', 'sick' country, youse got to tap into what the truck drivers and what the hairdressers know, because friend, it's gospel; know what I mean, jelly bean?"

Professor Sorentsen smiled, saying, "You've become such a professional little Lip Flossie, haven't you?"

To which the columnist replied, "Why are the shortsighted always the most long-winded?"

"Be leery of Institutional provincialism, Chaz, as it will squelch any possibility of change." Both, for a change, in the presence of the other, reflected, remaining quiet until the professor spoke again, "Manipulating another's misery is a miserly path to philosophical profit, can we agree, that both the DNC and the RNC are DOA for the USA?"

With the clinking of crystal and the generous sips of 'the bubbly', the discourse softened immediately. Then, after an appropriate pause of time if there ever is such a thing, the student spoke up again.

"In Egypt, ancient Egypt, the words for "teaching" and for "punishment" were the same." Both smiled.

"You know, professor, I do keep part of you with me at all times." Prof. Sorentsen was quizzical as Tripp pulled a tattered piece of paper from his wallet.

"This is from one of your lectures about the land of the Nile and it's, as you said, snooty schoolmasters."

"Did I now?" The professor's eyes revealed the affection he had for the speaker.

"The writers were perhaps right as they applauded the life of a scribe and were contemptuous of smaller skills."

The educator playfully chided,"And this is the cause of you casting a plague on all readers of your columns?"

Chaz returned the grin, continuing, "The referred quote goes,' I have seen the metalworker... He's stank more than fish roe... The weaver in the workshops, he is worse than a woman, with his thighs against his belly... The embalmer, his fingers are foul, for the odor thereof is corpses... Behold, there is no profession free of a boss except for the scribe: he is the boss."

Professes Sorentsen visibly moved, recovered, "Thank you, I selected that from a national geographical Society book, late 1960s, I believe, about the Bible... and look how it saved your sorry soul!"

"And a Jew at that, huh?"

Cade Bartholomew entered master control. "Thank you, Senator, for your support for the kids at Jude's and at Ronald's."

"The warriors too."

"Yes."

"Exes are like balks, Cade; wrong move and poof, married, single, stupid, smart, it doesn't matter,"

"The women?"

Senator put his drink down near the audio board, realized his ill conceived move and quickly picked the glass up, bringing it back closer to its comfort zone, his mouth, and after this happy reunion, he continued," No. They just get a free pass to second base otherwise known as ownership of the majesty of scoring the big scorn, all because of a simple teensy little flinch."

"I appreciate your understanding of my natural bent."

"Republican?"

"No, Senator; women before money. Republicans are more into adultery than the cash, whereas, Democrats, except for Clinton, are into the money."

"But they are 'dead broke', so... "

"Speaking of under oath, the next occasion you have to testify..."

"Ugly fat chance on that one, Senator."

"When orating, young man, you, ah, but first a fine sip of malice, yes," and the Senator did so and then, "Remember that public speaking really comes down to the fact, pregnant or otherwise, that 'pause' has cause."

"You said gauze?"

"Silence purports Wai-Mart sized gravitas to the occasion of any conversation."

"Listen, you aren't trying to tell me that you don't attempt to milk it until the utter truth is thoroughly and verbally drained from the teat, because I have heard you otherwise, sir!"

"Curdled cleverness there. But you're an excellent bologanist yourself. Ah, pour me another, will you please.." Cade tipped the bottle and fulfilled the Senators request.

"You know, Cade, I can drink good, I can drink bad, but, no matter what, I find this is good for the bad." Peering over the boards of electronics, the Senator stared through the glass down to the studio. "What is Odessa Gabrielle about?"

"Full frontal inflammatory, but with a heart."

"I've heard of the good things she does."

"Never dated," Cade said, as if this had to be aired out because of the many peccadilloes and rumored romances sported about unfairly about him as well as their topic of conversation. "Just perceptions passed on by directors and grips. Always ignore the producers."

Senator Bruce continued to look at the studio. "I hope Sean knows his way around the set." The Senators stock shot up in Cades estimation as Cade was sure that his best friend since college had another ally in life that gives a damn about something other than himself. Damn, pause does have cause.

Down on the studio floor the third act was nearing conclusion.

"Learn anything from the anointed one?"

"Hawkins-Burke?"

"The one and lonely, yes."

"Yes, yes, I did. I learned what I do not like about myself."

Sorentsen adeptly changed posturing by glancing up towards the master control suite, directing Sean's attention to the two bobbing heads within. "Nice to see they seem to have more in common than just the same air space."

Sean followed Sorentsens gaze and laughed. "Esoterical Nirvana, I'm sure."

After the professors approving smile, he turned on the 'serious' again, "Do you agree we live in disproportionate era…the highs and lows and the distance between being the steepest I can ever recall?"

"When have we not?"

"And have not veterans always overpaid for the 'privilege' of these times, yes?"

Sean remained silent.

"Listen, I respect what you, Moah and John have sacrificed for these banzai moments....but, I most respect your humbleness, your devotion to those who can no longer march towards the sounds of the drums, to those now deemed 'stragglers'; the result of others selfish designs, these misshapen beautiful beings … you guys have fought hard for them to not be short changed anymore .and this, this is the essence of you and the others too, the right thing to do, it's part of all of you..... always seems to be your guide and I am humbled by this majesty, this clarity, most especially in this age of obfuscation and no obligations...."

"We march in spring. That's history. That's when man gets it on, around the time the buds of renewal become the battle fields of human ... the seeds in the fields remind warriors of their childhoods when 'small' had meaning... but the taste of fruit is not so sweet anymore after you have slain your foe in the grass on the knoll."

"Or on the steps of a theater."

"Humm." Sean was among a select few that the agency pulls from the ranks. He had acquitted himself exquisitely and now, he remained an occasional consultant to this previous employer. He was presently in search of a position with a little more length and strength for career growth and a position with just slightly less hazardous job requirements. He hadn't involved himself in but two relationships of any weight or strength, both of which he curtailed, as he thought his 'lifestyle' did not portend nor rate highly on the favorability rating for a long term prospectus; quite unfair, he deemed, to the ladies aspirations and plans.

Most importantly, though, as he still didn't completely understand the lay of the land of matrimony, he thought it best then as well as now, to wait for advanced equipment to provide for improved reconnaissance of the situation. So Fabian delay was his preferred choice.

Sean heard the Professor speaking with another person. Good, as Sean was conversing within himself. He remembered being informed when Sean came of the age when he was considered able to understand things that his parents had died in a car crash in Mexico and that both his parents were 'orphans' and that he was the only next of kin. No family. No history. No feeling. Sean remembered a quote from one of Sorentsens classes. It was from Alexander Hamilton. "My blood is as good as that of those who plume themselves upon their ancestry." Hamilton was a bastard. He recalled his teacher from Mississippi, Mrs. Reeves, admonition, "Be Teddy Roosevelt, be Pete Rose, be a M. Twain, but for Gods' sake, Sean, never be an 'in between.' He rarely pondered his place in the Universe. And he rarely looked back as memory, for the likes of him, could be a sometime pus filled wound. Understandably, heterodoxy was more his fashion. He'd started to write his will, "I, being of what I believe is a sound mind"... but beyond this blood spoke passage and Sean could not 'ink' on. He'd left further scribbled down instructions and put it in his 'everything' drawer, planning on returning to it later. He never approached his mortality again. Perchance it was because he really had problems with his 'start', his origins, and the 'skinned knee days' that he had missed by not being somebody's son. "May I be bold?"

The professor intruded upon Sean's mental gymnastics.

"Why change now."

Ignoring the obvious, the Professor observed, "Fulgurous isn't she? Sean knew his 'date' was an obvious center of attention so as he had all evening, he just rolled with the flow, same as Odessa does. "You know, Sean, Warren G. Harding commented about his wife, Flossie, that she, and I quote, "She wants to be the drum major in every band that passes", unquote. And, Sean, please, no offence, but, as a man of many years notched, in all that time, Miss Gabriel's fundament is resoundingly firm topography with gentle terrain and slopes, yes, but the, well, not meaning any harm, son, just a general view of another evidentiary piece of God's existence, yes?"

Both men looked over to the news set, watching Odessa engaged in animated conversation with Senator Langtree, who was leaning against the stations call letters on the anchor desk.

In the most positive of manner, the word, 'avuncular', crossed Sean's thoughts. He allowed for the liquor loosened lip play, privately sensing it all as a light compliment to him as well as a major one to her. He turned back and continued to smile politely at his teacher, his mentor, his friend. "You know, Professor, it's been said that about a fifth of our brain is used up attempting to handle the visual world."

"Thank God it's only a fifth as nothing would ever make sense if it were more."

Sean's smile widens. The Uncle isn't finished.

"Is she a woman worth warring for, Sean? Like Helen, Helen, the daughter of Zeus and Leda, the wife of Menelaus, King of Sparta; why, her elopement with Orlando Bloom caused the Trojan conflict and Brad Pitt to get pissed off enough to go to war over it, so I ask again, is she a Helen?" Sean's smile tightened.

"Son, here's how Buddha viewed the mystery of the female....The sage had a question from his favorite student, probably 'disciple' is a more apt description, anyway, Ananda was the questioner in this vignette and this Ananda asked Buddha,

"How are we to conduct ourselves, Lord, with regards to womankind?"

Buddha responded, "As not seeing them, Ananda."

"But if we should see them," Ananda continued," what are we to do?" "No talking, Ananda."

"But if they should speak to us, Lord, what are we to do?"

"Keep wide awake, Ananda." Professor Sorentsen eyed his friend for a 'read' but wasn't sure if Sean was irritated or amused.

"Time to go elsewhere." It was Odessa Gabriel and she was next to the men, who were surprised by her unnoticed arrival.

Sean recovered, "Saint Elsewhere?"

"If any place is sanctified," Odessa postured," I don't want to go there now."

As hard as he tried, Dr. Sorentsen could not disguise his contented look.

Odessa acknowledged this 'comfy peepage' with "And by the looks of you, Professor, I say you need a little Joan of Lark to help you come to God again, don't you?"

The professor, appearing as if he were a lad in awe of the candy in the window, was stunned silent.

Sean was pleased with Ms. Gabriel's coup de grace and then she followed up, saying, "Sean, let's get Godboy and go."

Sean smiled 'alright'; while the professor, still tongue-tied, could only nod his head, in a shaky "Good-bye."

Chapter 7

"High Wire Drains Back Alley Brains"

"Washington D.C. is a city of magnificent intentions."

Charles Dickens

October 9, 2015

Tripp despised this part of the process of writing a book, the part which, in common parlance is known as 'the start.' This especially since he'd just finished a semi-biographical book presently with the publisher and the editor. It had proved wearisome and yet, as Mr. Bellows said to himself, brings on the bamboo shoots and the prods.

'What is wrong with me? Why am I doing this again so soon?' Chaz drank another shot of his double caffeine java. He stared at his office desktop covered in a mish-mash of raw memo sized notes and headline clippings from both Washington D.C. newspapers.

'Title? What do I say? Snappy of course; whip a word out now, asshole! Hey, yes,' "Clip Notes?" "Sideswiped?" Maybe a chapter title but not a book title, hell no!' Mr. Bellows sorted and selected 10 clippings and laid them out to the side of the pile. He placed them, alternating The Times clippings with The Posts clippings. They read as follows:

"New Tax Break For Largest Drug Makers Allows Payments At Fraction Of Normal Tax Rate"

Washington Post

"Legal System Creates Chaos And Distains Traditional Values"

Washington Times

"CEOs Fatten Profits To Increase Stock Value, Sell Options At Inflated Price"

Washington Post

"Commerce Dept. Shakes Down Businesses For Campaign Contributions"

Washington Times

"Corporations Get Wishes, Freeze Internet Taxes + More Work Visas"

Washington Post

"Campaign Finance Laws Treated As Nuisances"

Washington Times

"Lawmakers Cocktail With Lobbyists. Receive Big Campaign Checks"

Washington Post

"Felons Sentences Shortened. Police Punished. Criminals Set Free"

Washington Times

Chaz backed away from the desk. 'Too bad humans are not immune from being human, but, hah, whatever would I have to bitch about then. These idiots believe that their escapades will never catch up to them. Kind of like a rock band. Come on 'Isaac', focus! Work with me, words, work with me. Only the insane would understand, could appreciate how I approach these torturous type faced torments and trippingly on the tongue trials. Focus, Tripp, focus. Didn't Aleixandre Dumas say something about these large moments of authors distrust? Yes, that bloody anxiety over what you've just written and whether or not it is worth the time to scribble it down. When you believe something is really 'good', apprehension always seems to pal along. Will anyone like this 'icky-inky' thing? How can it be read the way I meant it to be? Damn, I wonder what Shakespeare felt sitting in his space before diving into cleaning up the delivery of his thoughts. I bet he loved the ale. Isaac Tripp Chaz Bellows was irritated with his meandering mindlessness...Hey, maybe song title here, 'Meandering Mindlessness'. Country or teen angst? Work it Tripp, Work it.'

"Double-double, toil and trouble, my sweet." Tripp laughed at how that sounded out loud. 'Best witch ever, that Margaret Hamilton, yes, indeedy.'

Chaz placed the final two headlines down in front of him.

"Religious Leaders Preach Confession/Atonement While Hiding Wrongdoing Within Church" Washington Post

"Parents Demand School Board Change Grades Despite Children's Cheating"

Washington Times

"Thank you through the tears, you bastards."

Hey! Hey! There, that's, that's a song! Yes, "Thank You Through The Tears"!

Mr. Bellows swept the notes and headline clippings off his desk. "Pulitzer can wait. The rest of the afternoon it's lyric time, baby. Now where's that Fender?"

Chapter 8

"Beckon To Be Known"

"Tender moments and ticklish times."

Francis Bacon

The restaurant walls are partially decorated with portraits of the variety of the faces and the hues of humanity. Intertwined between these pictures are expensive hand carved wooden and 'in your face' neon signs, representative of all the local dining establishments that had, within the last fifteen to twenty years, gone out of business. This was the owner of The Floozy Malthusian, rocker turned columnist/restaurateur, Tripp Bellows, not so subtle visual reminder of the precariousness of life in the dining industry; how the slightest thing, from inconsiderate service, acting as if the public should be serving you and not the other way around to failing to keep the water glasses filled, linens clean or meals prepared to the diners specific requests, can take any eatery to the dumpster in a flash.

In the owner's private library/office, distinct from the crowded interior and the sounds consistent with a booming business, Chaz commiserated with true blood friends; two of his buddies from college, Cade and Sean. The other two of this male cohort were absent, with Moah working the airways and The Navaho away in Tulsa, assisting in preparing for next summer's pow-wow, pitching local oil business's for contributions.

"White elephant, definition being,"... Tripp paused, eyeing Sean, attempting to read whether or not his friend was in mood for frivolity and, as usual, failing, continued anyways, "...a rare, pale gray type of Asian elephant held sacred by the Siamese and the Burmese ...which, in word play, means, anything rare but expensive to keep....any burdensome possession."

Sean did not respond immediately, then, "Your point being, Isaac?"

Cade opened the cage door wider, "God designed, no assembly required. She's the Cha-Cha, wow, wow woman, and the man in uniform strikes again."

"It's well known that you have no taste, Cade," Tripp noted, "But continue the habit, babe, just go with it."

Men rarely reveal all. This group did. Mostly. One among them, for a rather lengthy period of time, had withheld something important from the others because he had made a blood oath with the lady who now was at the center of their "playful" conversation. He'd pledged to her to keep their "mattress" moment private for as long as possible. He had assented to assist her forever in the care and love of the beautiful result of their youthful 'exuberance' now residing in North Dakota. The pact had held. And now he was continuing the 'cover' by participation in the ribbing of his friend, her most recent attraction. He could not do otherwise.

"Ah, ladies, ladies."

"Yes, Cade, they spin the top that never stops. Always have." Tripp then referenced something he had discovered during a rare instance when had studied for one of Sorentsens' tests. "Do you know, gentlemen, that two thousand years ago, longer actually, according to ancient Chinese historians, in late Yayoi Japan..."

"Ya what?"

"Yayoi, like ahoy, alright; well, anyway, according to the records..."

"Chinese writing about Japanese doesn't sound kosher."

Ignoring Cade, Tripp pursued his point, "300 B.C. or so, I tell you, what a life those dudes had.

They did..."

"The Chinese?"

"No, Japanese, Jack wad! Listen, women outnumbered men and men of importance had four to five wives while the rest had to settle for two to three spouses. The women, and this is according to the Chinese chronicles, mind you, were 'faithful and never jealous.'

"What about all those mother-in-laws?"

As I was saying, Sean," Mr. Bellows purposely ignored Mr. Bartholomew," these Japanese had it made. There was basically no thievery to speak of, but, when a man did break the law, guess what? Their wives and their children were confiscated! Instant bachelorhood! Over and over again."

"And the mother in law problem is solved."

"This, from Mr. Moral Compass his self!"....

"How did I become so right when all my life I thought I was so left?"

Sean beat Tripp to the reply," Bargain basement reasoning and an expensive divorce." "Some vigorous discord here, what?"

"Well, you both are drinking a wee bit earlier than usual."

They stared at Sean. Tripp let loose first," Friction and fire, soldier and Diva, oh Lords to boards, what's a situation supposed to do?

Sean shrugged. "Hers is a dance, sing, dinner thing. Yes, we're so different but that's, there's the attraction. Now I want to..."

"Are you the moth or the light?"

Sean waved the two away. "Leave me be. Time to bite, not bitch." The two waved him off in return and began to clinch and spar over politics.

As Sean savors the initial quarter piece of the 'Monti Cristo de Flooze'. he recalls the last Cristo he had had. Was it at a party in Bel Aire or was it Beverly Hills? No matter, just as fatuous as the silliness he was a party to now. Odessa is radiant tonight, isn't she. He remembered that she had chided him about the truffles. "Sean, dear, they are from the Piedmonte, $1,500 a pound; for God's sake, you've got to at least try them!" And he had and he knew that he never would again, but not before he'd uttered, "You equate taste with money too often, my dear." Sean knew he was 'meat' as soon as he said this. Wrong place, wrong time thing. Fortunately, Odessa had chosen to bank his directness away for later returns as she had acted as if she hadn't heard, commenting instead," These parties don't blow, Sean, they inhale; a collection of vacuum mouths sucking in whatever resembles 'with-it-ness' in this four cornered bore." Odessa had honed her ability to act above it all as only a professional in Hollywood could. "Jesus, yes." Sean concurred. "Who really gives a lick about diaphragms, cat lovers, Levi's, Brian Williams, or cloning?"

Odessa had circled her arm in his and then, with 'reckless' revelation, "I hate myself for parking my eyes on you so often, soldier boy."

"Then you're disgustingly foolish. I don't leave my eyes on anything for long, or as Chaz says, except of course if it's naked, and not a Jewish holiday."

"How outre".

"Well, it is Tripp. Come on. Let's leave."

"What about your eyes?"

"They're coming along too ... in the trunk."

"Au contraire lite!"

Sean had then, along with Odessa, turned to review the action around them. He observes aloud, "See the people thinking and living as if they're free only if they play the blind man game...the one that, if you don't see the indignity that goes on in this toy called life, then you get to continue playing with it with a 'clean' conscious. But once their eyes have witnessed how the game 'pieces' are made, the gory of the glory of it all; they throw the keys to their own locks in the in the trash because, don't you know, a good society imposes conformity on everyone so everyone is as miserable as everyone else is and that hear nothing, see nothing, say nothing pacification of the plenty is maintained. Sickened saddened souls, spirits in tatters, even these well-heeled things we see flitting about us now, Odessa, they too bargained for more when they came through the door and it shows...no matter how hard they work to mask the pain." Sean recalled that Odessa remained silent, concern very apparent on her face before she had commented," What's wanted really doesn't work well in the world of 'what is', does it?"

Sean played both 'parties' back in his mind; the ugly one presently playing, consisting of Cade and Tripp, oblivious to his scrutiny, entrenched in a vigorous effort of besting each other and the other one, the kissing on the cheek greeting gathering, the party from the beautiful recent past in reality challenged California.

Enjoying another quarter piece of the Flooze's Christo, Sean recalled Odessa's critique of the" La-La" gathering as she had commented, "Appears, mon ami, we wade amidst loquacious agrarian groupies; no better yet, we weave within a chez abattoirs, a mise-en-scene of harried proclamations, no tropes, tropes capering about as aphorisms with nary a hint of apercu or logic in attendance, oui, do we not, Seanee?"

'Oui, Seanee' tickled him. The 'then and now' mind play halted abruptly as Tripp and Cade brought his fancy flight back to the landing pad of the present.

"Yes, Mr. Linden," Tripp opined, "a woman of commanding beauty and unfailing consequences, yes?"

The 'yipper' and the 'yapper' were staring at him awaiting reaction. Sean smiled and took another bite of sandwich, patiently chewing as if it were a last meal before swallowing, then, "What is wanted doesn't really work well in the world of 'what is', now does it?" Their quizzical faces pleased him almost physically as much as the knowledge that the lady in question would be meeting later for brief interlude and more. Cade waive his empty hand, a brush-off towards Sean's direction. Tripp got up to retrieve another liquid pleasure. Sean watched him and then his attention went to above Tripp to another neon vestige of another failed dream hanging on the Floozes' wall and Sean was back in Bel Air again as more of Odessa's words echoed in his head," Your idea of a delightful gathering is 'doggy' and don't you deny it, you devil." To which Sean had replied, "You back into genius often, Odessa, and I definitely respect and appreciate your approach to smarts." They then had left the party without another word.

Sean watched as Cade and Chaz continued their never-ending battle over the press versus the people. What a pair, but a man could not ask for any better.

Chaz Isaac 'Tripp' Bellows certainly lived his name. Sean remembered from his studies of Hebrew history that 'Isaac' meant "He who laughs". As for 'Bellows', well, Tripp had been a Rocker singer in his earlier 'mellower' career. Now, as a columnist, Tripp had distanced himself little from traveling the galactic good times of the Circus Cures and their road kill nights of voluptuous debaucheries.

The only time that Chaz Bellows ran away from home was when he was upset with having to get another crew cut. The Beatles had long hair success and girls and he wanted the lucky locks now too. His dad had said no. Young Chaz made a scene and ran out the front door and then proceeded to wander the suburbs of Norman, Oklahoma, returning six hours later for water, a late lunch and a trip to the barbershop and an appointment with contents from ajar of Butchwax applied to his close-to-the-skull cropped new doo.

In those very rare and very nice 'alone' moments, his memories replayed the parties at Thunderbird Lake, the football Saturdays and most especially that magical time in life when youth overcomes the 'can't do's with the 'why nots' as he had begun his first guitar lessons with the able Mr. Palmer.

Just under six feet tall, trim, with blue eyes women still fell into even as his hair hinted at age, Tripp, often, before going out to belt out his lines, returned to that humid 'run away' day in July of 1969 as he habitually would glance in the dressing room mirror one last time, checking to see if his dark ponytail was tied his certain way and whether or not his 'hobo of the rails' beard completed the look he desired. He usually smiled, and with a wink, would say, "Whose your daddy now," and exit for the stage.

The elder Mr. Bellows was a wildcatter and land man who provided for his family as did Mrs. Sally Bellows. She had worked part time at Dinkos Diner, a traditional favorite of the collegiate set, an establishment which served two plates; one with the entree on it and the other, a clean plate for the customer to drain the grease on to it from the first plate. Mrs. Bellows remained Tripp's biggest fan, loving him no matter the year, no matter the look or no matter the words to a song, as 'Bravo' always played in her heart for her talented boy.

Now Mr. Bellows was playing a new venue, that of columnist. He had worked this gig ever since the Cures decided to retire. Tripp knew when his epiphany of 'it's time to mosey elsewhere,' struck. It was during one of their last drawn out recording sessions, (are there any other kind) when he sensed himself flying above the studio, seeing himself, as nothing more than a 40 plus year old trained seal waving his flippers, barking and performing for that next herring and for that next sound of mass approval, applause.

The other members of The Circus Cures agreed that the time was proper for 'de-staging' and they did it; retiring early, wealthy, and most critically, remaining friends and alive without too much accumulated brain damage amongst themselves.

Tripp remained true to family, paying for his sisters children's education as well as underwriting in love and in money for, as he privately called them, his 'stepping out' children, 'Mag' and 'Pie'(Maggie and Pia Bellows) the surprising but pleasing results of two weekends of love with their then groupie mothers. These relationships stayed out of the limelight. Mag and Pie were in their mid-twenties and wholeheartedly supported their fathers' mid-life career shift. "Just another lyric in life, Dad," Pie had pronounced.

His volatility, a regrettable remnant, a tiresome calling card from his early crash and burn days, still arose, or maybe, more precisely stated, evolved, within the workings of his new venture as he vigorously attacked political corruption and the sponsored attacks that it breeds; as he railed against the 'theft of thinking clearly' by what he called the simpering 'whimsical 'wise' ones, they of little note or regard for the 'actual' sinews of everyday survival; as he railed against the bias of big and small bigotry; railed against greed and its playthings, manipulation and massage.... 'Classless caresses for a lazy mind' Tripp called it.

"What would your mother have told you to do?"

Sean watched Tripp ponder Cades question, rolling his eyes, exasperated with the mogul...the same face Sean remembered Tripp expressing when Sean first asked the 'rocker' what 'type' music the Cures 'indulged' in. Mr. Bellows had responded to Mr. Linden's question with, "Indulged? Why, our music, oh hell, Sean, generally, I call, well, it's a glorified dumpster dive of The Moody Blues on acid, with a sprinkle of The Mothers of Invention thrown in for ill mannered measure and all marinated in a saucy squirt or two of Inagoddadavita, baby!, How's that for you, mister marshal music himself."

Nevertheless, Tripp had often called Sean to go over freshly written lyrics, to get, as Tripp summarized it, "a true layman's opinion, raw and uncultured."

"She'd told me not to hang out with the likes of you, Mr. T.V. Big shot."

Sean continued consuming his sandwich as the other two continued their lightly absurd arguing. Sean thought of one instance when Chaz called him with the news that he had just received inspiration from, of all places, a trip to a shelter for strays in Encino. Chaz had picked up "Jelly Bean the baby Boxer number one" and "Jelly Bean the baby Boxer number two" for the then young, Mag and Pie. Chaz shared with Sean that, as he was driving home with the puppies, he'd spotted a rather oversized young lady walking a Newfoundland and the thought crossed the artists mind," God, that lady damn well knows that I am looking at the dog and not at her, and Sean, then, why, I really don't know, maybe something about the sadness of this thinking, you know, appearance as first judgment and how 'thin' is in and here this giant dog gets my notice and the lady, because she wasn't desirable in 'societies' eye, or mine either, dammit, that sadness of her knowing, at least I took the liberty of her thoughts, wrongly, I know, but the line "Greyhound My Love" flashed; silly I know, but I think I can work through to sensible story rhymes...what do you think?" Sean told him that "if anyone can work with your thinking Tripp, you and The Cures can pull something reasonable out of your brain patterns, I'm sure." Tripp had taken Sean's comment as complimentary and the band did go on and make a hit out of guilt of their conscientious yet oddly put together "front man."

"Your mother obviously didn't ever, ever, teach you the etiquette of allowing others to catch up to your way of thinking, did she? No, I didn't think so, Bartholomew!" Smiling wide, Sean considered

Tripp's latest adventure; print boy. Tripp called him before his column pieces had began publication, asking Sean's opinion on "getting too heavy with history and whether it was a good thing or not?" And not waiting for Sean or himself to take a breath, he quoted Aeschylus, yes, Aeschylus, which goes, "The blood that mother Earth consumes clots hard, it won't seep through, it breeds revenge."

Sean had told him," possibly good, possibly nightmarish, if you want to read or feel what the 'raw uncultured' masses think, you know, those people like me, right, it really depends on the content, what the reference point is...but go for it; how much philosophical fallout and more damage can you possibly do to your reputation anyway? If no one understands your view, let alone why the hell the quote, you can always whirly bird backwards and say Jelly Bean One or Two ate your notes and you had to scramble something down as you were about to miss your deadline or just go to the old standby of...,

"Which is what?

"I did not have sex with that woman."

Tripp had uttered an expletive and Sean had told him that he was glad that he "could be of service" which prompted more profanity and this had pleased Sean even more. Among the Circus Cures many hits, mostly written by Mr. Bellows, were "Methodical Melodical" and one of Sean's favorites, "Flower Face". Sean had watched Tripp put its beginnings together on scratch paper as they drove through the streets of Los Angeles to L.A.X. when the rocker had missed the bands jet to Chicago," due to circumstances within my control," as Tripp had described the "liaison with an artist in waiting who couldn't really wait, Sean, a Lady with a talented brush stroke and the agility of a Mona Lisa", which Sean, to this day, did not understand the meaning of. Tripp was deep into a small book on flowers that "the artist" had given him. As Tripp was waiting on a corner in Culver City for Sean to pick him up, he'd opened the small book to the first picture and the name of the flower captured him and after jumping in the car, Tripp read its description aloud to Sean, making notes as he talked. "Pleasant aroma, used to be strewn on the straw in the castles ...Queen Elizabeth the First loved it, how about that and, let's see, flavored wine, made a tea out of it too..." Sean had then interrupted as they stopped at a light, "What is the name of the thing, Tripp?" "It's called, and I love this, called 'Meadowsweet', a creamy white flower, June to early September are its blooming' days; also known as the Queen of the meadows." Tripp then had taken a pause to write a note and then, as Sean had finally reached the freeway, Tripp read more, saying, "Listen here, in Welsh mythology, Gwendolyn and Math created a woman out of oak blossom broom. They named her 'Meadowsweet' or in their words, ah, I believe it's pronounced, "Blodenwedd" or, yes, to us, "Flower Face." Wow. "Flower Face," that's, I can song that out with a name like that, Seanny! It's a beautiful tag, don't you agree!" Sean remembered impatiently giving his friend a hasty nod at the same time as Sean quickly maneuvered to miss a driver cutting in front of them. Tripp hadn't noticed, as he had already become lost in the passionate paper and pen pursuit of perfecting fresh 'hooks of the heart', an exercise that Tripp himself described as, 'Mad Cow narcissism", the result of which had made Mr. Bellows and the other Cures 'crazy' wealthy for life.

Sean finished his last quarter of sandwich as Cade and Tripp were discussing whether or not "Be My Me", the Cures most recent album, was 'creatively' as ringing a success as some of their earlier efforts. The Trades and TMZ and others were currently abuzz with the apparent breakup of the band which the bands representatives had frankly not been too adept at handling and it didn't help that none of the members would talk to anyone about it.

"Loved it, Tripp, but I hope the rumors of your group demise are nothing more that promotional urges.. That you get back to work one more time and not stuff, just hype to sell more of what you're already living off of now because I think you can be so much..." Tripp cut Cade off, "Hear it here first Cade, you too, Sean." Tripp paused and reached into his briefcase he'd left open on the serving table behind him. "We all now have kids, babies. Chaz Cures, my brudders of other mudders and I are going to work together, at least one more time, maybe more, to attempt the elevation of kids, boost their lives if we can do it." Sean and Cade listened without comment as Tripp dropped some legal pads on the table. "Were going to make, hopefully, make childhood and learning fun again."

Tripp motioned for his friends to get up and come stand with him as he spread out the work papers.

"These are some of my, our research, our raw lines and first stabs."

Tripp's hand printed notes could be mistaken for the clean lines and craft of a trained scrivener, easily readable, no straining for understanding. At the top of the first yellow page was written, "Herodotus of Halicarnassus". There's 'Hero' in His Name..."

Tripp had researched, dug deep, into historical figures and historical names and their meanings in order to generate, as Tripp shared, "Prompts for fresh pathways to the lyrical paradise of prose gone rightly rogue." Sean and Cade, along with 'the author', silently read the following notes.

Meanings in 'Greek' for name such as 'Ulysses' meant "hater" Common names (not sure of which language, need to find later) but Steven meant 'Crown.' Richard meant 'Strong, like a ruler;'...In Hebrew, 'Gabriel,' meant 'Man of God'. Sean spotted this item quickly as Tripp had written after 'Gabriel', the notation in parentheses, "(Odessa?)" then followed Tripp's rambling in words, searching for rhyme with ... 'bus, buzz, fuss, muss, plus, pus, truss, us, discuss, blunderbuss, omnibus...a fabulous impetus, intensity of motion for the time in the mind, for the mind in the time of Herodutus??? Wha...

Beneath this, circled in red ink, as if to distinguish from the other writings, read "The Opera Of The Overwrought Octopus" or "Ink Me Tonight Baby!"...then, back into blue ink the notes continued,..."Satyr Of The Saturnine", "Solonic Colonic", "Rodomontade Marinade", and then listed in order beneath these 'titles' were definitions....

"Absolution" formal forgiveness of sins.

"Absolutism" those in government should have unlimited power.

"Acrobatic" spectacular gymnastic feats.

"Acronym" word formed from the first letters of other words e.g." laser".

"Ambrosia" food of the gods.... In Greek, "Elixir of life" Scribbled next to this, standing out from the other writing because of its messy style, "I needed an ambrosia ambulance a few times, doo da, doo.da.."

"Ambulance" vehicle taking sick and injured people from hospital.

"Apotheosis" the highest point, the raising of someone for the rank of a God.

"Ride Of The Roaring 40s" stormy ocean areas between latitudes 40° and 50° south 'song this one out sometime soon, yes.' Next to this, in purple ink," Courtesans To Courthouses", adjacent to these words in green ink were a couple of more definitions.. "Laudable" deserving praise and commendation.

"Landunum "solution prepared from opium and formally used as a painkiller. Beneath these definitions followed apparently rough beginnings to a song...titled "Martin Man"

'A Lutheran man who nailed it

Laid it on thick, loud and clear,
Landunum and Liturgy in the air,
Oh Lay those hands on, oh Martin Man, lay those hands on,
Lay those hands on the Tiber band,
Conform and control, you dare to object,
Oh Martin Man, conform and control,
Landunum and Liturgy,
Oh Martin Man, Handyman of God,
Landunum and Liturgy,
How grand, how grand...."

"I like the route you are going down with this, Chaz ...need to finish and..." "Cade, will get to it, yes, but I'm probably, no I am going to finish Herodotus song first; as the others and I at least agree on that as priority if nothing else." Tripp noticed Sean looking at second pad. "Sean, again this is all pretty rough, but," "Mentalscape murals for mayhem, I'd call em," Sean joshed with Chaz, "but worthy of more of your mind, yes, that's true."

Chaz read the remaining, "Herodotus" "page notes, aloud. "Head poppin, heart throbbin, the mural metalis of Cryptoman, of Tecumseh, sad Chief of Chance and woe, neither acquainted with the long ago cavemen of Lascaux, ancient long hairs working their magic in charcoal, clay and iron, their bison, mammoths and horses still parading across walls of sandstone, ere long before Cleo saved Caesar, centuries ahead of Alexandria's Library in ashes on the ground, and yo, Bro, even previous to Cato, Euripides and Cicero's dire prose, before discounted divinity and Saintly offers of salvation vying with other ear splitting pleas from primping savages of nobility...It's history, It's mystery, It's Lemurias' seams splitting apart to the lands we now know...It's mystery, it's history, Blame it on Herodotus of Halicarnassus.. the mystery, the history ...It's you, it's me, its truth be told, hail Herodotus, it's time to break mold, from Halicarnassus to Hellespont , it's the story of us, it's a story for the bold." Tripp looked at his friends, "I want to close some way, need to nurse it, but think I can close it with something I've decided to end my columns with too."

"Which is?"

Well, some clarion call for common sense, common sense in a world gone slummy..."

"Is 'slummy' a word?"

"That hasn't stopped him before, Sean."

"True."

"Guys, want to close with this, so listen, please...goes..." Deo Volente, Latin for 'God willing', so the complete line goes, "Deo Volente, and hold the relish." Mr. Bellows looked for approval from Mr. Linden and Mr. Bartholomew. As hard as the two tried, they finally relented, smiling their "okays". Mr. Bellows was well pleased, which lasted just under two seconds as Cade asked, "Hey, band boy, what time is that book burning, I mean 'signing', book signing, tomorrow?" swiftly followed by Sean contributing, "Yeah, will you be robo-signing or mailing it in as you do in concerts?"

Tripp looked at his friends and shook his head.

"Just kidding, maestro. You'll shake them up tomorrow, Shakespeare, I know you will." The owner the Floozy Malthusian, squinting against the bright skylight sunshine, grinned wide in true appreciation of Sean's comment.

For some inexplicable reason, Sean thought of what Tripp had told him the day before yesterday about Tripp's visit to an odds and ends store off Vine where Tripp had purchased a turquoise and gold statue of a smiling Buddha; a happy, contented, and squat figure sitting beneath a Bhodi tree; which, according to the most recent fashioneesta in Hollywood, Mr. Bellows, was "a very pleasant arrangement for a very unpleasant time." Tripp further informed Sean that he'd chosen to place it next to his bed on his nightstand because, "It brings peace of mind, my man; peace of mind to start any day." The modem day Gautama then had declared, "Fung Sui to the max, right, Sean?"

Now, two days later, Sean decided, 'what do you know; a Rock and Roller now a Gentle Souler. No need for Ambien forever more.'

****

Sean Linden waited alone in a private area of Odessa's friends' restaurant, "Starved Times 2." The restaurant was on Pennsylvania Avenue. Hopefully the actress's arrival would be subtle. She had landed then checked in at her favorite place to stay in Washington DC, the Ritz-Carlton on 22nd St. NW. Traffic would probably cause her to be slightly delayed... With the Navajo gone and Godboy traveling with him, the townhome was available for the one night the lovers could fit into their schedules. The aroma of the grill heightened senses and Sean's were on red alert. He'd had kept intake for the day to only the Christo at the Flooze as he anticipated that his 'plate' would be scrumptiously overflowing later in the evening...after dinner.

On this occasion, the actress had the limo driver wait outside. She had her subcontracted body guard escort her to the restaurant front door only and then asked him to remain on standby with the driver. The maitre d' welcomed Odessa and escorted her through the crowd of stunned stares and dropped jaws to the private corner area and Sean. Her phone rang as she quickly glanced at Sean. He welcomed her with a smile and stood to hug her. "Damn things." Odessa looked at her phone screen then shoved it in her purse and she returned his kiss and hug. "So sorry, my sweet, but these answering things, a voicemail, then we don't allow them to do their job right, Sean."

"Answer?"

"I'm turning it off now. But it's the only thing to turn off tonight, soldier boy." Sean kissed her cheek again and she trembled at the sensuality of being in the arms of a man of propriety. The maitre d' waited the professionally perfect beat, then asked the couple as they unclasped and began to sit across from each other "Liquid refreshments, Maam, Sir?" The actress, without hesitation, "Your best Irish whiskey, Karl; right, Sean?" Sean winked at her and then to the restaurateur, "You heard the lady; thank you very much, Karl." They turned, focusing on each other, gently reaching, touching each other's outstretched arms.

"Do you know why St. Patrick's Day's on the 17th?"

"No, tell me, ol' Celtic one..."

"Well, the Irish argued..."

"Kind of a redundancy, wouldn't you think?"

"The Irish argued amongst themselves."

"Keeping it in the family shows class."

"They heartedly discussed whether their Saint was born on the eighth or on the ninth of March. People fought and died over the damn date."

"Why not say both days and the debauchery would last longer, right?"

"Well, the Pope, uh, Pope, oh Hell, can't remember which one but..."

"Well, honey, they all have, they all use names other than their god given Christian names anyways, don't they now?"

"Pope whatever his name the twenty-third stepped in and decided the issue by making the date the seventeenth by adding the two disputed dates together."

"Proving again that co-mingling can be tingling good in the most delicate of times, yes?"

Then, Odessa, seriously, "Sean, is it true, I mean Saint Pats' birthday and all that bashing to get to a date to celebrate?" She took measure of Sean's furled brow, the type response Odessa was all too familiar with; the male, 'would I lie to you' look. She instantly recognized her mistake. With this man it was different. This man did not insult easily nor act insulted as physical testimonial of 'innocence'.

"Your honesty is refreshing and frightening."

"Is there any other way?"

"Honesty?"

"Yes."

"Other ways you'll never touch. You are obviously not devious" then, with slight smile, "Unless, perhaps, in the service of your country." She had drawn blood. He had smiled. "Perhaps, too, 'un poco' naive. I have not met a person like you, Sean, let alone a man." "Do you always need entertainment?"

"Not on my private stage, no."

"What don't you have now? Is it weighty? Or is it as ethereal as a rainbow, a colorful draft of a mirage, textured but never touched? What is the quotient in your world, Odessa?"

"My quotient in my world? Wow. Counting coup now are we."

Karl arrived, served the whiskey, and asked if they needed anything else. Both shook their heads 'no'; he slightly bowed and left.

"Well, Sean, I know that I'm not an insipid etiolated jejune starveling, one of those screamers of the screen, unnatural, with the steamy stats of propped up boobs and bozo sized lips, if that's what you're asking. How's my math so far, Archimedes?"

Her left leg nudged his right leg beneath the table.

"It's adding up."

Flirtation continued between "a beautiful individual and a thoughtful beast" as Odessa's gay director friend had called her (in his opinion) most recent, "life toy".

Odessa Gabriel's approach to celebrity 'success' meant managing the challenge faced in the panicky prickly panoply sphere of pushiness and engineered provocation otherwise known as public opinion, or, according to Odessa, the world of "her"; meaning winning at any cost with disgrace viewed only as excess baggage to be discarded at first opportunity. She considered all the clamor and 'cheesyness' a centrifugal necessity, a mandate for any 'star' for said 'star' to maintain balance in the expected 'line dance', the glorified steps the public pays big bucks for, the waltz between ardor and abandonment, between desire and disaster, the accident no one ever can look away from... a business model she'd never shied or strayed from ever since her first appearance, her first audition, her first casting couch.

Inherent in most 'getting to know you/I know I'd enjoy being loved by you' 360° open ended conversations are meanings waiting to collide; issues, in the infancy of relationships, hidden in the leftover smoke of that ageless blue flamed burn of anticipation chasing temptation and its inevitable capture.

"Personally, I like two faced deities, more maneuvering space, if you know what I mean. Take Ishtar; the Sumerians worshiped her as goddess of love but the Assyrians worshiped her as a goddess of war. Now what could be handier to an actress than to come off as both? Keeps agents and producers at bay and the public eternally intrigued. Push the demiurge, darling, push the demiurge, stay in front and riant will follow."

"The ria?"

"Creative power to peddle gaiety, my man." Odessa took a bigger than average sip of the Irish joy juice. "Stay sapid, Sean, and you too can become an arbiterselegantiae; the judge and the jury in matters of style, in preferences of fashionable thinking...God know that's why I am invited to so many celeb weddings, don't you know."

Sean thought he loved her when she was on a roll.

"Of course, these are purely anticipatory antics preceding the subpoena for me to appear in court for either the ex bride or the ex groom in the requisite fiscal fist fight that all Hollywood celebrity divorces entail...they being just about as regular as the day beds down the night."

Karl arrived with salmon for the lady and tenderloin for the man as Sean had ordered before Odessa's arrival and had told the server to have the meal ready about a half hour after the first drink was served. Karl left to bring more liquids.

"Manny has excellent Chinese cuisine too. Recall reading background for some script about a warlord who ruled Szechuan and he was infamous for his cruelty as well as his for his excellent Chinese cuisine... a little sweet, a little sour... a little good, a little bad, keeps the boys happy and the girls sad." Odessa savored her first bite and watched as Sean cut into his meat. "You know, Sean, I almost got waylaid by a Christian man once in the most unmissionary of manners." She watched as he seemed to chew his meat a little more forcefully. They laughed. The whiskey was succeeding in its wonderfully wandering mission of accelerating a devil may care and even if he did, so what attitude. "So breaking into hell with Elmer Gantry, huh?" Sean paused, took another small bite of baked potato, then, "What about God's gift to women you've been with, I read about, with, what, for the last few couple years or so?" It was the first mention between them of any serious "ex's".

"We all get our roses, "our" songs catered to ourselves with lyrics others think we will buy that takes some time to silence in our heads. It's the nibbles at the bait, or being nibbled maybe, which excites me more. But damn, hooks leave scars so it's always dangerous fishing in those first rippling waves of lust, wouldn't you agree, Seanee?" Odessa took another bite of fish and saw that Sean was serious. "I met him in Venice. Location."

"Let me guess. You met at the Bridge of Sighs."

"More like the Arch of Ache; but no, elsewhere. Sad symbiosis."

"Like fungi and algae in the wrong field of lichens?"

"Leeches, yes." She noted the teasing still 'on hold' within him. "Sean, he's so soidisant, come on, he's nothing, nothing more than a, a farrago pastiche, a..."

"So just another..."

"...Teachable moment, yes." She noted some softening. "He was a turkey cock, strutted around, and grew very pompous, conceited; which I found for him was second nature..." "So it was a mutual attraction?" and the tease was back.

"No." Odessa smiled. "Because he didn't have what it takes to make a woman put up with such garbage... He needed a stuntman for the bedroom, for Gods sake. He hadn't done his homework in the art of being an understudy or a stud-under-the-covers in the vernacular verite' of Hollywood and Vine. But he did have a face with a view, if you know the type."

"How long did it take you to reach this conclusion?"

"Two years of premiers, one Time magazine cover, two interviews in Rolling Stone and 1000 pages of blissful negative publicity and when Viagra was rumored to be in trouble, I knew it was time to move on to bigger, better plans."

"Did you play tennis together?"

"What on earth!" She was pleased to see the glint in his eyes again. "Don't think we, maybe once, charity event, just appeared to but what the blank that has to do with..."

"Read a survey done by Club Med once which found that's couples who compete against each other, play opposite sides of the net, enjoy romance and what follows three times as often as couples who play together as a team."

"All in the groundstroke, baby, all in the groundstroke, no lobs allowed, right?" They momentarily indulged in bites and sips and the happy faces of people in pursuit of the same goal.

"Well did you know, Mr. Linden, that 74 percent of women love boxers over briefs?"

"Why?"

"Well, I don't like either as commando's more preferable, more to my tastes." Sean was not shocked by anything anymore with Odessa. Why bother.

"Listen, my dear, I'm one of those women who don't put on any underwear before 9 a.m. west coast time."

"Even for early calls on a set?"

"Even for early calls on a set, yes."

He took an even bigger sip of whisky as she did the same.

"Privacy, aye, 'privacy', there's the rub. In show biz, I feel ones got to maintain some mystery, I tell you, if you are going to remain at the top in this crazy vocation, Sean. Because once you become "common", starring in the lights of the 'spectacular vernacular of the mundane,' you're dead. Or worse, forgotten." Odessa leaned closer to Sean and acted as if she was blowing," The kiss of death." She retreated slightly. "But privacy, ha! Every word from your mouth is a target of bugs, cameras, lip readers; even when you are free of your prison. Hell, you can't sunbathe nude anywhere in Hollywood. I think they have drones specifically designed to zero in on private parts of public people. You'd be, Sean, if you were a male actor, they'd be after your loving thing for certain, Photoshop's definitely not necessary as you are a prime cut of prime time, my darling." He obviously reddened and she adored it. "Have people ever told you that you're a snob and dangerous? One of the two? No, then you're not alive." Odessa put her index finger to her chin. "Shyness is really action to hide the private self. And you're still heavily peppered with it, Mr. Sean, what are you hiding? Is your memory romantically impaired?"

Mr. Linden was not in stride as this path was in unfamiliar territory, no training for it. "Yeah, I probably go against the grain, so..."

"Oh my, not that I haven't noticed that, right." Odessa motion to the maitre d' and gave him orders to "Dismiss the limousine and the bodyguard, Karl, would you please." She'd never felt as protected or as guarded as she did now, now with so much at stake.

Sean quickly stopped the maitre d' mid-turn, grabbing his arm. "And then, Karl, please set the Escalade taxi pickup for 5 minutes from now, please."

Odessa laughed, "Shy, my ass!"

Sean caught himself, "I'm sorry, Ms. "O", did you want dessert?"

"I rarely do. One can only indulge in what's bad for you for only so much... Besides, 'desserts' spelled backwards is 'stressed', and darling, we'll have none of that now, understand."

The professional driver expertly guided the couple inside, closed the door, and proceeded to drive without paying any further notice to his passengers as he headed towards the location with the directions the gentleman had given him.

The lady clasped his hands in hers. "Sean, let you in on a little succulent trade secret of mine, which you may know already...but with the proper person, I'm proficient in protrusiling passion to almost unearthly pitch."

"No doubt of that ever, Oh My Gee, Gabriel."

"Mind you, I'm not succubus incarnate, because I despise doing all the work. In other words, you better be awake when I jump your bones, baby". They kissed and laughed and kissed again, in both instances just long enough not to ruin 'lovemaking' later, which, according to the actress is, "all about the excruciation, the gnawing wonderment of delightfully delayed pleasure."

"Oh, Sean, I want my tongue wherever you imagine it should be, comprende compadre?" He kissed her his 'yes', then, softly he said, "Habeas corpus, baby."

"What?"

"It's semi-Latin for, 'you have the body', baby." Their hands began to play for real as the vehicles sound systems music segued from Crosby Stills and Nash's "Glad That You've Got It Made" to Pink Floyd's "Same Old Fears, Wish You Were Here." Her lips, lush and receptive, welcomed his exploratory adaptations and gentle concerns. Seconds later, she slowly pulled back, just an inch, eyes attentive to only his as she said, "Welcome to my nightmare..." and she kissed his clef chin before concluding, "...because, you see, dearest, nothing's real when you're in bed with a movie star." They laughed and they wished they were 'there' already.

The Escalade stopped. The professional promptly opened the door, assisted the passengers over the curb to the sidewalk and with equally appropriate nonchalance, accepted Sean's generous tip and just as professionally, quickly dissolved into the background.

Sean opens the townhomes door. They both aim for the living room and the large light colored davenport, seemingly overwhelmed by numerous and various sized blue and green pillows. Sean was thankful that Thucydides was at the neighbors as this was the feline's usual domain and she would most certainly be disturbed by the scent of another female within her realm.

"I love your place, Sean."

"That's whiskey speaking; speaking of which, little more?"

"Yes. Please." She settled on the largest pillow as Sean quickly moved in the direction of the bar.

"Did you know, mi macho grande that the average man laughs 69 times a day?"

"69?"

"Significant numero. Humorously entwined design, 'tickler' serifs at each end; the possibilities, mathematically, are endless, yes?"

Sean Linden had never operated a decanter more swiftly.

He brought them and sat next to her as she sampled hers.

Finished with the taste test, Odessa cocked her head and with lifted brow, "You may find it interesting to learn that the word "Glamour", you know, the thing the business I'm in claims as its mantra, well, 'glamour' comes from a medieval belief that it stems from a witches brew, no, no, make that, a witches 'spell'."

"Spell?"

"Yes. A witch's spell to rid men of their favorite magic...'wands'." Odessa's brows rose even higher.

"Has your wand ever been bewitched, Sean?"

He could only laugh. She asked, "Is that your 69th? If you don't watch it, you know, we're going to go over your limit." As if she were a physician listening with her stethoscope, she leaned down and put her head on his chest. "I'm a renown auscultator and I can tell your heart is bold, and by the bass in its sound, ...horny." He fought hard but lost and grinned wide. She gently pushed up from his heart and laid her head back on the cushion. He did the same. Both strained to relax.

"It's difficult avoiding intimacy, isn't it?"

He didn't move a muscle, unsure of the next move, hers or his.

"You and I both know it's a game, right?"

Sean smiled but did not laugh as he didn't want to go over his 'average man' quota. "It usually goes man makes move then lady rejects man... Shows that woman's not, quote, a bad girl. If woman's sitting with legs crossed, dangling shoes or shoe on toes, usually its first step at undressing or, or, as if she acted as to resist, and if she brushes her hair and smiles at you, Sean, that's when a man better get ready for mattress magic; verstehen, darling?" Odessa kicked her low cut heels into the air, and before they had the opportunity to fall to the parquet floor, Sean swept her up into his arms and they were on the move upstairs.

Amidst a flurry of kisses, buttons busting, zippers breaking, Odessa went combustible, the white hot igniter being one Sean Linden. They retreated for air and she, ala M. Monroe, breathlessly, "Have you noticed the shape of a pubic hair?"

"God, what the..."

"That the shape of a pubic hair is a 'question' mark."

Sean squinted through sweat streaming from his forehead.

"That's why I shave, Sean. I don't appreciate uncertainty. Don't want you going Robert Frost on me at 'the fork' and taking the wrong path, swerving on the wrong curves."

He put his hand to her mouth, lovingly, and his other hand seductively elsewhere. They laughed and kissed, pleasantly and delicately, not unlike those of adolescents' first experimentations, those ccurrences of youthful discovery that often happen in those long grasses on those rolling hills up behind many a rural town's water tower.

She pulled him close and in his ear she whispered," I find it preferable never to be shocked by behavior in bed." She kissed his lobe. "I want to stun you hard, my love." She moved to his neck and lower, her perfumed breathe pleasing him softly as if a butterfly fluttering a winged 'adieu'. "And you're all the energy I need." The scintillation, the oscillation, the quaking akin to aspen in September breeze, stretched the length of early evening into the late dawn of detumescenses' last dalliance and the mornings copper rays of unwelcomed stabbing light.

CHAPTER 9

"I Know The Results And I Still Yell At The Screen"

"If women didn't exist, all the money in the world would have no meaning."

Aristotle Onassis

October 11, 2015

Magdalena Marconi's 'Wag The Blog' bookstore sat in the middle of the waterfront district. Tripp Bellows sat in the middle of Ms. Marconi's store beneath fluorescent lights; his least favorite illumination as it tended to accent the lines in his face and highlight his 'spots' of grey, (not 'shades' of grey, his preferred description for his locks) more prominently or less desirably than any celebrity used to controlling the staging of any event they are at the center of would prefer. Per his publishers contract demands, though, Tripp is participating in the first of two book signings for "What The Ringmaster Didn't Tell Me- Is It Net Or Is It Gross?". And even though Mr. Bellows advocates for improvement in the human condition, Mr. Bellows, in general, prefers, almost phobic, separation; whether through the use of roadies or maitred's or the stage upon which he plays, partition from public contact was his usual goal. So sitting and signing, while albeit a different kind of 'charge', still took some getting used to for the 'fresh' author.

He was pleased that Sean, Cade, The Navaho, Moah, Godboy and Senator Bruce attended as familiarity softened his fears of actually socializing with actual strangers. After the first fifteen minutes of flourishes of autographs and perfunctory 'thank you's', Tripp glanced up to the Peter Max clock above the stores front door as if to give a visual cue to the seconds to speed up, and then, he saw her standing there. She stood at the back of a long line of what he now viewed as impedimenta. She obviously had a few less years on earth than the center of attention she had come to the Wag The Blog to see. Mr. Bellows put his head down and sped up the process to near fever pitch. Then, as if the 'seconds' on the Max clock had agreed with Mr. Bellows earlier mental request, he looked up and suddenly, she was in front of him.

"Thank you for coming." She nodded. He trudged on, "How, uh, what can I sign ...I mean, what, what would you like me to sign in your book?"

"No, sir. Thank you, thank you for helping the children and the charities." He fought hard not to fall through her hazel eyes.

She thought his eyes more gentle, his smile more genuine, so much more so than his pictures ever portrayed them to be.

Her book remained unsigned as he struggled and finally, "What do you do?'' was all he could muster.

And Ms. Emily Pinckney told Mr. Isaac Bellows, "My name is Emily. I'm an edgy environmentalist, a practicing dendrochronologist ..."

"Dendrochro?..."

"...with a full time job in the Senate as an assistant parliamentarian because, Mr. Bellows, I'm on top of it; I mean, I understand the proper procedural, the 'how to' of handling the nuances, the nuisances and the numbers involved in legislature."

"I'm sure you do, Miss Pinckney."

"Ms."

"Yes, Ms., uh Ms. Pinckney, what is a dendrochro what?"

"Dendrochronology, the study of tree rings."

"Tree rings?"

"Yes; what thick ones mean, what thin ones mean."

Tripp swallowed as he also took notice of the line behind Emily; fans disgruntled, stirring restlessly, waiting for the author to finished with the lady ahead of them. Noticeable concern registered on Mrs. Marconi's and the publishers representatives faces, so he acted, saying as he stood," I apologize, the session is over as I have new previous engagement that must be attended to but, but," as the crowd let out a collective groan," I will purchase all your books, sign each of them and then send each of you signed copies of the Cures upcoming album too," which surprised all and pleased all as this bit of news was not public knowledge, nor hinted or even speculated on in the media. "I'm shutting this down as I now have new previous engagements. Thank you for your patience. Please talk to Mrs. Marconi, leave your address, phone numbers, names, you know, the particulars and all will be mailed to you at my expense. God bless and good night." The "Blogs" workers ushered the crowd towards a hastily set up work area in order to fulfill the rockers sudden announcement. Tripp motioned for Emily to follow him and she did as they moved away from the mild hubbub. Tripp's friends remained in the background. They knew it best to allow their friend space, at least for five minutes.

Tripp asked for more from Emily...about tree rings. She detailed to him that, "Cracks develop as old bark dies. There's sapwood, then, Mr. Bellows..."

"It's Chaz or Tripp or whatever you want it to be, Emily."

Emily's big 'OMG' smile was the first indication that she too could indeed embarrass as equally as he could and this heightened his level of wonderment about what was happening as she recovered responding," and there's also heartwood in the center of the tree, Mr., uh, Chaz."

He smiled at hearing his name from her lips as she continued.

"Wood is added to the trunk with wider rings meaning rapid growth that occurs or I should say, that happen during periods of special growing conditions, bountiful years and then there are those naughty narrow rings meaning slower growth, very poor conditions for expansion."

Tripp's friends remained a polite distance from him and his newest 'friend.'

They would come to understand more later on as the ripening relationship showed its metaphorical "hand."

Senator Bruce mentioned to the others that he couldn't place the woman, but he felt he had seen her before.

The couple sat in two chairs meant for readers, near the 'cooking and diet' sections of the bookstore.

Tripp struggled to look 'cool'; thinking to himself, 'whatever the fuck that looks like'. And then he said," You sure that you're not a tintinnabulator in disguise, are you?"

"I ring them at Christmas, yes, and maybe, metaphysically, in other circumstances too, perhaps."

They were both ready to range wide and range weird.

"I did study campanology, yes."

Not knowing, ignorantly, what that had to do with 'bells', Tripp announced, "I'm anti- bowdlerizing, if that's somehow related to what you just said."

Through their laughter, Emily decided, "So you are a censorious type, are you?"

"No. No. Never soil your sources. Besides, I can take scolding; say do you know that 'scold' in Old Norse..."

"What?'

"Viking talk."

"Oh."

"Yes, it meant someone who writes or recites epic poems."

"I kind of favor Zoroastrian theology myself. Zoroastrians recognize four classes; priests, warriors, scribes and, as always, pulling up the rear, peasants, and you see, most men are four class guys. You have the spiteful fervor of a man of God, you have the killer instinct, you have the creative ability in some men of a Pan, and finally, you have those with the habits of pigs roaming beyond their sties."

He thought her a walking 'illegality' and he dared wondered if he would ever share this with her later. She thought him a bundle of beautiful inconsistencies and knew it wouldn't matter. He thought of what she would later think of his places. His condo was sparsely furnished as domestic was something he'd never read about or wanted to hear a definition of. He knew he leaned towards the Oscar Madison type rather than the Felix Unger type. When Emily eventually visited his D.C. domain and saw his bare walls, except for the expertly hung expensively framed exquisite drawings of some mighty fine furniture pieces accompanied by a giant old beanbag and a giant 'those were the days 70's' waterbed, complemented by a plasma screen television that Tripp believed would be a waste of time 'and dinero' to improve upon, she fell in love with the Isaac Bellows approach to minimalist design theory. The 'dessert' was when she walked into his work area as he called it, a room with portraits of renderings of bars and velvet paintings of dogs playing poker in smoke-filled harshly lit environments inherent in many undistinguishable dives she knew were probably part of his early days. She knew then that he would never cheat on her as she knew herself to be a special singularity, a 'Mrs. Job' with almost apocryphal patience, a female with guts enough to allow for man boy antics but never for disrespect of any nature; and combining this with the Holy Grail of a man's perspective, that of the male meeting a female so sure of who she is that she would never try to change the male, Emily knew that any man with half a lick of sense would never gambled around with a woman like this, like Emily, as women like Emily are as rare as, well, as rare as an Annie Oakley in chaps with the heart of an Athena. And in her opinion, she would chance that the odds were in her favor as Mr. Bellows seemed to be, at the least, a little less than half crazy. Maybe.

Their space within the confines of Wag The Blog remained private. Their conversation wove and stuttered through various levels of intrigue, innocuousness and fun.

He: "Straw-up-your-nose lyrics make sense only when you're ripped."

She: "Wimple days are really those 24 hour blocks when you squeeze them dry of everything you possibly can."

He: "Love the strings of the ukulele, the original Hawaiian jumping flea."

She: "My, my, how men remember and women never forget."

He: "How do you feel about this song I'm scribbling over, call it the, and this is only a working title, of course..."

She: "Of course."

He: "Manicure of the Measured Magician?"

She: "Uh, why not call it, "The Addiction of Marginalia", instead?"

He: "I do write notes around typed words, yes; so how'd you come to know..."

She: "Chromosome intuition."

He later confided to Sean and Cade that, in this 'getting familiar time' that, which happened much more swiftly than usual for him, he had read the small print on Emily' shirt, professing to them that he had initially missed this detail as Tripp explained, because," Emily's eyes and Emily's 'prominent points of contention' which had stressed the limits of her pink T-shirt, apparently, in Tripp's professional opinion, had" disarmed my usual ability of attention to detail, if not, boys, totally dismantled it."

Cade then asked the obvious, "Well, what the hell did it say, son?"

"Honest and Horny."

"And you missed that early?" Cade was befuddled.

Sean then added, "A thorny thing for the screechy preachies, right, Chaz?"

"Dammit, guys," Tripp pleaded, "Isn't flirting an over decorated thing, come on, at our age, I see no..."

"Our age?"

"Bite me big, boys, bite me big," and Tripp's commiseration with his 'hoodmates' thus would end but not before the rocker added, "But dang, men, did you see that ponytail?"

Eventually, in meaning and in effect, the relationship figuratively got up, elevating from the soft oversized chairs presently occupied by Mr. Bellows and Ms. Pinckney, to a higher place, which, at this moment in 'The Wag', neither could ever perceive destiny would allow.

For instance, in these first moments of the mind mob called 'first interactions', he had no clue that he'd find her collection of bonsai trees, which face South in Emily's mini atrium, such lovely things. The bonsai surrounded a pink chaise lounge upon which, again, he'd later learn, she enjoyed meditating in the nude listening to Joe Cocker's "You Can Leave Your Hat On," as she reclined, enjoying her view of her no maintenance greenery. Tripp would also notice, during this initial visit to Ms. Pinckney's townhome, a black mahogany framed white bordered Fleetwood Mac "Trees" album, signed (Pre Stevie, pre-Lindsay) by the band members. But the creme de la creme in Tripp's heart was when he spotted all of the Circus Cures albums on a corner table in a 'can't miss' part of Emily's living room. Tripp smiled as would recall the band's decision to record only on vinyl, precluding any other method of musical delivery, digital or otherwise, and they ordered their attorneys to pursue and sue all who tempted to fraud the band of their intellectual properties returns. Their decision became a marketing coup, that is, until their recent decision to stop the music, become more family men and do 'things' outside 'the group'. Vinyl and this decision to split, except for Tripp's push to do something lyrically in an effort to enhance the thought processes of Americas youth, it added value to the bands throwback to the olden way, to times without duplication and theft without consequence, to those days before today's leach field of relativity ethics and the easy disdain for borders or restrictions by those that steal against the rights of artists simply defending the results of their creative efforts. Tripp would later write in a column, "We live in an era that now, what was proper is now pooh-poohed, passé, shoved to the side as an anachronistic tendency, out of date with, God help us, 'the times.' We live in the moment of sad dismay when the word "we" has been replaced by the word "me". "We" is hiding in the contrived weeds and flowery pedals of political correctness, where it's institutional to rant on the limb that no one should be insulted, where no one can be called to account for their acts because origin excuses them or someone must have held them back somewhere, right? Where no one is above the holiness of relativity thinking which strives to excuse all ill results, right? Don't we live, America, where "We" live in days where the frothiest voice of tribalism wins the moment and wins the headlines in the compliant and complacent soft peddlers residing in the once great residency called 'the press?'; if this be so, we will continue to endure, to allow these lazy, indulgent ignoramuses to set the topic of the day and land will be worse for it, mark my written words." Emily proved to be the kindred soul of the "ancientness" that traveled within the veins of her newest, and, as it would turn out, her most sincere and fabulously talented lover. She proved a 'simpatico vibration'; almost devilishly so he'd later think, an amorous tuning fork of a sort, with an understanding of the proper pitch within the heart of her lovers pace through life. She'd indeed judge him correctly as she would, in the future, ask, "This is why you write, isn't it, baby?"

"It's all Sorentsen's doing."

"Who?"

"My university professor, Elliot Sorentsen."

"Hoity high mighty sounding name there."

"No, no, he's as far from that, Em, as Lake Titicaca is from Timbuktu; he's the antithesis of mile high snobbery...that's my, my, hell, my attraction for, well, him. Point being, in class that afternoon, he said to 'you muddled skulls of mush,' as he often called us,' that, in order to participate on all cylinders in life, to improve upon whatever God loaned you at birth to work with, you got to dig deeper than a mud-jacking mad hatter, you got to break through the cozy foundations of your most comfortable beliefs, and then, and then, you children in adult bodies, then you must diamond cut even deeper than these first shovelfuls and you must become furious upon the discovery, the miserable knowledge that you still don't know 'jack' about the jewels which still lie deeper below you in the gooey sands of studied time. Your ire should grow as you realize, with even more clarity than when you began this, that you are still incapable of answering, with any authority, the questions not 'of' but 'for' your lifetime...which is, 'what's my footprint going to mean to anyone else and will it lead to anything important ten million days from today? Make your mark and make it count, people.' Sorentsen then wrapped up with, "Furor Scribendi", Latin for, "A passion for writing"; for this is how you march through time, but only if you embrace the bountiful mud and never sling it. Class dismissed."

That's why I write, Emily; songs to release, I suppose, what is in my heart and now, well, this, whatever this is I do today, the column, to free some burdens of an uneasy soul; oh hell, to leave my footprint and to not lose my mind."

As would become her habit, Emily waited for the last drops to fall before taking her umbrella back.

"God, Em, I do love the new competition," and, with hint of Odessa-speak barging in, "sparring with these wide-eyed soi-disant baby Cronkite's and toothless tigers of the blogs, it's; man, I sound grumpy, don't I?" He hated when age bounced around in his head.

She knew the rain gear was ready for folding. "I suggest that you school zone down as you always seem better reigning in the terror of your first thoughts before they become printed finalities, don't you?"

She followed with what he called her "Phrenology Fugue", as she massaged his head, knowing thumbs accompanied by barely there fingers, orchestrating calmness and a melody for the mind he adored.

"Don't ever stop being my fan, Em."

"Don't ever go after another groupie, actress, intern, feminine savants and I will light my Bic after your every performance. If not, I'll set your hair on fire, break your guitars and destroy your velvet voodoo Elvis doll." To which Chaz retorted, "Could you not obfuscate, just let it hang out, dry in the air a while and see if the softener does its job?"

Near "W.T.D."'s 'Cooking/Self Help' aisle, The Navaho and the Senator, oblivious to the musicians and the parliamentarian's soiree of the heart across from them, attempted more familiarity with the other. The Senator knew from Sean Linden and from Moah Halas that their eponymously named friend was indeed one lodestone of loyalty, straight talk, and very dangerous to double cross individual. The Senator had had only cursory 'hellos' previously with John Truefellow and now the politician wanted to peel back more from this never say die spokesperson for something very dear to the Senators heart, native America.

"We are a Third World territory, a shoved to the side hovel in the Temple of the USA, Senator; it is not deniable!" This was said in controlled firm manner which the legislator from Oklahoma was impressed with, mentally noting the conviction in the words as well as the take no prisoner attitude in the tone of the meanings shared. "One way to clear the unwanted, if not by theft, is to demolish their traditions, kill their languages," and Truefellow glanced over to the crowd waiting to get their mailing addresses collected by the bookstore since 'their' person of the moment friend was involved in other than agreed to 'actually' obligated duties as Tripp was involved in a moment with his own person of the moment. He smiled as he turned back towards the Senator." I say this in a bookstore, only 20 maybe 25 of 170 or so surviving American Indian dialects are expected to make it, to survive another four years maybe. In fact, Senator, nearly sixty native tongues face impending extinction because they have may be maybe five maybe six less people who can speak them and these are elders all in their mid-to late later days."

Sen. Bruce remained silent, unnatural for him.

"Were more than just blankets, buckskins and baskets, so much more, sir, more than the modern-day icons of the Noble Savage draped in the solemnity and in the purchased penances as only victors can write about their victims....awash in the balmy therapeutic froth of 'white' mea culpa swirling in competition for attention with 'white' rinse-the-sin -away waves of 'How so nice of me,' donations."

"As you know I'm from Oklahoma, John. I have tried, I've done my best to help, from the Cherokee to the Chickasha, from the land grab assignment of being a guilty white as you call him and I try hard for funding I hope you're aware of funding for the tribes. I have not accomplished the goals of my heart but I will never quit trying to succeed at. I know you have recently tried to get more monied sponsors for powwows, schools, health, and I tell you, John, I will try to improve, to dedicate more of what little power I have to help you in any way I can."

The man from the land of the endearing Canyon de Chelly and the sacred Tse Bit'a'I or 'Winged Rock' called "Shiprock by the conquerors" as The Navaho would often described to guests to the lands, John knew the older gentleman's word should be taken as faith, that Strong Bull Bruce is a man worth dealing with.

"50% unemployment is an American tragedy, John, I know."

"Do you believe in omens as a God-fearing Republican?"

"There is no correct play to the base answer for that, son. I'm no Nostradamus, if that's what you're talking about."

"Then there's Custer, George Armstrong."

"Goon."

"Pay attention to omens. Modern men don't. They've seen it all. And then they've seen nothing. I saw the painting, Senator, by Ole guy, Ole Peter Hansen something or other. ..name like some Indians like "He Who Stands Alone," hard to remember many named men sometimes... I don't know, but this, it is painting, it's called, maybe you've seen it, 'Grant And His Generals' and painted in 1865, it shows Gen. George Armstrong Custer, second from the left, next to the flag standards spear held by a trooper on the generals left. It is a red flag decorated with the images of a white spear, its arrowhead sharp head tied tight to staff and draped in ceremonial feathers and three white stars bordering on its left and some sort of banner running left to right across both the stars and the spear. If you follow it's, the 'flagpole slash spear' vertical line in the painting, it runs right down to where Custer's, well, right to his privates."

"And?"

"The 'and' is, the same year, 1876, the same year that the major leagues began playing baseball, the same year the first phone call with Alexander G. Bell happened, to that year is tied to this Custer Battle which is really the battle of the Greasy Grass Creek in June of '76, 11 years after this painting's premiere in 1865. The other 'and' in the room is, if you're still with me, Senator?"

"I am."

"After the battle Custer's body was found with bullet holes in his breast and his temple 'and', and with an arrow shot into his privates, same target rich area as the red and white standard 'flagpoles' as seen in the painting that you tell me of omens don't have meaning get this I just remember the name the painters name, yes, Ole Peter Hansen and his last name, figuratively, the kicker, his last name is 'Balling'."

The Senator would not laugh first nor was he sure that he should.

"If that isn't sticking to the truth ahead of time, Mr. Bruce, I don't know what ever an omen could ever be...and if not, what, senator, what does an omen have to do to be an omen other than to show up later in some big way, you know, omen sized and obvious?" "Quite a grouping of historical figures I recall, John, at the battle; Chief Gall, Crazy Horse, Two Moon and Hump and the others, Sitting Bull, Crow King and Custer." "Custer and his brothers."

"Ah, yes; the 'And.'"

Truefellow continued, "Gerrymandering writ large on reservations, sir, permanent majority of paleface people on school boards, on city offices. Identification grievances not in Navaho favor, also no small things as there are no translators, with registrations of Navajo voters; it's a farce, discriminatory. Raise some problems with race, oh yes, long time gauntlet for us and every other wonderfully colored fugitive from the White Play Book, 1887 Dawes act could be considered the first chapter...but, it being but one disgrace among many injustices, each deeper than the previous one. The actions of the overly concerned with the business of others sect of white people explained that its pious goal was to infuse Indian culture into the wonderful world of white. Actually used, they did, the words "gradual extinction" meaning of tribe's and reservations, so we, The Dineh, in order to preserve sanity and the sanctity of the tribe, cannot, in good conscious do as you and learn the habits of civilized life. We, The Dineh, ask who invented the word 'civilized'; the killers or the victims?" The sheriff paused. "Have at that battle, which, the Battle of Greasy Grass Creek, or "Big Hom" to Caucasians on imposed special occasions, well, the battle lasted maybe forty five minutes."

"Custer's?"

"Yes."

"It would seem I need to go at this painting again sometime, might I?"

"Senator, I know you push hard for veteran's rights and I appreciate. Now being as selfish as I can, I want to request, I want you to put that much effort for Native rights." Senator Bruce nodded but that was the only discernable "tell" Mr. Truefellow could see. "By the way, Custer wasn't scalped."

"No?"

"Might have been difficult thing anyways as the general had had his locks cut short before departing the fort. He was balding too."

"Epiphany's are expensive these days."

"Ah, the balm of a Savage blessing...white men's way of wash away guilt is to donate, some much more than others and some much more real,....all is still cast in present tense, easier for all to work that way.. Not against anything...I just raise funds on the killed." The Navaho knew he was on the proper path to the Senators good side as both Sean and Moah had told him that the Senator digging, taking a somewhat irascible tact bordered by a few knowing winks that you had made a very favorable impression on the man and you had made a friend.

"Mr. Truefellow, I know you're aware of Thoreau, 'Civil Disobedience?'"

"Yes."

"Thoreau, yes a saying of his, a passage, something to the effect of quote,' I saw to what extent the people among whom I live could be trusted as good neighbors and friends, that their friendship was for summer weather only."

"That's very unlike what happens at the intersection of Good Hope Road and Martin Luther King and Acosta waterfront quite frequently…someone helps those that need help, so I've read it about it being told."

"Charmed by that, thank you." The Senator appreciated considerate conversation. "I am certain that if you are hanging around with Moah and Sean that you are a four season friend for they would have no others than friends knowledgeable about the cost of commitment and the fatal attraction of unrestrained values."

"Senator there's enough negativity and I say it's increasingly hard for individuals not to question their validity while others are slipping away here and there around them, falling foolishly to Mother Earth which was made for our pleasure and for our stewardship, how wasteful this overflow of stranded souls, agree?"

The Navaho's dire assessment found a home in the Senator as he sadly concurred... John Truefellow noticed the older man's consternation and slightly shifted the atmospheric gears with, "Senator, we're all more alike, whites, natives, which is perhaps uncomfortable for both of us. Ever notice how John Wayne and Sitting Bull have resemblances to each other, yes, and their faces next each other in black-and-white pictures side by side, same rugged outlook on the faces terrain, same bones, I swear it." "Kevin Bacon six strikes or times removed again, huh?"

The Sheriffs laughter almost caused mishap. He recovered. His attention now looked over at the WTB's interior hovering over and around the author and the fan, commenting, "These colors were right time, right place in store; they are good omens quite good medicine for Bellows and his book."

"Do tell."

"Navajos," as Truefellow pointed towards the interior design, "believe yellow to be the mountains, the Western mountains and also yellow brings the twilight, one of the two magical times of day, the other dawn. See the off-white or eggshell as they call it now, that's the Eastern sky, the creator of the day."

The senator continued in that vein of conversation. "So all around good luck day; dawn to dusk, for Master Chaz. Once, early in my career, had a union leader tell me to always sign anything in blue ink, because blue was equated with trust. I later read that in religious representations the color communicates truth too and that it an example of fellowship too with the creative power of God! The creative power of God! Ha. Therefore, Mr. Truefellow, I'm sure that the term 'blue blood' came from the likes of these perks of thoughts and really, the only blue I see here today, Sheriff, is Tripp's suit." "Senator, I know you're good stock, gentle nature, and indomitable will,"

"Well, John, I'm not all that close by the…"

"And I feel you would agree with me that we should take the largest smudge sticks to this abomination..."

"Washington?"

"You knew the answer as you asked."

"Yes, this cesspool now on Algonquian native land."

The senator was about to interject but could not find a reasonable response that made sense with his heart as he agreed again with what the younger man said.

"It's just that, Senator, I do not put anything and I mean anything pass anyone that's been in this town for even an hour."

Sen. Bruce interrupted the uneasy silence, "Looks like a very good lad,'' indicating towards Godboy, "your nephew."

They both glanced at the teenager engaged in conversation with Sean Linden, Moah and the Mogul. They also took note of Bellows, chatting from the big chair, sitting in larger-than-life conversation with an attractive lady in a green dress and, as Sen. Bruce said, "and an oh my! Pink T-shirt."

God boy is serious, "Does Odessa Gabriel believe in God?"

Sean Linden was quiet, stopped near silly, by this, their new younger acquaintances directness, but Sean caught himself as he considered the teenagers recent blood memories as shared with Sean by the Navaho about this young man when The Navaho was asking for Sean in helping with his, the Sheriffs care of the" nephew." Moah smiled, a rarity recently, as the Mogul leaned in closer to see how their friend would respond to this young man's focused morality quest. Before Sean Linden could respond, Godboy continued, "My mom told, rather taught me recently that three fourths of Americans believe God had forgiven them for any past mistakes or wrongdoings. I see Americans a confident people here in this survey my mom spoke to me about the way the lessons were ignored. Only half, 50 percent...that's the percentage of respondents who had forgiven other transgressors in their lives other people so many convinced of God's forgiveness unable half the time forgive their fellow man. Some practice the type of pseudo-forgiveness to manipulate others I've seen, my mom had to have too. You know, 'I have forgiven you, now you owe me one.' That mentality, that meanness."

"In spite of what you may have read about Hollywood what I've heard about this Gabrielle persistence from participants in the lunacy out there she's not like that is she Mr. Linden?"

"I've told you, call me Sean, please... I've only known her for a short time but I can tell you she is not lazy with her beliefs."

The mogul almost worked himself into a knot holding back a smirk, snicker or smile and he succeeded.

Godboy's deceased mother used religion to teach proper techniques for decision-making, the calm passion necessary when facing and respecting the unknown and the fact that man does not have all the answers. ..and that spirit in the art of forgiveness are gifts from God and not the tainted by the dishonorable notices of the average soul, identifiable, quickly by the contamination of selfish thinking. She left her son many teachable moments and she advocated questioning all things man-made but never to question God's test and trials for us. Dios Nino knew from her loving efforts that about a third of the people were religious which he had come to understand even more clearly, recently, as he battled with God about the 'Why' of his now. She had taught him that while religion leads to service the great needs of humanity it also wrought horrible inhumane acts and as an example of the devil's salads from all benches, teams of Protestant, teams of Catholic, teams of Muslim, Jews, each of these divided by separate intentions and death dealing dissent. Steadiness in the face of doing the easy, evil thing, she believed to be the goal for those desirous of a character worthy for consideration for reaching the grace of The Almighty. His mother was cautionary at the conclusion of talks with caveats most memorable for Alexjandro Jesus Buddha Simon de Mejas being was his mother statement that, "fault finders can be good people too." And she continued with the example of "Copernicus theory of the earth revolving around the sun and not the opposite way and then in the 16th, 17th centuries, Catholics and Protestants assailed full throatily and rudely argued against it with notable man like Shakespeare, Milton Pascal even Francis Bacon disavowing it as well.. Again these were not with you does not mean that they are not decent beings... Jesus?!"

Sean Linden stopped Godboys somewhat rambling road memories with a blessing of distraction as he answered, "We are each a Temple of the highest ones making, are we not, God boy?"

Via the quizzical yet firm response, the young man understood that now was neither the time nor Wag The Blog the place to continue any further with this topic.

Moah turned from Godboy and the others to continue fencing with the only senator he respected, Sen. Dunleavy Bruce, been advocating and sponsoring for funding anything that assisted veterans forever. Always remember the friends of the military. Previous to Union Station delivery for the signing, Moah had traveled by train (always, when he could, when he was not working at his two-year-old job as Air Marshal). He had flown in perhaps one too many mini choppers, warthogs and other military aircraft over the years and opinion now formed that the odds of his safety in life were less than before the many years of flight.

"Ah, the moxie of youth." he addressed the senator, who responded," Mixed in with a fresh balmy Tiffany epiphany of mortality and how are you undulating these days?" Moah had visited Arlington that morning, a habit, a ritual within his being of his schedule his way about life as he needed this cleansing as exoneration for his existence, and he meets this demand every time he was in town, in the District of Columbia. He knew the 600+ acres of rolling hills as well as the Sioux knew the Badlands. Arlington averaged now about 20 to 22 burials a day. This autumn morning had not been unlike any other in that sacred territory as the grounds played host to backhoes and bulldozers clawing for fresh eternities, mobile canopies fluttering in the unusual heated whisper of the wind, hovering, covering five green soft material chairs settled in for services later this day. A functioning without waste, a final fashion statement from military, a runway for eternity, which, when the show is over, is easily and quickly forgotten by distant patriots, but not this one.

Just when Moah gathered his thoughts to step back to the present, both he and the Senator are interrupted by the fresh author from wagging the dog in the Wag The Blog restroom acknowledging the senator and the warrior with a near breathless, "Nice to see the two branches of government together," to which the targets of Bellows raised their glasses as the fresh published pressman hurried by them to the obviously appointed spot for further adoration.

"Perfervid. Very or excessively fervid. Ardent. Zealous." And the Senator then turned his attention again towards Mr. Halas.

"You have to remain as constant for us as ever, Senator. For Vets, times are furious with our decisions. Yes, you have always had, but you inhabit such a den of..." Moah hesitated as he noticed the Senator posture straighten a little more evenly, more erect and even seemingly bracing, "not that I am demeaning your efforts because of your work atmosphere."

Senator Dunleavy released a little tightness and sipped on his comfort.

"What I mean, well, Japanese old saying 'the strong eat and the weak become the meat', that's as for our military, I think military is seen as sometimes viewed as nothing more than ground shock chuck. Hell, Congress has treated service people like stepchildren of the state, God, they've exposed us to HIV, hepatitis, life infections, damage even unsterile colonoscopies at Reed and others in unemployment after seeing some figure still problematic, Senator, like 10,000 homeless vets just in LA, Christ's sake, and it's worse now with 30% higher unemployed that still and if you're honorable need I say more?" Sen. Dunleavy nodded. "An old Egyptian saying goes 'We live on one fourth of what we eat, and the doctors live on the rest.' Well, mordant Mullah Moah, this pyramid still exists."

Both were silent. As Moah looked away from the Senator, glancing about the bookstore to no one in particular he mused aloud, "War makes you wise in a hurry and angry forever." Moah glanced over to the silent Senator. "I am a consequentialist by nature. What's the worst case, you understand, what's the worst that can happen because of action I take, you understand? This is how any plan should begin, should begin by cruising to the baddest that can happen fast and you; you'll do some clear research if you've experienced mistakes by mis-routing before.

The Senator interjected, "I've forgotten, no, I've got it..goes...nullum beneficium est impunitum .. No good deed goes unpunished."

"Support and defend, Senator."

"Yes. Always."

"And thank you."

And you too, sir."

The two friends turned, making their way towards the others as Moah concluded, "Your biggest enemy, really, Senator, is being not remembered."

Moah halted their progression in the direction of the signing-desk now turned waiting-desk, pulling up short and with kind perceptions the intention, glanced from Sean and Godboy and then stared the Senator straight on, "One more thing on the veterans. I'm not for illegals, you know that. But your party and the other one I dislike a tad more for the hypocrisy of the situation you put these poor souls in. The illegals. Democrats think illegal's are beggars in training, votes in waiting while the Redubs think illegal's are peons to push around, always the pitiful players for maintaining 'The Clubs' solid bottom lines. But 70,000 immigrants, sir, 70,000 serve, one third not yet citizens mostly Mexicans, Senator, try to legislate fairness would you, well even illegal's, if they fight it means to me the same uniform I've want to legalize it, make it faster rail for them to hammer their way through to their dreams in America well it would be a equalizing the dream act too. It's simple, you be sweated blood, tears and bad memories in military service meant to protect average Americans that they serve, they serve, they deserve." Moah was more verbose than usual. "Hell, Congress still creates laws we have to abide by but you skate. Not you, necessarily but damn near Marauding manipulators, I mean, that you hang out with."

"Moah, it is well what you say. I can only strive for what's right in these times of punctuated ethics, unquantifiable 'what ifs' and smiley denials but I will not falter, I will continue to try. I promise I continue."

"Party be damned?"

"Damn straight."

"Hey, you two ram rods." The author was calling them, "Toast time." Bellows had taken a break from pink blouse green dress girl who was not to be seen as she apparently was being sanctioned elsewhere for the moment.

Moah asked Tripp, "Avid reader?"

"Yates and Emily Sue..." They pressed each other as always, as only BOAM's could. Tripp judged, "Look at you. A beautiful attempt at reasonableness, sadly gone fishing in Little Loon Lake."

"Should have finished what you started."

The author turned from his beloved nemesis and spoke to Mr. Bruce. "Dear Senator, I did not finish college."

"So you have told me."

The author nee loud rocker, took the distinct ingredients from the glass champagne flute again as Moah concluded his opinion, "Should have finished."

Mr. Bellows attention remained with Mr. Bruce. "Senator, I read that there are two types of individuals that never get it. Those who never listen or do as they are asked and those that always do as they're told." Tripp took another sip before engaging again, "Especially when it's involving a woman..."

"What a dreary dude you are, Moah. But now, to the owner of The W. Blog, Mrs., make that Ms. Carmoni, thank you, my child and thank all for coming, friends and other persuasions, those inelegant disasters, my agents and publishers, whom, I hope they recall I selected for their magnificent senses of humor. The staff, the fans, of course." The lady with the pigtail returned and Tripp spotted her and blurted out, "Sports logos are our hieroglyphics, people, our most sacred carvings." He watched her sit close. He took another drink of champagne.

As the young lady with the pig tails became more comfortable, her lettering on her t-shirt came into focus, and "Horny but Honest" became a source of crowd control all its own as it quickly became common knowledge that the pressman would not be writing a column that evening. With a little more volume then previously, "And here's to justice in America, especially if you can afford it. You know, that kind of velvety attraction you pray above for, a personal request from whence you do not recall, a surreal plea that sweet justice goes ahead and stumbles, trips up for you for just one more night, leave consequences searching for just one more time."

As Bellows publishers lost count of the toasts and other vested participants squirmed, Cade could not resist a perceived advantage.

"Justice? You're kidding! Celebrities get away with mayhem and murder and worst of all the mundane, frequently then leaving the garbage of their ways for others to study as these ungenerous ones happen to be more than understudies at pulling solid alibis out of somebody else's arse. I mean, isn't at all about assisting in the downfall of another famous 'other' that this is a cherished sport throughout the cine and the polo clubs of America?" The publisher and agent succeeded drawing crowd away from Bellows and friends by offering and Ms. Carmona led in this offering even more discounts, free drawings for books and Wag The Blog gifts; anything to draw them away from the author and now the mogul too.

"There's a systematic insipid stretching the truth here about these days, rich defendants buy their lives back while the poor are put to death. Here can we agree, Cade? Take a swig that bubbly so you're on my par, will yah?"

"Bad things happening to good people and its legal." And Cade put his flute out for more. The others recognized that all was well as Cade and Tripp were visibly satisfied that they had conducted their signature argument and agreement conversational style to the best of their abilities considering the brand of champagne and all.

They sat in the oversize leather chairs. Cade pulled out an oversize Cuban to suck.

"She's very pretty. So, oh my God beautiful."

"My cigar?"

"No, you decadent dick, Sorry, Godboy, but you know what I mean."

"The lady is slobbering downspout beautiful. Yes."

Tripp frowned towards the Navaho. "Takes her sweet time pattering her nose." "Wondering who she's with now, I bet." Sean contributed.

"That will come, I'm sure," Moah chided.

Cade appeared puzzled. "I wonder if any woman from my memories, if they ponder, if she ponders if she is with if she would have been better off with me?"

"Whoa, heavy load there, my man".

Isaac, with the perfect timing of a musician trying to time a pause for emphasis, "Probably not."

"Never forget, Tripp, as a man that what if I think what she thinks is what I think that I think than I know I am thinking so wrong. See, I found that out on my first marriage."

"You were only married once, fool."

"It's sad crazy what you say."

Women have an edge when it comes to reading someone....our reads, though..."

"Man reads..."

"Yeah, Cade, for instance, legs crossed; feet flat on the ground arms crossed they are convinced that you're really not what you say you are... Woman drinking from a straw as if this movement is a transferable talent, now there's a 'tell' there."

"Only sorry cowboys would ever miss that."

"Yeah, Thomas Crown affair with Queen Dunaway and the Bishop getting fondling practice going on the chessboard as McQueen took notes."

"Worldwide, woman with down cast eyes, men will look at her. She looks down before she looks away, that's submission."

"What part of the world are you talking about with this mess?"

"When the women cross her ankles under chair they like what they see."

"Yeah, and if they have both feet flat on the floor it means they're ready to meet troops somewhere."

Ms. Carmona brought a decanter and put it on the table, nodded and left for more productive areas of her business... As Chaz poured the first glass some kind of healthy looking punch, he almost shouted, "Livingstone."

"The lost English dude, Africa?"

"One in the same. Or was it Stanley? Did you know, Cade that the man reported on the tribe of the Makololo and the women of the Makololo tribe... They lived by the Zambezi River and these women were shocked to hear from Livingston that in his home country of England a man only had one wife, and this was shocking to the Makololo ladies, because as Livingstone, yes that's the one, he wrote that to the Makololo to have only one measly wife was to have no respect, to be a poor man indeed. And with this in mind, I say to a toast to Mormon men and their strength to endure the burden of respectability for all the rest of us."

"That's mind blowing." And Cade raised his glass. "To desirable perspiration's!"

"Indeed."

The others had poured the mango appearing refreshment into their glasses and tasted it. Godboy wondered if Ms. Carmona had made it an adult punch but he wasn't about to ask, just in case she had.

The Navaho spoke, "Here's to living where life is large and living American is the only charge."

All followed the pleasant wish and drank to the request.

"Excellent smoothies, yes."

"Yes, and you can't even discern the rum." Sean observed.

"I thought it was vodka," countered Moah.

And Godboy was pleased.

"There's a home in my soul for the crafty, not the cunning, mind you, that's only healthy respect, but no, I mean 'crafty'." Tripp waited for response.

"Such as?" Cade could not help himself.

"Something justice this way comes."

"I take that as possibly negatory vibes towards authority figures and I salute you, Mr. Bellows."

"Thank you, Mr. Halas. But remember, I'm speaking 'crafty', that talent that shines, beating proud with the risible perseverance of a religion thoroughly versed in endless confidants and Fabreche confederations. For example, my children, I present the sect called the Lothardi; lived sometime in the 1300's.

"In their approach to a moral life, conservative trappings certainly ruled but they also believed that moral lives could be above ground practices only."

"What?"

"They cleared their consciences by putting in stone that if you were at least 27 inches, not 25, not 26, but 27 inches below the surface, and anything goes. Hence, all the Lothardi meetings were held in caverns and they were orgies. All, I assure you, below 27 inches beneath the floor, all those prudes pimpin' about on the downlow." Tripp spotted the girl slowly making her way towards him. "What are the odds of religion actually being a cleaner game than politics? Fifty-fifty? People used to think that you didn't have to be born into wealth to be in government. How sad."

"The more I read the more I become disgusted. And what is said these days," Moah continued, "Mouthed magniloquent malignancies, that's a lot of what I hear."

The Senator appropriately frowned again.

"My network is multifunctional. Heroes and Hell. Cover them both. That's what I sell. For instance, rocker boy, you know that this nation of ours is completing an average of the construction of a new prison every week?"

"And making you more money than Midas."

"Now there's justice for you, boys."

"Yeah, right, Moah. Child services can take the child away because they're trained to regard the parents as abusers first, they can enter a home even pick up the child away from the parents presence and then the fathers first to be disposed or how about the Supreme Court allowing police to search more freely? Your car, your trash?"

"One favorite specimen never leaves my memory; largest mass murder Rhode Island history, 1996. My dad pointed this baby at me before he passed. Guys name Tapia, set this fire four children died playing. He received, since liberal robed child judge sided with the defense attorney who threw the baggage of bad childhood and single parent home in the presentation of a highly polished excuse. Guy is eligible for parole in 20 or so years? That's how it ended. Justice? Another guy, again my dad highlighted this about guy in New Orleans."

"Nuns love that city."

Moah continued, "The guy shoots two, robs the bodies. He's caught literally red-handed. But the law, the Almighty balances the scales has the freedom to allow him to plead guilty to manslaughter and with added sugar did this killer sees eligibility for parole after only four years, yeah, four years."

"Justice, right? A couple of brothers beat and rape a woman in Atlanta. These are previous offenders, mind you, and they get one-year sentences all this to save time and trouble the prosecution with the ugliness."

Clenching his teeth Cade responded, "Justice this way comes when a guy grows pot in his basement to treat severe arthritis. An informant tells police that the guy is a meth head. Police raid home, find pot. This is a true one, Chaz, the guy gets 93 year sentence."

"That can't be recently?"

"That cannot be serious, Cade." The Senator was truly incredulous.

"Justice this way comes when a teenager attacks a guy with an ax. The perpetrator serves a third of his sentence. He gets out and murders someone's loved one. Guy cost taxpayers in the tens of millions of dollars. Serves half his sentence and repeats. Contrast thousands of Americans who have hard time for possession."

"Giving head to the vapid. Sorry, Godboy."

"Heard it before." Moah gauged correctly.

Tripp, down stage once again, "Equal justice doesn't belong in the same breath, the same orbits of meanings as something to be taken really seriously. Aw shucks populists head to D.C., all acting like a Mr. Smith while doing the dosey dough, servicing with lobbyists, licking each other saying they both are really clean."

Moah engaged, "Sooner or later children will wonder why, Chaz, the children will wonder why, right, will wonder whether or not it is really alright to be brought up by people who cheat and steal?"

"Liars elected by pacified dupes. That's the game board now, gentlemen."

"Yes, Sean, and they're just waiting for dissent to die, Chaz, Cade, that's all." The Senator's insight, welcomed, wrapped in significance and sadness, bulls-eyed big time. Chaz watched as Ms. Pinckney returned from another quick soiree around the grounds and she looked at him and smiled and shrugged and then said, "People are lacking in the brushstrokes of life. The uninvolved, the sweet abstemiousness of groups among us these days, the allegorically challenged counted on by the high and mighty to dutifully ruminate on the unimportant, on trash stamps, and on the absurd, purpose being, why to assist, no, to frame life in such a way that whatever the dealings of the wealthy they are always mythic and therefore they are always untouchable and sacrosanct, because, you see, life on a 'how do you want me' basis is never assailable and with a ready supply of the socially tattooed at the beck and call on standby, ready for the stake of easy blame, all's revealed for its nature, for all is divergence, gentlemen ,and all is wound tight to keep all the collective eyes off all the collective balls in the air and nothing more."

Tripp broke the men's stunned silence. "Wow, I could not have described it more evenly considering the condition you're in."

Emily laughed and signaled, "Will get us two to go."

"For the limo?"

"Perhaps." And she was into the distance and moving well.

"She's preparing to make her escape to me."

Cade let this slide as he well knew his friends habit of unleashing unbounded fondness for the quirky and for the beautiful and this lady, this bookworm in bob tails was assuredly a breathing, clear thinking, leave a giant sized footprint representation of what Mr. Bellows felt kept Mr. Bellows young and Cade was happy for his friend.

"We'll survive, you and I, Cade, as we know how to roll with the pandas in the bamboo; been in more cultural exchanges, let's call them, than the alphabet has letters, right?"

"You love her lots already, mucho correcto?"

"She's uneven while simultaneously off the charts smooth. She's related to Charles Pinckney."

"Who?"

"Nearly won presidential election; from South Carolina, 1800 or so."

"Ah, Emily."

Chaz turned to greet the lady, "Drinks to go, oh honey, you should have!" All right, shall we?"

"Yes."

Cade waved his rehabilitated half filled flute. The others signaled happy adieus with their mango smoothies as Tripp, leaving with Emily in hand, returning the waves couldn't help himself as he lifted to another time, to an assortment of concerts and trained roadies, artisans in setting up the quick and the easy from the front rows, only the ones you dipped your guitar towards would you accept, mind you, yes. His staged memory of how he would usually be in waiting arms and iced therapy of chilled alcohol within four minutes flat, from the last bow to the driver opening the door, four minutes flat, and now back to now, he had on his arm the potential of 'The Bomb' in beautiful quirkiness, and as his friend, Cade, across over there by Sean, of all gathered, Cade, understood better than the rest the circumstances unfolding, saying to no one in particular as the couple left to fans applause, "Now, that's, that's justice."

In four minutes flat.

CHAPTER 10

"If You Have A Fast Car, You Can Get A Lot Done"

"I hope we shall...crush in its birth the aristocracy of our moneyed corporations, which dare already to challenge our government to a trial of strength and bid defiance to the laws of our country."

Thomas Jefferson to George Logan
1816

October 31st, 2015

Sixty nine feet in elevation, approximately thirty miles from Washington D.C., Mount Zion, Maryland, is headquarters for Magi Incorporated, presently hosting its annual Halloween charity party; a costume and candy fest for underprivileged children, children that needed all of about five minutes to quickly change into spooks, demons, and other meaningful frightful attire, so very important for children still alive with belief in mystery and miracle. Donors were given a choice of masks handed out at the party entry as well as given golden envelopes expected to be used sometime, in the midst of wonderfully swirling freaky streaks of color and material, giggly disfigurements and the clamor of child joy, as vessels of kindness, because enclosed within the envelopes are spooky sized donations placed into huge barrels posing as witches brew pots with all proceeds dedicated to easing the future of the little goblins sugaring about the room as well as semi pacifying the collective conscience of the donors, with most wondering if they should be feeling guilty, embracing it, because as they consider their golden situations in life, the 'there but for the grace of God' line keeps playing in their heads and somehow they sense a kind of shame at their fortune. At least most do. Not all.

The CEO-CFO stood on a raised platform with his new legislative friend. Both smiled at the scene of "nice" parading around below them.

"I arrange destinies and it sometimes fun."

The senator remained silent, now grown used to the audaciousness of her newest lover-in-waiting.

"And he coordinates fate."

She followed Hawkins-Burke's pointed finger down to a man a couple hundred feet away on the right. She looked at the older man then back to the younger. "The craft of his engines hath passed his dream, in haste to the good or the evil goal."

The owner of Magi allowed bewilderment to sample his face but just as quickly it was gone. She noticed.

"That's Sophocles, darling, from Antigone."

"Ah, a woman thing of course."

Orange and black crepe streamers fell on them from an overhead beam and as they playfully unraveled, Senator Langtree pronounced, "It should've been a pumpkin on you, Ichabod!"

Undeterred, he continued, "He's an artist."

"Who?"

"Hyde."

"I've dealt with him a couple of times. Through third parties, always."

"Of course."

"The artist illuminates the inspiration but not the source of the light. Manipulate, agitate, postulate, that's Hyde's acronym, MAP, MAP for success." The Senator maintained her distant stare. "Toynbee argued that the greater the technological triumph, the greater the risk of spiritual devastation."

"As you well know the lay of the board game, Senator, lobbyists overseas, they assist; they are the insiders who help build new futures in new places."

"The henhouse for the foxes."

"They save welfare for stockholders, save productive America from tax, fines, and pliable claims and spurious charges, hell, they know their turf, and they can take this climate out of climate change and put the worst pollution as a positive agenda. And Hyde's an incomparable agenda setter."

"And the shiftiest among us is that man you have harped on for the past, oh, four minutes or so?''

"Yes, the one and the same you have been staring a hole through, yes, that's him."

"Well, he's in his costumed best, in a three piece look at me, suitable for framing others. Jansen Hyde. Stuart, I can unequivocally state that he is one of my least favorite Irishman."

"Some natives insist true Irishman distinguish between 40 shades of green."

Hawkins Burke again indicated towards his business associate.

"That is why he handles all my green efforts."

"Environmentally, Mr. big bugshot, what do you advocate for?"

"By greening up I mean my financial gardens, Ms. Langtree, and, oh, those of the shareholders too."

"But of course."

She sipped a small amount of juice, then, "The strong are not easily influenced by morality." Still eyeing Hyde, the man with the reputation of managing manners with money equally as well as he massaged, cajoled, and prophesized in tireless effort to help along, get passed strings-attached regulations and other benefits for the taking from those with the power at the stroke of a pen. Hyde pushed his way, his benefactors' way, as far as any non-elected citizen ever had been able to before. "Fete those with the most to lose, correct, Stuart?"

"Least resistant, yes." Hawkins-Burke was an adoring fan of Hyde's ability to cloud, to portray opponents of Magi as enemies of America while simultaneously defeating broad consensus and other bothersome alliances to secure not what was necessarily best for the majority but contribute to the good health and welfare of the Corporation. Hyde was thoroughly versed in making potential grievances expensive, perplexing and massive regarding the scope and size of the projected amount of the courts possible waste of time, enough so that any judgments by the peers usually went down black holes because of time expansion, pleasing mistrials, if circumstances even reached that far, would always be the pleasing result. The CEO-FFO excused himself from Sen. Langtree in order to make his way to the temporary dais to give perfunctory comments about helping the gathered downtrodden climb the ladder to success and use the phrase of promise that Hyde had concocted, "Donate, Germinate and Celebrate." Hyde had instructed early in their relationship that, "Charity promotes smaller fines and reduced jail times." And Hawkins-Burke proved an effective student with his instituting a standard operating policy of non-business-related giving and because of the Hyde 'work,' at the same time, effectively avoiding the appearance of self-aggrandizement.. As Hyde had summed it up then, "If I ever do something to the worst of my abilities in your behalf, the worst you might ever get is six months of home detention." And this, Stuart had shared with Lilith, was the deal maker.

Sen. Langtry watched as Hawkins-Burke stepped up to the raised platform but she could not help but remain curious about the mentor now standing off to the left of the mini stage, unobtrusive, nondescript, and as she knew, dangerously proud, not easily penetrated or friable. Nicknamed "The Great Lubricator", Jansen Hyde was a diabetic with the George Hamilton tan clothed in the Alexander Hamilton elite brutishness of denim, who believe there was way too much sweetness in government, an overabundance of pushover phraseology and not enough pumping of fists. "Focus on the contrivances of men and make them work for you. Adoration with purpose can never be dismissed."

His gray eyes could deliver the ice if the desires of his clients were not met or if his self-taught impeccable approach to the business of commiseration and compensation were interrupted by orders of discontent which installed or blocked anything or anyone that negated Hyde's control of both sides of any issue in the money tree that has always kept the District of Columbia and surrounding suburbs the lowest unemployment levels, Congress... Hyde was Magi Inc.'s level one transactional closer slash fixer, a last option in a corporation's business policy plan when something is not written down for present guidance from previous experiences. His career choice had become even wiser when George Bush was elected and 9/11 happened. The defense industry money pit became God sized; fears wallowing in fervent patriotism just as the press suddenly became docile about the subject of conflicts of interest and zeroed in on the claim of weapons of mass destruction....hence, prying eyes were off the ball as newspaper 'peepers' preferred shades to magnifying glasses.

At 5'10", still naturally dark hair, muscular build for a man 56 years old, Jansen Hyde was an imposing figure accompanied by an almost lyrical smooth voice, folded in a playfully diabolical tone, steeped in mischievous possibilities, always present in the man when he found himself in the presence of an organized, brilliant woman, whom, he anticipated in positive light, would possibly be a difficult lover, his favorite type.

Senator Langtree chortled to herself. Hyde was rumored to be quite the paramour. Ah, the cultivation of another rough-edged, paper thin truth, syruped up mightily in thick bulging lies and, as usual, balance takes a fall. She amused at the effort everyone around her puts forth to attempt composure, to try and ignore, but, one can't help but stare. It's the DC way. It's the scene of an accident that never fades away. It's the brown tips on the green blades of grass; it's the assumption of attraction being taken for granted.

It's the disgruntled always racing in first to distance themselves from the disgraced. She watched his posture, and even from her distance of observation, he carried well. Hyde was born in the Virgin Islands. Family had owned a Hilton in St. Croix, St. Thomas market. His father was friend to many administrations and their personnel. Contacts came quickly and at the earliest of stages for the young Hyde.

He was divorced by his now ex-wife, Annie Nickman, after the last of his three daughters graduated college. Their hobbies had been polo and other activities the privileged did well. They remained in contact through their respective C.P.A.'s and through infrequent phone calls. Annie was a brilliant lawyer, but, in Jansen's opinion, unchanged from day one of their first contact, Annie's weakness's were that she led with her heart; that she had values, and that it was hard for her to be 'conditional' on anything.

He stayed in touch with the daughters and lovingly doted on them as did Ms. Nickman. The daughters frequently acted as go-betweens between their parents which actually did save the family a lot of money that otherwise would've been spent on high-priced attorneys and other over glorified mouth pieces. Jansen Hyde always seemed to know which shell the ball was under. To Hawkins-Burke, he appeared almost hypnotic in his dedication working for his clients and for his benefit: how the man used the special power of a fear whose time has come to work bottom line, well, magic. One of Hyde's responses to one of Hawkins-Burkes questions during the getting to know each other period was ingrained into Stuart's mind. "There can be profit in most problems, most especially if one expands the problem and then solicits the solution and gets credit for solving the deal much like a gun dealer who is instigating crime in his neighborhood in order to boost sales of its weapons and ammunition while simultaneously, he's profiting from pushing, as Hyde phrased it, 'in terms the young and devious can comprehend' the 'phat of fear'.

Hyde's home in the Islands, tile of every hue, linear lines; 'Minoan', a friend deemed it,' everything Minos would appreciate,' except Hyde's waterfront domain did not include large wall murals of bare-breasted attractive women flipping themselves over the horns of charging bulls nor did it include a Minotaur. Hyde had many options the day before meeting and tying up with Hawkins-Burke. As an ex-cabinet member, he could command a minimum of $60,000 on lecture circuit or he could've brought out his law degree out of the storage chest and earned a few million per annum, but Jansen had not come to this junction in life to fail at opting for the biggest opportunity yet, and it was with Magi, Inc., and the intriguing, Hawkins-Burke.

Ms. Langtree, from bitter experience, knew that, unless it would assist her election, and even, then it had better be monumental to do so, not to antagonize a man such as Jansen Hyde; a fixer that wields such influence and he could see to it that none of her bills would ever see the light of day if she were ever a participant on his shit list. She wasn't listening to Hawkins Burke's closing marks, instead calculating the future; how she might benefit from a little closer association with Magi's mentor, the eminent practitioner of late and not debated for even a minute additions to spending bills, the chief instigator of loopholes of so 'Oh My God' proportions, it left even envious Wall Street speechless. She noted Hyde's apparent humbleness and rectitude in public is nearly impregnable to assault, and had assisted magnificently in the working of seemingly legislative miracles beneath the dome of rumbling redundancies, Solzhenitsyn subtleties and blood matches of the truly misinformed, the Congress of The United States of America.

In a city where maneuvering is as daily an exercise as brushing your teeth, the authority on manipulation and charm with a smile to match was Mr. Hyde and it had been such for a notable length of time.

Sen. Langtree watched him and watched Hawkins-Burke as he waved to the assembled needy's applause at the completion of Hawkins-Burkes short 'commercial'. Through the clapping noise and other high pitched distractions, the Senator recalled Stuart's sharing of another of Hyde's observations. Hawkins-Burke told Lilith it was during their first interview about going into business together. Stuart had said, "Mr. Hyde quoted Plutarch to me, Lily, within 5 minutes of our first contact! Nobody quotes anyone anymore least of all, something with sinew in it."

Lilith continue to watch as Hyde shook Hawkins-Burkes' hand as the leader of Magi, Inc. made ready to slowly make way up and away from the skeletons, the hobos, the princesses, and transformers buzzing around him and below her.

The quote used by Hyde was attributed by Plutarch to Alexander the Great "God is the common father of all men, but he makes the best one's peculiarly his own."

Hawkins-Burke neared and she grinned. He shared with her that he thought the event was going well and that all was good as could be hoped for at a charity event. She interrupted him.

"Tell me more about Hyde, Stuart."

"The blade cuts clean, exquisitely sharp without blood or splatter, so precise it is. Now mingle with me, my lady, if only for a few tidy meet and greets, shall we?"

"Just the appropriate amount of face time for a man of the people, right?"

Hawkins-Burke acknowledged the sarcasm with a hint of highbrows, "Absolutely, but damn, wealth is in the giving, right?" As they turned together to play "public", his mind meandered, brought on by the chemical biological workings of memory and repetition, and unfortunately for him, the repetitiveness of his inability to escape his one big private question, the origins of his existence. Who was his non-stage, non-superstar parents? He never pursued the question in too much detail or in too much depth for fear of finding and attempting to confront the actual reason for abandonment and subsequently failing, not being able to control it for the remainder of life. What the Hell, I turned out fine in my own little pursuit of happiness. Why mess it up with silly little superficial bouts of regret anyways. Stuart felt good. "Jansen's unlike you in that he is not one for ornamentation," and quickly sensing the urgency for rapid recovery, "but, dear, that's of course because he doesn't have the goods like you to succeed in that league, now does he?"

She knocked away a couple of floating orange black helium balloons tied to a table. And she asked him, "What's the best arrangement or deal he's produced for you, for Magi, or," and she smiled, "...maybe the most devious that he's accomplished for you?"

He paused. Her coolness was a turn on.

"The ability to repeat, to recycle though, to grow currency, that's the cloak of his worth, Lilith." They both looked at the photographer and smiled for the picture which would make the circuits of the society pages and blogs the next day or two then they returned to each other.

"He shorts the market when the small guys fiddle. Short a countries currency, watch the bankers flee. Hyde's perfected the most painless methods of performing this."

"Painless for whom?"

"For us, of course. Make currencies crazy and time it for later to purchase everything back for pennies on the dollar. Clean, legal repossession of a good thing gone badly and make it all right again. Leave others to sort out what happened."

"He is brilliant man, yes." She nodded towards Mr. Hyde.

"Well, he is the gatekeeper, maybe, but he is not the king."

She tingled when she struck the jealous cord in vain men.

They watched Hyde at the exit door standing, surrounded by swarming trick-or-treaters and their doting parents, still patiently posing for group photos by thankful participants. "He's taught me, Lily, that the supercilious always dances the same steps as the serendipitous, that history is an arch of humor and hurt and that it doesn't pay to stomp on the toes of either as it will always trip you up as well." Stuart paused to take another drink. "As example number one of toe stomping catching up to people, Hyde presented to me, Pompey and Caesar. Pompey the Great knew Greek. He wasn't an uneducated soul, mind you, worked hard at appearances, showing deference in public to Roman vogue and to the most popular arts. He certainly made a big deal about the ceremonies; worshiping all the correct gods and making sure that his deference for said deities were duly noted. Simply stated, Pompey was a very decent soldier who became counsel. Wanted to be liked and respected, thought of in a good way as all of us do."

"Seems smart, but how does this wraparound Hyde's thinking, again?"

"First, Pompey, well, was not, well, very 'street' sharp."

"Oh? He did rule, didn't he? How?"

"Good God, Lilith, he married five times, how intelligent is that?"

She cackled at his pose of exasperation.

"Pompey, Hyde says, you can get sense of by simply remembering to connect his name to the word, 'pompous'. But here's the 'rub of time' as Jansen calls it. Pompey and Caesar grew apart and fought. Eventually, in 48 B.C., when Caesar was in Egypt pumping Cleo, he was presented, as a gift from King Ptolemy of Egypt, the head of his rival, Pompey. Caesar, stricken, ordered it taken away. He was horrified at the vision.

I'm sure it pleased him that his enemy was no more, but it probably reminded him of the potential of this happening to him too. Fear is never arm's-length proposal, Jansen says. But here's the kicker. Four years later, Ides of March, you've heard of?"

"Caesar had a bad day with Brutus, I believe."

"In the Senate, correct?"

"Yes."

"Wrong. Caesar was assassinated in a theatre."

"Like Lincoln?"

"You can say that. He was stabbed, though, knifed by traitors in a theatre that was built as a gift to the people of Rome, the benefactor, whose statue Caesar bled to death beneath the base of, was none other than, yes, you guessed it, Gnaeus Pompeius Magnus, Pompey the Great."

The Senator drew a breath. "And the song remains the same."

The titian haired senator and the capitalist enter a hallway leading to another of his offices.

"Jansen could've taught, professor emeritus, anywhere. He is the best I've ever seen at pellucid presentation with a posture, a physical warning that 'here is an individual that will suffer no bumptiousness whatsoever, even as he mollifies them, the targets of his disdain. That's talent Washington gets, bows to, isn't it?"

She nodded, slightly.

"It's alchemy for achievement, mix the soft with the firm and leave only one choice, no stinking options needed. Jansen knows where to tap to get the sap."

Ms. Langtree watched as Mr. Hawkins-Burke carefully opened the cabinet behind the small desk as he pulled out a bottle of top shelf cognac.

"There is a God." He opened the liquor and poured it out for her. "Jobs said it best." He raised his glass to meet hers. "Oh wow. Oh wow. Oh wow; now that's genius way of saying, I told you so."

"Bewitchingly beautiful, yes."

CHAPTER 11

"Don't Sit Under The Boa Tree With Anyone Else But Me."

"One's real life is often the life than one does' not lead."

Oscar Wilde

November 7, 2015

Above the fold and above the eye-catching red and yellow lettered bigger stores' display advertising pitching Black Friday specials sales offers, premium positioning in the desired bottom borders of page one, the headline in The Tulsa Worlds Special Pre-Thanksgiving Day edition read, "Preacher Killed By Light From Above". The newspaper story describing the preacher's new wife as saying she found him prone on the floor of their multimillion dollar production facility with a Klieg light on his "much fractured skull." Details were sketchy as the tragedy had occurred just before the papers deadline for going to print.

What Tulsa, a city frequently cited in reports as America's town for cheapest gasoline prices with the most churches per capita in the country as well as reigning one of the communities in America with the highest divorce rate, would not be made aware of for months is what the Tulsa County authorities found at the scene.

The preachers third wife was not helpful as all she could cry was, "He said to 'go sit, to wait in the Cadillac' as he had to go over minor funding details with a new donor and that 'it would only take the time to sign the agreement, no more, no less and then dinner at Jamils.' Those were his last words to me, detectives."

According to one detectives interview notes, which were scheduled to never be released to the public, detailed the preacher's third wife as 'a mix between Tammy Faye with real lashes and Dolly P. with nearly normal sized 'palm pilots' preceding her every move.' The preacher never conducted the profitable business of being an electronically inclined evangelist in her presence. The preacher, a flawed account executive in his early career, had soon found his niche in promoting compassion, pity, and salable blessings in the shape of 5 inch by 5 inch, guaranteed suede replicas of the Shroud of Turin material at $50 per "Righteous Rag" as he called the items in private. "And praise the Lord, tax free too." The court would eventually revealed evidence that tended to the occurrence not being accidental. No fingerprints or DNA separate from the third wife or employee list were gathered. Detectives documented, still withheld from the public, that a row of overhead stage lights had been rigged with wireless electrical magnets used as clasps and that they had been apparently released to fall on the victim by distance control upon the receipt of a transmitted wireless signal.

Saved or unsaved, it really didn't matter when the lights fell on the man of the "cloth." It also gradually leaked out that two items had been left on the body. A type written note which simply read, "He could not see the light for the gleam of the gold." And placed with obvious emphasis on the dead man's groin were a pair of expensive white bright gloves, with each finger and thumb stretched out as if 'pushing against a demon seed', as a female detective had commented at the scene. Check of security cameras were of no use as they had been turned off. A creature of habit, the preacher had kept the cameras turned off the day of the homicide as he always did when he was involved in raising funds that were, well, not for broadcast campaign purposes and not to be recorded for the Almighty nor recorded for posterity nor for the agents of the Secretary of the Treasury nor for the attorneys on behalf of previous soul mates, his ex wives. The story would grow and eventually compete in interest level with both the continuing decades' long community saga of the city attempting to develop the Arkansas River with a series of expensive dams and with the story of the seemingly never ending efforts for the city of Tulsa to seriously consider competing in the bid for bringing the summer Olympics to the Sooner state.

The preacher 'story' would grow larger than local in soon enough time.

CHAPTER 12

"Touch The Note"*

*Bellows quote #1

> *"You are literally touching musical notes on guitars, more so than other instruments, because, with a guitar, it's the closest thing to the gut and to the groin when being played."*

Bellows quote #2

> *"Always watch out for the player with two necks on the guitar."*

November 29th, 2015

> *"For since their votes have been no longer bought,*
> *All public care has vanished from their thought,*
> *And those who once, with unresisted sway,*
> *Gave Armies, empire, everything, away,*
> *For two poor claims have long renounced the whole*
> *And only ask - the Circus and the Dole."*

Juvenal, Roman Poet, CA A.D. 55-130

Minerva's Taverna was Chaz's second restaurant. It presently hosted the owner and Ms. Pinckney.

"No, I'll never be a politician. You asked that and you say you know me? I cannot lie and smile. I either do one or the other."

The ring counter studied the fresh blood purple ring on her wine glass, grinned, and said, "Why not? People have applauded your skeletons already and I..."

"Politicians hire consultants to enhance the politician's ability to state the obvious in a new way. That's all."

Minerva's evening crowd was thickening. Chaz hailed his manager, Jackie, "More vino the gods, all right? And some shrimp, please. That's all right, right, Emily? Good. And Jackie, put up the velvet cord. Keep em at bay, please. Thank you, yeah, thanks."

He turned back to Emily to hear, "The women or the critics?

"What?"

"Fans and pans, Maestro, keep them all a king size bed distance from you, yeah?"

"You are a wise woman for any age."

"A definite compliment coming from one of such a swollen sample size." He laughed and he was young again. She felt life was light hearted again and laughed to that hope as they reached for each other's free hand.

"I couldn't deal with the focus groups like a Clinton or an Obama, whether to use the word, 'invest' and not 'spend'. When talking about taxes, people's cash, politicians are cavalier with the subject because it's not their subject 'matter'. They dispirit so many, so fast."

"Whoa, boy, there was meaning somewhere in them thar words."

"The journeys got to be fresher or people will just ignore."

"And you can walk the walk, Chaz."

"I swear three fourths of Americans are addicted to something so why would any political beast worry about people paying attention to what they do? Shit, it's perfect for the perpetually jaded because the other 25% of the population has been dumbed down by our system, so much so, that they don't have opinions they trust themselves, leaving only emotional strings which are easily strummed and drummed by the media and other accomplices on a daily basis; all, all of it predicated upon which masters bid the highest for the media to caddy, to carry the water for them that particular news cycle!"

Jackie unhooked the velvet cord and served the iced shrimp.

"Appears quite devourable." Emily judged, "Real word or not."

The owner thanked his faithful manager and asked, "Jackie, you're smarter than anyone for now in Minerva, accepting, of course, my favorite tree bee here..."

The women blushed slightly as women had for years in his presence, or so he thought.

"So I ask you; someone wise once said, and I sincerely wish I could recall the human that said it, quote," Until war is outlawed and overcome, civilization is a precarious interlude between catastrophes."

Jackie poured fresh wine, paused and said, "According to a Dutch dude I read about in Smithsonian or was it Scientific American, oh, well, he said something like that, he said, our technology, affluence, our population extinctions of plants and animals in the past half billion years there's been something like five catastrophic 'goodbyes'; asteroids, and other natural roughhouse events and he says this is what he called it, ah, the new Anthropogenic epoch, with the sixth wipeout coming on strong, so yes, yes, I think as Pogo might say today "I have met the dilemma and the dilemma is us."

All grinned in agreement; Tripp, impressed that Jackie knew about Pogo, the swamp character of long ago comics sections and Emily; impressed that Jackie's view of mankind was the same as hers.

In playful 'Southern', Jackie checked, "Anything else now, yaa all?" Emily responded, "No thank you, ...Scarlet." Jackie returned both their smiles and then was off to the front to greet Minerva's most recent arrivals.

"She's as talented as any Cleopatra, as beautiful as Queen Nefertiti and is God damn soulful as anyone I've ever encountered, Chaz."

"She's a single mom with four superb kids and try as I have, I can't find a way to duplicate her so she could shipshape The Flooze too."

Emily sipped some more. "I'm serious about you running, not just commenting. We are stuck, I mean all of us, everyone with two pusillanimous parties, Chaz. By their acts they've squelched the quest for value. Tripp, it's these times, these ways, they cannot be allowed to go on."

"Absolutely bull's-eye, babe. Politicians spend bucks on some polls and on some special people called consultants telling them what not to say and that's why I write instead and am not a politician. I say what I think needs to be said through the narrow detonations of perfectly-used words."

He took a sip. "I don't need a poll to pronounce what's pissing me off." "You can't put a price on defeating the unimaginative, the ordinary, the dull, can you?"

"Scuttled preconceptions work, always have, always will."

"Unfortunately, it can take years for people to catch up to "smart", doesn't it?"

"Terse, pithy, but sometimes distracting, detracting entanglements, though."

"Jesus, woman; you should have been the one with the book signing!"

Emily horse laughed, "Well, you do know that the first author poet known by name in history, was a woman, right?"

"What?"

"Of course you do, right? She was the first feminist too."

"Oh, God help us!"

"A Mesopotamian priestess, the daughter of Sargon the Great."

"Now, I've heard of him."

"But, of course, and not heard of her, though."

"Well, not..."

"She was Enheduanna of Sumaria from the city of Ur, rhymes with 'her' and don't you forget it, buster."

"My God, I've grabbed a buzz saw by it blades, haven't I and to pile on, you're a cat lover too!"

"Don't go insulting Stella. She'll get used to you eventually just as I will, I suppose." He smiled above the rim of his glass, sipped and, "Do you know that dogs appear in the Bible forty times and cats, only once."

She sat back from the table and with a serious pose but with give-away-eyes, "Tripp, your business is nothing more than commenting on earthquake imbroglios, purchased peccadillo's and rare instances of intelligence by accident, while all the time you are curled up with your sorry comfort of barley and Zen; now how tough is that, really?"

Then, so uncharacteristically for Emily Pinckney, "And I love you."

The front man for The Cures, noted columnist and, now, published author, stumped, stone cold silent and so very, very pleased, finally responded with (what would eventually become a private joke between them), "More shrimp? Probably needs more ice; yes, I'll call Jackie."

"You do that, Isaac.'

And he laughed. And they laughed together and they laughed well aware that love is ticklish, pleasurable to the point of pain and frequently, fleeting. So peel the crustaceans, Emily, down the vineyards' gift, Chaz, for tomorrow, life may take it on the chin and we may never laugh again.

CHAPTER 13

"Mattresses, Mirth and Madness"

"My particular inner desire to fly the Atlantic alone was nothing new with me. I had flown the Atlantic before. Everyone has his own Atlantic to fly. Whatever you want very much to do, against the opposition of tradition, neighborhood opinion, and so-called 'common sense'-that is an Atlantic."

Amelia Earhart
American Aviator

December 1st, 2015

The week of November 24 through November 30 had been another engaging body high time between lovers. Ms. Gabriel was nearly finished with describing what happened to Ms. Vanessa Ricks, Odessa's personal assistant and ready confidant.

"A soldier with a romantic streak, I'm telling you, Rikki, Sean's found locales for le amour, well, Rocky and Adrienne found it in alleys and in a pet store in Philly. We found it by geysers, ports and the sea and Jackson Hole, goodness. I see why Native Americans thought Yellowstone a sacred mystical place, even more so in winter. I told you I did love Port Angeles and Sunset Beach, but, girl, being in the grasp of God's ultimate goody bag for human enjoyment, just you and your lover in a snowed in cabin, fire roaring; there's no better, no way.''

'Rikki' did not remind Ms. O that Sean and she had actually stayed at director friends vacant for the holiday 13,000 square foot 'cabin'.

"We had our bird for T-day, and then we ate."

"God, you're a nasty witch, aren't you?"

"We nibbled on giblets and gobbled way more than even I thought possible."

When their laughter settled, Rikki reminded, "Please excuse, chief, but I've got to go take a schedule of marketing call-ins, so."

"Yes, time to go. I'm going out to get little golden rays to rinse the snows away. 75 degrees on the 1st of December, Vanessa."

"Yes, and smog be gone."

"Yes, see you later, bye."

Odessa, watermelon and coconut smoothie in hand, moved outside, gravitating towards the Jacuzzi side pool, resplendent in the Southern California shine. She relived his smile as she stepped in.

'At least he is as far from coquet as, well, I seem to attract those. No, Sean's 'demiurge'. She tickled herself as she thought of her sobriquet for him, 'Mr. Sober.'

The water felt wonderful and the jets satisfying and she replayed some of their conversations.

"I watched a little of the Series last month."

"Yes?"

"What's 'Hey, batter, batter', supposed to do? And why do ball batters blow on their hands when they are wearing some of the most garish gloves, and its 70 degrees out? How are they paid so much when they do things like this, Sean?"

Sean had just remained still until he didn't as he reached and held both her arms in his. He then had said, "Habeas Corpus, baby." Odessa remembered his eyes as he answered her knowing look with, "It's retrofitted Latin for, 'you have the body, baby.'" And then Mr. Sober had targeted Odessa's nape with a kiss and then her hand too and with this, the time for conversation ended and Odessa replayed it as she leaned back slightly more against the pool wall. She was focused on the recollection of his admirable puissance. She smiled at how they had spent their first day in Jackson Hole away from the world doing unworldly things.

"De la grande petite morte, mon ami. I'm fracturing two languages, but what the hell, who cares." And he didn't as he kissed her again.

"No one's laughed easier nor loved me harder than you, Sean."

She remembered his quietness and the blood finally returning to his smiling face.

"You are the best man that ever has happened over me," they then had literally giggled and embraced in another joyful release and it lasted.

She sat up and sipped the watermelon and the coconut.

The days in Key West in the Hemingway B and B were nice and unkept. They'd rented it out for themselves. Made love at the southern most point of the United States. A week later, we get up to the northwest point of the country in Port Angeles. Ha, need to head to the most northeastern point and make it happen in a light house in Maine. Four comers, even I haven't done that.

Pondering the possibilities, Odessa sipped more smoothie and let the remains decorate her lips.

She was now full relaxed and her mind wanted to play.

He'd half seriously inquired, "You're just a little disenchanted with reality like I am, aren't you?"

"Of course, "she'd replied, "it's my moneymaker." And Odessa recalled the thought she had as she watched his response, his kind face, his grin, and Odessa remembered her vision of a baby being tickled, laughing so hard, you are made whole by the tots' smile, you are changed.

Odessa opened her eyes. She stared skyward. Crosby, Stills, Nash wind-milled through her mind and she replayed more of what pleased her.

Sean was not inquisitive of family and, as she had said, "My mother is a minefield and I'm her little detonator, so don't go there." He'd dimpled a grin. "You are a bear of a man. You know, grizzlies, females, three years after birth, ovulate only by attention from potential mates. One third of all of their cubs survive the first year. First year! One in five of the little fur balls survive three years, so grizzly women want to make sure of the virile gene in the jeans of their grizzly man."

"We've been what a friend of mine would call, 'mating fools,' you know that, don't you?"

"We all fuck differently. You fuck with fascination and care for me. I fuck like an actress. Most women try to. Our deepest desires are carnal, Sean, at least in my world." She had then leaned close to his ear and whispered, "And by our experience, I'd say you are always the delicious tease and pretty randy."

Odessa put her hand above her brow. There's a noise in the air. The noise in the air is a banner plane. The banner, flagging, folding, ruffling so much that it wasn't clear as to what the letters were on the yellow background. 'Damn noisy' and then the long miles to SeaTac, Seattle's airport, came rushing. It was the most serious part of their trip, the inevitable time of questioning, and an all too familiar exercise to Odessa. In the limo, Sean had been silent for a while when I vocalized for both what intelligent people do; I've been pondering on as I'm sure you had too?"

"Do you know what the earth's speed is as it travels around the sun?"

Sean's inquiry had peaked Odessa's interest. She'd responded "Oh, of course, even Einstein's come for me, for my opinions, because I played a scientist on the movie screen, so sure, I've got that number right here on the tip of my... tongue, right."

Odessa recalled his seriousness. "What is it, Sean?

"Odessa, the earth races around about 67,000 miles per hour, and truthfully, I wonder if we are going even faster than that?"

She had slumped back in the plush leather and had glanced out the window at the passing cars and passing lights. Then she'd turned back to Sean who was looking straight ahead. "Maybe, Sean. I've seen enough real-time, real insane and relationships between two dominant personalities, it's tough, if not a nut cracker of a mistake."

Sean remained silent. "It's thought both are better alone or with someone they can dominate. That's what experts say."

Sean had turned to her with the shade of the smile, "It as with the Irish and Scots. They love hard and, Odessa,"

"Yes, they certainly do!"

"And, and they fight hard. And they never forget how much they put into a match so they have the hardest time forgiving the loss they feel."

They traveled the remainder of the ride in silence but had held hands. They kissed and hugged tightly when they had to head to separate concourses.

Odessa got out of the water, heading indoors. As she pulled the sliding glass doors to enter, she recalled the one thing worth remembering from her one and only session with a psychiatrist. The lady doctor had told Odessa, "You tend not to respect or have any admiration for a man you can dominate. So you fall in love, become attracted to Godzilla sized type "A's" such as yourself and you resist their need for control as they do yours and like the Roman candle, the fireworks are beautiful as they go off but the experience is not long-lived and when it's over, it's all ashes and bad smells and brittle sized memories." Then Odessa, thinking humor would mask her vulnerability, had replied to the doctor, "Well, what do you know, and here I thought it was all due to inadequate wicks."

As Odessa closed the patio door behind her, she wondered if the psychiatrist is married to a producer or to another psychiatrist. No worries; watermelon coconut, your mama's comin' home and Odessa zeroed in on the half filled blender resting on the kitchen island.

CHAPTER 14

"Do The Children Need To Know This?"

"(It) places a young person under a kind of compulsion to produce impressive quantities of scientific publications-a temptation to superficiality."

Albert Einstein, commenting about Academia

December 1, 2015

Sean called professor Sorentsen. He asked to attend class and have lunch afterwards. The professor eagerly agreed. When it was time, Sean sauntered into the theater styled lecture room a few minutes early. He had a four day beard, sunglasses and a still rumpled demeanor of someone, if the observers didn't know better, would say that Sean appeared to have been in bed for a week, at least. These pajama pundits and blog blasters would've been surprised to discover that they had finally been correct in one of the many youthful assumptions coexistent with university life and their generation, that 'bed' is the new 'religion'. Sean wore his favorite pair of frayed edge Levi's, completing the 'Non-descript me now' task. He noted that the professor remained the same at the podium, unmoved as ever by the cacophony of another self important generation coming through the class doors. It hasn't changed much from Sean's college days except for the technology, which has increased the rate for self absorption masking insecurity by twenty fold, if not more. Prof. Sorentsen had previewed the lesson plan on the phone. Sean was pleased as the topic was a favorite. The Professor waited until all were settled in. He flipped the switch and, with a noticeable preference for bass from the player, Joe Cocker's "Lie To Me" began the class. The actual lecture began with the last echo of the last lyric's fade to silence. Sean looked to his sides in the last upper rows. As the professor began, speaking very softly, Sean smiled as he saw the student's lean forward as the professor knew they would have to in order to understand him. It only took a sentence or two for the professor to ensure all would hear him clearly, front row to back row.

"Exam next Monday. Remember, green sparks inventiveness. Don't wear red for tests. But, for those of you that care, if you are playing intramurals this weekend or involved in a trivia drinking contest at one of the many bars mistaken for study halls around here, more matches are won by teams wearing red than by wearing blue. Blue makes you more comfortable but make it green, if you can, Monday, because from our first attempts at measuring what you've learned this semester, well, I dare say that it should make you red with embarrassment and green with envy at real student's efforts."

All gathered laughed, as all knew that the teacher really did care about them and that every word he said to register for longer than the attention span of a gnat; hence, the rock song and the humor.

"Today, we talk 'heroic'. Today, we talk 'Gracchi."

The professor began to turn towards the blackboard (he despised PowerPoint) but was interrupted as he noticed the reason University freshmen have keggers, sitting in the front row.

"And, no, the Gracchi were not fashion designers, Ms. Bonbo."

Sean noticed that Ms. Bonbo did not dislike the attention and he quickly surmised that Ms. Bonbo was an obvious philosophy major with a minor in tormenting boys and tenured men. No, no change. Freshman coeds still consumed all the air out of a class as males almost suffocated not by lack of oxygen but by swallowing their tongues.

"You do have your requisite notepads, of course." Professor barred laptop's, iPhone, iPads; any electronically driven device that interfered with the his proudly 'old' fashioned platform for learning; the establishment of an atmosphere by the professor in the classroom in which quietude lends success to more attentive minds, thereby lending a hand to instructions working hard to reach through the swirl of the noise of the day, just the brain, the pen, and the notepad, legal or regular sized. The laggards finally finished putting technology in its place beneath their desks or into their nearly weapon sized back packs. Sean noted that it appeared all 300 or so students understood that the rules of this lecture room also meant that even a hint of 'multitasking' would be considered profane by the person in control of the room.

"There will be no questions until I require them of you. You will write your thoughts as to what I say today about how what you hear from activities and commentary maybe a couple thousand years old or so and what you hear from, what you make of them? How what happened so long ago is relevant in how many ways and in how many manners to your world, the one you wade through today?"

Professor Sorentsen moved to the center of the walking area in front of the podium. "Joe Cocker's, "Lie To Me": would the Romans rock to that? Would they immediately recognize its relevance to their particular journeys through their particular time and their particular place? Again, I will segment parts; give you a moment or two to put in a sentence or two how what I say about the brothers Gracchi relate to buying into your world, today, maybe. Please sign your name and date at the top. You will be graded on clear fashion of your thinking, advocacy for your position, and your ability to write cursively, not cursive at me."

Groans are noticeable.

"Print, if necessary."

Sean recalled the first time the professor did this in Sean's class. Cade, Chaz, The Navajo agreed with him later that the process momentarily unnerved them all. But, after a couple of similar sessions and red ink adjustments by the professor on their paperwork, they became at ease with the suggestions to "Get comfortable with your thoughts, ladies and gentlemen. Don't be fearful of putting them down in print, cursively or otherwise, naked to review, rebuke, celebration or a combination thereof. It can only help you if you allow it."

"Number one." The professor had Sean's attention in the here and now once again. "This is from Plutarch; he is quoting parts of a speech by Tiberius Gracchus. Ready?"

Dr. Sorentsen peered over his half-glasses to see if he had the attention of the 300 and he did. "And it so goes, quote, "The wild animals that range over Italy have a hole, and each of them has its lair and nest, but men who fight and die for Italy have no part or lot in anything but the air and the sunlight. It is for the sake of other men's wealth and luxury that these go to the wars and give their lives. They're called the lords of the World, and they have not a single clod of earth to call their own." Again class, this is Plutarch putting down information about the Gracchi, this being Tiberius."

The professor looked up towards Sean and nodded. He took a few minutes perusing the heads bowed with a few raised, looking heavenward, possibly a passing grade inspirational somewhere up there, yes.

"Number two. Tiberius Gracchus was stirred to action by more than just a problem of how the state, the Senate, treated the needs of the returning fighting men of Rome. Basically, ladies and gentlemen, poverty in the land set Tiberius off. He proposed, I think he was a Tribune, and please, look that up, see what the Tribune position in rank means. Mr. Gracchus pushes the idea of assignment of public land. He promotes blocking the rich landowners, senators and their families and friends from what we would call insider trading these days; amazing, more things remain the same, right? Tiberius also hit on the fact that the lawmakers acted above the laws that the Senate makes for all the rest to live by, and yet, for you in for the Senate, the laws are nothing more than something to skate by."

The teacher paused. All heads are bowed except Sean's.

"If Tiberius gets his way, the propertied would no longer be able to encroach on public lands. Whoa, mining claims, grazing rights today, public development on private property, that's Kelso decision, yes, trouble sure can be a time machine, can't it, class? Same situations through thousands of years, perhaps. Tiberius proposals were welcomed in adoration by the majority, the majority being the unconnected, the disenfranchised, the ones savagely opposed by the efforts and mechanisms of government by the Senate and by the rich. Tiberius, being pretty cool dude as you will find, was from a wealthy family both he and his younger brother, Gaius, were from the Roman elite class.

Tiberius wasn't finished blowing smoke up the senators Toga's. He reformed voting in Rome too. You see, Rome, until around 139, 131 Before the Common Era, and look that up to find out how the abbreviation, B.C.E. evolved; anyway, voting in Rome had had its intimidation factors. Harassment of voters was an accepted method. The powers that be had the populace, in order to vote, they had them go up narrow passageways, ramps, to cast their preferences...and then these voters were bothered, offered bribes by various paid political 'advisers', who threatened, cajoled, ridiculed, they would even try to inspect what the voter had written down on the ballot as to which voter had in mind for which candidate. And you thought we had it tough with all the mental fog arts of the campaigns we face today right? Even though a lot of us feel like we are going to explode after a year of the screeching and the preaching, we at least don't have to face the possibility of physical harm protesting your vote as you would find back in Roman elections. The Senate angered also at Tiberius expanding the voter's paths. He widened the walkways so that those intimidating voters could not really hinder them as much and as malevolently as before, nor could the consultants bribe or reach out and abuse the electorate as easily as previously. Tiberius tested the powers and that must've been a bitch for tradition, you think?"

The classroom responded positively again and when they settled, "Yes, Tiberius and then his conspicuous brother, Gaius, were considered by those with the goods so to speak as raucous, as turbulent traitors to their heritage, terribly upsetting those of their own class who felt it was their God-given right to oversee, manage the control, the weight of each day in the lives of the undeserving masses, the foolish unwashed. How dare anyone think they equal to us, the clean and the godly?"

The teacher walked back to the blackboard and, in white chalk wrote 'Number Two or Number Three, your choice.' Prof. Sorentsen turned to face class.

"The Gracchi and other likeminded populists really established that grand term for action, the 'last straw', by starting to go to the people directly, take proposals to the plebes; look that up, 'plebeians', and then they, the Gracchi, as I said, took the laws, the proposals straight to the plebes and the plebes decided to put legislation right through without need for the approval the pretty boys in the Senate."

Professor Sorentsen sipped a hint of water from his glass and after setting the glass down, he stared at it for 5, maybe 7 seconds and the class leaned forward.

"What happened, you ask? Well, the Senate put out contracts, hits on political abusers and unneeded reformers and the ones loved by the many were going to go down.

Political assassination, yes, but there, well, the senator group as is the case in much of today's election efforts also assume the need for a reason for such dire acts, so character assassination precedes the continued excruciating exercise culminating in the final bloody deed.. As in most cases in history, money was the root of evil. Tiberius had bucked the senator's view that all things financial in the empire were their province; everyone else, keep your grimy unwashed hands off! The robes know best. Tiberius said 'no' to this and when he proposed to stand as Tribune for a second term, proposing for the second year grander scale plan for even larger reforms, well, the Senate decided it was time to dismantle the danger. Of course they need to be the "victims" to carry it off.. The senators said that Tiberius was pushing towards something entirely different. They accused Tiberius of the Holy Grail of accusations in Roman politics, that of being someone in pursuit of 'kingship'; this was Pavlovian in its effect on the Roman elite. Tiberius wanted to be dictator. So it went. The Senate's set up the ambush with contrived effrontery to The State of Rome. Why, Tiberius, they said, had the crown and even a purple robe, the color purple being considered by ancients as the color of royalty, only royalty could own it, mind you, so Tiberius was really a felon now as he had dissed the fashion police too. Sidebar here, class. Look up Phoenician dyes, inks, alright?"

The professor rocked ever so lightly on the balls of his feet.

"The Senate had publicized through the appropriate channels that Tiberius had been seen motioning towards his forehead while on Capitol grounds which was a sure sign that he wanted a crown on his noggin and the very liberties of Rome were at stake! The accusations were hideous deformities. The brothers Gracchus were of noble lineage. But kingship was not in their blood. The Senate ignored this so they could follow up on their charges and make them real with judgment settled early. They used these pretenses to kill a man. The chief operator of the nefarious plan was man named Scipio Nasica or something like that. After murdering the populist, this Scipio character was acclaimed by the Senate as, what else, a liberator acting for, what else, freedom. Gracchus, along with three hundred supporters, was murdered, beaten on Capitol Hill."

The professor paused again to let this sink in and to take his glasses off to rub his tired eyes.

Glasses in place, he continued," Your mothers probably told you about how sticks and stones will break your bones but names will never hurt you, right?"

The students remained silent.

"Well, being described as desirous of kingship and being named by jealous and envious greedy individuals and powerful entities as one who's going for the gold and then being killed with stones and sharp sticks, in fact, Tiberius, it is reported was killed with a smashing blow to his skull, with a broken chair leg. Yes, your mom lied to you and history tells you so." The teacher came closer to the front.

"Gaius Gracchus beseeches the government to give him his brother's body. The government refused. This, even after the mourning brother, Gaius, promised to bury Tiberius privately, hidden, anomalously located as to belie the fear of his burial ground becoming a troublesome shrine and a painful, agitating thorn in the paw of the Roman lion. The situation gnawed at Gaius. Guess what? Gaius gets elected Tribune, around 123 or year 120 B. C. E. And he proposes even more challenging legislation to the

Senate than his dead brother had. Gaius, it seemed, took up every suffering thing men and women of Rome were putting up with. Good guy, Gaius. He subsidized grain prices. He kicked the senators out of courts and away from the systems of voting, yes, Gaius basically was going against the grain of his own class just like his older brother had, the younger questioned his classes system, style and their detestable pleasure of taking from the masses, the pirating of others earnings, the general acceptance of ill-gotten privilege and it was suffocating to the conscious of young Gaius. He was as if a Jesus to the poor and a Judas to the well-heeled perched parasites on the Palatine hills appeared.

Mr. Gracchus was the Mr. Smith of his times. Hopefully, some of you know of Jimmy Stewart and what thereof I speak. If not, research! It won't hurt your grade; believe me, to add to your scribbles the correlation of Jimmy's condition of an honest man in a place gone badly rotten, just like the younger Gracchus. I read, class, somewhere and again, I don't know the source to attribute this to; hints, extra credit possibly here, come up with a name, nevertheless, it is said that Gaius presented his actions as a quote," Dagger in the ribs of the Senate". He moved the senators out of courts that oversaw extortion cases. He made this the job of non Senators to oversee these cases. This put Senatorial pride in the Avian gutter." The professor took a few more steps towards the middle of the speaking area. "Gaius didn't stop there. He opened the, retooled the justice system, opening up more participation to the common people. All major civil and criminal adjudications had always been judged and advocated by senators only until this Gaius guy came along. His equal liberty, as he tagged it, or hash tag for you, was a direct reproach to the self-styled dignity and self avowed sanctity with the Gods used as cover for their mistakes, and hence the power of the Senate. So guess what? The Senate had to construct another excuse to kill the latest threat to their worldview and their world size fortunes. Honor probably came in third place with this group. This Senate came up with something like a Patriot Act, declared emergency powers with act called the" Last Decree. What did it do? Well, basically, it was set up so that senators could suppress those people declared by the Senate to be public enemies against Rome." The professor waited for note taking to come to rest before, "Wouldn't want that on your resume now, would you, enemy of the State?

Pretty handy way to make to dissent die, and 'change' take flight, wouldn't you say? Results, Gaius went down as did thousands of his proponents. Gaius lost his head, cold blooded murder. Most likely, because the Senate, in its infinite treachery, proclaimed that anyone who brought in literally the head of Gaius Graccus, would receive blood money payment in gold based on the weight of the head."

Professor Sorentsen walked to pick up his water container, ignoring the half full glass, takes his second drink from the container. He pauses to let the picture of the decapitated heroes head imprint in the minds he was attempting to improve and expand. He knew this generation well as he deftly drove attention towards the gore and to the rewards and to the forfeitures caused by humans in history. His attentiveness to the stimulation needed for today's cohort to grasp, retain and expand upon with lessons learned featuring impressions not soon folded up and forgotten is key.

"According to a few sources, a nefarious individual with name reminiscent of one of our months, Septimuleius was his name, finally ended up with it and after making a hasty modification, stuck Gaius's head on a spear. He then went to Gaius's enemy, Opimius, for payment. In fact, it was said this Opimius was one of Gaius's attackers. Septimuleius proceeded to place the head on the scales and, according to Roman lore; it weighed 17 and 2/3 pounds. Talk about big heads, right! Not your usual weight for a head, but this Septimuleius was not your usual unprincipled rascal either. You see, he had removed the brain of Gracchus and filled the cavity in the skull with lead. Opimius, who was a counsel, paid old Septimuleius the gold. By the way, the attacker, Opimius; yes, he stood trial for the events, the murder, and yes; the standard operating procedure for the law of Rome was on full display with the all too familiar open palm and envious eye guiding the court, a true jury of Gracchi foes, which acquitted Opimius.

The locations where the brothers Gracchi perished were regarded as Holy ground by their followers. Cults sprung up. The Gracchi became gods to their most ardent fans. And the Senate, well they had their claques, their groups, what today we would call the hacks in the media, positioned them, that is, promoted the Senate as quote, "The Optimates" or "The best, good men". These shallow, cynical and hypocritical miserable excuses for humanity, fought challenges to their prerogatives and formulated pre-eminences and voices that were loud, fiery, and antagonistic to change of any permutation or persuasion. History, my muddled minds of mush, is untidy and always uncomfortably lurking in the proximity of 'the present' and no matter the level or volume of denial of its worst moments or scrapes with propriety, any attempt to portray it otherwise trashes the facts of our origins and does our future no favors. I ask you, is it not then as it ever is now?"

Sean noted that it was a rare occurrence that in any gathering of three hundred collegians students that you would ever be able to hear a pin drop on the floor at anytime let alone when a teacher had concluded his presentation. The teacher crushed the silence with, "All right; please note a change, class."

The professor went to the blackboard. He wrote the time and date of the next class. "Here's what I require by this deadline. Take what's you've noted today and do more research on these characters that I've introduced to you, from the killers to the killed, find out more and then type up a one-page, yes, no cursive this time; please type your thoughts about what I have been talking to you about today, you're lucky, yes, as I was saying, a single space paper, a one-page remembering in your own words what you have sampled here today and what you dig up in your highly anticipated and diligently executed research." Mr. Sorentsen pointed to the chalk board, "Then we will...." The professor hesitated, "Why, yes, Ms. Bondo?"

"But, you said, your rules were, that these notes would be the source for the exams. I took good..."

"Rules, Miss Bondo, rules? We don't need no stinking rules! We're Academia, Miss Bondo!"

All tittered, including the inquirer.

"Remember, bring in today's scribbling stapled to one typewritten page; all thoughts, concerns, protests, all hopefully presented in clear, precise terms, and notably indulgent in what one might surmise could be generally mistaken for intelligence. Thank you. Class dismissed."

Sean waited for the students to file out, pleasantly surprised that he had not been recognized. Glad that people are so involved in themselves. As he made his way down to the professor, Sean was greeted with, "Ah, sweet prince, another day of edifying emendations, revising the world as it should be and not as it is, don't you think?"

They shook hands and made their way outside into the brisk December air and light. "I always appreciated the Gracchi. I heard it first from you."

"I'd like to have met them, Sean. Don't really think too many alive today could carry their water, do you?"

"Not in politics, no."

The professor saw his opening, "Have you given any more mind time to what the old Pol, myself and you yakked about at my humble hacienda?"

Sean did not immediately respond, then, "Not too deeply, no."

That morning at first coffee the professor had espied a small entertainment side story on AOL that referred to possible sightings in various locales of Sean's activities and company for the Thanksgiving Holiday, but the professor knew it best not to get nosy, no matter the snarling curiosity tugging at him. Must be a teacher thing.

"Guided confusion is the governments' ace in the hole, Sean. Keep the culture uneasy and you keep it controllable and the powers that orchestrate forever safe, if not actually sound."

Sean was used to the provocative pronunciations and the purpose behind them. He kept pace with the peripatetic friend, listening for the next utterance.

"There are no unobstructed views of the truth; one must look around the angles today to get a glimpse of reality and then circle back to make sure the evidence still exists. That's the real 'string theory' there."

The professor opened the large dark wooden doors, entering the faculty office and lounge areas as they needed to travel through the building to shortcut to the taxi pickup.

"Henry James's, Sean, says it better than I do, something to the effect, quote, "constant rapid cultural change and the frantic pace at which all culture is experienced, numbs the individual's ability to be conscious.""

They entered the atrium/library of the building.

"Welcome to that domain."

Sean picked up his pace to keep up with the professor.

"It's the federal formula, mass stimulation of apparent need for governments overbearing assistance as catastrophes are portrayed daily in spoon fed two minute news bites. Negativity waves throughout the atmosphere. People weaken these days and the government steps in as their Ovotine, their Red Bull, and voila, election uninterupptus. Oh, the mug shots may change every two to six years, but, the shiny ball of confusion twirls and everything remains perfectly and politically the same."

As they made their way through the archway, a couple of professorial appearing individuals nodded towards the professor and he nodded back as they passed.

"Proud esoterically inclined, slight of mind polemicists, prime examples and protectors of an educational area 51, the University of Alice, a studied wasteland of tempting varieties of aging agendas dressed up in fancy new duds of updated deceit and fulfillment comes on as fast as an easy maiden and the fast food generations eat it all up. Problem is, not an hour later, they go looking for more food in that what they were fed earlier had no substance, but since they have been taught not to discriminate, not to overly compete; to actively be hammered for semesters, drilled with a philosophy of extinguishing excellence and it's clear why 'get it and go' fulfillment is an easy achievement for a government fearful of a insightful electorate."

The professor smiled his 'adieus' as they exited the room.

"You could be an actor or pretty fair country lawyer, doc; you mask well."

The professor gave a quick side smile.

"Used to be that the one thing both sides were proficient in was smiling through their difficulties and their contempt for each other and now that's blown to smithereens too."

They stopped at the professor's corner office, obviously inhabited by an individual comfortable in his surroundings. "We still have a few, a little time." He moved to clean a stack of paper and other oddities of his profession, an old blue cover dictionary and a thesaurus off of the old brown cushioned chair for Sean to sit in. "Our government profits from the outrage of the hour. It's the perfect instrument to truncate debate, stifle unrestrained opinion." The professor headed behind his chair and desk. "Obama is a good man, caught up in himself too much, but that's our selfie society, no? He cannot help it." He opened a cabinet door and retrieved a box of sugar cubes. "Do believe he does feel the pain of others too... Affordable Care Act was ramrod beast through, wrongheaded with the ideology of idiots as a guide. Consequential, raw moment in history, that. Interesting character within that frame, yes; but he feels, still feels abandoned, Sean, like anyone would without a parent or parent who leaves when one is so fragile and young. Probably leaves behind some scars that reopen at the most inauspicious of moments." He moved something and reached. "Yes, a treasured travesty he, and that's the rub. Ah, here it is." He turned, "I'm having green tea. Want some?" "Sure. So you're part of the green revolution now too?"

The professor gave a scowl and turned his attention to the teabag. "Yes, sir, people do want fresh, want honest, want humble, because all they've experienced recently is the aroma of pretense and the grip of cynicism in their lungs. They want a person who serves with a purpose that stretches far beyond the borders of that nasty realm of what's in it for me."

"Not listening. Not interested. Got it?"

Ignoring protestations, unperturbed, Sorentsen surges on, "Remember, from your learning days, the Greek, Cleisthenes?"

"Yes, but what does..."

"He, Sean, was a rarity, a spasm in society. He too refreshed, successfully caused and sustained a plan for fairer treatment and a more just situation in life for more Greeks... Why? How? He did not go the old Bastille or village against the Castle and moat ways, no. He avoided civil war by building up local governments and councils first. Got the 'hayseed' experienced way of looking at the world into as many ancillary administrative positions as he could; gave 'chops' and 'props' to the peeps to decide things locally and gradually, eventually, get them equally in line with the power of the aristocracy. Amazing!

"No dirt bag demigod, correct?"

"Yes, it was a democratic revolution by integrated pushing to the front of the bus without running the bus off the road. Cleisthenes was the reformers reformer. Without rancor. Or ringing necks. He leveled the playing ground."

"And the dirt?"

"The dirt is planted, germinating seeds, patient seeds, sturdy when full grown, and hardy with nourishment for more in Attica than ever previously."

"But, didn't that same dirt, that same plowed field of Cleisthenes, also produced the bitter harvest of ostracism?"

"Well, not documented, but likely."

"Ostracism was used as a tool to thwart, to send away any citizen, anyone, deemed by the Demos to be a threat to the democracy, right?"

Again, not waiting for interruption, "Someone looks around, wants to set up business as a tyrant, well, ostracism kept democracy, would you say, free?"

The professor continued to sip his tea.

"But didn't Cleisthenes "darling" turn nightmarish, as people begin ostracizing and punishing any person they could gang up on and were opposed to for reasons other than the sanctity and security of the city states. Target your enemies for exile on trumped up charges, place appropriate bribes, and it's,' adios, see you in 10 years, right?"

"Yes, Sean, efforts are made to overreach the boundaries of our better natures. That's man. But that can't block another attempt in a long line of basically good people trying to do the better or the right thing, can it?"

"No, but didn't you also mentioned in class that Cleisthenes might've been ostracized too?"

"Well, it's still speculative, but..."

"Bit him in the ass."

They sipped simultaneously.

Sean looked up from his cup. "It's not on my horizon, Doc, so please, don't block the view of my future even though I'm not sure what I'm seeing ahead anyways, not what's on the next mountaintop nor what's in the valley below, I'm not sure yet. I know you know this."

The professor set up in his swivel chair put his feet up on the desk blotter, scattering some paperwork to the floor to join the rest... "Were talking lifeblood here, Sean, not only yours, but the countries."

Sean rose to stretch then reached down to take another drink.

"We don't educate by the illumination of factual fire anymore. Instead, we get shish kebab medleys of simpletons thinking as leads for lesson plans. God, these highbrows don't get it. Maybe they don't want to. For Christ sake, Sean, in the most used recently published history book for public schools, Abraham Lincoln merits one paragraph. One paragraph on the rail splitter! There's another educational publication were there are three mentions of the last name of 'Washington' in the index and two of them are George Washington Carver. Now George Washington Carver's a great man, yes, but only one mention of the father the country?"

Sean remained silent.

"Sean, we've allowed intellectual dishonesty and prefab elitists to enter our teaching ranks the last 30 years, besides me."

"Of course."

"These minions are given way to trash and lie about our God damn beautiful beginnings and our singular foundations unlike any damn country in the history of our world and it's a tough nut to crack." The professor looked at his ex-student, "We need a lawgiver who doesn't know he or she is a lawgiver and whose ethics are unimpeachable and who also doesn't have to say something twice for others to understand."

"Professor, you're a piece of odd works and good thoughts. But politics is high-priced profanity, about as valuable for self-fulfillment and as tasteful as graffiti on a monument." "You know, it's noon. I think it's past tea time, so, it's by-God Brandy time. The taxi's still twenty minutes off, right?"

"Yes."

"Whoa, professor, stop. Don't you have classes? And I don't..."

"Nope, and it wouldn't matter if I did. Ah, the temerity of the tenured few, don't you know." He eyed the color in the glass and was satisfied. "Don't worry; lunch after liquidity is on me. Can't dine on a dehydrated stomach, can we? No!" The learned man began again as he poured Sean's drink, "Here, in these musty mausoleums of mental malfeasance, everything has or matters evenly. All is equivalent, so nothing is truly important. God help us, God help you, if you're a singularity in scholarland. Sheep hate to be shown up or sheared by logic. Whatever is venturesome, tingling or has rapid pulse is blunted or stripped of its individuality, its unique wholeness. I'm telling you, Sean, universities are voluminous sized incubators for the 'go along, get along crowds,' those youngsters baking and shaking for employment within the elliptically challenged orbits of general un-relativity and foolishness, another name for what goes on at that voracious interchange, that black hole at the junction between the joined-at-the-hip orbits of the Corporate and the Governmental worlds. That's the 'ring' they go for, not something without a price tag on it. That would take some thought." The Professor paused, lifted his glass in semi toast position towards Sean. "All the lost talent is sad. The biggest secret to success is to give kids the opportunity to be kids. Need some tricks, yes. But you must let understanding sneak up on them."

He nodded and took another taste. Sean followed suit.

"According to that man, Herodotus, Croesus of Lydia, another king from way back, planned to battle the Persians. Old Croesus thought he understood the task at hand but results would prove otherwise. The Persians defeated the Lydian as the ancestors of Iran won through the superior stench of their camels. Yes, camels; you see, the horses of the Lydian cavalry could not bear the aroma of the enemies animals. The horses tore off, fled the field; ending in the Lydian's being routed and their capital, Sardis, put to ruin. Goes to show that the sweet smell of success can be a tricky thing and that it doesn't always have to be flower sweet, now does it? Of course the kids like the story about camel stench winning a battle. These things make sense to them at this age. A lot of them, though, graduate from high school with little useful information, factually challenged." The teacher stared at his half empty glass. "You know, the struggle to recognize self, its something, Sean, which never ends. Especially when you can push button your 'smarts' and fool the other push button boobs that everyone is in conversation with other intelligent beings without even having to lift your ass out of a chair to greet and touch another opened hand." The cognac is lapping the green tea.

"I'm glad you taught me and the others when you were less full of it."

"That's because I'm finding less things to love, Sean." He noticeably sighed. "Reform, such a flexible word, no? Most necessary now that it comes and as Solon noted... allowing reasonable chance for stability and acting on shifting the blocks of power will undoubtedly spark some tastes, acts among the haves and additionally frustrate the aspirations of the have-nots... The old Greek said the experience of his time in office was as bad of a wolf set upon by a pack of hounds, but as the sage would say, "Dike", justice, as you recall, did eventually come to Attica as Solon destroyed the aristocracies peculiarly structured benefit packages of privilege which in turn improved the general welfare for all. That man charged downhill, flaunting traditional immunity from the "real world" and "real world" consequences for the ruling minority, just by the assumed virtue of their station or office. Steadiness, good sense, experience and force of personality, these do leaders make. Solon had the math right 2500 years ago. In a world so disheveled as ours, dismay is not an option. 'Long term' must be voiced again."

Sunlight reflected a rainbow prism from his cut glass. It moved on the wall to the professors' side. He was oblivious to it.

"Equations are more important to me, because politics is for the present, but an equation is something for eternity." There's Einstein for you, light makes might, right? Shine on the truth, no matter how many black holes surround you."

"Agreed."

"Sean, you're an honest tactician. You do not hug limelight." Prof. Sorentsen paused. "Exceptions like Thanksgiving week, perhaps, maybe?" The teacher got the smile he had anticipated and continued, "But, Sean, generally, today, clarity of purpose is lost. No one's focused on why they should win! They don't see..."

"Pardon the interruption, professor. I do appreciate the considerations presented, but for me, I think it would, it still is so far safer and saner work where measurements are black and white and half measures are due to get you killed. This is me. Yes, I know I'm at a crossroads, but, politics, hell, it feels like an inside joke that really lacks humor when you break down the punch lines."

Sorentsen arose.

"Time to tack to 'Twenty-Two Times Turned', what do you say?"

"Sounds very good. Who knows, Cade may be there for a late lunch."

"God, its great fun to have students as owners of restaurants. They cut me slack on the 'hash' they dish up. Noggin knockers too."

"Brandy?"

"Yes."

As the professor led the way, they were engaged in an eyeful of merry go round in color and steel and some plastic.

"Hey, Sean, quite the Woodstockian evoking Boomer stationary metal toy parade, huh, otherwise designated as the faculty parking facility..."

The professor hesitated, Sean too.

"VW bus, perfectly restored, isn't it?"

The professor started, then momentarily halted, as if to emphasize, "Feels on wheels, we called them, "and he moved on past another row, Sean in pursuit.

"That's the Dean's Barracuda and..."

"Dean of...?"

"Sociology, of course. Oh, here's a Tesla. Look, here's a BMW, Volvo too; and a, a Smart car. Here, another not so good shape VW van, not sure, but probably a teacher's assistant. And, of course, a Volt, and a, yes, that's a Prius. What do you know, not a clunker among them even though our generation is now living the clunker stage ourselves no matter how much Rustoleum we use trying to restage ourselves."

Sean noticed first and waved the distant taxi forward.

"But, no sir to the blasphemous; ain't no Hendrix around these days to heal the unloved, I tell you, Sean."

Mr. Sorenson winked, his signal to Sean, 'everything's in control even the teacher, all gonna be okay."

"You're incorrigible."

"Why, yes, but aren't you happy with your life that I am?"

"Where to, gentlemen?"

The cabbie wanted to get his fares on their way.

"Twenty-Two Times Turned, please."

"Yes, please driver, sir, speed us away as rapidly as possible from this arena of parked cliché, would you?"

"Ah, yes, sir."

Medium, that's how I want my steak. Sean's lips moistened. No, make that medium rare.

CHAPTER 15

"Lovely Labors"

"Virtue and talents were alone sufficient to elevate to office, instead of hereditary rights derived from men whose meanness or vices were the principal causes of their grandeur."

William Thorton, 1786

December 4, 2015

"God, you're more of a hoarder than Sorentsen!"

Sean was sitting in Chas Bellows combination office/playroom, a.k.a. notes, records, CDs, one old organ two broken Stratocasters and boxes of other things representing his past existence.

"Whore, maybe. Hoarder, no."

The mahogany wooded room, besides clutter and unsorted 'to-do's' everywhere, the desk sat in cheery bright sunlight and remained that way for most of everyday. Upon the medium-sized oak piece, Tripp's Underwood typewriter was centerpiece and appeared immaculate in condition. The friends were drinking without any remarkable additives such as Kailua or Baileys. This is to be a serious 'review' meeting between friends about the lifestyle change of major proportions for one. At least, this was Tripp's plan.

"So the curmudgeon suggested, speaking of painted ladies, politics? Hell, you'd knock it dead."

"The professor and you in agreement? That's omen enough to flee."

Chaz grinned, but as looked over the steam of his coffee, he took in his friend's posture and appearance and he knew Sean was perplexed. "How about big consultant on plants, facilities, security for them or their critical response plans or a speaker series with..." "Integrity in the workplace; well, at least somewhat familiar with that."

Chaz frowned. "Look, Sean, I know you're still stumbling mentally around accepting the fact that people pay handsomely for people like you to talk to them in a comfortable atmosphere about uncomfortable things."

"That's, it just seems as unethical as any politicians appeal, that I am, that you should be do the right thing over and over again at speeches that's syrupy shameful shift to a lower standard of life is all I am saying."

"Saw a news clip once, years ago, when a lady, after major river flooded her neighborhood and her response to some urbane know-it-all reporter's question of why she, the lady, and this was up in Yoggee's North Dakota, summertime, yeah, well, the quote, journalist, unquote, asked why the lady had opened her place to strangers who were the victims of the rising waters?

Sean, I loved her response as it's exactly how I imagine a wise, tough inhabitant of that part of the country would react as she measuring the fiber of the city 'slick' as she asked the reporter, "You're not from around here, are you?" And that's you, Sean." Tripp turned on the exaggerated haughtiness, "You're not of Decree, you see, and that's good, man." "Not sure of your example."

"Sean, the old man might have it on the head."

"Look, I've told you, told him, it's a bunch of crock."

"Here's the deal. Here's why I think the town's ready: hell, the country is ready for honesty which, frankly, doesn't need promotion."

Sean squirmed, than got up to pour himself more caffeine. "Warn me if I'm about to step on something important, okay?"

Tripp, ignoring the comment on his level of cleanliness and filing except for," There's enough spare parts of the floor to get by for now. Hear me out. Modern pols, with rare exception, are married to or born wealthy. They do not depend on the good heartedness of unfamiliar acquaintances or strangers, only the money managers of such people. They understand perfectly the who and the why of the energy possible, the lifeblood of the contents within the bulging, stuffed envelopes and they can never be ignored. Ergo, with the price of holding office escalating faster every election than Higgs Boson does the splits, the friendly strangers do get the legislation they pay for and we get ballyhooed overpriced freight charges for the power trips of these predatory peddlers; the backwash of humanity and I blame JFK for it."

Sean returned to his chair. "Believe me, I'm listening."

"He and his compliant press corps of the time became entangled, ethics, secrets all at play in an unhealthy for the country relationship and it continues today. When they weren't covering up for the dalliances, the press boobs, falling in line to promote Peace Corps, other service opportunities, all were stamped with approval as part of the concept of glorifying politics as a career, a profession, investing in a lifetime of enabling pushy pseudo-philosophies to be called legislation and become laws. All this from the unholy eyewash that we are stuck with today; a bunch of office squatters who can't afford to lose elections as they might have to actually drive a car for themselves or dial a phone and speak to someone that has absolutely nothing to offer them. How frightening is that? Its endemic of these coreless apples, most, do not have a good read on what "average" really is and this is what these "Can't Do Withouts" face if they lose a campaign. One benefit though, I'm sure, is that they do increase the employment levels of the psychiatric industry, I'm positive on that score. And then, Sean, you mix this with a sycophantic press corps we been yakking about and recent experiences say otherwise regarding that much touted notion of journalistic skepticism and investigative suspicion, it's all now burdened in the delivery by ideological selectivity and by woeful misdirection and omission. Flourish, seasoned with bombast and daily misery, plays well if your mission every day is to keep everybody occupied and at bay."

"And ignorant."

"I swear, Sean, the only thing you can gauge with certainty in D. Ceeee, is miscalculation and predicament is well represented in the neighborhood."

"I'm glad you write when you're sober."

"Who says I'm sober? Who dares to cast aspersions and says I'm sober?" Tripp, lifted, and pushed back from his desk, lowering his legs to the floor. "Sean, I now have two careers in businesses where substance abuse is part of the resume; rock 'n roll and journalism." He maneuvered around the chair. "Music is loud and messy; the press, prissy and passe." Sean agreed with raised coffee mug.

"Let's add some spoon bender to the Java, shall we?"

Sean knew from past experience it was fruitless to protest his friends proclamation, as it was not a request.

"Irony is stretching my patience, Sean. We live in a free country, the press can pick the topic and what do we get for the most part? Bad is what we get. That is what we get! In dictatorships like Castro, Chavez, Gaddafi, they all wanted to be the press's' Shirley Temples', and low to any press person that didn't like the curls on the stars head as they may well lose their access if they didn't say it was a curl which could only be styled by God.." Tripp hesitated at the window, staring at the wintry mix. "Remember how the press softens their protests about war when the "O" man came in the White House door? The substitution of fiction for fact took off and as things went south for the Lefts view of the world, they just as unscrupulously as ever, the tide turns and the Democrats turn on their leader so they can write him off, make Obama the biggest scapegoat they can for their failure and as rapidly as it can be typed and spewed out they..."

"Public confidence seems to me to be a tool only allowed for use by the press."

"Manipulation has many fathers."

"Listen, Tripp, I don't think consulting, I don't have the fire for it. I can't wrap it up and greet the concept. So it's not a target, a soft target by no means because it's me, it's the rest of my walk..."

Its infrequent Chaz witnessing Sean Linden dealing openly about what his 'withins' were about. Chaz recalled only one other moment. It was after a Greek fraternity party. Both agreed never to join a group such as a fraternity but they both agreed they would drink their beer and eat their food. Sean's eyes were as intense now if not as bloodshot as then. They'd sat on a Lindsay street curb that night after the party. Chaz remembered Sean mentioning growing up in an only child situation, as his parents, they were killed in accident when he was a baby. The distinct aloneness of his friend was vivid and painful that night. He stared at him. "My true view, my true friend? You may not be receptive but..."

"Never stopped you before."

"Obviously not in a grade AAA receptive mood for my beliefs but I bet you, the Navajo, Moah, Cade would agree that, well, the country still needs service from you, dude.''

Sean looked past Tripp to the outside.

"In so many ways I do not see much hope for this country and unless people like you engage and I'm not talking your service, jeez, no, it's the other fights, you know what I mean." Tripp had sat with his drink and now, fidgety, stood and stretched before continuing." Hell, my epee is my pen and I piss off as many lunatic fringe legislators as I can get away with. If I could legally somehow close out the jackals clear out of my world forever, I'd sell what I have left of my soul I swear I would."

Tripp move to shelf and poured more Baileys.

"Here's my world view. Mine you, it's from an ex-acid head, self-styled Casanova wanna-be rocker boy, but at least, I wasn't a student body president."

Sean smirked, raised his mug in approval then relaxed back into the brown sofa... He glanced above his friends at the gold framed, gold selling Circus Cures first album. Looking below that, he saw the etching in marble of the words, the name of Tripp's newspaper column, "Panem et Circenses." Sean's eyes wandered up to the clock, whose hands never moved as it was stuck on 4:20. "Why the clock, the wrong time, all the time; never asked you that?"

"Not the wrong time, hombre. Did you know that all the clocks in 'Pulp Fiction' were stuck at 4:20?" Chaz saw it wasn't registering. "It means to you and it means to me that it's high time to act, yes, how's that?"

Sean switched topics. "The book's selling dynamite, isn't it?"

"Enough so that I can buy lunch."

"That's big, you, the owner of restaurants."

Tripp ignored him. "It's paying for itself. My biggest hope, my marketing Nirvana would be that it gets put on the Papal Index of prohibited books: yeah, jack's up profit like a rocket to be singled out as a racy, caddy writer whose tongue's tasted a bit of what the world has had to offer and for this, your humble scrivener, is chewed on by the Holy See."

"I can't believe it, with your life, that you haven't been banned by religions everywhere already."

"Funny, grunt face."

The rocker's face scrunched up, brow wrinkled, eyes squinting, saying, "Between the lefties to the far left of my Libertarian comfort zone and a press calculated in deceit and obfuscation and motivated by the tearing down of the gutsy, it motivates me, but not enough to ever vote Republican, but that's the price of a restless heart, I suppose. The Left work through the schools and through the media and the Right works through the banks; hell, Sean, one breaks down morals while the other one hides behind them. Demise is nigh if we allow it, I'm telling you."

Tripp drank a little more dark firewater.

"The watchfulness, the almighty leveler of the past, the self glorified industry called the press; the fourth something is out there, the fifth or they drink a fifth because or not the fourth; I don't know, but there were, they were the watchdogs of government supposedly. What happened? I tell you, the majority of them are up the government's ass and they are perfectly content with the smell. That's pretty pricey access. The 'Indulgent Indignant'; and with them it really is about what they opt not to do more often than what they do." "Agree."

"Hey, how about finding a way through the thicket of what I do?"

"What?"

"Writing! Listen, if I can do it pulling stuff out of fruit boxes and make it seem fresh, and get paid for it, why, you got the actuality behind what you might put down on the paper; you got facts, you got experience in things that almost got you killed. That's of interest. The bullets in the realms you've dealt with, I dare say you know pretty factual stuff other people probably need to know, right?"

"Some worlds are rather thin and other worlds are rather fat, I have just worked in the borders between both."

"Yes."

"You know, Chaz, the war correspondents: I can't figure, recall names only the stands, the postures, the way they go about things, ladies and men today, some great, brave individuals in pursuit of what's the hidden behind the what is. They're about the only, the guys and gals in the swirling middle of man's disasters and redefinitions, that can sometimes adequately share with other men and women what it's like and doing a much better job of it than I ever will."

"All right."

"Something Jefferson wrote corresponding with friend said, "Were it left to me to decide whether we should have a government without newspapers or newspapers without a government, I should not hesitate a moment to prefer the latter.""

"Good words from a brilliant, sometimes conflicted, sometimes odd man; but could not be all bad is he was into the vineyards and into the unexplored."

"Most of what I've read or recently heard on the airways is purchased demonization, stories that rely on nothing but quip, innuendo, and assassination by anecdote. And all the while, in the background, 'Rail Against the Machine' sounds on the boom box, right?" "It's not 'rail', okay; it's 'rage', Sean. More Baileys or its Kalua?"

"God, in the last couple weeks, I think I've had the Vikings quota for booze."

"The better to axe away the fat, right?" Chaz relaxed against the counter.

"Writing, Sean, perhaps, yes."

Sean sipped, remaining quiet.

"Did you know longhand writing, grandma's cursive, is what the early printers based the characters of their type faces on, the longhand writing of our ancestors? The flowing beauty of an exquisitely written letter, whether an A or whether a Z, it is pleasing to the eye, quite the delicacy, a rarity still stirring us from the era of "B.C.T.""

"Alright, I give; what?"

"Before Common Texting, the downfall of mankind."

Sean leaned just a smidge forward.

"First publishers in Venice, Italy, wanted to crowd more words on a page to save printing costs, paper, labor, so these smart people compressed the type. They came up with animated look of "italic"; italics tightened the page and that read more 'moola' for infant industry." The speaker took a drink for the cause. "But now, you get things like newly rich celeb journalists reporting on their newly rich friends in newly filled positions of power; friends from their overly ripe glory times together at University. Talk about the inequity of capitalism and income disparity and its collateral damages regarding the ability to think clearly; just channel surf and you will see the evidence pixilated perfectly, irrefutable, on a nightly basis."

"And they are only interrupted by calls from their CPA's."

"It's contributed to a government picking winners and losers and thinking they can get away with it."

Sean nodded 'yes'.

"You know I'm a liberal at heart but a conservative in my head, right?"

"I know you rank up there with a few friends with posttraumatic stress syndrome, but they don't have the acid flashbacks such as yourself, but if you allow that in your comparison standard, then. Yes."

"Both sides tend to throw meaning overboard and this is one aspect of my angst. That and government attempts with our tax money to help failures to continue. Informational streams should never be damned but they can be scary ass damning in a flash. There's no time for scrutiny when food is getting cold. And dogs, they get tired of the same dish in the bowl too, don't they?"

Sean thought they might need to indeed think about something to chew on to blend in with the liquid of special effects they held in their hands.

"Sean, you can't take anything as five-time per day ritual anymore, no matter what it is - everything seems worn."

"Wonder if hogs get tired of the same slop?"

"This crew of taddy-tale tadpoles just wants to hang out on the biggest lily pad with the biggest toady, using other toad tax money to subsidize their career mistakes. The giant toad provides access, and you think reporters will challenge officials whom the publishers are teammates within the donor/benefactor Scrabble game? Any vibrations otherwise by the salaried wordsmiths' on the lower floors brings the rough touch of control from on high, comes down turd thud hard; no edgy, unshackled press, dag nab it! Can't have it, can't use it."

Tripp moistened his lips, which seemed odd to him with all the Kailua intake. "Founding fathers saw the press's reason for existence as being a check, a gadfly, a Socrates with bona fides; why, the boys of Philadelphia decided that with a press doing its job, a government would never become comfortable or expected or assume 'word lackeys', then or now, could be use at governments' leisure and caprice. The wigged ones thought that government should always have to concern itself with the effects of the press looking up its dress.

"That was probably a Franklyn, Jefferson preference."

"What?"

"The dress part."

"They weren't the only randy dandies. But what I was saying; the press should work against the governments preferred positioning of the public which is 'missionary'." "I was taught that the press came about to shed illumination on the unreasoned, the unchallenged, the usual in government. But, I agree with you; they wash the hands of the other, Pontius cleansing Pilate."

"Recently, oh, a few some years ago now, saw story about media titan who's about to default on $1 billion debt. Still haven't had details together for story but it deals with the complexity of modem ways; involving Obama, geeze, I had so much hope for him..." "Many did, most."

"Well, it goes that this tycoon in the communication business gets a prepackaged Chapter 11, reducing his debt from nearly $1 trillion to $265 million. Why? Because the tycoon's creditors happened to all be banks that had received federal funds, the acceptance of which, required the borrower banks to rewrite regulations, pushed again by the administration, remember, and lo and behold, these regulations set up to clean up banks fudged books and miserable balances by actually forcing these banks to write off bad debt in bulk size, such as those on their account books with campaign donor-sized debts, for instance. My, the play of the pen is mighty indeed; a billion down to 165, and remember, November is just around the comer. And it isn't one party that's poisonous; the system is a game of rotating spoils and roils. And as you know, no good liberal diatribe is complete without a quote from V.I. Lenin..."

Sean slightly shook his head 'no'.

Tripp reached into the drawer and pulled out a second, smaller piece of yellowed newspaper.

"Lenin said, and I quote, Comrade... 'Germany will militarize herself out of existence, England will expand herself out of existence, and America will spend herself out of existence.'"

"Tell me you're out of clippings."

"No, no more clippings. Only a quote from Camus."

"Got in the wrong car on the wrong day, that guy."

"Camus, and I'm paraphrasing, so maybe not full-on quote; he says that a journalist who does not judge himself or herself daily- if they don't, why, they're not worthy of this profession, journalism. Camus says he or she in this business bears the heaviest of duties, responsibilities in their eyes and in the eyes of their country."

"Pithy. He wrote 'The Plague'; read that early. Didn't fully appreciate it."

"Could be the press is the plague of our era. Judgment is permissive, lazy, fawning for the attention of importantly positioned people..."

"... Who are as 'missionary' with gusto as they are themselves." Sean finished his drink. "Righteousness, these days, Tripp; what's the bid price for it?"

"Sean, whenever you begin to agree a little more often than you normally do with me I know it's time to either, one, secure harder liquor, or, two, quickly refer to the Torah for guidance, or, three, both."

"Again, the going price?"

"A clear eye, a tumultuous heart and a tormented soul."

Sean raised his empty glass. "Da, I thought so, Comrade, da."

CHAPTER 16

"O Temporal O Mores!"
(Oh the times! Oh the manners!)

"Every saint has a past, while every sinner has a future."

Oscar Wilde

December 7th, 2015

It was Chaz's idea. He organized the trip. He'd told Cade that, "Really, you're not the old Caddoo that I knew, bud! And you haven't been, since your last serious 'experiment' in dating, months ago. What was her name? No matter. It's just that 'Too much funk and not enough female,' will stunt your growth." Sean was surprised at Cades response. Mr. Bartholomew agreed with Tripp.

And so off to D.C.'s most posh, most elegant gentlemen's club they went.

They entered 'Horace's' with only one of the three knowing what to expect; women in expensive evening gowns serving exquisitely tasting cuisine and top shelf, turn-up-the heat liquor, whom, after fulfilling menu requests, dance and interpret the latest sound, attired less formally in neon bikini bottoms and moving in such manner as would be expected for ladies less encumbered by clothes. The owner is a friend of the rockers and Tripp thought it might do the media man good to meet her. And selfishly, although he never would own up to it was the fact that Tripp was curious about the consequences of such a proposed meeting. Tripp had intended to make this happen earlier when Cade was first coming down from the recent relationship gone sour. Tripp considered then that it was probably unwise and very unfriendly to force feed something that could have likely evolved into a rebound predicament with both parties sorely disappointed. Tripp knew the bad taste of these mishaps all too well, so, 'no go' until now, today, Pearl Harbor Day.

The club had just opened its doors for the day's business. The men entered and heard a soft but firm voice speaking in a level manner.

"It's never better to be someone else." The focus of the words was a petite, very attractive woman and the speaker was the owner of the club.

"Listen, Doc Holliday stood 5 foot two, weighed 115 pounds. Monika, you're taller than Alexander the Great too, he's a 5 foot three Spitfire and don't ever forget that he was 5 foot three and conquered the world. All you need to do is conquer this stage and the friendly slaves seated around it. You tower over them, girl, and you own their weaknesses. Taller and better. Don't ever forget it!" The speaker sensed the midday arrivals. She turned, smiled and waved to Tripp. Tripp glanced over towards Cade and could tell his friend was happy with what Tripp had got him into. As for Sean, Tripp still could not read whether or not he was pleased or perplexed.

"I don't have nearly enough mouths." Cade was impressed.

The men were seated. After hugging her employee, the center of attention, strolled their way.

"Cyrano and Cicero, nose and prose; how's my favorite scrivener doing today, Trippee?"

"Chardonnay, I want you to meet Sean Linden..."

"The hero? Yes, I recognize, how are you?"

Sean blushed, "Very well, thank you."

"And this is Cade Bartholomew."

She recognized the face from television and the stance of maledom from experience.

"Char, to my friends."

"Alright, Chardsy, very pleasurable to meet you." Cade Bartholomew couldn't resist his habit of quickly tagging someone with a nickname when the individual was obviously and uncomfortably his equal, if not more. Raven haired, turquoise eyes, stunning how they played with him; the lady owned all present options, firmly in control of the power stick.

"I have a nickname, thank you." The silence of the males, she loved it. "My father, in the minimum time he was around, called me, 'Calliope,' 'beautiful voice' and, as I saw later, it also meant 'muse of eloquence'."

"You mean 'calamity' or..."

"No, Calliope."

Tripp winced at Cade's rapid descent, playfulness seemingly failing his almost flailing friend.

After the 'sweep me up now eyes', Cade had noticed the voice of Ginger Leigh Crownover aka Chardonnay Hooray, second. The 'whispered heat' in her tone, velvety close to primeval, baked in his current unevenness.

Ginger Leigh 'Calliope' Crownover always began her professional introductions with "Independent and you?" She'd worked endlessly in a seemingly never see the light occupation of stripping; but now, she never remove clothing except on her terms. She owned Horace's, D.C.'s posh 'play' for the powerful and the pitiful. The only scar in her considerations of her life was that she had been a preacher's daughter, which, upon discovering, Cade's mind unfastened in endorphin heaven.

She was an honest achiever in a vocation of deceit and fantasy. She worked out but did not like to work out with others; so, after success, she purchased her own midsized health club which many times, when she was otherwise occupied and not muscling her arms or age proofing her abs, she'd open the facility free to single mothers and other women on tight budgets.

After the attractions of eyes and sound, Cade was intrigued as the deal closed, with Chars posture, a natural Nefertitiesque strength within grace, adorned in poise.

Ms. Hooray's goal as a young runaway was to grasp the ownership of her dreams away from the rigid life at home; which had been entirely too much for a child of the wild. Not much had blocked her way once the course was charted. Vegas had been the home, where her parents had eloped, stayed and then found God. Her father evangelized and her Mother became a professional martyr. As Ginger eventually would share, her mother was the dutiful wife, a closet Gothic trash novel paperback enthusiast that, along with her days of secretly sipping deep iced liquored Hosia's, pleasantly aided and abetted her mother's escape.

The rebel teen from Vegas turned women raconteur in the devils playground of Washington DC, made her early budding fortune by promoting charity strip-offs, tastefully done, for Veteran care and for the Make-A-Wish foundation. Mr. Bartholomew had been aware of Ms. Hooray's efforts. Her determined way, her public avoidance of conformity, bewitched him from afar.

Mr. Bartholomew was now pleased that he had acquiesced to Mr. Bellows suggestion that the time was right, Pearl Harbor Day, for Tripp, Sean and Mr. Bartholomew, to 'boy it up', at least during happy hour, and, "Have some fun sneak up on us again like it used to."

Ms. Hooray leaned slightly towards Cade. He leaned towards her. Sean and Tripp quickly acted otherwise occupied.

"If you weren't devil appealing, I'd think you a ratbag."

"Not a compliment, I assume."

"No. Just dated a British rocker for too long."

"And I've," Cade rolled his eyes toward Tripp, "been saddled with this misguided Karaoke miscreant too."

"But not dating?"

"No."

They leaned back.

"Gentlemen, your glasses seem wanting. Carly, come get the boys orders, please, dear. Thanks." She returned to the most tortured one. "Now, Cade, I know Tripp's preferences as there are none and Sean, I see, enjoys Coors. What's to your liking, broadcast boy?"

"Anything straight up."

Chardonnay purposely missed a beat, then, "But, of course. That math equates." They leaned in towards the other again.

"The only math I thought I knew was 'rhombus'; thought it meant fracas on a rumbling bus as a kid. And then there's the ever ready and I might add, my second favorite tongue twister, the ever odd, 'quadrangle trapezium.' Fun to say, yes?"

"I imagine." She sipped her water and gave a nibble to the cucumber slice before, "I've read you're a college graduate."

"Yes, Oklahoma; a short spurt to Colorado before then..."

"So, incompletes at the peaks? Well, I did not college up; but funny, in high school, I was partial to math. I majored in vulgar fractions and the theory of Pi."

"You're the most beautiful woman I've seen sober."

"The woman or you?"

"It's probably the women with your past, right, Cade?"

"Assistance not necessary, Tripp, thank you."

"Yes, any sober woman with interest in you is, well, please."

"You too, Sean?"

Sean ignored Cades protest, "Miss Hooray, your banner says tonight's amateur night.

What is that?"

"Yes, Sean, regular girls, amateurs, come in and strip for prize money, isn't that correct

Char?" Tripp seemed quite familiar with the process.

"Gentlemen, there are no amateurs." Ms. Hooray then directed her eyes on Mr. Bartholomew. "There are no amateurs anymore, anywhere."

Chardonnay witnessed the familiar deer in headlight countenances of males whose constructs are crushed, especially prevalent in groups of two or more of them. Time to feed them.

She turned and asked, "J.C., please; some soft tacos, cheesy nachos with buffalo and some waters, iced. Thanks."

Tripp and Sean silently watched as the mogul and his equal happily tested their boundaries. Bacall came to mind; the type woman that would add 10 years to your life, no matter your age.

"How's the landscape of your heart, Cade? Is it rugged terrain, crags and hidden canyons or is it a desert which blooms only once a year?"

The men were transfixed.

"And when do you expect it to change? The next earthquake, perhaps?"

Tripp assessed the nonverbal between Cade and Chardonnay. Their palms were flat on the table. The physical distance between the two became smaller. As any trained eye such as Mr. Bellows could see, obligations were forming.

Cade moved from himself to herself. "I've seen you called the "Ambassadress of Undress" in press bites; where did, who; is that even a word, 'ambassadress'?" "I prefer the 'Ambassadress of more is less', Mr. Bartholomew."

He hesitated at stepping into the next sentence and being revealed as a full frontal fool.

She didn't. "Imagination, sir, is kindling, stoking the embers of embraceable possibilities and the fuse, sir, the length of it, is up to you."

Chardonnay moved a few inches closer. "Peel and reveal more than the charm of speculation allows; not prudent, not profitable...no, Mr. Bartholomew, I'm rather the ambassadress of the properly undressed." She leaned in even closer. "Wouldn't you concur?" Her coral turtleneck was as equally penetrating to the senses as were her powder blue eyes and her ever so stark as to appear unnatural ebony locks. He felt unclothed. "You find this unflattering, Cade?''

"No. I find it weak in description for the wonderment it attempts to describe."

Her body language moved in favorable ways, physically approving of what he said as she patted, brushed the soft hairs on the top of his hand, before slowly retreating back into her chair, smiling generously.

"How did you, where did the name for your club, where's it from?"

"I can tell you like history too. Horace was a poet. And sometime, if I recall correctly around the time Cleo and Mark Anthony died and Rome had Egypt for its own, being a good Roman, Horace, in one of his odes, wrote something to the effect, "...the time for drinking and dancing had come." I'd liked that since the time I first heard it and hence, years later, a gentleman's club where ladies feel at ease in impeccable decor and attire, scrumptious dining, no tramp stamp tattoos, nor midgets lip-syncing the blues and there you go, Horace's."

Tripp chuckled inside. No androphobia here. He motioned to Sean that they should get up and leave Cade and Chardonnay alone until the food arrived. They excused themselves and headed towards the bar and the bartender 'J.C.'. Their excuse, "To get a closer look at the large saltwater aquarium that circled part of J.C.'s station area, right, Sean?"

Cade and Chardonnay barely acknowledged the other two's absence.

"The girls, their names, no stage names, diamond girl nicknames, no..."

"No, it's their own; no nicknames except for me, of course. I want them in their own skin, no changing to please others..."

"Men?"

"Yes. Nevertheless, we do make profit on the misapprehensions, on the primacy of the primate philosophies of average males and their ancient drives, both automatic and stick shift."

Cade had never before felt so good feeling so uncomfortable. He swiftly shifted the topic. "Your hair is, well, it's so deep, I mean so dark and so rich and..."

"I was called "Raven" as a girl. I liked that when, in class, I read that it was Sam Houston's Indian name. Early, I liked anything that dealt with Texas and with our red sisters and our red brothers."

"The Raven by Poe was one story I did not resort to Cliff Notes for."

They laughed and Cade continued, "Were you aware that Edgar Allan Poe was paid the mighty sum of two dollars for The Raven?"

"Figures. Some publishers are still not princesses or princes of propriety, are they?" Chardonnay brushed the hair from her brow, perhaps subconsciously.

"The Romans also thought brunettes, 'Rave' girls to us hip 'dark' ones today; they thought brunettes were the virtuous ladies in the Empire. Oh, yes, and they reinforced that by making a law that made the prostitutes dye their hair blond so that it was easy to distinguish between the girls that do and the girls that say they don't."

Cade finished his drink. "You give Romans, I give you Greeks. As an obviously knowledgeable devotee of the past and it's relevance to today, you probably know that the Parthenon is named after a virgin, Athena Parthenos."

"I know my virgins, yes, because there are so few, it's so easy an accounting."

"About as easy as counting amateurs, right?"

Drinks for two were delivered by another evening gowned beauty.

"Thank you, Molly." Ms. Hooray focused on the man again. "Ah, the sanctity of Holy Sinners, huh, Cade...Romans, Greeks, multiple Gods for multiple mea culpa's for simply being human. Cade, men are as different as the Greeks and the Romans; you know that, right?"

Cade really did not feel comfortable about this subject, 'men'.

Ms. Hooray noticed. She liked her position. "Oh, please. You can talk about women. This is not about either sex alone. Good God, that would be almost Opera-sized boring!"

Cade almost spit his drink out in mirthful agreement then quickly recovered after Ms. Hooray evenly followed with, "No. It's just about sex! Always!" Her ocean blue eyes punctuated the comment as perfectly as billowing clouds accent a bottomless sky.

"Men are as different as the Greeks were to the Romans. Greeks are Democrats. Romans are Republicans. Greeks were viewed as inclined to levity, superficiality, spendthrifts, quite unreliable. In Roman society, proper citizens, which were male only, I believe; they were supposed to have sexual relations with only male slaves and non-Roman inferiors and not as the Greeks practiced, where free male citizens went at it with each other." Cade winced.

"Look at the Romans, inhibited, wound tight in cloth togas, whereas the Greek men competed and exercised in the nude."

Attempting to appear at ease, Cade contributed, "So prudes and dudettes, yes?"

"My broadcast boy, are you a member of the movie set party, the Democrats; they're all false fronts. Or are you a member of the big flop-eared party, the Republicans? They all wanna be hunks who really wish they were all trunk. Which are you, Cade?"

"Probably, Miss fandance, I'm like you. I hate the props of a stage and I never thought Dumbo was a cute thing either."

"Very good, Mr. B'meau! Toast to G.D.I.'s everywhere!"

Cade toasted Chardonnays offered glass, amazed how long it had been since he'd last heard the term 'G.D.I.'.

"Pleasure to meet another, 'God Damn Independent,' Miss Hooray." "You can call me Calliope."

"All right, beautiful voice."

"Goodness, you remember well." They sipped the toast. "Now back to the subject in hand."

"Which was, is?"

"Sex. We both sell it. You've seen my place and I have seen your shows."

Ms. Hooray finished the remainder of the coastal waters, then, "I have a hunch you love haunch."

Cade hesitated again as was his approach when he was about to cut open a part of himself. "Perhaps." He attempted a return serve," Too many women, in my humble estimation, flaunt their breasts for notoriety and self acknowledgement, esteem."

"Really?"

Cade felt he needed to right the boat quickly. "Well, yes, and as Tripp and I both believe..."

"So you have an accomplice in this thinking?"

"We believe that women fail in understanding that really, that men, at least Tripp and I, that women do not truly understand that, in the true nature of gallant men, butts win!" "So you do lean Greek after all!" And before the man could respond, she concluded, "I knew I still have the touch. I knew you liked walking behind women and as for Tripp, well..." Cade impish smile acknowledged her judgment.

"The senses must be part of any game plan for good old fashioned gitchee goo, don't you agree?"

Cade sensed the boat might be taking on water.

"I read a study a while back that revealed that lying down can squelch sensitivity to sound and smells...so the position of the church, 'missionary' may not be the best position, not as invigorating as say, sitting up."

"Or bent over?"

She eyed him closely. He hoped she knew that that comment was meant as an attempt at levity but she showed no 'tells' whatsoever.

"I read a few years ago that only one in five men consider sex to be the ultimate pleasure in their world; were you aware of that, sir? Your look says 'no'. That may be good."

The word, 'maybe' always concerned him.

"And about a third of males believed that 'being in love' is the 'bomb'. Where are you on this scale?"

"I'm in the ever equivocating 'I'm not sure'. I did read recently though that one in ten men shared with researchers that 'love', per say, is an idea whose time has past, old fashioned, not modern. These guys, and not me, necessarily, they said, well, that sex was better without it."

"Without what?"

"Love." He grabbed the wheel at the helm tighter. "Do you believe this, that amour is dated, unfashionable?" The current was becoming stronger and he wondered if he'd strayed away from leeward.

She put her index finger to her chin. "I suppose I am with you, undecided and happy with that decision."

"But you like the way it was, don't you? So why not the romance of lore? Too restrictive? I thought you like your ancients?" The maelstrom was near now and he knew it.

"Yes, I do see many of them in here with their nieces, spending boo coup in hope, I'm sure, of getting the "no can do" switched to the affirmative, and, as I'm sure you can attest; if one don't got the moolajuice, the hideous die young." Her eyebrows slightly arched but her eyes hinted amusement.

He continued. "Speaking of ugly men..."

"Yes?"

"Would as brilliant a male as a Socrates even have a shot today to grab some very ill bedside manners if he was without moneyed pedigree or pricey toga?"

"I read that his eyes bulged and that they sometimes swiveled."

"Swiveled?"

"Yes."

"Listen, there's a lesson here, my dear..." He suddenly sensed that perhaps he'd misspoken, but this concern past when he saw her jovially seal her lips with her free hand.

"Xenophon, you know the..."

"Greek historian, yes..."

"Well, according to him, Socrates was married to a woman called Xanthippe and according to the "X" man; she was, well, complicated."

"You mean difficult?"

"How 'bout independent?"

"I like that better, yes."

"The historian quotes Socrates as saying about his wife that, "I want to keep company with the human race and so I have acquired her"...the 'acquired' part, by the way, Miss Hooray, is what Xenophon put into Socrates mouth..."

"Uh huh...I've heard worse."

"Yes, well, again the complete thought, quote..."

"According to Xenophon..."

"Yes. It goes 'I want to keep company with the human race and so I have acquired her, for if I can put up with her, I will easily get on with all the rest of mankind.'"

Would the whirlpool claim another victim?

"Touche." Her smile signaled that he had made it to the breakwater.

"And another 'beaut' of a Greek, so my Professor Sorentsen taught me was..." "Is that Norwegian or pickled Viking?"

"Probably the latter. Anyway, he shared a ditty from Aristotle that went something to the effect...that basically, quote, 'that for women and barbarians, freedom, is a wholly inappropriate state.'"

"And they made busts of him? I've got your inappropriate state for you right here, mister!"

Their laughter gave notice to Sean and to Chaz to stay put, remain in conversation with J.C. and to continue admiring the fish.

"You've apparently met too many harridans whilst dating, haven't you?"

God, Cade surmised, she has some vocabulary on her, doesn't she.

"Speaking of hobbies..."

"You think dating is a hobby?"

"It's expensive, consumes much and in plenty of cases, when it runs its' course, more often than not, you are left wondering about when it began to lose its' attraction and what the hell was all the commotion about anyway, right?"

His silence meant he knew that she knew she had him.

"Hobby is a great cover, both for preferences and for perversions."

She had him even tighter. He leaned on the table with his hands now folded as if it would help relieve tension, good tension, which, in fact, it did not.

"Perversion as hobby example one; Kinsey, the sex studier slash researcher, whatever his title, one of his lab reports was concerned with the issue of determining whether men dribble or spurt..."

"When they are eating?"

"And Kinsey discovered that 70 percent of men...dribble."

He didn't move because he couldn't.

"Mr. Bartholomeau, I have a feeling that you are not in the majority ...although you do have a little...dribble of wine at the corner of your mouth."

Cade understood audacity was the requirement for the moment. He feared that if he didn't flirt dirty now, she might very well reevaluate her initial readings of his daring and of his 'devil ride south' persona. At least that is what he thought she thought. Most certainly, he did not want to lose her because of what, for him, was unnatural; a lack of temerity.

"Calliope, your hobbies; are they Keynesian in nature too? And I don't mean economics." "I get pleasure from many sources, Mr. B. boy."

Cade held back. "Expressions in color and in form; I guess you would call it, art." She sipped the remainder of her wine. "The subtle and the not so subtle skewed portrayals; the paid for nuances of the naughty and the haughty, yes, I find these the most attractive and nearly the most fulfilling of hobbies, the study of them, yes, I do."

"Nearly?"

"Yes, 'nearly', as I hold my heart in reserve for the most satisfying objects, presentation and protest, the defiance in the works of the artist against 'what is'; the allegiances to lost causes draw me in the deepest and the final tragedy of what could have been inspire me the most. They come in various shapes and in various sizes; the lost causes, I mean." Cade adjusted his posture.

"I have many of them sitting here in my club, knowing if they're really reflective, which is not why they enter my doors in the first place, mind you, that the truth is that they stand no chance to prance with my ladies of the dance and yet they return, keep showing up knowing they can never finish the dream. Now, is that a habit or a hobby, because both are repeat actions, must be something likable or you throw away the smokes or you burn the stamps; the collecting becomes a burden and not an escape."

"And the hobby loses mystique and the search begins for another source of comfort?"

"And avoidance..."

"Yes, very possibly."

"I work arts, I attempt creating in paint, do dabble in small clay works, sometimes. It is sometimes a balm to savage memories, sometimes."

Cade listen as professionally and as carefully as only trained negotiators can, trying to pry open what really is a motivating factor, what is that which is not revealed and to understand the 'why' of the deal and the 'what' which is in the air and needs answering. "...And it, the process of pushing against the world, Cade, I am lost in this delicate existence without clocks, without deadlines, as it is just me in the canvas or in the clay, it's the 'doing', not the done, yes, I'm happiest then."

Cade knew his mother would approve of the flame burning in front of him now. Finally, a woman, she would tell him, with talent to persevere, to stand and deliver in an arena of action where the material comes a calling as a slave to the spiritual; far, far away from this silly, sad time and place where 'ho' means 'humm' and where recognition is vastly over rated by accommodating fools. Yes, Lady Bartholomeau would most certainly find a fellow champion in Ms. Chardonnay Hooray. Damn.

"Years ago, a television producer who frequents my establishment when he is in town, gave me advice that stuck."

"A producer with something to offer besides a scheme; I am impressed." "Pepi said..."

"Pepi?"

"Yes, Pepi said that 'it takes a second to reveal the one, an hour to greet the one, a day to love the one, but forever eternity and a day to forget them. Life is too short to clothe yourself in bitterness, Chardonnay. Dance naked and the music will never stop.' So I do." Cade sensed opportunity to be 'bad' Cade.

"You have a make-love-all-night body, Ms. Hooray, and while I know that I am not the first to comment as such, I do know that I'm the only one that can promise would never hit the snooze button, once."

She smiled and he knew she was pleased with his 'vow'.

As she grinned Chardonnay waved towards Tripp and Sean to join them as the orders were being served. She then turned her attention towards Cade again.

"And you wonder why I sleep in."

As Sean and Tripp sat down, they recognized their presence was mere formality. Cade was beaming and the source of their friends' happy discomfort was glowing as well. Both men attempted to appear as if nothing uncommon was occurring. They failed.

They hurriedly ate the tacos, drank the drinks and tried to stay out of the way.

"You can be a slave to riches, a man in your position, Mr. Bartholomeau, but I know that you are not of that ilk. I believe you a generous soul or you couldn't possibly have the smile that you do."

Oh, God, Tripp thought, Cade's a goner but he is definitely going out in style.

Cade moved into the chair next to Chardonnay. She protested not. The Mogul and The Stripper attempted to keep their conversation on the down low without appearing to ignore the 'extras' at the table. They were unsuccessful. Ms. Hooray leaned close to Mr. Bartholomeau's left ear, which happened to be Cade's most sensitive lobe.

"Warm, genuine, you're obviously a man who goes for seconds and I like that."

Cade struggled not to let on to how ticklish he was nor how rapidly he was, shall we say, becoming motivated by the moment. He attempted witty repartee in effort to relieve his lovely tension.

"Nothing conducts heat better than diamonds, you do..."

She, still positioned a hairs breath from his skin, whispered, interrupting in soft sweet tone, "And nothing can cause such monstrous blackouts either, Cade."

She leaned back into her seat to give him air.

"Is Icarus falling?"

Tripp and Sean wondered what Ms. Hoorays comment implied.

"I do hope you are a different type of Titan, Cade."

Tripp finished his drink. "I have to be heading back to write tomorrow's column." This, for a deadline he really did not have, but a suitable excuse nevertheless. Sean took the cue and told Chardonnay, "What a pleasure. Thank you for your hospitality, but I need to be leaving too."

Since Cade had driven, and since he knew his friends well, he sensed they knew what they were doing, which he actually welcomed, as he was presently questioning his own reasoning ability.

Chardonnay arose and made as if she needed to 'return to running the place'.

She hugged each at the door and made sure each embrace was of the same length, but her smile, while polite, belied that her glance rarely wavered from Mr. Bartholomew's. She waved and disappeared as her bouncer or professional policeman of politeness as she called Burleigh, the perfect doorman/manager with undersize sleeves on oversize arms, held the door open.

As they got into Cade's Hummer, he couldn't contain himself. "GOG!"

Sean, from the back seat, "What the?"

"GOG," Tripp interpreted, "my dear man, Linden, is Cadeese for..."

Cade interrupted, "God ol', with an apostrophe, gorgeous!"

You're like an ostrich, Cade," Sean softly reprimanded, "Your eyes are bigger than your brain."

"Trash me all you want boys, but that lady, I swear, they're scarce. There's no assembly required!"

Laughter, then silence.

Sean Linden returned to considering the complexities of his future. Chaz Bellows wondered if Emily would see him that evening.

Cade Bartholomeau broke the silence. "Oh, shit!" He'd suddenly realized that, one, he had not given his phone number to the woman, and that, two, she hadn't asked him for it.

CHAPTER 17

Momentarily Pious

"Between the ideal and the reality/ Between the motion/and the act/ Falls the shadow"

December 7th 2015   T.S. Elliot

Hawkins-Burke is alone. He is aloft, flying west in Magi's jet, Moody 1; destination, John Wayne airport and two meetings with bond traders. Hyde was already on the ground in Orange County.

Nothing like a threat to attack a currency or dump bonds to bring rapid requests for face time. Get the large financials salivating at the prospect of a Magi move, short or long, and they want to ride with him, leading to Magi's position with the Corporation's preferences taking on larger than actual strength thereby making the bean counters efforts more likely to contribute to the Corporation's success. Maximize returns or feel the wrath of one Hawkins-Burke. Keep the potential in global finance continuously on the edge of crisis, make it every day news that a currencies failure is nigh and the stampede of the stupid continues and millions are ready for the taking. Pain and defeat can be hidden assets and bumbling managers and not enough investigators equals God's blessing on the activist Corporation, right? Ha! What God!

Hawkins-Burke turned away from the window and asked the attendant, Jillian, to fix a Caesar salad with "lots of garlic croutons." Jillian had been the Moody 1's 'mistress of the heavens' since the day the jet was purchased. Competent, circumspect, loyal, and paid handsomely; neither did it hurt her future prospects that she was also a very attractive individual. Hawkins-Burke played at making a pass now and then, but both understood that there were "no dice on this table, mister" and Hawkins-Burke knew that even he couldn't afford the price of losing her so Jillian was, in actuality, the 'sister' he wished he'd had, more so now than ever because the 'blood' one he was now mourning was gone.

Only Hyde knew of the gnawing, the mental abstracts, and the 'what could have been', his boss was contending with since Hyde had confirmed her death but not much more. Hyde had withheld the sad information from Hawkins-Burke while the CEO was on vacation in Spain.

Hawkins-Burke read the handwritten note above the memorandum for the meetings. 'Rebus sic stantibus'... 'Every treaty contains the unwritten clause.' It was a quote from Bismarck. Hyde had added ... 'Danger often beds down with opportunity.'

Hyde was referring to the upcoming meetings and to the workings of a special section of Magi Corporation, the currency division and to the unpredictability of the worlds half a trillion dollars a day money play in the financial markets.

Hawkins-Burke recalled Hyde's final comment during their conversation about the Magi mans sister's death. "Whether you are wealthy or you are overly poverty stricken, Stuart, goodness and evil have nothing to do with the situation."

Hawkins-Burke stared down at the passing clouds. Ha, this is, according to those foolish enough to believe, representative of the almost laughable domain of a thing called heaven.

Jesus, what a crock! He was surprised at the size of his hurt and how he was failing to manage it. Through a break in the clouds, Hawkins-Burke spotted what appeared to be a multiple car train of coal running across the flats of the mid-country. So much cash in that thin dark line. He was pleased that Magi had holdings in both domestic and overseas extraction properties. Overseas worked the best, especially in countries with the least governmental oversight and scarce indigent resistance; read here, enviros. Magi investments overseas centered in locales which offered low costs, relaxed regulations; and, most suitably for the corporations needs, in places of high unemployment with no dearth of dismay and poverty. "In the black lands," Hyde called them. "Danger dancing with opportunity in the muddied terrain of trampled dreams; we can be heroes' to these people, Stuart."

The head of Magi stared down at fields in winter array, a hodge-podge of straw and rust colored circles and rectangles bordering the slow moving rail cars.

What an ugly pastiche. Bonds and death. Both crush without rush. Both, just parking spaces, right God? One might take six months, the other, 66 years. No matter, the ultimate evidence of real term limits, right, Lord?

"Do you want ground pepper, sir?" Jillian placed the salad on Hawkins-Burkes' tray.

"Yes, please. Thank you."

Jillian finished serving and returned to the front work area and Hawkins-Burke returned to staring out the window to the view from 25,000 feet.

Damn it; she'd been so remote, so distant, the last years. Christ, I don't know. Was she married without children? Hell, he was Mexican; Catholic, I'm sure. Of course there are kids. An Uncle, really? Hyde's got to dig deeper when there's time for such trivia. Trivia? Why do I dismiss this? Because it's convenient, Stuart, you fool.

The Magi man took a bite of the Caesar. The pepper was just right.

Not so easy to condescend down what hurts the most, though, is it? What had it been, 15, maybe 18 years?

"Jillian, please; a strawberry daiquiri and make one for yourself. You know I don't enjoy drinking by myself." Jillian knew not to object and began as requested.

Estranged from his only known blood relative, how? He knew how, his ego allowed it to happen, that's how, you fool. An escape hatch, a descent into relativity and rationalization had kept these present feelings submerged until, until now. He felt the same pull at his innards as when he let loose on Hyde about redundancy in Magi's employment pools; when he signals his ire with his pat phrase of disgust, "Too many G.D. sinecures in these halls, Hyde!" Hyde would then customarily about face and quickly head down another hallway. Hawkins-Burke smirked, the closest thing to a smile besides when he addressed Jillian.

The Rockies appeared on the horizon, jabbing at the lower edges of the western sky, as unremitting and as uneven as the pangs now pulling at what remained of the CEO's conscience. Suddenly, he considered his habit of repaying generosity with tempered viciousness. It had been his method for excusing himself of any sense of obligation to anyone, a survival technique he'd believed from his earliest days on his own; but now, this too, rolled over him like the locomotive running heavy on the rails below.

"Your drink, sir."

"Thank you, Lillian. Did you pour yourself a double?" Lillian noticeably blushed.

"Just joshin', Lilly, just joshin."

Lillian excused herself. Hawkins-Burke turned again to the world outside his window. He took a small sip of the perfectly executed concoction; sip slowly or ice headache, here we come. Its 'Golden' good as only Lillian can assemble a liquid glass of 'recovery' juice. Golden was the color of his sisters' hair.

Toria Hawkins-Burke and Barrett Burke were king and queen sized producers in Los Angeles and they, like many other celebrities at the time, got the adoption bug. They adopted Stuart and his sister when the siblings were only three weeks old. The consummate Hollywood couple de jour sped up the adoption process with the alacrity that money in proper hands can accomplish when a deed needs doing and the deed concerns the image of 'very special' Americans; those types, then and today, who need everyone else to recognize their obvious grace and grandeur, those individuals constantly desirous of feedback commending their obvious generosities, a force as potent a drive, as equally as weighty, as the weary addicts whom need the silver hued needle of nirvana juice to validate their pain.

The Hawkins-Burke 'foursome' became the latest 'Perfect Family' in La-La land. Jesus, 'Jet,' why did you leave me? God, I know our first steps were boorish, self- centered but look where we came from! But we had to run, Jet; you know we did. When Mom and Dad weren't focused on the next script, they did love us, in their own way, as you said. 'Jet' was the 'wild' child, eventually leading to her ultimate act of protest in her desperate search for distinctiveness when Georgette Hawkins-Burke careened away from one of her packaged overseas treks to instead alighting in Mexico and marrying a handsome man of observable wealth who fell in love with the charming and spirited 'gringo loco'. Toria Hawkins-Burke and Barrett Burke publicly disowned her, although, in press releases, they obfuscated the real reason for their dismay. The step parents investigators did not find much that was verifiable about 'Jet's new mate; only that he was rumored to be one of the most successful drug lords in his state and that the local population was protective of him because, and this confounded the parents, he was considered benevolent to the impoverished and a bulwark against particular squads of corrupt Mexican police. Through the ensuing months and years, the producers attempted contact with their daughter up until the days of their deaths. They were unsuccessful.

Stuart Hawkins-Burke had pursued her too, especially after he had inherited the family wealth. He wanted to share, and for the first year or two of their separation, he never felt more alone, or the 'High Lonelys', as his favorite bands number one song at the time was titled.

Hawkins-Burke slowly considered the taste of strawberry and ice in his mouth and looked at Jillian in the forward cabin. Yes, The Circus Cures had hit it out of the park with 'High Lonelys". How odd now that he viewed Bellows as adversary, but this was in sync with Hawkins-Burkes view of the majority of the press. But give the 'front man' credit; Issac Chaz' Tripp Bellows or whatever he was calling himself at that hour, his lyrics did contribute to young Stuarts formulary conclusion that he wasn't unique, that he was like all others; "come in alone, die alone...the high lonelys cause many to fall, don't moan about it, don't groan about it, before the boatman shadows your heart, child, give mortality its due, sweat each drop out of the life you got, because, darling true, in the high lonelys, no one else will ever do it just for you." But, the complexities of being human being what they are, Hawkins-Burkes' greatest horror still remained, and that was to be thought of as a 'common man.'

Jillian noticed him noticing her but she was not affected as she recognized that her boss was staring right through her as he was wont to do when troubled or bemused. She knew it best to move on to other duties and not inquire.

Hyde still did not have much on the vanished life of his sibling and the CEO-CFO of Magi had no more rabbits to pull out than other in the hat of his house magician, Hyde, and this discomforted him.

Rumors, faint traces from few sources, were that there were children with the Mexican. Was he an uncle of dead nieces or nephews or both? In the first snippets Hyde was able to obtain, the word that seemed like fire to the eye, as piercing as the flame atop the colossus at Rhodes, was 'massacre'. This implied others besides his beloved 'Jet', right lord? The lives of drug lords and their families are guarded issues, mostly couched in cornered speculations leading elsewhere than the truth, but more often than not to lead and dead for those unfortunate enough to get too close to the fire.

Moisture gathered at the edge of his lids. He hadn't teared so much as he had this past week since a decade ago when he'd become emotional over what he thought was, "lost love." It begun with sadness, then anger and now, revenge...but against what, against whom? Georgette Hawkins-Burke was the only one in Stuart's life that had ever brought him the spirit lift reminiscent of a child's joy; pristine, unabashed, honest. She would be missed forever. Who perpetrated this on him?

He laughed at himself. For once, the 'monster of method', as he was known by the talking heads in the mimicking media, didn't exactly know what he wanted and did not precisely understand how to get what he did not know.

The first step came to him as he sipped a little more of what was now more ice than berry. He decided to do what any other notable mourner would do; he would establish a charity in her memory. She'd like that. Probably. Maybe. He felt somewhat sure that, at the very least, Jet would like it better than the first project he had undertaken which had been inspired by his sister. When Jet, in an act of defiance, in an effort to outrage their, as he came to view them too, self-indulgent, promote anything, anywhere, step parents, opted to pose nude in Playboy. As she shared with Hawkins-Burke during one of their last conversations, "I got the last harrumph, didn't I, Stewie", and then she had laughed and told him, "I love you, brother dear. Know this, even if you never hear it again from me as I tend to travel light, don't you know..." Stuart began to respond, "What do you..." and then being interrupted by the phone line going silent and a deafening deadness. He'd prayed for his sister's safe journey. He'd also thought of her other protest against their guardians, the spread in Hefner's glossy and then he had damned himself for thinking how good she looked naked. That was perverse and coarse and frightening to him that he would even consider this perspective and he had quickly scrambled to erase it from his thoughts and he had not thought of it since, until now, when she was dead. He hated these small acts of strangeness. This one, though, in the 'past imperfect' time of finding one's own path, did initiate one of Hawkins-Burkes earliest profitable ventures. Haunted by his sisters' audacity, her bite, and at that time, by his lack of it, he decided to have others 'pay' for his peculiar fear of being taken as not as shining a 'star' as his rambunctious and headline initiating sibling. Young master Hawkins-Burke paid a ghost writer to co-author (paid rather handsomely as there really wasn't a need for a large word count for the publications chance of success) with him and a noted photographer to combine in producing a handsome big hardcover coffee table-sized book, a "Now and Then" retrospective, presenting interviews and photographs with women in their sixties and younger, (Forty-five years old was the minimum age requirement) who, during their heydays of heavenly bodies and hopeful hearts had posed, it should be said, in some rather 'unreligious' publications..."just this side of porn," as the 'holy thumpers' had labeled them. The book investigated how the women's lives had changed since their controversial at the time acts so many ages ago. Better or worse? The publication sold as successfully as a cake recipe that called for edible marijuana as frosting. Hawkins-Burke had purchased the rights to all the ladies photographs and their stories and the young businessman additionally had provided above average royalties to them for their efforts. He thought his sister would approve, and at the least, he had hoped that she had been made aware of it even though he wasn't sure until finally, last year, in the only instance since their separation, he had received a Christmas card, let alone a short note, only the second written correspondence in fifteen years.

Hawkins-Burke reached for his briefcase. He eschewed the preparation folder for the upcoming meetings Hyde had compiled, selecting instead an odd shape envelope. He took the contents out. It was the Christmas card and the note. Had it really been a year already?

Georgette did comment that her brother's book, "Snap Back", was "delicious," but, oddly cryptically for her, she added, "...wouldn't put it out where children might catch sight of it as children must have space to grow old and dirty on their own terms."

She hadn't said 'her children.'

Jets' focus of attention centered on perhaps the most famous of the women from "Snap Back", a blond with a still wondrous posture and ponderous profile, a flaxen haired attractive lady who had come from pictorials to politics, becoming one of the most sought after lobbyist in Congress.

Jet had included a copy of the woman's short blurb from the book. Stuart had kept it folded inside his sisters' greeting card. He re-read the lobbyist words again.

"Tell me, young man, do you know...

What is a slave to wonder and yet often in your pocket?

It's not promised or owed to everyone, and often,

It's fire behind the rocket.

It's 'times' mistress and a handmaiden to history...

Though often pitiful, it can be forgiving too, the saving grace of mistake well taken... It's the 'why' of the 'how'... It's the 'then' and the 'now'...

...these reflections in black and white from youths' roar, its careless prowl... I embrace, dear man, for they measure the distance I've traveled...

Cocoon to butterfly beautiful, wonderful and new...

And what is this that drives me, that which puzzles you?

Why it's 'Change',

But of course,

'Change', I now growl... 'Change', my darling Stu,

'Change' for all we folly through...the final measure of Gods pleasure if we handle "it" as he would approve... 'Change'".

Jets' note read, "If she's a bimbo, I'm my mothers' child! God damn, why ever did she climb down the ladder to politics? A lot more than a little leg has gone a long way in what she wants men to legislate over, hasn't it, though? Yes, she stoops to conquer, obviously, but she has the brains to push the boobs, both hers and the ones she must deal with, to make it seem so effortless.

P.S. Men still salivate at the women they want to change, do they not, dear brother?" Stu grimaced again at this line.

"From what I've heard, I trust your life has healed and this pleases me so. Make your new year about more than just 'self'. I know you will. All my love and with whatever charge is left in my heart, know this, it's indebted to the kindness of God for having him plan for you to be in my blood, and brother, for having you being there at the beginning when all seemed so blue. Jet on!"

And she had. And the Magi man fought hard to foil moisture from forming in the eyes again.

The captain of 'Moody I' announced to his only passenger and to the only person the captain was allowed to fly for that they would be arriving at John Wayne in approximately ten minutes. Hawkins-Burke asked Jillian to go to the cabin and thank the captain for 'smooth flying as always.'

Hawkins-Burke looked out the window at the sunset framing the top of the planes left wing. He glances below at the twinkling 'whites' and the flowing 'reds' of what used to be his childhood home. He buckles his seat belt tighter. He promises himself he will not stay one minute longer than absolutely necessary. He wishes his sister was landing with him.

CHAPTER 18

"Outer Mongolia Is An Equal Opportunity Employer"

"It is a true old saying... that make yourselves sheep and the wolves will eat you."

Ben Franklin
on appearing weak to the crown.

December 19th, 2015

"I say it once more. No politics. Look guys, I don't wish to sell my soul at the Congressional cash register, just another government mule packing it in my pocket from the public purse! And before you say it, Military is different and you two know it."

The speaker was among friends, but friends not used to the speaker hemming and hawing. They knew him to be decisive and this recent bout of indecision was mildly unsettling to them.

"I'm reviewing options for in this odd time for me, abominable options as I see them, utterly mind numbing; Hamlet has even dabbled across my thoughts...yes, if it doesn't smell, why not?"

Sean was sitting across from Moah and The Navaho, both of whom remain consistent in feeling about what's the best for the situation their friend is in.

Moah suggests that, "You can't turn from the woes of this country, Sean. You have it, you have been vetted by the country in the blood you have bled; Hell, we all have, but you, you, Sean, have more to..."

"It's no use, Halas. I would feel two-faced and I can't really pinpoint the nexus of why I sense this, not yet, but I see..."

The Navaho nearly yelled, his frustration verging on outburst but he regained control with a slow building "AWuUUugh', these miscreants in office exploit the masses, man, and these with the wads get bigger wads; they behave in ways we the people would be criminalized for if we did what they do because these philosophers of sleaze and squeeze make rules for themselves...flittering from one camera to another, above the rest of us, grabbing for glory where it has no place being. They are part of the caste system in America, oh yeah, they are the untouchables when they conduct insider trades, and they are the untouchables when they forgive the student loan debts of their families and their workers, America's untouchables ..."

"What?"

"Oh, yes, Moah. These are just a few of their favorite things we would be in the slammer for while they and their cronies feed off these 'deeds'. Hell, they then get accolades for such actions from their aid and abettors in the bordellos that pass for the press today." "Excepting Tripp."

"Yes, Sean. We know Tripp is a fighter like us... but he's chosen infiltration and more power to him, but he serves in a corps known for crooked letters, operating in a working environment that's in a standards free fall."

"Remember, we were selected for physical prowess and mental resilience. Right there, Sean, you're ahead of 99% of these bottom feeders."

Sean waved it off, but Moah choired in, "The source of action is never the community itself; it's always, Sean, always the act of the separate soul, the against the current kind of man or woman, always in the minority because creative forces never originate en masse; it comes from the expression of one and how it illuminates and affects others to as critical a point as the 'thinker tinkerer himself.'"

John Truefellow didn't miss a drumbeat, "You've lead where others fear to stroll. You've been painted in the blue red of your own blood. The rank and file, the great mom and pops of American, don't need any more treasured travesties like the one's we have now." "The parties are perverse, Sean. We know, and sadly, I know they know this too and that is the truly disgusting part, but they are cowards."

"Dammit, enough, fools!" Sean's voice and the others had continued to slowly increase in volume until Mr. Linden's loud request. All seemed upset but all knew it was only momentary, but it still bit like the burn of being shot or the gut pull when the words arrive to the heart that someone loved had died. And the fact that their discontent was prompted by those they despise, had caused them to be near downright discourteous to each other, angered them more.

John Truefellow lightened it with, "What happened to the quiet professionals, huh?" "They quit drinking," Moah observed as he got up and headed in the direction of Truefellows and Lindens refrigerator. "It's brewskis time, my hearty boys to men."

The bottle caps popped. Sean was the only one who didn't initially sample the results of the decapping. "Really don't like either party, but I know I wouldn't be a participant in one of them for certain."

"Well that's a start, a decision. Hell, I've voted both ways, twice." Moah continued between sips, "And I've been disgusted and disappointed always."

Sean attempted to switch topics. "John, when will Nino get back from your moms?" "Comes back the 21st."

"And when will you come back from rudderless land, brother?" Moah's impatience was never camouflaged. "This country, I swear this as I swear to cover your two backs; the disenchanted, the disenfranchised, the Americans with their guts in the mud, they don't understand all this money for nothing that's rampant in their land nor do they comprehend the dignified ignorant that are ramrodding this country now, those that are grinding it all down into a shell of what it once was. Sean, Americans will tune in to an accountable, understandable detailed plan for achieving greatness again."

"Yeah, Sean," The Navaho took in more hop juice before continuing, "All they need is a man who can't be bought to show them the way to supply the many with what the few cling to today. I tell you, my white man, all would move in closer to the fire to hear that call, to take those one's with the secret guilt by the balls or the by the short hairs if they don't come equipped with the center of an average mans universe, to make the way-too- smug wish that, when all is said and done, they were back in their unloving mothers arms again!"

Moah raised his beer to The Navaho's vision and Sean slowly touched his to theirs.

Moah finished his beer 'gulp' and burped, not unlike the pounding of a gavel by a judge; it's the primitive call of Homosapiens, not exclusive to the male of the species, frequently sounded when one male wants the undivided attention of the others. Rarely fails in its goal. "Only in D.C.'s political insider culture can you find the disorder of thinking that lends credence to the postulation that working for anyone for under $200,000 is sub- human, a type of deprivation and suffering only a fool or imbecile would endure.

Once a great notion, shot to Hell again."

The Navaho, more emphatically, "Once a great nation shot to Hell again!" He turned towards Sean. "You know how Vets feel about this shit that floats on top. You know they would support you to..."

"Stop the noise, guys. I've told you and probably will again that I am leaning towards some sort of consulting work. I've resolved that by the first of next month to have a clear path laid out. And politics..."

"You make that word so perfectly profane, "Truefellow approved, "another reason you'd make it all happen right, Sean."

"If it sounds like a duck, "Moah added, "...clip its wings."

"Listen, dear roommate, our opponent is mighty. It's greed."

"An almost insurmountable foe except for the brave..."

"Or the uninformed." Sean's patience began to lose to the beer.

Truefellow did not pull back. "It would be the quest of a lifetime to meet the challenge of changing the conscious of a nation, would it not?"

"God, we're in mighty tall cotton with that lofty verbiage, aren't we?" Sean did not hide his growing frustration.

Sheriff Truefellow forged ahead with intensity, speed and force. "The national alienation of the purchased from powerless is widening every day, Sean. It has become all too familiar, the corruption that precedes most legislation and any election. I get sickened by its potential for even more damage by the graft, that when I think of our government, I get indigestion and sense I'm about to have the runs."

"You sure that it's not the beer, Braveheart?" Sean's attempt at humor fell flat. Moah broke in. "This is serious nature time, Sean."

"Thanks for the cabinet meeting, boys." And with Sean initiating the move, the friends raised their bottles and finished the contents. Moah excused himself as he was scheduled for an early flight in the morning. The Navaho said he needed to return phone calls and went upstairs. Sean remained alone. He began to wrestle with the 'what ifs' of two uncertainties; his future employment and the outcome of his relationship with the lovely Odessa. No 'body' slams in sight, he tapped out as the beer was telling him to take a dive into the waiting warmth of his forgiving friend, his beckoning bed, a welcoming oasis from the crowds in his head. 'Time to recover, hero boy, for tomorrow, we bleed anew.' In minutes, the pillow is declared victor; the arena empties, the trash cleared and the venue readies for the jumbo weight matches scheduled on the card for the next event. And Macho Man is nowhere in sight.

CHAPTER 19

"Foiled Flowers"

"Far better it is to dare mighty things, to win glorious triumphs, even though checked by failure, than to take rank with those poor spirits who neither enjoy much nor suffer much, because they live in the gray twilight that know not victory or defeat."

Teddy Roosevelt

December 21st, 2015

He'd been awakened by a call from the left coast the morning of the 20th. It was a whim invite from Odessa and he surprised her and himself too by booking the next flight available. He flew into LAX and immediately was taken in the hired automobile to Odessa's domain in the hills above the city of angels. They'd been at it; the good, the bad and the ugly, since he'd thrown his bag on her foyer floor.

Now, he was scheduled to return flight mid-day, and "last call time" worked its evil to warp all decisions and desires.

Sean escaped to Odessa's kitchen to prepare coffee... He flipped on her radio player next to the grinder and Donovan's voice crisply set the day, "Sunshine came through my windows today...", as Sean reached below for the cast iron pan to begin sausages and eggs, he stopped to take a finger swipe from the whipped cream atop the pie they had forgotten to return to the refrigerator in their haste for last night to close the 20th hour of their visit with more of the same of what had filled the previous nineteen hours of their time together. Still childish sweet; the whipped cream.

As Sean lifted the cookware, Odessa appeared. "Pumpkin for my pumpkins pumping ways, hey?"

Sometimes Sean thought Odessa beyond crude and sometimes he enjoyed it. "I read, honey, pumpkin pie and lavender gets men's penal flow stoked and I say you've proven the lab boys right, baby."

Sean sheepishly planted a peck on Odessa's cheek as he reached for the eggs.

"That article also said that the smell of cucumber and Good and Plenty candy got women good and ready." Odessa was topless. She wore short pink bottoms with purple fringe. Sean's attention is confused, not certain where to focus, but he managed," I understand the cucumber."

He turned to cracking eggs as Odessa open the freezer to get the sausage out. They knew they were superior bedmates but both separately questioned the grade and the durability of their happiness. What about those 'non-horizontal' moments as Odessa had come to think of them? Sean wondered too about the more important times away from the lovemaking: it seemed to him sometimes as if he and Odessa were looking for cues offstage. As in most early segments of the ga-ga goo-goo world between potential mates, the hearts were not listening to the heads and the participants sense it as it happens, but it's sent off, pushed away as the animal overwhelms the prey of thoughtfulness, freshly caught in the steely eyed honey trap of emotional stress and exhaustive release. The inexperienced call it bliss.

Odessa separated the sausages and prepared to fry them. "Pascal, you heard of..." "Always French, right?"

"Oui, oui, mon ami." She turned slightly three quarters and leaned softly against his shoulder. "Pascal, a beautiful thinker, he said, 'the Heart has its reasons, of which the Reason has no knowledge.' Comprenez vous?"

"A wee bit. Sensible, I think."

"Well then, "The Beauty Spot"; have you heard of it?"

"No, but I feel I feel it on me now...one of them."

"Ah, you sweet thing; no beauty spot. Alfred Louise Charles De Masset would think you not alive, Sean."

"Things are starting to indicate that I am."

"That checkpoint was hours ago, babe."

The sausages begin to sizzle.

"De Masset speculated that, 'Excepting idiots, lovers alone find no monotony in repeating the same thing over and over again'."

"Such as quoting French dudes?"

Sean added a splash of water to the glass measuring cup and began whipping the eggs. They enjoyed the close proximity of their skin. Sean's body was perfectly fit for briefs and Odessa's, well, her body was always prepared for anything on the menu, because, as she shared with confidants, she defined lust as 'nothing more than a preference for the divine with an amendment; you know the one, ladies, the clause that says that when the 'sumptuoalities' are over, there will be no aftertaste.'

"Oh, biscuits! Sean, flip the oven on, 350 please."

Sean did as she asked and moved around her and turned the oven on to the requested heat. He sensed origins arising of what most males would prefer to avoid it any cost, what to the majority of men is exhausting and nearly the most debilitating forum between a man and a woman there can be...discussing the meanings of love. Moahs' thoughts on the subject careened through Sean's mind. "If it needs talking about, it eventually walks out the door with nary a regard for the dust it tracked in."

"Offers seem to ...I'm not getting near the quality or the quantity of scripts I did before. My touch is no longer in vogue."

Sean vetoed his better notion for the situation and responded, "Please, that is outrageous, you..."

"I'm over 30. And even though I know the better brainy beautiful women that I portrayed in the movies are forming differently now; their characters are sadly conforming to the changing woman of today... Ebert said that the industry is led around by its nose by the teenage male who's lost interest in sex altogether. They want tough woman who kills everyone and destroys. Do you believe that?"

"I'm not a teenager."

Odessa eyed him carefully. "That's where you can come in and help me reboot my career, right?" She was teasing or so he thought. "Bang me up, Sean. Make me that one in a million bitch that movie boys admire and pay to see in their juvenile dreams; you can do that big boy, right? You know the type, those tykes that salivate at destruction and the avoidance of romance."

Sean had delayed the eggs completion until the oven was right for the biscuits so he whipped them one more time and maintained silence.

"You know, I've often thought of something Rosanne Barr said years ago. She thinks all the celebs, all of the famous are mentally deranged damaged souls."

Sean opened the oven and put the flaky Grand's in. He smiled at the actress and returned to giving the eggs another whipping.

"She says that we're indulgent freaks, selfish, petty people."

"Well..." Sean engaged as he poured the liquefied eggs into the hot and ready cast iron pan.."...you are the masters of the circus, in the center ring where crowds want to see the next downfall, dance or disaster, right?"

Odessa listened.

"It's like a, a 24-hour buffet of bluster and cluster fuck, topped with croutons of crazy, finishing at the end with the desert that smacks with the sweetness of the fact that 'they', you know, the 'watched', are so much more dumber than those doing the watching. The question I have about this cafeteria where 'self is the main course, is, where does all the grease go?"

Odessa frowned playfully, a soft glower supported by a grin, as she finished setting the utensils. "So I take it you're not too enamored with the smoothly elegant 'misses at adulthood' that I work with, are you?"

"Never told you my favorite song, have I?" "Not that I recall, no."

"'Smooth', by Santana."

"I thought it would be something by Dire Straits."

"But you don't want me to have chicks for free, do you?"

"Remember in Dakota that the first common ground we found there besides the parking lot was Blue Oyster Cult?"

Sean paused before answering. "Yes."

"When we agree or better said, we knew we were working our way to sinful love; oh come on, we both knew."

"Perhaps."

"Perhaps, my arse!

They sit down to breakfast. Sean gets up again for the orange juice. Odessa enjoys a bite of well done sausage as Sean returns to his seat with juice in hand.

"I'm talking red meat here, you understand."

"Of course." Then, Sean, almost singing, "Love you like sin, and that's the hard of it all, I won't be your pigeon nor you my second in command, both can't afford the fall." Odessa doesn't still.

"I'm talking about eating more chicken here, you understand."

"Biscuits are ready and I think its mimosa time too, darling."

"No thanks."

Odessa got the biscuits out of the oven and placed a couple on their plates and then heads to the bar to get the object of her next desire, the finery of alcohol.

"Liquor's Gods' little noggin knocker to remind me of death and that there is only so much merriment left on the kitchen timer, don't you know. And since I'm a religious little lass, I'm devoted to the teachings; dogmatic drinking, I call it."

Sean put peach jam on his biscuit. For some reason, the music began fading in and out, evidence of atmospheric interference.

"Chinese are known for many things, many insights such as this one, my love." Odessa finished the touches on her mimosa and headed back towards the breakfast table. "They say that a marriage gone bad, basically, my dear, is two humans sleeping in the same place but they dream different dreams."

"The indeterminate ground between love and hate is unmarked territory, isn't it; no matter how hard we try to find the metes and bounds..."

"I'm beginning to see once again that luck has nothing to do with love."

"I do not judge myself by others calculations."

"I've seen too many promised lands produce only mirages."

"Your Tinkerbelle is coming out and its, well, toilsome."

"You know, soldier; yes, people do become too attached to dreams and then they tire them out by their frothy efforts to make them real, yes they do."

Odessa smiled without hinting at the 'why' behind her apparent pleasantness. She was considering a term she'd learned early in her career. It was 'tiring room', as archaic a term for the 'dressing room' in a theatre as 'let's play pepper' is for baseball. Yes, the 'tiring room', made up clothes for the staged reality of exaggerated sound and the visually boisterous poke-in-your-eye color that is the Theatre. She sipped more mimosa. Sean finished his scrambled egg. He looked over Odessa's right shoulder to the painting she had done. She called it 'expressionist.' He thought it 'apropos.' It reminded him of a dripping poinsettia, rages of red streaking down as if tugging the color over the white backdrop, not unlike the loop rings of a tent held in place by stakes in the ground. The pointy 'petals' seemed tense, taut, discomforting and dangerously sharp.

"Is it true, Sean, that we are the only animals that can cry?"

Sean shrugged, but not in a rude manner. Odessa nodded ever so slightly. Both proceeded to finish their breakfast.

Sean's' thoughts flashed to a Marine friends lamentations upon the brave man receiving a 'Dear John' while on tour in the 'Muddled' East; the chiseled face struggling to show no change nor chink in attitude but failing miserably as the pain of sharing disaster could not be held back. Sean had never witnessed Clarence rupture under fire, ever; but this day; this 'fight' was different.

"Sean, she says that she's fallen in love with a felon. Now that's about as fucked as it gets! Pen pal in prison! Jesus Christ, that could be one of your white boys' country-assed songs, couldn't it?"

Sean had tried to lighten it up with, "Or Charlie Prides'..." but this hadn't played well during the burning of a breaking heart in the screaming heat of Afghanistan.

"Do you believe this, man?" Clarence, after a deep inhalation, had continued. "Damn shrink she went to during my last vacation over here. Told her she had a 'sexual disorder' and she paid him for that gabby garbage. With my money!"

Sean had not asked for more detail as he was satisfied that he had already heard enough but you don't leave or push away another man gone through the broken guardrails of the gender gauntlet; never.

"I called the degreed asshole when I got stateside. You know, I knew this letter had the potential of being delivered but I had to try to understand the failure, you know? Sean recalled silently assenting and even putting his hand on the big man's shoulder. "Shrink told me that my choir girl was something called a love advocate; no, I mean avoidant, a love avoidant. Said some women, my wife, fantasize... found inaccessible man more attractive, more desirable, more dangerously exciting, and more stimulating than the actuality of a meaningful relationship with a willing colleague. A willing colleague! What the shit is a willing colleague, Sean?"

God what was, where was Clarence from? Tuscaloosa, no, Tulsa; no, Tuskegee, yes, the airmen town, eastern Alabama, Tuskee..."

"Sean." Odessa sliced through his cerebral play. "Sean, I swear, you're on some kind of mission overload when you want to be."

Sean eyed the most beautiful woman he had ever seen without makeup. "You misjudge my reticence." Sean folded his hands in front of himself, elbows on the table. "It's both of us, Odessa. You think the sky when I'm thinking down to earth. Our wavelengths are frequently not the same width. Either I'm above or you're the one in the balloon. It seems it might never be the same champagne flight, no matter how many bottles are popped."

The morning felt sluggish, aching with the expanding weight of goneness.

The interference of the radio stopped. A commercial for a last minute Christmas sale blared through, clear as the sight on a snipers scope.

Sean couldn't shake the image of Clarence's swan song; a swan song, something from ancient Greek fable that said that swans, black or white, I suppose, sing a last song before they die.

"Shoddy dismissal is just this side of easy acclaim, don't you know, soldier boy?" Odessa drove it on home. "Yes, I've screwed up so many times. I've caused the people I love so many agonies...But, Sean, its kindness or coldness with you; there's no win, place or show, is there?" Odessa fought not too well up. "And because I've never felt so much on the line as I do now, you are unquestionably, my biggest mistake."

Sean found it odd, if not obscene, how glamorous Odessa looked in her refined dismay. She finished her mimosa before asking, "Whatever happened to happily ever after?" "Where does that come from, habit or hobby?"

"You forget, Sean. Stars always get to lick for free, even if it's the last sucker in the jar." "And you forget, Odessa that I never stay through the credits."

Odessa got up, heading to the landline. She tried to stay off cell phones as much as possible especially at her residence. "I'll call the car."

"Believe me, I will be ready."

Odessa finished her instructions to Melinda and hung up.

Odessa pushed her kitchen chair in. She left her hands on the top for support. "You will always remind me of why there is a God, Sean, for only a God could provide such pleasure and such pain as you do."

"You're right, except for the 'God' thing." Sean pushed away from the table and stood. "Not a low bar for me regarding emotional leaps of faith, I agree. But Ms. Gabriel, it's a required 'good bye' for both."

"For now."

"Yes."

Sean regretted it after he spoke it. It was the first time he recognized tears forming at the sides of Odessa's stunning eyes. He was at lost for words. He thought an actress without lines or without a script sadder than an unwanted puppy in a metal cage. He immediately left to dress.

Instead of confronting the actuality of it, they attempted to act as if it was just another December day; they failed, as two more scarred hearts broke apart in a world which didn't have time to referee nor even notice.

In the short term, each would work hard to keep the one from entering the other ones thoughts. And both would approach this task from different perspectives.

The actress reverted to her preferences for indulgences in 'whispered only' varieties of sex; penance by penis, she deemed it, trysts with contingencies and whomever she was with understood the ritual well, with Odessa in total control; from the communion at the comfortable alter of a firm mattress to the offering plate that never went empty, the deity had you by the balls and you best not forget it. The parishioners knew also, that when the sermon was finished, they needed to vacate the church quickly as these were the commandments in Ms. Gabriel's cathedral of the 'Could of, Would of, Should of, Church of the Holy Gone Wrong'. Odessa believed that she was on the right track again and that God heard her prayers and that God had always forgiven for her improvident paths to his glory or why the Hell else would she be graced with all her orgasms, if it wasn't proof of 'high five' Hallelujahs from the Lord Almighty himself, of course.

The soldier's path, well; Sean would swear two oaths, one, to never fall into the devils trap of taking the bait of foolishly believing love exists, biting into it full throated and not giving a damn about how an overabundance of sugar can kill and, two, he would never ever make the mistake again of believing that men and women were of the same species.

They hugged and Sean got into the limo. Odessa turned to get busy cancelling commitments for a week, planning to stay home for time to privatize her pain as only she knew how. Sean did not turn to look at her walking away. The first song on the limos sound system seemed Hitchcockian in its perfect sting. Sean smirked as The Doobie Brothers 'Without Love' stretched the limits of credulity. He shut his eyes as if it would provide relief from the testimonial of what they had just witnessed, one of the saddest moments in his life. It did not work as 'play' was stuck on an irreversible loop and continued without abatement for the next six hours it took to get to D.C.

* * * * * * * * * * * * *

The Murky Mayan was at 'code red' celebratory level. Its proud owner triumphantly acknowledged the restaurants three year anniversary, particularly noting the establishments' track record of having survived opening day and that The Murky Mayan had not only weathered the mumbo jumbo of the planet alignment on December 21st, 2012, and the attendant dire predictions of disaster and woe that were foretold for the day its doors opened, but that he was most thankful for the fact that the restaurant had survived in spite of his, Cade's, inadequacies as an owner and also "Thank God that 'The Murk' had a staff that knew what the hell it was doing or the Murky Mayan would have had a treasured place on one of Tripp Bellows restaurant walls."

Cade Bartholomew did not share that he was big time happy that Sean Linden made it back from La-La land to celebrate with him. Sean had called from the cab to ask that Cade meet him at the delivery entrance as Sean was tired and did not want to face a crowd the instant he entered The Murk "after a tiresome trip," but that he did indeed wish to have one drink with his friend to share in Cade's joy in spite of weariness from travel. Cade greeted his back door guest. "How's the drama queenie?"

"Not funny, Cade."

The mogul knew body language. Sean's enunciated 'serious', not humorous. "We're heading to my office; let Tripp and the others alone for awhile, right? Except for those we love, the Murks' is packed, as usual, with a whole lot of the 'expensively odd but rich' in the joint and I can tell that's the farthest thing from your mind right now."

"Thank you."

Cade handed Sean a shot of J. Beam and they made their way to Cades' 'haven from havoc' as he called his soundproof, comfortable, plush chaired, no desk, one fire proof file, private domain, office.

"A little tight on the light, a lot of been there, done that, before you got there and done that, right? I mean out to Cali?" Cade couldn't help himself and Sean understood.

Nachos Gigante arrived, escorted by two expertly devised mujetos. The waiter left. Sean responded. "You know that men don't talk about 'it' like women do?"

"Define 'it.' Is it like a Clintons 'is'? Of course he lied about 'it' too. Most men do. Most women don't."

"I felt I loved, Cade."

"Most men do. Guacamole?"

Sean had concluded on his flight East that maybe the women, few as they were, were replacements for a mother; momentary icons for a special kind of softness he'd never felt, but had speculated on often as to how it should feel. Maybe. He pounded the mujeto dry. "I fell in love with her laugh and tender pleasures."

"Must be; better than with her pout, yes?"

Cade emptied his drink. "She's an actress, for God's sake, Sean. The blood in her veins runs on perfected coyness and adept contriteness and her heart is on a maintenance schedule that hardly, if ever, allows for it to be broken. Hell, her eyes cause more mischief in a week than I have in all my wanderings on the avenue of scoundrelhood with my entire body! Listen, son, perception must be clear, precise, early in the proceedings. Your aura must sweat bee-bees with the gleam of another's dream...and the sale goes down, brother; usually, but unfortunately without a warranty, though. Remember, Sean, 'touch and go' eyes have the longevity, the half-life, of unrefrigerated sour cream."

"She quoted James Madison to me, Cade, first time we get together."

"She had you at 'Hello Dolly', right? What she say, what?"

"Quote, 'The truth is, that all men having power ought to be mistrusted,' unquote. And then she said, 'excepting you, Sean."

"Maybe she was just laying out the ground rules...that, no matter whatever executive privileges were stirring up between you two, she was going to be as frank as the fourth president and that she would be the one that would caste the initial fly in the ..." "What does that mean, Cade?"

"Just saying that the hook sunk deep into your lip. Listen, listen, my ex, and by that I mean my ex-wife..."

"Kirsten?"

"Yes, you ingrate. Only married once and you know that, bastard. Nevertheless, I learned during the paradise days and nights of unholy matrimony that if I think what she thinks and she knows that I know this, that I'm, well, wrong. Doesn't matter. Kirsten did teach me one thing worth remembering though..."

"And that is?"

"Never envy a sheik or a Mormon man."

"Excepting Tell?"

"Of course."

Sean took another bite of Nacho Gigante. Cade followed suit.

Sean finished first. "You think Tripp and the others wondering where you are?" "No. There's plenty of walking foolishness in the house to keep him and the others occupied for a little longer." Cade stared at Sean with slowly building concern for his friends' demeanor. Rare to see this man this, well, down. "Aspirin's probably out of place now, right?"

Sean laughed for the first time since four o'clock that morning.

"Vixen? Hear of it?" Not waiting or allowing time for response, Cade smashed on," It's a female fox and the other meaning in Webster's is a turbulent, quarrelsome woman, a shrew."

"A turbulent fox? Yes, that was your weakness, your attraction then seemed limited to innumerable occasions of misinterpreting your early plays of the heart, wasn't it?'' "Harsh, but true, yes. So I speak of what I therefore intimately know thereof. Be weary, Sean, it's never easy to completely escape unscathed the travails of amore."

They both paused to allow for the nicety of silence.

"Look, Sean, after meeting Chardonnay, I feel, well, I don't think about them, the others, I mean. Maybe its heavens' way of getting us to move along I suppose. I tell you, I'm sitting here amazed at humanities talent for forgetfulness. My current indifference over all the 'what in my life is a godsend, really."

"That's just a losers cry over one too many loves taken downhill on one too many black diamonds, on one too many pairs of the wrong skies with the wrong wax..."

Cade saw Sean's smiling and heard him insulting. This delighted Cade as this is a good thing in the unfocused blather of male bonding, which only males recognize as such. "Ah, but you got to love the faceplants, my son, the faceplants are sometimes messy good, don't you agree, Mr. Linden?"

"...Or better than that, Mr. Bartholomew..."

"Yes?''

"...It's the yelp of a certain media mogul with a penchant to pursue, affection certainly, for things that come in pairs..." Sean raised his hands chest high and began turning his hands, fingers and thumbs pinched closer together, as if he were adjusting unseen knobs on something other than an old Silvertone radio. Then, in mock German, Sean raised his brows and, "Komen sie here, come in Berlin; wie gehts, vist you, darlink, Helga?"

"Yes, yes; you're right. I'm a sucker for. .."

"Suckers."

"Yes, Jackass! That and women with meaning behind their walk, yes." "Uh-huh."

Yes, like Danica's strut that time in pit row where she was god awful pissed at some driver that had cut her off or something...a direct stride, an 'out of my way' movement; now that's a meaningful walk in a woman and yes, I like the 'watch me' gait too, but the one I respect most is that other stride which approaches and says to any man with a clue to hide your manhood quickly...yes I respect that even more than the second movement mentioned, yes."

"You speak like a man of experience."

"Sean, ex girlfriends are like balks; they come back to haunt you just when you think you are going to get out of the inning unscathed. Hey, you know, Sean, Helen of Troy..."

"Yes?"

".. .in my youth I found it damn near impossible to believe her story, the Iliad's and then, upon further reflection..."

"And how many harassment suits?"

"...and I became older, I could see how it could happen, I mean a war over a woman." Cade's cell phone rang. "Yes. Yes. Uh-huh. Well, Sean and I needed to yak. We'll be out in a few minutes, yes, thank you." He turned towards Sean. "I won't mention the Odessa thing to Char or anyone else. I'll just follow your cues."

"Don't say 'cues' right now."

Cade smiled at Sean's feigned indignity. "Sean, bud, just remember there's no infield fly rule on the diamond of love either. Nothing's automatic. Nothing. Except when you hit one out then the next one's sure as shooting' going to be high and tight and you wake up with the taste of the batters box in your mouth; that's a no doubter, for sure."

The pair of friends arose. Cade put his arm around Sean's shoulder. "Shall we muster forth to the marvelous sounds of a happy Murk where better moods await us, Watson?" "Only if there are more mujetos, Sherlock."

"Tallyho then to the sound of, of, well, a pair of mujetos!"

"And drinks too, right?"

"But, of course. What else but the best for a pair of chums, dear man."

"Or for a couple of bums, right?"

"Did you say buns, dear boy?"

At that instant, Sean could not think of another place he would rather be than in the company of another self inflicted wounded man; it's a healing thing old chap, don't you know, what!

CHAPTER 20

"White Cuffs And Corduroy"

"To be a man is actually to be responsible to know shame when you come upon suffering not caused by you; to take pride in the success your colleagues have won; to feel, as you apply your strength, that you helped to build the world."

Antoine de Saint Exupery

December 22nd, 2015

The location did not matter. The event did. Senator Dunleavy Bruce rotated his annual charity event among various ballrooms, slash, high ceiling seminar rooms, to host his annual wintertime "Children's Time Now" charity extravaganza.

The Senators' adopted familial foursome, Cody, Josey, Dakota and Shane, were in attendance acting as auxiliary and trusted 'protection' since they were old enough to assist their stepfather, not only as co-sponsors but, additionally, as on-site co-security with the hired off duty enforcement authorities, whose regular job was in the employment of the District of Columbia's politicians, otherwise known as, D.C. capitol police.

Add to the Senators son's, the usual-unusual suspects attended too.

Representing, among many corporate donors, Magi Incorporated, was Jansen Hyde. He presented a rather large monitorial check to Senator Bruce, an action conducted as professionally slick as usual, specifically timed to highlight the generous action by Mr. Hyde to insure, early in the proceedings, that the press were sober enough and able enough to properly and duly report the largesse of Hyde's employer, publically bending over backwards to help the single-digitally aged humans in need and that such act of kindness would be properly reported in the next day's 'news chomp.'

Tripp, Cade and Sean, nearly recovered from their Murky Mayan celebration of the previous evening, were, to the best of their abilities, acting sober and, in the case of two of them, to fend off the way-too-close scrutiny of two new "suspects," Chardonnay and Emily, attending the festivities for their first time and accompanying their men in grand style, hangovers be damned, not allowing the men's foolish ways to interfer in the ladies approach to the sense and the step of the occasion.

The Navaho, Godboy are in attendance as well as Sean and Moah's Cranium Fill's co- owner, Mr. Drummerman, who had flown in on a late afternoon flight. Professor Sorentsen always appeared to assist his best friend, Mr. Bruce, in any of the Senators charitable endeavors and this evening was no exception.

The large room became a stage for the serial 'otherness', endemic to D.C.; a contrived arena of self awareness swirling with misrepresentation guided by disinterested inquiry and all nicely wrapped in the deceptive gloss of polished fawning and distorted decoration.

Senator Dunleavy Bruce stood besides Sean Linden, giving him a blow by blow description of the Senators most recent interaction with the master lobbyist of the town, the man who had just finished donating a princely sum, Mr. Hyde.

"I swear, Sean, he has a sibylline touch at the end of most of his sentences; a scurrilous tone more often than not, given to coarse jocularity at times, yes, but, as Brits say, a bit stroppy for my blood."

"But he did pay you handsomely for the privilege of his company, did he not?"

Mr. Bruce smiled at the younger mans' sardonic observation. "Well, just remember, no matter Hyde's 'talents', he is saintly compared to his boss..." The host of the event allowed no further interruption, nor hardly a breath, as Mr. Bruce continued, "When that Representative begins a speech, Sean, dyspepsia begins and doesn't quit until his mouth stops emitting sound...and that couple over there, well, they think they're the end all, be all of atavistic asses, but they are really just asses...and God, she, while she is an able bodied foe and I have respect for some of her tricks, but she's a full mouthed source of crapulence more often than not..."

"Full mouthed?"

"Something I used early days in Oklahoma; term for cattle, for judging how healthy, how they have a full mouth of teeth, understand?"

"Piranha must be in tip top shape then."

"And even though that committee chairman standing next to what I assume is his daughter goes on and on like Methuselah, we have combined for a few bills, he mostly works on the tarra diddle side of the aisle; just look how he is doing all the talking while his escort, uh, daughter, speaks volumes' about what his real priorities are, right?" "Some things will always be the same."

"By the by, Sean, I thank you for attending, supporting the future, kids..."

Sean nodded.

"...and for suffering the foolhardy among us paper pushers and for hearing out my unbiased commentary on all of it too."

Sean caught the twinkle in the Senators eye and raised his virgin orange juice to touch base with the Senators "of age" glass of rye. As Sean sipped, he spotted Cade with his new lady engaged in animated conversation with Chaz, but he thought it would be rude to excuse himself from the Senator at that moment. He needed to drink a little more with him than just the one toast and then maybe, sooner than later, he could politely exit. Chaz studied his friend, the mogul, and his other friend, the stripper, as they interacted. Since the couple's introduction at Horace's, Chaz noted a change in Cade. Cade usually had gone off like a school boy about his previous 'fem fatales par excellence,' with each lady always having been tagged by Cade as 'the one.' Now, whenever Ms. Hoorays name came up, Cade is reticent, even almost damn near a gentleman.

Ms. Hooray excused herself to the powder room.

Chaz immediately charged into the world of 'righteous kismet.' "Fates happy fickleness, Cade; you believe it, I believe it, right?" Before Cade could utter an attempt at an educated response, Mr. Bellows continued, "You know that Jefferson and John Adams died on July 4th, same year, 1826, right? Well, did you know that Shakespeare and Cervantes died on the same day too, April 23rd 1616? I'm telling you, Cade, 'serendipity' is the 'capital letter' at the beginning of the sentence of life and its' the 'period' at the conclusion of its' term too. Its Gods toy, I swear it. I bet you don't know that Jack Benny liked the age of 39, what he always said his age was, because, if I remember correctly, it was his favorite psalm: no, wait, maybe, something with the Bible that dealt with David and his son, Solomon, that dude of wisdom and queen of Sheba fame; well, he ruled for, you guessed it, 39 years, and Benny, somehow, attached to it. Did you know?"

"You are a veritable source of frilly laced 'what's goin' on's,' aren't you? And what does this have to do with Chardonnay?"

"As always, we must provide venues for vivid expressions of the intimate and the ultimate, don't we? It all goes together as if it were all planned, that's what I mean about you and..."

"And you smile with the vague pain, Tripp, of Mother Teresa, Mary Todd Lincoln,

Jimmy Carter and Andy Kaufman rolled into one big furball of deke and freak pandering philosophy about the destinies between women and men, and I think it's a bucket full of..."

"So you don't believe the story of Rome is not repeatable?"

"What?"

"Empire in decline, happening now and it has always gone this way, Cade; just as a God would have his toy continue in its same ways to satisfy his need for mirth and release from the stress of being the deity; playing with time and with measureable amazing effects that seem incongruous to us mortal mites but fit perfectly into a tired Gods scheme of things to provide him with amusement and a break from his other required duties."

"Jesus!"

"Look at the exaggerated art in our galleries and the spectacle on T.V. that your network frequently contributes to...you think none of it is meant to be; you think Chardonnay wasn't in Gods heart, way before you both were born, that you both weren't part of his heavenly equipment devised by him to please him with what you call 'happy luck', of you both making the acquaintance of the other, when it was, in actuality, God enjoying his toy, his proudest invention, besides life itself, the occurrences of accidental discoveries, which really aren't so unintentional at all? It's destined."

"And this coming from the composer of "Dogpile With You, Girl."

"I never released that on an album! A single, maybe, but, dammit, Mr. Bartholomeau, I'm just saying, its righteous serendipitous fortuity that you met this woman of our times, just in time, camera boy."

"God, Chaz, you really love me, you really do..."

"Shut the schmooze, schlemiel. Serendipity really means even slobs can get fortunate." "I think it's a Zen lapse, your thinking, I mean."

"Well, I've always said that foolish chakras can be good for even people like you...and a stripper with brains is a businessman's personal pah-pah dream become reality, isn't it? And before you say anything, I know she is a business woman, not just the easy cliché of having the handle of 'stripper' attached to her."

"Did you two men of the cave figure out which of you found out that the earliest known recipe was for beer? And now wine. Come on, which one of you gets the bone?" "Gentlemen and lady," Tripp looked at the others; could not remember what he had wanted to say.

"I'm sure you know that primitives initiated boys to see if they were ready to be men, ready to take a bride." Chardonnay picked up speed.

"Jesus, that is..."

Chardonnay cut Cade off. "And the brides demanded that the prospective grooms prove their manhood, publicly proving the males boundaries for pain for which marriage..." "Which marriage certainly can be," Cades' smile faded as he adjusted to Chardonnay's disapproving smile which he knew really meant 'laugh if you dare, please; but do so at your own risk, buster.'

"Among many, initiation required circumcision." Chardonnay took a sip of her drink. The men took shots of theirs. Chardonnay pivoted on her heels to face Tripp straight on. He still hadn't thought of what he had wanted to say. "Yes, Tripp, the brides get to watch the ceremony..."

"I thought ceremonies were good things."

"...and during the celebration as the brides watch with keen attention..."

"I bet."

"... because if they witness a groom to be, flinching or saying anything out loud as the knife does its duty, the bride would refuse him, not wanting to be stuck with "a girl" as they called it, for a lifelong mate."

Tripp was pleased with his judgment that this woman was finally, yes, 'the one' for his best friend. He remembered what he had wanted to say before Chardonnay's sharing of what pleasure means to primitives. "Give her of the fruitage of her hands, and let her works praise her. Proverbs 31:31."

"God quoting now, are you? Speaking of men becoming men by the good works of women with good hands, did you know that the Spartan males were forcefully made aware in their prepubescent days and nights the arts of survival, the techniques to take hardship, very hard circumstances and turning them around with demonstrable endurance learned from youth, so entrenched in a Spartans' mind, his soul, that no matter the weight of said 'hardship', the Spartan, if truly a Spartan, would ask for more." Before the men could catch a breath or utter some ignorance, Chardonnay concluded. "Yes and these warriors in the making were taught to steal if necessary, lie too: to keep to the short use of big words, bravery, trained thoroughly in the careful observation as to what works and what doesn't, but most importantly, the Spartan youth were taught reverence for the justice of God, or Gods in their time of reference. Always got something to do with God, boys, no matter how it arrives, if anything good is going to come."

Cade was the first male to become untangled as he espied two 'friendlies approaching. "Ah, Chardonnay, please meet another friend, John Truefellow and his nephew, Alejandro Buddha Jesus Simon de Mejas"

"Well, my pleasure, Mr. Truefellow."

"The Navajo." Tripp added.

"Yes, Cades told me and you... "Chardonnay hesitated, attempting to recall Godboys many worded God-given name. The young man rescued her.

"Just 'the nephew' is fine for now, ma'am."

Laughter welcomed the humbleness. A waiter appeared with wraps and as the others indulged, Chardonnay focused on Mr. Truefellow.

"Your proud nation, John, if I may call you that..." "You sure may."

"It's, well, when I was first planning my business," Chardonnay carefully eyed Godboy and did not think twice about forging ahead, "I considered another name instead of Horace's and its, in it's odd way it was in my mind because of reading stories of your canyonlands, reading of, well, the tribes poverty in general, and what I saw as the complete failure of this government, with the alcoholism, the lack of electricity, and running water so scarce, I could think of nothing but great sadness and I ,somehow, when I thought of your reservation I thought of Pandora and her story... eons old tale of woe and ill outcomes...and, of course, 'Pandora's Box' for a gentleman's club might seem forward but ideal for marketing... nevertheless I backed off then for Horace's, but..."

"So you saw Pandora, tied it to what Native American has put up with?"

"Simplistic, I know but,"

"I think not, Chardonnay. I think you're arrow on target." The Navajo turned to Godboy asking, "You've at least heard of Pandora, right, Nino?"

"Yes. To me, she's Mexico."

"Pandora was the first mortal woman sent to earth as punishment to man for Prometheus's theft of fire. It's always the woman to get blamed, isn't it?" Ms. Hooray didn't wait for affirmation. "The box she was sent to earth with held all the ills of humanity within and when the lid was opened, all wretchedness imaginable was loosed throughout the world, and as the fable goes, after the punishing act, leaving only Hope at the bottom of the box."

"Poignant and painful."

"Life and childbirth," Chardonnay responded.

"Navajos and Mexico," the youngest member contributed.

The Navaho was impressed. She talked 'other dimensional' as if she really meant it.

"Animal spirits speak. It's the human-animal duality. You have your power animals, you dance to them, your pow-wows, their power, your drums...do you know they produce changes to the central nervous system, low frequency results in more energy transmitted, more spirits in the sky; yes, drums, are best for trance states because of their wonderful effect."

"Yes, that and peyote."

Through her laughter, Chardonnay spotted Cade and Tripp, still a distance away, talking to a reporter acquaintance they both liked and the lady was obviously maintaining their attention. She saw Moah join them. Odd, how so often, men hate to hear the words of a woman unless the woman is new. Didn't matter now as she was pleased with her company as Mr. Truefellow and Ms. Hooray verbally indulged in numerous topics, from the worship of stars, sabaism; stripping and women as the more powerful of the sexes. Godboy remained a silent but keen observer.

"Look, John, without Wokatanka, God, Yahweh, we would all be naked, right? We'd would then all die first from overpopulation because what else would we do? Eventually equilibrium would occur as nudity would become common, and the intimacy of feeling, that high as you feel approachable to the universe hand in hand with another; it would all get damped down, become work, not wonder; and the less frequency of attempts to reach deified heights through sex and the failures to do so would proceed the downfall of life, of us, and why? Why due to the new 'sexy', celibacy. Of course, you understand, women would fare better than men."

"Oh and why would that be?"

"Because we're more sophisticated in our denials and in our desires."

The Navaho knew when to remain quiet. Godboy knew his mother would like this strong style of one Ms. Chardonnay Hooray. Near the St. Nick ice sculpture and in dangerous proximity to the oversize punch bowl full of swirling Bailey's, three "wise men" were in full throttle mode a la Holiday. "I can see by your face, Moah, that you don't agree with the concept that the proposition for today's Americans is 'I give you my freedom, now give me back my safety."

"Chaz, on the contrary, I agree with you partially."

"Do tell."

"The Patriot Act was meant to give cover to the government for its acts as well as shall we say, extracurricular powers that everyone said they would come back later to and argue the legalities after threats are contained. Threats can sure last a long time in the air, forever sometimes. Politicians gave it intrusiveness because of their own cowardly thoughts. Now we experience warrants without findings; and forfeitures, a technocrat term for robbery, outrageous for its scale and for its scope, the size of which is certifiably a brigand's wet dream. With the data basing of every breath we make and every leak we take, Sam's going to become even more unreasonable as his understanding the fundamentals of each of us is enhanced, fined tuned and we are then shepherded into even more unfamiliar and unwanted corrals for new brands."

"Do you hear that Cade, Moah's come around to...?"

"Come nothing. I partially agree, I said you're a systems guy and I'm a person's guy."

Moah smiled at his false categorization as did Chaz.

"Politicians, except for Dunleavy over there, they are the reason for our developing demise. They allow this dismantling by the DEA, the FBI, EPA, IRS, and every other asshole alphabet agency that the politicians like to say they're on the side of when the politicians feel the crush of making any heavy-duty decision such as, oh, I don't know, what about the security of every mother's daughter and son in this country? Go overboard of protecting freedoms by squelching them. That's the reason you never give a politician an even break. They'll take that as a mistake and act according on a perceived weakness; yes, this gung ho patriotism by the pols has been cause for, shall we call them, modifications, to civil liberties, pleasing everybody but the people who are paying for their enslavement, us."

"Modifications?" Cade questioned further, "You mean strangling the life out of all our rights, don't you?"

"Yes, just trying to low key it in the spirit of the season."

"Yeah," Chaz added, "it's Children's Now Time, don't forget."

"Yes, it is, Chaz. Our freedoms and how we fight for them and how we go about protecting them against the distinctly different forces, internally and externally, which we face in this modern era of mans more costly and most deadly errors; so yes, this function's for their futures and don't forget to cross your fingers either."

"The terrorists..."Cade inquired, "...or the politicians?"

"Look Moah, we agree on the direction maybe but not degree because..."Tripp paused, then in a low but firm affected pitch spiced with Country Music vocal twang, "... you see, my prickly pals, Sturm and Drang just ain't my Lovin' thang." Tripp finished his Baileys again. "My 'Lovin' thang' is unscrewing, revealing the touch the ground truth about the 'importants' in life; reporting, yes, it's the 'It' for me and yes, I still caress crooning too, but..."

Cade rarely complimented but now was, after all, the time of Noel. "Tripp, we have our polar opposites but you're the only press person I can stock trust in. Of course, in these desultory days of imposed despair and cleverly produced catastrophes...even warthogs can be glamorous, so I..."

"Cade's right, Tripp. You haven't the traits of a coward or a sorry wannabe idealist." Tripp rarely embarrassed, but the compliments, diverse as they were, did the trick, and males complimenting males added to the discomfort for Tripp as it usually does in most average male groups. Humor is frequently attempted to escape the focus of the true feelings between men so Tripp sought to lighten it all up with levity. "And here's to you Tiny Tim and to you, Citizen Kane, and to all, a grand good time of a night!"

"For the children?"

"Of course, Moah."

"Tripp, I'm serious. Cade is too. You're a student of history and you have put down words that bring 'what was' to 'what is' and tie it together in what needs to be done in the future to make things more sensible then they are now, does that make sense, guys?" "Hell, yes. Tripp, that column, what was it, couple of months ago, about the Senate of Rome and the "thing" we have today?"

"Oh, the exemptions from their own edicts, their shamefully luxurious ways, that quote?" "Hello? Anyone seen my friend, John? Yes."

"Yes, did get one, well it was one of my best social network days and I..."

"And elaborating about buying up justice, how sick is that?" "Moah's on fire."

"I'm working now on a column about DNA and DNA tests: maybe a series, and how

DNA could be manipulated against someone, put an innocent behind bars." "An entry 'drug' of a different sort."

"My fear... "Tripp presented, "... Is that this is an assembly line for the powerful to even more efficiently set up scapegoats in waiting. All you add is structural motives and perfected means to dignify the goals of the strongest bias's, to preserve and use DNA dropped around in nefarious acts by the naughty and the nasty and 'known new facts,' here we go. And drones, Jesus; Justice today, hold onto your hats for tomorrow."

"What a tricky Dickie word, justice." Moah stared at his glass. "Often I have found it, justice, is nothing more than someone is getting screwed at someone else's obscene pleasure."

"The law today ..."Tripp continued, "...is unfortunate in its reptilian skin, its shedding away layers of laws that harm the billable futures of the practitioners of ever expanding, ever intruding, 'justice'. Ha, justice and its documented nature to vandalize ethics for the right prejudice or price or both, really needs an about face and soon."

"All the shells are empty. There's no ball beneath any of them anymore, is there?" Tripp poured another glass of Baileys. "Guys, I've been thinking of adding a new sign-off statement to my column. This is from a Roman, Juvenal, who asks, 'quis custodiet ipsos custodes?'"

"Which means?"

"Quis custodiet ipsos custodes meaning, who is to watch the watchers?" "Use it." Moah urged.

"I got your neo Latin for yous guys," Cade was now louder than Moah, "... thanks to Sorentsen: 'lo to these panjandrums of provender for the proletariat, to these dejecta excrementas."

"Don't know what that means exactly, but" Cade added, "but it sure sounds right." "Means shit and animal fodder." Moah turned towards the writer. "Tripp, I'm with Cade on the part about trust. You fight for vets. You fight for those that gave integrity to my existence, to my warrior sisters and brothers. You've written about the vacated, the unknown damage, the unaccounted, vet suicides, the unemployment we still battle through after duty, and for all this, with the exception of your music, I hail."

"Of course."

"I salute you, Tripp Bellows" and Moah raised his glass.

Cade toasted the others. "Scat and Skol"

Tripp took his gulp and then, "You know what Einstein said about war? It's an illness of childhood, that's what he said."

"No matter..." Moah caught himself. "...look, well, of course, it matters. What I'm saying is that I like the people I work with. There are only certain types of individuals that work at four in the morning without complaint, UPS and the military."

"And criminals," Cade juiced back.

"Touche, TV boy, touché." And Moah touched his glass again to Cades.

Tripp finished his glass of cream. "The press today, of which I'm but a parking lot attendant and whose industry I participate in name only separate from common din, because no one's paid me for my accountability. It reminds me of reversed hagiography, why our Congressional report is the study of lives, the heavy priced study of today's sinners as saints, when in actuality, the body of the report reveals that the subjects of said report are nothing more than small printed barely visible almost infinitesimal footnotes at the bottom of the last page of such a monumental waste of so many trees and so many people's lives." Tripp espied a walking enigma approaching the trio. "Speaking of sinners, the man made it!"

Cade and Moah turned around to see if it was whom they hoped it was.

"You know it's damn hard to get a connection this week from North Dakota!"

Moah quickly retorted to his business partner, "Hell yes, I know; because I've had to go there to save your ass, holiday or not."

As he himself proclaimed often, 'the face that launched a thousand complaints, the man with perfect teeth, (the man with a stab wound in the back that he never discussed with anyone but once with Moah Halas) the man with the sometime rusty throated voice earned while stationed on the West Coast from one too many drags from one too many illegal rolled ones during my body surfing the wave existential tour days, yes, the man with a classic Jaguar up on blocks in the garage of a bar, Leonard Samson Drummerman is within the walls and how are you?'

Yoggee is in the event hall.

There were rumors of an older brother Yoggee argued politics with living in Bend, Oregon; tales of lots of aunts, uncles, cousins, two nephews and a niece, and all, except for the children, Yoggee said he'd never climb a mountain.... He remembered the nephews and nieces on their birthdays. He sent them books about archaeology and history as he truly believed this reading material 'revelatory because of the sorry nature of what now passes history and for music and these nieces and nephews schools.' And in what he believed a true statement of his affection for these youngsters he also listed the best music for them to grab a bit of ear time with, including but not limited to The Allman Brothers, The Doobie Brothers, the Moody Blues and Johnny Cash. It is not known how well the youngsters took to these suggestions. There is no record of military service. The cause for his unrelenting passion for his country is shared on a need to know basis with trusted friends only. He publicly would resort to the claim that he was 'an innocent astrophysicist with occasional systems analysis tendencies or what you might call a shrink for the inanimate in animate things. His business partners knew the subject matter best. Their partner was actually best versed in wheeler dealer encryption, the relevance of mental torture and how to apply it without leaving a trace of its existence and they also knew that their associate was an early initiate specialist in the governments study of remote viewing, something that dropped off the social radar for decades and its supposed eulogies in public helped keep the actual process secretly progressing in private. Yoggee was frequently still called upon to contribute his 'talents' in a consulting capacity for employers unnamed. Yoggee, the scion of hardy perspicacious Swedish stock, hadn't allowed space in his 'tour' for many serious relationships. Only recently had Sean and Moah learned that Yoggees' sister-friend with benefits, as Yoggee affectionately described her, had broken it off with him, an eight year relationship now gone, and Yoggee had not shared a thing about it with them or apparently anyone else for two months since the fallout. The partners never noticed a pivot whatsoever in Mr. Drummerman's personality and habits, so it had surprised them, but upon reflection, not really. As Moah had shared in private with Sean upon hearing of the split, "When the benefit supplier weighed the cost of non-commitment and found the price too high, a wearing exercise at the least, she concluded that the only other thing she valued more than her love for Leonard Samson Drummerman was her own sanity."

The co-owner of the Cranium Fill had arrived to "help children and adults too." In his wake, Sean, the senator, The Navaho, Chardonnay, Emily Pinckney, the hosting Senator, the professor and Godboy moved like the crew of the Minnow, taken up in the swirl, following the ripples in the crowds, where Yoggee' was making way, a good bet to put into port near Cade, Moah and Tripp, harbor masters all.

Even the inimitable Mr. Hyde interrupted his 'leaving early' apologies to look at Mr. Drummerman's entrance. When Hyde assured himself, estimating that, one, the new arrival was not a threat and, two, it is the arrival of someone that couldn't be assuaged to assist or benefit Mr. Jansen Hyde; he closed with hasty but polite 'byes' and exited.

Cade saw Yoggee heading directly towards him "This will get the elves ears upright."

"As oaths are made to be broken, I vow, Cade, truckers drive down the road with tears in their eyes with what they see in this country. Why, they, we, I'm telling you, are all just one air brake malfunction away from any moment becoming destinies calling card." Leonard Samson Drummerman rowed through life on his terms; his canoe, his paddle, his schedule, his unchartered waters...and this was both his attraction and his distraction. A self-described 6 foot five mass of holy unruliness, whose nickname, Yoggee, he said, was an amalgamation of Yogi Bear, Yoda and Yogi Berra; but in fact, it was what his father cried out, "Oh Geez!" ('Gutt' in Swedish, but elder Mr. Drummerman was heard to exclaim his shock in English so the name stuck) when Yoggee was born weighing 10 lbs.

1 oz., a 'man-child' his father called him. He is attractive with Peter Otoole eyes and Kenny Stabler hip; a revolution in human form still stocked with teenage merriment as well as middle-aged wonderment at all that there is still yet to learn.

"Well, well, see the three things my daddy told me about..."

Cade, Chaz, and Moah waited. Sean arrived with the others close behind.

"Mr. Drummerman, my dad said to the young Yoggee in waiting, he said, 'Leonard, remember this: only a flagellating, flagrant fool heart argues with a grizzly," and Yoggee pointed at Moah, "...a chuck wagon cook," next indicating towards Mr. Bartholomew "...or a porcupine." as he put his right hand on Mr. Bellows left shoulder, adding, "Well, someone had to be the prickly one and I figured you had the spine to take it to make the adage work and pertinent to you three today." Yoggee took a taste from an offered glass of Baileys, then, "Now the chuck wagon cookie and the porcupine, they're interchangeable as you both work in the messy smellies of cooking up news, of mediadizing and you both claim restuaranting on your supposed resumes, correct? And as for the grizzly, Moah; determined, not afraid to say 'no' or 'never' to anyone, anywhere...so Daddy Drummerman was right, gentlemen; it's fruitless to argue with a porcupine, a grizzly, or anyone who cooks for cowboys, but most especially, it is fruitless to argue with little old me! How are Hell and you too, boys?!"

Chardonnay arrived with the others. Cade introduced his new BFF, "Ms. Hooray, this is Mr. Drummerman."

"Miss Hooray, Cade's description of you is an injustice as the boy is sincerely lacking in any language or vocabulary to give your beauty the proper bouquet."

A veteran of many a man's advance, Chardonnay feels this one actually means the words and she approves with a real smile in return.

Tripp rapidly follows Cades gentlemanly way and introduces Emily Pinckney, to which Mr. Drummerman announces, "My lady, you are as wondrous as any lyric in any song he ever wrote." Then, after an appropriately timed mini pause, "Except for 'Dogpile with You Babe' or whatever that thing was called."

The melting of the ice sculpture of Santa Claus appeared to accelerate.

"Ms. Hooray?" Yoggee asked.

"Call me, Char." He nodded towards the lady while noting the Navaho and the teen and the senator and another man now completing the scenery.

"Char, strip clubs, sorry; gentlemen clubs, why, you are wise in the business you're in, no doubt. But many an American married man checks it in for what they have at home for free and he goes there to where it's a very money thing and away from where it's something for nothing. It dazzles me that."

"Yoggee, may I call you Yogz?"

"Certainly."

This surprises Mr. Drummermans' friends as they know him to despise this 'prick name' as he called it, but Mr. Drummerman was adept at managing calculated exceptions when faced with such a beautiful explanation for such an atypical act.

"Yogz, it's simple. I perfected what to do with knowledge earned by never underestimating the activities of the two heads of a man, especially when the smaller head leads and the bigger head is drunk and full of. .. rum."

"I agree with you as I've been too headed, I was with my first wife."

Moah informed further, "His ex-wife was a Greek woman, named Iris after the Greek goddess of chaos and strife."

"The most well named woman I've ever fallen in love with." Yogz paused briefly. "The problem, as I now see it, Char, is that both of my wives, they were both Christian women with drop down on your knees bodies, and nocturnal too, both of them."

"I didn't take you for such a religious man, Mr. Drummerman." Chardonnay enjoyed this man, one who could laugh at himself.

"Oh Miss Hooray, believe me, I become a heretic in the morning. We eventually escaped, the three of us, I mean; boarding up, shuttering up botched sermons and invasive catechisms in stony places of the heart where they wouldn't hurt as much."

Moah observed, "I'm sure both ladies, Yoggee, found God again when they were delivered from you too."

"You're one crazy agnostic ass, aren't you?" Moah toasted his older partner and Yoggee in turn, Ms. Hooray.

"Yes, Char, Iris was perfect pitch for the tone in my life at that particular stage, but I almost lost all faith because her pews weren't polished but her phobias were and I realized then that I needed to read the fine print more closely when it comes to mythology."

"Litanies, lies and love and never in that order, right Yogz?"

"Why yes, Char, whereas, fight, fart or fib, that's men. It's easy with us, but with women, well now, they always seem to be the keepers of a special secret and smiling about it and that's tough for the Cro Magnum mind....there's great mystery even when they are naked. But that's women; haunting, haughty good, but full-on heart rending if you're the man misfortunate enough to feel the bite from our gender that supposedly needs protection when they have been wronged. It hurts like a bitch. And for certain, longer than it takes for the average wound to heal."

Cade and Moah had alerted Yoggee about Sean's change of status with Odessa. He paused and leaned in, whispering to Sean, "Keep your heart in glide position, Sean, and you'll never run out of gas."

Ms. Hooray had taken the break in conversation to quietly ask Cade, "Yoggee really loved his wife and hates the memory, doesn't he?"

"The Greek or the Russian?"

Sean, smiling straight at Yoggee, "No, you mean the Polish one."

"So three times the charm, Mr. Drummerman?"

"When necessary to do so, I lost count, Ms. Hooray."

Tripp took Emily's hand and entered the fray. "Sigmund Freud and I quote..."

"That's kind of like a takeout bid in bridge, the Freud play...huh, Tripp?" Chardonnay teased.

".. .and a quote I respect goes as follows, quote, 'the great question that has never been answered, and which I, Freud that is, is that I have not yet been able to answer, despite my 30 years of research into the feminine soul, it is,... what does a woman want?" Tripp glanced at Emily. "Emily, shall I do the honor of educating these ill-bred miscreants of masculinity?"

"You hike up your skirt and you go girl," Emily urged.

"You see, Yogz and others, neglect by a man reinforces a safe perception for him of the ordinariness in women, a way for his heart to keep skating along. This, among many reasons, is why women initiate 75%, 75% mind you, of divorces. Women keep track of things; details are of vast importance to women. You say a woman's beautiful she wants to know what's behind the particulars of how do you measure beauty? Cade? Moah?

Navaho? Sean? Is it how she's dressed, is it her body, perhaps the way her hair is playing in the light; what is the special in the special about her? Women want to know; from every cell, every molecule, every atom, it's much deeper than dimples with women, guys, they want to understand why they are special to you."

"Women..." Char, concurring with Mr. Bellow, "...intensely, and it doesn't take long for a wise woman..."

"Are there any other kind?"

"Thank you, Emily. No, it doesn't take long for a lady worth her standards to build a passionate dislike towards the aloof, the withdrawn male. Hell no. Give me a guy that's bold enough to share emotions and I can pretty well let anything else slip by. Having command of language is tool number two for the sensual man and don't you forget it. And humorous men, well, I want a man to make me laugh as well as being the courageous sexy one who can laugh at himself too, in bed and elsewhere."

Emily and Chardonnay smiled at their "fresh" men class.

Yoggee was the first to bring his jaw back into normal operating position. "Another school of marketing might be to be going against the grain, anti social media, anti electronic royalty; it's all pixilated narcissisms delivered in pornographic proportions. Why accept this? Look at me, look at where I was, at where I am and the sham of me telling you where I am going; trash on the curb rubbish, is what it is, so empty the bucket, don't line up like everyone else and don't stand perfectly behind anyone else ever again either.

John Muir said something more than gibberish about trees..."

Ms. Pinckney jumped in feigned offense, "Trees are not subjects for gibberish or jive, mister." She smiled wide. "Nor John Muir."

Tripp added, "She's a noted dendrochronologist."

"My apologies, Emily, no slight to neither tree nor Muir. Love Muir. He said, and this is elegant in its truth, a bargain for the brain, said that..." Yoggee glanced Moahs way then quickly back to Ms. Pinckney "...talked about what he called 'soul hunger, the torment of not knowing who you are.' The 'self is eaten alive with all these cannibalistic social tech touch paths, the sterile mindways that inhabit the rituals of our times, noisy intrusions, which hardly, if ever, allow for the 'self to hear 'itself, to feel 'itself breathe deeply, to take in the gorgeous separateness that signals to 'self, yes, you, 'self, you have successfully overcome the stigma of not being connected and survived to tell about it. Fear sells. It's a fallback position for the greedy, you know this Tripp. The tragic and the terrific; you're telling me there's not 'tudes in type or tunes with these overtones than I say 'why you're not marketing, man! And as you know, Circus song man, the best marketing men were of, still some are, from the '60's and the '70's when they obviously had the real good stuff. Look, if you were at Woodstock, '69, you'd still test positive in drug test today, even if you hadn't taken a direct tote at the concert. Now that's real second hand smoke there, yes, during the crazy summers of foolishness and experimental grabs at making sense of it all."

Yoggee abruptly caught himself as he spotted The Navaho and the young man for the first time again.

"John, sorry. Good god, young man, just remember I'm just a rambling romantic and you can see by my meandering musings that weed is wicked, drugs dig graves early and that I especially have no earthly idea about the meaning of women for that matter; and how are you?"

"This is my nephew, Yoggee. You can just call him NinoDios as his real name is too long to remember for now."

"Diosni? Godboy! That's a wonderful tag, boy." Yoggee shook the teenager's hand. The young man responded. "Thank you, Mr. Dru..."

"No misters; it's Yoggee, son."

"Thank you, Yoggee. And believe me; I'm intimate with the fine line results of drugs, present company excluded."

John Truefellow knew he'd just witnessed the birth of a friendship and it gladden his thoughts.

When Yoggee recovered from hard laughter he responded," For the beyond your years knowledge and perception, you deserve a toast, but since the nog and the Baileys are not legal for you, I will give you something ever better, advice."

Cade, groaned. The Navaho turned to NinoDios. "Now we will see how tough you really are."

Yoggee, per usual routing system, ignored all comers of quips; instead plowing ahead to his promised land of posing the question of what, to Mr. Drummerman was dead serious obvious to anyone with a pulse, and that is... How can you or anyone else not be anything but helped, be persuaded by what I have to impart?

"In my humble bakery of laymen acumen, most held in reserve I might add, I have one peculiar property, one bordered on five sides with crudely scrawled 'No Trespassing Unless Invited' signs hanging on the cross fence protecting this fertile field of considerations now overrun with philosophers stones, often randomly rearing their hard parts amid and above the carefully cultivated roles of the richly soiled, where the fertilizer is ripe with seedy permutations and acre-feet of pugnacious preponderancies."
Mr. Drummerman leaned slightly forward to get a closer glimpse of Mr. de Mejas.

"My condensed version; not everyone talks a good walk in the lark and that's why I laugh late and I cry early. The day seems to go better that way. Just don't become part of the sales pitch and usually all works out. And number two..."

"There's more?" Sean nudged Yoggee.

"And two, when you're young, you remember even the foul balls, so make a basket catch on every detail now, so you have that habit when you're no longer young enough to wear a glove anymore." Yoggee stood back a little. "Make big things small, small things big! Sells every time. Big ass? You want it small and you buy to that bad boy. Small weenie, I mean, Beanie, promised big! That's what we sell at the Cranium Fill. The dreams of having both, the grand scheme and the quiet tingle too. It's marketing, man, basically, remedies for the remedially inclined, make big things small; make small things big. In a marketplace known for dominance of dummies, you have got to sell the smell of high things that match the aroma of their dreams. Kind of funny thing though, in steps in that magical process called 'serving others', and those you help to contentment will actually contribute mightily to making the big and the small of your dreams happily workable for you as well. I tell you what, Mr. de Mejas; successful marketing is merely pissing off the wrong people at the right time. All the others will love it then too. Hell, son, I mean, shoot; our bars best advertisings been refused as not suitable by every media outlet in North Dakota. Now I ask you, what's wrong with this, 'The Cranium Fill, where thinking takes a back seat to drinking'? Huh? Yeah. People upset with me for years, twenty plus years and ten years because I was 'gone fishing' in the lake of life for my happiness limit and they couldn't get in the boat with me but the heck with them!"

Godboy, The Navaho, Sean and the others couldn't help but smile approvingly. Yoggee appeared pleased with the reaction to his 'bites of wise' as he called his shared thoughts. "Yep, we set up solar generated electric promotional signs around a section piece or so of land in the Williston area, drink specials and special thoughts for the day, they run continuously. We get our notoriety from these signs, from the public and the sign code police and from the howling media right on schedule when we may need to remind the public of our presence in the community again; yes, it all seems to click when the 'indignity' glass needs topping off on days devoid of real news, it's the best marketing for gratis imaginable.

"So the media's," ventured Godboy, "a marketing godsend, you say; and not a burden of bile as I've heard many posture?

..Mr. Drummerman stared at NinoDios, stood straight, putting both hands on hips, saying, "Jury was still out on you, son, until now. I adjudicate and find you guilty of good taste and for your ability to make one forget their headaches."

Senator Dunleavy Bruce approached Yoggee. "Everything I've heard about you, sir, has proven true tonight. You have humor, big healing thoughts and I thank you for the Fills donation. And to you Sean, and you too, Moah, my appreciation. To all of you to make it here tonight, thank you. I got to thank others but I'll be back verily. Merry Christmas, friends." And the senator continued on his appointed rounds of gratitude.

"Good man for a politician." Yoggee confidently observed to Tripp.

"Yoggee, he is, and so is my friend here, Professor Doctor Elliot Sorentsen the Third." "You taught Chaz Bellows! Good God man, you must have the patience of a Job on speed; how'd you do it, how'd he do?"

"Somewhere, somehow that makes sense; I'm sure, Mr. Drummerman."

They laughed as only men in on an assumed secret to life laugh; loudly, near obnoxious. "I've heard about you from Sean, Moah, and the critic."

"The rebel rocker, cum scrivener?"

"Yes"

"I've read about you too and I like your words in Time, "Not easy being a conservative in a strange land, by which I mean academia."

"Nor is it easy being a personage stranger than fiction, I'm sure." They clinked glasses and Yoggee added, "Little too much meg and not enough nut."

The professor looked to his side to his ex-students than back to Yoggee. "Cade, Tripp or Sean? I leave The Navaho out because John was and is smarter than the lot of them." "Apparently, I'm not the only snail in the ivy and this pleases me."

"A fork among the spoons as I see it."

"Professor Sorentsen, was Mr. Bellows here a decent pupil in your stead?"

Both Emily and Chaz move in closer to hear more clearly over the din of the continuing festivities and Ho Ho merriment. Chaz is mildly amused whilst Emily and the nog considered the professor and the 'philosopher' enlightened.

"Chaz, you were special, Emily, he was really, when he showed up for class. Yoggee, he was the only student I ever had that used or even knew the meaning of the word, 'boustrophedon'."

"Ah, Professor..." Yoggee acted as if he were guessing, "...isn't that, let's see, as the ox plows once to the right then plows once to the left; kind of like the hemispheres of the mind, right, left hemispheres, right Doctor.? Right, Tripp? Take what your other mind thinks and write it down, don't you?"

"Well, yes, the direction of the ox turns is correct but the left and right brain theory is now viewed as invalid."

With that Yoggee spun to his left. "Professor, nevertheless, I'd like you to check out a Web portal I'm working on. Voice your opinion on, if you care to. Call it Brainjerks.com; the 'J' is silent. Will laser in on the Cosmos, Costco and the retirement homes of famous communists."

The professor was on his game. "Or intelligent design, rouge and ruse."

Tripp dropped his hat in the ring. "You learned and liquored up jingoistic loveable young at heart people, I want..." The professor silenced the student with compliment, "Chaz, in all seriousness, Yoggee, you see, this man is writing things that we, that I agree with. He stands, he states, and I respect his view that we as humans are better for what we don't say then for what we do. And that..." Emily hugged her rocker man as she saw a happy rarity, his embarrassment full-blown, as she knew her man admired the man speaking and his meaningful comments complementing Chaz were more valuable to her man than another gold record, "... that you have also lived on stage and now in print the rule that it's always dangerous to do the right thing." As he finished, Professor Sorentsen raised his mug, "Salutes." Yoggee followed, "Scat and skol." Emily and the men downed the nog. Yoggee couldn't resist being Yoggee. "But, I swear, Tripp, no matter what you got to do you ought to get away from those damn 'Udopeians'..."

"Udopeians? What the...," The professor's confusion emptied as Tripp interpreted, "Environmentalists, professor, Enviros to you. Yoggee's always, Cade too, ripping on me about being green and Earth's restorer in chief."

"Man," Yoggee, almost sounding on the verge of blurting or burping, "I can no way control the environment of this ancient orbiting thing, this Gaia, globally or even locally, as I could dang well diddle Lady Gaga."

"Is that your personal big bang theory, Mr. Drummerman?" Emily was pleased with her response as well as with Ms. Hoorays' glass of approval raised in Ms. Pinckney's direction. Emily wondered the question she returned to more than one would think necessary; however through the eons of time has Mother Earth ever been able to put up with demands of men and other morons and survived.

"You know, you are my favorite Indian, besides Gandhi." Moahs amount of hair-of-the- dog intake level had apparently reached the 'nice' stage.

"I am not an Indian. I am Dine, nee native American." The Navaho was not upset. He knew Moah Halas and he knew that holidays could be argumentative times as his friend wrestled with his now dead wife and happiness lost and it seemed to ripple within Moah more so at holiday time than others. Mr. Truefellow understood those verbal challenges and light bombast as pressure releases. Mr. Truefellow had experienced these exercises with Mr. Halas before. With Godboys presence, Moah was not as demonstrative as during previous occasions. Godboy believed the bark and froth friendly.

"Isn't that right, Nino?" Mr. Truefellow had turn towards the teenager. Moah straightened up. He was included in the circle of the comrades of the Navaho that knew the details of the boy's arrival; that had the capabilities and the understanding to properly take on the load of another's plight besides their own.

Godboy knew when and where he could speak freely. The three had separated a short distance from the crowd.

"I do not want to forgive the killers of my family. So leave my tears alone."

"They're dead, amigo. My connections have told me the Policia have killed as many as they and the Federales could."

"Only because the bastards, the gangs, backed out on their payments, their bribes to the law; not because they were wanted for murder."

Moah was now back on the same track as John.

"It helps though, doesn't it?"

"My Mom taught me, all of us, that it often takes humor to deflate the feeling of needing to immediately understand the unknowable."

"You will eventually learn to modify your everyday thinking in order to compete as comfortably as possible with the discord, the punch line of being human." Moah hesitated, sizing up the younger man before staking out a more muscular image. "Revenge is as potent as love. Genghis Khan is quoted as saying, and it is among my favorites, 'Man's highest joy is in victory: to conquer one's enemies, to pursue them, to deprive them of their possessions, to make their beloved weep, to ride their horses and to embrace their wives and daughters.'"

"Yes, Nino, this is Moah's way of expressing empathy."

The Navaho knew Moah did concern himself with the welfare of young Mr. de Mejas. He recalled Moahs' descriptions, heart rendering, of Moahs' times in Africa and about the fighting mans impressions of the faces of Africa's children; their 'ever after' frowns, their faces nothing more than skin to bone staging areas for the constancy of flies and interchangeable expressions of forlornness and hopelessness. The Navaho also knew that Godboy did not know, nor would possibly never know of Moah's pain from Moahs' loss five years earlier, of Maria, his wife. Maria had died at a Denver hospital after the event, Moah had exploded waiting in line for admittance behind, what Moah to this day describes as, 'fifty illegal's'. Moah did not have a racist bone. John knew this, but 'illegals', whatever the constructed image Moah had formed to wade through the numbness of those dreary early hours upon hours of 'what ifs'; he hadn't been able to shake his reaction of still bone chilling coldness to anyone, any look, any words that brought the image of that night in the emergency room back. Moah battled with this searing disgust and angst and as he shared once with John, "Hell, I'd come here too, by hook or by crook, to feed my children, my woman, but dammit, John, the line was so long and English seemed so foreign a vernacular and Maria was trying to be so brave, but God, I hate hating!" That was the last it was ever spoken of.

"Maybe a Genghis is needed. I cry for Mexico. I cry for my fathers' participation in the sadness."

They remained silent until Moah pondered," We live in tribal times again." To which the Navaho responded, "We've never left them."

Godboy looked away and saw Senator Bruce and Professor Sorentsen coming towards him. They were stopped by an apparently influential woman visibly wanting them to share her valuable time with her. Keenly observant in what often is mistaken for obtuse and yet, upon further investigation, isn't;

Godboy commented, "That woman with the Senator, doesn't she, well, she has a young mouth but an old nose."

Moah and John looked not too far away at the subject of Godboys' attention standing between Mr. Bruce and Mr. Sorentsen. Moah wasn't completely in tune with the younger mans words but the woman was speaking and the two men closest to her were listening so she definitely had the youthful energy it takes to tirelessly work the jawbone towards positive consequences, although the nose did have large but strangely attractive nostrils, Moah still puzzled at Godboys' comment which reminded Moah of dealing with the meanings behind another friends observances.

"You sure you're not a long lost relative of Yoggee's, Nino?"

The professor and the Senator excused themselves. The lady, a representative from Maryland, appeared satisfied and released them.

"Did you get enough to eat, young man?"

Godboy nodded in the affirmative to the Senator from the land of tribes, Oklahoma.

"I do know you two gentlemen and I know I need not inquire as to your condition, right?" Professor Sorentsen answered for them. "The Christian condition, righteously full of good cheer, right boys?"

Godboy covered for his new big 'brother' and newly minted 'Uncle', smiling the look of an innocent jester indicating no harm intended, "So professor, they tell me you are the one with all the answers."

Mr. Sorentsen had not been taken aback by anything in twenty years as when he was surprised by his wife's infidelity which had been prompted by his own. Such a wonderful antagonist, this teenager; blindsided me, nearly as surprising as finding Rafina in bed with a student majoring in Zoology, but not quite.

"Far from it, young Mr. Alejandro Buddha Jesus Simon de Mejas, political refugee that you are."

Godboy did not give away the nerves he felt inside. He remained still.

"Don't be surprised. You are among friends. Senator here included." Godboy looked to John Truefellow.

"The Navaho did not betray you. He knew that in order for you to succeed, you need this network as motley as we are all, Sean, Cade and even Chaz Bellows too. Understand that if Truefellow says something, it's important for us to respond as he would to any of our needs or requests; promptly."

Senator Bruce contributed, "What better time, better place to lay all the cards out on the table than here at Children's Now Time and while you are definitely nearing, if not already, the age of majority and this is indelicate, but where is your family now?"

It took the strength of a giant for Godboy not to well up but he managed to be bigger than the wound. Confident it is time to get more out, seek release from the significant pressure cooker the pain of loss is, he asks, "What does one do when confronted with wayward ones actually doing a good deed or deeds? How do you rationalize this seemingly contradictory fact? My father pretended not to be in the cartel and my mother pretended not to be married to a criminal, that's how." He opened up; talking about his Mexican household and father's hypocritical devotion to the Roman Catholic Church. "My mother secretly illuminated in my mind the possibilities of alternatives to my father's foundational beliefs. He was a person who most certainly did not practice what he preached. He was cartel as his father had been cartel. But my mother and father loved each other."

"Even Hitler had Ava." Moah reminded.

"My mother never back down from her beliefs and she was a person that wanted me to be more of her than the man she loved, married and was devoted to. I remember when she gave me a small red book. It was the day before my thirteenth birthday. The hacienda was festively adorned although the mix is blurred in my memory because of what I saw on the few pages before me. I was sitting at the island in the kitchen with my mom. It was dusk, that 5 minute time of amber pink mixes of ethereal light and preciseness which somehow heightens the senses in unknown but ancient ways, you know what I mean?''

"Yes."

"A flash thought streaks across my consciousness; I am merely a participate in one of the Master's universal fits of fun; and momentary as it is, the color is so head clearing, we are thankful models, sincere, and hoping we present well."

The professor asked, "What on earth did you read to cause such a mark on the mind?"

"It was from a reformer, a Catholic reformer, from the Middle Ages. It was called Ditatus Papae, 'The Sayings of the Pope'. It was attributed to Pope Gregory VII. It asserted the power of the Pope against emperors and others who might be of mind to challenge the Papal sphere of influence, jurisdiction and control."

"Probably ghostwritten," Mr. Sorentsen snorted. "Are you familiar with it?"

"Yes. What specifically caused your expansive thinking, besides your mother, I mean?'' "Just two things. One, that, quote, 'the Roman Church has never erred, nor ever, by the witness of Scripture, shall ere to all eternity.' The second eye catcher, quote, 'That he himself may be judged my no one.' We're talking about the Pope here. When I finished these remarkable observations, the magic five minute period had about run its course as it was early evening in Mexico, that time when the western horizon's a thin streak of navy blue cutting into the bottom of the dark above, and from that moment on, I thought of my father in a different light." Mr. de Mejas paused to drink a sip of orange juice. "Most churches have accomplished good things for many people. Catholic charity is renown, but, like other denominations, so is their extravagance. My mother said that the finest quality of a productive mind is to be more than just good, better yet, be good for something. You are measured, she said, by how you stand up to the blows and bow downs of fate; that's the real talent gauge, Alejandro."

"It's all about how one goes about their walk in the universe, and how, with one twist of the screw in the mechanics of God, the path you've chosen can completely spin around the future to the other side of the cosmic carousel." Moah was not finished." It's God standing logic on its head sometimes. Take the swastika for instance. It's derived from Sanskrit. 'Su' meant 'well' and 'asti' meant 'being'. The swastika, among many primitives before the Nazi's deformed it, was a symbol of good luck and yes, well-being. Then here God goes again, upside downing again with original meanings; do you know what the word 'meek' meant? Well, instead of timid, 'meek' originally meant 'well prepared.' This stand on head logic is nothing more than the rapidly rotating galactic gyroscope of God, spinning for his amusement, as well as for sticking to his script for the laws of change." Moah turned his head to see the surrounding movement and sounds. "The eternal nag of life, NinoDios, is not unpleasantness and ailment." He turned to face Alejandro. "It's unwarranted unpleasantness and ailment. Like prejudice. It's a killer. Early, maybe after a church Sunday school, I was single digit, maybe 6 or 7, dad told me about a teacher he had had and admired who'd shared an example of the pigheadedness of man that stuck with dad and he wanted it to stick to me too. He told me about the caste system in India; or as he put it, 'Another example of the disease of the mind.' The wretchedness of mans heartless treatment of fellow man; the sadness, that I share with my dad. He was always distraught at the racism in this country. The tale he told me that afternoon, he said that there was a child of a rich Hindu family, this is in India, and this family was positioned at one of the higher rungs of the caste system. The child, not a swimmer, goes near water, dumb; and falls into a fountain. And what do you know, but that the worst of the worst, an outcast, is in the vicinity and hears the Hindu mother's frantic screams for help for her child in jeopardy. The outcaste offers the mother aid, to leap in and rescue the child; but, but, the mother, pride before prejudice or is it prejudice before pride; she refuses his offer. She refuses aid as it would interfere with the mother's frame of reference, the caste system. So, essentially, this proud vane thing preferred the sad end of her baby over the defilement of the 'killing waters' by an outcast leaping into them. Ah, the tenuousness of maintaining soothing 'realities' of superiority and roll-over- everyone holiness; it costs, and well, I may be prejudicial here, but it costs oh so much more than those without knowledge of value will ever understand."

"That's one unfortunate fortunate son, Mr. Halas."

The Senator, Mr. Sorentsen and the others chuckled at Moahs' stunned amusement with the teenager's peculiar precociousness.

"Mr. de Mejas, please don't subjugate your talents on being either a teacher or a politician." The Senator wasn't asking, he implored. "You actually have 'live' ability. With your tools, theory would be a waste."

The senator noticed Cade Bartholomew's eyebrow signaling him. The mogul was surrounded by Chardonnay, Emily and two chattering D.C. socialites and was requesting 'man help'. The Senator abetted Cades retreat, loudly stating, "Cade, want for you to meet some people. Pardon me, Chardonnay, hope I..."

"Go on, go on. I can see mogul turning blue." She turned back with Emily to hear what was roiling DC that news cycle. The senator took and introduced him to the senators adopted sons, who were stationed throughout the ballroom assisting their father. They impressed Cade with their courtesy and obvious devotion to the senator. All had military experience and all presently employed with capital law enforcement in one capacity or another. They found a less occupied corner of the room and Shane, the eldest of the senator's sons, hovered nearby to politely fend off interruptions of any kind.

"Thank you, Cadie, as always, for your support and even though you do not have any children..."

"That I know of, sir," Mr. Bartholomew replied playfully but still with an intimation of caution.

"Yes, but you still donate as if kids were your own."

Cade Bartholomew, uneasy with compliments, changed topics. "Your boys, they're a proud thing for life, Senator, and you are to be commended."

"Thank you, Cade. Not about us, though. Your business must have been good for the year...the size of your donation is the grandest yet. I imagine, well, the kids will get real good things from this; to start with, their spirit back." Mr. Bruce noticed Mr. Bartholomew appearing uncomfortable. "On other sports, I must say you have stepped up your game with this business woman, mister!"

Mr. Bartholomew smiled big.

"Miss Hooray; she's a charitable soul too, Cade. I will have to return the favor. I'm well aware that she too has her from the heart projects."

"Well, yes, Acappella Barbell and children's..."

"No, I mean dating you."

"Yes, Senator, the network has done very well. The right lighting, dozens of gourmet conspiracies to choose from, spokespersons that appear smarter than they really are, throw in a little pinch of hope at the end of each night and bingo go the ratings."

"Wiley E. Coyote, who can't catch a long-tailed ground cuckoo, also called the chaparral cock..."

"Do tell."

"Yes, well, the Coyotes inability, his failure to succeed and his inevitable beatings and yet he still goes for it; his failures give hope to the tenacious, even to the most dismal Looney Toons among us, which is good for the likes of little ol' me as I perform my tasks in Congress where there are no conundrums, don't you know, there are only sides."

"You know, Senator, watching an hour or two of CSPAN while back I saw politicians speaking trippingly on the tongue, leads me closer to understanding why the Islamic whirling dervishes want to kill the West."

"And why animals eat their young, right?"

"The coverage of the Brits in Parliament is a marvel, just how they are so neat and they are so tidy in their oh so cool style of lambast and insult...'To my right honorable child- molesting, lamb loving, devil seed of a Lord from West Humpfullshire...very envious of their insulting way of being polite, I am."

"Ah, the high art of low insult. Set the bar low and then crawl under it. It's only mud." "My father would not believe the people you hang out with, Senator; at work, I mean. He'd use dark liquor on them in negotiations, that's what he used on the other side in negotiations held at altitude. He reserved the Cade Bar The Vodka good stuff for only when it was time to celebrate."

"Cade, how negligent of me, thank you for the case, larruping good vodka it is!"

"My privilege, sir. We sell vat loads of the 'mindsauce' at Twenty Two Times Turned. Now, excuse me, sir, as I promised Tripp Bellows ten minutes before we leave to give him some yakking on the record, you know, bits of wisdom for his New Years column or as he calls it, 'A Capitalist Cleans Up His Act At Christmas Charity Event."

"Break a leg, broadcaster. Say, isn't that a term of..."

"Break a leg?"

"No. Broadcaster; it sounds like sorting through manila folders of files of women for future roles."

"Why, Senator, I do believe you are a male in spite of what the papers say!"

"Damn laser straight, son. And Cade?"

"Yes sir?"

The Senator raised his glass full of the freshly poured and toasted, "Hooray for Hollywood. You two go together. Congrats."

As he got up to go to his rendezvous with the pressman, Mr. Bartholomew reached out and shook the hand of the only politician he actually considered as a friend. Mr. Bartholomew was then off to appear witty with the only person he considered as a friend in the press, Mr. Bellows.

Cade and Tripp edged as a unobtrusively as a media magnate and a lead singer can towards a small alcove off the main lobby, their two drivers acting as subtle but firm blockers for their run, steering the curious, the clammy and the contributors to the children's charity who might desire proximity to the famous; their goal being a mention, a notice of their existence in the 'who's who' sections of next mornings papers.

Cade sat across from Tripp; an average sized square oak table with inlaid chessboard positioned between upon which, the reporter put his tape recorder and pushed the red record button.

"So this whole process began because of Guttenberg, right?"

"Whoa, there. Do I have in an uncooperative witness on my hands?"

"You know how I feel about interviews. I'm only doing this because it's the giving time of the year and what I will give you is a ration of..."

"Hey, they're children here, somewhere?"

"Well, I think fabrication in news about news is expansive. It's the only thing that could have happened with social media. So many more corrections these days, it seems but that's to be expected when it's become common to flirt with the truth and flatter the fictitious. In spite of this, Tripp..."

"Yes?"

"...you are the only wordsmith I will sit down with, so fire away. This capitalist is on a schedule."

"All righty, then, Mr. Bartholomew..."

"Call me Cade."

"Well, Cade, what gets a consumer wet?"

"What? You're not going to print that?"

"What gets someone to buy your shtick, what makes your shtick standout in the digital express lanes?"

"Advertising the benefits of jumping on it, maybe."

"Come on."

"Well that is the idea."

Tripp waved this away with a smirk and then his smile hardened. "No more kidding, at least for five minutes. Let's make this worth our time, bud, alright?"

"That surprises me as I thought you knew that I thought of you as one of the few people on earth I would feel I was wasting my time with."

"Mr. Bartholomew, what's good marketing to you?"

"Show what you sell in the first 5 seconds. Remember, the eyes are like a chicken furiously pecking at the ground in front of them, digesting data at light speed, so don't make ads that make the chicken think too much; don't get in the way of the attraction. It's 'HISS', baby. Habits, imitation, suggestion and sex, these are the ingredients of a sale. Prosaic, I can hire. Creative you have to corral and not corrupt. We are attracted to bright colors and sharp edges, not unlike the sensation, the caress we can't hide from of the devil red lipstick on the pouting parted mouth of your multifarious dreams."

"I can see I will need to edit some with your preapproval, of course."

"And Tripp, Chaz or if you're going by Mr. Bellows at the moment, do you remember what our professor preached but did practice?"

"Today's media; your thoughts, observations?"

"First, Sorentsen said that consideration and competent editorial placement of stories and ads was the key to success. Where has that gone?" You know Chaz; he is more right today that he was when at school. There's no oversight. I still recall an improperly positioned ad in Denver years ago, upper right hand side of page; maybe it was the Rocky Mountain News before it was no more, don't recall, but the upper right hand side of page, sales headline read quote, 'The Best Sex Of Your Life.' And what's next to it in the outside column? The obituary of a fallen service member from Durango. There's some good taste going on there you betcha! Used to be on television, you would never place car dealership commercials in the same two minute block of ads. Never. And that went for jewelers, appliance stores, whatever, never next to each other in the same commercial break. And now, it's not just two minute blocks, hell, I've seen 8 ads back-to-back in some places. There's no discretion. Everything's been Clintonized and Bushified, finely tuned obfuscations abetted by shoddy relativities."

"Hey, Clinton did some good while Republicans done a lot of bad too, so don't..."

"May I continue, Mad Marx, Junior?"

"Yes, go on, proximity and placement of ads?"

"It's not just TV; it spread to print."

"Accepted, go ahead."

"Anchorman, and now women, Chardonnay would let me have it if didn't include some women in my ranting as she tells me that she then knows it's the real me speaking..."

"I have no doubt of that."

"Anchor people; they were the most believable in the most disbelieving of times. That's nearby been destroyed for viewers too. They believed what they were sharing was gospel."

My dad's dad would be flipping out if he found out that Cronkite was a flaming liberal because Walter was a professional and maintained as such when granddad watched him at least until the Vietnam war. Then the mask dropped. But he had kept the personal away. Now, we have bobble head reactionaries who haven't the vaguest clue as to why their heads move, I swear. Packaged news is boring, territorial, and predictably similar in intros and outtros; frequently, word for word. There's no limit to the dangerousness of unexamined intuition let loose upon such a reactionary mob as the audiences we play to today. Caution and deliberation and then decision and action; what's wrong with this picture? Where has it gone?"

"Although I mostly agree with you, more than usual, some might find self righteous."

"Then don't watch or listen to us. Digital's not done away with the dial yet, has it?" Before continuing, Cade asked a passing server to 'please bring more 'Noggin Knocker Juice'.

"Philosophy is a thirsty vocation. I know you agree with me, Tripp, that the diversity of sources today, blogs, twitter, face whatever, photo phones: all have contributed to the dismantling of the stranglehold of the ABC's, the CBS's and the NBC's had, far too long, they were gatekeepers of the nations airways, structuring what they thought we should know and what we should not know for the day, with all efforts mostly redounding to one political party; well, not any longer."

"Well, to some degree, but today the forms expanded, yes, but your opinion, I must disclaim, comes from their main competitor, you; so I would say your opinion on this matter particular area of conversation might be a little, oh, deformed."

"Goes to show you, Tripp, that if you lecture in lies long enough that even if you have the brightest and biggest choir, the mass media, gee, that is an appropriate name, mass media for the religion of liberalism, or you have the biggest pipe organ, the unions too, no matter, when your sermon becomes less and less relevant, your pews will empty, your offerings will become strained and stained and your teachings will be left without the dignity of remembrance; this is what the networks fear and the Left too. They abdicated responsibility. They are getting what they deserve."

"Damn it, Corn, I asked you not to hold back for this. When you gonna open up, come on. Aw, good, noggin juice cometh." Tripp attempted to tip the waiter, but was refused. They both drank the fresh delivery. Tripp smacked his lips when finished then, "Could you, in short form, offer your thoughts as to what a good advertisement consists of, and what about its target, the consumer, the nature of the viewer?"

"Viewers don't really know it, but they share a proclivity for one special letter of the alphabet."

"Do tell."

"It's the letter 'D' as 'D' seems to headline what watchers tend to watch; drugs, derangement, dysfunction, divorce, death and mixed with a dash of the divine thrown in for appropriate measure and you have the ingredients for commercial success because, you see, Tripp, most people are more informed about other people's maladies than their own as it helps them feel more than adequate about themselves, if even for a short period of time. These are the ingredients that stir pocketbooks to action, the mighty D's, almost as forceful a drive as the draw of cult or of a religion, both of which seem at times to have a touch of another 'D' in them, dastardly."

"You can't say that with a straight face, can you?"

"If it's good enough for Denny Crane and good enough for Boston Legal, it's good enough for me."

"Cade, you really ought to consider hanging out with a higher level of CEO's." "Ready for another critique about your brothers in charms?"

"You forget female correspondents, didn't you?"

"Oh, Char will notice that, so please, add lady newsmen, will you?"

Mr. Bartholomew took another sip of the noggin knocker. "Look Tripp, I believe American newspapers today are what you get when you combine responsibility with vanity. It's what you get with..."

"Sorentsen said the mind, it's not controlled by contrasts that are logical or clear but instead by the fluttering thing we call links, such as are your kids on my soccer team; are you in my carpool?"

"Now it's how well you advocate not appearing to be advocating although most of the ones love to hear the sounds of their own voice, causing diminution of any meaning from what they have to say. "

"The crowded mouths long ago shredded the mantle of impartiality. Maybe editors of newspapers should return to the past when..."

"If you mean dealing with the credible, the unaccommodating, the accountable and the reliable, then yes, I agree, back to print VERITAS."

"Well, yes, but I was referring to the days, mainly in the old South, where, if editors wanted to continue breathing, they had to be damn near angelic not to offend anyone in the close proximity of their home. You see, then, it was sissy boy to sue someone; to get a judge to rule on whether you should go after someone for slander or not. The community at large thought you weren't a man if you needed legal services to defend your reputation. I read that's why editors defended their right to put their words down as they saw fit with a helpmate, a gun and in some cases, a dueling weapon to go after someone perceived to have maimed their reputation. Better be damn certain of whose foot you stepped on or whose feathers you plucked..."

"I like that, Chaz. Probably make a bundle investing in shooting ranges if that were the case today. Ha, Ted Nugent and Paul Krugman having their skills come together at a shooting range, who'd think it?"

"Let's end this talk and go to our favorite profanities..."

"Politics?"

"Yes and Wall Street and I'll start."

"What? I thought I was the interviewee?"

"Thanks to Ronald Reagan's corporations...."

"Here we go again, always back to Reagan or Bush second."

"Corporations got larger subsidies and lower taxes and it only got worse. They got a hell of a deal. Send less to DC. Get more from DC and the middle class struggles mightily since there was no lobby for 'the rabble', same as today."

"Is this where I ask you a question?"

"Your thoughts, please, on the 'far right' for instance?"

"Here's my question. What did you think when the left got their panties in a bunch when Mike Huckabee ran for office and his faith was foremost, a cross symbol in a commercial caused the indulgent indignant hair to go on fire. Your buddies howled that you can't use religion to promote your politics and on and on and on, but when Obama, the icon of idolatry, conveniently spreads Jesus around at prayer breakfasts and ceremonies to scapegoat others, the interchangeable sycophants for the fooled don't cackle at him for throwing in with the God bit, now do they? Oh, no, they just go into the conforming mode of hear no, see no, know no evil as their cherished leader carries on."

Tripp, as customary, allows Cade to fume, as this too will pass. And it gives Tripp more to work with for final edit.

"They say Jesus would 'want you to pay your taxes', just ask the leader of the free world, that God fearing Christian himself, who, for twenty years, sat in Reverend Wright's caldron of 'camp' Christianity, but he hasn't needed to worry as the majority of your comrades in tomes have already kissed his ring. The template must not be tarnished. Huckabee was portrayed as almost a sinner. Obama, then and now, is portrayed as someone even the Almighty should take notes from. And you're not disgusted with the Left?" Cade put his unoccupied hand up. "Don't interrupt, I'm still rolling. The Far Right, well Hell; both parties join in the fudging mix of the perpetually prostrated, bowing down to the punctual prostitutes, nee lobbyists, on site offering services equally to both the 'Dems' and the 'Pubs' with only the price of souls to be negotiated."

"Amen brother. And the Tea Party is..."

"Tripp, the Right prefers to redistribute costs from themselves while the Left likes to redistribute other people's monies. The Right often resides in states with more churches than establishments that push the demon brew but also in states with the highest divorce rates..."

"There go those 'D's again."

"...and pregnant children and other like kind results from one too many Camels enjoyed after one too many Country songs come true."

"And the Left, yes, Cade, they have gifted us with bankrupted cities and morals diversity, yes, and sex that is not sex when it's more convenient to change its meaning for ones justification and preservation, they are and were okay with that, I will give you that." "Both sides constantly appropriate for less than the good of the general welfare. The speed of the robbery is the only difference between the parties."

"The noggin juice is full throttle now, isn't it?"

"Ah, the sweet Wall Street. When has it been in the past that CEO's can write their own meal ticket when they can run their business into the ground, losing millions and millions and still get not only millions in salary plus a bonus, but when it becomes so untenable as to be ludicrous, it becomes even more deliciously delirious; I know, 'D's again, but it comes to a head and the chief is paid millions more in severance to basically get the hell gone. Wall Street has been and still is able to write the rules by which they play. Accountability? You got to be kidding. I ask you, Tripp, is there any more room in the Hatters hat? And how many are still in jail or even went? Right, zero; not a one deserves freedom."

"And a lot of these barons of banditry get corporate welfare from the government and still crash their business and the average Joe and average Jane, they are the dismissed, the statistics, where do they to go to assure justice? Gilded Age all over again with more dangerous people."

"These lovely examples of God's best efforts; so discouraging, its border line suffocating I ask you Tripp, where are today's heroes for today's kids? Where are those inspirational few every generation needs? I know we aren't fathers but..."

Tripp, as if uncomfortable, adjusted his position in the chair. North Dakota vibrations came and then left as swiftly as they had entered.

As Cade finished he saw Mr. Drummerman coming their way. The drivers stood aside as they recognized Yoggee as a friendly. "Speaking of a timeless piece of walking La La; Yoggee, Merry Christmas!"

"Gentlemen; and I use that phrase only because it's the season to be polite and good cheer, goodbye, good night and God bless. Didn't mean to interrupt an obviously highbrow jawbone moment."

As Tripp searched in the distance over Cades shoulder for available server, he implored," Mr. Drummerman, time for nightcap. We finished smarting up each other here, Yoggee." "No. No, got early flight back to icy reality in the morning. But thank you, man." Yoggee looked around saw that they were still separated from most of the others. "This is been a fine occasion. I'm pleased to help the Senator mucho much. But I must share with you that the level of density and disingenuousness I've been introduced to tonight is mind altering! Not from our friends of course. Near borderline depravity."

Yoggee shook Cades hand first then quickly shook Tripp's.

"Frustratingly numbing to witness this cellular collision of inch-deep, mile wide gulf of gullibility I've been wading in tonight. Border line depravity."

"Whoa...," Cade, intrigued as he usually was when Yoggee was within earshot, "... this view comes from the practicing victualer of grog, gadgetry and morality glitches; and other people are strange?"

"My cab should be about here so I will encapsulate my experience with this." Yoggee waited made sure that the audience of two was attentive. "Please note; I hope the taxi is soundproof and the driver deaf." Yoggee turned to exit, paused and turned back towards his friends. "It's a mother of miracles."

"What?"

"That there are two good women on earth who think that you're both worth their time... but they are from DC now, aren't they?" And before they could respond he was out the door.

"There goes Mr. L. S. Drummerman; the 'L's for loose, the 'S's for screw and the 'D's for delightful and I wouldn't have it any other way." Tripp nodded agreement.

CHAPTER 21

"Never Live Downwind"

"...not merely to keep aces up sleeves but to insist God put them there."

Benjamin Disraeli commenting on the
audacity of his foe, William Gladstone.

December 23, 2015

His is a Beaux Arts mansion, built during the Gilded Age, located in the vicinity of Massachusetts Avenue and DuPont Circle on one of the friendly appearing tree shaded streets. It is hard to miss. The granite and marble multi storied building is surrounded by a high brick and cast iron fence, trimmed in security cameras. The massive front doors are gold plated and for a short span each day when the sun is shining, the reflection can be blinding. The foyer is curiously average sized, but opposite the front, he has a vintage elevator, a beautiful mahogany and copper and steel conversation starter, which is one of only two methods to go upstairs.

Hers is a smaller Northumbrian styled home in McLean with more land than building, less ostentatious and more seclusion by owner design and natural inclination. Both were now seen as Washington's newest "couple toy". Privilege, power and FrontPage personas made it catnip for the coveting curious; the feral thinking participants, vying daily within the metaphysical free litter box of D.C., clawing, cloying contests of accusation or claim; DC, the 'drag you down to my level' gossip market of all gossip markets, a channel through which these sojourners of say-so seek a sense of relief, of comfort from the realization, finally, that they will never ever live the lives that they dreamt they would live when they first came to this hashtag town. Therefore, everyone else must be made to pay. There are already too many I cannot look down on as it is, seemed to be the prevailing mindset.

The most provocative lady in the Senate had never met Mr. Hawkins-Burke previous to the charity event, which was odd in that both had been in near proximity of the other for nearly 4 years. Lilith Langtree's mother gave her the name of Adam's first wife, the one before Eve, because her mother projected and wanted a girl to grow into a woman who stood alone, no assistance necessary nor need of aid by any man that would come along. Mother Darla Langtree claimed the famous performer as "I've heard it told a distant relative," unverified but still colorful addition to origin story. Darla wanted her newborn to know her namesake with one "L" well. She taught the younger Langtree that the biblical Lilith was later conceived and portrayed by early church as 'evil', most certainly, as Darla shared with her daughter,' because Lilith was feisty and independent so they denounced her as a demon who stole children.' Darla Langtree had researched further and had found Assyrian and Babylonian legends about Lilith being a 'female demon who haunted desolate places, the same empty spaces that inhabit the area between a man's ears.

And don't forget how Mary Magdalene was portrayed by these couch philosophers too, *Lily!'*

Darla Langtree was a lifelong waitress and a damn good one. She gave birth to Lilith on a bus just outside Blythe, California as Darla was running from an abusive relationship from the father, "A one night stand from Armadillo that lasted one morning after one day too long." Darla was personal and earned good-sized tips, enough to cover some small additional costs to send her now six foot Lilith to college on a partial volleyball scholarship. The daughter received her degree in international business in three years. Lilith also worked as a waitress to help with costs. She, like her mother was very good at personal service and she did quite well, making larger than average tips. Lilith first worked as a consultant to firms for a major headhunting group before devoting more and more time to advocating for women's rights, which eventually strained her relationship with her conservative firm and she left them to become a paid worker and spokes lady for groups she felt needed someone fighting for them that wasn't afraid of going for broke. Ms. Langtry marched in demonstrations and parades; contributed and helped with charitable events for assistance for abusive women programs; for breast cancer awareness rounded out by seeking donations for medical programs for needy children.

These steps seemed a natural progression to her when she first considered elective office. And so it was. When not in her presence, male Senate colleagues called her 'Lilith of the bust' as a takeoff of her press promoted bio nickname of 'Lilith of the bus.' 42, tall blonde with attitude, trim with strong upper arms, Lilith 'of the bus' was glib and knowledgeable of the topics of current momentum. Often rumored in affairs, she dismissed with a beautiful smile and the words, "Never documented, not one of them." She'd been linked to an actor some years previously, but for the majority, she'd successfully kept her private ways off the record. Her demeanor insured that any possible suitor/wooers understood clearly that she was a take no prisoners lady, a tough veneer with a heart that is never on loan. One hidden vanity competing with this core of toughness that Lilith liked to wrap up in was her inexplicable shame and embarrassment at her scoliosis scar, the sole reason for the senator to always wear one-piece bathing suits which cover her back; this even on such a body as would have brought a blush, a breathless sigh from da Vinci himself at the prospect of her acquiescing to modeling for the master. She relished the simple "C"s; Clapton, Coldplay and her pink Corvette convertible 'Sachet'. She thoroughly valued independence, volleyball, poker and perusing past issues of Soldier of Fortune.

She demanded men respect her and to fear the consequences of causing her ill. Secretly, she desired a person to share her scars with and theirs with her but so far to no happy success. She strives to stoke gobs of foo-foo coverage for her concerns from a compliant press, but recently, this was becoming a wee bit more challenging as truthful reportage seems to be gaining a foothold again. She'd adapt. She nearly always executed pivots as precisely as a prima ballerina should. She demanded men respect her enough to fear the consequences of causing her ill. She even secretly longed for a man to share her scars with but this recent slight shift towards using even handed wordage was gaining a foothold in the foreground of her thoughts so sharing anything of value with a man now was the farthest from her thoughts today.

She was a cautious optimist who, when impatient, sometimes would give away her edginess, playing with her hair and moving her crossed leg slightly up and down such as when she came to the conclusion that the government was not doing more than what was called for helping the poor. She had made waves as such in her short time in office, for the poor, which were a constant reminder of where her mother and she had come from.

The 'toy' is touring the 'playthings' hallway gallery and sun room on the top floor. The plaything is wound up.

"Perfect politics is exquisite resonance," Hawkins-Burke postured, "...a finely tuned approach to the proper calibration of humanities harmonics, the desires, the dreams, and of course it helps that the crowd is culturally insular and not subject to nuance." "Uneducated you mean?"

"Some what, yes. That way you purchase both sides of history.

"Ms. Langtree's silence was commentary.

"I'm a bad boy with moola, Honey." His attempted humor fell flat. "I did not think that it needed mentioning as I thought it would be an insult to your intelligence, I mean the way I am with money?"

Lilith smiled small. She liked it when men squirmed to explain. Amazing how an arched brow or tightened lips can bring this in males. Hawkins-Burke tried to finalize it.

"You have your opinions. I have my ways."

"I'm no hobbling hobereaux, Stuart. I know how the most profitable acts are frequently carried out in the penumbra of others."

"Geishas in the shade, right, of course."

Hawkins-Burke handed Lilith a cup of fresh green tea.

"Were working now in the sectors of soft insurgencies, how to prevent, how to initiate; sugar, dear?"

"No thank you."

"We're susceptible to cyber terrorism, the grid, banks, bribe or blackmail, hacking in R&D accelerates as more villains get a hold of more of other peoples work." Hawkins- Burke took a sip of his sweetened tea. "Ah but the lasers, love, lasers..."

"Is this like plastics from The Graduate?" Already, Lilith loved tweaking him.

"It's rather an indelicate science, dear, undeserving of sarcasm; especially when its mastery can lead to the death of satellites, missiles, and men."

"Ah, play serious for me now, will you."

"At Magi, the policies simple; always cover all bases." They stopped in front of a still life, a brilliantly colored floral splash.

"Our management approach is ever as a flower, a flower when the divisions in each world, each petal, which are of the same number and multiples of the same number itself and you use the wonderment of the harmony of form to your benefit in a planned symmetry for profits. You like the colors in this one, right?"

"Yes". And they moved on.

"Acquiring art is maneuver and manipulate; you maneuver in preparation to execute a skilled stroke in manipulating men either away from their emotions or towards their emotions, whichever is necessary to hang what I want in my hallways."

"And am I the subject of your most recent maneuver and manipulation, Hawkins-Burke?" "No. Although you have become my current obsession besides lasers."

"Lasers?"

"Yes, lasers, the final degree of influence challenging all aspects of matter, one atom after another atom crossbreeding in the material world."

"You're talking dwarfs now, right? Nanotechnology, heroin for Hawkins-Burke, or so I have read."

"There are over 400 or so commercial products, probably more, where nano plays big. We are working on improving the bounty box that this technology holds; expansive possibilities for photovoltaic's, batteries, and in medicine, smart drugs, gene and here's that word again, manipulation in ways not imaginable even a handful of years ago. We are breaking up things once thought unbreakable and..."

"You're almost drooling you're on such a spittle high."

He laughed and motioned for her to follow. They entered the large second living room with the wrap around view windows. "Never get tired of this."

They were just in time to see the last splashes of coral, pink and purple softly washing away the Western sky as it welcomed the tender part of the night, dusk.

"The key, Senator Langtree, is carbon and how to use it effectively, how to maximize connectivity and tensile strength. Listen, Lil,...,"He had never been this informal or intimate with her before and she was please as it made her feel distinct from what she could tell of his life of otherwise strict formality and protective standoffishness.

"... Nano means trillions, in Greek or any other language in the global economy. We are reaching accords now with development organizations and governments, then..."

"For subsidies? I sense Hyde, his fingers on the keys for this rhapsody; am I wrong? Of course, you supply the sheet music; I know that, but..."

"The governments' allocating almost two billion to move the industry to critical mass and Magi want to be in on the big bang." Lilith giggled, "I bet you do!"

"The CIA's, one of, shall we call it venture firms, an investor with us."

Lily was listening closely to see if she needed to give a warning to the CFO CEO that he was in a zone that she as senator did not want to share. She thought it too early for conflict of interest to intrude just yet.

"This division, I'm calling it; it's a separate entity from Magi, we're calling it LifeSpun Incorporated or L. L. C.; depends on what Hyde finds out as to which offers the least tax exposure."

"Prudent and predictable."

Hawkins-Burke offered his hand. Ms. Langtree took it and they headed towards the hall. "Lilith, only a handful, maybe two handfuls of people knows this; what I want to share with you. You've heard of Tom Swift? Well this is Swiftian in its scope."

"I know the books, the inventor boy. I was more into Nancy Drew and Cosmo, but you're getting at?"

"Just that we are close, very close to perfecting cloaking." "You mean improved stealth?"

"In a way, yes, but I mean the ability to be invisible."

Reserve filter fails miserably as she nearly shrieks, "Really? No!" She gathered herself. "How does it, the uses could be, why, they can be..."

"Triumphal."

"Yes, and toxic."

"Listen, its gods finger-painting in lightplay. It's opaque and transparent wonderment, together, as never before. We pour a form of coating for cloaking. 'Liquid Gone,' we call it."

"And the Word was light."

"In Greek, 'nanos', does, as you referenced earlier, does mean 'dwarf.'" Lilith and his sister could be soul mates; both unconquerable.

"You remind me of someone I used to know."

Georgette wearied him still. No leads on in-laws or funerals or burials; the dearth of details still haunted. And now these concerns competed with a woman who was much more than passing weakness. Hawkins-Burke had not dated in 4 to 5 years. When he had 'nighted out,' it was strictly business based, broad, and bottom line fine and beautiful as there were no commitments. He answered her unasked question.

"No, not someone I was romantically in the ditch with."

This is a true-nature response one would expect from an individual with two bullet proof vehicles, who employs unprepossessing men reclassified as 'cultural fixers'; men with specialized skills in extracurricular needs and deniability.

She knows that, behind the unfolding goodness from the man she wants to know better, there is a willingness to hurt others for profit and that there is a not so insignificant track record, if press reports mean anything anymore, of his proclivity for getting away from bedplay once he had become bored with his playmate; but it didn't matter with Lilith, for she was on a sensual safari too and opposite what the rumors were about her private life, she is energetic about someone else for the first time in years.

"Delightfully amorous, aren't we?"

Hawkins-Burke softly swirled as he took her hand and guided Ms. Langtree back towards the dining area and the conversation back towards nano nano.

"No one has yet produced the way to make nano tubes long enough, a better length. That's their optimum form to handle the workloads of a new era. We're close. But we're still rolling the atomic dice and still crapping out but you know, Lilith, if you pressure carbon, squish it hard, stretch out every square issue, make it work in your favor; carbon becomes diamond."

They stopped at Hawkins-Burke's favorite antique. "This credenza is from the Renaissance. This significant piece was a useful tool for executive decisions. It was where food was tested for poison before a meal was served, furniture with a purpose other than style or comfort."

Hawkins-Burke opened the drawers and brought out the most beautiful display of natural 'poison' Ms. Langtree had ever seen; cognac diamonds mixed with blues.

"Mythically rare," Hawkins-Burke proudly observed," ...worth up to 1 million or more per carat."

"Where do they come from?"

"The saturated pink darlings are from down under. The supplies dwindling, hence, the sweet poison of scarcity will kill any chance of their devaluation. Waiting on another delivery this week; held up by the holidays, but worth the delay."

He leaned in to better see the reflection of the stones in her eyes. She did not give ground; instead deflecting his intrusion into her comfort space with, "Splendid and expensive, Stuart Hawkins-Burke; Babylonian extravagance on Alexandrian scale, yes?" following quickly with, "Colored diamonds; which sex has the more discerning eye, Stewart?"

He was mesmerized by the depth of her delivery and the sparkle in her words but recovered to respond, "Men aren't close to women when it's about color."

"Have you shown this collection to many?"

"You know, Lilith, I had not thought of this, but, no. No, I haven't, it's, I've never wanted to until..." He caught himself again and he hated it.

"Why have displays if not for show?"

Again, Hawkins-Burke pause to calculate, uncomfortable with how often this woman had caused this unaccustomed search for words within the past hour alone, finally, "You women, your preference is to showcase them, the diamonds, drape in them, while, men, you know, me, I like to shine light on them and to handle them and..."

"Just like testicles, right"?

With all that swirls in the usual calamity of the minds battle with emotion whenever the heart is on approach to refreshed destiny, alarms do go off. Lilith's countered these qualms with the surprising yet calming knowledge that she still had not been introduced to the Magi man's master bedroom, nor invited to this symphony of the of the sexes that it is most noted for. Her anticipation of the final landing grows even more intense and yet she senses shyness returning as well. Hawkins-Burke, a gentleman! Who'd believe it? Game changer. Was she the only one that could perfect this diamond in the rough to the state or quality of a gem worthy of her promotion and adoration? Why'd the others fail? This meant effort and this meant something new to a woman who had never had to sweat to get a man to sweat for her.

The ETA's still speculative. The passengers, used to being captains, don't object. They are enjoying the flight without worrying about having to steer, and it wouldn't work anyway if either tried. Both are at the state of lift where they hope the 'fasten the seat belt' announcement will never sound as they aren't ready for the ground just quite yet.

CHAPTER 22

"Dreams On The Bottom"

"Like all Americans, I like big things: big prairies, big forests and mountains, big wheat fields, railroads and herds of cattle too, big factories and steamboats and everything else. But one must keep steadily in mind that no people were ever yet benefitted by riches if their prosperity corrupted their virtue. It is more important that we should show ourselves honest, brave, truthful."

Teddy Roosevelt
July 4th speech

December 25, 2015

The grounds in the vicinity of the Constitution Gardens adjacent to the National Mall and northeast of the Lincoln Memorial are covered in December bleak. Skies are flat gray with no depth and dirty snow completes the somber tenor.

The three men are in the company of the only family they had in town to spend the hallowed day with, themselves. They are walking the path of pathos which is the Vietnam Memorial, a polished black granite tribute to fallen American warriors founded by Jan Scruggs, an infantry corporal who served in the 199th light infantry in Vietnam; "a go get em' grunt" as Truefellow described him.

The Navaho had thought it best for Godboy to be with Truefellows' mother on the reservation as the Navajo, at the last moment, could not find a flight out until the next day and he did not want his mother or the boy alone. John Truefellow also considered that his roommate might desire some private time after the breakup with Odessa. That had gone to seed with Tripp's call to the condo on Christmas Eve. Emily had flown out to be with family and Tripp invited them to join him for dinner the next day at The Flooze.

Now they stood still. They look down the ends of the wall and noticed one other couple in the distance and that was it for crowd. "Guys," Chaz ruminated aloud, "my prayer for today besides for these significant souls etched into this dark reminder of glories past visitations is that in the new year I finally do not need to write another word again about the ruinous folly of what has become our of country that these brave people died for." Sean notice the vein on the Navajos left temple before the sheriff spoke up "Hey, these men and women gave it up for each other, gave it up for their families, gave it up for the America that is not this government and don't you mistake one with the other."

"Well, Navajo, I misspoke. You are right. These politicians are so deep in swill that stench is viewed as a cost of living in this sty. You read me. You know my heart. You know it's broken; the gnawing cynicism is the new victory garden. We are being run over by clowns without a sense of timing, who have notoriety without achievement and improprieties revealed which would conquer you or me."

"Fair play is passe." Sean interjected. "Bags of cash shouldn't excuse inexcusable behavior."

"You know, I recall a character I read a piece about when I was at the precipice of jumping into the press pool or not..."

"Cesspool?"

"Press! Press! Writing instead of piping vibes. Anyway, a guy in Texas and the Texas Senate, name of Pilgrim; yep, Bo Pilgrim, from East Texas parts that's hilly and green. He was from the non-alibi throwback era when bribery was in the open. This Pilgrim moved around passing out money to get other Texas politicians to vote for him or for his cronies. It was acceptable. Up to 10 thousand dollars to the people's representatives in the middle of hearings or in the middle of votes that were of interest to this guys desires, this Pilgrim's. This is nearly 25 years ago maybe, more or less. And just, have we, is it any better now because it's gone to the subterranean caves of quid pro quo and that batshit lawyers hired to fly out and say, "It's okay, we aren't really sucking the blood out of all you.""

"Me?" Sean had turned around to face John and Chaz, "I like Pilgrim's Pride of being open and honest about his motives, ulterior or otherwise; refreshing."

"I may not know much, dumb Indian and all; but one thing I've learned from my time with the councils, budgets are the four aces at the table. It's when you find out who's the dealer, who's going to get screwed and who's doing the screwing. And when it's over, how will they graft us the next time? And what will the rules, how will the rules of the game be changed? They always are."

Sean had moved closer to the wall as he'd spotted the name of a friend's father; the father being the reason Sean's friend had joined the military.

"Huh, Bucks dad." John moved closer and agreed. "You know, the sun's fighting to come through but I swear it's colder than when we walked up." Chaz pulled his jacket collars up higher.

"It has 58,000 reasons to be uncomfortable here."

Truefellow had stepped away from their friend's father's name on the wall and was looking at Chaz. "Isn't there a law on the books, Tripp, against government-sponsored propaganda?"

"Well, yes, in the 50's there..."

"Then, couldn't the networks be indicted for being nothing but house organs for the government?"

"Uh?"

"And since the press corps in this cerebrally challenged slum shun the effects of these acts; the first, the second, and the third acts of this strewn about tragedy of purchased remissions and gratuitous dignities and the resulting damage done to the decent in America because of it, can the citizenry, Jesus, can they go after and sue for fraud, that's what I'm asking, for malpractice impersonating journalists or how about the ability for them to be sued civilly by whores and pimps impugning their reputations as well? Now, Tripp, I excuse you from this rant because you don't cut comers."

With exaggerated hurt, Tripp replied, "Well, I should hope so. Every day, I..."

"I excuse you, Tripp, because, one, you have thoroughly covered, in detail, Congress's abandonment of any affectation of representing on behalf of the people; and two, you are hosting Christmas dinner and for both, I am thankful."

"This talk of all these ethical mutants in our lives is giving me a slightly upset stomach and headache." And then with a low groan, "Then, again, it might just be the twist of fate place we're standing in."

After a stretch of silence, Tripp gathered himself. "Look, still have short time before dinner will be ready at the Flooze. Got ham, turkey and maize for you, Native boy!" The Navajo ignored Tripp. "Hush. The time for long memory is back."

The three walk together along the remainder of the Memorial and John Truefellow continued his thoughts. "The goal of the powerful is to make us forget our past, our origins, erase our histories and fools will turn to the convenient use and words of the uninformed. The status quo becomes a borderland not to be trespassed on by intolerably ordinary folk; Wakantonka forbid this ever happens!"

"The inability to concentrate is key." Sean Linden had paused at the end of the Memorial. "YouTube, Facebook, Google, keep people occupied with the most important thing it seems these days in their lives; themselves. And the teeth gnashing cacophony of the 24- hour crisis by the minute and the polls of immature significance from news outlets that

aid and abet in the softening, this white noise 'blessing' for the powerful. The resulting retreat by the ruled from having to face any cumbersome thought of what really matters in this world is planned. It's structured for the people to throw up their hands as if all is confused and not wanting to be occupied with anything else except your own skin is permissible."

Sean flashed to the questions of his youth; of his entire life; the 'who', the 'what', and the 'where' parts that still perplex.

"It's harder than ever to know the right path even when you're on top of it. Now, others say they have the answers and it's become a popular choice to say 'yeah' and put decisions into automatic pilot, again, good way for the greedy to inherit the weak."

The sun snuck a few rays in as the moisture moved towards the East.

"Security is fragile. Got to take it into your grasp. Judgment must improve or growth is only a word listed under G in the dictionary, if you live enough to get past F, that is. And who reads dictionaries anymore?"

Tripp spoke up, "We have, Sean. That's because you, The Navajo, me, we are cast from an era when 'imagination' wasn't just a reference to the past. Yes, John, we were and still are, I bet, curious as we ever were; want to know why 'starts' stop and other mysteries." Tripp, too late, realized that maybe, hopefully not, but maybe, Sean had just heard the whistle for the depot named Odessa.

"Sean, all women cause ulcers. Just like I think we give women their gray hair." Always the one to ignore warning lanterns, Tripp put more wood in the locomotive firepot.

"Sean, I mentioned to you that I knew Odessa. Way back. She does have the good parts of humanity in her, really pronounced, I think you'd agree..."

"Yes, or I would not have taken the time."

"No, none of us would."

"Unless we are interested in nature's course and whether or not squaw and brave are going to work, then maybe, but?"

Tripp waved Truefellow away. Sean half smiled, saying "That's probably true too."

"I know I should have better controlled my urges towards anatomical anarchy like you have, Sean." Tripp was serious and that made it all the more humorous.

"Listen, Yoggee, geez, he taught me a couple, had a few thoughts about well, remorse." "Remorse? Jesus, Tripp," Sean protested, "no one died!"

"Mr. Drummerman shared this with me a while back, Sean. He said you can't tell which way the caboose went by just looking at the rails and..."

"God, there's more?"

"If you think everyone has something good in them, then you need to get out way more often than you think you should."

Sean smiled as Tripp added, "The Stoics believed that passion was a human misery which came from the mind just going into a steely mental irrational contraction. They thought passion to be a disease of the soul."

"Sean," the Navajo had more to import,"...if it makes you feel better, the Cherokees changed wives three or four times a year. My Uncle once told me he wished this were so now for Navaho too. You see, my ex step-Aunt, was, according to him, one of those whose loci is loco. Now that's my ex step-Aunt, Sean, not talking about Odessa here, no."

Tripp looked at his watch. ""It's time for the 'floozen' to commence." But before Tripp could utter another sound, both military man turned about-face and slowly saluted. Tripp bowed his head as the breeze kicked up. When he saw the arms come gently to rest he suggests "Let's turn the problems of the world loose, gentleman, at least for Christmas dinner, right guys?"

John and Sean both gave Tripp a hug. Tripp gave one last look over the shoulder.

"Wonder if Jan..."

"Who?"

"Scruggs, who started this; I wonder if he's a relative of Earl Scruggs?"

Sean and John were blank.

"You illiterate infidels; Lester Flatt and Earl Scruggs! Banjo's the dirty work in music and they were great at it. You know, tough instrument to play like a man and you said this Jan guy was a grunt, tough on the ledge, so I say the two, Earl and Jan, got to be blooded, right? Get my sizzle drizzle, Bro's?"

Laughter echoed. They girded themselves against the arrival of a more pestering wind, walking towards the Floozy Malthusian and a feast suitable for royalty, if not three musketeers, and towards a situation far enough away from the granite wall of ebony and woe as to allow the 'present' some space within which to stretch.

CHAPTER 23

"Mathematics Seemed Perfect Until The Equation Man"

"Spherical bastards..."
What Swiss astronomer, Fritz Zwicky, called colleagues at Mount Wilson Observatory, because, as he said, "They were bastards anyway you looked at them."

December 29, 2015

The two friends sat at their usual table. And as usual, the owner of the establishment would not let them pay. For the record, the owner would charge customer number ones' credit card and then reimburse the learned client the tab; noted in the owners books as a cost of advertising under 'personal appearance fees'. This accomplished two goals. First, the owner repaid what he considered a lifelong debt for what the owner had learned in customer number ones classroom and two, it kept the other customer, number two, from ever being accused of quid pro quo chicanery if the owner ever had business or concerns that became the center of attention before one of customer two's committees or investigative bodies. Sen. Bruce and Prof. Sorentsen sat in '22 Times Turned T-bones and Chop Shoppe', another one of their friend Cade Bartholomew's restaurant successes. The concept of 'T Times Five' as Cade called it, was a computer program that precisely calculated the exact timing required for 22 revolutions of the pricy pieces of prime center cuts skewed on rotating spits above roaring fires; achieving, no matter if rare, medium rare, well or well done, pallet perfection bar none, or as Cades' advertising promoted, 'as pleasing a smooch to the mouth as a kiss'. Cade avoided advertising agencies. They reminded him of previous mistakes with women and other promises or endearments or was it endurances; anyway, he was against them. In fact, Cade authored his two signature campaign phrases. "22 Times Turned T-bones and Chop Shoppe, maybe a mouthful, but isn't that what you want?" as well as "22 Times Turned T-bones and Chop Shoppe, new age technology cookin' up the savory taste of the old age when pride was part of the recipe and meals meant more than just sustenance."

Apparently, something made sense as reservations were required months in advance. Cade responded to compliments about the success of his efforts with his customary diffidence, "Even a visually impaired mentally challenged squirrel can stumble into acorn heaven once in a while."

The conversation at the usual table was the usual exchange, politics and education, and what both lacked.

"God bless the Tea Party for beginning the process of reining in the kissing of the rings that occurs after elections, Gunner."

"So the rusty tradition of bowing down by the fresh catechumens continues on in other forms and the Cardinals by other names, right Dunsey?"

"The enfant perdu; these freshmen and women would be even more forlorn if the voters, by God, had not help pushed earmarks to earth and staged dogged eared madness, pushing for change in the workings of my place of employment and now we have this incrementally sillier and sillier excuse for an independent press which means more battles to come."

"Except for Tripp."

"Yes, professor, except for that lovable miscreant, they are all caught up in saying the Emperor is clothed, that his laws do protect common good, and that it's all for the children. I don't know how they can read their manifestoes at night without vomiting!" "Ah, thank you for reminding me I need more sour cream for my spud."

"They're tiresome, termagant nannies, Gunner, consistently squeaking from their holes about what they don't have and what they see misarranged in others."

"You're on a roll, Senator.

Their personal waiter arrives.

Ah, thank you, Ronald, for the sour cream. And the Senator just reminded me; will you please bring some more Kaisers? Thank you."

God, think what the 'worries' would do with Earl or Huey Long."

"They would never run out of things to fill with."

"Men who knew corruption and how to move it around the board."

Sen. Bruce took another bite of filet mignon. "I think it was Earl Long that pointed out to prospective investors in his, shall we call them, ideals, that if they gave funds at the outset of his campaign, he'd make an effort to consider their desires and then he said that big contributions at the white-hot moment towards near the end day of the voters decision making process, late money from these donors would be given only quote, good government, unquote, on their behalf."

"I have another name for that money. It's hush money for 'we the people'. Keep our mouths shut, our minds shut and keep sucking on that tootsie roll and only respond when the bell rings."

"Squamous fidget midgets, spawned in sporting houses of venality, that's the mire I wade in."

Sorentsen sensed his friend's disgust. The senator, now silent, sips a small wash of cool water, paused, stared out at the activity on the street and to no one in particular, "It's called rotten and I've seen it done." Mr. Bruce stared at Mr. Sorentsen. "Lobbyist writing legislation to exempt them from possible environmental hazards, efforts to shortchange royalty payments, grazing fees, sticking it to Uncle Sam on mining laws, mostly done out of the glare of public oversight and debate, executing all in the opaque cages of conference committees, where there's no reconciliation, only origination of a separate version of the bill than was initially brought them. Its payback time for donors and their psyches. I swear Americans would shutter."

"Jefferson quote seems apropos, Dunsey. He said, "Anyone who would pretend that a campaign donation is unrelated to a desire for political influence is either a liar or an idiot."

"Forgive me, my friend, but I fear for the future. I fear it because, well, our education is flawed. Were training, teaching a crop of idiots who can't recognize the state of Mississippi on a map, let alone a crook trying to get their votes! I ask you, doctor my love, why are the teacher unions still in business?"

"Educational bureaucrats and their protected interests are flaming good marriages for them even though one third of students fail to finish on time, requirements are inadequate, contributions count more than choice, cheating's not shamed, teachers impacts considered more important than kids impacts, student loneliness, alienation, too much television not enough face-to-face time, it adds up to our times."

"A few years back I saw somewhere, it said that every 30 seconds or so, 1000 students, kids, drop out of school."

"Vouchers can be part of the solution. Spend equal amounts, on all races; kids first parents second; teachers last. Unfortunately, parents have also been dumbed down along with their kids."

"I'm glad I grew up when scoring mattered; grades, games and dames. It goes back to who do the kids have to emulate, the proven path? Not for promotion but for personal enlightenment and progress? Athletes cheat, couples cheat, why it has come down to its okay to be a thief. Concentration of power means everything; checks and balances are considered ancient. Corporations buy legislatures and judges and they buy them to block proposed regulations which harm their schemes and the executive branch acts oblivious to it all when the debts come due for the finery wrap of re-election time."

"You've heard; you are aware of Hesoid?"

"Yes, the Greek, what was he?"

"A poet writer; he wrote something called 'Theogony' which dealt with the myths of the Greeks and how they related to people. It also was the story of the gods, the birth of the gods and goddesses at Mount Olympus."

"Who were his sources?"

"Cute. What I am saying is that Hesoid had a term for the nobles of his times and I think it is as equally appropriate for the ignoble ones of ours, you know, your associates that are steeped in the shimmer of their own shine." The professor put his spoon to a cherry and scooped as much Kirshwasser and Bluebell homemade vanilla remains as possible. The Senator followed suit.

"Hesiod said, that the Greek nobles, that, they are 'dorophagoi ', gift-hungry."

"He wouldn't get an editor's job today, "Dunleavy observed "...he's too honest."

"Ain't that the sad truth."

"Had a cousin, settled up in the Ennis area of Montana; good fishing in that place; anyway, lost track of him recent years. A while back, well, God, years ago, he told me about a local legend from a neighboring town, Virginia City. This is hundred plus years old story about what happened with the sheriff there. Lawman's name was one Henry Plummer. Here's the kicker; not only was Plummer sheriff, he was the leader of the largest group of desperados and robbers too!"

"Hell, he'd be in familiar territory in Congress today. Write laws for everyone else to obey but you make sure they're written so you don't have to."

"Insider skating."

"Yes."

"Nepotism."

"Yes and think of the clean thefts he could commit in Congress. He wouldn't stand out."

"Yeah. It went on for some time for ol' Henry. Stagecoaches held up, people killed, spoils split."

"And what happened to Plummer?"

"They hanged him. Say, Doc, what was that saying ascribed to Cato the Elder, the Roman, who ended all his orations with the same epithet is, something that..." "Delenda est Carthago!' meaning, 'Carthage must be destroyed'."

"That's the one. How 'bout 'Delenda est Fidget Midgets' for the conclusions of my speeches from now on; you like?"

"You can write off the vertically challenged, I can tell you that. Hesiod's 'Theogony' should now be called 'The Agony", if this keeps up."

"I wonder, have we answered our calling, Gunnar?"

"I wouldn't know, Senator."

"I never answer the phone anymore."

"So you're saying leave a message if we've done the right thing?"

"It's just the, well, we participate in the bitching, high-volume, ever think of that? And never, never do we get to stitching things back together the way they were when they were fresh."

"And one other thing; tell me why, professor, that music seems louder, in malls, barber shops, restaurants, everywhere these days; why?"

"Either you recently cleared your ears out or your feet just don't want to tap to the beat they used to or because they can't."

"Damn you, Gunnar, I will tango again."

"Is this the bitching or is this the stitching?"

"It's a fair warning, I'm climbing back into my youth again and taking big boy ammunition with me."

"God, they must really love you in Oklahoma."

"No. They love me out of Oklahoma; that's why they keep reelecting me." "Keep the boy in DC?"

"Yes, as far away from OKC and Okmulgee as they can get me."

"Just shows a man's got to know his constituencies, Senator."

"Yes, Gunnar, that and a good bartender with a short memory."

CHAPTER 24

"La Politique Napas d'Entrailles"
(Politics Have No Bowels)

"Men are not corrupted by the exercise of power or debased by the habit of obedience; but by the exercise of a power which they believe to be illegal and by obedience to a rule they consider to be usurped and oppressive."

Alexis de Tocqueville

December 30, 2015

Hawkins-Burke had committed to a rare interview for the 31st of December. He wanted it face-to-face. So, he'd moved up his invitation by a day to the "beautiful one"; the nickname Ms. Langtree knew co-workers called her when they thought she was not in earshot of their sarcasm and envy; a name Hawkins-Burke adored and recently, he had begun to let her know it.

They were awaiting the arrival of an 'associate' or perhaps, as the evening would progress and the situation would develop, a more apt description is an obviously indebted soul who would act in her man's presence, obsequiously; with a kind description being what could be best defined as the tortured look of a wounded animal..

Sen. Lilith Langtree surveyed her surroundings. The heated tent was canvas and large. She would be spending New Year's in Nevada; but not in Vegas and not exactly on New Year's Eve. She felt some minor internal discomfort as the location they are in is not a far distance from where she began life's journey. The memory is not always a harmonious one.

Hawkins-Burke had flown them to Nevada to an area of a national park, which the CEO CPO had paid mighty handsomely for to have privacy. Hawkins-Burke paid for security, and will pay for improvements after they leave. Four in-house Magi men were near. It was a one night safari to the stars, he'd called it. He explained to her that, when he could get away with it, he was partial to sunsets in the desert, and he'd entreated her to join him by asking her, "When was the last time you were able to do some fun on the spur of the moment? Just 'here we go, with no plans, no clocks and no clothes." He'd promised to have her back before "we turn into pumpkins." She'd liked that he had become more familiar with her.

And now, here they were. Air's crisp; the stars are minimal and faint as it is onset of dusk; western clouds coloring their good byes in mauves, purples and small soft circles of orange and coral, as resplendent and equally hypnotic as the delicate diamond bracelet she's wearing, a gift from an appreciative Hawkins-Burke for her saying, 'Yes; Boulder City, warmer than D.C., so why not.'

As she watched Hawkins-Burke instructing his four Magi men, she noticed other workers erecting another not as grand canvas tent, not a great distance from where she was standing. Maybe for the men.

An Escalade drives to the gathering of males and parks. All but Hawkins-Burke disburse as the passenger door opens and the Senator recognizes the man approaching Hawkins- Burke, Hinton Moss.

Hawkins-Burke had informed Lilith during their flight that he was meeting an important associate for a short while, only necessary to renew an old 'understanding' for the New Year as Hawkins-Burke described it. Stuart told her that he wanted this face to face, same as the New Year's interview. Lilith accepted this without qualm and she wasn't surprised that it was a politician, nor that Hawkins-Burke did not consider introducing the newcomer to her. Deniability is always preferable.

She was surprised at the brevity of the conversation between the two men and also that, upon conclusion of their momentary discussion, Hawkins-Burke escorted Mr. Moss to the newly erected second tent, slapped the man on the back and with a noticeably loud tone, Hawkins-Burke declares, "We will have breakfast at 8:30 so we can get you back to the ones you love so you can welcome in the new year right, right?"

The other man nodded, glanced in her direction and entered his tent for his night in the desert.

Very robotic Lilith sensed as it appeared to her that the other man's movement was seemingly weighed down by an ill tailored suit in sack cloth of itchy impuissance, complemented by a buttoned-down look of what might've been. She would not ask Hawkins-Burke about any of it as she knew Hawkins-Burke would expect inquiry and Lilith now well knew that it would agitate him no end and this pleasured her. She wouldn't reveal her curiosity or comment upon the scene just played. She also understood Hawkins- Burke could not resist tantalizing the one he was tantalized by; or so she calculated by the few experiences of the interesting times they'd already spent together. He stood beside her. She threw them him off by kissing him on the cheek.

"Sorry for the interruption but I did alert you that I might need time for business and now..."

"And now?"

"And now the eve begins." He lifted the bottle of champagne from the ice and poured their flutes full. Still, no notice from Lilith of her awareness of the proximity of their other tented guest for the night. The turning over of his cards began with generic gabbing.

"I don't believe much in life to be adventitious or aleatory; sensuous, yes, especially with the corrupt ruling class, do you?"

"If you mean that in order to succeed today you must invest in both bordello houses, so no matter what, you get laid, then, yes, I agree. I agree that there is no luck involved in the love you ride in on, don't you?"

Stupefacient, beauty as narcotic, it dripped from her and he knew he wasn't sure if he liked it because he felt he may love it.

Surefooted, a frontloaded lady, he thought he grasped her mentality at least well enough to know that any weakness, any denigration of self would only encourage scorn, so as he lifted his drink towards the direction of the other tent he spit out, "It's good to control those that think they have control." He noticed her eyes and face betray interest.

"Known him to be asset for me for couple of years; very beneficial on the West Coast." She finally flips her queens over. "All right; what do you have on this man, this asset that would cause him to travel to this place on this date to kiss your ring?"

"Ha, I knew you couldn't help but wonder? You're a lovely temptress my lady, who knows how to gain a slave's attention, don't you?"

"Don't mouth syrup me, you bastard, I'm not one of your usual flapjacks."

"And if I were to use butter?"

"I'll ruin your eggs forever."

Hawkins-Burke circumambulated slowly around Senator Langtree. "I never tire of this walk, do you? I got someone's future by the balls and you can relate to that and that part of you I find a luxury."

Finishing his 360, he gently but firmly took her hand, escorting her inside the heated tent. "We'll see how the web is woven and whether Charlotte is really responsible for it all." "Selfish slave, is that possible?"

It was time for satisfaction of their trust in each other to be caramelized in each others agitation and sweat. Shared fears are abandoned in desperate tenderness; hands become distracted by each others body.

"You are my sinful excess."

She continues the exploration of his lips as he cautiously lays her down on the soft beige bedding, an ineluctable beginning framed in faithful scorn on the canvas of Satan.

She was more than a one of a kind 'collectible' and as was his custom with women, he satisfied himself with the power he thought he had over them. She knew he would never look at her the same now that they were nude. This is the magic of power portrayed and of power exchanged. It is the most effort he has ever needed for the chase and she knew it and she loved it. She mewled and he moaned in mutual thralldom, nasty perspiration everywhere, soaking them in moist memory of the night they both lost control of their fantasies.

All security were well enough off the 'premises' so that sound was not a consideration, that is, except for the one for whom the process of humiliation was intended; of being taken for granted as much as if a sagebrush or a cactus, of being in the heated tent close to a tent seemingly aflame with the sounds of the growls and groveling of love-aching and love-making, thereby insuring Mr. Moss would not sleep for hours. Disdain permeated his starry night and the delights of joy airing across the sands rubbed him so raw that he couldn't close his eyes. My God, he thought, they sound like monks and nuns casting religion into a pit of fire!

She was unfailingly attracted to men that could get away with anything and not give a damn about the consequences or propriety and duly go about stuffing the fact of their arrogances down the throat of anyone that doth protest too much; LBJ sitting on his toilet giving orders to his minions, Clinton flaunting his infidelities, Obama, his unrelenting narcissisms. This is 'mud sexy' and tonight, she participates in the rushed crush of the screaming purity of unbridled power, that pushy lust akin to the musky dalliances of animals. She is tingly with the fire of its cry. Couple this with her sinfully pleasurable consideration that other men were hot that night, unable to escape the airwaves filled with her love cries and the fact that they could not call or caress her, but instead, could only retreat to some later hideaway of their own to release on the numbing nagging memory of this night and their carnal discomfiture and their future imagined surrenders of her to them especially charged her. Oh, Stuart, such silly boys.

CHAPTER 25

"Judgment Cum Laude"

"Hypocrisy is the tribute that vice pays to virtue."

Duc Francois de Rochefoucauld

December 31, 2015

Mahmud Sulee Arnu was known as a boisterous advocate for the rights of Muslims in America. As an instigator openly and notoriously pushing the limits of United States laws, promoting Sharia and the right of cultures to maintain their cultural reliefs and traditions, ' Even as guests in a foreign land.' This included the view of women through the lens of the strictest of formalities of Islam, inclusive of stoning for adultery and honor killings.

He'd refuse, upon every request, to comment on ISIS, except to say that, 'I would not go about praising Allah the way that they do.'

He assisted nationally in the positive fundraising for the construction of mosques. He'd suggested that America's Constitution should be interpreted so that "Madrassa's should be defined under the law, with the same guarantees as Temples, Tabernacles, Montessori schooling and churches are allowed. I say, if Americans can have vegans, wiccans, Scientologists, and the Ku Klux Klan, why, praise be to Allah, are our madrassa's being discriminated against; schools where actual learning is occurring instead of training the young materialists in the making on how to get the highest ranking on Twitter or Facebook or on how to properly cheer on an abortion!"

The federal authorities had included him in indictments for allegedly aiding terrorists and/or associations with charities charged with funding groups on the terror watch lists; but he was cleared twice, as evidence of direct ties and verifiable records were, without difficulty, ably deflected by Mr. Arnu's high-priced defense team, especially the lead attorney; a man of posturing high standing, a cabinet member from a previous administration who, after serving in government, had built his legal legacy defending the most 'against-the-grain of clients. Arnu's defense costs were supported by the ACLU and other groups in the libertarian pantheon of think tanks. The most notable or notorious, depending upon which paper you gather your news from and where your prejudices reside, when a picture surfaced, an iconic moment from the case which rapidly became headline leading, showing the lawyer kissing Amu on both cheeks upon hearing the decision that his client was being cleared from any further court proceedings. The attorney brushed it aside, stating, he was, "Merely performing the traditional sign of welcome at the oasis."

The Right were timely in their dismay; as they promoted this 'act' as insulting to veterans and another case of liberal judges getting it wrong.

The Left played it as testimony to America's practice of inclusiveness and welcoming diversity and as a deal worthy of the world's approval.

On the morning which proved to be on the last day of Mr. Arnu's spirited life, his body is discovered by his American born wife, Krista, as she arrives back in town from visiting her relatives for the Christmas holidays, which Amu never would join her in, having told her that 'it would be a bad business decision'. He did join Mrs. Amu in selecting gifts for her family as Mr. Amu did love her parents and welcomed when they visited.

Krista Amu, a registered nurse, discovering the scene, stifling shock as best she can as training kicks in, frantically tried to revive her husband by mouth to mouth, dialing 911, and compressions.

Mrs. Amu is sworn to secrecy by the investigators about the evidence and the details at the crime scene. Krista didn't need to be told this. There were tapes in a box by the body and that can never be good, especially since she knew her husband had, without hesitation, pursued his fantasies of harem and young women and she had allowed this as she enjoyed the celebrated life he'd provided her and because she did not ever want to work in a hospital again and now, she was overly distraught with the looming possibility, that, besides a dead husband, the killer had apparently left tapes of her husbands peccadilloes.

Insurance would continue her lifestyle, fate would have her called the martyrs widow by many.

The authorities found a note, a memo book, the previously mentioned box and a pair of white gloves.

The detectives initial impression when they had arrived at the crime was that this was a disconcerting sight with no apparent cause of death, "professionally clean" was the predominating thought; "Autopsy will have to justify its existence on this baby," was the other.

The notes message is formed and pasted in cut-out letters of various fonts and pica sizes. It reads "He was as mean as he was unclean. The prophet will never allow him his virgins as deceit angers Allah." Next to the note is a small memo book with what turns out to be escort services and call women's phone numbers, all written apparently in the deceased's handwriting. On top of the small black book are the white gloves. Sitting along side the easy boy lazy chair, in which the body sat, is an open UPS delivery box, and 'the tapes'. The origin is unknown as address and tracking numbers are torn away. The box is hand stamped in fresh red, "Handle With Care."

The Detroit Free Press would not find out about any of this for weeks, but the Tulsa police would know about it that New Year's Eve. They had sent out an earlier general alert, November 27, to interested authorities, Michigan law enforcement among them, about the private details of preacher Posey's case. The lead detective remembers the e-mail. He eventually will receive a preliminary autopsy report that a hypodermic injection point has been located in the victim's neck. An injection of poison or an overdose of some sort will be suspected as the cause of death.

Detroit and Tulsa police speculated that last day in 2015 that a possibly new serial killer was loose upon the land and that this was probably not the work of a drifter or vague loner but rather, a calculating seasoned taker of lives whom now, twice, has left bodies and left a begging question as large as the western sky; 'how'? 'Why' will come later.

And, coincidentally the same as the Oklahoma victim, Mr. Amu did not believe in security cameras because Mr. Amu feared that the United States government or some other foe would, in the future, possibly obtain copies of uncomfortable digital memories and use video against him and, except for his pictorial documentations of portrayed conquest, Mr. Amu maintained physical evidence of his sincerest weaknesses the old- fashioned way, he memorialized them in ink in his precious memo book.

As he had positioned with Krista, "It's a difficult world in which to be properly understood; just look at the sex tapes of the celebrities. In this crazy country, it enhances their careers. It would kill ours."

And so, the American-born husband, Mahmud Salee Amu, christened at birth, Alonzo Carver Cutter, left the American-born wife, Mrs. Amu, christened at birth, Krista Kirkpatrick, in good stead financially and wondering as to which of the women in the videotapes had killed him.

CHAPTER 26

"My Current Obsession"

*"Not only in the race and the contests of the circus but also in the arena of life,
we must keep to the inner circle."*

Seneca 4? B.C.-A.D. 65
Roman philosopher/Dramatist

December 31 2015

Odd, how couples meet. Holidays are frequently part of the tableau as Holidays are the time most people break up or hook up.

His friends were not gathering until later in the evening.

Her friends were in other states; family too. She had returned the day before from overseas and was still fighting the lag from the flight and the thought of cooking was furthest from her desires. She would head to Jaw Jammers, get their number one seller, 'The B.S.', the Blame Shame Burger,' as the establishments advertising announced each work day at 7:30, eleven and noon, 'The most tasteful excuse for being a devil you will ever, ever bite into!' She planned to enjoy the early hubbub and then, before the crowds become messy, back to the house.

He is in his comfortable for public consumption attire, striving for 'usualness', he relaxes in shoddy denims, pants and jacket, gray t-shirt, ball cap, beard growth, and pitch black- in-the-light transitional eyewear. His hair has become longer too. He is on his second one thinking about a third and also that he should began to think about getting a 'B.S' now as the party eats would be late. He looked at his glass of amber and he imagined philosophers coming up with ideas much like the bubbles rising in his drink which 'pop' when they reach where they need to go.

Ah, the sparkles of my contemplations; a friend in every gulp, a nemesis in every sip, laughing at invisible merriment and actions, yes, 'action', the inner directors plea for us, his contrarians, to 'about face and in a hurry, mister.' He is glad that he is cabbing it tonight.

Her hair is autumn; silky waves of copper, her locks shimmering in the winter light, the woman walks in as an owner would; not overbearing but confidant. Sean momentarily forgot about the 'B.S.'. Madison Avenue strut, I've got the power walk and yet, she is smiling and apparently meaning it. Can there be too many Goddesses for America's good? Who does she remind me of?

Appears the only seat with some room is at the table with the guy in the jeans. Will sit to order and get it to go. Have one drink.

"Care if I sit to get order to go?" God, he's more handsome than I'd imagined from over there; slight scar over his left eye. Wonder if he got it from dueling with himself?

"Why, yes, please do." He stood to assist with her seat.

Robbyn Bancques McGrew's mother is of French descent; her father, a more nuts and bolts man, Irish with cutting wit. Robbyn is the blended gem of her parent's best settings. Many a self styled suitor had become tangled up in her pleasing heart and graciousness and had mistaken her kindnesses for more than she ever had pondered with one, let alone any.

Her eyes, her turquoise eyes; he knew he would never forget them. Sean wondered if things like this really happen.

She never had met her sense of a champion; a man who could be the origin of lovely concerns, a man who could cause Robbyn so much anticipation that quaking as an aspen in a brisk wind would not be out of realm of possibilities. Would he allow for her inherited fire? Better. Why is he so familiar?

It's got to be her. Father, a grocer mogul, mother, of European wealth; and from what I've seen, she does charity in the best way; big. One thing, she, if it's her, handles the damn miscues and mayhem of the media better than I do.

If it's him, he's certainly not grunge and grind alone or that lady would have had none of it.

What did she say in one of her talks for battered women; oh, yeah, it stuck, something to effect, 'We're turning into a punctuated punk society. Lord help us if we have to put up with one full frontal, full throttle sentence of serious thought! No heart plus no soul equals who gives a damn about others if I have mine! I say, that if these are not the most profane words of our age, they are, at the least, the saddest.' Sean remembers how he had wanted to meet her then.

"Hard to get the waiters' attention..."

"I will try to get mine. I just ordered before you came..."

"That's alright. I'm not as much in a hurry as I thought I was."

Whether in the boardroom crusading for her causes or, in the rarity of the case of a contest in the boudoir, she well knows the mark of the devil and what to do with sulfur. Damn, he can't stop dancing in my mind. Well, girl, it is New Years.

Her preferred vehicle is a Jeep. She had traveled the world in her mid-twenties and became noted as a photographer with 'guts', capturing peoples hidden voices and silent concerns in the least cherished places on earth. From her earliest recollection, Robbyn acted on her fathers' admonition, "Everest is merely a steppingstone. Always nudge on." What is a man such as this, dressed as he is, again, if it is him, doing out tonight? He isn't acting like any man who'd just split with an actress or she with him, however that's supposed to look.

"I don't mean to be informal, Maam, but, and I don't know your name, but, I hope you are as good as you smell and that the scent is mutual." Damn, Sean, get a grip, don't act like a dandelion in the wind!

Good God; if he likes Jackson Browne, appreciates Dickens and Dickens' disquiet for all those that walk alone in life, it's all over.

"Sean Linden, isn't it? Is this your formal dress; ball cap, stubble, manly mumbles?"

"Well, I've heard of you too and I wouldn't comment on the attire, Ms. McGrew; you're styled in laid back landlady, yourself, don't you think?"

"Did not think I'd need to fuss up the face; didn't plan on late night. Didn't really want to be known and look what you do, Mr. Linden."

Sean hailed a waiter. "Please, two glasses Pinot Noir, two B.S. Jaw jammers with all the shame you can pile on them."

"How'd you know what I came here for?"

"Jawjammer's 'BS' an easy guess."

Robbyn smiled. "No shame, no blame, is that your game?"

As a teenager and when she had time to give it presence, she'd fantasized that the man for her would be a man sentimental (which she still finds seductive); a man with quiet dashing and humble way, a man with morals more than 'looks'. Of all the things to come to mind... 'why in all the world of all the gin joints and all the dives, did I ask to sit here?' ... Mr. Linden is more than I bargained for.

"Is that your game, Mr. Sean Linden?"

"How about this, Ms. Robbyn Bancques McGrew; we are who we thought we are and no game is ever going to change that."

Ms. McGrew lost a beat and then recovered, choosing humor.

"Gee, have you ever been told that you look so much drunker in real life?" She smiles with the focus of the perfect mouth and he is so pleased that he is here now.

"And Happy New Year to you too, miss bumptious boop!"

Robbyn reaches into her purse. She looks up from the bag, asks, "Boop?" as she brings out an object a friend had given to Robbyn as a gag gift after a relationship had gone bad. She places it on the table and leans in closer to look at it more carefully.

"I thought I would test my first impressions."

Sean recognizes the construction stud finder.

"Yes, you measure up." And the perfect mouth of Ms. McGrew gladdened at hearing the sound of the perfect laugh from Mr. Linden.

"Have you had to put up with being a redhead with a blonde brain all your life or is this an acquired mentality?"

"I'm just wondering, Mr. Linden, were you breastfed, because studies show that breastfed babies are more intelligent and the juries still out on...." Robbyn caught her breath as she notices a hint, a change, a perplexity perhaps, appear and, just as quickly, disappear from Sean's expression. She recalls a piece she had read about Linden's past and it didn't include much about his parents or upbringing, God, what was his...

Sean rescues her momentary embarrassment. "I'm not sure if I was breastfed, but as a matter of fact, Ms. McGrew, I can assure you that I am now not at all adverse to the prospect in my later years though."

"How rustic, how boorish, loutish, churlish, unmannerly and how it's everything I want!"

"How come you left out devilish?"

"I knew there had to be a reason reminding me to go to church this Sunday."

"Rarely really talk about sex much, Ms. McGrew."

Robbyn suddenly has visages of someone from the past who didn't talk much about sex either; and while the aftertaste lessens over time, there's still no sweet in the bitter.

What kind of truth or dare am I stomping into this time? Robbyn waited for the waiter to serve wine and leave. "Well, what do you know; a shy boy in D.C., a hood pickled with full-fledged pricks."

Sean quickly took his first drink of wine. 'My, she gives dirty talk a proper sheen.' Robbyn sipped the grape too and both are silenced by the abundant 'loud' in The Jaw' and by both feeling the need to collect their thoughts.

'Quiet strength and humor, a man's best evidence to be adjudged second date worthy and this man, well...' Robbyn lifted her glass a bit higher. "My dad taught me about wine early, sneak me some at family events, well before legal and he pointed out that if red wine is served much warmer than 65 degrees, flavors even out, become flat and the alcohol will smolder in the mouth. Why 65 as cap; well, as dad said, because 65 degrees is the ambient temperature of damp chateaux's in the best vineyards of France."

"Is that true?"

"I hope it is. Now see those 'tears' on your glass? Yes, there. These tears on the glass are thick and slow over the surface which is always a good thing, but regarding wine, it means the wine is maxed out in sugar or alcohol whereas if these tears were thin and swiftly streaking down the stem, Sean, the bangs not as big for the buck. Please notice the stemware curves and angles display the prominent and distinctive fundamentals of the liquor they hold within their subtle clear grasp."

Sean peered at his glass. "These seem to be fat tears to me."

"Thick and slow, way to go." Robbyns eyes completed the sentence. Sean wanted to read more.

The appulse smoothly enters endorphic gravipause without either traveler jarred in the slightest by the trajectory or by the landing.

"Music can energize the same areas of the mind as food and sex. Yes, the euphoria of eating, and well, the other, are cathartic."

"So Beethoven, Bach and the Beatles make us want a Big Mac and a night in the sack, or Lead Zeppelin, or Jackson Browne, huh?"

Robbyn nearly spits wine out but manages to maintain. She changes subjects. "How come you have never married? Never mind, I never have either. Ever been on a chat line or placed something on one of the match making wiz-bang now-you-are-two-instead-of-one gadget groups?"

"No, on all counts." "Me neither."

"So we're both just good old fashioned stumble bumbles in the dating lane?"

Robbyn thinks of Odessa Gabriel but Robbyn knows out of bounds when she encounters it.

Sean thinks of the actress too then thinks better of it. "I'm a man. I'm not complex."

"Most men fall into that category."

"I guess I just want a woman without body piercings and ..."

"Are ear lobes excluded?"

Sean ignored, continuing,"...no ink and at least most of her teeth."

"And navels?"

"Navels?"

"Body piercings...and she needs to be as virgin as Mother Mary, right?"

"Frankly, my dear, not sure if that is a positive or a negative."

Their laughter is interrupted.

"Blame and Shame is served." The waiter places the iconic American edibles down; onion rings for Robbyn and French fries for Sean follow soon after. "May I get you anything else?"

"I would like mayo, please."

"Certainly, Maam."

Sean put his B.S. Jawjammer down, savoring the first taste of 'well done'. He reaches for water and asks, "The little I do know of you I'd think as a traveler, you appreciate cultures, histories, the ideas from other places..."

"You mean like Bollywood and Kama Sutra?" 'Damn, slow the wine down, girl!' Sean blushed. She notices and likes. "I'm sorry, Sean, I'm usually not such a blatant hussy but you make it so easy to be rowdy, randy and not concerned about it...not a lick." 'Oh, my, lady, what are you doing?'

Sean turned his cap around backwards. "I'm leaning in to get hit by the pitch." "I'm serious. It's rare that I, or anybody for that instance can be, well, comfortable enough to feel they can be given an honest chance as a person with someone else and not have to pretend that they aren't needy, that they don't fear loneliness or that they still might have some damage, no matter how minuscule or how much space it takes up in their mind that comes from a love gone down the wrong rabbit hole."

They haven't yet touched but the current implies that they have.

"Mayo, maam."

"Thank you. And will you please bring two more wine; okay, Sean?"

"Yes, of course."

They both take bites. Sean finishes and asks, "History, like I was saying, your favorites, things, peoples, myths?"

Robbyn pondered an onion ring. "As a kid I like an enchantress from the Arthurian stories. She was Fata Morgana, of Avalon. May have been Celtic. Morgana was expert in changing shapes and healings."

"Bet she was a carrot top."

Robbyn ignores him. "I also found romance in the tale of Middle Easterner, a Kurd the Crusaders could not keep up with..."

Sean froze. "You know Saladin?"

"Yes. His style is timeless."

Saladin is one of Sean's kingpins from childhood; right at the top with Sean's other favorite, the outlaw from Sherwood Forest.

As the sun sets, prancing rays streak earthward through skylight windows, scattering asteriations, a sparkling within her locks takes hold, and the weaving of light lends a playfully brilliant lambent to her presence. Sean breaks trance and returns to Robbyn's words.

"...a sacred warrior, honest, chivalrous to women and to the poor, the children, tolerant; he showed mercy to even those that killed his kin."

"The Afghans have a saying, 'Friendship is born in sorrow.'"

"Were you there long?"

"Short durations; long moments." Great God sweat! She knows Saladin, Arthur; has a definite sense of military... What day is this? Ah, yes; New Year's.

Robbyn stared at him over the rim of her wine glass. He's worth pacing over, dammit.

"One of the most beautiful things I learned while in Hawaii is their ancient way of saying 'Hello'. It's called 'Honi'. You have to gaze into a newcomers eyes and walk through this gateway to their soul, touch foreheads, and like Eskimos, touch noses, then, together, inhale deeply and you are sharing what Hawaiians call the breath of air, the 'ha'." Robbyn considered the safety of embrace, the caring without cause, the knowing before saying, the head to toe pulse of possibilities before her and asks, "You wonder, Sean, do animals, I mean besides man, do animals fall in love?"

"No, but I am wondering what you are doing for the rest of the night and if you would wander through the wonder with me?

"Why, I do believe you're asking me out and I am game for it."

"Great. We're heading to my friends place, Minerva's Taverna; heard of it?"

"One of Chaz Bellows' fooderies, yes."

"Won't stay until the witching hour; promise. I'm not really used to staying up late drinking this much in the same day."

"Agree on the first part. I don't believe second."

The Jawjammers remain unfinished. Sean pays amid Robbyns' protests and tips the waiter and then, for the first time, as they stand to leave, Sean takes Robbyns' hand. She responds with a firm return grip. Anticipation rising, they proceed outside amidst dusks' last sigh. The concept revolving in both that the future changed today predominates. Although both would not share until later, on this day of initial acquainting, they both harbored the hope that this would be different, that it would not end as numerous explorations of the heart often do in stifling regret and clinging 'whyness'.

** * ** *** ******

They had landed early afternoon at Reagan and had immediately hurried to her place to catch a nap together; something neither had done with anyone or themselves in decades. Recovery from the jaunt in the desert is a must before making an appearance. Lilith had again challenged the importance of the scheduled interview and the questionable efficacy of 'a face to face yak fest' when a phone in would make their life so much easier for the night.

He is asleep. She moves the sheets up and over both. She kisses his hair. The pillow is cool, working perfectly.

The alarm sounded at four p.m. Eastern Standard Time. A surprisingly soft hand is caressing the curve of her hip to her waist.

"That was too quick. You're absolutely on for this 'market lark' as you call it?''

"More than ever. Nap helped. Been years." He almost shrugged his shoulders. "Look, I must submit to at least maybe once, twice a year, to fulfill an unwritten Board directive to talk to someone important, to be somewhere important about something that is supposed to be..."

"Important?"

"Yes. And viola, this year, since I have not done any, get it in the last day of year at Tripp Bellows New Year's Eve gala at Minerva's and I'm good at Magi for another three sixty- five." He sat by her on the bed. "What do you think of this, I mean to use in part of the interview?"

She leaned on him. "Go ahead."

"My actions give money a good name." He looked at her as she sat upright.

"It has potential to be remembered, yes." She arises and heads towards her shower. She halts and turns to face him, now stretched out lying on the bed. She notices his eyes are not looking at hers.

"You just need to know the consequences of your dreams, Mr. Hawkins-Burke, because, you see, yours come true."

He is impressed with himself for selecting such a woman.

She is pleased that he believes that he is in control.

"Remember too, that the divinely inspired often become exorbitant and precious ewes for the mighty insular and the proudly bucolic to feast on." Lilith pivots. Stuart senses Aphrodite in the house. Just before Lilith enters the shower, she calls to him, "Class will resume in the limo. Have you done your homework?"

"No cheat sheets necessary," he replied. "Your student's ready for the exam, oral or otherwise."

Lilith laughs. The sprays temperature is perfect. How odd how one can feel so 'dirty' in the steam and clean. How odd. How nice.

CHAPTER 27

"The Toll Roads Of Golgotha"

"Your laws do not pertain to me."

Mick Jagger
Rolling Stones lead singer

December 31, 2015-January 1, 2016

Minerva's Taverna is on the seventh floor. The ground floor valet is nuts. He has more than he can effectively manage. He directs the cabbie, not without protest, to deliver his fares to the basement parking elevator. Sean opens the door for Robbyn, tips the driver. and then reaches, touching the button on the door panel with the seven on it. They enter Mr. Otis's contraption of ease and effortless loft, and are welcomed by the haunting voice of Dusty Springfield and the wistful lyrics of 'Windmills of Your Mind'.

The elevator begins skyward and, just as promptly; bell dongs, announcing intentions to stop at the next floor which is ground floor. The elevator slows to a halt. The doors open to the lobby. Sean Linden recognized Stuart Hawkins-Burke recognizing Sean.

Robbyn Banques McGrew thinks Langtree a pouty bitch with perhaps a smidgen of positive possibilities.

Lily Langtree thinks Linden is taller in person. Never had met. And he's in a ball cap for New Years? Novel.

Hawkins-Burke verges on ogling as he takes the measure of Ms. McGrew and she knows it before he knows that she does. He attempts congeniality. "Ms. McGrew, what an accomplished philanthropist, I can understand why."

Lilith knew that Stuart was sincerely attempting to mask innate shyness with this macho machismo cha-cha crap.

Sean Linden battled against even a glance towards the Senator and wished he wasn't wearing a ball cap for New Years Eve.

"Windmills" plays emotional deep ball for many generations and the couples in the cramp space are not special or immune from its intrigue. Talk must commence to overcome the lyrics.

"Senator Langtree, this is Robbyn Banques McGrew."

"Thank you, Mr. Linden. Pleasure meeting you, Ms. McGrew."

"Mine too."

Hawkins-Burke reaches for Sean's hand. "Happy New Year."

"And to you too, Mr. Hawkins-Burke."

"Call me Stuart."

The Magi security group made sure the door shut tight. They then proceed to follow their boss up in the adjacent elevator; the seventh floor exit already secured by Magi's advance team.

In this atmosphere of surprise and coincidence, the Maginot's are up. Each believes their appearance inadequate to the occasion and each is visibly uncomfortable.

Lilith and Stuart thought themselves too formal, too much tight body drapery in black and white; while Robbyn and Sean thinking otherwise; they are too casual, too live and let live, too loose for present company. Nevertheless, the four get down to the business of being human casting aside the knowledge that the full truth of an individual dish is if the impression is meaningful in its effortlessness at delivering good taste without the usual merciless additives requiring sluggish promotion and thuggish persuasion. None can afford the cost of silence. The 'stepping in it' begins.

"Sean," Hawkins-Burke inquires, "I have gathered through grapevines that you are entertaining new options, is this true? Magi can use a man of your talents."

Lilith engaged Robbyn. "I admire your work, Robbyn. Strength for others, right?"

Sean responds to Stuart. "I appreciate your considerable offer, Mr. Hawkins-Burke, but my choices are still being measured."

Robbyn spoke. "I'm fascinated by your back story, Senator..."

"Lilith."

"...Lilith, of how you got to where you are in a ..."

"Man's world, Robbyn?"

"Look, Sean," Stuart seemed almost pleading, "we compete with the Lockheed's, skunk works and others, the Boeings and here's the kicker, we sell to them too. Multiverse of markets. We're in solar enhancement, drones, dimension shifting..." Hawkins-Burke became curious. "Usually, that, the dimension thing usually gets a 'what the fuck' when mentioned but you're probably familiar with exotic research, aren't you, yes?"

"I know enough to know when not to know."

In a rarity for the wealthy loner, Hawkins-Burke desires to know Mr. Linden further, maybe even on a social basis.

Robbyn Bancques McGrew is mildly amused at herself, pleased that Lilith appears the opposite of soulless.

Lilith Langtree did not have many, if any; close female friends, only acquaintances and aides. She wonders what McGrew might think if Lilith looked upon her as a friendly territory?

"Sean, I have read about, well, curiosity and rudeness, I am told, are part of my DNA..." They both smiled at the self debasement.

"...did you experience what physicians call 'angor animi'; the smothering conviction that death is imminent, a sick sixth sense?"

"Well, Miss Langtree, there's nothing more visionary than violence, the clarity of mortality is never sharper but, and I've not really thought about this, but, no, death didn't detain me from my duty. I cannot explain it more."

Finally, a man of no pretense; worth Hawkins-Burkes' ear. The Magi owner, to no one in particular, "America, Sean, is one magnificent manifestation of exceptional originality vying, neck and neck, daily, with the disposition of the conquered for survival."

They reach the seventh with each occupant separately wishing they had figuratively taken the 'fifth' instead. The desire for more time together would seem defeatist so it remains hidden.

"May the worst of times be behind you," Lilith wishes Sean.

"And may the best outdo your dreams," as Robbyn returns the kindness to Stuart. Magi security walls off the CEO and the Senator, but before their grand entry, both turned and as the men shake hands, the ladies hold each other's hand gently, in a physical rapprochement for peace.

Chaz and Ms. Pinckney approach their friends and Hawkins-Burke and the Senator. After the preliminary hubbub of loud chatters and lazy flatteries, Ms. Pinckney leads Sean and Robbyn to Chaz's private table. Simultaneously, Chaz escorts the CEO and the politician to the room selected for the interview, the interview with the man from Magi and with perhaps a contribution, a snippet or verbal dessert from the only legislator that the rocker has ever experienced lustful considerations for. But that's for another conversation. Shrimp cocktails and mini steak kabobs are ready. All fill plates. "Home reds are fine," is Hawkins-Burkes response to server's question. "Sam Adams will work for me initially," is the restaurant owner's response.

"Tripp, you have supported my charities events and for that, first, thank you for that, even though you haven't always supported corporate America." Hawkins-Burke notices Tripp's' slight freeze face. "Besides, you know that I'm a Cures fan; so is Lilith."

"'Be My Me' is delicious, Mr. Bellows." The Senator almost melts him again. "Love it, since you did it."

"Thank you, Senator Langtree, 'Be My Me' is, well, if I had known you then it well could have been about you, if I had known you then."

Hawkins-Burke hopes his double take goes unnoticed as he quickly becomes fatigued by the absurdity of the flirtation. He asks Tripp what he wants out of this interview. Tripp tells him, "Random topics, wishes for the New Year, political changes, you know, how all the game pieces jump into place."

"Keep the same knowledge train on the same track. Neophytes will only muck up the works; they will cost us more in 'mistake' money while at the same instant squashing the unconstructed, the unfocused hopes of the majority; so 'no' to, no matter how screwed up everything appears through the sometimes dangerous sloppiness of Democrats and Republicans, 'no' to Third Party's. Yes, the time may be ripe, but not yet. Not all is properly prepared for an untainted by affiliation virgin yet untamed president. The system will fear itself being targeted, because, you see, the system is not presently sophisticated enough to handle even a hint of adulthood." Stuart notices Mr. Bellows consternation. The CEO adds, "But, if not now, Tripp, I, we are seeing an acceleration in passion, in protests, the awkwardness of misplaced hate and its sad remainders and what it causes and these add up to maybe a minor tremor the next decade; but quite honestly, I think America having a rumble in the night sooner than later. No estimates of time frames, though; have to be prepared for all contingencies as estimates tend to keep fools employed. Napoleon criticized with careful attention and cleverness and observed everything and while a short stint, still longer than our Presidents, initially, the man made things happen which were good for his country, short term. Basically, we need a Napoleon with a heart; observant, clever with good intent, detailed but not anal as that kills any chance at humor and in humor therein lies the quality of our best presidents, the ability to laugh at themselves. The very best never unjustly blame someone else or trump up ghosts as excuses for their inadequacies. Those types are now used as just reference points in history books, human base lines in the measurement of the basest of people." Stuart turns to Senator Langtree. "More shrimp?"

"Ready, yes, thank you."

"The Corsican let nothing deter him from his ambition. But he didn't have the 'good heart' and it was his downfall."

"He would have made mincemeat of Machiavelli." The Senator had the men's attention but she decided that the plate and bowls of Indian appetizers were more desirable than continuing her point. The cuisine was requested by Hawkins-Burke in that he knew Lilith loved it and because Mr. Hawkins-Burke is borderline hypochondriac. Before they had engaged in the purpose of their gathering, he had complimented Tripp on the curry.

"Our compliments to the chefs, Tripp. Do you know that something in curry might have an enzyme that's effective against dementia, curcumin specifically?"

The Magi mans concerns with mortality often play through the fairways of his thoughts, partnered with and competing with the panic is his belief that even the wisest can be foiled by the intervention of chance, sand traps grabbing your balls just when you think you have broken par. Also unknown, except to a now deceased therapist, is Hawkins- Burkes' astraphobia. The therapist told him that the fear reaches back to Hawkins-Burkes earliest moments; maybe a lightning strike with the impact and concussion of a bomb blowing up nearby or thunder that roared and shook, that left an unforgiving imprint in the infants body and mind. No matter the cause; Stuart remains cautious of rain.

Tripp decided to just include bullet point quotes of the talk in his column as the session had swiftly turned free form, which Tripp doesn't view as anything but positive as he knows 'off the cuff ' is revelation time.

"But with what we have to work with today, Tripp, what can be expected when only one of four college freshmen last year knew that Washington, good ol' George, had been a president of ours, what the...is that?"

"It appears on good days that our youth have forgotten how imagination can bestow kindness in the void, in the emptiness and whose to blame them, look at what they have to play with these days; politics is all promotion and commotion, except, of course..." He smiles towards Ms. Langtree, "...for this gentle servant of the people sitting next to me."

She returns the kindness with a smile but with a caveat too. "Simplicity tends to offend, to prompt conflict, so, please..."she faces Tripp, "...factually, I am not as gentle as he would have me, Mr. Bellows. In fact, like Napoleon, I know that a good leader must convey the thought that I don't envy anyone who dares to go deep with me; that I don't need a myth to justify what I do. So, 'gentle'; it's a kind term for Holidays, but I would not describe myself as an overly 'gentle' individual when it comes to the line of work I'm in, no."

"Se non e' vero e' ben trovato. If it is not true it is well invented." Hawkins-Burke waited for the Senator to smile. "I'm joshing you, dear, that's all. Also, it's about the only Latin I recall. Rarely get to use it."

The Senator does grin, then, "Funny how things stick in your mind. For you, Stuart, it's your Latin whereas for me one of many oddities I've run into besides you two gentlemen; I'm teasing, teasing. But did you know that years back, seamen, sailors, believed that, in order to keep from going down to Davey Jones locker, not drowning, it was smart to ink in a tattoo of a pig on one foot and the tattoo of a rooster on the other foot. "I can't put it out of my mind. I have been thinking of doing the same to keep myself aboveboard among today's hogs and cocks, what do you think, Robbyn?" Ms. McGrew pauses.

"Not sure that I will use that one, Senator. Maybe, but probably not." And Tripp knew as he spoke these words that it would not matter to the lady one teeny bit whether he included this comment in the column or not.

"We place our bets accordingly, right Tripp?"

"Every day, Stuart; every day."

Hawkins-Burke slowly reaches for Ms. Langtree's hand, slowly so as not to offend, but still, suggesting in the move, that he was confident that he had fulfilled his annual obligation of personal marketing for Magi; that he now needed to get back with Lilith to the business of aloofness and his type of vacation called 'privacy'.

They thank each other. Tripp escorts his guests to the elevator. They repeat best wishes and the CEO and the Senator get into the elevator. The door closes. Tripp Chaz Isaac Bellows begins towards the celebration in the Minerva's view room. He projects the interview worth three columns, maybe four columns but only with a phone follow-up when both interviewee and interviewer aren't in a party atmosphere, and if Hawkins-Burke will take his call.

Now on to Sean and that someone new with him. Sean had informed Chas that Moah, as usual for his habit, doesn't celebrate New Year's as it is another 'reminder' notch on the post of time spent without his beloved Maria.

Tripp had fallen all over himself the day he met one Emily Carter Pinckney. She is a direct descendent of revolutionary war hero Charles Pinckney. The 31-year-old vegan would let anyone know; "That's vegan not virgin!" Her fashion is predominately 'Hippie' or 'casual lust' as she shared with Robbyn, "No color is beyond matching, because there are no bad colors." She cares not a whit about the age difference between Tripp and herself. She loves what he and The Cures created during Tripp's rigid rock days of early aging on the road. She agrees with much of what he writes in his columns, so what's the problem? She knew she'd get along with him before she met him. But she never had anticipated on Cupid stepping into the box. Her floating, flowery, Joni Mitchell tone softens the pounding bass within his heart. She works part time as aide in the Senate but the bulk of her income is derived from aromatic massage therapy. Her clientele include a few senators and representatives who pay well and flirt often; the latter part something she does. She drives a midnight blue Cooper which she keeps in her garage below her two bedroom townhome in Georgetown where she lives with 'the cat' and her tortoise 'Sal'. When her hectic schedule permits, she lends aid in charitable and volunteer efforts but a good amount of her time, she earns the big money during irregular hours responding to last minute requests for relief from the everyday aches and pains of overwrought and overpaid legislators. Sleep is frequently a premium for her.

Tripp is a changed man and his male friends see it and are happy for him. He shared with them early that he, for first time in years, indulges Emily's passion for gal pal movies. A Thelma and Louise poster hangs above her bed. He told Sean that, occasionally, it bothers him because he knows both actresses and in the least convenient moments, he swears to Sean, he thinks of 'them' watching him his every move, and, depending upon the position, whether Tripp was any good or not. Sean doesn't talk sex and he rather the subject is not brought up again and let Tripp know this when the rocker had stated this particular piece of unwelcome information to him. Mr. Bellows views Ms. Pinckney's' musical tastes eclectic; except for her preference for The Cures. They tease-argue over it. Tripp counters any challenge to his, 'I'm the professional here' attitude. Emily stands her ground, always. "So its argumentation time with a bloviating front man, is it!" And they love it so. Their 'tiffs' usually lead to peace between the sheets and between the generations and makeup come-to-Jesus moments that shut down all discourse until their lungs catch up to their breaths. Tripp discovered Cajun washboard and zydeco music because of Emily. He'd heard of it, but she really endorsed it. Tripp thinks the sound seems to push her buttons faster, except for The Cures, of course.

Emily pivots to Robbyn. "I just want to tell you again, Robbyn, that it's my sincere pleasure meeting you. Don't take this as a curse but I think we are alike in our humor and in our excellent tastes in males."

"Thank you, Emily; but I just met Sean a couple of hours ago and..."

"Yes, I can genuinely attest that I have learned a lot from this loveable beach ball romanticist in a very short time."

"How'd the word fest go with Hawkins-Burke?" It is a rare contribution from Sean, who has been very reserved and evident to all, very happy as well.

"You know, it's odd; the Magi man reminds me of someone in my past and I can't break the bank on it yet. But as to the 'word' fest, well, y'all have to read it in the papers." "Rubbish!" Emily protests.

"What, my column or the paper?"

"Both!"

"I'm just saying here's my perspective on this." Chaz sits.

He scans his guests. His eyes settle on Emily.

"Well, I want you to read me so you can understand me and the Magi man clearly, in two days as I will not have a word in print tomorrow..."

"Praise Jesus!"

Tripp ignored Emily's jab. "...in that I have always refused to accept deadlines on the first day of any year and this year coming is no exception."

"Em; may I call you Em?"

"I am insulted if you don't, Robbyn."

"Besides massage therapy, you are also a dendro, a den..."

"A ring counter, our natural links to ancestors."

"And Montana lady too; do you hunt?"

"Did in early teens, then I grew differently than my brother. And my father too."

"I'd hope so."

"Brother's great; but if he eats anything opposite the color of pink or medium rare, his world's not right then. My dad's definitely a different slice of the same cake; helped me catch my first trout on the Madison. Better yet, one of best memories is when my father introduced me to Pete, and then a year later, Gladys. And dad eats vegetables."

"Were they relatives, neighbors or..."

"Two bluejays."

"Bluejays?"

"Yes. I was eight, maybe nine, when Pete flew into our lives. Dad had been feeding him. I didn't know until one day Dad calls me back to the garage and there on his workbench is Pete the Bluejay. Dad had gained Pete's trust enough to fly through the workshop door when called and Pete would sit on the vice clamp and eat from my father's hand. I was apparently viewed as a sketchy piece of the scenery by Pete the first time I was introduced to him because when I first saw Pete perched, my astonishment formed in a loud, "Holy cow!" which was Pete's signal of 'adios' to a loud short human. He zipped past me and out the door. Dad did not yell or say a word. Just looks at me as if his best friend had done him wrong. All he said was, 'I hope Pete realizes you are with me and that he comes back, little lady.' That was all. As the tears ran down my face, he held me in his arms. Pete did not return."

"Oh, ever?"

"Approximately a year after, Robbyn, the kicker is, Pete flies into workshop again and surprises Dad as Pete is not alone. I'm working in our berry patch when I hear dad's soft tones calling to me across the yard... 'psst, Em, Em, come here, quietly, quietly, and quickly.' I was confused by his actions, why the whispering? When I slowly walk in, here's Pete on the workbench and on what used to be Pete's 'place' on the vice clamp, is another jay, and according to dad, a female. Her feathers, Robbyn, seemed to be brighter than Pete's. To this day I do not know why, but I instantly called her Gladys."

"Pete and Gladys; how cute!"

"Yes, and eventually, both let me feed them. It was the best of memories for me, and Dad too. Soon, we saw no more of both and I worried that I had done something to frighten them away. Dad told me, 'All is alright. They have other things scheduled, Honey. Be happy for their happiness, huh?' This suited me. Then, again, about a year later, dad and I are heading towards the garage to get fishing gear and suddenly, flashes of nearly neon blue blurs zip over our heads and into the work area. We edged slowly up to the entry and peek in. There, on the clamp is Gladys and on the benchtop is Pete, and close, next to him, are three little Pete's and Gladys's, three baby Jay's, old enough now to fly, the proud parents bringing them back to show off to the baby birds' grandparent, my dad.

It's among the best, as far as smiles in my memories, Robbyn, that look of my dad's joy at nature coming home again, unforgettable, the love in the lines of his face."

"What a good piece of growing up that is; Em, did they come back the next year?"

"No. After meeting the family that late spring, we never saw them again. For many months after, it was apparent that something had changed but I refused to accept it. I talked to every bluejay I saw, calling 'Pete', 'Gladys' to each and every time the birds would fly away. Eventually, I grew out of it."

"What did you mean earlier, Emily, about rings being 'links'?"

Emily grins. "I know you will get a kick out of this from the little I have read about you."

"Yes?"

"A few years ago, scientists from Switzerland had a big study researching tree rings from European forests and varieties of woods. They were checking climatology for 2,500 years ago, just the time during the period of Rome's glory, the grand empire. The research found that tree rings were widest then, evidence, that, at that time, there were better than necessary amounts of rain and the temperatures were moderate and the Empire thrived because of these factors. Scientists also found that the last 300 or so years of the empire, around 250 A.D. on, the tree rings are much thinner, lean years predominate and the empire begin to fold as nature seemingly cashed in its chips. The last years of Rome's glory were times of extreme variability and climate shifting. That's why I vouch that tree rings tell us most all of what we need to know the ebb and flow of empires."

"We are doing lunch soon, Em; agreed?"

"Was there any question?" Their laughter seals it; and the best kind of a friendship, those from out of the blue, is launched and off the pad.

"Emily, will you please help me with this?" Tripp has a brown shipping box at his feet and is motioning towards Ms. Pinckney. Emily stands and goes towards Tripp as Tripp opens the flaps of the shipping carton.

"Free for everyone, Minerva Taverna's apparel!" Tripp holds up a powder blue T-shirt with the restaurants' logo, and below it, a message in quotes, reading, 'Sine Qua Non', Latin for 'That which is indispensible'; literally, 'Without which not.'

Tripp hands the first shirt to Emily. "Dear Em, without you, Sine Qua Non, without which not, emptiness would become my daily bread." Emily, reddened, embarrassed but happy, kisses him quickly.

"All triple X sizes, not the kind that offends, just the only size that befriends, right?" Usually, from 11:00 P.M. on, New Year's always seems to slow time down, especially to people trying to fight the effects of liquid merriment and the bothersome tease of sleep, midnight seems to take forever to arrive.

After the disbursement of the shirts, Tripp held fort conversing about his new trades, journalism and authorship. "I get paid to rabble rouse. Not often, mind you. You got to remember that it tends to cheapen the value of the act if you act up too much. Journalists cannot break with their integrity. They become nothing more than ungrateful little Goebbels."

"If all you want to do is get cackles up, Mr. Bellows, I have a speedy way you can do that."

"And that is, Em?"

"Talk about the differences between men and women."

Warning, warning, Mr. Bellows; do you really want to step here? "Yes, go on, Em." "There's men's time and there's women's time. All you got to do, Tripp, is argue that a man's time has more meaning than a woman's and there you have it; let the noisy clucking begin."

Robbyn joins her 'sister'. "I've found that men's time comes in quarters; first, second, third and fourth while women are more productive as women's time is well spent in a mall without limits on credit or clock management. That's a perception, Tripp, that is sure to be noisy and there you have want you desire for increased readership, delectable disharmony."

The evening revelry played on until Robbyn is first to notice.

"Look, look, the ball; it's almost bye-bye '15'time!"

Tripp announces, "I'm in working stages for a song about you, Em."

Robbyn fist pumped Emily. Sean clapped as did everyone else.

"It's just a thrumming adumbration now, but I will get the perfect pitch of togetherness, believe me."

"That sounds like something, maybe the polite words for something nice and nasty, Tripp."

"Why, Robbyn Banques McGrew," Emily comments, "you got game, girl!"

Tripp, portraying exasperation, "No, no. It's the, a faint warning, a soft directional alert, a thrumming adumbration, get it?"

No one responded to his plea as the crystal ball on T.V. fulfilled its' yearly duty. The party confetti and balloons rain down. Kisses and hugs abound among most revelers. Sean hugs Robbyn and kisses her cheek. Robbyn adjusts the situation by kissing Sean's lips. She slightly pulls back. "Now that's where kisses are meant to alight, Mr. Linden." "Then prepare, Miss McGrew, because I'm approaching for another landing." They lightly explore the contours of the others smile when propriety interrupts as friends amid their own carousing, are cheering them on. Sean and Robbyn break, embarrassed but very pleased.

"Champagne call, get those glasses on your tables, people; one last toast. And then, it's adios time before we all pumpkinize."

Cheers and then Tripp concludes his wishes with, "Good night all. You'll be happy to know, I've been informed that your rides are ready downstairs. Be safe and whatever you do, remember, don't fall off.

CHAPTER 28

"Even Imbeciles Have Dreams"

"Sure there are dishonest men in local government.
But there are dishonest men in national government too."

Richard Nixon

January 2, 2016

His preference definitely old style, Jansen Hyde reviews his Day-Timer. The recruits sit patiently. Hawkins-Burke knows the routine. Hyde's lips are moving but there is no sound. He is about finished with the orientation.

'Let's see, Executive agents' grads 'welcome.' Easy access plans. Lobbyists; how to make them assets. Magi protocols. Trainer assignments. Wishes for New Year.' Hyde did not mouth to himself the last note which evolved from a phone call from Hawkins-Burke at 6:00A.M., New Year's morning. 'Boss not sure of whether he likes what Tripp Bellows will put in his column from the interview at Taverna. Assuage!'

Hyde is ready to speak again. "In conclusion, gentlemen, "Hyde's face evolves into what most would consider a sneer. "Wall Street!" It's a near yell; Hyde almost shakes for emphasis. He swiftly scans the recipients of his outburst. None flinched. Good.

He addresses the boss. "Looks like we have the potential for an A-list rotation for this quarter, sir."

"The bar can still be higher." Hawkins-Burke turns from the teacher towards the pupils.

"Correct, gentleman?"

"Yes sir!" the quartet choruses.

The maestro of Magi, Inc. gives no indication of pleased or unpleased.

"What did you think, feel; your response to hearing the words 'Wall Street'?"

Mr. Hyde waits two seconds for something cognizant to be said. It is not forthcoming. "Well, let us clue you in." This is Hyde's standard cue for Mr. H.B. to jump in.

"No conscious, calculating, unaffected by collapses they cause, empathy is not fathomable; these, gentlemen, these are a few of my favorite things about Wall Street, and from this utterance on, they become yours as well." Mr. Stuart Hawkins-Burke never asks if there are 'any questions' after he speaks as he expects his employees to understand precisely what his words mean or they shouldn't have been hired in the first place.

"Be keen, be very on top of every issue, gentlemen. Always frame the 'Big Picture' with a light touch." Hawkins-Burke reaches into his coat pocket. Out comes a Peppermint Patty mint which he carefully unwraps, but doesn't immediately eat.

"Gravity forms the massively sized scale of the universe even though gravity is the puniest of the four degrees of force. God tricking man again, gentlemen, and this is what we must become; shape everything we can without ever revealing the scaffolding."

Hawkins-Burke now enjoys the 'Patty'. Smiling, he licks the last from his fingers, lips smacking, almost in a joking manner, but no one is sure but Mr. Hyde and Mr. Hawkins-Burke.

Hyde begins covering in-house paperwork that still needs completion by the 'newbies'. Stuart's mind momentarily reverts to thinking about Mr. Bellows upcoming column featuring the interview. 'Damn Bellows; probably not going to be as bad as it could have been. Yet, the follow up text questions yesterday, though; should have called him on the phone with answers. No; would have taken too long. The short bites will work fine, right? He reviews the gist of the early morning call with Hyde early New Years' morning,

"Wish I could see what I say in print before I say the damn things. Always been a visual-first-everything-else-second kind of guy with everything, Hyde. And did you know, Hyde, Bellows had the audacity to use the term 'henchmen', in reference to a few members of our Board of Directors? Yes, as he phrased it, said he was referencing, in some quarters, the public perception of Magi operations, and that these were not necessarily generally his own views; but, of course they aren't, right!

I correctly informed him, Hyde, that 'henchman'; the first definition of it is 'trusted follower' and you best not omit that, Tripp,' I told him. I acted like I was teasing but, as you know; I only tease when I don't care."

Hawkins-Burke snaps back to the present. Mr. Hyde is wrapping up.

"Never forget, gentlemen, that there is no unified public morality. This can be of benefit to you and of benefit to the company if you train to your utmost capacities.

Believe in what you are taught, and together, we will each reach what Magi Incorporated requires of us and you will be compensated well beyond your greediest desires."

Hawkins-Burke picks up on cue. "In a nutshell, what Mr. Hyde is telling you is that you must never take bended knee in any religion which is woefully barren in faithful consequence and which exists only for intent and nothing more. You must know what is necessary for being a professional. This means understanding the involvement of eloquence and charming indifference and how they relate to your success. This means understanding the dynamics of loopholes; big ones and small ones."

"What Mr. Hawkins-Burke is saying, gentlemen, is that there can be just inches between morose and morals." Hyde let this settle before continuing. "Hundreds of years ago, speaking of religion, there was a sect; perhaps a better description, a cult, in Russia, the Lothardi group, which preached that, while a man or a woman is above the land, literally, topside earth; that man and woman should aspire to higher things, righteousness and devoted acts with the goal, of course, of hightailing it at the end of your days through the gates of pearl. This is the 1300's and people have not changed much, as you will hear. These Rus, the

Lothardi, set up a rule to survive their faith, yes, they went 'loophole' on themselves. How? Well, creatively, that's how. The leaders told the congregation that members could still be considered people of god and righteous even when doing the most unrighteous acts. It is proclaimed that hence, that if a member of the church was at least 27 inches below the surface of the general terrain then everything goes, literally: clothes, conscience, guilt and everything would be dandy with the Almighty. Why, you ask? Well, because under the new 'intent' or edit, the congregation desired gatherings be conducted in natural cathedrals, settings in caves, because one, the gatherings became underground orgies and two, they weren't sins, as everyone is way below 27 inches depth whilst pursuing the worst of free will. Talk about donations, gentlemen. Say 'Amen' to the whopper of a difference a few inches can mean;

loopholes are adaptations and adaptation is survival."

Jansen Hyde scans the faces. He likes what he sees. "Even Popes adapt, gentlemen. Year is 1484 and a man is elected Pope and is named Pope Innocent the Eight. His nickname is 'honest', Pope Innocent the Honest. He is seen as such a commendable chap and such because, it turns out, that while the Pope is the father of illegitimate children, he is the first in the Papacy as Peter's heir to admit that he fathers babies out of wedlock. It proves so refreshing to the masses then that they immediately lay the tag of 'honest' on the Pope who actually turns out to be not so innocent after all, right? Loopholes; loopholes are updated to today's standards in that they have become wormholes of a sort, wormholes for the wise and the sly to spread money with alacrity as well as access in head spinning relief."

Magi security operators' identities are on a need to know basis only. Hawkins-Burke is no exception. He only knows these four 'fresh' men by the skewed non de plumes of Donner, Blitzen, Thunder and Lightning. Deniability is never off the burner in Magi's kitchen.

"Finally, one must tease out the full measure of every issue; and then one must purchase all the answers that can possibly ooze out later from this matter so you can move on to the next issue unimpeded by some nagging thing you left undone or which you have left with no opportunity for denial." Hyde visibly straightens. "No questions? Excellent! Please report to the next manger on your schedules. Thank you."

Donner, Blitzen, Thunder and Lightening exited. Santa Claus and his main elf are pleased.

"I like your choices, Hyde; degreed and discreet."

"Thank you, sir. They will be ready for field in a month."

"You've already replaced the two that came from the 'golf' division, correct?"

"Yes, Thunder and Lightening personally trained the new members of the 'links' team before they were allowed to advance to where they are today."

"Good man, Hyde, good man!"

"Thank you, sir."

CHAPTER 29

"Politics As Unusual" or "Truth Be Told"

"There is no distinctly criminal class except for Congress."

Mark Twain

January 4th, 2016

The men have met briefly twice before at charity events sponsored by Senator Dunleavy Bruce. And in answer to a request by one of the men, Senator Bruce has arranged today's gathering.

The Senator had given no indication in his 'invite' to Sean Linden as to why Mr. Casey Hardin O'Hara had asked the Senator to have Sean meet with Mr. O'Hara for something with more meat on the bone than purely a perfunctory meet and greet for public consumption; and, in spite of Mr. Lindens curiosity surrounding Mr. O'Hara's request, and even though the legislator had been informed by Mr. O'Hara two weeks earlier of Mr. O'Hara's meaningful yet highly surprising intentions, the Senator would give Mr. Linden no clue as to subject matter when Sean had asked, "What does he want with me?" The Senator knew it better that the "what?" could best be conveyed to Sean directly from the 'horses' mouth; besides, the Senator had told Sean, "You know I don't discuss specific details of anything, if I can help it, over damn pipsqueak phones, cells especially. I'll just say this, Sean, the man has bold plans and, if publicly revealed now, they would draw the standard catcalls and condescending themes from the usual purchased pundits in the usually unreliable media. Hell, Sean, I can see the headlines such as "Simplistic" or "Stretches Credulity of Reasonable People Everywhere," if this is not handled properly." This had piqued Mr. Linden's interest. He'd readily agreed with the Senators wishes. The hope by the senator for the goal of this get-together is for Sean to enter the fray with first man. Senator Bruce knew they would complement each other; that would not be a problem. Besides, in the Senators opinion, Sean needed to decide sooner than later his next stage in life, post military career, regardless of the younger mans protestations to the contrary.

They meet at McDonald's. Both are in dress-downed nondescript attire; consisting of dissimilar ball caps, unfashionable sunglasses, wrinkled but clean shirts, faded jeans, with the final touch, both sporting two day plus stubble. Happily, they draw no attention amidst the noisy camouflage of spilt Happy Meals, protesting kids and weary-eyed parents.

The noted doctor and the national hero stand at the counter unrecognized. Mr. O'Hara orders Big Macs, fries and Coca Colas. Food secured, they make way to a booth warmed by sunshine.

"Thank you for meeting me, Sean."

"Well, the Senator made it important, that was clear in his tone, so I could not refuse; and I would have come anyways based on the few words we've had before."

"Nice. Well, I sense you know what I am investigating?"

"Fair idea."

"I am going to run for office and I am asking for your help."

"Senator's good enough vouch, but I am unsure how I can help. Not political, but maybe fly in a couple of times to your state if you think the local community would see it as a benefit for you; so..."

"Been working since November, quietly, mind you; use scouts to set up offices, pursue completion of ballot conditions in all states, maybe May, probably June and..."

Sean's mind races. Did he mishear? States? "Which Party?"

"Neither. Sean, I am running for the honor serving as Commander In Chief and I am running as a G.D.I."

"A what?"

"A God Damn Independent."

Sean took a bite of the Big Mac. Moah will like this. John; Tripp too. Even Cade. So why the smell of ambush? You must go for this Sean, you must help.

Casey works over a couple of fries with ketchup. He speaks first.

"Just review what we have in office now. There's apparently no upside to honesty anymore because there's' no shame in the life a liar anymore. They appeal for reform as they systematically corrupt the system even more." Mr. O'Hara paused for more Coke, then, "Oblivious has become obvious as the preferred excuse. Plato said, 'Those too intelligent to engage in politics are punished by being governed by those who are not.' Example one, for your careful consideration, Sean, I offer this from among innumerable others...a few years back, the Congress blew off the poor, the sick, the disabled, senior citizens, laws were purposely not enacted for these peoples, these voters needs in case of emergency were ignored as no one provided or brought to the floor. Plans, evacuation plans for the most fragile among us, but what these brave legislators were chest pumping over is that they did pass a law, a Federal law that required local municipalities to design a scheme for the evacuation of, you guessed it, pets."

"Well," Mr. Linden, smiling again, "Alex de Tocqueville did say that we Americans are motivated, as he called it, by habits of the heart."

"The American dream is no longer safe from theft."

"So many thieves..."

"So much time..."

Sean sat up a little straighter. "Seizing properties in vogue again, isn't it?"

"I will, Sean take all measures to squash the octopus that eminent domain has become because property is king and if anything can be turned into a, metaphorically speaking, mind you, blood sport, it's government overreach, a grimy grab by bureaucratic blue bloods to take what is not rightfully theirs.

Among many, shall we call them subjects, I will platform out measures to squash the octopus that eminent domain has spawned.

The ink of red tape spewed out by the beast will not stop me. This is an issue that wounds both parties. Their fingerprints are all over the shovels. We're talking peoples 'dirt' here, Sean; their toil, their soil. Wedge issues on steroids with boomtown potential for an honest broker."

"Not to be rude, Mr. O'Hara, but…"

"Casey." It had become a joke between them. Both didn't dig formalities.

"Yes, right. The funding, how you pay, Casey?"

"Are you wired?"

"Of course."

"Then I will continue. A mix of my money, the majority, presently, and we've already quietly established twelve regional offices. Done the paperwork and disclosures, still not coming on Press radar yet, thank the Lord. Mrs. O'Hara is focused on structuring the youth vote; she's sharp and considerate of Social Media's nuance and paths of persuasion better than anyone I know. Not going to unleash anything until the starter gun should be loaded and fired, not when the others hear it. Turtle will defeat the Hare."

"So, and I know you've earned every penny, but you literally are putting your money behind the promises?"

"It's an especially giant promise when it's made to countrymen and countrywomen in a land of freshly broken promises, wouldn't you think that worth a large investment?" Mr. O'Hara sits back in the booth and reaches beneath his ball cap and smoothly pulls a laminated piece of yellowed paper with words, and from what Sean's trained look could discern, scrawled out in faded blue lettering. Sean's tickled. 'Another quote collector in his closest circle of influence; unnatural.'

"Keep my soul under my hat these days one might say, yes. Please indulge me as I believe you will concur with me as to the beauty, the conciseness of these thoughts."

"Please do."

"As Ayn Rand says, and I'm paraphrasing, since we must co-habitate, it's imperative, that in order to have any law at all, boundaries, you must have the least amount of law if you can. This assists against The States' unethical underhandedness, because the State extorts allegiance. It wants your sweat, your living and your unwavering fealty even though it may not be deserved. Each citizen is targeted. The resulting civilization, or lack of, as she calls it, it is in direct proportional worth to the scale of extortion administered."

"You remind me of other people I dearly respect. And each of these individuals values the words of Rand as I do too. They; well, they are always carrying around some sort of compass or reference points on themselves too. Clippings, scribbled notes, just like you. It's a good 'tell'.

"We both know the question in the air, Sean; is America prepared to risk change on an almost unimaginable scope; it is too far away, too hard for a country which now believes almost everything has a back story; that most everything is of delusional origins at best, a country which hears cleverness and commanding deceit in most governmental communiqués and to these concerns I say 'Yes', yes, you have a right to be on razor sharp alert, America."

Tall, dark brown hair and eyes, above average in height, Casey Harden O'Hara is athletic. In between surgeries, the physician works at smashing 'whitey' on fairways, performing with expert skill in both venues. His agitation at recent efforts to pigeonhole Americans into comers against each other through hired promotion of unimportant issues and overhyped by unnamed sources for nothing more than achieving the goal of maintaining those in power whom pay for the propaganda and for the tar in the first place. Why can't I stand up and yell, 'Enough!' And so began the search for plausibility of the act; is success even of reasonable consideration, and if not, is it still worth the odds? As the doctor never got in a 'rough' he didn't figure he could handle, he doesn't hesitate on this. He shares the plan with Mrs. O'Hara. She is not surprised. She endorses it.

Shawna Wayne O'Hara is Casey's 'lodestone, his angel with an attitude. Mrs. O'Hara's always been the keeper of perspective in the foreground of their lives. Shawna, which in original Celtic Irish means, 'still waters', is not sure of which clan or tribe is original with the meaning of her name but Casey told her that it fit her perfectly as Mrs. O'Hara, in her husband's opinion, is 'always on top of her emotions, no matter how dire or trying the prickliness of a problem, she mirrors the waters of a lake at dawn, reflective and smooth.' Both envision applying hometown sense to countrywide politics. Both O'Hara's are adept at reading 'charts' and both think the patient named 'Sam' is almost bled to death by the gorging leeches. "Sucking for others", Shawna tagged it. "The land is losing its love, Mr. O'Hara, and can you blame them? Everyone's occupied with rising blends of glee and gloom. Stability's become mythic or so the paid-forlorn posture, Casey."

The O'Hara's, as they worked their incomes to comfortable levels, began early to donate to all charities they could find that dealt in reputable and heart first ways for children in need. Both O'Hara's chewed up Science Fiction in bulk. Casey, early in their relationship, had joked about becoming President for the sole purpose of learning about the truth behind UFO's. Hendrix is a weakness for both, Hank Williams too. They subscribed to the Wall Street Journal, The Economist and the New York Times, because, as Mrs. O'Hara said, 'just want to see if they have changed their stripes.' Casey had once checked his ancestry as his parents were not too forthcoming as to origins when he was growing up and as best as he could find, his O'Hara's very likely came from the Lymrick area of green Eire.

"Sean, it's now evident to me that whether or not our society can survive is the question for the here and now; can we remain intact in the age of the glorification of the self. I wonder how many of us realize that sometimes luxury is actually a noose or that introspection is now considered a rumor or that the pleasure evocative in our modem day colonnades, baths, and dinners is mistaken for things of value, how many see these things who know they are viewing the constructs of their own demise?"

"Subjection through suppers and sex, Casey; I think many make that trade off, yes." "You said that, not I," Mr. O'Hara clarified. "By the way, do you see coherency anywhere on the menu. No? Probably too small of print, if you ask me."

"You're right. Problems need examination, remedies need fashioning." Casey reaches across the booth to shake Sean's hand.

"At least one thing not changed in this country, Sean."

"And that is?"

"You need a shake to make the Mac go down."

"Oh, more bravado than tomahtoe, huh? Funny, Casey; I haven't eaten McDonalds in years."

"All I know about that, Sean, is that McDonalds is as ingrained in the American psyche as revolution is."

The men toast Cokes. Both are pleased. It is always time well spent when people discover other people deserving of trust; certainly sad commentary on society that such occurrences are so precious and scarce.

Mr. O'Hara, to no one in particular, "You know, Ronald McDonalds expression hasn't changed in decades. Big Mac neither. The secret to their success is the fries, skinny fries, thin little pieces of potassium that fit perfectly into children's tiny fingers, no burly sized adult fries here, no. Kid sized fries made Ronald a king. Quality of the taste of the rest is secondary. Kids felt big, grown up, older when eating the skinny fries...perception, proportion and scaling; necessary for fast food success and for insurgent campaigns too." Mr. O'Hara took another sip of soda. Mr. Linden remains silent.

"You have not inquired as to, 'position' is not the proper word, but how you..."

"What do you think I can contribute to help you? I have no background in politics and no death wish to participate in it now, really, if truth be..."

"Death wish! Ha. You're right; no logical thinker should consider what I am considering, can't argue."

"I did not mean it that harshly."

"No, no; it's just that you spit out the word, 'politics' like you were about to have a stroke; and that, Sean, says to me, your participation is critical; screw me, I mean for the land, the communities whose days are colored for in drab array and the sad grays of life. The pulse of potential must be introduced to the body electorate again. 'Aspirations'; Sean, I ask, when did you last hear that word in conversation or broadcasts; doesn't come to mind, does it?"

"All the bitter non-voters, Casey; this is where the tinder must be placed." "The self disenfranchised are large in demographic."

"I am sure the good Senator updated you as to my ugly limbo now, so without definition for the immediate on my horizons, I will help in any small way that is appropriate, and I do not know what this means either, so ..."

"Thank you, Sean. Thank you for considering this at all."

"Love sports, doctor, because I love underdogs and I love their possibilities for unsettling things. And I have tended to fight in an increasingly bullying world that draws me to the 'dog' even faster. I tell you this, Casey; the Senator must be crazy to put the universe in someone else's hands besides his own."

"Ha, yes! Strong Bull he is. Definitely hard to see him tormented by this choice so it must be honored by what comes next and how all is managed."

"So he is ready to leave his party?"

"A little crazy wouldn't you say?"

"Yes, maybe but I see crazy like a fox, Casey, crazy like a silver fox who knows where all the rascally wrabbits live."

"Do tell, Elmer. Well, let the Fudd begin!"

The fries were about gone. Mr. O'Hara wipes his mouth with napkin and rinses with water. "Do no harm is my life, my condition, I suppose. This doesn't mean don't buck the trend; on the contrary, buck the trend seems absolutely a requirement; circle the wagons, race tight to the barrel; it's time to have the clowns at the ready to misdirect the standard campaign 'bull' and if you can rope the wayward, crowd the strong and do it all with the accuracy of Annie Oakley and the vision of Crazy Horse, I believe, Sean, that proper compulsions will prevail." Mr. O'Hara smirks, then smiles like a kid. "Nice to be in the company of people who can laugh at themselves, right, Sean?"

Before Mr. Linden finished recovering from laughing with his mouth full, Mr. O'Hara digs deeper.

"Metaphors aren't what they used to be, are they? I'm just saying when the grandstands are populated by chapless asses and syrup stirrups..."

"Syr...?"

"Syrup stirrups; wanna-be buckaroos take the sweet but not the sweat; syrup stirrups, you can tell them by their hands; softer than a baby's behind and as about as useful."

"I suggest that you engage the country in a conversation about the philosophy of dreams, Casey; see whether or not our country can still enunciate 'the unseen but the hoped for' in meaningful terms ever again, and if not...you better be a wizard or Merlin himself." "That's gospel, yes. True. Damn, Sean, I wonder if the self-absorb have good dreams, I mean dreams 'normal' people would consider good or valuable."

"Because?"

"Because self-sacrifice, to the majority of people today, means lending your cell phone to someone else for that someone else's friends' 'need' for a "selfie" because this over inflated egotist has just exited the dentist's office, puffy lips, slobber apparently unfelt, as novacane still present in neighborhood, and all this the world breathlessly awaits this unselfish act, this sacrifice by so many to show, thank god, another survivor of the dentist chair and the spit glass! The next thing you know the author of the 'look' will be upset to find that Google owns the rights to the proud posting. Sacrifice, 2016 A.D."

A baby, four booths away, screams in joy, perhaps a first lick of sugar kick. Mr. O'Hara waits for the echo in the ears to soften before continuing. "If action is delayed longer, the next generation is going to be ground down, finite, so crushed they will come to believe that there never could have been a golden age in America for how, they'll spat out, 'how could this place ever have held greatness when now, look at it, so littered with ill resolve and caddy calculation, so dried up of any freshness or bold bitching, how come?

Sean, I'm running for president and I need your help to keep me aligned. At this moment, only a close circle and Mrs. O'Hara know of my developments."

"They are private with us as well."

"Yes. It is true that the press will fondle their favorites, dems, pubs...I will be the target."

Mr. Linden is still. He is digesting more than thin fries.

"Sean, we've become a country of orphaned spirits. I feel it's time for a gut check without anyone telling anyone else how to do it. Has to be individualized into a national calling or it will never be accepted."

"Remember what I said about Merlin."

"The way I see it, it comes down to we have got to reach both the cowpunchers and the cowtippers to have a chance, because people like these know that Bull is the only animal that doesn't look good, coming or going; they never forget the smell either and, no matter how many sycophants in a media intimidated by its' own prejudices that you have looking the other way, the punchers and the tippers know the aroma is really an odor and that smell is the most powerful memory of all and that memory can be a double edged fury in politics."

Sean finishes his last fries. "Know what I believe, Mr. Casey Harden O'Hara?"

"No. What?"

"That Irish people really talk a lot, don't they?"

"Yes, we do, Mr. Sean Linden. In a McDonalds, dressed like urchins, eating potato, well, fries....so I guess it begs the question, 'do you know where your cliché is tonight, right?'" "By St. Peter, I bonny well do, Mr. O'Hara...Scottish, I know but ...cliché within sight, down on the corner, there, it's clapping hands with irony, it's keeping pace with the mad leprechauns' jig, even twirling a time or two with blarney, a pint and with a prayer for new shoes! Still not a fan of Notre Dame, though."

"Me neither."

"Must be an Irish thing."

"Of course."

CHAPTER 30

"The Devil's Seen Better Days"

"They will say this; that the Righteous Man, being what he is, will be scourged and racked and shackled and will have his eyes seared out with red-hot irons and finally will be impaled after having gone through every lesser torture to discover on the stake, that the right aim to set oneself is not to be righteous but pretend to be."

Plato 'Respublica'

January 14th, 2016

Getting to know each other is proceeding more smoothly than either party had anticipated. They're also beginning to receive media attention, which both abhor. They sit in the private dining room at '22 Times Turned T-Bones and Chops'. The businesswoman respects the man she sits with, but she ponders if he respects women. "The Aztecs know the value of a woman. Proof is..."

They had small-talked themselves out during the mini taco appetizers. They've just entered the ever-possible conversational pitfalls of equality, justice, religion and sex. Politics, they discovered early, they were very simpatico, so no courteous discord there. The lady continues, "...the words for 'wife' for Aztecs, it meant "one who is owner of men", did you know that, Mr. Bartholomew?"

"Ja. Ja. Femi-power." It was a lame attempt to make light of something that had the potential to turn into something meaningful that he did not want to make room for discussion for now. Far from it. Need to hear more of the businesswoman. And she obliged.

"The only reason you are here is because of a woman." Chardonnay took a sip of her drink. "Powerful women; The Oracle of Delphi powerful enough, I'd say. Her role as Pythia, she could cause bothers to the construction of cities and their destruction too."

"I know the Oracle; enjoyed history to the point of paying attention. History does teach one thing that many a thing never changes in nature. Take your priestess; originally came from aristocracy, and she had to be a virgin, comely, and oh, the catch; 'chase' forever. With young looks which can kill right, and what do you know, the expected happens; Man loses the battle with nature trying to change nature. Again, all it takes is one Pythia not digging celibacy no more when she sees a drop-down-oh-my-God-handsome warrior man. The scandal caused change as man did nature wrong again. The Pythia now has to be old, the homelier the better. Nature wins again, Ms. Hooray."

"You know, since we're talking about women naturally being sex objects and nothing more..."

Cade knew a road in need of repair when he turned onto one. He also knew he needed to immediately maneuver into a smoother, smarter lane and be quiet.

"Do you know what men's favorite fantasy about women and their occupations is, what the combo is that men swoon over, what men would like to mess with most?"

"I know mine is a strip club owner.'

"Cute, quirky and expected; you."

"Me?''

"Men. Men fantasize about nurses, executives, teachers, cops and 'whoa' brother cowgirls."

Chardonnay smiles at Cades obvious thoughts. "I do have chaps if one prefers, and a body temperature stethoscope for improved osculation if that can be of assistance too." As his mind and his eyes were at lost for directions, she switched his gears hard.

"This is my first opportunity to tell you, but your restaurant, make that restaurants, their reputation precedes them. I do appreciate the minor sound adjustments, you listening to suggestions means a lot. Do you like this better than broadcast?"

"Both." Cade answered, pleased that Ms. Hooray is a shoot from the hip straight talker and also that they were off the subject of 'sex.'

"Restaurant; it's simple. Just fill brains more than stomachs. Your place should tell people that they belong, that the wait staff loves them. That and age proven marketing. Place menu items that are the most profitable in red borderline boxes on the upper right-hand side of the menu. Grabs attention because the nature of the eyes scanning process."

"Yes."

"And tables: look at ours, what do you notice?"

"Round, clean tablecloth, nice."

"Tables speak to us. Round is better than square. Square tables are formal. Steaks and chops, its engaging time, not an Escargot or spitting spurts from vineyards time; Hell, no, it's 'round', says round says 'reach out to me', that's one other thing my food man..."

"Food wha...?"

"My consultant's par excellence. You know, Chardonnay, consultants; one of those high falootin people who state the obvious and charge people outrageous sums just so people think it worth it."

"Yes I do."

"Well my special consultant has really helped.

"And she is...?"

"He. It's Yoggee, Sean and Moah's business partner."

"Yes, remember him well."

"Yoggee helped me with the background music and acoustical planning for both here and The Mayan. Yoggee said that scientists had found that it is harder to read a menu in a loud place. Harder to read the print too and this gets worse as voices and music rise higher on the V.U. meter."

"Is all this because boys will be boys; because you are in competition with Isaac's Flooze and Minerva's?"

"Yes, Yoggee came up with a new sandwich for the Fill which he shared for the Mayan, calls it the 'Rye Reformation; as he puts it, 'One Ginormous Corn Beef Monstrosity', which, as Yoggee wrote in the tagline, 'Is so heavenly even Luthor couldn't protest!" What Yoggee did not tell me about was how his 'Luthor' campaign pissed off so many of the appropriate Protestants from the Fill to Bismarck and beyond to Fargo even that it spawned a contest thought up by Yoggee, of course, for one listener of the radio ads to come up with another less annoying name for the sandwich which must, as requirements of the hastily thought up contest made succinctly clear, leave any and all religious figures out of the sales pitch."

"I still heard an ad a couple of days ago, I swear, for the 'Rye Reformation' with the Luthor line."

"Yes, you did. D.C. is opposite universe different than Williston when it comes to levels of offence and offence taken. Char, I figure half the crowd here is on par with religious lightweights and that I still have another quarter or two campaign time left because of this fact. We have also gone Co-op with Yoggee on our first batch of electronic sign boards. I call them hi-tech Burma-Shave billboards. We have set up a satellite connect and, as of yesterday, we have ten signs about to go on line. We can change specials instantly, we can update local road conditions, we can do much to maintain an advantage in marketing to travelers on a minute by minute basis if need to. We've paid very good lease fees to our first farmer clients, in six states so far, more on the way. The Fill, The Mayan, The Flooze, Twenty-Two Times, and Minerva are going to rotate promos."

"I love your enthusiasm and it sounds credible."

"It's like those signs for Little America in Wyoming, the hotel restaurant slash truck stop and they have signs up promoting their business, signs sometimes hundreds of miles away out in the middle of 'where in the hell are we America, you know the land. You see a sign in lower Utah or somewhere and it says, you're only 813 miles from Little America! Smile!'... or something to that effect. I always found that stuff, a sign out in the never lands promoting a business ten mountain ranges away as exotic if not dam romantic for some reason. That's never changed."

"Advertising for something in Washington D.C. thousand miles west of the Mississippi and beyond, something else this way comes, I sense."

"Yes. These electronic messenger boards are our little network in waiting. Very precise; your observations, Ms. Hooray."

"It could be a warning system too, but for whom and against what?"

"I want you to come to Colorado with me."

Ms. Hooray is taken aback, but, recovering, "Someday, maybe, but not in the near future. We both have much to do for the New Year."

"It' inexpressible, fall walks on colorful leaf laden pathways, winters playground, nature's sumptuary, where God vacations when he's got the time. Colorado, it's rainbow colored smooth rounded lake rocks shining through clear shallows of alpine waters, granite grandeur framing the tops and sides of peaks originally known as the Stoney Mountains, yes, the Rockies were once the Stoneys..."

"And so they are again, it would appear."

"Oh, yes with..."

"We will sometime, Mr. Bartholomew."

"Ms. Hooray, be aware that the Persian word that best fits Colorado, I know you love the rugs, the word is 'Paradise', in Persian meaning hunting parks, palaces and harems and what more could one desire, excepting for the harems, sure."

"Thoughtful."

"In May, paradise is the rushing of the hummingbirds and maybe confused robins as snow can trick the best of the red breasts. It can be four seasons in one day."

"Cade, maybe in a few months, not May though." She reads the slightest of disappointment. "Listen, Cade, in recent years, I've become, well, I feel that mountains, even skyscrapers, high rise things, they cause me to feel, well, heavier, more cumbersome..."

"Heavier?"

"What I am saying is that I have with age become, I suppose, somewhat claustrophobic. I appreciate 'flat' more than ever now. Elbows have room. There, dumb, maybe, but me." Cade orders more sour dough bread and butter. He knows she is not joking.

"Okay. I can kind of relate. I'm, well, I am opposite; opposite in that I understand what some would consider the extremities of our thoughts but from an opposite perspective. You see, if I am in D.C. for longer than usual or in some other vertically challenged environ such as Florida or Kansas, I find myself pulled towards the nearest hillock or interstate overpass just to get above twenty feet from zero altitude. I like height like you apparently like sprawl. Now, I like grand sweeping vistas too, but I like them from high up."

"Private jet elevation level?"

Cade pours more wine. "See more animals that way, yes. You love animals, Ms. Hooray; animals love Colorado, elk promiscuous but beautiful..."

Char, amused, "Go on.'

"They're polygamous. Bulls might gather fifty cows just for the mating season." "Sounds like something you would like; incessant over-familiarity."

"Whereas, coyotes; they are urgently monogamous, but they too, love Colorado.

"Urgently monogamous! Really?"

"Among other lovers of Colorado, specifically among raptors, females are powerfully clawed and mostly larger than the males."

"There you go." She notices some laugh wrinkles for the first time. Suddenly, he seems just a bit nicked up mentally, but, she challenges herself, who isn't? "You've been in broadcasting for how long; I can see years in your eyes."

Without hesitation, Cade reveals, "Just had my dad cross my mind, that's all."

"Go on, please."

"He taught me to diss-learn, know that assumptions are going to be wrong more often than not and, ha, here I am thinking of the little placard, oak framed, he gave me and on it was the secret to television."

"Is it that 'assumption' is deadly in banks and in love and in reruns of old themes?"

"No, but hand stitched in green yarn, sewn by my Mom's loving hands, is the Latin phrase, 'Paucis Verbis'." Cade stared at Chardonnay. "It means, 'in few words'. And Dad was a man of his word, literally 'word', as his were infrequent, yet they were powerful because of their rarity."

"Good marketing, tease the eyes more than the ears."

"Yes, the best tales, the greatest promotions, deal with unresolved issues which get resolved. In fact, the best "mind-grabs" are those that incorporate a willful disobedient act that exhorts, in touching and reasonable sentimentality, an echoing call to correct the wrongs, whether it's the stains of burgundy wine on a pink dress or the indiscriminate mayhem caused by the soulless among us; words tend to get in the way in these unalleviated moments.

Dad said a bad story is like elderly men in old style strapped white t-shirts with tattoos of 'mom' and old flames 'names' settled into fleshy misguided places, notable for all the wrong reasons; unforgivably unforgettable."

"Now that's a picture that's not easily replaced."

"My dad warned me years ago about where this broadcast business was heading. It will consist, he said, of simplemindedness and single-mindedness. The winners will know the difference. Instant celebrity will become tiresome and anchors with short leashes will see themselves through the wrong monitors. And on this topic of talking heads, Bartholomew Senior furthered that 'as management, Cade, remember to invest in their, the anchors, their insecurities at the proper time in the proper crisis in their rather improper lives and you, Cade, can be their Colonel Tom Parker for life."

Chardonnay playfully winced and slightly bowed her chin.

"My H.R. Department has simple protocol. Short and easy; they ask prospective employees to rank four items in order of importance; determination, hard work, education and four, treating people with respect. H. R. is under my standing orders to automatically give second interviews to those applicants that selected number four on the list to be listed as their top item. There's a foot in the door."

Chardonnay Hooray raised her wine glass as if to agree.

"Senior said, 'the owner's job is not to be the Einstein in the palace. Second, deal with only those on the ground that only tell you what you need to hear, not what they think you want to hear."

Ms. Hooray is pleased that Mr. Bartholomew is easing into friendship with her; she's pleased that she can see that he senses her to be a good fit as a friend and potentially more. A man doesn't talk to a woman about his father unless this is true. She knows he knows she's there too.

"Just before he started to fade, rather quickly it was, dad came into my office, and he noted something so foolhardy but illustrative of the times we live in; he walks in, saying, 'Maybe we can charge for palm readings on the news or charge for reading efficiency in presenting words and concepts in terms that are billable to the non-attentive clients, commonly called, 'The Public.' My curiosity is on red alert. Dad has the targets' attention."

"Yes, and he says?"

"Tells me, 'You must tell accounting to set up a chargeable for what that guy, the architect that walked away from the D.I.A. thing, the south airport terminal, Cade, set up on billing sheet like he did.' Unsure exactly of dads point, I remained silent and Dad asks me, 'you know the guy, resembled Gene Simmons with short hair, the guy stops his participation in the project and then bills the City of Denver nearly a half million dollars for, and this is typed in on the bill, mind you, he types in half million dollars for, are you ready, and of course I nodded that I was, he says, 'bills the city fathers for "visioning." A half a million dollars for 'visioning'. Oh, really now? And the hourly rates for such 'visioning' rang the bell at a half a million dollars, for Christ sake, Cade! Can I have a witness! I want the bookkeeper and the beekeeper too, if necessary, to find a lawsuit proof manner for us to charge for 'visioning; got it, young Bartholomew?! I can see it now; tell clients, 'I am visioning you signing on the bottom line. Thank you Mr. or Mrs. Business person and here's my bill for a thousand dollars for my 'visioning' of you completing this agreement.' Chardonnay, saying this, he wheels on his Buster Browns and is out my door before I could grab my next breath."

"I am sorry that I didn't meet the man or your mom either."

With certitude, Cade attests, "They both would have appreciated the essence of you."

Cade sensed it a 'home run' even though he hadn't been swinging for the fences as Chardonnay seemed to actually shine with the compliment and responds with the hint of a kiss blown his way.

"Dad had a plaque; yes, I know; lots of things on lots of walls and atop lots of desks but that's seniors' way. The lines are from Petrarch from the 14th century. Dad had originally handwritten a note with the words scribbled out and given it to me the first week of my internship at the station. Goes as follow, "I have always possessed extreme contempt for wealth; not that riches are not desirable in themselves, but because I hate the anxiety and care which are invariably associated with them." And just beneath the quote in the note my father gave me, in bold red ink, were the words, 'P.S. Don't ask for a raise!' Char, he had the good sense to level me frequently, once sharing with me that, in his opinion, his accomplishments are gist for the comics and my failures, son, are the mornings headlines...so if you can handle this style as you walk through this life, I feel you will do right more often than not and that the stations will probably survive the weaker parts of your humanity. This comforts me somewhat.' And this, Miss Hooray, was the nicest observation I ever received from Senior. As you can see, Dad had many mind ticklers and he tended to print them on small business card sized, well, cards, mainly for ease of reference as he had so many favorites, many apparently passed down by my great grandfather to my Uncle and dad. The favorite philosopher, by far, for my dad was and is, Mark Twain. And these words from the author kind of summarize what my dad wanted his children to grasp; quote, "It is better to deserve honors and not have them than to have them and not deserve them."

The son learned well. After struggling for a time with mourning the death of parents, the son took the network on new trajectory as expansion and content development coincided with the signing of an exclusive agreement with the top 25 airports to have all the televisions set to Cades channel. These efforts to project a 'grandness' proved successful on a scale that Senior would certainly be surprised by and yet, perhaps too, one he would have envisioned all along.

"Thank you, Chardonnay…"

"For?"

"…for being the best listener I have ever met, I promise you the same."

Chadonnay can only say, "Yes."

"While Senior was a wealthy man, he was a rare wealthy man in that he had immeasurable thankfulness." Cade pushes a little distance from the table and sits back in his chair. "I know I was a disappointment to him early. Dated numerous women, lost sight of what was important. Now, what do you know, I'm alone and single. The early marriage was a miscommunication awaiting fiasco. Senior had told me that if I had kept it up that I would eventually end up alone in old age. How about alone in mid-age! God, I hate seeing dad right sometimes." Cade shutters as he realizes his vulnerability is showing.

"So what you are saying is that you are upset that you are not Jesus?"

"No; what I am saying is that I wish my early besotted times were more condensed. I wish I had not wasted those days looking and not knowing what I was looking for."

"You mean years?" Chardonnay made him smile no matter what and this strikes a cord with him as she continues, "I make money because men like to look; all men do, even if they are gay."

Cade thinks of the press 'feeds' about him being a man, when romantically inclined, who has a propensity to dive into the shallow end. Damn, I am on the high dive board now, aren't I? Attempting humor, "It must be the females fault, right? I mean, didn't the Old Testament teach that, "Thou shalt not suffer a witch to live?" Why, even in Elizabethan times, with a Queen leading them, they had executions for witchcraft. So there must be something to…"

"You sound like a recalcitrant puissant pussy."

Cade straightens in the chair, surprised by Char's vociferous judgment.

"No, better yet, you sound more like the heap big angry white man whose cackles rise when you hear what to you is the unmelodic call of a Hillary or some other strong appearing female. She still has gravitas in some circles. I like parts of her attitude."

"Look, Char, I'm just teas..."

"You are lucky women are in the world. Women authored the first computer program; did you know that, 'Everyman'? Lady was named Lovelace, of all things…"

Cade struggled hard not to betray a smile.

"Hypatia to Madame Curie, Rosa Parks and Tubman, heroes all and listen, toy boy; did you know that over half the injuries in high school sports that lead to paralysis or even death are happening among cheerleaders, did you? Who's tougher now? Huh?"

Cade is relieved to see that Chardonnay is unable to hold back a smile which begins in her eyes and quickly trends to her lips.

"This is one of those 'what do I do now' moments, isn't it?"

"I am as down and dirty as you, fellah. I make my living on the weaknesses of the male and all you can use is religious toddy tripe on me, on women.'

''No, that's not..."

"You know what my bread and butter is; you know why I did not end up as just another amanuensis, a note taker, since your face says you haven't a clue as to its meaning. I've got your religious footnote for you ...," Ms. Hooray is at maximum 'rev' and would likely beat Mr. Bartholomew if she knew how turned on he was becoming, specifically because she was edging towards feeling the same way too. "...Do you know what the Bible means by "stolen waters" and why they are 'sweet'?

"Because that's why every glass has wine?"

Chardonnay stopped. She let the language of her body soften. "Bible uses waters, refreshing clear waters as metaphor for the beautiful intimacy which can only belong to married couples. The Bible goes on to say that 'Stolen waters' are those waters where someone is dabbling, shall we say, more than just their toes in someone else's waters; it goes on to say these 'stolen waters' are also 'sweet' because, for all the energy and the fear wrapped up and expended in such an immoral act as adultery and then to successfully get away with it; it is a high for these are the sweetest of waters then, so the Bible says, because they break the forbidden bounds of conscious, and pleasure seems not so attached to an overabundance of words when everything seems to be flowing just right, correct? At least until you get around the next bend and reality's heard in the distance as sweet waters are now sounding loud and hounding and you wish you had never stolen a drop, if a million. Comes down to whether you are an individual who can work your time well to get the time you deserve and not at the expense of any other person or ego, or, if you are a person thirsty for a new taste all the time who has never been taught the proper techniques to handle the spigot in the first place."

"Well, I agree that not all ..."

"I say you have to fill the potholes in your personality before commenting on the gaps in others."

Cade chuckled, saying, "Bug off."

Chardonnay returned the grin. "No. 'Bug on' is much more preferable, sir."

Cade opens as if hard to breathe.

"What's the problem; can't think, can't ad-lib for once? In Latin, 'ad libitum' means 'according to pleasure.'"

He is done for.

"You know, Horace's bottom line can be encapsulated by a French word, 'frisson.' Body friction causes 'frisson'. It means 'thrill' and that's what I am the vendor of, but, you, young Cade, don't need a ticket to ride."

"You must come to Colorado with me. I won't let the mountains close in on you, Char, I promise." Cade squints a little and in almost boyish terms, "I just want to show you my pride and my never ending joy, my hidden dingle..."

She couldn't resist laughter. He recovers, explaining, "...it means my deep wooded valley, my dingle."

Ms. Hooray is on top now. "Call the driver, Cade. We're going to Shalimar."

"Where?"

"In Sanskrit, I think the original, Shalimar, meant 'abode of love.' In today's Kings English, it means, my townhome."

Cade would not remember much after leaving 'Twenty Two Times Turned T-Bones and Chops' this January night; except for the small snippets that will flashback during the upcoming week. He will remember Chardonnays' welcome mat. It is colorful. It is Maat, the Egyptian Goddess of balance and truth, set with feathered wings outstretched as if to say it is okay with the Goddess if you enter Ms. Hoorays' threshold. He will recall also that, as Chardonnay was opening her door, he remembers thinking as he stared at Maat that he was, in fact, not balanced too well at all and how on earth did Maat ever miss this detail?

He will remember Chardonnays' large foyer, with numerous seraphim on numerous glass display shelves. He will note that Miss Hoorays bedroom is aglow, a bright pink lettered, turquoise trimmed neon sign with Chardonnays' 'Ocapella Barbell' logo shining bright as the source. Cade will recall a bust of Casanova on Ms. Hooray's nightstand and Chardonnays' expounding on it. "His style was abominable but his life was big, Cade. Casanova said, 'the slightest constraint spoils the greatest pleasures.' God," Ms. Hooray had continued, "The sweetest tongued devil. I know I would have enjoyed his company; and probably conversing with him too." The piece de resistance, in Mr. Bartholomew's groggy estimation, is the Official Department of Transportation oversized sign that hangs above Ms. Hooray's oversized waterbed. The bold black lettering, which once advised drivers of possible dangerous conditions, now warns observers in the general proximity of the sign that conditions can become "Slippery When Wet"; so proceed at your own risk if you wish to continue...and Cade certainly had.

As bodies recover from the nights primal trek into the 'oh and ah' hinterlands of libido, lust and lace and as their limbs strive to refresh from the strenuous requests of such hikes of numerous ups and downs, Yang lays wondering if mortals are deserving of such heights whilst Yin lays opposite and speculates whether or not this is mental derangement, the kind ancients believed depended on the changing phases of the moon, the one the ancients called 'lunacy.'

CHAPTER 31

"Tempus Fugit"
(Time Flies)

"Those who favor freedom and [criticize] agitation are [people] who want crops without plowing up the ground, rain without thunder and lightning."

Frederick Douglas

January 18th 2016

The event for charity rotated locations annually; from Mclean Gardens Ballroom to the Chevy Chase ballroom to this year's event in the renovated Wonderland Ballroom in Columbia Heights, the MLK 'Swing and Bling for Scholars Dance' sponsors, Senator Bruce and Ms. Katherine Starr Mulhane are exceptionally pleased with the turnout and with the initial reports on the size of donations for scholarships.

Sean Linden and Robbyn Banques McGrew are in attendance as are Mr. and Mrs. O'Hara. Senator Bruce's sons are working with seating and serving and general crowd 'assistance'.

The Senator finishes a short 'thank you' to everyone. Then, as personality cannot help it, the Senator announces, "Reminder, buffet is to be served until eight, then the 'balling' will commence at 8:10; any questions?" Senator Bruce smiles large until he spies Ms. Mulhane's frown; and playful though it is, it demands a response. "Well, heck, Katie; I could have, at least I did not bring up religion!" The Senator continues the banter of a happy hearted man, reasons being, besides Miss Mulhane in attendance at another successful event for needy kids, is that the Senator is very pleased as well to have made Miss McGrew's acquaintance; especially when introduced by one obviously enthralled Mr. Linden; 'so good to see a friends light turn on again, yes sir.'

"Yes, it was called grandpa's doodlebug, his divining rod, whatever it was, it served him well, my Grandfathers' generation, yes, his generation being the only generation that's' gone from outlaws chasing outlaws in Oklahoma to Okie's flying around in space. Biggest amount of stuff happening in the shortest amount of time in history, that's grandpa's generation.'

Ms. Mulhane is glad that Mr. Bruce and she are lifelong friends. She's glad too that he is still light on his feet as they always open up the 'Ball' with the first dance, and, as it happened again within the last couple of minutes, the two to three minute annual rendezvous in rhythm with Dunleavy is ever so pleasurable as it never fails to remind Kate of their first dance together, so many years and so many trials ago. 'And he's never stepped on me once. Lord, knows, we can't tell a lie without the other aware of the speciousness because we have been in it together since forever!'

Katherine Starr Mulhane is wealthy, generous; a quietly transformative agent in many individuals lives; thankful souls who'll never know the name behind the kindness.

Mr. Bruce continues. "One of my favorite facets of Katherine's loveliness is that she honors me by allowing me into her sacred circle of closeness and comfort. Let's just say she narrows down the odds of disappointment to zero, and always has."

He is known for legislating from the hip and from the lip; 'naysayers, go scuttle yourselves' he views as a positive affirmation. He is loved by the voters for his unmitigated and risible style and by Katherine for his grip on reality for the long term; she'd never known him to be a man of the short game, ever.

The man is proudest when his sons are near. The boys had recently completed their five year vetting process for acceptance as members of the Capitol Police. Each has served in various branches of the military. All are sedulous souls; each considerate of the honor of their father in all that they've each ventured so far in life and all the young gentlemen apply an equal level of respect to whom the boys know the Senator adores as equally as he does them; Ms. Kate Mulhane, or, as the boys called her when they were of single digit ages, 'Mama Katbird'.

'Mama Katbird' is presently amused at how 'youthful' the Senator seems to shine into when in the company of such a lovely individual as Ms. McGrew. Good for the man to stretch his imaginations.

"In response to your inquiry as to what I am proficient at, Ms. McGrew, I'm a troubadour of tauromachy."

"The art of bullfighting..." Ms. Mulhane inserts, "...and don't forget, Robbyn, he can be a Master of the 'ole', if you let him."

"Like most of them, right, Katherine?"

The Senator and the military man are pleased that the women 'appear' to like each other.

They both believe 'smart' men should always hedge their perceptions about what women like and dislike, and frequently, if not always, they both adhere to the approach that advocates waiting for more clues before ever even mentioning or venturing a single view out loud on the subject of female friendships during their evolutionary stages.

Sean softly takes Robbyn's arm, then her hand. "Excuse us, but this is slow enough that Robbyns' feet will be safe." Sean and Robbyn smile 'adieu'. They head towards the ballroom floor as an easy waltz begins.

The Senator and Ms. Mulhane watch the young couple. They are pleased with Sean and Robbyns' cheery way; and they are near giddy with the bounce they see in the younger couple's first steps of discovery. It is impossible not to notice that Robbyn and Sean obviously intend to forge ahead into the unexplored worlds of each other. Kate will later remark to Dunleavy, "The pleasantries between those two are refreshing, Dunsey. They remind me of good and full memories of my own and can one suggest a greater gift than that? I dare say no, Dunsey; I dare say no."

The pace livens. Verticilation accelerates. Kate sees it first. "Senator, they're Gable and Leigh, isn't it; look at their movement, right?"

The iconic dance sequence in 'GoneWith The Wind' always strikes them as a romantic bond. It had been the first cinema they'd seen. It was a second date. The first date had been at a hay ride.

"They're in focus while all about is blurred, whirling and they are the universe and there are no others."

Senator Bruce concurred. "Rhett and Scarlet, Robbyn and Sean, so high beam, so in focus, so clear, so hard not to notice their merriment and confusion." The Senator grips Ms. Mulhanes' hand a wee bit more firmly. Ms. Mulhane returns the commitment with a quick grip too.

"Never forget, do you."

"No, Dunsey; never do."

The Senator spots them first. "Welcome once again, O'Hara clan."

"Not sure, Dunsey," Katherine suggests, "...if Irish have Clans; maybe."

"Don't care. I know they drink. That's Irish enough, isn't it, Kate?"

"Nice to see friendlies!" Casey O'Hara elaborated. "You are looking at two of only the most recent escapees from the fleshy cage of a..."

"...A fleshy cage of a madding messy press corps," Shawna O'Hara finished. "Messy in manners, messy in 'purpose' misplaced, messy and flummoxed by messianic egos; yes, and then toss in messy with the facts and heck yes, maam, heck yes, sir; you got the makings of a beautiful 'stunt' relationship, a task for daredevils, and as I tell Casey, with the only participants allowed being those that cause what is to be written about and those that see cause in all that they write."

"A woman of my own heart, welcome again, Shawna." Ms. Mulhane, quite unlike her usual nature, dove into conversation. "It's evident that a currency of some sort is rippling throughout the gossip and gloss of the 'self-registered', self glorified D.C. punditry in attendance; I see it. I recognize 'herd' when I see it too."

The newly arrived sit as do the Senator and Ms. Mulhane.

"I'm telling you, look around; the churning is different; a noticeable head-turning 'hum', 'potential' has a way of doing this, it draws attention in the mind with the sharpness, the keenness of an old man remembering the ease of catching up to a baseball in flight during his halcyon days in the centerfields of his youth. He remembers this because now there is pain where origins of memory once lived. Now, there is only comfort when he lowers his reach, unable to even paint a level line on a wall without clicks in the bones and spurs that catch in the shoulder, in unison going, 'whoa boy', you'll never make that greatest catch ever again, even though you see it, spotless, the ball so white against the sky, so perfect against the blue, your back to the crowd, you have a bead on it, your glove completes your move and the catch that stays for a lifetime has caught up to you once more and who says potential is dead, right?."

The Senator reaches over and kisses the top of Ms. Mulhane's right hand. "If you will allow me, Ms. Mulhane; Kate, Shawna, Shawna, Kate!"

"Yes, Kate; my pleasure, and if I may be so bold, that we have the 'potential' to be more than just cursory friends and I..."

Ms. Mulhane stops Mrs. O'Hara. "Oh Hell, woman; don't you know? I just like hanging out with future first ladies."

The women laugh as if they've known each other from Gerber days. Odd, how at this moment, the men think the music in the hall is becoming better and say so.

All move towards the doorway to better view the action of the band and the dancers. The invitation for the event was explicit. 'Dress is mandatory informal/formal.' Apparently, the attendees are a literate bunch as evening gowns, tuxes and perfectly coifed manes mix with Levis, longhair, short hair, no hair, Mohawks, bling, Afros and one Pink Floyd black light t-shirt. The band kicks it different with Doobie Brothers 'China Grove' and space on the dance floor disappears. The lead guitar plays witty and hard while the bass is telling all, 'let loose, you fools, let loose1' and so they do.

Robbyn and Sean arrive and are greeted by the others.

"Too many people high stepping in a teeny place means a little too much booty banging for me." Mrs. O'Hara is not one to mince words.

"Good God, yes," Robbyn agrees.

They retreat a short distance into an unused meeting room offering less noise and least notice. It has the smell of new carpet and fresh paint. Cody, Josey, Dakota and Shane Bruce maintain the group's privacy.

Mr. Linden and Ms. McGraw decide to lean against the commercial kitchen island bar as the others sit.

The 'Intendee' is responding to an inquiry from the 'Interviewee'.

"The Parties are hostage, as I know you are aware, Senator, to the most base and the most vocal, to the most vicious of orchestrated noise and bluster and to the near Neanderthal precepts ever witnessed by so many, *so* often, so hourly, everyday. Can you still be moral and can you lead and still use power effectively and be true to your foundations simultaneously?" The doctor places his drink on the table. "It's as Cicero's brother admonished the orator, something to the effect ... 'make a habit of developing the 'influential' carefully. Cicero's' brother adds that his sibling should 'take notice that the slaves in the households speak well of him too.' Senator, you've heard of E.F.

Schumacher?"

"Unsure. Maybe?"

"Well, a title of his always stuck with me from college. Called "A Study of Economics As If People Mattered"; isn't that a nail it on the head dinger! A quote of his, Dunleavy, excerpt that I recall is about weakness of politicians...something about 'politicians corrupting themselves by practicing greed, and they corrupt the rest of society by provoking envy.'"

The music is louder through the wall and is now lightly vibrating the fire safety doors.

The Senator finishes scribbling on a drink napkin and passes it to the 'Intendee.' "Senator, I will let you know early. No need now."

"I don't mean to be indelicate but I am. There are sometimes seismic shifts in selections, first to be picked in tag of as member of team, last forever. And so do errors as to second bananas."

"It's your floor, literally; please," Mr. O'Hara urges.

"Take no one whose stories verge on the hemline of veracity. Need someone who makes other's lives more important than their own or at least the perception." The Senator reaches with his drink glass and toasts his with Ms. Mulhane's. "And nowhere is it written that 'she' must be a 'he' either."

Ms. Mulhane's eyes indicate to the Senator that he is getting points.

"Do appreciate you hearing me out, Casey. Continuing, second banana selection process; do not choose anyone that voted 'present' more times than taking stands. Don't need head in the sand safe, God forbid, just remember that an ostrich's eye is bigger than its' brain. Please note, also, just because someone might have a hefty block of voters from a hefty state, look very closely at the shine as these individuals tend to have more than a pedestrian opinion of themselves. I can help with the structure and communications, if you like. Let people know what they should expect of you early is key. I know that you are already ground working your ass off on the ballots and I can help here too, state by state, delegate by delegate. Eventually, my party will squeal. Let them." Senator Bruce leans in. "The public is disgusted by the abuse of both parties."

"Senator, I still need to describe our decision and the conditions behind the roll of the rocks and begging question, 'why me?'"

"Moving mountains brings a lot of scrutiny, I'll give you that."

"I've never bowed to pitter patter philosophies requiring credulity on bended knee at the alter of chicanery, nor will I ever."

"Sean, Casey, Robbyn, anyone, can you quickly name or show how many people in history have been tagged with the last name of 'The Great'? Well, there's Catherine of course, spelled incorrectly with a 'C' I might add, then Alexander, Ivan, Alfred..."

"I believe that it is long overdue for Cleopatra." Ms. Mulhane is the 'challenger' now. "She deserves the title of 'Great' as any man does, don't you agree, Shawna?"

"Yes, Kate, and you know why they were 'great'? They were either so terrible that others were afraid to call them anything less than 'Great' or, they were so far-seeing for their epoch, acting differently than others before them, often constructing their precepts with visions so discomforting and so riotous versus what preceded these individuals entry onto the bloody stage of mans inconsistencies and intemperate manners, that disaster is always the final calculation of history, so if it were me, Kate, I don't know if I would want to hashtag 'The Great' after my name any time soon, in this century or in the next."

"You are right, Shawna, the value of the word's meaning has been diminished by over use."

The music seems to amp up again as not a word is spoken for about five seconds until, "One other thing on the Veep..." The group makes mock appearances as if fending off an unwanted beast.

"Oh, come on. It's important. Casey, never trust anyone who hasn't fallen off a bull, electrical or otherwise and never trust anyone who doesn't like to fish, fornicate or fight and your campaign will be successful."

As the O'Hara's laugh with the others, Casey O'Hara suddenly recalls snippets of an interview he had given a couple of weeks previously. He'd shared that he had "found my Waldon upon meeting Shawna.,;

When Casey and she met, Shawna Wayne, the land developers' daughter from Naples, Florida, was beginning her teaching career as speech therapist and sign language specialist.

Her soft Southern accent reassured the pupils who could hear her lovely sound while her smile spoke volumes to those who couldn't. It's apparent that as the lady of the O'Hara house is introduced, America is choosing to like her. Accomplished, she is reported as "commanding without commotion" and "trustworthy without the theatre of having to tell you so."

When he graduated and became 'M.D.' O'Hara, Shawna Wayne O'Hara became the leeward port during the white capped storm of emotional turmoil in Casey's cumbersome first months of his career. She'd stood ready to calm her love's unrelenting sense of loss, of the pain of a young doctor, just beginning, too attached, losing patients to the hands of God, coming to the realization, sincerely shocked, that he or she isn't God and that, "can not to do what we are trained to do; save the patients damn lives!"

"My, that seems years ago, girl." Mrs. O'Hara comes back to watching the two men. She chuckles to herself. 'Well known fact that a Senator and a Doctor, no matter how chummy it appears, they both want the other to know that they are on the planet too! Outsiders might consider the scene argumentative. Pshaw! It's a male thing. Mostly.' "Americans are disgusted with this most recent bulging batch of saviors on the cheap, Casey! We both know this."

"It's easy to accomplish when the facts are trampled by emotion; when the social condition is confusion, when trust is seen as a rusty thing; so, as ever again and ever before, the benefits inure to those that own the earplugs."

"Just goes to show you that humor does involve tragedy, doesn't it?" Shawna had their attention. "You both know voters begin as chatty Cathy's believing anything; they then become Barbie and Ken and the 'what's in it for me, I mean us,' takes over. Bargain with the dolls about their dress and it's a losing proposition, gentlemen."

"In Rome, you ran for office literally wearing your campaign on your sleeve. White togas, you see, announced that you, the wearer, are "pure", decked out in the color of honesty; today it's 'step right up and get your pure here' in light blue shirts, red ties, variations of navy blue suits and non threatening fashion for lady candidates as well as the proper hues; these of the 21st century togas for the 21st century candidates, so bargaining with 'dolls' works both ways; for voters and candidates."

Senator Bruce turns from Ms. Mulhane towards the O'Hara's.

"Candidate, unusual origin, a word, Latin, 'candidatus', meaning, you guessed it, 'dressed in white.' Any questions, class?"

"Well," Mr. O'Hara concludes, "could it be any other way; of course not." Mr. O'Hara softly places his hand atop Mrs. O'Hara's. "Yes, the sheen of propriety brought to you by all those men of the past who wore white sheets lying to everyone else about why they were the only ones wearing these white sheets, these togas, these finely garbed instruments of pimps for purity through the ages." Mr. O'Hara turns towards Shawna. "Is that what were working for, Mrs. O'Hara?"

"Let's see; new wardrobe, new friends, new home, unlimited 'miles', yes, Mr. O'Hara, I think these are a few of a pimp woman's favorite things, yes."

Ms. Mulhane horselaughs; it's the cue for release and all do.

Mr. O'Hara recovers first. "Way too much 'me' for a dolls world these days; Shawna, you're on it."

Mrs. O'Hara near blushed.

"The lady, listen, everyone, if you will indulge me just a wee more; she got to me early. And for once, I wasn't a dumb mick. I paid attention. She knew then, as now, what is and saw what ought to be and conveyed this to me in such clarity and beauty that it's never left me. She's my blessed reminder every day of why I am lucky to be alive for she could have been a 'contender', an actress, a governor, yes, and not that working miracles in kids lives everyday isn't a magnificent destiny, but she settles for a wet-eared doctor instead." Casey appeared to tighten his lips, then, "Listen, Shawnee, will you do the 'Patrick Henry' for us, for me?" "What is that, a dance?"

"No, Kate; it isn't a dance. And Casey, 'no' to you too! I sensed a buttering up for something coming on, Mr. O'Hara, about the time you said 'settles for a wet-eared doctor."

"Tell us, Shawna," Robbyn implores,"...curiosity's at cruel stage now."

"What's this breaking ranks, girl?" Mrs. O'Hara teases. "Oh, well. What Casey is talking about is..."

"She closed the deal for me with this. I'd known you maybe two, three..."

"It was two weeks, Casey." Mrs. O'Hara looks towards the floor. She begins, "This is a work from college; I minored in Drama and dabbled in history." Shawna sits up. "I had to come up with something quick and quirky enough to pull at least a 'B' out of a teacher that thought himself a professorial Romeo. Ladies, you know what I mean."

"Oh, yeah, do tell, girl."

"I remembered a part of a speech from high school, a speech my teacher had said 'moved a country'. I decided to spice it up for teacher boy on the prowl by incorporation of another piece of history into the patriot's speech, another presentation that, shall I say, had moved men too." Mrs. O'Hara stands up. "Ladies and gentlemen, this is Marilyn Monroe channeling Patrick Henry. And this is from a book in the sixties written by, oh, what is, yes, by one M.C. Tyler; with liberties from Marilyn and myself."

Mrs. O'Hara stands up and pantomimes applying blush, eye liner, puckers up her lips ala M.M and, in 'dirty word syrup' as Casey in private coins it, Shawna O'Hara disappears. "I was addressing the boys in the Burgesses and I asked them 'what...'" the breathy play works, as Marilyn rolls out trippingly on Shawna's tongue, "...what are you waiting for?"

Shawna playfully pushes her hips out; places a fist on hip and with the free hand points. "Our brethren are already in the field hoeing down the right lane. Why stand here idle and empty handed?" Shawna tiny steps a few feet, accent on the hour and on the glass, of course. With orotund perfection, 'Marilyn' continues, "What is it, gentlemen wish? What would they have?"

Senator Bruce broke. "I can sure as hell speak for them if you like."

Ms. Mulhane playfully elbows him. "Shut up, fool. A stateswoman is speaking!" Laughter subsides and 'Marilyn' is unflappable. She gracefully lowers down on her knees. "I kneeled, some say, like a manacled slave and said, 'Is life so dear, our peace so sweet, as to be..." Shawna wiggles as if a chill is playing with her spine. "...purchased at the price of chains and slavery?"

"What, no whips?"

'Marilyn' ignores her husband's commentary.

"Forbid it, Almighty God!" 'Marilyn' turns and vamp walks the ten feet back to her chair, pivoting with a smoothly executed flourish. "I bent to Mother Earth, my hands crossed across my, well," Shawna looks down at her breasts. "...well, you know, and I remained posed, then suddenly," Shawna drew out the word to where 'suddenly' came out so slowly, so lush, as if to refute the meaning of the word. "Yes, suddenly, I sprang up and shouted 'Give me liberty or give me death' as I flung my arms wide open, paused, lowered them and then I made a fist of my right hand as if I held a dagger at my, well, well, you know...and I said, sepulchral tones: 'or give me death." 'Marilyn Henry' blows a kiss towards Casey. "I then beat me, well," Shawna points downwards, "you know. She slowly moves an invisible blade back and forth from herself. "There was silence around me until a fine gentleman who had been listening to my plea at an open window, shouted, "Let me be buried on this spot." Frankly, I was not sure if he meant the courthouse or ..." Shawna again indicates 'south' "...or, you know." 'Marilyn' bows. Shawna lifts her head to smile at the applause.

"As you all can see," Mr. O'Hara is beaming, "...she had me at, well, well, you know." Mrs. O'Hara leans and kisses her husband on the cheek. Senator Bruce leads the clapping again. Mr. O'Hara is not finished. "Seriously, though; with all that we've, the country, have been saddled with, citizens bombarded with never ending mesmerations fashioned in burnished biases; a country reined in by designed negligence and subtle diffusions. It seems capricious of nature to allow the liberating, to think that an act of impulsive courage is yet still a possibility with all the odds against it today." Casey nudges Mrs. O'Hara. "You know what this means, Mrs. O'Hara?"

"Do tell, Mr. O'Hara?"

"That we're not long shots, no; we are actually just fricken freaks of nature. So what's the worry, we're not supposed to be anyways, right?" The group agrees with various vocalizations of support.

Dakota Bruce politely interrupts. "Senator, pardon me, but it's probably time for your closing remarks, Sir." When Senator Bruce seemed to question his son's comments, the younger Bruce, shrugging, elaborates, "Dad, cabs are waiting!"

"Good job, Koda," Ms. Mulhane commends.

"Yes, yes, son, thank you." Senator Bruce acknowledges, "Adios time is now. Need to send everyone that's need of with our thanks, check to see if the kids are still having fun dancing with grownups. You know, Katherine, I've heard we are ahead of last year's amounts."

"Good, good; good get together on many levels, Dunsey." Ms. Mulhane stands as does everyone else. "If you ask me, and I do not care if you don't," turning towards the O'Hara's,"...I think it's good for a country to lose a little control once in a while. You offer, humor, a casual manner, you're considerate and careful but not fearful.

You are able to look in the mirror and understand the lines...and add your blood heritage in the mix, and whoa; it's certain to me that the time for bottled sweet water is over; it's time to answer every 'why' with 'why not', answer every 'can't' with 'can'. Yes, it's time for 'sass with kick ass' and may I say again, and I will anyways, I think you both measure up for the proper amount of mayhem required for the task at hand."

Senator breaks the pleased silence. "Katherine, I say lady, when you're talking dirty, I know its way past the point of flirty and it's definitely time to go!"

"Why, Senator, whatever are you suggesting? Just remember, Mr. Bruce, all urges don't necessarily come with happy endings!" Ms. Mulhane spins on her heels.

"Robbyn, Shawna, shall we show the men how it's done?"

"Show how what's done?" The 'Bruce' is confused.

"Why, 'control', dear, 'control.' And actually, gentlemen, the better question might be, how can you lose what you don't have?"

Dakota Bruce escorts the three newly minted friends towards the music; the ladies gracefully gliding ahead of the men and the evidence is clear, the proposition of 'control' and who really wields it is not in doubt, nor, upon honest reflection, has it ever been since time primeval.

Yes Maam. No sir.

CHAPTER 32

"Littered People Of The Peace"

"..it is plainly contrary to the law of Nature, however defined, that children should command old men, fools, wise men, and that the privilege few should gorge themselves with superfluities, while the starving multitudes are in want of the bare necessities of life."

Jean-Jacque Rousseau
(1712 – 1778)

January 25th, 2016

The trend is clear. Las Vegas Police contact Michigan and Oklahoma authorities. This one is a money manager hyphen banker considered by many, or was, as a Nevadan of pitted ethics, ripe reputation, and unknown wealth (but everyone knew he has; had it,) who is discovered dead, white dress gloves stuffed in the hip pockets of the victims youngish jeans. A note is discovered pinned to a jester doll the deceased, Caleb Trivian, used as a paperweight on his home office desk. The note consists of variously sized cut out letters in picas and fonts of all types.

"Very tedious; very industrious to assemble such a communique." Detective Geyer is speculating aloud to his subordinates. "No apparent cause. The torso is in chair, slumped, and I bet you that we will not find any DNA, prints; now, it's Vegas. So we have tight times. The items of interest here and the complete note, allegedly left by the killer, will be leaked within 48 hours. We all know it; so full ride on this one, ladies and gentlemen." Caleb Trivian had believed himself untouchable. Security was only considered as events warranted. Unfortunately for the player, today's bet went south. Literally.

"Listen up. This is private that does not get leaked, understand? Scratch that.

I'll make copies for those that need further reference. Note goes...

'He didn't care as families were laid bare on the courthouse steps. No, his time was too golden to be bothered with their heartbreak as he had grander pursuits of easy avarice and acreages on the cheap."

Detective Geyer looks up at his team. "Clear so far? Good. Now, the public will soon be peer reviewing, just like authorities, the victims to date; who they were in life that ties them together in death? What was thought of them to make them targets? And 'did any of them deserve this' will begin to swirl for churns sake, we all know this."

Detective Geyer returns to the note.

"Talented in managing meanness, men and money, no lawsuits in loss columns for you, oh no, your lawyers beat everyone....until today, the 25th of January, your debt is paid in full with penalty because as you are a Shay late and a dollar short because you just 'stood by!"

Detective Geyer waits for questions. There are none. 'Smart group.'

He glances in the office southeast corner, peering at Trivians' statue of himself. The policeman's eyes can't help but quickly refer back to the body slumped in the chair. He steps outdoors to the relative pleasantness of Las Vegas in January.

'No forced entry. Gloves, apparent ease of travel and covering costs; sponsors maybe? The only item Mr. Geyer had kept from his team (except for his assistant/partner) is the second folded note found in the grasp of one of the white gloves. It has Geyer and others reviewing the dates of the other similar cases as they could be specifically important in association with the 'why' of the act. The detective assures that he is alone in the garden area and putting on proper glove ware, he then takes out the 'rest of the evidence'.

'In 1787, in the scrambled times of discontent since the Redcoats defeat, Daniel Shays civil disobedience evolved into Americas first civil war, a civilians aggravated act for the debt-ridden, the over taxed and the empty handed. Seek him out, America. You need to

re-introduce yourselves to Mr. Shays again. Quickly!'

Detective Geyer carefully folds the paper and places it in an evidence baggie. He immediately goes to the net on his phone. He learns that Daniel Shays and his rabble in arms biggest victory in the rebellion was at the Springfield, Massachusetts Arsenal. No

coincidence that Trivian is killed on the 25th. 'Dates' are definitely in play to attempt to gain 'meaning' of a sort for the actions of the White Glove killer.

"Rocky, check the dates for Tulsa and for Ypsilanti murders. Then, check the historical significance of each date, what happened on those dates, all the way back to Moses if you have too, understand?"

"Yes, of course." Geyer's partner leaves.

The detective looks to the distance above the estates walls and stares at the familiar skyline of the electronic Lego world of light and dark, the world's foci fun house of small satisfactions and large let downs, otherwise known as Mr. Geyers' birthplace.

Thoughts race; better bone up on history, let's see, a televangelist, a Muslim advocate

and now, a banker. Where's the pattern? All controversial, yes, who's not in this age? All three winners of victories in celebrated lawsuits, and hated for them, could this be glue? In two of the three trials, the public seemed almost as pissed as they did about the O.J. verdict. Jesus, this killer could find so many dates he sees as times government screwed the people. I know he feels no one is accountable. This is the reason for his being. Think so, yes. A target rich environment for vigilantism, that's for shitting sure. People may begin to root for this guy. Have we gotten this bad?'

The phone rings. It is the coroner with word that Mr. Trivian died of a broken neck. Geyer hangs up without commenting except for 'thanks.'

No signs of break in or struggle. Great. It's professional with a messianic complex. Double great. Odds this ends on its own; bet the house that it's 'zero.' Chance I can still begin vacation in a week; 'zero.' Chance I'm still married after this news, fifty-fifty.'

CHAPTER 33

"Living On Angel Time"

"Those who say that we're in a time when there are no heroes, they just don't know where to look."
Ronald Reagan, 1981

January 25th, 2016

As soon as the announcement came that it is okay to use cell phones, Ms. McGrew calls Mr. Linden from the plane.

"Change of plans; hope okay. Meet me at the National Gallery of Art, Sean."

Robbyn has just landed from West Coast engagements. She had left the morning after Senator Bruce's MLK event for a week of advocacy for children's rights, victims of rape and promoting legislation for legal aid for the poor. She'd used her 'celebrity' and public likeability for these special causes in her heart for a few years now. She always paid her way and demanded that all money that comes in because of her appearance would go to the groups in need and not one cent to administrative wages or costs. She drew capacity audiences because Robbyn is selective, only conducting these appearances maybe once, twice at most, per year. Robbyn's constant preference is to shy the limelight; it tends to body slam her stomach as she always feels faint before these public forays, rarely getting a full nights rest before the appointed day of departure for said occasion.

And she always felt the same within; that she should be in a children's hospital or what stands for one, in some forlorn place on earth instead of, as she classified it, "Throwing my mug out in front of cameras on display for the national press, the massively uninvolved; waiting for me to hurry my words so they can make their deadlines in time for fricken happy hour!"

"Yes, I missed you too. Good. It's just that I need ASAP to get wrapped up in the distraction only the masterly and mania of art; no, correct that, that only art and now you, Sean, give me."

They agree to meet in front of the Rubens. Sean arrives first. He has two day stubble, a Nationals ball cap with signs of sweat, older jeans, a muted gray shirt and his standard cheap sunglasses. No one paid a second glance in his direction as he leans in to study brush strokes more closely.

"Amazing that such a small country could have such a large impact in behavior and spectral compositions, wouldn't you agree?"

She strolled towards him wearing a pink 'hug-me-tight' top and bright white pants.

He forgets Ruben's, Rembrandt and reason as they embrace. She surprises him with more than just a hello on his lips. When they realize that they are becoming subjects of growing observation, an 'organic' display in a hall of inanimate attractions, they release. "Long week, Miss McGrew?"

"Ah, the stories, Mr. Linden, the stories." They turn and began strolling.

"I can really only try to push so much, since we still do not have court enforced charity yet, probably around the bend, though, the way things operate these days. It just seems, Sean, that problems are often mistaken for rabbits, there are so many." They continue a few more steps. "Thank you for meeting me here. I usually come here after one of these weeks. It calms me, the fantastic play of light and dark, the atmosphere, the smell of the gallery; peaceful, an addiction, I suppose.'

They pause in front of a Winslow Homer. Robbyn opens a side pocket of her roller luggage. "These are good. Have one. For airline chocolate mints; not too bad." Sean accepts and pops the sweet into his mouth. Robbyn enjoys her third piece. "Chocolates taste, smell, yes, the smell stays forever, doesn't it? I think of my Mother going to her sons', my brothers condo to, as Mom said, 'to smell the scent of her only son, now gone." Robbyn did not reveal the circumstances of her sibling's death.

"You see, my mother brought chocolates that day, box of dark chocolates, because Mother said men prefer dark chocolates."

"In shock?"

"Oh, yes. Like that for a while, but strong for Dad. That's Mom. And that's chocolate to me." She feels this might be too much heavy much too soon. She directs Sean's attention elsewhere. "Look at Homer's use of the touches of colors, where he has it orchestrating themes and ..."

"Newton proved white light is composed of all visible colors of the spectrum and..."

"Yes, but some painter said 'white' doesn't exist in nature; Renoir, I believe, yes, and I like him, almost a Newton, but not quite."

"I did not thank you; this mint's good, but I'm more partial to vanilla. Hope this isn't a deal breaker."

Robbyn, smiling, "White vanilla boy, well, you know evidence suggests the smell of vanilla may cause the man to relax. Scientific."

"I do like Bluebell homemade the best, true."

"So it is the smell, the indulgence of contentment, back rub and candlelight notwithstanding, ice cream is, vanilla is your 'museum', right? That's good. You have potential after all."

Masterpieces become backdrops only as they walk on, cherishing the 'taste' of new togetherness. They pause at a sculpture.

"Look, they say it's a nude, but I say, pity the modern woman if this is the 'mod bod', right?"

Sean doesn't commit, instead pointing towards a free bench for them to sit. They look at the 'nude' from a further distance. "You know, Robbyn, she does look better from afar." "Still appears as a waste of granite to me. Gender misrepresentation; what's fashionable about that?"

Seam chooses correctly. "Not a thing. Seems old style."

"I had a raving feminist for professor who actually taught me one reasonable thing that I kept. P.S.; she turned out to be randy for men, probably a nymphomaniac; but that is another story."

"Tell that one now."

"Cute. No, the woman the randy lady taught me about is a twelfth century genius. Her name is Heloise. Bear with me, it's a hell of a lesson and I had it down pat in school. Let's see, speaking of memory...it goes, yes, quoting Heloise, 'For it is not wealth or power that makes a man great. Wealth and power stem from luck. Greatness stems from merit.' Funny how things stick, isn't it? Continuing, Heloise closes with this, 'To marry a rich man in preference to a poor man, and to value the advantages of a husband's rank more highly than his innate virtues, is tantamount to selling oneself.'"

Sean is transfixed. She's so lovely in her passion.

"Certainly, a woman who is prompted to marry by any such covetousness deserves to be paid rather than loved, for it is obvious that her attachment is not to the man but to his riches and that, given the opportunity, she would gladly have prostituted herself to an even wealthier man."

"She was on top of it, yes."

"More ways than one, Sean. Let's restroom now; I think they are, I know the closest." They stand.

"And Sean..." "Yes?"

"Heloise is a female hunketta, right?"

"I think whatever that means, I agree."

"Good to hear as you continue."

"Continue?"

"Your odds are improving. Majority of women say they cannot enjoy sex with someone who is not as smart as they are and I think you're near me in 'smarts', so..."

"Is that an insult or near insult?" They walk.

"You do know that museums do not count as 'third' dates?"

"Oh?"

"No. They are more of a buffer between the second and the 'actual' third date because third dates usually consist of smatterings of seriousness nesses asses..." Both laugh louder than premises recommend. They halt mid-guffaw as they notice everyone is staring at them. They move quickly to their respective havens otherwise known as the ladies and the men's bathrooms.

Upon reunification, Robbyn asks, "Now, I may be dealing too deep here, but, when we met at 'Jaw jammers', you said, you never knew your parents."

"So this may be an official third date after all."

"Accident? Is that what I have read?'

"Yes."

They begin to walk slower.

"Do you know that the name 'Linden'; it's probably like McGrew, Celtic?"

"Funny you say that, Robbyn. It's always what I have felt."

"No brothers or sisters?"

"None, at least in my early years at Omaha, none on record."

They walk a few more feet in silence.

"From what I learned long time ago, parents were only children too. Their parents apparently deceased and I really could not trace much else and really, I just put it all out of my mind in my teens. Have not given much thought to it since because what does, what difference does it make now? Zero. But I do feel you are right, that I am 'Keltoi'."

"Keltoi; Greek?"

"Yes. What they called the wild ones, the Celts, yes."

"Hobbit, you like Tolkien, right?"

"Books better than the movies, yes."

"Well, Tolkien said, 'Celtic of any sort is a magic bag, into which anything may be put, and out of which almost anything may come.'"

"Love that."

"Another Greek, Arrian, says the Celts were people of great stature and naughty disposition."

"Well, that settles it. They got to be 'blood'."

"English and French restricted, even banned the Celtic language. Despite these prejudices', despite the poverty and isolation of them, they weather through. So, Robbyn, if we are Celtic, we are lucky."

"Now, don't shake rattle or roll, but, years ago, when I thought about children; I almost see you shivering, Sean," Robbyn jests. "I had picked out Celtic Saints for names too, Kieran and Finian."

"Boys would love the fact that Celtic fighters hung enemy heads on their houses as a show of prowess and Gods grace."

"Which head?"

"You can be disarmingly dirty, can't you?"

"Yes, rarely; but with the right audience..."

"It's odd, but I have found that, if you are Irish, Welsh, Scottish, it's assumed you have Celtic blood even though, just 300 years ago, no one called someone a 'Celt.' Not recorded anywhere."

"That's Tolkien for you."

"A mountain of mystery, yes."

"My aunt Opal sparked my interest early about ancestors. She and Mom were school teachers in their first careers. My Auntie taught me my first Irish ditty."

"Ditty?"

"Yes, ditty; and I damn well love this ditty. You've heard it probably. Goes, 'May your neighbors respect you, trouble neglect you, the Angels protect you and heaven accept you.'"

"My favorite, yes; walked me through a couple of woozier moments, absolutely hung in with me."

"My Aunt Opal was definitely a singular entity on the personality scale. Married once, short time. When she became single again, she began a habit that lasted until she moved to, well, let's just say, moved to better digs."

"And that was?"

"She used to hang over-sized, I mean, jumbo sized old style white granny panties on her clothesline. She also would include a bra seemingly built for four instead of two 'occupants' and hang it up on the line to complete, as she called it, the 'security asset'. You see, she thought a rapist would think twice about dealing with a woman bigger than an Amazon with beer kegs for breasts and possibly forearms bigger than a man's waist. I thought Opal cooler than my Mother until I got older and my Mother suddenly became

'hip'."

"You could put together a book, a good book, on female leaders and maybe..."

"Yes. I have doodled on this. Maybe."

"You; I am sure you know of the Alexandrian genius, Hypatia; she's a must include, right?" For an 'unofficial' third date, he'd hit a bank shot.

"Yes, yes; outdo any man in government or Temple procedures."

"But, for your leading ladies book, in alphabetical order, you have to include Aspasia..." The shot is now a 'swish' and a winner.

"Yes, God, Sean. You know these names?"

"Aspasia, taught Socrates. Married Pericles in spite of the Greek law then. Sage councilor to anyone that had the sense to listen."

"You really want to get into someone's pants tonight, don't you?"

Neither spoke for another minute until Robbyn asks, "Food, modem, remote and female access at a bargain price and not necessarily in that order; I ask you, Mr. Linden, are you one of those males?" Robbyn's smile provides the answer but Sean plays through anyway.

"So, that's a fact, huh? Men are tools?"

"Yes. And you'd be even grumpier..."

"Grumpier?"

"Yes, if you knew that the tiny ants, you know those that can lift twenty times their weight, if you knew that they are female! Yes, more grumpier."

They face each other smiling. Robbyn reaches out and Sean meets her hands to hold. "Robbyn Banques McGrew, I am lucky, yes. Because, you see, for a man like me to find a lady like you; oligarchic beauty with a plebian heart..."

"I think I like this."

"... and humor too; reminds me of Mark Twain saying, 'I wouldn't have a girl I was worthy of.' Remember, this is Twain talking. In fact, that's more up Cades' alley than mine."

"So this is your view of singlehood?" As expected, he's slightly perplexed. "Thank you for the lovely thoughts. Truly."

She wanted to pull him closer but they release and began walking again.

"Did you know, Sean, that many primitives still believe that monogamy is unnatural and immoral?"

'God, where is this trek heading?'

"Yes, you would have liked to have lived in Babylon, Sean."

"Oh and why is this?"

"Because Babylon is where, before a woman would be allowed to marry, it was demanded of a woman to give herself at the Temple of Mylitta to any man that asked her."

Robbyn's tickled that Sean seems dumbfounded.

"What would Vegas do, huh? Herodotus records that every woman was obliged, once in her life, to sit in the temple and have intercourse with some stranger. Oh, yes! When a woman had once seated herself, she could not return home until some stranger has thrown a piece of silver in her lap and had lain with her outside the temple. As part of what they call a ritual, the stranger would say, 'I beseech the goddess, Mylitta, to favor thee.' Herodotus goes on to say that 'the silver may be ever so small, for she will not reject it, inasmuch as it is not lawful for her to do so, for such silver is accounted sacred." "So a quarter would have..."

Robbyn ignores his reference. "The woman follows the first man that throws the silver..."

"Wealthy or poor, the women did this?" "Yes. And they refused no one."

"Nerd heaven."

"When she has had intercourse and absolved herself from her obligations to the goddess, she returns home. Those, and again, this is Herodotus detailing, those that are endowed with beauty and symmetry of shape are soon set free; but the deformed are detained a long time from the inability to satisfy the law, for as the first historian says, some wait for a space and time as he puts it, of three to four years."

"Oh, come on!"

"No, they did not, at least for three to four years!"

"How sad. But years, helpless and lonely..."

"And no gitchy goo-goo on the side either."

As they continue, the pace slightly quickens.

"Goes to show that anything is possible, doesn't it; like, very 'ordinary' meeting very 'extraordinary' in a museum for instance."

They keep walking. Her glance at him tells Sean it's time to think ahead. He considers his townhome. He thinks of things he hadn't given thought to fifteen seconds before. Is the bed made? Got to put anything of Odessa away. Glad that Thucydides is with Godboy and The Navaho. They'll be gone two more days. Yippee. Crap, what will she think of the furniture?

"My cab is in the vicinity, standing by until I call him. I will...'

"One selfish indulgence, yes?"

"Yes."

"I want to show you my place before entertaining any thoughts of seeing yours. Don't ask me why. Just feels the better way."

He is down for the count. Ta-Ta to townhome 'To Do's.

"Absolutely."

As Ms. McGrew opens her front door, she flips on lights, revealing a 'sock it to you to your eyes only' color splash of the world's priciest spice, the yellow gold wash of saffron.

"I love returning home to this. It's better than caffeine."

Sean nods but he is focused elsewhere, on a bust. "Always wooed by her."

"Oh, yes. Nefertiti means, 'Beauty's arrival'. Nice welcome, no?"

"Ego enhancer, right? Instead of a mirror, I mean."

"Maybe for you, but not for me."

"The casing around the girl; what is that, paint?"

"Hardly; compliments her well, though, agreed?"

"Well, yes."

"It's mummy pigment; mummy remains ground up into this rich brown. It was popular in Europe for a few centuries."

"I'd heard of this. Never seen."

Ms. McGrew picks up a remote and switches on a preset musical selection. It is what is now called Celtic music. "You like, I see."

"Very."

"It's the first sound I want to encounter after being away, a lift me up, like the saffron room." She crosses the room and motions to him to follow. She opens a door Sean hadn't noticed. "Welcome to my vice, Mr. Linden." Ms. McGrew stands back so Mr. Linden can see into an obviously temperature controlled space inhabited by racks of wine bottles.

"Oh, my!"

"No; 'oh, ours', if you like." She leads him in. "Washington state has excellent whites and Oregon, pinots, fine vineyards both. As I said, got into it during my first major, international finance; was told wine would definitely be integral part of a career in moving money."

"In vino veritas."

"In wine, truth, yes." She motions for him to follow her again. "Welcome to the rest of Robbyns' Shangri-La, which I've seen defined as both 'paradise on earth'..."

"Sounds promising."

"...and 'abode of love'."

"Is that, Shalimar? I've heard that..."

"Either way, it defines 'good'. Do you disagree?"

"Foolish, if I do. Right?"

Robbyn adjusts the lighting in the green room. Sitting on stands and shelves of various heights, plants line two walls. An oversized lime green loveseat is bordered by two oversized matching color bean bag 'chairs'. The ceiling is a skylight.

She sits on the edge of the loveseat. Sean looks past her towards two porcelain Buddha's with jovial countenances; their mouths acting as springheads for the soothing sound of babbling waters.

"Ripple of contentment in the air, no? I come here often."

Sean is stuck on how often he finds himself just staring at her. Stop it.

"My family owns this building. Sure you knew that."

He did not.

"This penthouse was Aunt Opals. Mom said it was left it to me because, 'your Aunt saw integrity in you at early age, and because she knows you will never sell it to, as your Aunt put it, little bird, just another dirt bag in D.C.' Mom can do 'sailor' talk when least expected."

"Edgar Cayce said the color green was the 'healing' vibration. In China, they believe green denotes 'East', and to Muslims, it's a sacred color."

"And da Vinci said green represented water."

"Enter the Buddha's?"

"Yes, you fool." Robbyn arises. "It is my room of good consequences where I can hear myself trouble through things without intrusions. More often than not, my thoughts are defined here. It's here, in fact, that I concluded that we are living in heaven and hell and we are judged by what we do by whether or not our breaths are guarded or graceful. These are the judgment hours." She motions for him to escort her elsewhere.

"I've concluded that standing for, aiding others when others can only sit or crawl, putting everything on the ledge so others don't tumble further and the returns are immeasurable, Sean, these; it gives you just a slice, a gleaming of 'forever' and Sean, I daresay, 'forever' is never the same again."

She enters another room on the right and the lights come on, revealing a mixture of hot pink, mahogany and stainless steel. "Pink for a purpose, baby, right?"

"A Baskin-Robbins without the ice cream?"

"You better be good or you wont get to lick the cone. No, pink is another calming agent for me. Pink's used in jails to chill inmates, did you know that?" She guides him to the isle wet bar so they can uncork the bottle of Bordeaux she's brought from her 'vino' room. She gives him the corkscrew. "Please note, Mr. L., the isle bar sink is bordered by specifically colored tile."

"And?"

"Just a funky thing, a blue-based red, which happens today to be the preferred lipstick color of women with, shall we say, hazy motives."

The cork pops and wine flows.

"Red quickens the heart; did you know that, Mr. Sean Linden?"

Not waiting for his response, Ms. Robbyn Banques McGrew indicates that is time to be on the move again. As she leads him back towards the entry, she adds, "Red also releases adrenaline."

They pass the 'green' room and enter a hallway he had not noticed before. They come to a door at the end and upon Robbyn opening the door, Sean sees that it's a master suite with elbow room for giants. She turns to him. They entwine and drink from each other's glass. They slowly untangle. Robbyn moves towards a wall of her photographs and he follows to stand by her side and to admire her work.

"So easily lost, if not nurtured to their fullest bloom." The photographs are in color and in black and white. They are children's faces. They're all smiles. And they are prints of her pictures which she has sold to donors for raising funds for, as Robbyn calls them, her 'little petals of joy'.

Robbyn had considered adoption. She'd soon judged this as only inspirational; a hoax on her to placate the inner turmoil, the sense of not doing more than she already was to help. She knows her life has to downshift from its presently engaged gear of 'frenetic pace' to eventually the evenness of 'cruise control' before this consideration is to have any legs at all.

"I've always believed that, without fanfare or wallop, we've got to do more for the least pleased among us, don't we? Don't you agree that we have to attach ourselves to the squalor holes of earth where smiles are few and distant and where comfort and security are mirage, yes?"

"I've fought in these terrains and you are right."

"Of course; I did not mean to exclude your...well," Robbyn turns the lights up and Sean zeroes in on a photograph of one beautiful brown eyed girl, perhaps five or six, smiling, teeth whiter than ivory, skin of ebony wonder. "She's been brought alive by your careful eye and detail. She's beautiful, Robbyn. The meaning in her look is stunning." "Welcome to my heartland, Sean Linden. That's Rena. She's now fifteen, healthy and living in North Carolina with stepparents that give a damn instead of a shove off. These are the colors of humanities hopes and dreams, as many as ten million shades of beauty, my little flowers of love, God's bouquets, God's perfections, before we do our best to mess them up, that is. These are His reminders of what good can be."

"These are astounding. I'd seen some of your work but, the truth, what matters the most to you; it's here. The love is obvious in what you've captured."

She see's in his eyes the truth in his words and for once, she's almost afraid to conclude, but she might just be one hundred per cent correct about a man.

"It's a matter of what is our charge, what is our destiny?"

"I see the answers here, don't I?"

"Only God speculates that big, Mr. Linden."

"And over here; him?"

"That's Banta. He's an orphan from blood diamond wars. Both parents accused of stealing stones, so they went 'bye-bye' forever. He was placed with a well-meaning missionary that should not have been one as he was out of his depth as to managing the trauma of one so young and injured as Banta."

"Art for action; that's you."

"One of the Millers, Henry or Arthur, Monroe's ex, can't recall which, but one of them said that 'art teaches nothing, except the significance of life. You agree?"

"I'll tell you what is mastery, Robbyn; it's the art of men speaking without knowledge in response to issues that mere mortals will never settle or solve and actually believing everything they spit out; now that's art."

"Well, good news is that Banta is..."

Sean gently brings Robbyn to him and touches her lower lip with his forefinger. He will not find out more about Banta tonight as Robbyn responds with both of her lips surrounding Sean's finger. He kisses her neck. She attempts nibbling his ear but fails and doesn't care. All is good but she wants it better and knows that he does too. Robbyn softly unclenches. "Wait." She turns and lights a scented candle by the bed. It's vanilla.

The outside world is off line, nowhere to be found.

Ms. McGrew's back is to Mr. Linden as she removes her Columbine purple blouse. Mr. Linden has retreated to sitting on her bed. She turns to face him.

"Lay back."

Trusting her, Sean does as he is told.

Trusting him, Robbyn's jeans drop to her ankles.

Sean's unsure where to focus; stay on her face or go looking elsewhere.

Robbyn's sure their destination is the same; his eyes say so.

Her alabaster skin... teasing, topped with velvety wisps of Autumn-hued barely negotiable locks of hair, smothers his thinking. Her Lincoln green bikini panties and bra are 'agents' of distinctive distraction. Sirens of myth, fascinating and dangerous, come to mind and yet, it's the best he's felt in a 'fog', as it matters not which shore the current pulls him towards. He knows he will go on the rocks for her, no question now. She watches his eyes remain on hers. The bikini is slowly discarded. She's impressed with his control. His eyes haven't wavered. Time we send the 'gentleman' away, Lady, because when seduction tangles with grace, all bets are off; House (Robbyn) rules.

She moves closer to the edge of the bed, daring him to touch her.

"Iris delivered messages from the Gods, my charger; and I know she's saddened that she cannot deliver this one. Do you accept the fee...and will you tip?"

Sean begins unbuttoning his top button.

"It's not time for the faint-hearted, hero boy." Robbyn bends down. She unbuttons the rest. He's motionless. She hears his breath. She stands, she smiles. "The Arabs have a proverb, you may have heard it in one of your excursions; it says, 'the beauty of man lies in the eloquence of his tongue." She see's him unable to reframe from grinning. "Let that sink in."

Sean sticks his tongue out, 'raspberry' style.

Robbyn near cackles. She bends down again. She undoes his belt. She unzips him. She stands.

Sean stands and removes what remains of his clothes.

Her pupils grow larger for he is now as natural as she is and only inches apart.

He tenderly places his open palm on her cheek. "Your 'arrival' is well worth the delay."

"Patient and passionate; oh, whatever am I to do with you, Sean Linden?"

"Are you taking suggestions, Robbyn Banques McGrew?"

"Yes. I suggest we shut up."

As evening merges into morning, and for as long as they are able to avoid sleep, he calls her "Sweetness" and "Humble Pie" and she calls him every name in the book.

****

They are reposed and in embrace. Both pretend to be asleep. Their breaths eventually sync. It's too obvious. Sean's the first to giggle; Robbyn, a heartbeat later.

They greet each other with a kiss and then lay back and stretch.

Both are struck by how much laughter, how much joy, they'd shared under the covers. Both are excited. Both wonder, if at this moment, there can possibly be two people on earth more pleased than them. And, both question the meaning of sanity.

Robbyn glances at the gallery of her 'little hopes for humanity' across the room from the lovers. She perceives the faces as more 'alive', more illuminated in dawns first fawning rays than they had appeared many hours ago. She ponders why. 'Perhaps the petals sense their gardener's pleasure at seeds finding such verdant rows.'

"I'm a morning person, Sean; are you?"

"You couldn't tell?"

"Ah, a rogue you are, sir; even upon first light. Something to look forward to."

Robbyn leans over and kisses him on his forehead, then gets out of bed.

"You like your eggs scrambled soft, right?"

"Yes, thank you. I'll help."

"No. No. Stay, Sean. Don't want you in my kitchen."

"A little late for that, isn't it?"

"You sweet, sweet bastard." Robbyn turns, takes two steps and whirls around.

"Can God make life any better than this?"

"If so, baby; the good Lord better send Jesus back with an elaboration, cuz I sure don't believe it can ever be better than being with you."

Hard Charger and Humble Pie.

Who knew.

CHAPTER 34

"What Is Below The Bottoms Of Your Feet?"

"If you lose the past, the will easily crumbles

Meng Jiao, Poet 9th Century

February 27, 2016

The Navaho and Alejandro Buddha Jesus Simon plan on camping for two nights. They are riding through pinon and juniper just a notch north of the Arizona line on the western boundary of the Navaho Indian Reservation towards Rainbow Bridge. They thread their way through canyons formed by five million years of snowmelt and rainwater erosion through porous red, ocher, and gray sandstone rock. The sheriff points out chockstone 'wedgies' just above a mini plunge pool he admits to enjoying once"...when no one was looking and I was younger."

John Truefellow speaks of the Holiness of the land; of Monument Valley, of Canyon de Chelly and the massacre by Kit Carson. The younger man slows his horse to listen more carefully. When the Sheriff finishes, he motions to get the horses going again.

"You feeling okay on 'Baskerville?"

"Doing well, thanks."

"Still pockets of snow, so rein her from them as much as possible. Don't know what's under, how deep."

"Yes. Listen, your mother taught me well. I can keep up and be safe too."

Mrs. Truefellow, upon learning of the boys story and the boys fathers connection to her John, had quickly welcomed Godboy; accepting, without hesitation, her son's absolute need for her assistance. Mrs. Truefellow recognized the young man's pain behind his brave attempt to hide the hurt. She'd seen it in John's eyes before, once.

She knew her respected position in the community as well as her son's advocacy and volunteer work would enhance the cover story for the 'new' arrival. The family was clued in within 24 hours of Mr. de Mejas's arrival. The visitor from the south is 'blood' now.

The Truefellow's four horses on their twenty acre spread are John's mothers 'four legged fountains of youth.' Horses are still on the sheriff's mind.

"Feeding them, exercising and letting the animals know she loves them keeps her going and now, another being in need of affection, of reinforcement of self worth walks through her Hogan's door, so understand where she comes from, si; and why, also, I am particular about the horses."

The Navaho rises in the saddle to see ahead. "Not too far now. Rainbow Bridge is holy ground. Its 275 foot natural span, the longest on Mother Earth. It's said that 'Navaho', a leader, was trapped by a flash flood in this canyon."

Godboy eyes the sky.

"It is said that the Father of the Sky cast a rainbow before the turbulent waters and the Navaho, he uses his hands and his feet, scurrying, maneuvering across the arch to get away from the downpour and the Sky Father steps up and turns the rainbow to stone, and since it is sacred because it is said it is the place that all moisture is born."

They dismount and tie the mounts. They must walk the rest of the path in. February means the foot traffic is minimal. Finally, beneath, alone; they marvel at the Sky father's masterpiece.

"A white man, a good man, has proper words for this reminder of what is good. He is called John Muir."

"My mother mentioned him. A good man from her home area, she told me. Said he cared about ecology before ecology was cool."

They sit on an outcrop. The wind picks up.

"Yes, he was good currency, this Muir, warning about problems caused by man before man, white man, knew they were the problem. This man, Muir, I remember some of his words from school. These; they speak well of him. Listen, the teacher stuck this hatchet of humanity in my head and it's never left."

A gust nearly blows The Navahos hat off. He catches it. "Mr. Muir says, 'I'll hear waterfalls and birds and winds sing I'll acquaint myself with the glaciers and wild gardens, and get as near the heart of the world as I can.' Look both ways, Nino. Use your nose and ears too. Take in the mesas, the sweet smells, the uneven sounds and scratchy shadows; the light playing the angles on stonework sculptures from the fingertips of God. Man intrudes on all, Godboy, interloping without invitation and often without concern. Always respect the fact that we are the hostiles in the daily reckonings of Nature."

Rocks fall, crashing nearby to the west. They stand. The Navaho puts his hand on Godboys shoulder. "I suppose Mr. Muir is just one of those people who believe that it is best to never give up on doing the right thing, 'good medicine' and I like that, that's all." He motions to their left. "Mares tail; sudden, immediate storms come with the neighborhood. We best head back now before the origin of all moisture proves it." They reach the horses and mount for the couple of miles ride back to the campsite.

"Biggest mistake on the plateau or in the canyons is to not have choices for withdrawal, sometimes something really wicked comes quickly down the chute and you better know where and what to grab." Rumbles in the sky justify the decision to get to the tent. "And that means 'you have to be quick on the feet you move within your head."

Godboy's father's favorite ballplayer, Yogi Berra, comes to mind. Young de Mejas is amused and sad.

They reach camp about a half hour before dusk. As they prepare for the evening, moisture hangs heavy. The Navaho readies the fire beneath the sandstone ceiling of the cutout that will act as protection against the elements. Thunder now replaces the rumbles and in the distance, rain is evident and to the left of the massing blue gray cloud and its first liquid 'drapes', a rainbow shivers into a prism-blazed sheen.

"Do you see the second rainbow?"

"What?"

"All rainbows come in pairs." The sheriff squinted. "I don't see the faint one, probably the suns not right. It parallels the other rainbow, only its colors are reversed."

Ten minutes later, night begins its accelerated creep. The fire sounds louder and is definitely warmer. John is cooking breakfast for dinner. Temperature is dropping. Sausage, hash browns, and bacon sizzle in the caste iron pan. Mr. de Mejas watches sparks rise, mingling with early stars. Mr. Truefellow watches him studying the "above." "We believe, at creation, the sky, the heavens originally was set up by elders of our people in a sensible and illustrious shapes and then what goes on? Why, that trickster, the Coyote, ran across our elder's handiwork and the stars were strewn all over the heavens, making them a ceiling of modern art, no obvious form or message. That's your basic Milky Way these days, billions of years old stew of star mess compliments of the Trickster. That's why we see charts of lines to dots, stars, to make sense of Orion Belt, Ursa; these are mans attempts to put things in their place, Nino, as we, in our infinite wisdom, believe they should be. Dippers, bears, Zodiac signs, all to make us more comfortable as if we really know, know that things are the way we think they should be; yes, true masters of place and time, that be us!"

John stacks Alejandro's plate "with grub that even kings of the universe like us can salivate over."

The younger man takes a bite and compliments the older man's culinary talents. They focus on feeding. Eventually, the younger looks up. "So, what I see is the Tricksters design and not the elders?"

"An unplanned collaboration between the elders and a four-legged party crasher, yes?" The sheriff takes another bite. "The hash browns came out alright." The sheriff points upwards with his fork. "Remarkable. One hundred billion stars in our galaxy; billions of galaxies, and the spirit in the sky, the chandelier of God; twinkle, twinkles on. With a whole lot of dark energy up there with them."

"There's a whole lot of dark energy down here too."

The Navaho knew he had touched a chord he did not want to strum again. He pours a cup of coffee, takes a sip before musing, "Someone said something like this, it's good so I want to use it too, but when Grandfather calls me I want it said that I only desired to protect the visions of others, nothing else."

"Good medicine there, Uncle."

"No one acquires spirituality; doesn't wear well either if it's not meant to fit. I studied theology in school with your Uncle Sean, an elective."

As he felt safer and less alone picking his way through each emotional pivot point as carefully as he could for his age and for his circumstance, Godboy began to call The Navaho, Sean and Moah, 'Uncle', as it is so nice to 'attach' again if not equally as necessary for survival.

"Wow; what were you two after, some wayward preachers' daughter?"

"You're a little trickster yourself, aren't you?"

John swigs some water from his canteen before continuing.

"Among my studies we learned about a philosophy called theosophy, which says that through such things as contemplation, devout petition and reasoned awareness may knowledge of God be achieved. One thing I remember; in Greek, 'theosophos' means 'wise concerning God.'"

"Didn't the Greeks have many Gods?"

"Spiritual doesn't come gift wrapped from E-bay and that's a problem for our new societies, endemic with touch and go feelings, heartless in many ways." The Sheriff stands and stretches. "Spirit, my vision, is clear waters and below, rounded various sized lakeshore rocks, their colors blasting through the reflection of the surface, no color's absent beneath the face of the lake; reds, greens, blues, and not far away an eagle allows your intrusion as you watch it dive bomb the water and bring up a fish and trusting you enough to land on a big stone not far away from you, you watch him reward his spirit with blessed sustenance. The first sight of returning hummingbirds in spring, that lifts me; a mama fox with newborn kits poking their heads out of all things, a town culvert, the mama's choice for this broods upbringing, her spirit, in essence, dealing with the dilemmas posed by man as best as her life energy allows, these are the territories of my heart, the tender mercies that corner my rage and I am thankful for this kindness from He who Knows all." John Truefellow moves towards the horses to settle them for the night. "Douse fire time?"

"Yes. Thanks, Nino."

They complete their tasks. The lantern assists in setting the sleeping bags out properly. Just before The Navaho turns the light off a little more must flow. "Light travels around six trillion miles within a year's time, so I ask, 'how big are you', right? I mean the universe sizes up men pretty quickly, how inflated you are mankind, it says. That's why, poquito, when you look down upon the earth you trod upon, bow down big as the fact of your own insignificance humbles you, for as a native brother whose name I have unfortunately lost said, that for each day you walk on Mother Earth, each step upon her should be as a prayer, strong in purpose, soft in request."

"That's exquisite in sentiment, holy in meaning."

"Sounds so to me."

Godboy adjusts his pillow. He turns on his side to face in The Navahos direction.

"Sean will be in for breakfast?"

"Yes, he should be. Mom will drop off the horse and the white 'dude' early."

"Sheriff?"

"Yes?"

"At the end of two rainbows, are there two leprechauns with two pots of gold?"

"Only if you're vision's vast, Nino; only if you dream huge; then, yes, though I daresay that gold will be the least of your rewards, no matter how many leprechauns tease you with their charms."

"Lucky Charms?"

"Go to sleep. I'm done with this day."

****

Mrs. Truefellow taxis Sean and "Bluebonnet" to the trailhead, arriving at sunrise. Finished with helping Sean cinch up and mount, she hugs him.

"Now you three get back here in time for dinner tomorrow night. And I mean by the time I can still see your mugs in daylight, right?" "We'll get here, Mrs. Truefellow.'

"You better if you're going to get some rest before your flights."

He waves as the good lady drives off. "Bluebonnet" knows the way.

Not long into the ride, in one of the most isolated locations, the aroma of civilization, bacon, smelling the right side of crisp, causes Sean to urge the horse, where level and safe, to pick up the pace.

Mr. Linden arrives in camp bringing three six packs of Orange Crush, Diet Cola, and

A&W Root Beer, iced perfectly in large cooler which also contains 3 large frozen water jugs, treats for the horses from their mother of another species back at the Truefellow hogan. Hoagies are on top of the ice and three individually wrapped chocolate fudge cake pieces are on top of these, making it easy to think about eating a piece well before 8:30 in the morning.

"What's the password or words to join this happy repast, Uncle Sean?"

"Bacon, beer and brats?"

"He's one of us and he has Orange Crush," the Sheriff judges.

After ten minutes dedicated to chow, coffee and soda; Truefellow, curiosity rising, "Will this O'Hara, the tribes; how do you know he is trustworthy? What's his party?" "Hold it, Tonto. He's going with an independent run at the presidency, if he decides to run."

"He is. Let him know the things that are meaningful, I mean the next time you see him."

"Only have met on a couple of times."

"No matter. I'll go warpath, code 10 for this guy if, if he understands the tribes exiguous existences, the dismay on the reservations is disquieting, palpable. They're under patrolled and under regulated. Felony assault, rape, molestation, not guilty by loophole, you name

it, Sean, it's prevalent on native lands and this man needs to know these things. All we're asking is for him to assist in the tribe's survival. I think that's worth two white men's time, don't you? "

"You'll have help, someway. Let's get him into office first."

"Still too early for beer; more hash browns, Nino?"

"Please."

"Sean?"

'Load her up, thanks."

The sheriff does as ordered, placing heaps of well done hash browns and crisp perfectly burnt bacon slices on their plates, so much so, if not balanced properly on the knees, the edges are threatened.

"The crime rates at some reservations are ten times the rate outside the borders."

Between bites of second helpings, "Will he serve the, will he work for the first constituents in an honorable way?"

"He is one I can recommend."

"Godboy; more caffeine, please."

Mr. de Mejas reaches and begins to pour into Sean's mug.

"Sheriff gets to add Kuala to his java." And he does. 'It's time, Sean. It's after 7:45a.m. Have some jubilee juice with me."

"No. I'm not that good at horses' stone sober, so, no."

Mr. de Mejas pours the remainder of the brew in Mr. Truefellows' flask upon which the sheriff immediately caps his canteen/flask and shakes it. Finished with the rock and roll, he uncaps it and steam and the smell of candy permeates the air. The Navaho squints in the new rays of a new day. He is staring at Sean. "You tell this man who would be leader that our children, the Dineh battle immunodeficiency problems, that our teens, their anguish of not even having the opportunity instead of seeing their dreams dashed is killing our future."

A meadowlark signals its presence. All look in the direction the call seemed to come from.

"How connecting."

"What is that, Uncle John?"

"Just thinking of my placement in the Forest Service as a summer intern..."

"This is before the Common Era?"

"Still the trickster, aren't we? No, Godboy, I was boning up on animals, terrain, water management but spent more time with familiar things; coyotes, cactus, reptiles, scorpions, birds; Roadrunner to what we just heard, the meadowlark, my favorite songbird, of those I have had long acquaintances with." John Truefellow pauses to enjoy another satisfying taste of his morning 'high' octane before continuing. "Yes, the meadowlark, not only for its yellow vest do I pleasure its existence, but its species name is ponderously unforgettable too. Sturbella Neglecta. Sturbella Neglecta. Hell, we were interrupted by western meadowlark song not a few ticks ago. Could be a mascot for Native America, I've always thought. Haunting reminder of the past, this bird's call, a woeful plea in search of association, lovely and lonely and proud. The tribes; Sturbella Neglecta: fifty per cent unemployment. Sturbella Neglecta. Yes, Sean, you tell O'Hara about the bird we've been given for too long, will you please."

"More octane free coming up." Godboy pours a topping of 'hot' into Sean's mug.

"He must be capable of seismic change. I've never heard you promote, Sean, especially without reservation, except in rare instances." Finished with his morning jolt, the sheriff stands and refreshes his mug with non-octane fuel.

"Both parties pow-wow for no good. I like this party crasher, I think, Sean." His attention is now on the 'nephew' whom he tosses the last biscuit towards. The boy's father would have been proud of his son's reflexes with a 'looks like you have done it before' catch. The 'throwee' addresses the 'catchee'. "Son, you know what's behind the term, 'true blue?'"

Godboy takes a bite of biscuit before, "Genuine, always there."

"An elder chief told me that a white childhood friend of his, a paleface, Sean, who'd eventually became an union boss, or so the chief said, but that this white friend told the chief to always use 'blue' ink to sign anything, because you see, 'blue' is identified with trustworthiness. Well, the chief was a fervid believer; never used another color ink to sign anything, because, you see, he felt his obedience to his friends sage advice instigated the recent fortunate occurrences' for his tribe. You see, his people had struck oil in the same year during which they were approved for a casino."

"Shows anyone that the power of blue is in the making of green."

"And on that note, Uncle Sean, it's time to saddle up. Still pleasant."

"Know where blue blood comes from?"

"Speak up, donkey boy."

"Uncle Sean?"

"Don't know. Fire away. I can hear you."

"From a crab."

"Alright, follow me on. Go on, Nino. Sorry. Come on 'Blue', you too, 'Basker.'" The Navaho smiled back over his shoulder.

"Well, if you're something dinosaurs are younger than, and if you are something that has blueblood that saves human lives, I think you can pretty much claim the right to being called the first blueblood. I present the horseshoe crab, gentlemen. Its' blood is blue and is used in screening for bacteria, even has ability to do something good in pathogens work that makes them a collectible item to the sad tune for them of over a half million of them a year. Blue bloods save red bloods in big ways."

They are now engaged as man and horse accommodates each other in compatible manner again, moving at comfortable stride. The jump out of colors, the stony patina from recent rains nearly blinds.

The Navaho and Sean are in the lead and riding astride where the path is wide enough. "There's an 'after-effect' riding right here in reservation city, I tell you, son."

"Get away from me, you strange Indian."

Godboy is pleased that he can still understand most of their words from his mount. "Sean, it's just that we haven't met her, and yet, while you haven't said much, what you have said, it's pretty damn good!" Truefellow turns in the saddle. "Isn't that right, Dios Nino?"

"It's true, Sean."

"We'll all meet in due time. Now let it be."

Mr. de Mejas respects the request.

The sheriff doesn't need 'no stinkin' badge.' "I'm just saying," in a voice loud enough to reach any aeries in the vicinity, "that it's pretty scary when; hey, watch that boulder on the left, yes, there you go, good Sean, good Bon Bon, good Baskerville."

They are maneuvering around a small area of shard impedimenta. It's warm.

They lunch by a large drop pool. Finished, the sheriff leads the others up a short trail that leads to a small interconnected rock walled kiva-like structure, better described as more like a castle turret for defense, abutting the cliff, complete with a window for surveillance and arms fire, bow and arrow or otherwise. "Most speculate that this was used as a lookout for cattle rustlers with great views of the river from two directions, down two canyons, as you can see. See the Law coming and going."

As they mounted for the rest of the journey, it's spotted, and it's the wrapping on the gift of the condors riding the early thermals high above. The riders and horses stay still as if necessary. They watch the animal two ridges away.

"He knows we're here. They can smell for some four to six miles."

John gives the binoculars to Godboy.

"There was a guy who was a guide back home before the service. Tracked grizzly. Said they always make you stop. That black bear over there is a cub compared. Well, Ronny said he had this high priced client once, and together, they watched a grizzly, a male, attack, paw to smithereens, willows of all things, tearing the reed, the bark. The problem with this says, Ron, is that Grizz aren't moose. Don't eat willows. But this Grizz did. Why? Well, because Nature knows, that's why. Nature knows. Later, this particular Grizz got shot. Ron was one of the first on the scene and no, he did not shoot him. He said that he noticed the bear had a busted tooth. He also said to me that in the depression of the tooth, he found it stuffed with willow bark; yes, willow bark." The sheriff looked to his side at the others. "Who taught this bear, who passed this down to this bear when it was a cub? Did other illness prompt this response?"

"Why did the bear act that way, sheriff? What did Ronny say?"

"Salicylic acid," Sean responds.

"Aspirin, Nino." The Sheriff adds, "Nature knows, nature knows."

They late midday feast on Hoagies and carrot sticks. Conversation again moves through thoughts about the people of many ancient manners and many timeless myths, Native Americans.

"They put themselves, the men, the young; they set about testing their merit, eagerly placing themselves in precarious settings to weed out weakness and unnecessary emotions. Test of endurance, quest for relevance."

John gets up and stokes the small fire. Sparks flash upwards. "A Cherokee friend from the Pow-Wows shared with me a tale the Cherokee tell their children. He said these words he heard from his Uncle as his father, my friends, had been dead for years. It talks about a grandfather to grandson talk. Grandfather says 'A fight is going on inside me.' This is what he tells the grandson. 'The fight is between two wolves. One is evil. The other is good. This same fight goes on inside you and inside every other human being too. The grandson asks, 'which wolf will win?' The Cherokee grandfather simply replies, 'The one we feed.' The nutcracker, Nino, is what is a man worth who will not dare to die for the cause of their life, no matter, fair or foul, their ground of play? There should not be enough wampum in the world to purchase your integrity nor dissuade you from your desired destiny. Then and only then will you be worth remembering."

"Wampum, that's money?"

"Yes, Nino. They were beads used for value. They were black, white or dark purple, the dark beads having double the value of the white...were it so today, huh, Sean?"

From an area of the newly designated campsite for the evening which had been quite, comes, "So numerous are the manners in which we loath one another."

Mr. Linden takes another sip from his cup of high octane coffee that John had concocted for him as soon as their feet had hit the ground. Godboy and The Navaho quieted as sarcasm from Sean Linden is about as frequent an occurrence as the sighting of a Sasquatch and just as meaningful.

"As I know, Nino, you've been tested in as tough a trial of life as any warrior encountered. No family. I understand as some perhaps can't."

What sounds like a soft and distant 'who', perhaps an owl, sounds and all three act as if they were listening to this, but they are not.

"Never forget that one day, one hour, one minute can remain and matter mightily for the rest of your life, Godboy. We all know this is irrefutable. So I speak now of opportunity. The purpose of a problem is to fire up your imagination and forge opportunity from it. Bend it. Mold it. Hammer it into the shape of your best intentions and design will set you free, my brothers, free!"

Sean stands as if stretching will defeat approaching tipsiness.

"Sean, will you get us some more unleaded, more pop, please?"

"Sure."

After Sean delivers the sodas and is in the midst of enjoying another gulp of hot coffee, The Navaho looks at Godboy. "Are you ready?"

With the solemnity of a pastor, Godboy answers, "Yes sir, Sheriff."

Sean watches as they hurriedly down the cans of soda pop, the pop, cold and fizzy and most importantly, still fully carbonated. He sees the other two seeming to hold their breaths.

"You look like two bullfrogs a courting."

"Don't make me laugh," Godboy pleads but fails as he burps, a gravelly mature well rounded belch complimented by Orange Crush forthcoming from his nostrils.

The Navaho added a sounding of his own in attempting a 'besting' of the boys aural greatness. When competing serenades of competing gastrointestinal systems subsides, Godboy is first to recover. "Godzilla burps, Sean. They're Godzilla burps."

"Yeah, Sean. Get with it. Godzilla burps; it's a well known fact that the big guy doesn't like them along with bats, snakes and Mothra."

Godboy interrupts Mr. Truefellow with another monster throated belch, a Joe E. Brown mouthful of alarm, a released reverberation that only a shaken, not stirred Orange Crush can deliver.

They laugh themselves to eventually near slumber but not before The Navaho gives one more query. "So her name is Robbyn? We're hearing she's nice."

"You're hearing right. You'll eventually, both of you, meet her."

The tone at the end of Sean's words is recognized by campmates to mean, in most polite terms, 'end of subject for now, thank you.'

It is about all of a half minute before, "You think Godzilla would like her, Uncle John?"

Before Mr. Linden can utter an 'oh, come on,' Mr. Truefellow bellows a guttural call so firmly it seems the fire almost goes out.

Then, just as the fireside seems to be settling down, all laughed out, Sean asks, "I'll take that to mean a 'yes', right?"

With sunrise scheduled to be the alarm clock, laughter soon titters to nothing. The melody of the meadowlark will come soon enough.

Made in the USA
Charleston, SC
24 January 2016